Queens of Mist and Madness
Fae Isles - Book 4
Lisette Marshall

Copyright © 2024 by Lisette Marshall

All rights reserved. This book or any portion thereof may not be reproduced or used in any manner whatsoever without the express written permission of the author, except for the use of brief quotations in promotional texts and/or book reviews. This is a work of fiction. Any resemblance to actual persons, living or dead, or actual events is purely coincidental.

ASIN: B0CM6NW451

Cover design: Saint Jupiter

Editor: Erin Grey, The Word Faery

www.lisettemarshall.com

www.facebook.com/LisetteMarshallAuthor

www.instagram.com/AuthorLisetteMarshall

To Erin, who is always right.
Thank you for being there at 10AM.

Contents

Chapter 1	1
Chapter 2	12
Chapter 3	24
Chapter 4	40
Chapter 5	58
Chapter 6	74
Chapter 7	92
Chapter 8	109
Chapter 9	125
Chapter 10	139
Chapter 11	150
Chapter 12	168
Chapter 13	182
Chapter 14	198
Chapter 15	216
Chapter 16	227

Chapter 17	239
Chapter 18	256
Chapter 19	268
Chapter 20	279
Chapter 21	299
Chapter 22	318
Chapter 23	333
Chapter 24	344
Chapter 25	355
Chapter 26	365
Chapter 27	380
Chapter 28	393
Chapter 29	408
Chapter 30	422
Chapter 31	437
Chapter 32	447
Chapter 33	461
Chapter 34	472
Chapter 35	488
Chapter 36	499
Chapter 37	508
Chapter 38	521

Chapter 39	536
Chapter 40	546
Chapter 41	562
Chapter 42	571
Other books by Lisette Marshall	591
About the Author	593

Chapter 1

For one infinite moment, time itself stood suspended.

No more shouts. No more laughter. The allies and enemies behind me might as well have ceased to exist, their opinions and complaints no more relevant than the dust beneath my boots. The howling of the wind, the flickering torches, the shards of the shattered binding on the rocky ground of the Cobalt Court ... they could have been a million miles away, and I would not have noticed.

All I saw was Creon, dark eyes burning in the night, fingers gripping my arm with a strength that threatened to leave bruises. And all I heard ...

Em. Emelin.

The syllables hung in the air between us like the sweetest, hoarsest treasure.

He'd *spoken* those words. I'd *heard* those words. Guttural and gravelly, perhaps, his voice brittle from decades of disuse – but those coughs and rasps had broken the silence all the same, unfamiliar sounds yet brimming with an emotion that was far from new. I'd seen it smouldering in his eyes so many times before. I'd felt it in his fingers on my skin.

Emelin.

Hot tears suddenly stung behind my eyelids, threatening to spill over.

And then, in a flash of muscular limbs and velvety wings, the world snapped back into motion – movements so fast my mind didn't comprehend what was happening until Creon was already standing, until those scarred hands of his had already dragged me to my feet. Dark wings swept out wide, obscuring the starry sky. Someone sputtered some objection behind me, about things to be done and dangers to be minded ... but Creon didn't waver as he scooped me into his arms and flexed his fingers in a silent reminder of the explosive magic always lurking below his skin.

Whoever had unwisely opened their mouth hurriedly corrected the mistake.

We shot into the night sky so fast my heart plummeted into my stomach.

My cry was lost in the rush of air whipping past us, the whoosh of his powerful wings. Darkness swallowed us within moments. As soon as we soared past the first jagged mountain ridge, out of sight of the torches, nothing but stars and silhouettes remained in the pale moonlight. I clung to Creon's labouring shoulders for dear life as the cold wind tore at my dress and hair, squeezing my eyes shut so as not to see the gaping void beneath us; if I was going to fall, I much preferred not knowing in advance how bad it would be.

Where in hell was he *going*?

But he was already descending before I could ask, my vital organs now pulled in the opposite direction as his wings surrendered us to gravity – the descent so close to an actual plunge that I would have screamed again if not for his unwavering arms around me. My eyes flew open in a panicked reflex. Before us, the dark ocean stretched all the way to the horizon, the waxing moon accompanied by its distorted reflection on the surface. A small bay nestled in the coastline, and it was for that crescent-shaped beach Creon seemed to be aiming, his back and shoulders straining furiously as we dropped down the last dozens of feet.

He'd never landed so clumsily with me in his arms, not even after the Mother's ball, when I'd been lust-dazed enough to fondle him in deeply unhelpful places as he flew. Half-standing, half-stumbling, he regained his balance and released me, falling to his knees the moment I'd found my footing in the black sand.

'*Creon*,' I managed, my brain lagging several minutes behind.

'Sorry,' he rasped as his fingers reflexively twitched through the corresponding sign; he stared at them for a moment, then raised his hand to his throat, as if to rub his vocal cords. 'So sorry. Just—'

Another string of grating coughs overcame him mid-sentence.

'Alright,' I said, casting one glance at his convulsing body and shuddering wings and deciding that the questions and explanations could wait. 'Never mind. Let me find you something to drink. Don't suffocate in the meantime, please.'

The tense motions of his fingers were barely readable in the moonlight. *Will try.*

Thank the gods for the black sand: it offered plenty of magic to change a nearby rock into a workable, albeit roughly-shaped, cup and to remove the salt from the seawater with an experimental shade of deep orange. The result still tasted strongly of minerals, but no longer so briny.

Creon drank it down so swiftly I doubted he'd tasted anything at all.

'Thank you.' He dragged out the words like heavy weights – gods help me, that *voice*. Dry and croaking, as if he was recovering from a heavy flu after weeks of coughing and wheezing ... but it made my toes curl in my boots all the same, that damaged, glorious sound. 'Fuck. Sorry. What—'

Again his vocal cords seemed to crumple as his throat convulsed in throaty rasps.

'You know what?' I wryly said, dropping into the sand beside him. It was still warm against my legs from the sunlight of the day. 'Let's just stick with signing for now. We can try talking once you've worked your way through a bucket of cough syrup.'

The sound that escaped him was half-wheeze, half-groan. *This is infuriating.*

It was. Gods help me, it was. I wanted to hear him again, *yearned* for him to speak my name out loud again – *Emelin* – with that breathless reverence that turned the plain old syllables into a brand new enchantment. Then again …

'Would it be any less infuriating to cough your throat to shreds and have to wait for it to heal?'

No. He dragged in one more shuddering breath, then tucked his wings in against his back and rubbed a hand over his face, allowing his shoulders to slump. *What in hell happened?*

Right. He'd blacked out without warning, then woken up confused and vulnerable, suddenly in possession of a voice, but lacking any recollection of the past minute. No wonder he'd fled. Better to get the hell out of there than stay to beg Tared for an explanation.

'Thysandra attacked you,' I said, swallowing something bitter as the events played out in my mind's eye again with unwelcome clarity. If only I'd stopped her. If only I'd seen it coming. 'So you swung a knife at her and Naxi knocked you out before you could hurt her. You dropped the binding as you fell.'

A muscle twitched in his jaw. *Did it break?*

I nodded.

So … you had to choose?

Even in the near-darkness, those signs looked more grim than I'd expected. There was no relief in his expression, not the faintest sparkle of elation at the return of his voice; if anything, he looked like a male struggling to come to terms with a devastating blow.

I swallowed and whispered, 'Yes.'

He let himself sink back into the sand, black wings flattening out on either side of his lean torso. *Fuck.*

And that was all.

Doubt hooked its claws into me without warning, so swift and vicious I could taste it like bile in the back of my throat. Had I picked the wrong option after all? Had he wanted me to save his unbound powers, that advantage in battle that might have won us the war? Hell, he'd tormented himself to near-death for decades for just a chance to end the Mother – so what was a voice to …

Cactus, his fingers interrupted my spiralling train of thoughts. He didn't even raise his head from the sand to look at me. *There's no need for that.*

Oh.

Bloody demon senses.

I drew in a gulp of air. 'I just thought …'

Now he did come up on his elbows, supporting himself on one arm as he lifted the other. In the moonlight, the dark cuts of ink on his wrist and fingers seemed to twist beneath his skin as he signed, *Give me half a second to catch up, Em. It's not been the most uneventful of nights.*

'No, but—'

And stop looking for reasons to doubt yourself.

I froze.

Doubting myself. *Again.* Hell, why was I jumping straight to the worst possible explanation of that tightness in his face, as if none of his love and trust would mean a damn when push came to shove? He'd missed his voice. I knew that. He'd wanted me to stop denying my heart. I knew that, too.

So perhaps there were other options.

'Right.' I wrapped my arms around my sweaty self, shifting in the sand. 'Thanks. I … I suppose it's theoretically possible that you're simply unhappy about the situation in general, rather than about me.'

His grin broke through – that wry, skewed grin, not yet as overjoyed as I wanted to see it, but a thousand times better than the dull blankness in his gaze. *Would you think?*

'Oh, fuck off.' My chuckle came out breathless – both relief and the ever-familiar sensation of my guts tangling themselves into knots at the sight of that smile. 'Please just tell me what you're thinking, then. Optimistic guesswork isn't my strong side.'

I'm thinking way too many things. He brusquely sat up, pulling his knees to his chest and draping his arms over them; his wings drooped into the sand behind his back, the velvety surface darker than even the night sky itself. *Trying to figure out what this means for our chances against the Mother. If I should be pissed with Naxi. If the rest of the world is going to give you trouble over this decision and if—*

'Since when are you the one worried about the rest of the world?' My voice shot up.

He scoffed. *I'm worried about you.*

'Why? I know exactly what choice I made.' It was strangely liberating to speak the words out loud – to no longer be waffling, doubting Emelin, the girl who tried to want nothing yet wanted everything at once. 'And the rest of the world was accounted for when I made it. If they want to give me trouble over it, they can go fight their own fucking war as far as I'm concerned, and if they're stupid enough to try that, there's not much value to their opinions anyway. I'll be fine.'

Creon stared at me.

'Also,' I added, words pouring out of their own accord now that I'd started, 'you were right. And I've been an idiot. And I'm sorry – I'm so, *so* sorry – and I swear to all the dead and living gods that I'll stop pretending I don't love you to death – hell, I should never have tried to pretend in the first place, and ...'

His lips parted, but not a sound came out – not even the weakest cough.

The final part of my sentence drifted from my grasp. Only now did it finally sink in, the danger we'd only barely escaped. The choices I might have made. The depths I'd allowed myself to sink to, the desperate measures I'd somehow believed to be worth the peace among my friends.

I could have lost him today.

I could have hurt him so, so much today.

'I'm sorry,' I whispered again, throat tightening. 'I'm so very sorry, and I love you so very much. I don't know why it took a shattered binding to make me realise what I was doing. It should have been clear from the very first moment I realised I was hurting you.'

His grimy face was inscrutable in the darkness, his eyes pools of coal-black ink. But his mouth moved again as he held out his hand – those beautiful, sensual lips, the same lips I'd learned to read fluently without a sound to guide me.

'Come here,' he rasped.

I threw myself into his arms.

He pressed me to his chest with so much force I couldn't breathe for a second, his fingers trembling against my skin. As if he could erase these weeks of distance by simply holding me close enough. As if his rough breath in my hair and his lips against my forehead could undo every harsh word, every flare of frustration. I clung to him as if my life depended on it, wrapped my arms around him and all but pressed myself through his ribcage – *mine*, the blood in my veins sang, *mine, mine, mine.*

'I'm sorry,' I mumbled. 'I ...'

'It's alright.' A croaky, harrowing whisper, like the rough slide of calloused fingers down my spine – enough to set every inch of me on fire. 'It's alright, Em, I promise. We're alright.'

I still couldn't get my pulse to slow down. I still couldn't hold him close enough. Those sharp, bitter signs had etched themselves into my mind's eye, that desperate fight on the beach – *tell them what you want, but I'll be taking it for the truth ...*

I'd never been so desperate to shout the truth at every soul willing to listen.

'Are you really, very sure?' I murmured, my face buried into his shirt. 'Because if you need any other reassurances from me, I'm ready. Happy to go back and stick my tongue down your throat before Tared's eyes, if you think it'll cheer you up?'

His lips remained pressed against my forehead, his hands didn't loosen on my back – but a new sound escaped him amidst a small fit of coughs. It came out muffled, that unexpected hiccup, as if his own tongue was not yet quite sure what to do with it ...

But it was undeniably, indisputably, a laugh.

A *laugh*.

For the very first time, I could *hear* the mirth that vibrated through his chest, shaking his body against mine. It was just a single short chuckle. Barely more than an involuntary outburst of air. My guts drew tight as a clenched fist all the same, stealing the breath from my lungs – a fierce, explosive triumph so utterly blissful that it hurt.

How did a sound so brittle, so rough, manage to be as beautiful as all the rest of him?

I pulled back just enough to meet his gaze. His face was stained with blood and mud, his hair a tousled mess, dark strands sticking to his temples and cheeks ... But something trembled around the corners of his lips, something that made me want to kiss him and keep kissing him until the sun rose.

Something I might need as much as the oxygen I breathed.

'Is that a yes?' I whispered.

Another wobbly laugh escaped him. It fell from his lips with a sincerity that bordered on the heartbreaking, even these quiet chuckles bursting with awe and marvelling ... As if the feeling was as new to him as the sound itself. As if he was rediscovering every turn of his voice alongside me, a thrilling little secret to be shared by us alone.

'I'm serious!' I managed, laughter worming out of my throat no matter how hard I willed it to stay down. 'Whatever you want, I'm ready to do it. Should I make a dramatic declaration to the entire Alliance? Write the phoenix elders that I've been shagging you for ages? Tell Agenor he'll either have to add you to the family tree immediately or cut me out of it?'

He only laughed louder – then coughed, then laughed again, amusement shuddering down to the very tips of his wings. There it was, finally, that explosive joy I'd waited for, rising on his face like the unstoppable tide. 'Em ...'

'What do you want?' My hands were shaking. My heart was beating so fast the thuds were blurring together in my ears. I'd always thought him the single most stunning creature I'd ever laid eyes upon, yet somehow in this moment, covered in blood and grime and sweat, his composure folding in upon itself, his face a mask of every possible emotion and a couple more at once, he was twice as breathtaking as ever. 'Please. Anything I can do—'

He kissed me.

He tasted of salt and blood, of battle and victory, and I stopped thinking at the first brush of his mouth over mine, stopped feeling anything but his demanding lips, his hands tangling in my hair to tug me closer.

I grabbed his shoulders. His wings swept around the both of us like a dark cocoon of warmth and safety. I reached out instinctively, trailing my fingertips over that straining surface in an unthinking reflex ...

Creon moaned.

He *moaned*.

The sound slid beneath my skin like liquid fire, igniting every nerve ending in a roar of sensations. I did it again, and he let out another groan against my lips – a raspy, gravelly sound of need not unlike the taste of gooey warm caramel.

Sweet. Addictive. And gods help me, impossible to stop craving.

Fuck. I needed *more* of this.

Who cared that we were sitting on a beach, unhidden except by the cover of darkness? Who cared people might be looking for us? My hands were wandering on their own now, finding every sensitive place I knew so well, cataloguing every brand new audible reaction. A feathery brush over the sharp tip of his ear, and he let out a ragged breath against my mouth. A nip at his jaw, and he growled low in his throat, his hands tightening around my waist. A scrape of nails over the onset of his wing, and he *snarled* – a primal sound that left me lightheaded and gasping for air.

It was like drowning in him. Like drowning in desire. My eager ears seemed to render my skin and fingers twice as sensitive, every moan and whimper stirring flickers of need unlike anything I'd felt before – fanning those flames demanding more, more, *more*.

'Em,' he growled, and gods have mercy on me, there was such *wonder* in that single rough syllable. 'Em, I—'

His voice started cracking again.

'Shh,' I muttered, wrapping my fingers around his face. 'I don't think you need all that many words for this, Your Highness.'

His laughter was a surrender. I pressed my mouth to his, tasting the sounds that escaped him – part moan, part cough, part laughter, and each of them equally delicious. He moved back, and I moved with him, straddling him as he fumbled to shift his wings beneath himself and lie down in the sand.

Kissing him, I dug my nails into his chest. My reward was a hoarse groan that reverberated all the way down my body, heating the wetness between my thighs to a torturous fever.

I could have lost him.

But damn it all, I *hadn't,* and this ... this I could make right.

I tore myself away from his mouth and moved downwards, my lips tracing a trail down his neck and chest, my hands clawing at the buttons of his shirt. Two or three broke off in my hurry to unfasten them. The chiselled planes of his chest emerged smooth and silvery in the moonlight, the dark lines of his scars standing out like a map of battles and pain; I couldn't help but bend over to kiss every single one of them, lapping the salty flavour of his sweat off his skin.

The sound that escaped him was a guttural growl – pleasure as much as frustration.

'More of that,' I breathed, nuzzling his nipple. 'Please. I don't need words. I just want to hear what I make you feel.'

His rough exhalation was the only response I needed.

He didn't even touch me. He didn't need to. His voice seemed to have taken on a physical shape against my skin, scraping down my sensitive nerves, adding another point of friction to the hardness of his body beneath me – as if those gasps and moans had become tangible things, caressing me in places no finger could touch. He still felt like himself. He still smelled like himself, musky and sweet. But whenever I closed my eyes, he sounded like a stranger, and somehow the thrill of that brand new unknown only deepened the ache for him.

More.

More.

I moved down.

Licking and kissing, down the ridges of his chest, down his muscular stomach ... I paused to circle my tongue around his navel just once, tasting him. His breath came faster now, a desperate rhythm that matched my own frantic pulse; his hands tangled in my hair as he arched off the black beach, hips bucking up to meet me. I fought with the fastening of his trousers. My fingers were trembling and slick with sweat, and gods help me, why were these damned things still not giving way?

I tore off another button in the end, freeing his straining erection with a hiss of impatience. Such a familiar sight, the curved hardness of him, thick and swollen and glistening temptingly in the moonlight ...

But I rubbed down his length in one firm stroke, and the husky groan that escaped him was thrillingly, gloriously new.

Sound and sensation mingled. He arched up, thrusting into my fingers, and moaned again – that deep, fraying surrender I could feel in every fibre of my body. I flicked my thumb over the smooth head of his cock, spreading the moisture welling there. This time, the sound that fell from his lips was almost a whimper, a perfect match to the shudder that soared through him.

I leaned over and licked down his shaft, and *gods*, his cry of surrender made the emptiness between my thighs ache with need.

How would I ever get enough of this? They'd have to pause their damn war. The Mother would have to find something else to do instead of slaughtering innocent islands of people. I'd be too busy fucking her son for the rest of the year to make time for killing her – too busy making up for a hundred and thirty years of torturous silence.

These moans ... these glorious moans ...

I took him deeper into my mouth, savouring the silky, salty weight on my tongue, savouring every barely suppressed whimper. Hell, I wanted to hear him pleading for release. I wanted to hear him howl with pleasure. My fingers joined my lips and tongue, finding new spots to torment. Anything to stop him from ever going quiet again, anything to make him feel just how much I wanted and needed him ...

And it was then, just as I started wondering if it was possible to climax from the sound of pleasure alone, that Alyra's agitated squeaks abruptly shattered the delirium of my lust-dazed thoughts.

Chapter 2

I'D NEVER MOVED SO fast in my life.

My limbs launched me away from Creon before my mind had caught up, my familiar's alarm hitting me as intuitively as any of her thoughts. Next to me, Creon somehow managed to look lethally elegant as he shot up and buttoned his trousers in the blink of an eye, glazed expression sharpening into a narrow-eyed threat that even his unbuttoned shirt and sand-covered wings couldn't spoil.

The last of my arousal faded as Alyra's shrill chirping continued. Where *was* she?

Half a heartbeat could be a very long time – more than enough to imagine a host of disastrous possibilities, each of them more alarming than the last. Had more fae shown up in Thysandra's wake? Had the Mother herself appeared on the island? Had she realised how dangerous it would be for us to know the locations of the bindings and razed the whole of the Cobalt Court to the ground, destroying each crystal orb in the process? I dug my fingers deeper into the coarse sand, searching frantically for a glimpse of white feathers – *there*, bursting from the darkness and into the silver light of the moon …

At the same moment, a streak of fire soared across the cliffs.

An attack? Hell, a *comet*? And only then did I recognise those fiery butterfly wings, flames licking hungrily at the night air around her.

Lyn.

I sagged into the sand, heart hammering against my ribs. Alyra landed beside me an instant later, squeaking incessantly and glaring at Creon with obvious accusation in her beady eyes. *Do you have any idea,* that look said, *how long I've been flying around looking for you, you oversized bloody bat?*

'Never mind that now,' I sharply told her, hoping the hoarseness of my voice sounded like worry and not like my mouth had been full of fae prince a moment ago. I could still taste him with every word I spoke. 'What is the matter?'

She didn't seem to be entirely sure, or at least, no coherent explanation found me through her thoughts. People had needed me. People had been worried. *Lyn* had been worried, most of all, and since she was small and winged and therefore sensible, Alyra had taken her alarm to heart and set out to find me.

'For the bloody gods' sakes,' I muttered, jumping to my feet. 'Lyn!'

The comet-like streak of fire bent our way.

She landed some twenty feet away, wings sizzling out behind her shoulders as she hurried towards us. A new flame flared up in her open palm, shrouding her round, freckled face in a golden glow and illuminating the sand and rocks of the little bay. 'Oh, thank Inika's bloody heart – *here* you are.'

'What is it?' I threw a glance at Creon, who hadn't moved from where he sat – left hand in the black sand, right hand loosely on his knee, ready to unleash hell on whatever danger showed its face. In the light of Lyn's phoenix fire, his eyes glowed with inhuman intensity. 'Is anyone in danger?'

'Oh, no, no,' she hurried to say, wiping red curls from her eyes with her free hand. 'No one but my sanity, that is. How's the voice?'

Creon grimaced but managed a mostly intelligible, 'Rusty.'

She winced. 'Oh, good gods. Go look for some cough syrup once we're back in the Underground, will you?'

He gave her a half-shrug, half-nod – that gesture that said he theoretically agreed with her on the necessity of the medicine but wasn't yet sure whether his pride would survive having to ask for some alf healer's help. She rolled her eyes at him, then glanced at me and added, 'Make sure he does, please.'

'Of course,' I said, forcing a small grin at Creon's indignant huff.

'Good.' She plopped down beside us with a muffled grumble, tucking a stubborn curl behind her ear again. 'Alright. Where do I start?'

My pulse was slowly coming down in absence of any screaming panic on her side. In its place, the first slivers of annoyance were rising. Gods be damned, I didn't *want* to talk about cough syrup and trouble right now, didn't want to worry about anyone's sanity for the rest of the night. Was it really too much to ask for the world to leave us alone for a couple of hours, after days of battles and meetings with goddesses?

But this was Lyn, not some alf trying to cause trouble. And since most of my friends were currently not even talking to me, I should probably take care to keep the last few exceptions around.

So I swallowed my frustration, pulled on as polite a face as I felt capable of, and said, 'Did anything happen after we, um, left?'

'Beyla started relocating corpses to remove all traces of the fight. The rest of us took Thysandra to the Underground.' She scoffed, tossing her handful of fire into the sand. It merrily continued to burn there without any fuel. 'Which meant we had to explain where we found her. Which meant we had to explain that we found a castle full of bindings, which means people currently have *questions*. Of the rather hysterical kind.'

Of course they had. I didn't even need to close my eyes to envision it, the excitable masses of nymphs and alves and vampires below, clamouring for news and answers. Much as I was in the mood to loathe them for it, I couldn't even truly blame them. It was the survival of their kind on the line, after all.

Next to me, Creon had gone icily still – as if the mention of the bindings alone had been a declaration of war.

'So you want to give them some answers?' I said.

'Yes, and I wish that was all of it.' There was an apology in Lyn's amber eyes as she hesitated, her gaze shooting back and forth between the two of us. 'Someone apparently told the Alliance about the last message the phoenix elders sent us. People were shouting about that issue as much as about the bindings.'

It took me a moment to remember.

Zera's temple. Agenor's letter. *They told me they will reconsider their decision not to join if and only if Em makes a bargain to never exchange a word with him again...*

For fuck's sake. Life had been so much easier while I could pretend forgetting about it would be enough to solve that problem.

Who knows, exactly? Creon signed next to me, with all the slow, catlike grace of a predator about to rip someone's head off. *Just the Council? Or ...*

'Pretty much everyone, at this point,' Lyn said bleakly. 'It probably leaked through Agenor's advisors and the alves at the Golden Court, who ... well, they're alves.'

I'd never heard Creon curse before and didn't know the Faerie word he muttered under his breath, but even in that broken, gravelly voice, the feeling behind the unknown syllables was more than obvious.

'Yes,' Lyn said and grimaced at him. 'So there's some uproar. We managed to keep them from calling a full Council meeting for now, but in exchange, we were more or less forced to agree with the living room of the Svirla household as the location for our smaller gathering. The most important representatives will be there in about half an hour, and they'll want to hear from you in particular, Em.'

The Alliance's unbound little symbol, once again called upon to explain and justify herself. I could *feel* Creon's displeasure in the corner of my sight more than that I saw it – a tension that I now realised had always been there at these occasions, with every blatant expectation laid at my feet. Bracing himself for every knot I'd tie myself into, every lie I'd insist on telling myself and the world around me.

You're not a pawn in this game.

To hell with their hysterical questions. If I answered them wrong, if I didn't answer them at all, they'd still need me to save their arses.

'And you're sure you want me there?' I said, shaking my hair down my back. 'Because I doubt my thoughts on the matter are going to calm anyone down that much.'

She briefly closed her eyes; the fire sputtered between us. 'Em ...'

'I know. I *know*.' The weight I felt was resting on her small shoulders, too – over a century of desperate rebellion, thousands of lives hanging in the balance. But I knew where that weight would lead me if I let it. I'd allowed it to drag me far too close to rock bottom already. 'They won't like my refusal to make that bloody bargain or any weaker version of it. And then what? Are they going to hand me over to the Mother in revenge?'

Her laugh was wafer-thin. 'Of course they aren't.'

'No.' I shrugged. 'So then there isn't a problem, really.'

Except that the ones of them I liked might be furious, too – the alves I'd played cards with, the nymphs who'd accompanied me during my long hours in the library. Hallthor and Ylfreda. Beyla. Edored.

Tared.

Go to hell, Emelin.

I gritted my teeth, steeling my heart against the stab of betrayal. Even Tared's anger didn't change things – not *really*. Either he'd see sense, or he wouldn't. And if it turned out he only wanted to be a friend to the little human girl who hated fae princes and agreed with him on all matters of honour and morality ... well, then I would have to conclude that he didn't want to be a friend to me.

It hurt, that thought. But it was a sharp, clear sort of hurt – a clean cut, not the ragged teeth of doubt that had tormented my heart for all these weeks.

'As you wish,' Lyn was saying, watching me closely with those wide amber eyes of hers. They gleamed in the light of her fire. 'I hope you know what you're doing, in that case.'

'I think I've finally figured out what I'm doing,' I said wryly. 'I'm still fighting the fight, don't get me wrong. It's just that if I'm already risking my life for all of this, I'm not sacrificing my bloody soul, too.'

'Right.' She gave me a watery smile – pride and worry in equal amounts. 'Still, I doubt the others will stop harping on about that gods-damned bargain until they've heard your stance on it. So if you can find it in yourself to have a word with them ...'

She let the sentence die away, the rustling surf and crackling fire filling the air where her voice had been.

I looked at Creon, who hadn't moved – and yet his wings seemed to slump deeper behind his shoulders than a minute or two ago. Gone was the light in his eyes, that explosive joy of his laughter. Instead, all I found in his gaze was cold resignation, the look of a weary warrior once again called to the battlefield. No time to celebrate, to enjoy even a night of simple peace; this was the Silent Death again, born for nothing but bloodshed, his mind never far away from his schemes and strategies.

Was it anger, that feeling stirring in me?

I didn't want to go see the Alliance. Not now. But telling Lyn that we'd see them tomorrow wouldn't solve a damn thing either, not when the mere fact of her presence was enough to stifle all celebratory sentiments we might have felt. We could refuse the call of war, but we could hardly deny its existence now that it had landed at our damn feet.

And its existence was enough to reduce the victory of Creon's voice to little more than a small step forward.

For the gods' sakes. Would this never end?

'I suppose we can come,' I muttered, not breaking Creon's gaze. Expecting, perhaps, that he'd smile that confident, rebellious smile and announce there was no reason for us to go anywhere – that the Alliance could practice patience for a few hours while we finished what we'd started. When he didn't, I sheepishly added, 'If you don't mind, that is.'

The mirthless smile growing on his face was not the one I'd been hoping for. Too bitter. Too dark. *Obviously I mind.*

I let out a joyless chuckle. 'Obviously.'

But I suppose ... He sat straighter, ruffling his wings with another muffled curse. *I suppose it might be better to get this over with, if the idiots insist on making a point of it. We can't afford to lose days arguing about nothing.*

'We really can't,' Lyn said, sounding exhausted. 'Is there anything else we need to discuss, then? Because otherwise I would prefer to get back to the Underground as soon as possible to keep an eye on the mess.'

Back to the Underground.

Back, more specifically, to face Tared again.

Had she deliberately failed to mention him in the past few minutes, even though he must have been there during her dealings with Thysandra and the Council? I wanted to ask if she'd had any opportunity to talk with him after the fight I'd overheard on the beach. If there was any chance of him changing his mind about Creon and me – any chance I wouldn't find myself shoved out of the Skeire home before the day had passed.

But perhaps she wanted to think about him as little as I did, and either way, with less than half an hour to go, we didn't have the time.

'I'm ready,' I said, hauling myself to my feet with a groan and holding out my arm for Alyra. She let out a triumphant little squeal as she hopped onto my shoulder. 'Could we make a quick stop at home, though? I'm going to need soap and a clean dress before I'm capable of having a civilised conversation with anyone.'

Both to my relief and my disappointment, it wasn't Tared we found waiting for us by the shield around the Cobalt Court. Instead, some alf male I vaguely recognised as one of Edored's card friends stood lounging between the remaining corpses of Thysandra's people, appreciatively studying the cuts and burn wounds that had led to their demise.

His grin went a little tight at the sight of Creon and me flying towards him. It wasn't fear, that expression, but it definitely betrayed he'd heard the story of the Sun fleet and its destruction at our hands.

'Found them,' Lyn announced rather redundantly as she landed next to him, wings sputtering out with a last bright flare. The tone of her young voice didn't allow for any questions. 'If you could just get us home? You can come help Beyla here afterwards.'

As if she'd been summoned, Beyla appeared from thin air some fifty feet away, grabbed yet another corpse from the moss-covered slope, and vanished without even acknowledging our presence. Off to Oskya, to stage a battlefield on the other side of the archipelago and hope the Mother would not realise we'd ever set foot on the island of the Cobalt Court at all.

'At your service, Phiramelyndra,' the alf said brightly, chuckling at the scorching glare she shot him while she grabbed his elbow.

Creon put me back on my feet but did not let go of me as he took Lyn's free arm in turn. Alyra tucked her head beneath her wing on my shoulder, talons digging through my dress. Despite his carefree air, the alf didn't waste a moment; he faded the instant we'd all linked up, without so much as a word of warning.

In a flicker, the mountains and the ruins and the torch-lit night of the Cobalt Court dissolved.

For two thunderous heartbeats, everything ceased to exist except Alyra's talons and Creon's strong fingers grasping my forearm; the world swirled around us in darkness and flashes of crystalline stars, wisps of briny sea air and the roar of waves breaking on cliffs. Just two heartbeats, and then it was over. The ground abruptly turned solid beneath my feet, the colours stopped whirling. Roughly woven rugs replaced the rocky ground where I'd stood a moment before, and the smooth, iridescent walls of the Underground eclipsed the starlight and the open skies.

The smell of fresh bread and dusty wool hit me, a smell I had not known I missed but recognised in an instant. *Home.*

My knees almost buckled.

Rationally, I knew not even two weeks had gone by since I'd last seen the long table with its benches, the mismatched armchairs and couch, the green tapestries with the scorch marks Lyn had left in them. Beyla's chess set and Ylfreda's herbs and the sketchbooks with Hallthor's half-finished sword designs ... I *knew* I'd held them in my hands less than a month ago. And yet returning was like stepping years back into the past – a sensation so disorienting I barely noticed the alf male vanishing again, barely registered Lyn asking Creon another question or his signed reply.

Two weeks ago, I'd never laid eyes on the cursed, desolate continent above.

Two weeks ago, I hadn't known I'd find Zera. I hadn't known I'd return godsworn and with a bird familiar on my shoulder, wielding powers I shared only with the Mother herself. I hadn't known I'd hold Creon's binding in my hand and lose it the next moment – that I'd hear the sound of his voice, no matter how damaged, before I'd set foot in this house again.

The living room hadn't changed, and yet it felt smaller. Simpler.

I wasn't sure if I wanted to know what that said about me.

'Em?' Lyn said, and only then did I realise she'd called my name twice before. 'If you were still planning to go find yourself a clean dress …'

Right. The Alliance.

I gave myself a mental kick, forcing a smile. 'Yes, of course. I'll go change and see you there.'

She nodded and scurried out without another word, no attempts to hurry me or badger me about the details of my plans. Alyra remained perched on my shoulder, watching the dark walls and the flickering alf lights with distrustful eyes.

It was only as the door fell shut behind her that Creon turned to me, scarred eyebrow raised a fraction, lips curved into the wryest of smiles. *I?*

I blinked. 'What?'

Singular, he spelled, sinking down on the edge of the long bench beside the table. *Are you planning to go see them alone?*

Oh. *I'll see you there*, I'd just told Lyn. A sentence slipping from my lips without much thought or intention behind it – hell, I hadn't spent much thought on *any* part of the upcoming confrontation, except perhaps for some quiet grumbling and loathing.

Then again …

There was still that weary gleam in his eyes. His sagging wings – barely a few inches beneath their usual level, but noticeable all the same. It wasn't like him to show that much weakness to anyone, to lower the shield of the bored, invincible fae prince even for Lyn – so how close to collapse was he, to allow himself to be so unwillingly vulnerable?

And how much would it cost him to pull up that same shield again, for gods knew how long, in the company of far too many people who wouldn't be subtle about the depths of their dislike for him?

Perhaps my slip of the tongue had contained more wisdom than my conscious mind so far.

'Well,' I said slowly, 'it might not be a bad idea for you to stay here and have a few cups of honey tea instead. You could arguably do with some rest.'

So could you, he retorted.

'Yes, but they want to see me. No one has asked for you yet.' I rubbed my face and added, 'And I'll manage them on my own, I think.'

Even if you manage them just fine, they'll be pricks about it. The way his lip curled up a fraction was alarming – a sign of unravelling control that wouldn't be anywhere near constructive in the company of panicked, furious Underground rebels. *So either you'll feel forced to compromise, in which case I want to stop you, or they'll make you suffer for not compromising, in which case ...*

'You'll want to stop them?' I finished sourly.

He scoffed. *In which case I'll want to rip off their fingers and stuff them into their mouths to see if that might shut them up.*

Alyra squeaked approvingly on my shoulder.

'Right,' I said, letting out a laugh, 'and that is extremely gallant of you, but I can do all of that myself, if I find it necessary.'

He blinked. *Em ...*

'I'll be fine. I promise I will.' I crouched down before him, my hands on his thighs, and looked up at him – his face all lines and shadows, his shoulders slouched. If I'd felt any doubts about my opinions, the festering darkness in his eyes quickly did away with them. 'I'll have Alyra with me, too. If anything goes terribly wrong, she can always fly here to warn you.'

Alyra's accusing glare on the edge of my sight said she *absolutely* wasn't flying anywhere to warn anyone, and definitely not Creon with his unnecessarily sizeable wingspan; if anything were to go terribly wrong, she would be perfectly capable of gnawing off some fingers all by herself.

I pointedly ignored her.

'Creon.' I held his gaze, my fingers tightening on his thighs. 'Are you worried I might end up making some sort of bargain with the phoenixes after all? Because I'm really, really not going to ...'

'No.' The word was barely recognisable from his lips, his grating voice so rough I winced at the sound alone. 'I know. It's just—'

Another fit of dry coughs escaped him, sounding like bits and pieces of his airpipe might be coming out with them. Averting his eyes, left hand pressed to his throat, he bit out a curse and signed with tight fingers, *Want to help. Need to help.*

'There'll be plenty to do tomorrow! And I don't want you put in a situation where your throat starts trying to kill you while you're surrounded by people who'll delight in your suffering.' I gave a scoff. 'Imagine – I would have to break so many noses if they tried to mock you.'

His coughs mingled with laughter. *Cactus—*

'Please,' I interrupted, my voice cracking. 'I made you suffer their hatred for *weeks* without ever defending you the way I should have. Let me do this for you now. I promise I'll be perfectly fine, I promise I won't be taking any risks, and I promise I'll let you know if I need help. Just go inhale some cough syrup in the meantime – *please.*'

The guilt in his eyes cut straight through me – the look of the warrior who would fight himself to death before allowing anyone to harm so much as a hair on my head. He *would* have dealt with the Alliance for me, had I needed the help. Exhaustion and injuries be damned, somehow he would have managed it; this was, after all, the same male who'd survived centuries of pushing himself past all comprehensible pain limits for the sake of victory.

But I'd promised I'd have his back. I'd promised I would protect him, too. And I'd be damned if I let the expectations of the world get between me and that oath once again.

'Alright?' I whispered.

He closed his eyes, leaned down to kiss my forehead. It said everything there was to say, that kiss – an apology, a reassurance, a promise that he would be here and wait for me. The gratitude he didn't dare to feel. Most of all, lingering on his lips against my skin, the stifling guilt that eclipsed it all.

A problem. But a problem for later.

Right now, I had some allies to deal with.

Chapter 3

The house of Svirla was the largest alf family residing in the Underground, and as it so happened, my least favourite one, too.

Part of that had to do with its representative on the Council, sour-faced Valdora, who disliked me enough to disagree even with any compliments I tried to offer her. Part of it had to do with the handful of household members who'd kept objecting to Creon's presence in the Underground for weeks after even Edored had made peace with the fact. All in all, a meeting in their living room was a *little* better than a full Council gathering with all of the Alliance watching, but not by a large margin; my mood hadn't brightened in the slightest by the time I finally left the Skeire family home and went on my way, clothed in a dark red dress that I hoped would properly convey my feelings.

I was late; the meeting had likely already started in my absence. I couldn't summon the energy to be at all worried about it.

A strange atmosphere hovered in the dark corridors – not panic, but something headier, the sense of hundreds of people holding their breath for news to arrive. Little groups were standing around wherever I walked, more and more of them the closer I got to my destination.

Some of them turned to ask questions – 'Is Zera *really* alive, Emelin?' – but most of them just whispered among each other as I passed, and none of them seemed surprised when I didn't stop to answer them. No one pressed for a response. I couldn't tell if I had my own growing reputation to thank for it or Alyra, who sat perched on my shoulder and glared murderously at everyone who made the mistake of coming within five feet of me.

Definitely me, her huffy look at me said.

'Probably you,' I muttered.

She contently ruffled her feathers.

The corridor that gave access to the Svirla home was, hardly surprising, the busiest of all. Without an audience, I might have hesitated when I reached that rune-covered front door behind which handfuls of people were waiting to tell me I was making the wrong choices in roughly every inhumanly imaginable way. Now, with a few dozen nymphs and alves staring at my back, I bit away my doubt and grabbed the doorhandle without faltering, pushing into the narrow hallway beyond.

A cacophony of voices washed over me.

I slipped inside and hastily closed the door behind me, even though it seemed unlikely that anyone outside would be able to make out a sensible word from the noise, let alone a full string of thought. It took me a minute and a half of standing there between the boots and the coats to get some idea of what the fuss was all about – not the phoenixes, surprisingly, or even me, but rather …

The bindings.

'… deserve to get priority …' a shrill nymph's voice shrieked on the other side of the door. 'After that massacre …'

'… no children before the battle anyway …' someone else was arguing – a vampire, judging by the guttural accent.

'… perhaps a lottery …' a female voice sounding on the brink of tears weakly suggested.

The order. The realisation rose in me too slowly, with an incredulous, strangely detached sensation of bewilderment – they were fighting about the *order* in which they might be unbound. Which would presumably have to be decided at some point, for practical reasons if for nothing else ... but good gods, was that really the first thing to start bickering about?

Then again, at least it wasn't those gods-damned phoenix demands.

I sucked in a final breath for courage and opened the last door to step into the brightly lit, glittering heart of Valdora's territory.

The Svirla living room was like a magpie's nest, every free inch of it filled with spoils of war and ancient heirlooms. Against that backdrop of swords, helmets, and richly detailed golden armour, the mayhem of the conversation seemed even more surreal: vampires stood shouting at each other with fangs bared, nymphs were banging their little fists on the marble table, and several alves gave the impression that nothing but guest rights and house sanctuary was keeping them from shedding blood. There couldn't be more than twenty people in the room altogether, but they *sounded* like half an army, and through the throng of sweeping and gesticulating limbs, it took me a moment to make out any familiar faces at all.

But they were there. Of course they were there.

Lyn was sitting on the other side of the room, quiet but with a glower that suggested she wouldn't need much encouragement to set some coats on fire. Next to her, Tared slouched in his chair, staring unfazedly at his nails as a blue-haired nymph wailed about her mother's legacy. Naxi had curled up in a leather chair in the back of the room, looking small and morose, and Nenya was sitting straight-backed on the left side of the table, back to her usual impeccable and mildly frightening look – bright red nails and lips, perfectly drawn eyebrows, black hair braided into a crown-like structure. She looked ready to gnaw a few more heads off, and after the state in which I'd seen her at Zera's temple, that was oddly reassuring.

None of them seemed to notice me.

'I'm *telling* you,' a blond vampire male in ruffled shirt and waistcoat bellowed, every word sharp with frustration, 'that it makes no sense to start with anyone but the vampires! We can create new vampires in *minutes*! If we need a larger army before the battle starts—'

'And what about our magic, then?' snapped a nymph with scaly skin and pearls dangling from her ears. 'I'd rather have ten nymphs who know how to use their unbound magic in a fight than a hundred brand new vampires who haven't even figured out how to bite yet!'

'Has anyone considered,' an alf female drawled, 'that we aren't getting anywhere if fading turns out to be restricted by binding magic, too?'

'Fading has *never* been restricted by—'

'But didn't Lyn say the bindings might start taking wider effect as the war progresses? Lyn? *Lyn?* That is what you said, isn't—'

'Evening,' I said.

They whipped around as if the Mother herself had blown open the door to join the discussion.

If I hadn't been tired and furious and frustrated, it would have been amusing to see the lot of them inelegantly fall silent – eyes widening, jaws sagging, their furious stances suddenly comedic as they froze in their places. It felt like interrupting a poorly written play. Like catching a bunch of children red-handed with their fingers in the cookie jar, spoiling their little game ... except the children were immortals with centuries of life behind them, and the cookies might or might not be the advantages we desperately needed to win a war.

None of these people, my thoughts decided to remind me in that moment, had been drinking tea with a goddess mere days ago.

None of these people had ever carried the hurt of the world in their hands.

My tired, overburdened mind seemed to spin away from itself as that realisation spiralled out of control. I could see myself standing in the doorway all of a sudden, in violent red, my little familiar on my shoulder – in no way resembling the twenty-one-year-old girl I knew from the inside, the girl still wrestling to make sense of the world around her. The woman standing there, head high and back straight, looked like a godsworn mage in all her glory. Like a weapon, like someone who knew exactly what she was doing, like—

Alyra's talons pinched sharply into my shoulder.

'... you've made it,' Lyn was saying, her young voice reaching me from miles away, and only then did I realise that she must have been talking to me for a while. 'Take a seat. People have some questions for you, as I believe you may have noticed.'

Right.

Questions.

'Of course,' I said, even the sound of my own voice a fraction distant. Thank the gods my limbs knew what to do; my body walked itself to the nearest chair as my mind adjusted to the dizzying change in perspective, the grotesque discrepancy between the me I knew and the me the world was seeing. 'Sitting. Such a wonderful thing to do during a meeting.'

Those who had jumped up in the heat of the argument at least had the decency to look a little ashamed of themselves as they hastily slunk back into their chairs. Lyn pressed her lips tight in a suppressed grin; Nenya threw me a quick, fanged smile. Naxi's quiet greeting was more of a whimper.

Tared still didn't look up from his nails.

Not even the shortest glimpse – as if he'd never exchanged his wryly amused glances with me during so many escalating meetings before, those conspiratorial looks reassuring me that I was not alone in my exasperation.

It was his motionless silence that did away with the surreal detachment of it all and plunked me right back into the reality of the moment – my annoyance focusing my thoughts, as always. Damn him, then. If this was how he wanted to play the game ... Well, as long as he didn't jump up to declare me a liar and a traitor, he and his grudges could go enjoy each other's company for all I cared.

I was a godsworn mage, for hell's sake. I was not a pawn in this game. I did *not* need his bloody approval to deal with this meeting exactly as I saw fit.

'Wonderful,' Lyn said as I took my seat, just enough bite in her voice to shut down several others who had already been opening their mouths. 'Let's see – where do we start?'

'Seemed to me like you had already started a rather lively debate,' I said, smiling sweetly with my glance around the table. 'Very interesting arguments. Did anyone bring up the point that we're not exactly ready to start breaking bindings yet?'

I shouldn't have felt so good about the ripple of agitation that ran around the table – but hell take me, it *did* feel like a triumph, seeing their faces go blank for another moment.

'I have mentioned the possibility, yes,' Lyn said, a pointed undertone to her words that told me she had likely done so several times, using increasingly explicit language, with consistently little result. 'What is your estimate of the situation?'

'The main issue is identification,' I said, leaning back in my chair a little more comfortably. Alyra impatiently shifted her balance to stay in place. 'As far as I've been able to see, there are no labels or catalogue books to be found anywhere in the Cobalt Court. Which means I have no idea which of the bindings belong to which individuals.'

A few disconcerted murmurs went up on the other side of the table.

'I see,' Nenya cut in, glaring at the blond vampire who seemed about to launch into another dramatic monologue. 'So what you're saying is that, unless we want to risk matching random bindings with random people—'

'I don't want to end up with fire magic and some phoenix male's wings, Nenkhet,' one of the nymphs snapped.

'Well, that's the most optimistic outcome,' I said, smiling even more sweetly. 'We don't even know whether magic can be moved around like that – whether some random binding could be compatible with anyone else. The fact that the Mother has never granted herself alf or phoenix powers seems to suggest it's not possible, I'd say. Worst case, we might be losing all the magic in that binding or harm the receiver's health.'

The murmuring had quieted into a back-and-forth of even more disconcerted glances.

'And you don't even have a theory of what exactly would happen?' Valdora broke the brief silence, her lips pursed into her distinctive look of unimpressed annoyance. 'I thought you said she was the authority on the matter, Lyn.'

'I've had this magic for three days,' I said coldly.

Her nose wrinkled impressively as she scoffed. 'Some expert you are, then.'

'For the gods' sakes,' Lyn muttered through gritted teeth. 'Valdora—'

'Oh, it's alright,' I said, clinging to my saccharine smile as if I might drown the wiry alf female opposite me with it. 'I'm well aware I have plenty to learn. Why don't you tell me how we're going to solve this problem, Valdora, with your long and plentiful experience on the subject of texture magic?'

She froze for just an eyeblink too long. 'Of ... I beg your pardon, *texture magic*?'

I smiled even more pleasantly.

'Look.' Her chuckle was joyless and sharp as the blade on her back – almost sharp enough to hide her confusion. 'Clearly, *I'm* not the most knowledgeable person here. I'm just saying we should perhaps look for some actual experts, rather than an inexperienced child whose loyalty to the cause is still unclear. That's—'

'A lovely idea.' Had this been any other occasion, I might have flung the insult straight back into her face and reminded her that perhaps the head of the house infamous for its startling illiteracy rate was hardly in a position to doubt anyone's scientific opinions on any matter. But I *had* felt her pain with Zera's bag in my hands, I *had* understood for just one heartbeat what old hurts were driving every word she spoke, and even if the words in question made me wish I'd brought Creon after all to make good on his threats, I knew damn well that retaliation would only make everything worse. 'I would agree with you, if the actual experts existed. Which doesn't seem to be the case.'

She narrowed her eyes at me, distrust written in every line on her face. 'Of course you'd say that.'

'*Valdora*,' Lyn hissed.

'Well, I suppose they *do* exist,' I admitted with a shrug, letting my smile dwindle. 'If you prefer to go ask the Mother for advice, I wish you the best of luck and recommend taking a good sword. Alternatively, you could go look for Etele on the continent. She's quite possibly dead, and even if she is alive, she's certainly insane, but if you like those chances better than having to rely on me, I once again hope fortune is on your side. It would be nice to have a goddess's guidance in this matter, admittedly.'

A short silence fell. Nenya let out a cough that suspiciously resembled a chuckle.

'Here's the thing,' I added, holding Valdora's gaze as I leaned forward and planted my elbows on the marble table surface. She inched away from me ever so slightly. 'I know you're worried about the safety of your people. I know it must be infuriating to have some twenty-year-old show up and start bossing you around after you've been fighting this war for centuries. I *know*, alright? I understand – I really do.'

She stared at me as if I'd starting sprouting antlers. 'You … what?'

'And I didn't want to end up here either, if you want to know.' A gamble, that confession – a degree of vulnerability I would not have risked if I hadn't been so sure about the nature of the pain hiding behind that scowl. 'I'm frightened, too. I'm lying awake at night just as often as you are, worrying what will happen if I fail. But having this power and refusing to even *try* would make me a coward, and if that's the alternative, I'd rather be a failure.'

Some fine alf reasoning. I wasn't surprised to see a few blond heads nodding along on the edge of my sight, although Tared still hadn't glanced my way.

'So please allow me to explain my thoughts,' I finished, spreading my hands. 'If you disagree, just tell me why, and I'll be more than happy to reconsider. But at least do me the favour of believing I'm doing the best I can, too. My life hangs in the balance as much as everyone else's, in case I needed to remind you of it.'

Her lips were parted a fraction, as if she'd been about to speak but realised halfway through that she had lost track of her thoughts – had possibly lost track of whatever the hell words were supposed to be.

Lyn was covering her mouth on the other side of the table, small shoulders trembling dangerously.

'Right,' Nenya said firmly, sitting up even straighter in her black leather-and-lace corset before anyone could break the spell by firing some insult at me. 'So, what are your thoughts exactly, Emelin? I don't presume you want to leave that whole castle full of bindings lying about uselessly until we've lost the war.'

'Oh, no.' I settled back in my seat, drawing an annoyed squeak from Alyra as she once again had to adjust her position. 'There are a couple of options, I would say. First of all, I'm pretty sure Thysandra knows how the bindings are categorised.'

'Yes,' Lyn said slowly, sending me a warning look, 'but—'

'I could see if I can make her talk?' Naxi burst out before I could interpret that gaze correctly, jolting up from her armchair with such vehemence that she almost bounced onto the floor. 'If you just tell me where you're keeping her, I could—'

'Naxi.' I'd heard Lyn annoyed and exhausted before, but rarely quite like this – an edge to her voice that reminded me I was not the only one who'd seen Creon's binding fall and shatter in those moments of chaos. 'For the fifth time: I may usually be agreeable, but I'm *not* an idiot. You're not getting anywhere near that cell before we've ruled out every other option, and you should be counting your lucky stars that we haven't yet chained you down on the opposite side of the Underground. Drop it.'

Naxi sagged back into her chair like a wilting flower.

I might have felt sorry for her if the sound of breaking glass had not still been echoing through the shadowy corners of my mind. Now I forced myself to look away from her teary blue eyes, turn to Lyn instead, and say, 'Did Thysandra give the impression she might be open to a bargain of some kind? Her freedom in return for this information, something like that?'

'She informed me she'd rather be tortured to death than betray the Mother in any way,' Lyn said sourly. 'Don't think she was exaggerating, either.'

I had to admit that sounded likely, from all I knew about her. Still … 'She may not be prepared for more humane approaches, of course.'

'Yes.' She rubbed a curl from her eyes. 'It's worth trying, I suppose. Anything else?'

'We could look for the Mother's administration.' I pursed my lips. 'We know she's able to break individual bindings, so she must be keeping the paperwork *somewhere*. Agenor might know if it's at the Crimson Court, and if it isn't, we could take a look at some other likely locations, which would hopefully be a little less secure.'

Lyn sighed. 'Yes. Let's ask him in the morning. And we can send some people to the Cobalt Court ruins to double check for clues, too. We still have that magical key we took from Thysandra.'

'Yes,' I said slowly.

She raised her eyebrows. 'Doubts?'

'No. I mean, no, we should look for all the information we can find. Just ... we should be extremely careful not to leave any traces.' I grimaced. 'I have no idea how frequently she sends people to take a look, but we'd be in serious trouble if any fae arrived and found our lunch wrapping lying about.'

'So why don't we just move them?' said a willowy nymph I thought was called Kiska, worrying her purple bottom lip. 'She can't destroy them if we're keeping them in the Underground.'

'The identification, though,' I said.

Nenya frowned. 'You think we'd lose information we need to identify them even if we keep careful track of where we found each binding?'

'Well, we don't know what information we need,' Lyn said wryly. 'And I agree with Em that there is a chance. Even if it's small, I don't think I want to risk losing track of everyone's magic and fertility like that unless we truly don't have another choice.'

The room was quiet for a moment as people digested that argument. A few heads nodded in agreement; Valdora remained coldly silent, which amounted to the same thing.

The blond vampire broke the silence. 'So how will we know when we truly don't have another choice?'

'We'll need people on the lookout,' Valdora said brusquely. 'Someone to keep an eye on the court from the outside and alarm everyone as soon as any fae arrive. Svirla could take that upon its shoulders, if needed.'

I thought Lyn would protest, but all she said was, 'Thank you, Valdora. I greatly appreciate that.'

The expression that crossed the alf female's face was not a smile yet, but there was a little more warmth to it than before. *Gratitude*, I realised. Some job to be done – some way to be useful. Who cared if it was not the most exciting, adventurous task, as long as it might at least contribute to the greater cause?

Hell. I really might have underestimated her.

'Alright,' Lyn said, straightening in her seat to her full four feet. 'I think that's all there is to be said on the bindings right now. If any developments occur, I'll let you all know, of course. So that brings us to—'

'The phoenixes,' a grim alf male interrupted.

The room seemed to cool a smidgeon in the silence that followed.

Again, all eyes turned to me – those eyes that had been full of approval a moment ago, now abruptly reminded of yet another reason to distrust me and my motivations. The gods-damned phoenixes. *If and only if Em makes a bargain ...*

Fuckers.

'The phoenixes are a little complicated,' Lyn said, sounding like she was treading on thin ice.

'The phoenixes are rarely *not* complicated,' Nenya mumbled, which seemed a rather worrisome observation to me if her idea of average complications consisted of vampire kings sucking people's veins dry at their convenience. 'Is it true, then? About that bargain they demand?'

So they hadn't told her about it, that night at Zera's temple when we'd received Agenor's message. I shrugged and said, 'Afraid so.'

Someone hissed in a sharp breath next to me. The narrowing eyes around the circle seemed to convey similar opinions.

'Cas has tried to get them to make another suggestion,' Lyn hastily added, drawing the attention back to her own small figure. 'But ... well, we all know how they are. The current stance they're clinging to is that it's our turn to act now, and that they are not offering any new proposals for an alliance until they have received a formal response to their previous one.'

'I'll be happy to send them a formal response to stick that bargain up their arses, if you think that'll help,' I said.

For the shortest moment, I thought I saw Tared's shoulders shake in the corner of my eye. He was studying an enormous silver sword on the wall when I fully turned to him, though, and there was no trace of amusement to be found in the placid expression on his face; some stupidly hopeful part of me must have imagined it.

I gave myself a mental kick. Tared really shouldn't be my main source of worry in this room.

'They are going to be extremely unhappy about that,' Nenya said stiffly, and she certainly wasn't smiling now – *I had myself sucked dry by my worst nightmare to ensure an alliance*, the coolness in her eyes said, *and you're not even considering a compromise?* 'Even if we word it a little more diplomatically. Are we sure there isn't any way around this? If we just bargain you won't *talk* with him and we make sure not to exclude signing ...'

'No,' I said.

'Emelin' – Valdora pronounced my name like an exasperated mother about to send her child to their room for the next three days, with no books or games allowed – 'do you fully understand what's at stake here? We *need* the phoenixes. Fighting fae without any winged forces is—'

'—impossible. I know.' I gave her an apologetic shrug. 'And I'll try and get them on our side all the same, don't get me wrong. I'm just not going to make that bargain.'

Her huff said I'd just lost any and all goodwill I may have fostered with my vulnerable little speech, and then some. 'Is that what *doing your best* means to you? Giving up on your noble intentions the moment you need to make an actual effort?'

Alyra let out a sharp squeak on my shoulder.

'Oh no, you've figured me out,' I said, rolling my eyes. 'Fighting myself to near-death against the Sun fleet and almost drowning as a result was no effort at all, of course. Nor was breaking into the Cobalt Court, actually. Walk in the park.'

'Well, then, what's the matter with that bargain?' one of the vampires barked. 'Surely if you were willing to do all *those* things ...'

'It's the bloody Silent Death we're talking about,' Valdora added with a sharp laugh. 'Even if you consider yourself a ... *friend* of his for whatever unfathomable reason ...'

Oh, damn it, then.

Something seemed to have broken within me this night. As if I was a thread that had been pulled tighter and tighter for weeks, stretched inches past my limits – and now I had snapped, and there was no going back to the lengths I'd once managed to go. What did I care if they all thought me a madwoman, if the few people whose opinions I cared about already did? *It's not that he's a friend of mine*, I opened my mouth to say, the words crystal clear at once. *It's more that I love him so much I'm not sure I can breathe without him. It's more that he's a better person than all of you with your petty fears and grudges combined, and I'd rather lose the war to give him the peace he deserves than sacrifice him to win it. I—*

'It has nothing to do with friendship, Valdora,' Tared said.

I snapped around.

He'd sat up straight in his chair for the first time, grey eyes calm like a ripple-less water surface, that faint, mirthless smile I knew so well around his lips. Still he wouldn't meet my gaze. Instead, he had turned towards the alf female opposite me, his voice a soothing, reassuring contrast to the acidity with which her last words had left her mouth.

Next to him, even Lyn looked a fraction surprised.

'What?' Valdora snapped.

'That bargain.' He shrugged – that nonchalant shrug that could have placated a roaring wildfire. 'We'd be absolute idiots to accept it. Do we really want to grant any of our allies that sort of influence over us?'

I stared at him.

He still didn't look my way.

'Please elaborate,' I vaguely heard Valdora say.

'Here's the thing.' I'd forgotten how reassuring he could sound when he wasn't muttering insults under his breath – how perfectly, naturally in control. It didn't fail to silence a full circle of murmuring immortals now, as he leaned forward and planted his elbows on his knees with the air of a male who has considered a subject for months 'We should keep in mind that whatever we decide here is going to set a precedent for every single one of our allies above. Apparently this is a demand they can make now. So what if Em makes that bargain and Bakaru shows up tomorrow, insisting that Nenya never exchanges a word with a single alf again?'

The room had gone icily, eerily silent.

What in the world was *happening*? I gaped at Tared, not sure how to reconcile the male I was hearing with the male who'd told me to go to hell in the quiet darkness of Tolya, who I'd been all but certain would have me removed from his household the moment everything settled down enough for me to pack my bags. Was I being an idiot and entirely misunderstanding every single word he spoke? Or was he actually …

Defending Creon?

I'd sooner have expected Edored to develop a taste for fine arts and high fashion.

'Well,' Valdora muttered defiantly, 'but—'

'We should remember,' Tared continued, as if she hadn't spoken at all, 'that far too many people out there are quietly but deeply unhappy about the Alliance existing at all. Far too many kings and rulers strongly dislike the fact that we have found a loyalty here that doesn't adhere to their strict lines of species and islands. They won't do anything about it now, while they have a greater enemy to worry about. But I'd be willing to bet the bones of my ancestors that many of them would be very, very happy to see some cracks appear here once we get closer to the end of this war, and bargains to literally forbid communication among us is the most blatant example of it I've seen so far.'

Wolves against wolves, Lyn had said. I glanced at her and found her sitting with closed eyes now, small hands balled into fists in her lap – something to do with the phoenix elders, I suspected, with the island where she had been born yet hadn't lived for centuries.

'So.' Tared's joyless smile might have looked like it was aimed at me, but his eyes continued to stubbornly avoid mine, trailing over the wall behind me before swerving back to Valdora. 'I suggest we don't make the mistake of considering this merely an innocent proposal to guarantee their own safety. Let's not allow the people who have never given a damn about *our* safety to drive a wedge between us and our friends.'

Wait.

Had he just called Creon a *friend*?

It didn't make sense – *none* of this made sense – and yet around me people were nodding hesitantly, muttering words of unwilling agreement. Why was no one calling him out on this obvious nonsense? *Was it even obvious nonsense?* Or was this just how Tared Thorgedson ruled the alves whose leader he'd accidentally and involuntarily become – by sounding sensible at the right moments, and maybe even meaning it, too?

I had been awake for too long. My thoughts seemed to be blurring around the edges, tiredness slowing everything down. If he was truly, sensibly defending Creon here – then hell, why would he still not bloody *look* at me?

'So what do you recommend, then?' someone was saying.

'We reject their proposal.' A hint of that skewed grin slid over his face. 'Perhaps a little more diplomatically than Em suggested, although I see no reason to make it *much* more diplomatic. We remind them that we don't want them harmed any more than they do, and that none of us would let Creon anywhere near them if we suspected dangerous intentions on his part. And then we see what counteroffer they make.'

'That's hardly a *plan*, is it?' Nenya said sourly.

His grin broadened a fraction. 'You should know by now I'm shit at plans.'

'It all depends on their response, anyway,' Lyn added, managing to make her look at Tared look as though this was a topic the two of them had discussed for hours. 'And I can think of a hundred ways they might react, off the top of my head. There's no sense in obsessively working out strategies for all of them if they'll have a message back to us before we're done.'

The group seemed to accept that with surprisingly little protestations.

'So I think we're done for tonight.' The relief in her words was unmistakable. 'Please inform your houses and your bloodlines of all we discussed, and we'll let you know if new information comes up. Any questions?'

A handful of last questions were swiftly dealt with; Tared's intervention seemed to have taken the bite even from those most determined to cause trouble, and none of them directly targeted me. Then people were walking and fading out with muttered greetings and goodnight wishes, leaving just a handful of us behind in that glittering treasury. Naxi slipped out the door without looking anyone in the eyes. Nenya swept out like a stately empress. Lyn skilfully manoeuvred Valdora to the other side of the room, circling back to the subject of the guards the Svirla family would be posting around the Cobalt Court.

That left only Tared and me at the table.

And still, *still* he wouldn't meet my gaze. Watching Lyn and Valdora a few feet away, he absently gathered some loose documents from the marble surface, adjusted the buckle of his sheath belt, raked a hand through his tousled blond locks. Busying himself with absolutely nothing at all. Avoiding me so pointedly he may as well have told me to bugger off and leave him alone.

'Tared,' I hissed.

He stiffened.

'For hell's sake, Tared, could you just *tell* me what you're playing at, rather than—'

And just like that, he was gone – vanished into thin air like a maddening, cowardly puff of smoke.

Chapter 4

It turned out I wasn't so tired after all.

Who needed sleep when there was plenty of anger to keep me going? I could feel it sizzling in my veins as I marched through the now deserted Underground corridors, the culmination of weeks and weeks of worries and annoyances boiling to the surface. *Go to hell, Emelin* – did he really think he could brush me off so spinelessly after that? If he never wanted to see me again, the very damn least he could do was tell me straight to my face.

And if this was how he intended to play the game, I'd *make* him give me my answers, if need be.

But he wasn't in his bedroom, that sparsely furnished, almost austere room which whispered that its owner had already lost all he possessed once and would be damned if he suffered a similar loss ever again. He wasn't in the quiet living room or in the equally empty cesspit Edored called his bedroom. He wasn't in the kitchen, stuffing his face with bread or drinking himself to death on Hallthor's home-brewed honey mead.

Which didn't leave that many options. Really, assuming he hadn't faded into the world outside in some dramatic attempt to avoid every single person he knew for the rest of the night, it left only one.

The same place where we'd grown from wary allies into friends, all those months ago, where he'd grown from a stranger into the patient teacher proud of even my clumsiest stumbling. The same place where he'd called me a little fae brat for the first time, with that wry grin that somehow turned the insult into a brotherly show of affection I had clung to with every fibre of my being.

The bloody *nerve*.

I spun on my heel and sprinted towards the training hall, Alyra fluttering in wide circles around me like some feathery little moon.

'You might want to get out of here,' I muttered, teeth gritted. Something told me she'd try to dig her claws into Tared's face the moment we found him, and if anyone were to gouge out his eyes tonight, I'd bloody well do it myself. 'I'll manage this on my own.'

She did not seem particularly impressed by that argument.

'There are gardens around here,' I added, more hastily now, slowing my steps as we approached the last corner before the training hall. 'There's plenty of rooms to fly there. Some nice trees to take a nap. Doesn't that sound much better than this dark, stuffy place?'

I wasn't even fully sure *why* I wanted to face this fight alone so badly – why even the staunchly supportive, inhuman eyes of my own familiar felt like too much scrutiny. But it ran deep, the anger blazing in my chest. It seeped into parts of me even *I* barely dared to look at closely, and whatever I might end up saying, whatever I might end up doing …

It was *mine*.

'Lots of worms too, probably,' I added, throwing every bit of persuasion I possessed into my voice. 'You must be hungry, after all the excitement of the night.'

That seemed to hit the mark. She wavered, then fluttered down to perch on my shoulder, peering at me as if to determine whether I could still be considered entirely sound of mind and whether I might be joking about the worms.

'I'll be fine', I muttered, and forced a smile. 'Go get dinner.'

She huffed, ruffled her feathers one last time, but flew off in a storm of silvery white down, vanishing around the corner in the blink of an eye. I waited another few heartbeats, then drew in a resolute breath and marched on – rounding that last corner, finally, behind which the rune-covered gate to the training hall was waiting for me.

It stood ajar.

I didn't pause to knock, didn't check whether anyone else might be using the hall at this time of the night. Not even alves were generally mad enough to get up for sword training at two in the morning, after all. Barely slowing down, I flung the door the rest of the way open and stamped inside.

In the dim light, it took me a moment to make out the familiar outlines of the room, the high ceiling and the chests and benches along the smooth black walls. And, sitting on one of those benches in the most shadowy corner of the hall …

Tared.

I skidded to a standstill five steps into the hall, breath shallow, as my mind adjusted to align the sight of him with whatever I had expected. He'd been fleeing me, I'd thought. Had cowardly tried to avoid me, either because he had something to say I would not want to hear, or because he had something to say he did not want to speak out loud.

But the male lounging on that narrow wooden bench, long legs crossed and sword bared next to him, looked like he had been waiting for me.

My eloquent, furious thoughts crashed to a befuddled halt.

He sat up straighter in the same moment, untangling his legs with a sigh all too audible in the uncanny silence of the Underground. 'Evening, Em.'

It was too flat, his voice. Too resigned. In the shadows, his face was as good as unreadable, save for the grim lines around his lips hinting at an emotion I couldn't pinpoint, no matter how hard I tried. Was it anger? Annoyance?

Regret?

'What in hell are you doing here?' I snapped, rage trumping my confusion for a blissfully simple moment.

'Contemplating my sins.' He hauled himself to his feet, his sword loosely in his hand, and nodded at something behind me with that same unnatural restraint over his movements. 'You may want to close the door before you start shouting. People are still awake.'

And gossip *would* spread like wildfire in these nervous, news-hungry hours. Oh, hell take me, was that why he'd faded so shamefully from Ylfreda's living room? To avoid any appearance of a scene in the eyes of the people who'd be all too happy to take note of every possible weakness?

I took five steps back, not taking my gaze off him while I reached behind me and found the doorhandle with my fingers. The slam of wood against stone reverberated through the hall, the noise not nearly enough to soothe the boiling need for justice.

Go to hell, Emelin.

The words seemed to echo in the silence between us, growing larger by the heartbeat.

'So.' He broke the quiet, flicking his blade around once in his fingers – threat or invitation, I wasn't sure. 'Want to grab a sword?'

I blinked at him.

This was madness. All of it was madness. He was supposed to call me a little fae whore and inform me I wouldn't be setting foot in his family home ever again; I was supposed to tell him I didn't bloody care if he insisted on being a hateful arsehole for the rest of his life; and he was supposed to believe it even if *I* knew damn well that it would be a lie. So what was he standing there for, looking like a warrior bracing himself for a losing fight?

'What are you planning?' I said, narrowing my eyes at him.

His grin was mirthless as the grave. 'You know very well ...'

'... that you don't make plans.' I scoffed. 'Yes, I know. Convenient excuse. So what in hell just happened, then? Am I supposed to believe that you just decided to defend Creon because you happened to feel like doing him a favour?'

Tared shrugged. 'Something like that.'

I let out a sharp laugh. 'You're being ridiculous.'

'Am I?' Another flick of his sword. 'I thought this was roughly the change of mind for which you've been arguing for a while.'

'Yes, and it's rather absurd of you to suddenly make that change after centuries of clinging to the same opinions.' My hands were itching, clenching to fists by my side – inches away from the brilliant red of my dress. 'What changed?'

He hesitated a fraction of a moment. 'Lyn shouted at me for a couple of hours.'

I snorted. 'She's been shouting at you for decades.'

'Admittedly.' He briefly closed his eyes, fingers straining around his sword hilt. 'I've never seen him smile like that in all those decades, though.'

I stared at him.

'So' – another shrug, this one more tense – 'I figured—'

'His *smile*?' Thank the gods that I had closed the door behind me, because my soaring voice might have reached all the way into the fields around the Underground. 'You saw him fucking *smile* and all of a sudden decided to stop hating him with a passion? Do you have any idea how utterly laughable—'

'It was never about hating him, Em,' Tared interrupted flatly.

I snapped my mouth shut, breathing heavily. 'What?'

'The hate was not the point. Just—'

'You've been going out of your way to provoke and insult him every minute of the day for *weeks*,' I sputtered, forcing myself to be rational even when all I wanted was to throw my words into his face until it hurt. 'What else was it about, for hell's sake? Was he supposed to take all of it as a slightly misguided attempt to befriend him?'

It seemed for a moment Tared would say something else, but in the end, all that left his lips was a heavy, 'No.'

'But?' I snapped.

'I never said I didn't ...' His eyes flicked down to my red dress; again he seemed to swallow whatever exactly he'd been about to say. 'I never said I didn't strongly dislike him. Just that it was never the point of it all. The main thing I've always been trying to do is protect Lyn and protect you and—'

'*Protect* me?' My voice shot up again. 'You were trying to *protect* me by being an absolute arse to him?'

Tared hesitated. 'Well ...'

Oh.

Oh, gods help me.

Pieces of the puzzle fell into place with such force that it felt like being slapped over the head with them – Tared Thorgedson, forever the older brother to a young alf he hadn't been able to save, head of a family he'd sworn to guard at all costs. Of course it was never as simple as a broken mating bond. Of *course* it wasn't.

'You were hoping he'd leave again.' It wasn't even a question, that sentence stuttering over my lips. 'You knew I would be too stubborn to go anywhere, so ... so you hoped *he* would vanish and leave me alone if you just made his stay with us unpleasant enough?'

His cheerless pause said all that needed to be said.

'Oh, for fuck's sake – Tared, you bloody *idiot*!'

'Look, I'm not saying I disagree,' he said, rubbing his face with agitated, restless fingers, 'but could you try to see for a moment what I was seeing? He was obviously trying to keep you close all the time. You were obviously tense as a bowstring whenever I saw the two of you together. *Something* was making you uncomfortable to the point that you barely smiled for days on end, and you kept refusing to tell me what on earth the matter was. Was I supposed to take all of that as a sign you were totally, blissfully happy to have him around every minute of the day?'

That shut me up for half a second.

'And Creon continued to be so very much ... himself.' Tared's voice remained level, but his overly restrained inhalation betrayed the feelings stirring behind the words. 'The version of him that I remember, I mean. The person who once cheerfully informed me nothing would stop him from using his demon magic to make Lyn simply forget she once cared about my existence. So trusting his good intentions when he seemed just as determined to reopen every old wound between us ...'

Those gods-damned letters. That gods-dammed act of the evil fae prince, all arrogant smiles and vicious quips, an eternity away from the male who would not hesitate for a heartbeat to sacrifice his life for me.

Walls Creon had kept up every waking moment *because* of the others … but that didn't change anything about the side of him they'd seen since the day he'd returned.

'Right,' I said, clenching my teeth so tightly it hurt. I wanted to curse. I wanted to *break* something – stamp on it until there was nothing left of it but shards and dust and perhaps the blazing frustration within me would finally have dulled a little. All those good intentions, all those stupid old fears, and I'd nearly ruined the love of my life. 'And you changed your mind now because …'

'When you showed up with that binding.' Tared averted his face with another deep breath, parting his lips once, twice as he faltered. 'I … I never imagined …'

Creon's smile.

Good gods. I'd all but forgotten that moment, the triumph of it washed out by the panic that had followed – but I *did* remember now, the memory a defiant warm glow just beneath my midriff. A smile that had bloomed on his face like a flower unfolding its petals, offering its incomprehensibly vulnerable heart to the harsh, merciless world outside.

Not the smile a calculating villain would be able to feign. Nor one that villain would *want* to feign, for that matter.

'Right,' I managed again.

'I'm not a demon, you see,' Tared added, a hint of wryness in his voice as he met my gaze. 'I can't tell what's in people's hearts if they refuse to show me. But I know the face of a male in love when I see one, and even if I still think he's a self-conceited bastard with too much power on his hands …' His joyless smile was an apology and an acknowledgement all at once. 'I couldn't in all honesty keep believing he was a danger to you once I saw that look on his face. So that changed matters a little.'

'I'm going to need that sword,' I said.

His smile broadened into an equally joyless grin. 'Chest to your left.'

I was already moving. Violent frustration was buzzing in my limbs, or perhaps it was my pent-up anger losing its sense of where to go; if I forced myself to hold still a minute longer, I might end up losing control over my generous supply of red and accidentally bringing down the ceiling.

The chest contained a good number of slightly rusty swords – *real* ones, not the sword-sized training sticks I'd been swinging around at imaginary enemies for weeks. They were old and unused and forged from common steel rather than alf steel ... but it still felt alarmingly good, wrapping my fingers around a coarse leather hilt and lifting three feet of whetted metal from its resting place to do my violent bidding.

'Keep that wrist straight,' Tared said behind me.

I quickly adjusted my grip as I turned.

'Excellent.' He sauntered closer, sword in his hand loosely swinging back and forth with his steps. 'All set to murder me, then.'

'I don't want to *murder* you,' I said, rolling my eyes without taking my focus off him. If months of training under his guidance had taught me anything, it was that I rarely saw his earnest attacks coming until it was too late. 'Just hurting you a little will do.'

He chuckled. 'Impress me.'

As if we were back at training, back at our usual games and challenges. As if none of this journey had ever happened – as if I was still just as much at home in the Underground as I'd ever been, no nagging fears that perhaps this world had never been built to grant a haven to godsworn unbound mages.

As if he'd never snapped those words in my face. *Go to hell, Emelin.*

I took a swing – too quick, too reckless. He blocked it easily, retaliating with an attack I only barely dodged.

'You know what the problem is?' I said between gritted teeth, eyeing the seemingly nonchalant circles of his blade as we both retreated. 'I'm pretty sure I told you several times that I was fine and didn't need your help. Even if you were worried, you could have done me the honour of treating me like a bloody adult and *believing* me, rather than running off with your own prejudice and taking matters into your own hands.'

'Which is an interesting argument to make,' he said, sword never faltering, 'given that you've technically been lying through your teeth for months.'

'Oh, you're going to blame *me* for that now? You're—'

He lashed out so swiftly his sword blurred into a silvery streak of light. I interrupted myself with a blurted curse, fending off the attack in a reflex so intuitive I didn't realise what I was doing until our blades bounced off each other with a metallic shriek.

'Don't throw too much weight into the move,' he said, drawing back again. 'You'll lose your balance too easily.'

I nodded wordlessly, shifting my hands on the hilt as I regained my footing. My elbow was hurting a little from the force of that clash. I easily ignored it; the spinning fury of my thoughts was a far more urgent injury.

'So who should I blame for the lies, then?' he added, never changing his tone of voice. 'Did anyone force you to tell them?'

'No!' Too shrill. I couldn't let myself get carried away now; he'd just attack again if I allowed myself to lose control. 'For the bloody gods' sakes, Tared, don't you see I was lying because of *you*?'

He faltered. I shot forward – two could play that game – but he'd recovered before I could complete my swing at his left shoulder, dodging with an impossibly quick turn to the right. His voice did not waver. 'Please elaborate.'

'What in hell was I supposed to think after you spent hours nobly and helpfully insulting the person I happened to be madly in love with?' I feigned an attack. He didn't bite. 'For all I knew, you'd kick me out of the house if I told you, and that—'

He stiffened.

My strike forwards – no more than another half-hearted attempt, a challenge more than an attack – shot straight past his defences, past an alf steel blade that barely even *tried* to stop me. I only just managed to change direction, to twist my own weapon away from the path straight to his heart. The steel edge bit into his left arm instead, meeting the sickening resistance of skin and muscle before swinging free again.

I cried out.

Blood sprung where my sword had been an instant before, spreading through his grey shirt within moments.

'Oh, *fuck*.' I staggered back, weapon clattering from my hands. *Hurt you*, I'd said, and only now did I realise how little I'd meant that threat;

the sight of that wound was the fastest antidote to the brewing anger inside me. 'Fuck, Tared, I'm sorry. Let me heal—'

'Kick you *out*?' he interrupted, his own blade sagging.

'Tared, your arm!'

'To hell with my arm – where in the world did you get that idea, Em?' That was genuine shock in his voice – as if an executioner was merrily enquiring, axe over his shoulder, why I had ever been so silly to fear for the state of my neck. 'Did Creon—'

'No! And stop blaming him for everything, for fuck's sake!' My voice shot dangerously close to the point of shrieking. '*You* are the one who told me go to go hell the moment you found out! Was I supposed to take that as a friendly invitation into your home? When you were angry enough to—'

'Yes, of course I was angry!' he bit out with a wide swing of his injured arm. Blood was trickling over the inside of his elbow now. 'I'd just found out you'd been lying to me for months, that you got *Lyn* to lie to me for months, and I couldn't fucking figure out why. How does that have anything to do with—'

'It wasn't just that fight! You've been doing it since we got here!' I clenched my hands into fists – anything to keep them from trembling as the bitter truth finally poured over my lips. 'You never went a day without reminding every person in the world that you could barely stand to look at him – so how was I supposed to tell you the truth when I knew damn well you'd disagree with my decisions and might do gods know what in response? Did you ever even consider what that might look like to me, your stupid hateful campaign to get him out of here when I told you so many times I didn't want him to be going *anywhere*?'

He stared at me for a long, bewildered second, then turned away with a sharp intake of breath, sliding his sword into its sheath in the same movement. The trickle of blood had reached the wrist of his left hand now; he either hadn't noticed or didn't care.

'Tared ...' I started.

'Alright,' he said, raking a hand through his already messy blond locks. His voice was unusually unsteady. 'Seems like I have underestimated the misunderstanding and overestimated my own clarity of communication. By a rather significant margin. Give me … give me a moment to figure out what's going on here.'

'It's rather clear what's going on here, isn't it?' I ground out.

'Not to *me*.' A small groan. 'You actually thought—'

'Tared, you were an arse! And also really very angry!'

'Yes, but …' His voice caught; he shook his head as if to chase off a nagging fly. 'Look, I've been living in the same house with Edored for centuries. What part of that gave you the impression I make a habit of kicking people out over a fight or two?'

I scoffed. 'That's different, isn't it?'

'Is it?' His eyebrows shot up. 'I can assure you he's pissed me off *much* more over the years than even the ill-advised lies of some little fae brat ever did.'

'Half fae,' I grumbled reflexively.

He grinned. 'Irrelevant. You have a long way to go if you ever want to reach those levels of exasperation, Em.'

'Yes, but …' I swung a frustrated gesture in the rough direction of the Skeire home. 'Edored has been family for longer than I have lived. He's … *blood*. That's not … you know?'

Tared didn't move – didn't even blink. 'What?'

'What, what?'

'I … I'm afraid I'm not following you.' He rubbed his sleeve over his wounded arm, frowning at me. 'What in the world does blood have to do with anything, exactly?'

'Well, some people care about that sort of thing,' I said shrilly. 'Valter and Editta did, apparently.'

'Valter and Editta,' he said with a groan, 'are human heaps of shit who don't have the faintest fucking idea of the daughter they could have had if they'd pulled their heads out of their arses for half a minute. Let's just assume the rest of their judgement is equally flawed, alright? I feel that'll be more efficient than having to disprove every other bit of nonsense they decided to instil in you over the years.'

My throat clenched violently and without warning, turning every gulp of breath into a lungful of thorns and brambles. Fuck. I was *not* going to think about that moment of understanding with Zera's bag in my arms, the fear and hurt I'd sensed in the hearts of the people I'd called my parents – I was *not* going to curl up on the floor and bawl like a lost child. But my voice came out like a squeak all the same. 'Alright.'

His frown deepened. 'Do I need to find a slightly kinder way to describe them?'

'It's not that,' I managed. 'I'm just ... I'm trying to understand how alves define their families, if blood doesn't have anything to do with it.'

'Ah.' He blew out his cheeks. 'Well, that's easier. You've eaten at our table, you've slept in our beds, you've risked your life for us and we've risked our lives for you. Which means you're one of us now, as far as I'm concerned. We're simple creatures, really.'

I stared at him – couldn't stop staring at him, as if the sight of his slender face and tousled blond hair would make the words he was speaking any more comprehensible.

One of us.

This was entirely too simple.

'But ...' Words had come so easily a moment ago, and now I just found myself gaping at him in silent astonishment, feeling like I was slipping – sliding away over the smoothest ice, grasping desperately for any grip or support. It *couldn't* be this easy. He had been much, much too angry for it to be this easy. Surely he would tell me next that he was no longer joining me for sword training from today on. That he wished me good luck telling the rest of the Underground about this nonsense on my own. Or worse, perhaps he wouldn't *say* anything, only treat me with just a hint of frigid distance at breakfast tomorrow and never again grin as broadly at me as he used to ...

'Em,' he interrupted my frantic thoughts, head tilted a fraction, grey eyes examining me closely. 'What is the matter? I'm telling you you're not going anywhere. There's no reason to be scared here. Why are you looking at me like I just announced your dying day?'

'I just ...' My voice came out like a child's squeak. 'I'm trying to understand ... You're not going to keep holding it against me? That I lied to you? For ... I don't know, theoretical eternity?'

He stared at me.

I stared at him.

An endless stretch of silence ticked by. Contrary to the usual nature of time, I felt myself grow younger and younger with every moment of it – shrinking, shrivelling into a little creature that could be crushed with a single barbed smile.

Tared did not smile.

'I suppose,' he said finally, slowly, visibly searching for words even as he spoke them, 'that that explains a couple of things. You never told me the worst of it, did you?'

'Of what?' I yelped.

'Those human parents of yours.' His lip curled into a small sneer as he repeated, voice sharp with disgust now, '*Parents.*'

It was that disgust that hit me like a fist in the stomach, and at once I knew the nameless dread bubbling up in my lower belly, the poisonous claw of failure – the sensation of not even knowing *what* was wrong, just that *I* was wrong, that I'd failed and disappointed and turned out to be wholly unsatisfactory. My anger had seeped out of me like sand between my fingers. I couldn't even joke anymore. It was too sharp, the memory of Valter's letter pressed into my hands – it still stung too deep.

My parents.

My gods-damned parents.

'Orin's eye,' he muttered, and as composed as that curse came out, his expression suggested vivid visions of Valter whimpering under his worktable while an alf sword cleanly and efficiently sliced the workshop to shreds. 'Alright. I suppose it would have been helpful if I'd adequately grasped from the start how different our frames of reference are here.'

A shivery laugh escaped me. 'I'm still trying to grasp whatever your frame of reference is. Even if I'm one of you ... if you don't want Creon around and I'm determined to keep him with me ...'

'Did Lyn ever tell you why she left Phurys?' he said slowly.

My heart thudded. 'What in hell does that have to do with anything?'

He let out a joyless chuckle. 'That's a no?'

'She didn't, no, but—'

'Ah. Well, here's the short version.' He sucked in a slow breath as he turned and sauntered a few steps deeper into the hall, leaving a trickle of blood drops behind on the dark stone floor. 'There had been a number of ... incidents before everything exploded between her and the elders. But the one thing that eventually made the bastards inform her that it would be better if she left the island and took up living somewhere as far away as possible was that they were unhappy she was getting a little too involved with some primitive northern barbarian.'

'You mean ...' I blinked at the blond back of his head. 'You?'

'Yes.' The suppressed fury in his voice was tangible. 'Of course, she insists that it was not my fault and that she made her choice knowing what the consequences would be – but I've seen her wrestle with those same damn consequences all the same, and three centuries of guilt are a long time to build resolve never to cause anyone that sort of anguish. So' – he threw me a glance as he whipped back around, lips a thin line – 'I'm not kicking *anyone* out over their dubious taste in partners, Em. Not even if it's Creon we're talking about. Do I need to be any clearer on that?'

My thoughts seemed to come in stutters now.

That haunted gleam in Lyn's eye whenever the phoenixes were mentioned, her paling face at the suggestion they might want a word with her in person ... Signs Tared must have known and recognised for hundreds of years. I'd seen that quiet anger inside him and misunderstood it all this time – had thought it was a threat, waiting to aim itself at me at my slightest misstep, while in truth it had always been my ally, ready to destroy anyone who threatened to pull me away from the safety of my home.

My limbs were no longer buzzing.

'And if it *is* Creon we're talking about ...' My voice cracked. 'You're not angry about the damn fact that I love him? Just ... just about the lies?'

'Well, I don't *like* it,' Tared said, his sour smile a more outspoken confirmation of the fact. 'Quite hate it, really. But if you're sure this is what you want, I can either make peace with it or never see you again. So I'll make myself handle it somehow.'

'Oh,' I managed.

'That seemed so obvious to me,' he added helplessly. 'I didn't realise you'd think ...'

'That you'd tell me to go pack my bags instead?'

'No.' He let out a slow breath, meeting my gaze with a slightly frayed version of his usual stoic equanimity. 'I suppose that renders the anger a little misplaced, in hindsight.'

And then the tears were leaking from my eyes anyway, rolling over my cheeks in hot drops of shame and relief. I didn't *want* to cry, damn it. I was a grown woman, not a snotty, snivelling child in need of cuddles and reassurances …

Then again … what if I was?

One of us.

The tears flowed harder.

'Em …' He stepped closer, holding out a slightly bloodied hand. 'I'm so very sorry. Come here, little brat.'

I all but flew into his arms.

His hug was tight and protective. *One of us.* I buried my face into his shoulder and cried as if my tears could be an antidote to that poison still festering inside me – the memories of an empty bedroom on Cathra, of a letter trembling in my hand. The fear of every damn thing I'd thought I'd been about to lose, and every desperate decision I'd made in my attempts to save myself.

'It'll be fine, Em,' he muttered, patting me clumsily on the shoulder. 'On my alf honour. It'll all be fine.'

Which sounded impossible, laughably so, and yet … Something miles deep in my chest uncoiled for the first time in ages, maybe for the first time in my life. A very first inkling of understanding. A very first notion of what life might be with that certainty of family in it, with that ever-present safety net waiting beneath my every step.

A loud, violent safety net with a tendency to recklessness and excessive drinking … but so very safe all the same.

'Do you want me to inform the others about Creon and tell them to behave?' Tared added quietly. 'If you prefer not to do it yourself, I mean?'

Even now, my first instinct was to flinch – to imagine Edored's explosive fury and Hallthor's stoic disapproval and Ylfreda wondering out loud if she should check me for brain damage after all the battles

I'd recently survived. I didn't want *anyone* to tell them. The fear was still there, rotting in the marrow of my bones – a sensation like being perched atop a narrow ridge, where every wrong move could send me toppling down into the depths.

But the safety net was there. And if I never fell, I'd never learn that, either.

'Please,' I whispered. 'I would very much appreciate that.'

'Will do.' He finally let go of me, the gleam in his eyes betraying every emotion that familiar skewed smile of his was trying to hide. 'We're alright, then?'

I let out a teary, snotty chuckle. 'You were the angry one.'

'You were the frightened one,' he retorted, squeezing my shoulder before he stepped back and slipped his hands into his pockets. Half of his sleeve was soaked with blood now. 'So if there's anything else worrying you, I would very much like to know. Anything else you've been too afraid to tell me?'

'Don't think so,' I muttered, and when he quirked up an eyebrow, I sheepishly added, 'Promise. On my alf honour.'

For the first time in days, his smile looked like his own again – that laconic, perfectly composed grin that said there was no trouble in the world we wouldn't solve in the end. 'Oh, we'll make a decent alf out of you one day, don't worry.'

And for some reason, that was enough to loosen another knot sitting tight in my chest.

'Am I finally allowed to heal that arm, then?' I said hoarsely.

'Oh. That scratch?' He glanced down at his soaked sleeve, then stripped it up to his bicep to reveal a small, clean cut that still bled ferociously. 'You should let Ylfreda stitch it up and taunt me about the scar forever as the first time you managed to draw blood from me.'

I huffed a laugh and grabbed his wrist before he could object. 'I'm not *that* much of an alf yet. Hold still.'

He looked amused but obeyed. A single quick flash of blue from his shirt was enough to stop the bleeding; when I cleaned off some of the blood, only a pale strip of skin showed where the wound had been.

'There.' I let go of him, wiping my fingers on my bare forearms. 'Ylfreda will be unhappy enough with me for nicking her contraceptives. Don't need her to think I tried to kill you, too.'

'The true way to infuriate her would have been *not* to steal them when you needed them,' he said wryly. 'It'll be fine, Em. I'll have a word with the family. The best thing you can do is go get some sleep in the meantime.'

Sleep. When war was looming so close I could smell it. When we still had to figure out the bindings and manage a handful of obstinate phoenixes and somehow make sure not to die in the process.

But Creon was waiting for me in his bedroom – *our* bedroom, damn it – and no one was going to kick me out of it.

'Right.' It came out a little breathless. 'If you're very sure there's nothing else you need me to do right now …'

'There'll be more than enough on the list tomorrow.' He ruffled my hair, then stepped back, nodding at the door I'd slammed behind me when I arrived. 'Go to sleep, little brat. And thank you for stabbing some sense into me.'

Thank you? It seemed we still hadn't reached the deepest depths of this madness – but I was tired to the marrow of my bones, my thoughts a tangle of emotions I likely wouldn't fully understand for a while, and I couldn't muster the energy to point it out to him. If he had decided I'd done him a favour by falling in love with his worst enemy and injuring him over it, who was I to cause trouble?

'You're most welcome,' I said weakly. 'See you tomorrow, then?'

'See you.' He gestured in the direction of the Skeire home – the direction of Creon's room – with one eyebrow raised ever so slightly. 'I'll knock before coming in.'

If I hadn't been so relieved, I might have thrown something at him.

But good gods, it was *intoxicating*, this sudden lightness as I floated back into the shadowy corridors. The Underground still felt too small around me, the dark walls surrounding me like an ill-fitting coat on my shoulders. Passers-by still glanced at me with too much unease. Whispers rose quietly behind my back wherever I turned, loud in the absolute silence of this buried realm.

But I still had my friends.

I still had my family.

So surely I would soon feel at home again in this place, I firmly told myself. *Surely* I would.

Chapter 5

For the first time in months, I slipped into the Skeire home and then Creon's bedroom without feeling like a burglar. No more wincing at creaky hinges or backward glances before stepping into this forbidden place; after all, if loving a monster wasn't the crime I'd feared it to be all this time, who cared if they caught me?

And with the way I'd left him behind, I had more urgent things to worry about.

'Creon?' My voice echoed in the midnight silence, and I couldn't be bothered to keep it down, to guiltily close the door behind me before I started speaking. 'Creon, are you—'

I interrupted myself, two steps into the room.

He wasn't there.

He must have been around since our return to the Underground: his boots were standing next to the old desk, wet and sandy from the Cobalt Court beach. His favourite knives lay next to the books on his nightstand, too, and his travel bag had been flung into the farthest corner. But the chairs and bed were empty, and the bathroom was dark behind the half-opened door; the Silent Death himself was nowhere to be seen.

I blinked, too tired to instantly make sense of the observations. Where else could he be? My bedroom? But we *never* met in my bedroom, and—

'Looking for something?' an unknown voice said behind me.

I shrieked and whipped around.

And there he was, leaning against the doorframe with a steaming earthen mug in his hand and that most mischievous of smiles on his face – shirt half-buttoned, dark hair spilling loose over his shoulders, looking so astoundingly like he'd always done that it took my drained mind a full three heartbeats to figure out what had just happened. A stranger's voice. Coming from behind me. Coming, more specifically, from the exact spot where he was standing …

Oh.

Oh.

'Creon?' I said again, breathless now.

'Tea helped,' he dryly added, nodding at the mug he was holding – full lips moving in perfect synchronicity with the words I heard, and *still* it barely seemed real, that rich, hoarse baritone emerging from his mouth. 'And a whole lot of blue magic. It's still not exactly where it used to be, but all things considered …'

Some sort of sound fell over my lips.

His smile grew into a devilish smirk as he took a sip of tea. 'Anything wrong, cactus?'

'No.' It came out frantic. 'No – absolutely nothing wrong. Keep talking. Are you alright?'

'Bit of a sore throat,' he said and shrugged, stepping into the room and inching the door shut behind him. I didn't seem capable of moving – as if even my feet were too busy listening, soaking up every drop of that husky drawl through whatever means available. 'Which I'm sure will heal itself soon enough, and even if it doesn't, it doesn't really matter. It seems a rather decent price to pay.'

He spoke more slowly than I'd expected from the speed of his signing – not an air of slow-mindedness but rather of thoroughness, or perhaps the languid confidence of a male whose audience would generally be wise enough not to wander off or interrupt him. His Faerie accent was just a little more pronounced than I'd anticipated, too, lending a melodious lilt to my human language. For the very first time, I found myself wondering whether the Mother may have taken his voice as a sensible precaution, rather than for the sake of petty revenge – because this velvety timbre, this mesmerising cadence ...

Gods help me, this was the sort of voice that could make people *do* things.

'It ... yes.' I wasn't even fully sure what I was saying anymore. Who in hell cared about my words when *he* was talking – those lips I'd kissed so many times, bringing forth those breathtaking sounds? 'Very ... very decent.'

He put his tea on the desk, set himself on the edge of the wooden tabletop, and cocked his head at me with eyes that twinkled alarmingly. 'Glad you agree. Why is there blood on your arms, if I may ask?'

'What? Oh.' I glanced down, blinking at the finger-shaped smudges on my lower arms. 'I had a chat with Tared.'

'A ... chat,' that husky voice repeated.

It was unnerving, to hear him speak without seeing his expression. I realised in that moment I had no idea how to interpret the emotion behind those unhurried tones, not without the facial clues to help me out – was this what his suspicion sounded like? His incredulousness? His amusement?

I looked up and found him studying me with lips pressed tight – straining against what I knew must be a grin about to break through. Amusement, then.

'You know,' I said weakly. 'Alves.'

'Did you ...' He faltered, a delicious little hiccup that must be the sound of laughter about to overcome him. 'Em, did you *fight* him?'

I grimaced. 'I might have?'

He burst out laughing.

Zera help me, his *laughter* – it rolled over me like magic, a melodious sound so rich and full of life that I could do nothing but stand there and drown in it, soaking it in like warm sunlight on the first day of spring. He laughed like a male set free. Like all the weight in the world had been lifted from his shoulders for the first time in centuries and he could finally breathe again, the music of it resonating not just in the air between us, but in my very soul.

And somehow, the emotion that bubbled up in me in response was ... anger?

It was sharp, that feeling. Bitter and disconcertingly violent. Aimed not at him – at the shaking of his wings and shoulders and the crinkles of mirth around his eyes – but at these years and years of silence, every single time I'd seen him laugh and believed I'd known the depths of that scarred black heart. Most of all ...

At his mother.

His gods-damned mother.

'Oh, I'm going to *kill* her.' The bitter promise burst over my lips before I could think twice, the only way out for that fury building, burning in my chest. At once my feet were moving again; I stumbled towards him with a wide swing of my hand, flung up at the world above. 'The bitch – how could she? How *could* she? I—'

His hand closed around my wrist.

He pulled me against him with one swift movement, and then his lips were on mine – a kiss smothering my every bloodthirsty oath, drinking in the fire of my rage. His free hand knotted in my hair. His mouth was hot on mine, seeking entrance. I opened up to the coaxing demands of his tongue, and he swept in, releasing the roughest, quietest moan as our bodies melted together.

It turned out I had not yet forgotten those messy moments on the beach.

Heat stung my core, not anger but something far more dangerous. I nipped on his bottom lip, and he growled into my mouth in response – a brand new sound so ferocious that I had to grab his shoulders to keep my knees from buckling. His hand vanished from my wrist. Fingers clawed into my bottom the next moment, yanking me flush against him, pressing me so close I could not fail to notice the hardening bulge against my lower belly.

I gasped. I couldn't help myself.

'So violent,' he muttered, his warm breath brushing over the skin just below my ear. His fingers were inching down over my thighs, all the way to the hem of my dress – the strangest thing, to feel him and hear him at the same time. 'Did I ever tell you how utterly irresistible you are when you're threatening bloody murder in my name, Em?'

'It wasn't a seduction attempt!' I managed, the words coming out on a moan. 'I *am* going to kill her.'

'Oh, I know. It's just ...' Calloused fingers found my bare skin, slipping below my skirt the next moment. His wings flared out around me, enveloping me in an embrace of shadows. 'You don't have the faintest idea how relieved I am to have my little warrior back.'

There was just the tiniest crack in his voice – an almost inaudible catch, yet gods help me, it hit me like a fist to the throat. His signs I was used to. His wounded glances I'd seen before. But that little tremble, the hurt in it that he didn't fully manage to suppress ... As if every shield had fallen from around him and I was speaking directly to the fragile creature inside, that child so starved of love it had believed itself unlovable.

Guilt burrowed its claws into my heart so suddenly I winced.

'I'm so sorry.' The words came out on a choked whisper. 'Fuck, Creon, I was such a fool to ever think—'

He kissed me again.

'Hey!' I tore away from those sweet lips, breathing heavily. His arm around my waist wouldn't allow me to put more than a handful of inches between us, but his fingers stilled on my thigh as I glared at him. 'You'll have to at least allow me to properly *apologise*, Your Highness. I'm not going to let you pretend I didn't do anything wrong when I almost broke us up over—'

'You didn't break up anything,' he cut in – hell, that *voice*, the edge of roughness and the warmth below. 'You made mistakes and fixed them. Entirely different story.'

'I shouldn't have made the mistakes in the first place,' I flung back, 'and also, what do you mean, fixed them? You don't even know what I told Tared!'

He shrugged, the gesture too languid for my agitation. 'I know how you feel.'

I speechlessly stared at him, those almond-shaped eyes so close I could distinguish every sliver of colour in the black of his pupils – stared at him, and *felt* him look back at me, the weight of that demon gaze piercing far deeper than my bland ditchwater eyes and the lines of my face. Seeing me. Knowing me. Reading me like an open book.

The whirl of my emotions quieted obligingly, like children skittering off under a stern gaze.

'I barely know how I feel myself,' I breathed, standing unmoving in his arms. 'I haven't had time to figure it out.'

He sighed, closing his eyes. 'You've been a bundle of anxiety for weeks – no matter what else you were feeling, it's been brewing beneath the surface every moment of the day. Whereas right now ...' He parted his lips, hesitated – as if to taste the air around me. 'Exhaustion. Anger. Guilt. Little bits of arousal. And triumph, mostly. Blazing triumph, no fear to be found.'

The breath had caught in my throat.

'So ...' He smiled faintly and opened his eyes, gaze wandering down to my arms against his chest. 'I assume the blood isn't yours.'

A shivery laugh escaped me. 'It ... it isn't.'

'Excellent,' he muttered, and gods, that was an entirely new tone of his voice – like the deepest, richest cherry wood, unpolished but brimming with fire. 'No need to break every bone in his body, then.'

'Oh, no.' I managed a grimace. 'He apologised.'

'Even better.'

'Said he was just trying to protect me from your lecherous wiles – not in those words – by being an arse until you would leave us all alone. Without informing me of it, of course.'

A muscle trembled at the corner of his lips. 'I take it you told him what you thought of that strategy?'

'Hence the blood,' I said sheepishly.

His grin broke through. 'Then it looks to me like there isn't that much left to feel guilty over, wouldn't you say?'

'No, but you don't get it!' This time he did allow me to break away; I stumbled half a step backwards, regretting the move as soon as the cold air found the skin that had been pressed against his muscular body a moment ago. 'Even if we're fine *now*, I can still blame myself for all the hurt I caused you in the meantime, can't I? I messed up so much of it. I ...'

'Well,' he said, settling both his hands on the edge of the desk as he tilted his head at me again, 'you never saved the world before, of course.'

'No, but ...' I squeezed my eyes shut, fighting for words. 'Look, I want to save *you* as much as I want to save the bloody world, alright? It's bad enough that I can't magically undo three centuries of suffering with some clever blue magic – I shouldn't be adding so much as a single bloody day to it if I can help it.'

'That *is* a little ambitious, Em,' he said, some emotion in his voice I didn't quite recognise yet.

I scoffed. 'We're not going to win the war without a little ambition either.'

'Cactus ...'

He hesitated. I didn't look his way – didn't quite dare, unsure if that had been disappointment in the hoarse tones of his voice, and very sure I had no desire to see proof of it had that been the case.

'They are entirely different things,' he eventually said – speaking even more slowly now, no unhurried confidence but careful contemplation of every syllable that left his lips. 'The past few centuries as opposed to whatever pain you could cause me. I spent half a life assuming that what my mother felt for me was love, and the other half believing I must truly be a monster if I wasn't even worthy of *that*. So having you here after all of that, just ... just *feeling* ...'

Again he faltered. I looked up before I could stop myself, meeting his gaze half a step away – dark eyes reflecting every shard of old hurt I could catch in his voice, every twinge of regret.

Not disappointment.

Definitely not disappointment.

'You could never hurt me like she did unless you abruptly stopped giving a damn about me,' he said quietly. 'Which was never the case. So you're in no way bringing back those years – I just don't want to lose you. I don't want to feel like ... like I may not be quite worthy of you either, in the end.'

'Like when I started betraying you to a bunch of alves,' I grumbled.

A chuckle broke through the restraint. 'Who's the dramatic one now?'

'I'm not trying to be dramatic!' My voice cracked. 'It just feels like I'm nowhere close to putting things straight. You can't just shrug this off and pretend nothing happened when—'

'Your problem is you're waiting for some punishment,' he interrupted, leaning leisurely as ever against the edge of the desk as he ran a hand through his long hair. 'Which I suppose is natural, given that you grew up with parents who wouldn't allow you to forgive yourself for a mistake unless you'd suffered appropriately first. It's just nonsense, too.'

I blinked at him. 'What?'

'I said it before, Em.' He folded his arms. 'You're not some pet I'm trying to train.'

'I feel like you're oversimplifying this,' I said, sucking in a deep, barely controlled breath. 'It would be extremely natural for you to be angry with me, yes?'

'Is that what you want? Anger?' A small, wry grin. 'Because that will reassure you I won't quietly continue to resent you, if at least I've been allowed to hurt you back?'

'You're impossible!' I sputtered. 'I'm just—'

'Let's reverse the situation,' he cut in, waving my objections aside with an elegant gesture of those calloused fingers. 'Remember that time I fled the Underground and left you on your own because I couldn't get together the fucking guts to face my own magic? You never really got angry about that, if I recall correctly. Are you still waiting for me to set things straight there?'

'What? No!' I bit out a laugh. 'You hurt yourself plenty in those weeks, for a start. Why would I ...'

He just quirked up an eyebrow.

My jaw fell shut.

Hurt yourself. I heard myself say it again, a strange echo in the back of my mind – like these weeks of fear. Like months of denying what I wanted, denying *who* I wanted, for some dream of peace that turned out to be as impossible as it was ridiculous, a burden far too heavy to be carried by me alone.

'Oh,' I whispered.

There was a dangerous air of victory in the little smile he sent me. 'Made my point?'

'I ... I suppose so?' The room seemed to tilt around me a fraction, my legs suddenly no longer so steady as a billowing relief knocked out the ground below my thoughts. 'I mean ... if you're really, really sure ...'

'That there's no reason for you to keep apologising if you could be kissing me instead?' he dryly suggested. 'Pretty sure.'

And at once it was no longer a stranger's voice, finding me through the motions of those sensuous lips. No one could sound that much like him and still be a stranger to me – I recognised him not by tone and timbre but by the sheer sensual arrogance lacing those words, by the teasing quality that somehow resembled his every wicked smirk. There was a challenge there that I knew all too well. I hadn't been able to resist it since the first day he told me to calm down and stay out of sight – the overwhelming allure of his reckless confidence, of a game to play and a battle to win.

Or lose.

I wouldn't mind losing, either.

'Bold of you to assume kissing would be the alternative,' I said with a little snort, taking another step away from him. Damn it all, then. No more apologising. If he wanted his challenge, he would bloody well get it. 'Who says I'm not crawling into my own bed as soon as I'm done saying sorry? It's been a pretty long day, all in all.'

His gaze followed me even though he didn't move a finger, the weight of his attention a thrilling caress on my skin. 'Oh, I'll be the first to agree sleep would be your wisest choice.'

I narrowed my eyes at him. 'So?'

'So I assumed that wouldn't be your preference,' he said innocently. 'But correct me if I'm wrong.'

If we hadn't been at war yet, that would have done the trick – the pleasant, doe-eyed audacity. Gods help me, but I'd missed the sudden, addictive rush of this game, just the two of us and no force in the world to stop us; no armies to command, no diplomatic niceties to observe, and most of all, no consequences to fear.

'What,' I said and scoffed, 'you think *I* would be tempted into foolishness by that moderately agreeable face of yours? Pinnacle of wisdom that I am?'

His eyes glinted with devilish amusement. 'Could you tell me more about the inconceivable wisdom behind sucking people off on beaches, or is that beyond my immortal mind to grasp?'

'I'd never do such a thing, as you know very well,' I said indignantly. 'The notion alone fills me with horror.'

'Could fill you with some other things?' he blithely offered.

It was so dangerously exhilarating, the ease with which we found this brand new rhythm – a dance as much as a sparring match, back and forth, dodge and strike. Armed with his voice, he was somehow even more effortlessly provocative; my body responded to the languid sensuality in his tone as if it was a physical touch. It took all I had to keep my voice from wavering as I rolled my eyes at him and said, 'You'll have to be a little more specific for me to even consider that offer. I don't make blind deals with fae.'

'Some wisdom at last, Thenessa,' he muttered.

He pronounced the title as if he were tasting some exotic delicacy, lush lips shaping the syllables with an almost indulgent pleasure – making it sound unbearably sensual, suddenly, in that melodious accent of his native tongue. This time, there was no denying the shivers running down my spine. I just managed to huff and turn my back on him without sinking to my knees on the spot; even though I knew he could feel the heat gathering below my skin, at least my pride remained mostly intact this way.

His laughter behind me did not help the fraying seams of my self-restraint in the slightest. 'Oh, bad news, cactus. Looking away from me is not going to shut me out anymore.'

'Why would I want to shut you out?' I retorted, scowling at the wall as I untangled my braid. 'I'm not *afraid* of you, much as it may surprise you. I'm just preparing to go to bed, since you've so far failed to propose anything more substantial.'

'On the contrary,' he dryly said, 'I'm offering you something rather substantial indeed.'

I huffed. 'Your self-esteem?'

Even his chuckle somehow sent my toes curling in my boots. 'I can feel every stutter of your heart, Em. Scoffing at me is not going to save you.'

'I'm not here to be saved,' I informed him without looking over my shoulder, shaking out my loose locks and kneeling to untie the laces of my boots. 'I'm here to win.'

He didn't reply.

Something rustled behind me – wings against shoulders or hands over wood, I couldn't tell with my back towards him. Was he moving closer?

Or had I just imagined that feathery sound?

I cautiously straightened, skin tingling with merciless anticipation, ears straining to catch every breath and whisper. Could that have been a footstep behind me, that near-inaudible tap?

I'd *never* talked to him with my back towards him before. It had simply not been possible. The newness of it was enough to send my heart rattling against my ribs, the sensation of his presence behind me with nothing but his voice to cling to. My hips, my shoulders, the back of my neck ... they seemed to burn under the potential of his gaze, the knowledge that he was *there*, possibly about to touch me, possibly a full five strides away.

Was that the sound of a quiet inhalation to my left?

It took every ounce of self-control I possessed not to spin around and find him, sitting on the desk or sneaking up on me or anything in between. Instead, I stepped out of my boots and stripped my socks off my feet, suppressing the urge to hurry. Sooner or later, he *would* have to say something, wouldn't he?

Would he?

My eager ears couldn't catch the faintest clue – nothing but a slamming door in the far distance, a shred of shouting beyond the walls of this buried home. Wrestling to keep my breathing even and controlled, I freed myself from my fiery red dress with slow, deliberate motions, dropping it on top of my boots in a rustle of fabric. In nothing but my underwear, the temptation to stand still and let him ogle me was almost too strong to bear – but I wasn't *waiting* for him, damn it, and I hooked my fingers around the soft linen of my drawers almost without pausing.

'So tell me,' he murmured – suddenly so close behind me I almost shrieked and jumped, 'what victory are you looking for, exactly?'

Was that his hot breath against the back of my neck? My heart was racing so vehemently I feared it might burst through my ribs at any moment, heat creeping up my skin wherever his eyes might be wandering. My voice had gone hoarse, but at least it didn't tremble as I said, 'Your surrender, mostly.'

I felt his laughter more than heard it – both the gossamer brush of air over my bare shoulders and the sparks stirring in my lower belly in reply. 'Ah. Planning to make me beg for you?'

That purred suggestion licked down my spine in flames of ice-cold fire, leaving goosebumps in its wake. I squeezed shut my eyes, grateful he would at least not be able to see that little sign of weakness, and managed an almost natural chuckle. 'Would you?'

'Do you think there's anything I *wouldn't* do for you?' Another faint rustle behind me, like velvet sliding over velvet; when I hurriedly opened my eyes, the dark shapes of his wings were slowly folding into my sight on both sides, like a snare closing in on me. Yet he didn't touch me, not even as his voice slid into a flowery, almost theatrical declaration. 'My loveliest, most terrifying cactus ...'

'You're mocking me!' My voice wobbled all the same.

'I wouldn't dare,' he muttered, and suddenly there was a new edge of hoarseness to his words, a raw quality that had nothing to do with sore, unused vocal cords and everything to do with the reverent way his wings curled slowly around my naked body. 'I'm fully fucking honest when I say no one has ever frightened me as much as you do. I've never had this much to lose before.'

My breath hitched. 'Creon …'

His wings wrapped around me, velvety edges brushing down my collarbones, my breasts, my nipples. I gasped, and his hands followed around my waist at the same moment, sliding over my skin, creeping ever so slowly down my belly, His solid chest was there behind my back as I arched into his touch. I sagged against him, resting my head against his shoulder with a sound that was a plea as much as a moan.

'Then again …' His whispered words were hot against my neck, barely audible over the roar of blood in my ears. The strokes of his wings against my nipples sent my body throbbing with desire. 'I've never had this much to win, either.'

'Please,' I managed, squirming against him, trying to get some friction, *any* friction, over that burning spot that so desperately needed his touch. Gods, the rough sound of his laughter stroking over my skin …

'Very well,' he murmured, and finally, *finally* his hands slid down those last inches, beneath my underwear, through the dark curls at the apex of my thighs. 'Take your victory, Thenessa.'

I exploded at the first touch.

Like a coil wound tight enough to snap, my body unravelled under his fingers, coming sweetly, beautifully, powerlessly undone – weeks of secrets, weeks of fears and frustrations all shattering to pieces the moment he brushed over that hankering core of my pleasure. I cried out, convulsing through my blistering release as he held me to his chest and drained me with slow, gentle strokes.

Gods help me, I *had* won.

A surge of triumph had me moving before I became aware of my own limbs again, wriggling around in his arms to free myself. This time, he let me. I dragged him to the bed by the sleeve of his half-buttoned shirt, and we toppled into the blankets in a tangle of limbs and wings, my fingers fighting with his buttons as he claimed my mouth with his. Rough groans answered my moans. A muffled cry escaped him when

I dug my nails into his hips. I tore off his shirt with frantic eagerness, stripped off his trousers as if my very life depended on the sight of his bronze skin and straining muscles; his cock jutted free like a voracious beast, ready to devour me.

'Keep talking,' I breathed, pressing him onto his back as I struggled out of my underwear. 'Please ... *anything*.'

He came up on his elbows, wings spread wide over the blankets. 'Is this the moment to tell you how utterly bewitching you look in the blood of my enemies?'

I crawled over him, laughter bubbling out of me. His answering grin was positively wolfish – not the look of a predator finding his prey, but rather ...

Rather, a predator finding his match.

I knew every inch of that warrior's body below me. The lines and bulges of his muscles. The scrape of his nails and the silken softness of his skin. The musky fragrance of his arousal and the slick hardness of his erection as I wrapped my hand around it. And yet all of it felt thrillingly, gloriously new as I positioned myself over him and guided our bodies together, his chest rising and falling rapidly as he watched me with dark, ravenous eyes.

Mine.

War would come. Blood would spill. Empires might fall before the year was over, and we could only hope they wouldn't be ours. But the archipelago itself could sink into the sea tomorrow and it wouldn't change a thing about *this* – our perfect little world, two minds, one heart, and enough power to challenge the gods themselves if need be.

'*Our* victory,' I whispered.

He let out a guttural breath. 'Our victory.'

I sank down onto him in one fast slide.

A raw, broken grunt tore from his throat, and if I hadn't been soaked yet, that would have done the job – that throaty cry of lost control. His wings unfurled, sending a faint draft of air down my back. His hands tightened on my bottom, lifting me off him, dragging me back down, filling me to the hilt in that one deep thrust.

I smothered his next groan with my lips, our ragged breaths mingling.

Coherent thoughts lost their meaning. I rode him hard, desperately, steered by his fingers on my hips and the rhythm of his moans; every other sound fell away around me, drowned out by that intoxicating melody of his pleasure. His cock was throbbing steel inside me. My body strained, stretched by his need – a sensation that was neither pain nor pleasure but something far more glorious, something that smouldered hungrily at the core of me.

And nothing else mattered.

Just him.

Just me.

Just the flames under my skin, ready to burn the whole damn world to ashes.

He came with my name on his lips, flooding me with hot seed as he slammed me down over his cock one last time. I followed half a second later. We clung to each other as we rode through our release in a haze of moans and trembling limbs, hands clawing at slick skin, tongues tangling in breathless kisses – until I was nothing but a sticky, sated mess and so damn happy I could explode with it.

And *still* his voice was there, grounding me even as I sobbed and trembled, even as the bed and the night ceased to exist for one small eternity.

'Emelin. *Emelin* …'

He did not let go of me as he lowered the both of us into the blankets, arms and wings wrapped tightly around me, face buried in my hair. He did not let go of me as he whispered my name once more, as if he couldn't stop testing whether his voice was still there, whether there would be more than empty air in the motions of his lips.

A hundred and thirty years of silence, and he was talking again.

One day, I swore to myself, I would make him sing again.

We curled up in the bed together, huddled close in the darkness, my back pressed so tight against his chest that I could feel his heartbeat like my own. His fingers brushed along my shoulder, my arm. And just as my eyelids grew too heavy to keep them open, just as my thoughts began to scatter into dreams, I heard his voice one last time.

'*Liria.*' Even breathed so quietly, I could make out the Faerie word. *My love.*

And I slept.

Chapter 6

A SHARP, INCESSANT KNOCKING woke me, forcefully dragging my mind from the depths of my dreamless slumber and into the bright, noisy reality of wakefulness. I was sitting straight up in the blankets before I'd even opened my eyes, grabbing for the nearest black surface.

Only then did other sounds reach me. Running footsteps in the distance. Clamouring voices within the home. Next to me, Creon shot out of bed with feline swiftness, snatching his blades from the nightstand before he seized his trousers from the floor – taut bronze skin, rippling muscles, yet I couldn't quite marshal the usual appreciation for the deeply alluring vision of his naked glory. The knuckles against our door hadn't paused their urgent, pressing rhythm for a second.

'What is it?' I yelled, shoving myself out of bed, shooting into my underwear, and plucking my dress from where I'd dropped it last night.

The knocking abruptly stilled.

'Developments at the Golden Court.' Tared's voice made its way into the room muffled by the layer of wood separating us. 'The Moon fleet finally attacked fifteen minutes ago. We've started evacuating.'

I froze.

Attacked.

The word seemed too far removed from this safe, quiet room with its piles of leather-bound books and its plush, roughly-woven blankets, too far removed from the safety of Creon's arms. It took a determined effort to drag my mind back into the deadly world above, where the Mother's armies swarmed the archipelago – that world that wouldn't let me escape, no matter how hard I tried to forget about it.

'Do you need help?' Creon sharply said, and I jolted all over again at the unexpected sound of his voice.

'We're managing so far.' Tared sounded tired; I vaguely wondered if he'd had any sleep at all tonight. 'So not urgently, no. I just figured you would want to know that Agenor—'

Agenor.

The paralysis shattered.

I yanked my red dress over my head so fast I almost strangled myself and hurried to the door on bare feet, flinging it open. Tared stood behind, slightly dishevelled but with his sword still sheathed – no urgent danger, then.

Not *here*, at least.

My heartbeat refused to come down in the slightest.

'Is he safe?' The question burst over my lips with a violence that surprised me. 'Agenor? Did he—'

'He's fine, Em. He'll be here …' A small, unexpectedly ominous grimace flickered over Tared's face. 'In a moment, probably.'

'What?' I bit out. 'Is that a problem?'

Tared parted his lips, hesitated, then shifted his gaze over my shoulder without a word – into the corner where Creon was calmly and meticulously buttoning his shirt.

Something shifted in his eyes in the same moment. Something old and dark and very, very tired.

For just one staggering heartbeat, the room seemed to still between the three of us. I spun around, abruptly a helpless, powerless onlooker again – like that afternoon in Zera's forest, flashing blades and magic, my presence nowhere near enough to soften centuries of bitter hatred. The air between them grew just as charged now, the silence just as pressing. Their gazes met with the exact same weight to them – or rather the *awareness*, so very alive in both their minds, of every old wound inflicted between them, every hissed insult and heartfelt threat exchanged over the course of centuries.

Creon's scarred eyebrow twitched up ever so slightly. Not an attack. If anything, it looked like an invitation.

I could swear even the walls were holding their breaths around us.

'First of all,' Tared said, and he spoke the words with such visible effort that I wondered if he'd spent half the night rehearsing them to himself, 'I owe you some overdue apologies.'

Creon's expression didn't change.

He continued to fasten his shirt, scarred fingers slipping button after button into place so excruciatingly slowly I wanted to shake him – as if it had been little more than a comment on the weather, an empty remark not even worthy of the faintest reply. But his eyes didn't stray. And there was something in that look on his face that spoiled every attempt to believe him uncaring and unaffected – the shadow of an emotion held tightly in check.

I waited.

He lowered his hands, finally, and nodded – a single, barely perceptible nod, but there was no venom in it. His voice was carefully level as he said, 'Appreciated. And mutual.'

And that was all?

My heart stuttered back into motion, relief flooding me as much as confusion. Tared merely nodded, too. Creon averted his gaze and began rolling up his sleeves with short, snappish motions – a clear enough message that anything of importance had been said and it was time to get on with the actual order of the day.

Weren't they supposed to … *actually* apologise?

Or was this enough, a hard-won mutual declaration of intent, and had they quietly reached the unspoken agreement that there was no need to push themselves through the embarrassing work of actually *speaking* the apologies? Were they just planning to save each other's lives a handful of times, get drunk together once or twice, and consider that enough of a truce?

Perhaps that was simply the way all emotionally constipated warriors understood each other, I decided at just the same moment Creon looked up from his busy work on his sleeves and added, 'And second of all?'

There was a hint of relief in Tared's joyless chuckle – as if he had been bracing himself for a painful conversation about both of their past failures and would rather stick his sword through his limbs a couple of times. 'Second of all, I should perhaps have informed Edored about the two of you *after* he ran off to help evacuate Agenor's people. Looks like he was so absorbed by the news that—'

The front door slammed.

And Agenor's voice, louder than I'd ever heard him before, bellowed, '*Where is he?*'

'Well.' Tared grimaced, an apologetic gesture at the heart of the house. 'That. So I thought you might appreciate a quick warning. If you feel like getting out of here and postponing the joyful reunion, let me know.'

In the living room, I could hear a decidedly unamused Ylfreda snap something about manners and no bloody way to behave as a guest.

'Ah,' Creon said, the unwilling amusement in his hoarse voice so tangible that I had to make an effort not to laugh out loud with hysterical relief. 'Much obliged. I doubt I'd calm him down much by vanishing on him, though.'

Tared gave half a shrug – *on your head be it*, that gesture said – and turned, raising his voice ever so slightly. 'He's here, Agenor.'

The heated exchange in the living room abruptly broke off, brisk footsteps hurrying closer.

Creon threw me a quick grin, looking utterly undeterred by the fae equivalent of a rumbling volcano marching in for his head – looking *amused* more than anything, the bloody madman. I might have informed him of my doubts on his sanity if Agenor hadn't stamped around the corner in that same moment, appearing impossibly more murderous than the thick red snake coiled around his neck.

'You!' my father snapped, slightly out of breath and looking unusually unkempt with his short dark hair in tangles and streaks of dust and dirt marring the sapphire silk of his shirt. He barely seemed to register my presence at all. Every sliver of his furious attention lay fixed on the six feet of princely magnificence next to me, Creon's state of half-dress adding fuel to what had already been plenty of fire. '*You.* What in hell did you think …'

He faltered, visibly struggling for words that would even *begin* to convey the depths of his fatherly wrath. I might have felt touched if not for my slumbering annoyance, which seemed to be the main emotion the events of the past night had left in me – exhaustion, triumph, and a deep, almost unnerving eagerness to stamp every tiny nuisance in my life into the ground, risks or consequences be damned.

'I'm off to go settle a few hundred fae in their new homes,' Tared said, unfazed. 'All your remaining limbs are most welcome for lunch in an hour or so.'

He faded without waiting for a response.

Agenor barely seemed to notice, glowering at Creon with narrowed eyes and his gold-flecked, godsworn fingers clenched into fists. Creon must have noticed but merrily pretended not to, smiling his most innocent, most infuriating smile at my father like some snot-nosed little boy determined to get a rise out of the adults in the room.

I met the gaze of the snake around Agenor's neck. She seemed about as exasperated as I felt, resting her narrow head on his shoulder with an expression that suggested she currently regretted not having been born a constrictor.

Time to intervene before she did, then.

'Is this some prelude to, say, dowry negotiations?' I said, breaking the mounting silence with all the insincere lightness I could throw into my voice. 'Because in that case, I'd like to have it stated for the record that I think I'm worth at least several pieces of cattle. Probably a nice little farm, too. Just for your consideration.'

The corners of Creon's lips twitched dangerously, ruining that insincere, uncaring air of his in most satisfying ways.

'Em,' Agenor said through gritted teeth.

'What, am I supposed to modestly retreat and leave it to the men to determine my fate?' I said, rolling my eyes at him. 'Don't be a prick.'

He drew in a slow breath, closing his eyes for a fraction of a moment. 'Creon?'

The gleam in Creon's eyes as he leaned back against the wall and folded his arms was nothing less than alarming. 'Yes, old friend?'

'Oh, go to hell.' I'd never heard anyone pronounce that curse with so much heartfelt hope that its target may actually obey the command. 'Could I have a word with my daughter? In *private*?'

'Hardly my decision,' Creon said dryly. 'Ask your daughter, I'd say.'

Agenor's fingers twitched ominously near Coral's leathery red skin. 'For the bloody gods' sakes—'

'Oh, stop it,' I burst out, flinging up my hands as I glared at the both of them. 'Do we really need to be so bloody dramatic about this? Agenor, I'm happy to have a word if you can stop pretending I'm some helpless damsel to be rescued. Creon, you *do* realise there is no actual need to keep up this bloody act for the rest of eternity, don't you?'

His grin was just a little remorseful. 'But he makes it so *easy*, Em.'

'I seem to recall some conversations about needlessly provoking the people supposed to be your allies,' I said with a scoff. 'Do I need to remind you, or—'

'Oh, never mind. You're probably right.' He hauled himself upright with a groan, away from the wall, and reluctantly turned to face my father. That unfaltering mask of the swaggering fae prince melted from his face in the same moment, revealing the expressive features I knew so well below – the exhaustion and the wry amusement and something ... something that may just be the faintest hint of nervousness. 'Would you like a cup of tea, in that case?'

Agenor blinked.

'Or something stronger?' Creon added over his shoulder, striding to the wardrobe to pick clean socks from the drawer. Even with the knives at his belt and the inked scars rippling beneath his skin at every flick of his fingers, I'd never seen him look so harmless as in this moment – rummaging through heaps of knitted items to find his favourite pair. 'I could probably get my hands on Edored's mead supply, if you're in need of potentially life-threatening doses of liquor after this morning.'

'After …' Agenor's mouth opened and closed, his brows drawing closer as he looked back and forth between the two of us once, twice. 'Are you trying to poison me?'

'For fuck's *sake,*' I said.

Creon sent me a quick grin – not that cocky, overconfident grin of the Silent Death, that expression that spoke of nothing but seduction and murder. This smile was duller. Softer. Most of all, more genuine than anything I'd ever seen on his face in my father's vicinity. 'I told you it would be easier to just go on as we did before.'

'You're all idiots,' I grumbled, plopping down on the edge of the bed with another frustrated gesture at them both. 'Agenor, why in the world would he want to *poison* you?'

'In all fairness—' Creon started.

'Don't make it worse!' I desperately interrupted, flinging a habitual crackle of red magic at his face. He avoided it just as routinely, laughing out loud. 'Agenor …'

'I'm not *accusing* him,' my father said, looking bewildered. 'I'm just saying he hasn't offered anyone a cup of tea in his life, so how am I supposed—'

'Factually incorrect,' I cut in, waving that argument away. 'He did the moment I arrived at the pavilion for the first time, just to name an example. Anything else?'

'To be honest,' Creon muttered, sinking down in the nearest armchair to put on his socks, 'I was mostly hoping it would calm you down.'

I huffed a laugh. 'The first of many mistakes.'

He chuckled – a genuine chuckle with not a sliver of bloodlust below the surface. It turned out Agenor could look even more confused.

'I think he'll survive without the tea,' I told Creon.

'Probably.' He put on his second sock and got up, grabbed his boots, and squeezed my shoulder with his free hand – such an innocent touch, and yet under my father's disapproving glare, it turned into something heated and forbidden, sending my pulse racing no matter how hard I tried to keep it down. The wicked glint in Creon's eyes was proof enough he knew exactly what he was doing. 'I'll go take a look at the Golden Court, then. Try not to tear off his limbs.'

'That's your area of expertise,' I said sourly.

He sent me an amused and rather impolite gesture and nudged the door shut behind his back, leaving me alone with a vexed father, an equally vexed snake, and a room that showed just a few too many traces of the very naked, very adult activities in which we'd been engaging a mere handful of hours ago.

I plastered a patient smile onto my face and said, 'So?'

Agenor was looking remarkably like a winged, well-dressed thundercloud trying to be polite as he sucked in another deep breath, flexed his calloused fingers, and cleared his throat. 'So.' The strain in his voice betrayed there were about a hundred more aggressive approaches he was actively suppressing. It clearly took all he had to instead grit his teeth and settle for a barely restrained, 'Would you mind telling me what exactly is going on here, Em?'

'You seem to have a rather good idea of what is going on here,' I said with a snort. 'And don't you want to sit down?'

He did not give the impression he wanted to sit down but did so nonetheless, cautiously sinking into the armchair Creon had just vacated, as if he expected the wood and padding to erupt into flames any moment. Coral slithered from his shoulders, over the armrests, and onto the floor, meticulously avoiding my dirty socks and boots.

I braced myself. 'What do you want to know?'

'The full story would be a good start,' he said sharply, rubbing a restless finger over his temple as it to press back a building headache. 'All I know is that Edored suddenly stormed up to me and wanted to know if I knew whether Creon likes to play cards, because Tared ...' He closed his eyes, pronouncing every subsequent syllable with clipped, furious precision. 'Because Tared apparently dictated Creon was to be welcomed into the family as pleasantly as possible? Which—'

A choked sound escaped me.

His eyes flew open. 'What?'

'Oh. No. Nothing.' Nothing besides alves and their incomprehensible ethics, at least, and Edored and his unexpected enthusiasm were hardly a problem in the grander scheme of things right now. 'What else do you want to know, then? I can't think of anything in particular I'd like to add, frankly.'

'Gods and demons, Em,' he sputtered, dropping his hands to his armrests with a fluster that didn't suit his dignified stature in the least. 'Are you out of your bloody mind? I thought I made it clear enough that he's the *last* person in the world you should be getting involved with, and—'

I shrugged. 'You were a little late with your wisdom, I'm afraid.'

'A little …' He snapped his mouth shut, wings and shoulders sagging as the implications of those words registered. 'Oh, gods have mercy. All this time?'

I shrugged again.

'For hell's sake,' he said bleakly. 'What have you been *thinking*?'

'Well,' I said, 'have you seen what he looks like?'

The utterly appalled expression springing onto his face was worth every ounce of recklessness and then some. I chuckled despite myself, unable to help it. I was only making things worse – I *knew* I was – and yet there was a warped sort of triumph in allowing myself the freedom to be a brash idiot after all that time of cramped, desperate prudence.

'This is no *joke*, Em,' he ground out.

Something in his voice sobered me up faster than even the most vigorous outburst could have done.

It was the crack of helplessness, perhaps. The almost desperate plea in his eyes and the way his fingers gripped his armrests, struggling to hold on. I had prepared for anger and indignation, for fatherly disapproval that I could defiantly ignore. For threats and demands and attempts to drag me out of Creon's reach, no matter how hard I insisted my wishes were the opposite.

But instead, the male opposite me was doing the one thing against which I hadn't hardened my heart nearly so well: worrying.

'Oh, fine.' I looked away from those unnervingly troubled eyes, rubbing my face. 'I'll try not to treat it as one, then. What are you so concerned about, exactly?'

He let out a mirthless laugh. 'What part of "the most dangerous individual I have known in my life" is failing to get the message across? I don't want to see you hurt by—'

'He's not *hurting* me!' I protested, voice soaring. 'He never has! And weren't we all past assuming he was just looking for an opportunity to kill me or use me against you?'

'That's not what I mean.' He let himself fall back in the armchair with an uncharacteristically unrestrained gesture, wings folding uncomfortably between his tall back and the faded, floral cushions. 'I know he's on our side – as much as he'll ever be on anyone's side. I'm not worried about your physical safety.'

'Then what is it – bloody public opinion again?' I scoffed. 'Because I've thought about it for a bit, and I've decided the public can go walk into the sea with their opinions. I can't please all of them anyway.'

'Not the point either,' he said, pinching the bridge of his nose with agitated fingers. 'I'm just trying to understand ... Hell, what in the world are your plans with him, Em? Beyond this war, I mean? Is this just some ... some temporary fling? Or are you hoping for more than that in gods-know-how-many years down the road?'

I bit back several impolite answers welling up in me, settling for an icy, 'I don't see how that is anyone's concern but mine, to tell you the truth.'

He muttered a curse under his breath.

'Agenor—'

'Listen,' he interrupted, sounding as if he'd like to grab me by the shoulders and shake me until I obeyed that exasperated command. 'I know he can be charming, alright? I know he's perfectly able to choose the right words to get what he wants to get and achieve what he wants to achieve, and gods know you wouldn't be the first to fall for pretty promises. If you're expecting more from him, there's absolutely nothing to blame you for.'

I slapped my mouth shut, forcing the least genuine laugh I'd uttered in weeks. 'What exactly is your point?'

'What I'm trying to say ...' He paused, fingers fidgeting purposelessly. 'You should realise Creon wasn't born for peace and contentment, Em.

The war is in his blood and bones. He's not going to settle down and take up gardening for the rest of his life, no matter how peaceful the world around him, and I don't want you to expect some grand romance, only for him to break your heart in a couple of months when he runs off for fresh blood to shed.'

I was beyond the impolite answers now.

Through the deafening rush of blood in my ears, I could only stare at him – at the tired lines around his mouth and the cramped twitches of his fingers and those green-gold eyes, so full of worry, looking so very much like mine. All those good intentions. All that honest concern. And then these were the words born from those commendable feelings, all rot and poison – enough to make the godsworn magic itch under my skin in hungry ways I did not want to think too long about.

Pretty promises.

The fucking gall.

'I know you mean well,' I heard myself say, my voice strangely level against the anger thumping through my veins. 'So I'll be polite about it just once, alright?'

He narrowed his eyes. 'What do you—'

'Here's the thing,' I interrupted, every muscle in my body so tense it felt like I might snap in two. 'Until five minutes ago, you apparently weren't aware he drinks tea. Is that correct? While I can assure you he does – buckets of it. Preference for mint tea, with a slice of lemon if he can get it. I presume that's news to you, too.'

Agenor frowned, gold-flecked fingers rubbing the silk cuffs of his shirt. His voice was stiff as he said, 'I fail to see what his lemon tea has to do with the matter of—'

'What I'm trying to say, you log-headed idiot, is that you don't have the faintest idea of *who he is*.' My voice was rising again. So much for the attempt at politeness. 'You can proudly wave around the fact that you've known him since the day he was born, and I'd like to counter that apparently, in three centuries and a bit, you've never managed to realise there even *is* a person you don't know behind the façade he's always shown you at the court. Do you have any idea what he thinks about when you're not around? Do you know what makes him smile?

Do you have the faintest fucking clue of what he does in his spare time, when he isn't torturing himself to death or scheming against the Mother?'

Judging by the slightly hollow expression on Agenor's face, the concept of spare time in relation to Creon had never occurred to him in the first place. 'I ... I don't think—'

'No!' I snapped. 'Exactly! Much easier to assume he delights only in the sensation of fresh blood on his hands and has no hobbies but the seduction of poor, innocent virgins than to actually *think* about what you know of him, isn't it?'

Agenor huffed a befuddled breath. 'But—'

'He likes astronomy,' I said, biting out the words like arrows aimed at vulnerable flesh. 'Did you have any idea? He'll spend whole days puzzling over star charts if you let him – something to do with triangulation and oscillating stars, whatever the hell any of that means. I've never seen anyone get that excited about the connection between ellipses and gravity. You should ask him about his theories on Kothro's brightness someday – you won't be able to leave for the next thirty minutes, but I guarantee you *will* learn something new from the experience.'

Had I described the Mother as a gentle, humble lady with a particular interest in flower arrangements, my father could not have gaped at me any more bewilderedly.

'He likes to cook.' I counted the points on my fingers. 'He likes to read books by philosophers who argue endlessly about the true meaning of the word *meanwhile*. He likes flying at night, and in storms. He likes cats. I don't suppose any of that rings a bell?'

'I ... Good gods, Em.' His deep voice was cracking, as close to thinness as it could ever be. 'He's never—'

'*Exactly.* So my point is' – I underscored the words with the theatrical gesture of an illusionist about to reveal his grandest trick – 'that maybe you're not entirely in a position to tell me about his hopes and dreams and future intentions, you see? Which is the polite way of putting it. Please don't make me start a family feud by telling me I'm wrong.'

Agenor blinked at me. Then blinked at the floor and blinked up at me again, thoughts visibly spinning red-hot behind his eyes – making frantic attempts, doubtlessly, to match the words I was speaking to the Creon Hytherion he had known for three and a half centuries, ruthless and violent and hungry for nothing but blood and pleasure.

To his credit, he did not tell me I was wrong.

'I see.' The tone of his voice said the opposite. 'More or less.'

I slouched on the edge of the bed, heartbeat slowly coming down a smidge for the first time in this conversation. 'Good.'

An unsettled silence descended between us, broken only by the distant sounds of running footsteps in the wider Underground. The evacuation in progress, presumably. The lives of Agenor's people on the line … and yet the attack on the Golden Court appeared to be the very last thing on my father's mind as he sat there and rubbed the hard line of his jaw over and over again.

'And you …' He wavered for a moment, in spite of his visible determination to pull himself together to at least a semblance of his usual composure. 'And you're saying you actually … like him.'

'I'm saying I love him to pieces,' I pleasantly corrected.

'Gods help me,' he muttered, burying his face in his hands. 'Because you've *seen what he looks like*?'

I scoffed. 'No. Because he's the only damn person in this world who's never tried to make me more than I can be or less than I am. Because he makes me laugh when I'm frightened. Because he knows what it's like to be everyone's weapon. Because he stops me from doubting myself. Do I need to continue?'

His sharp inhale was a hair's breadth away from straying into the territory of hisses. 'No, thank you. I … I think I'm getting the picture.'

That seemed a little optimistic, but I decided not to tell him; he looked tormented enough in that ridiculous chair, his hands still covering his face as if he could hide from the truth that was slowly but irrevocably creeping up on him. On the other side of the room, Coral the snake chose that instant to slither back into view from below the wardrobe, glaring at the both of us with what I could only interpret as contemptuous pity.

I tried to imagine her in one room with Alyra and couldn't suppress a grin at the thought.

'In that case ...' Agenor started, faltering as he lowered his hands. He cleared his throat, then tried again. 'I ... I suppose ...'

Once again, he didn't finish his sentence.

'You suppose?' I said politely.

'I'm trying to figure out what in hell I'm supposed to say,' he blurted with a raw honesty that provoked an unexpected rush of fondness in my chest. 'I doubt you're in need of any edifying advice on love and related matters?'

I huffed a laugh. 'Correct. No need for biology lessons, either.'

'Thank the gods for that small mercy,' he muttered, drawing in another deep breath and holding it for a moment. 'Well. In that case ... congratulations, I presume?'

I blinked at him.

'Oh, gods,' he said, closing his eyes. 'That wasn't the right thing to say either?'

'What? No. No, it's fine.' I managed a bewildered chuckle. 'It's just ... you're *approving* of the situation now?'

'Well, you give the rather astonishing impression you're happy with it,' he said stiffly. 'And I'm trying not to cause any family feuds.'

'And that's all?' It came out more suspiciously than intended. 'I mean, I appreciate the change of heart, but it seems a little sudden. Since when are you so quick to overhaul your opinions over a bit of shouting?'

'One tries to learn,' he said with a grimace. 'And you seem to have inherited your mother's talent for shouting rather convincingly. Just ... could you promise me one thing, Em?'

I snorted. 'Ah, we're bargaining after all, then?'

'No!' He let out a strangled groan, hands gripping the armrests with obvious frustration. 'I'll try to behave regardless, for hell's sake. I'll just sleep better at night if I can be sure that you— Look, suppose you ever change your mind about this, or that you ever end up feeling unsure or unsafe around him—'

I stiffened. '*Agenor.*'

'Yes, yes,' he impatiently cut in, waving my interruption aside, 'you love him and he's perfect and you're going to make him a flock of tiny demon babies – it's all good, Em. But I've lived for twelve centuries and you would hardly be the first person to tell me the same things and end up disenchanted a few decades later, so please let this old codger talk for a minute, alright?'

I bit my tongue, although it took an effort. 'Fine. Go on.'

'All I'm asking ...' He briefly closed his eyes, gathering his thoughts. 'If you ever end up feeling stuck or unsafe or generally unhappy, and I don't care how impossible that may sound to you at this moment, will you please tell someone? Doesn't have to be me. Tell Lyn or Naxi or ... or *Zera*, for all I care. *Someone*. Can you promise me that? That you won't cling to your pride and decide to suffer through your troubles on your own?'

'You really think ...' I faltered. 'You think I'd do that?'

He threw me a sour smile. 'It's what people tend to do when making decisions everyone warned them against, isn't it? Avoiding the "told you so" at all costs?'

That, I had to admit, sounded like something I might be capable of doing.

'It's hard for me *not* to worry about this, Em,' he continued hastily, reading my expression. 'Even if I misunderstood him for centuries, that still *is* a history of centuries, and hardly a pleasant one. I'll try not to let that influence my behaviour too much, but it'll be much easier to trust him if I can be sure you're not quietly growing unhappy with your choices in the meantime. So humour me, please. Even if you'll never need it, could you just promise me for my benefit?'

Gods help me. There really was no way to hold on to my annoyance when confronted with that look on his face, with that infinitesimal crack in his deep voice – my father, feeling far too much, hitting my every weak spot all over again. I deflated like a leaking bag, the last of my defiant spite oozing out of me.

'Alright,' I murmured. 'If anything's wrong, I'll tell someone.'

Relief washed over his face, and suddenly he looked years older – no wrinkles, not a grey hair to be seen, yet something in the frail lines around his eyes and lips betrayed every single long year he'd lived in this world. 'Promise?'

'Promise.' A chuckle escaped me, wobbly and uncertain. 'On my alf honour.'

His laughter broke through the tension like a breath of fresh air, unchecked and filled with unexpected gratitude. 'I'm going to need a word with Tared about this, good gods.'

'I think he'll be tremendously pleased if you do,' I said, jumping from the bed and offering him a hand. He grabbed it without hesitation, allowing me to help him to his feet even though he was a good head taller than me and towered over me as soon as he was standing. 'I just figured fae honour wouldn't be all that reassuring to you, given that it doesn't seem to exist.'

'Not as such, no,' he admitted wryly, shaking his head. 'All the same, I feel your fae upbringing is rather lacking in some areas. Which I suppose is no one's fault but my own.'

'You're getting much better at being a father, though,' I said without thinking.

It came out so lightly, a throwaway remark blurted out all the more easily because of the sincerity with which it fell from my lips. Only as he froze in place did I fully realise what I'd said – and how many times I *hadn't* said it, had barely given myself the time to think it.

Father. I rarely even spoke the word out loud to him. He'd been so far removed from any sense of family when we'd found each other at the Golden Court, with his ancient mind and his fae heart and his never-ending schemes and plots ... But my heart *had* skipped a beat at the news of the attack on the court. He *had* stormed in to rescue me from Creon's wiles the moment Edored had revealed our secrets.

And then, for all his worry and objections, he *had* congratulated me.

'Oh.' His voice emerged a little choked. His eyes – that one part of him that had always been familiar, mirroring my own – gleamed with something that lay a fraction of an inch removed from panic. 'I— Oh. That's ... good.'

I managed a laugh, suddenly no longer quite sure where to look. 'Well. Yes.'

His answering chuckle was no less strained. He looked so lost, suddenly, more ill at ease than even that expensive silk shirt or twelve centuries of habitual dignity could conceal. I couldn't help but wonder, with unexpected, almost violent urgency, how long it had been since anyone had told Agenor Thenes, former Lord Protector of the Mother's court, that he was doing well; for all his prestige and respectable authority, hadn't he lived most of his life as starved for actual friends and family as I had?

'Well,' he said and cleared his throat, gold-stained fingers fidgeting restlessly by his side, 'I should probably be going. They're still evacuating the court – can't leave the alves to manage it all by themselves.'

Wait! I wanted to burst out, thoughts spinning, words aching on my tongue. *Damn the alves. Sit down and tell me about you. I know more about your titles than about your childhood memories, know how you fight your wars but not what food you like … Can't you stop being the lord of the Golden Court for a minute? Can't you just be my father for once?*

'Agenor …' I started.

Not *Father*. Never *Father*.

He frowned as I faltered. 'What is it?'

'I … I was just wondering …' It shouldn't be so damn hard, getting it past my lips. I shouldn't be bracing myself for mockery and refusals, not from the male who'd told me plainly enough that he *had* wanted me – and yet I found myself dragging out every word like a heavy boulder that might just bounce back into my face. 'If things have calmed down a little – with the Golden Court and the evacuation and everything – would you—'

A door slammed, no more than a corridor away.

Running footsteps. Someone crying out in shock. And Beyla's voice, sharp and urgent – 'Emelin! *Emelin!*'

In the blink of an eye, all traces of vulnerability were gone.

Agenor had turned and swept open the bedroom door before I could even shut my mouth, wings flaring out in alarm behind his shoulders. Coral shot after him with her fangs out. Now I heard Lyn in the distance, crying something about fights and blood and for Inika's dear sake, would we all be *careful*?

The Golden Court.

The evacuation.

There was no time to ask questions. No time to stop and think. Beyla stormed into the room in a flash of silver-blonde hair and drawn swords, a streak of blood running down her temple; the glow of alf magic pulsed around her in uneven flickers. She didn't grant Agenor as much as a look. Instead, she easily jumped over Coral and strode towards me, free hand reaching for my upper arm.

'What—' I started.

Her fingers closed around my shoulder.

Agenor shouted my name, eyes wide with outrage. Lyn sprinted into view in a sizzle of fire. But the world was already blurring around me, their voices already muted, and the smoky light and the books and the iridescent walls of the Underground mingled like wet paint as Beyla faded me out of that safe room and into gods knew where in the world.

Chapter 7

The world cleared around me with a flood of sunlight, the taste of briny island air, the smell of freshly spilled blood. Smooth stone beneath my bare feet. Familiar sandstone walls around me. The unmistakable clamour of clashing swords and agonised voices just around the corner, echoing down the empty halls.

The Golden Court.

If not for Beyla's hand on my shoulders, I might have tumbled over.

'What's *happening*?' My mind was desperately trying to catch up. There wasn't *supposed* to be a battle at the Golden Court at all, was there? All Agenor's plans had centred around that point – get every one of his people out of there before any blood could flow, because we simply did not have the numbers to justify a battle that would kill half of his forces and win us nothing.

And yet ...

The ferocious cries mere walls away from me did not give the impression of a swift and peaceful evacuation.

'Things escalated,' Beyla bit out, dragging me along by my shoulder as she strode down the deserted corridor. The floor was painfully cold beneath my bare soles. 'Don't ask me how. Tared asked me to get you to— Doralis!'

Only then did I notice the cowering figure of Agenor's right hand behind a square pillar, frantically flinging blue magic at a gaping wound in her leg. There had to be plenty of colour left in her pale purple wings, and yet the power seemed to come erratically at best – faint, useless flickers of blue sparking from her fingertips, doing absolutely nothing to slow the bleeding.

I was already running.

My red dress was useless, as were my bare arms and legs – but there was at least *some* blue in the brown of my hair, and I drew it without caring much about the unhealthy shade of orange that would be left. The wound grew shut at once, leaving only the pool of blood on the floor and a pale rash that covered most of Doralis' muscular thigh.

She slumped against the wall with a gasp of relief, breathing heavily. 'Oh, good gods, *thank* you. My magic—'

'I saw it,' I interrupted, too curt and too shrill. A crawling unease told me I knew exactly what the problem with her magic had been, but I shoved it aside for now – I would much rather be wrong, and either way, I had more urgent problems to worry about. 'And will someone tell me what for fuck's sake is going on?'

'Have they managed to reach him yet?' Beyla added sharply behind me.

'Reach who?' I snapped as Doralis shook her head – and then I saw the look in Beyla's pale blue eyes, and I knew.

I'll go take a look at the Golden Court, he'd said.

And then ...

No.

No.

Damn my bare feet. Damn my flimsy dress. I spun around and ran towards the noise like a woman possessed, down the sun-streaked hallway, to the high gate opening up on my left. Its carved wooden doors had been blasted from the hinges. The frame was marred by cracks and gashes – from swords or red magic, I didn't know.

Didn't care, either.

Not when I saw what was happening beyond that gate.

The courtyard of the Golden Court had turned into an arena of war, wings and writhing bodies wherever I looked. Hordes of fae soared over the castle, dressed in black, eclipsing the sunlight like swarms of insects bringing hunger and disease. A few dozen feet away, Tared and a handful of other alves were making desperate attempts to hold their own against that onslaught, fading back and forth, blood-stained blades circling without pause as they bit into wing after wing after wing.

And at the centre of the courtyard, separated from every single one of our allies by rows and rows of fae …

Creon.

Dying.

My heart stood still.

He'd been thrown onto his back on the rough stone paving, surrounded by two, three, four dozen fae attackers – all of them hovering well out of reach of the knife in his hand, circling him like impatient vultures as they showered him in red magic he tried to dodge in vain. His left arm lay bent in an unnatural direction. An arrow jutted from his thigh, another from his side. The stone tiles beneath him were stained with blood, and even if some of it was coming from the dozen dead bodies strewn around him rather than from his own veins …

There was too much of it.

Far, *far* too much of it.

The world went blank around me.

My feet propelled me forward before I could think, into the blistering morning air outside. The fingers of my left hand found my dress as my right arm swung up, aiming for the rows of fae who unwisely flew with their backs towards me.

Red exploded from my fingertips, bright with the force of my fury.

I took down four of them in that first outburst – four deafening thuds as they dropped to the ground with one wing cut off their shoulders, their agonised screams the only introduction I would ever need. For a moment and a half, it felt good. Heroic. Triumphant. Then the swarm faltered as every eye around the courtyard turned in my direction simultaneously, and my more sensible mind caught up – the part of me that could still count to a hundred and realised that the force opposite me was much, much larger than that.

'*Em*!' Tared shouted to my right.

'It's her!' a Faerie voice cried in the same moment, shrill with elation. 'It's the unbound one!'

Oh, fuck.

I stumbled back a step, trying not to flinch as commanders yelled their orders and the army started moving – a brutal winged wave rising over me, carrying the vicious force of the Mother's rage. On the bright side, at least they'd lost interest in killing Creon for a moment. On the more problematic side …

I needed more red than I could take from this single dress. I needed a level of cleverness I didn't feel quite capable of, staring in the face of my own looming death.

Most of all, I needed Creon by my side.

And where I stood, surrounded by pale sandstone and golden wood, I had none of those things.

I flung another desperate swing of red at the ranks advancing on me. Three of the most eager fae went down screaming, slamming into the courtyard tiles with sickening splats – but the others at their side barely even paused, and my dress had turned a pale watermelon shade of pink. I'd kill another handful of them this way, without doubt. And then my dress would go white and my hair would go white and I'd die a useless death minutes before Creon would, defeated by the bindings and a battle that was never supposed to happen.

So I needed something better than this.

I staggered back another few steps, back through the gate through which I'd come. On the edge of my sight, Tared made another strained attempt to reach Creon, only to find his way blocked by a few dozen fae too many.

Something better than that, too.

'Beyla?' I managed, not taking my eyes from the battlefield. 'Are you still there?'

'Of course I am, and what for Orin's sake are you *doing*?' The flicker of alf steel in the corner of my eye told me she was closer than I'd expected. 'Sacrificing yourself isn't—'

'I know. I *know*.' My voice cracked. 'Listen, I was supposed to be having breakfast right now, alright? I'm trying to catch up. Don't suppose you have any buckets of red paint around?'

'No such luck,' she said through gritted teeth. 'If you don't have any better ideas, I'm fading you out in five counts, do you understand?'

'No. No, *please*.' Not with the fae already realising they had forgotten about Creon; I watched the rearguard turn around with my stomach clenching, unable to pick between screaming or unleashing another storm of useless red magic. 'I'll come up with something. I'll—'

Beyla yanked me back. A bolt of crimson seared into the floor where I'd stood an eyeblink ago, slamming a crater three heads deep into the sandstone.

'Four,' she snapped, releasing me.

Another red flare came down. This time I had the presence of mind to dive away myself, withdrawing farther into the deceptive safety of that echoing hallway. Doralis shrieked a warning, and I spun sideways without thinking, landing ungently on all fours as a wooden beam splintered in the wall behind me.

'Three,' Beyla coldly said, unsheathing her second sword.

I barely even heard her anymore. I barely even felt the harsh sunlight or smelled the warm blood. My eyes had fixed themselves upon Creon, who had grabbed the nearest corpse in that moment and was dragging it over himself, a shield of dead flesh and wings to protect him from the magic raining down on him.

A shield.

A *shield*.

My mind jumped so suddenly I gasped.

Last night – a full eternity ago – I'd wrapped myself in a layer of motionlessness to cross the shield around the Cobalt Court. *Softness for movement*, except I had used it to create the opposite of movement. It had been softness for stillness – a little godsworn trick to fool the

Mother's defences into believing I wasn't there at all. So if I had been able to do that much ...

Iridescence for magic.

Who said I couldn't become a repellent for magic, too, and trick those red flares into believing there was nothing here to destroy?

'Two,' I heard Beyla say, the frail sound of her voice ages removed from my spinning mind.

'Wait. *Wait.* Doralis?' I spun around, finding her with her back pressed against the wall, eyes wide with fear. Not how I'd known her at the previous battle at this court, but then again, finding your magic suddenly malfunctioning was probably enough to make even the most battle-hardened individual waver. 'Please change my dress to mother-of-pearl, will you?'

'Change— What?' Her glance at Beyla carried obvious meaning – *has she gone mad?* 'To—'

'Mother-of-pearl,' I repeated, flexing my fingers. 'Yes. And keep changing it back if I manage to drain it, alright?'

She released a befuddled laugh even as she obediently flattened her hand against the pale yellow of the plastered sandstone walls. 'Why don't you do—'

'Can't do it anymore. Godsworn magic.' I leapt three feet back to avoid another blistering attack from the fae crowding around the gate; outside, their commanders were yelling at them to stop dithering, to go in and just *get* the little bitch. '*Now*, Doralis.

I hadn't known I could sound so much like Agenor – that same single-minded quality that wouldn't allow for delay or objections. It did the trick. Yellow flashed around me, and my red dress suddenly grew smooth and shimmering, reflecting the morning sunlight in a million colours at once.

'Keep renewing it,' I snapped and drew.

No magic. I imagined a flimsy layer of iridescence enveloping me, the same powers I'd used to deflect every ray of red sent my way during the battle at Tolya. Imagined how that shower of destructive magic would bounce off me, harmless as raindrops sliding off leaves – how I would walk and walk and walk, and none of them would ever harm me.

Rays of red burst in through the gate again, aiming for me and every spot around me.

No magic.

For a moment, I saw nothing but colour, nothing but violence as the magic struck ... and nothing happened.

No pain. No blood. Not a single ruffled hair on my head. I let out a high-strung laugh and stepped forward, welcoming the next surge of their attack with the iridescence tingling up my left arm – *no magic*, and here I was, the human equivalent of alf steel, walking through their firing line as if their powers were nothing but a harmless drizzle.

It *worked*. It fucking *worked*.

Cries of confusion went up amidst their ranks. I took another step forward, preparing to run. If I could just get to Creon this way – well, I'd figure out how to get the two of us *out* again once I'd managed that. A problem for a future version of me. For now—

Magic flashed again.

Pain bloomed through me, a venomous sting just beneath my left ear.

I jumped back instinctively, right hand flying to the injured spot and coming away red and sticky – *fuck*. Where had my magic gone?

No time to think. A sea of crimson lit up in the corner of my eye, and it was all I could do to dive out of the way, landing with a painful smack in Doralis' sheltered corner. Outside, people were shouting – *forward, go in, go get her*. The blood was trickling down from my neck onto my dress now ...

My dull, dark pink, decidedly non-pearlescent dress.

'Doralis!' I hissed, frustration burning under my skin. I'd been so close. *So* damned close, and then I'd failed for a reason as needless as a lack of fuel? 'I said you needed to renew it every time I—'

'I *know*,' she whimpered, trying desperately to heal the gash beneath my ear. Still the magic wouldn't flow well; only after three attempts did the pain soften a little. 'I tried to restore it, but all magic was bouncing off on you! Your dress resisted all the yellow I threw at it!'

Oh.

Oh, fuck.

'Emelin?' Beyla yelled from the other side of the doorframe, the undertone below my name a clear warning to either start thinking or prepare for departure. A fae male from the front line tried to jump in through the gate, only to find himself skewered on one of her swords the next moment.

So close. I only needed a way to keep drawing. Something not attached to me, but easily within reach of my left hand while I crossed an entire courtyard – hell, that didn't sound doable. Something better, then. Something—

My gaze fell to my feet.

My poor, bare feet.

Was I going insane now, or was it pure, undiluted brilliance turning the air in my lungs to fire? I'd only ever drawn through my hands. *Everyone* drew through their hands. But Creon had sucked the colour from every single surface around him, that day he'd nearly blown up Lyn's library, and if he could do it, then who said *I* couldn't do it if only I dared to give up on the safe restraints that guided my magic as I knew it?

I was quite possibly going insane.

But Creon was dying, and what need would I have for sanity if I didn't have him?

'Doralis?' I said, quickly taking down two more fae who were trying to work themselves in around Beyla. My dress was paling at an alarming rate. 'Change the floor to mother-of-pearl instead, will you?'

She did not even ask questions. The large paving stones before and beneath us turned white and lustrous with a single yellow blaze. I took another step forward, carefully flattening my feet against the silky surface – *iridescence*. Hell, how hard could it be? It was there, plenty of it, and if I could just draw it in through that rough, calloused skin ...

Doralis lunged past me, driving a long dagger deep into the neck of a fae warrior who'd been about to fire at me.

I clasped my hands together as in prayer, aiming every ounce of my willpower at the soles of my feet. The ball of my big toe, a little cushion pressed against that silky surface. The outer ridge, grounding me, digging in deep. My heels, strong and solid, keeping me from inching back even as that black-clothed swarm of fae descended upon me.

'Emelin!' Beyla shouted, not too far away. 'Whatever you're doing, best do it *fast*, will you?'

Something tingled through the bottom of my feet.

I closed my eyes.

No magic. That shimmering shield around me, again. It came easier now that I knew what I was looking for, knew what would work – I was the opposite of power. I was whiteness, the emptiest, palest shade of it. I was …

'*Emelin!*'

I looked up.

The world had gone scarlet and crimson around me.

I was standing in a whirlwind of red, magic nipping at my arms, my chest, my face … and yet I felt nothing but the intoxicating currents of iridescence up my body, fizzing from my feet upwards like bubbles in sparkling wine. One step forward, and still there was no pain. As if I was striding through a firestorm unburned, untouched.

The red faltered as Beyla's sword made quick work of the fae who'd drawn it in the first place. A temporary relief – the next group was already crowding inside.

'Doralis?' I had no time for joy or triumph. It was working. That was all I needed to know. Creon was still out there, and gods knew what had happened to him in the meantime. 'Change the rest of the corridor too.'

I didn't dare to look down and take my eyes away from the approaching fae, but the reflection of light against the walls changed ever so slightly, and the surprised hiss of my opponents seemed a good sign. Another step forward, and the magic kept flowing. Another one. I settled my right foot onto the mother-of-pearl with painstaking thoroughness before I dared to lift my left – the safety of the earth below me was the only weapon I had against the next round of red magic barrelling my way.

This shouldn't be taking so long. I wasn't looking forward to the moment they all realised they just needed to change the floor back to its previous stony state.

'Beyla?' My thoughts were spinning so fast they left me dizzy. 'Mind if I borrow a sword?'

'I do mind, yes,' she hissed, pressing Sunray into my hand as she shot past me, easily flipped Icebreaker to her other hand, and whacked the knees out from below a tall fae female. 'Lose it and I'll kill you. Anything else?'

'Fade Doralis to another side of the courtyard,' I said quickly, testing the weight of the blade in my hand. At least I'd held it once before, but it felt new and uncanny all the same. 'Somewhere that allows her to overlook the place. I need her to turn all of the paving iridescent.'

She scoffed, catching a ray of red on her sword rather than jumping away from it. 'And leave you here to—'

'*Beyla!*'

With a curse, she turned, grabbed Doralis, and vanished.

I gave myself no time to think or worry. They'd just have to manage. If they didn't, I was lost anyway; no use panicking over what I couldn't control. The only thing I *could* do now ...

I tightened my hand around the leather-covered hilt of my sword, making sure not to allow my skin anywhere near its alf-steel blade as I straightened my shoulders and looked up.

About a dozen fae had crowded around the open doorway to the courtyard, glaring at me with panic in their eyes and bloodlust in their sneers. What did I look like to them? Small and human. Half-dressed and barefoot. Clutching a blade that wasn't mine to hold. Most of all, destined to die in a few minutes at most.

'Fuckers,' I hissed under my breath and lowered my left hand to my pink dress again.

I had to let go of the iridescent magic as I drew – no mixing colours drawn through different limbs, I noted, in some faraway corner of my mind still capable of noting anything. It lasted just a fraction of a moment. Long enough for me to draw the last bit of red I had. Too short for my opponents to realise this would be the moment to attack.

My magic slammed into the wall beside the gate, leaving a man-sized hole in the sandstone.

I was already running.

Now they *did* attack, a bright vermilion blooming on the edge of my sight – but I had my floor and my feet, and the magic whizzed past me without leaving a scratch. One of them had the presence of mind to swing a dagger at me. I countered reflexively, Beyla's sword colliding with an unprotected forearm; its owner screamed out in pain as I tumbled through my newly created breach and onto the gleaming, many-hued courtyard outside.

Mother-of-pearl, as far as the eye could see.

I sent a quick prayer of thanks to whatever god or goddess might be listening and scrambled back to my feet, barely standing before the next wave of red magic washed over me from all sides. In the distance, an alvish voice I didn't know cried out in shock. Around me, fae faltered as they too found that their powers bounced off of me without the faintest effect, their triumph fading as confusion sank in.

I grinned back at them as I began moving again. Whatever the hell I looked like now, I doubted human or powerless was part of it.

'Little to the left!' Tared's voice shouted from somewhere above me – the battlements?

I adjusted my course without looking up, swinging my borrowed sword into a dagger someone threw at me. It clattered uselessly against the pearlescent tiles. There, *there* I finally caught sight of Creon's black-clad shape at the centre of the courtyard, surrounded but still moving, fending off attacks with what seemed to be a wing he'd cut off one of the bodies around him.

No more than fifty feet left between us. I ducked to avoid an arrow hissing my way and walked faster; around me, yellow magic blazed as Doralis restored the iridescent surface I was walking on.

Thirty feet.

Creon turned, eyes widening as he noticed me.

'*Behind you!*' an alvish voice I didn't know cried out, and I whirled around just in time to swing my blade up between the legs of a fae sneaking up on me with daggers in both hands. He went down howling. Tared appeared out of thin air some twenty feet to my left – as close as he could come, presumably, with the limitation he could only fade to where he'd stood before.

Through the next surge of red magic, I could only barely make out his words – something about the position of my wrist and covering my back.

Answering required a level of coordination I could no longer muster, every muscle in my body drawn tight, the magic coursing through my veins in a wild storm of power. I walked as fast as I could with one foot on the ground at all times, feeling like it was the magic that walked *me* now – trying to keep my balance as I made for Creon's broken shape with that unnatural, swaying gait. Another arrow shot past me, missing me by mere inches. I lashed out without thinking, left hand in my sickly orange hair, two fingers of my sword hand aiming for the unfortunate archer – feeling the iridescent magic beneath my feet falter as red whizzed through me and smashed into his bow and face.

Three, four flares of magic bit into my skin in that single moment before I pulled my shield back in place. Warm, sticky blood dripped down my upper arm, my thigh, my back.

I barely felt the pain.

'Stop her!' a female voice howled in Faerie. 'Keep her away from him!'

Had I been capable of talking, I would have told her others had tried that before.

But there was no time to talk, and no use to it, either. Before me, more and more fae landed inelegantly on the pearly tiles, faces contorted with unsettled bewilderment – a last wall between me and Creon. I raised Beyla's sword. They tensed but stayed where they stood – knowing as well as I did that even if I took down two or three of them, I would never cut my way through three dozen of them.

I could try, though.

Frankly, I quite felt like trying.

My blade swung down as if it shared my lust for blood. This sun-drenched mayhem couldn't be more different from the quiet, buried training hall in Orin's quarter, the frenzied battle cries of my opponents equally far removed from Tared's calm instructions … and yet it felt familiar, the lethal weight in my hand as I charged forward, blind to anything but unprotected wrists, throats, wings. They stopped being living creatures, the fae surrounding me. They were nothing but obstacles between Creon and me, nothing but targets to be destroyed, and if I had to kill every single one of them to reach him …

Well, so be it.

I did not *enjoy* the clean slide of sharp alf steel through the nearest wing in my way. But the fury driving me forward, that rush of battle … there was an addictive exhilaration to it.

With a fluency I could only attribute to months and months of training, I pushed forward past my falling victim, whirled around, swung again. Sunray collided with a fae female lunging forward, and the steel edge sank into her chest with a hollow squelch, sending her crumpling to the ground.

I was already moving again. Slashing, thrusting, slicing, until my arms ached and my hands were slippery with blood that could just as easily be mine as anyone else's. A sharp, nagging pain radiated from my side up through my guts, and I barely registered it – as long as they didn't reach my eyes or heart, was there anything a little blue magic couldn't fix?

A familiar voice – Tared? – cried a warning.

I turned just a moment too late.

Time slowed to a syrupy crawl in that fraction of a second, as if my senses felt the need to check and double-check the sight of the purple-winged fae male jumping towards me, wings slamming against the air to launch him forward, hand raised with a glint of sharp metal.

I was too slow.

I knew it even as I wildly flung up my hands, even as Sunray whistled a violent arc towards his neck. If I dodged, I would drop myself into one of his comrades' arms. If I stayed where I stood, his knife would lie buried in my chest before I could take another breath—

He froze mid-jump.

A single gargled groan and he slid to the ground, eyes rolling up in their sockets. The female next to him went down an instant later, and then *her* neighbour, a knife jutting from the back of his neck as he rolled over. I sprinted forward before I fully understood what was happening, bursting through the hole in their ranks before they could turn around and realise who was flinging daggers at them ...

Creon.

Creon.

He wasn't sitting up – not quite. But he'd hauled himself far enough off the ground to throw those three knives, a fourth already in his hand, and his eyes shone with a feral satisfaction that couldn't be dulled even by the arrows sticking from his thigh and waist. I hurled my last four steps towards him, all but throwing myself on top of him to shield him with my body. *Alive, alive, alive,* my blood sang, and at the same time ...

There didn't seem to be an inch of him that wasn't bleeding. Deep gashes in his neck and arms showed that his opponents had aimed to kill and made good progress on their way to his face and heart. A gushing wound just beneath his hairline sent a cascade of blood running down his nose and forehead. The arrows in his thighs and side had lodged themselves firmly in his flesh. A deep slashing cut ran from shoulder to midriff, an angry jagged line that wept scarlet at an alarming rate, and his wings ...

My stomach turned as he sat up a fraction straighter and revealed a gaping, tattered tear, large enough to send a flying male plummeting to the ground.

'Fuck.' The world was lighting up in fiery ruby red again, fae eclipsing the sunlight as they swarmed over us. I crawled over him as well as I could without touching the arrows, sword still in my right hand, keeping my left foot pressed against the mother-of-pearl paving – how long until I drained the surface? 'Fuck, Creon—'

'So sorry about this,' he groaned as he pressed his bleeding face into the hollow of my shoulder. 'And I'm fine, cactus – I'm fine. Don't let them see I'm talking. She'll know you found the bindings.'

That last point was enough to wipe my intended responses to the first two from my mind – that he should hardly be apologising for getting surrounded on a battlefield and that he was arguably farther from fine than I'd ever seen him since I'd dragged him out of the Mother's bone hall with chains through his wings. But his voice ... The bindings.

Of *course* he was still scheming, even on the brink of death – had I expected anything else?

'Fuck,' I said again.

A throaty laugh rose from his battered body. 'Could be worse. We could be dead.'

'We might *still* be dead, you bloody idiot.' As heartfelt as the exasperation was, I was overcome by an absurd urge to laugh at the same time – the sound of his voice alone lighting that reckless, ridiculous sense of invincibility in my heart again. At least we were together. If I were to die here, it would at least be in his arms. 'So unless you have any brilliant plans for getting us out of here …'

'We'll probably need an alf,' he muttered, and somehow he managed to sound disgruntled about it, even with half of his body's blood content on the wrong side of his skin. 'How close did Tared get?'

'He was about a dozen feet behind me.' I didn't dare to look over my shoulder – didn't dare to turn even a fraction away from Creon's face, just in case my iridescent shield would abruptly decide it no longer cared to cover him from the red magic raining down upon us from all sides. Around us, the ranks of fae seemed to be hesitating, doubtful whether they dared to come closer and finish us with blades and daggers or whether they would rather wait until my magic shield mysteriously gave in. 'But I doubt they'll happily let him through. Are you able to attack, or—'

He shook his head without looking up. 'Bindings causing trouble.'

'Fuck,' I said again, even though I'd suspected it from the moment I'd seen Doralis struggle with her own healing. 'Alright. I can take some red from your blood, I suppose?'

He was quiet for a moment in my arms – odd, how his silence had already started sounding wrong to me. I could fill in his thoughts all the same. Even if I had a sword, even if I used every last drop of red until he was bleeding white and grey, I still wouldn't be able to target more than one or two fae at once; they'd fill the breaches in their ranks before we could move anywhere.

And sooner or later, some of them would decide our blades would never kill them all and take the risk of coming closer.

'You deflected their magic at Tolya,' he said, so quietly I barely heard him.

I stiffened.

'Can you do it again? Instead of absorbing it?' He spoke so fast I had trouble following through the screams and shouts around us. 'If you somehow turn it into a ... a mirror of sorts ...'

I had already squeezed my eyes shut.

A *mirror*. I tried to see that pearly shield again, shimmering over my arms and legs, turning all magic that touched it to dust. Would I need more or less power to make it bounce back attacks instead? More iridescence had sent magic erupting in sparks at Tolya, and that seemed to be exactly what we needed today ...

I glanced at the large stone tile below my bare left feet. Under the steady shower of red lighting up the world around me, I had used enough of the magic to render it nearly entirely dull.

All or nothing, then.

I drew every last drop of magic I could find from that surface, working by nothing but intuition and desperate hope now, driven by nothing but the weight of the bleeding body in my arms and the burning need to make him survive. Damn the tempered, moderate defences. If they wanted me dead for my powers, they would *get* the bloody powers – not a defence now but a weapon as deadly as the blade in my hand ...

Shrill cries erupted around me.

When I jerked up my head, fae were staggering back and fluttering down wherever I looked, grasping for wounded faces and clutching torn wings. Crimson sparks still crackled through the air around us, a destructive halo of magic. Even the alves had stopped fighting on the edges of the courtyard, bloodied blades sagging in their hands – every single one of them gaping at me like I'd risen from the grave, my footprints sizzling with hellfire.

Tared was sprinting towards us, shouting something.

I stood before I thought of standing.

Creon dragged himself upright another few inches, holding out a hand slick with blood; I grabbed his wrist and yanked him towards me. Already, some fae were firing red at us again, their magic digging small craters in the paving around my feet. I half-carried, half-dragged Creon with me, stretching my sword hand back to Tared …

Calloused fingers found my bare lower arm.

The sun-streaked, blood-drenched battlefield blurred around me.

And it was in that fraction of a second, an eyeblink before we well and truly left the Golden Court behind, that a third arrow whizzed down and slammed with a sickening thwack between Creon's shoulder blades.

Chapter 8

He didn't even scream.

We emerged in the dusky Underground living room in a tangle of blood and limbs and torn wings, almost tumbling over from the speed with which we'd faded. Tared was cursing. I was still crying out in shock. But Creon dropped to his knees with nothing but a glower at the rest of the company, splayed his left hand flat against the dark floor, and began flicking blue magic at his bleeding wounds with such swiftness his fingers blurred in the dim light – curt, offhand gestures, as if this was a routine issue he dealt with every morning before breakfast.

'What in hell is *happening*?' Agenor snapped behind me, sounding on the brink of violence. 'Is the evacuation—'

Tared bit out something I only half registered, about the evacuation being the only bloody thing that *was* fine right now.

'Em?' Creon said between clenched teeth, not even looking up as he pressed his left hand to his blood-soaked black trousers and his right hand to the wound in his chest. Blue magic flared, and the gash stopped bleeding. 'The arrows are barbed. I'm going to need to cut them out. Could you—'

'What?' I heard myself splutter.

'They're barbed.' More blue. The wound at his hairline grew shut. 'Tearing damage is much harder to heal with magic, so I'm going to—'

'Cut them out?' I let out a shrill, joyless laugh, shoving Beyla's sword aside with a disregard that might have killed me under any other circumstances. 'By *yourself?*'

He looked up, expression showing no discomfort except for a mild, weary irritation. 'Yes? I've done it before.'

'I've also tried to kill you before,' I protested, my voice inching dangerously close to a shriek. 'Doesn't mean we need to do it again, does it? Ylfreda? *Ylfreda?*'

'She's getting her tools,' Lyn said – I hadn't realised she was in the room until that moment. 'I warned her the moment Beyla came crashing in that we might have injuries.'

Creon muttered a curse. 'There's no need for—'

'Oh, shut *up.*' My heart was beating at about ten times its usual speed, pumping more panic than blood through my jittery limbs. Why was he still bleeding? How did he even have any blood left to lose? 'You're not going to do a single fucking thing except sit still and let us get the damn things out, and don't you dare try and do it anyway. I *will* stop you.'

'You ...' His hands paused as he considered that for a moment, then groaned and admitted, 'I suppose you could.'

Agenor let out a choked sound on the other side of the room.

'Damn right I could,' I grumbled, managing a scoff. My head felt light – as if I'd stood up too swiftly and all the blood had sunken to my feet, except my ice-cold feet didn't feel like they'd been blessed with an abundance of it either. 'So you'll have to resign yourself to the coddling, villain that I am. Woe is you. You might have to start caring about your own comfort levels one day.'

On the couch, Tared let out a high-strung chuckle; I wasn't sure if it was a response to me or to Agenor, who couldn't have looked more dumbfounded if I'd grown wings on the spot. Creon glared at the both of them, then at the arrow in his thigh, and then at me again, visibly debating how much trouble he'd be in if he just pulled the thing out before Ylfreda showed up.

The healer appeared in the middle of the room before I could be forced to make good on my threats, thankfully.

One look at Creon and me, and she dumped her bag on the floor, snapped something about hot water and soap, and began pulling out a terrifying assortment of scalpels and knives as Lyn hurried off in the direction of the kitchen. 'Barbed?'

'All of them,' Creon said curtly.

She cursed and threw me an impatient glare. 'And you? Are you waiting for something before you heal yourself?'

I blinked and glanced down, realising only then that my pale pink dress was soaked with blood at my waist – a gash just below the lowest ribs on my left, bleeding fiercely. With a mumbled apology, I pressed my feet against the floor and drew out a bright azure. Too much: through the cut in my dress, the skin of my side grew pink and soft like a newborn child's.

Better than fainting, though.

Ylfreda set to work with commendable efficiency, grumbling all the while about reckless idiots and risks of perforated lungs. The arrow in Creon's back turned out to have lodged itself into a rib between spine and shoulder blade, which he called "a manageable scratch" and Ylfreda called "a madman's unearned good luck"; the resulting grisly wound was deep but at least clean. I attempted to get to my feet to help them heal it and found my vision blotting aggressively as soon as I did, black spots crawling over my field of sight like poisonous spiders.

Out of nowhere, Agenor's large hand landed on my shoulder, gold-flecked fingers squeezing tight. 'Best leave that to me, Em.'

I sank back to the floor with more relief than I wanted to admit. So close to Creon's spine and wings, I wasn't sure if I trusted myself not to leave any damaged nerves or muscles behind; after a few centuries spent dealing with the consequences of battlefields, my father might be the better candidate for this job.

Ylfreda quickly removed the second arrow, informing us with stern relief that it had just missed the liver. Creon healed the wound it left behind while Agenor worked on his back, restoring layers of bone and skin and muscle with grim-faced precision. Lyn trotted back into the room with sponges and a tub of steaming hot water, and by the time Creon had rinsed the drying blood off his face and arms, he at least no longer gave the impression he might topple into his grave any moment.

I sat and breathed. Lyn pushed a drink into my hand that tasted like molten iron, and as I sipped it, the black blotches before my eyes slowly crawled away.

By the time Agenor declared all vertebrae unharmed and Ylfreda moved on to the third and last arrow, my heartbeat was finally coming down a fraction. Creon still managed to look like there was nothing unusual going on as he chucked his bloodied sponge into the tub with equally bloodied water and began flashing blue magic at the tears in his wings; he barely even flinched as Ylfreda dug a knife into his thigh and began carving out the barbed steel that had buried itself into his muscles.

I didn't want to think about any of it – what pain levels he must be used to, for this to mean so little to him – and couldn't help thinking of it all the same.

He knew, of course. His dark eyes found me with just a glimpse of apology as he interrupted his work on his wings to heal the arrow wound that Ylfreda's handiwork had left in his thigh; for a moment, his smile was not so convincingly careless. 'I'm fine, Em. It's mostly scrapes and scratches from here on out.'

The remaining rips in his wings didn't look even remotely like scratches to me, but Tared cut in before I could reply, with a speed that told me he'd been holding back since the moment we'd faded into this room. 'If you insist you're bursting with health again, would this be the moment to explain what for Orin's fucking eye you were *doing*, Hytherion?'

That was *anger* in his voice – not the vicious grudge from before but raw, genuine anger, the sort of rage that sprouted from worry rather than hate. I turned and found him collapsed on the nearest couch, still holding on to his sword as if an army might burst through the front door before the hour was over. The small wounds on his arm were still bleeding, but he didn't appear to notice, glaring at Creon with a ferocity I had trouble matching to his vehement attempts to save the other's life a moment before.

'What?' I said.

Creon merely shrugged, looking not in the least surprised. 'Thought I'd try a little experiment.'

'An *experiment*?' I'd rarely seen Tared like this – furious with fear in a way that reminded me of the day Edored had walked into plague territory at Zera's temple. 'What were you trying to find out – what would happen if you threw yourself at an entire damn fleet on your own?'

'Beg your pardon?' Agenor said sharply.

'We were fading the last fae out, and His Highness decided that would be the perfect moment to charge head-on into the nearest battalion,' Tared snapped, finally flinging his sword aside and burying his face in his hands. 'Tried to reach him, couldn't, had Beyla fade Em in to save our arses. And then we *still* could have all died.'

So sorry, cactus. The apology in his glance. Slowly, the pieces of the puzzle started sliding together, leaving a gaping hole in the middle – *an experiment.*

What in the world?

'Consider it from the bright side,' Creon said, systematically working his way through the slashes in his wing. 'I'm pretty sure you've settled that life debt now.'

'Rot in hell,' Tared muttered, sounding just a little more relieved than he likely wanted the world to know. 'So what was the damn experiment about, then? Arrow sampling?'

'The bindings,' I said with a gasp, understanding everything and nothing at once. 'You wanted to know what the bindings would do?'

Creon sent me a wry, rueful smile.

'What?' There was an unmistakable edge of straining self-control in Tared's voice. 'You threw yourself at the entire bloody Moon fleet just to find out ...'

'If I could harm them,' Creon helpfully finished. His grin was perhaps not as deliberately infuriating as before, but the bite was still there, that unspoken challenge. 'I figured we'd better find out *before* our first actual battle, you see. Which I would say was confirmed by, well ...' A loose gesture at the pool of blood on the floor. 'This.'

At least I wasn't the only one gaping at him as if he'd abruptly started speaking Old Kurrian; it seemed even alves could be impressed by sheer recklessness. Tared let himself fall back into the couch cushions, cursing under his breath. Ylfreda glared pointedly at the blood-stained arrows on the floor. Only Agenor sank down in the nearest wooden chair with narrowing eyes, scooping Coral from the floor in a motion as ominous as an alf drawing their sword.

'Could you elaborate?' he said slowly.

'The first problem is that we were right the bindings would take wider effect once the Mother started caring about keeping people alive,' Creon said, sitting straighter, and at once every trace of the wounded, arrogant prince was gone. In the blink of an eye, he'd morphed into a predator with only one goal on his mind: to completely eradicate any enemy challenging him, in the most efficient, most ruthless way possible. 'They're protecting about a quarter of her army, if my sample at the court was in any way representative. Far too many people my magic couldn't harm. Furthermore, it appears my binding also blocked me from *healing* myself at regular occasions. Seems like merely keeping myself in a condition fit to kill them was considered enough of a threat.'

I'd known, and yet I felt the blood leach from my face as I stared at him, remembering Doralis and the gaping wound in her leg. Tared cursed again – an impressive string of muttered syllables that seemed to have something to do with the Mother's forebears and rats.

'Thirdly,' Creon continued, unperturbed, 'they are aware and were aware of it before I attacked them. They deliberately sent individuals my way they seemed to think were protected, and they were right on most counts, which was why they surrounded me so easily. Fourthly—'

'Gods have mercy,' Agenor muttered, rubbing his face. 'Do you have any names?'

Creon did – about thirty of them, none of them familiar to me, but enough reason for several darkening faces around the room. Not all of them were high-standing fae at the Mother's court, I gathered. If anyone bound wouldn't be able to hurt *them* …

It might indeed be a quarter of her people our forces wouldn't be able to harm. It might be worse than that at the Crimson Court itself, where even more individuals would be personally known to her.

'I see.' If my father had sounded on the verge of cursing before, he now gave the impression he might start screaming any moment. 'And fourthly?'

'Corydas shouted something interesting in an attempt to bait me,' Creon said, raking a blood-stained hand through his hair. 'If I understood him correctly, his point was that I would be able to harm him about as much as I'd be able to harm the Crimson Court itself. Which suggests to me that the Mother assumes we'll be hindered by the bindings once we try to attack the building, too.'

'Yes.' Agenor sucked in a breath between his teeth. 'Did he say anything else?'

'He was a little too busy dealing with my knife in his windpipe,' Creon said, half a grin growing on his face. 'Bastard always annoyed the hell out of me.'

Agenor's laugh was joyless as a mourner's wail. 'Well, that's one happy result, at least.'

'Hardly worth dying for, though, is it?' Tared said sharply. 'As useful as all of this is, would it be too much to inform us *beforehand*, next time you decide to bet your life on your overenthusiastic estimation of your own powers?'

'And maybe take an unbound mage with you if you ever try something similar again,' Lyn grumbled. 'Madman.'

'I suggest we just don't try anything similar again,' I said, unable to suppress a shiver.

'Yes,' Agenor said grimly, rising to his feet. 'I would strongly prefer that solution, too, but I don't suppose Achlys and Melinoë will hold back for much longer now that they have the Golden Court back in their hands. Once they start attacking the other islands, I doubt we'll have much of a choice.'

I swallowed. 'Unless we figure out how to identify the bindings?'

'That would be helpful, yes.' He elegantly avoided the pool of blood on his way to the door. 'If no one else is planning on dying for now, I should go see how my people are managing in Inika's quarter. Let me know if anything comes up, and— Oh.' He turned in the doorway, eyes finding me. 'One last thing. I presume that bargain with the phoenix elders is not going to happen?'

'You know me so well,' I said wryly.

Clearly, he didn't feel like smiling, but he managed to send me a quick grin all the same; it even managed to look quite genuine. 'In that case, I suggest you hurry up finding another way to get them on our side. If we want to fight that war without functioning magic *and* without any significant winged forces, we may as well surrender immediately.'

'We're meeting in the Wanderer's Wing after lunch to discuss the phoenixes,' Lyn said, staring at her hands, her lips a wafer-thin line. 'I'll let you know what we come up with.'

'Thanks,' he said, and with a last quick nod, he turned on his heel and strode out.

It didn't seem to matter to my heart that Creon was no longer bleeding, even the smallest scrapes found and healed with an ocean's worth of blue. Nor did it help much that the living room had been scrubbed clean with both magic and soap, no drop of blood left behind. I sat on his bed, watched him strip off his ruined clothes, and found my stomach turning all over again, every strip of paler, newly-formed skin another reminder of just how close I'd been to losing him between the sandstone walls of the Golden Court.

If Tared hadn't been around. If Beyla had cared just a little less. If they'd cared but been just a little slower. If, if, if ...

'Em,' Creon interrupted my spiralling thoughts, that hoarse, warm voice I still hadn't fully gotten used to. 'Keep breathing.'

He didn't even need to look my way, gaze fixed on the torn sleeves he was peeling off his arms. His demon senses noticed all there was to notice: my rattling heart, my twisting stomach, the aimless fear keeping every muscle in my body on high alert even as I merely sat and waited.

'I'm trying not to panic,' I said, voice small.

'Being angry at yourself over panicking is rarely ever helpful,' he wryly reminded me, flinging his shirt through the open bathroom door and rubbing absently over a smudge of blood it had left behind. Below those stains, the lighter lines of healed skin contrasted sharply with the crude black ink of his older injuries, the wounds the Mother had immortalised on his body for the sole purpose of teaching him a lesson – past and present, a macabre chronicle of scars.

My guts only clenched harder at the thought.

'I was just very much not prepared,' I managed, unsure if that was truly the root of the fear, but sure that it was at least *something* I wanted to say – something I needed him to understand. 'For Beyla to drag me onto a battlefield. For you to be dying without any sort of warning there would be a fight at all. I ... I don't exactly like the idea of having to worry about you every minute you're out of my sight, just in case you're suddenly battling people again.'

He quietly stripped off his trousers, then looked up again – gloriously naked, but even that couldn't persuade my heart to stop bouncing around my chest like a panicked deer. 'There really is no need to worry that much about me, cactus.'

'In that case, you did a pretty terrible job of making that point,' I said weakly.

'Admittedly.' He hesitated, glancing at the bathroom and then at me, and sighed. 'Want to help?'

I hauled myself off the bed, tore off my own blood-soaked dress, and followed him. Near-death experience or no, it would take more than a bit of panic for me to pass up a chance to rub soap all over him.

We worked in silence for a few minutes, in the dusky light of that small bathroom barely large enough for us to move around each other. I scrubbed the blood and sweat off his back with soap and warm water from the shallow basin, massaging the lather deep into his skin. He healed the last scrapes and bruises on my limbs with magic drawn from the dark stone walls. I brushed the grime off his wings, cautious not to put too much pressure on the newly healed surface, and he rinsed the filth from my hair, combing out the wet strands with his fingers with soft, heartbreaking tenderness.

They were safe, these silent moments. Sheltered. An intimacy so much quieter than the heated moments of last night, yet somehow no less intense – a slow, smouldering fire that ran as deep as any white-hot blaze had ever done.

It was in that steam-filled fog of lavender soap and warm bodies that he eventually quietly said, 'I suppose it's the curse of war that sometimes you have no choice but to take risks. And you never know quite how risky they are until you're standing on a battlefield with an arrow in your back.'

My stomach rolled at that image, but at least a little less violently than before; rubbing a fluffy towel over his shoulder blades, chasing every last rivulet of warm water trickling down his bronze skin, was enough of a reminder that right *now*, there were no arrows to be seen around us. 'I know. I don't think that's the problem.'

He was silent again, wings curling ever so slightly towards me as I continued to dry him off. I finished my work on his back, then knelt and continued down his muscular thighs, the back of his knees. His cock had hardened to a most alluring state under my ministrations, but I forced myself to keep my hands away from it, from the temptation of his slender hips and taut buttocks – it would be either fucking or talking now, and the talking was too important.

Instead, I dried his shins with gentle, circular motions and added, 'I'm well aware you're the sort of person to take ridiculous risks. I don't expect that to change. It's just ...'

He turned his head a fraction when I didn't continue. 'Hmm?'

'It's just that I don't get why you took *this* one,' I blurted, and suddenly I understood. Suddenly it had a name, the quiet dread burning inside me – incomprehension, unanswered questions, the rotting, poisonous seedlings of doubt. 'Usually when you take risks – when you hurt yourself and pretend it's nothing to worry about – you're doing it to save others, aren't you? You tortured yourself to spare the Mother's victims. You sacrificed yourself so I could escape the court. But I just don't understand ... I just don't see ...'

What he'd tried to die for this this time.

For a stronghold we'd all agreed we'd give up when the time came? For a castle stripped of all valuable shreds of information or sentimental possessions?

For conclusions we'd already expected?

It didn't make sense. He knew that we needed him more than we needed any of those things, didn't he? He knew *I* needed him more than that? This was what the lingering shadow of panic had tried to tell me, that the puzzle wasn't complete yet – that there had to be something else behind this reckless decision of his, something that truly justified the chance that he might not make it out of the encounter alive.

And that I had not the faintest idea what it was.

It flared in full force now, the anxiety lying dormant beneath my skin. I dropped the towel as I rose to my feet, mind turning in such frantic circles that my lips couldn't even begin to catch up. If I didn't understand ... that meant I couldn't make sure this didn't happen a second time. Which meant I could be caught by surprise *again*, another near-lethal fight without a shred of warning – or worse, that next time he might not be so lucky and I would not even know until it was too late. Which meant—

'Em,' he said.

'I just ...' The lavender steam, so safe and comforting a moment ago, had become smothering fumes in my lungs. The walls started turning around me. 'I just don't—'

Creon's hand clasped my wrist.

Strong, calloused fingers, pressing into my arm with the strength of a protective hug – and at once my thoughts uncoiled. His voice might be unfamiliar to me. His words I could ignore. This touch, on the other hand, was a language I spoke fluently, so instinctively that it no longer required a single thought to obey: skin on skin, power on power, the savage intensity of his focus radiating into every nerve ending of my body. I gasped in a breath, and the walls stopped turning, his grip anchoring me to reality.

'Cactus.' This time my mind did latch on to the sound of his voice – hoarse, low, but with an edge of sharpness to it I couldn't make sense of. 'Breathe before you talk.'

I gulped in another lavender-scented lungful of air.

'Good. Keep doing that.' He let go of my wrist and scooped me off the floor, cradling me against his damp chest as he carried me back into the colder, clearer bedroom air. His heart thundered against his ribs, a little too fast and a little too vehement, as if it was trying to break through his ribcage to reach out to me. 'I won't die so easily, Em. I promise I won't.'

'I know you won't die *easily*,' I managed as he sank down on the bed and installed my naked body between his thighs, my back against his chest. 'But if you start making a habit of throwing yourself at entire armies for something as trivial as a few experiments, you—'

He stiffened behind me. 'As *trivial?*'

Fuck.

I no longer had the faintest idea of what was happening – what he was thinking, what I was supposed to be thinking – but that, the abrupt bite of his voice told me, had not been the right thing to say.

'I ... I just mean ...' The words seemed to be elbowing each other aside on the way to my lips, tumbling over each other. 'No one was in immediate danger of dying, were they? There could have been other ways to find this information. Less dangerous ways. I—'

'Em.' His arms tightened around me. 'Do you really think I would have jumped into that if I'd thought there were safer ways to figure out the same information?'

Did I?

Not really, not *rationally*, yet perhaps a small part of me did – feared that I had so fundamentally misunderstood the sort of person he was at war, that I had overlooked some glory-hungry part of him that didn't care about sense or strategy. 'No, but—'

'And we had to know.' He was speaking faster than usual – as if he'd barely heard me. As if he wanted, *needed* to convince me of something and wasn't sure he could. 'People weren't dying *yet*, but they absolutely will be, and we cannot determine how to keep as many as possible alive if we have no idea of our strong and weak spots in battle. What do you think would have happened if Agenor had come up with some strategy hinging on magic use and we'd found out halfway through that the bindings were in our way?'

'No, I know!' I wrestled from his embrace to turn and face him, breath going shallow again. 'I'm not saying it's not useful to know – just that maybe it wouldn't have been worth *dying* for.'

'So you'd rather have sent others to die finding out?' he said sharply.

It would have been so easy for him to soften that blow. To turn it into a teasing remark, a joke to ease the mounting tension. Instead, it shot from those full, soft lips with the force of a fist to the face, a contrast that had me wincing in his lap – what on earth was he doing, turning that question into something so very close to a bitter accusation?

He knew I'd do worse to keep him alive, didn't he?

Hell, *he* would do much, much worse to keep the world from harming so much as a hair on my head – so why was he glaring at me like that, like I'd been ridiculous to suggest maybe he shouldn't throw his life away for unsurprising intelligence? *Something* was off, and it was no longer just the unanswered question of his reckless motivations. He wouldn't argue so harshly and make me feel like an idiot over nothing. He wouldn't push himself to the edge of anger over nothing.

Was he embarrassed he'd lost the fight? The Mother's invincible prince of death, not so invincible after all?

But that didn't make sense either. He'd been overpowered and outsmarted before – had nearly been killed by the Mother and put in chains by Agenor, and none of that had stopped him from being just as casually arrogant as before. So was it tiredness? Pain? Lingering frustration over my weeks of doubting and waffling?

All of that at once, perhaps?

And what was I supposed to say now?

I climbed off his lap, wrapping one of his blankets around my shoulders, hoping a little distance from his warm skin would bring clarity of mind. My head spun like a whirlwind. I could tell him I hadn't wanted any others to die, that we should simply have found a small fae outpost at the edges of the archipelago and conducted the experiment *there*, rather than against a full army hungry for glory. I could tell him that he should at the very least have warned someone or made me come with him or put some rescue plan in place rather than staking his life on a few alves' good intentions. And yet …

He had to know all of that. It was simply unthinkable that that scheming mind of his had not considered any of those alternatives before he charged mindlessly into a horde of fae.

So would any of those sensible points assuage him in the slightest, if I didn't have a clue why he was ignoring them in the first place?

'I didn't mean to criticise you,' I said cautiously, weighing every word. A safe start – but hell, I shouldn't *need* to tell him that. *He* was the one who always understood me long before I did. *He* was the one who loved my thorns and sharp edges – there should be no need for me to soften the message, to stroke his wounded pride. 'You simply scared the hell out of me. And … and I suppose this is making me realise how much I'm dreading this war.'

'Right.' There was a tinge of heaviness in his voice, as if he, too, had not expected the sharpness of his last words. 'I can see that.'

'And I don't want you to get hurt,' I managed, my artificial calm cracking. 'You do understand that, don't you? That I really, really need you to stay alive through all of this?'

His shoulders loosened a fraction as he closed his eyes, and suddenly he looked far more like himself again. Gone was that strange, haunted tension in his features. Gone was the cramped way he'd held his wings against his shoulders, as if this conversation might turn into a deadly fight at the slightest unfortunate turn.

Was this a surprise to him?

None of this conversation made sense. Absolutely none of it did.

'So …' I started, evaluating my options with frantic thoughts. There was little chance I could make him see right now, in the heat of the moment, how utterly nonsensical he was being. A temporary compromise would have to suffice until I could get to the bottom of this. 'Could you promise me you'll try to let me know when you have to take any serious risks? *Before* you do it? I promise I won't try to stop you – I just prefer to be prepared when things might get dangerous for either of us. Alright?'

He looked so gods-damned unbreakable, perched on the edge of his bed like a perfectly sculpted statue come to life – inch upon inch of wiry tendons and rippling muscles, a weapon forged from living flesh and bone. And yet the crack in his voice was unmistakable as he averted his eyes, dark hair falling like a veil over his temples, and muttered, 'I'll try.'

'Thank you.' I poked him in the side with my foot, the one spot where I knew he was just a little ticklish. 'To compensate, I promise I'll take you along whenever I'm planning on doing anything stupid. Don't want you to miss out on armies to decimate.'

That was his own laugh again – that husky, melodious sound I was still getting used to and had already started craving like an exotic but delicious delicacy. The fist around my heart unclenched a little. 'I'm once again deeply grateful, Thenessa.'

'As you should be,' I informed him with mock-lightness, poking him again until he whipped around to slap my foot away. That inflammable agitation had mellowed from his face, thank the gods ... yet at the same time, where in hell had it gone so quickly? 'Should we be off to lunch, then?'

He glanced at his own naked body, the planes of his chest and the carved lines of his abdomen luring the eye straight down to the magnificent, half-erect equipment below. 'Are you sure you want me to appear at lunch like this, cactus?'

'What? No!' Gods, it was a relief to feel the outraged heat blossoming on my cheeks, to hear the triumph of his laughter again. Nothing wiped away my discomfort like this most familiar of routines, his effortless provocations, these challenges I couldn't win no matter how hard I tried. 'Will you think of my poor old father's heart, for goodness' sake?'

'Your poor old father has seen worse from me,' he dryly said as he rose and made for the closet. 'Although he might take it more personally now.'

'My bet is on the bread knife,' I said.

He laughed. 'My bet is on Coral. Which is a fine reason to get dressed, admittedly.'

And just like that, everything was as it should be again – as if those arrows had never bitten their way into his body. As if he'd never snapped at me so sharply. As if I'd just imagined it, the fear and the confusion, and there was nothing to worry about but phoenixes and Thysandra's determined refusal to talk.

Still ...

The unanswered questions lingered, a taunting whisper in the back of my mind. Someday he'd see sense, wouldn't he? Someday, he'd talk?

And if I could do anything to help it, that day was coming sooner rather than later.

Chapter 9

Lunch was a hurried, haphazard affair: half of the family had already eaten by the time we arrived at the table, and we were kept company only by Hallthor, who spent most of the meal furiously scribbling a new sword design, and Beyla, who was similarly busy marking locations on maps. Both of them made visible attempts to be civil to Creon, at least. Still, I was glad to get away from the table as soon as I'd swallowed my last spoonful of soup; mere feet away from the spot where Creon had collapsed with an arrow in his back an hour ago, it was a struggle not to feel the urgency of all we had left to do.

Last night, the atmosphere haunting the Underground had been one of tense anticipation. The mood that now hung over the same buried corridors was almost the polar opposite – no waiting but acting, a feverish activity in every nook and corner we passed. Alves were fading back and forth wherever we looked, dragging luggage and food around. In the council hall at the heart of the city, a small host of nymphs was chalking a giant map of the archipelago on the dark floor, placing wooden blocks on the outlines of islands to represent the armed forces of our opponents. Others were sparring, writing letters, sharpening blades. As if the Alliance had been a waiting arrow all these weeks, its string pulled tighter and tighter as the days ticked by ... until the Mother had finally made her move against the Golden Court and sent us all hurtling towards our final battle.

I couldn't help but wonder, remembering the stark white hills Tared had shown me, how many final battles I would be fighting in the years to come.

No one stopped us as we made our way to Inika's quarter, where the newly arrived fae forces were taking up residence in what had originally been phoenix homes. But the eyes and ears were there at every corner we turned, and the whispers rose in a steady stream behind our backs. At first, I thought it was because of Edored's utter lack of secrecy, every single soul in the Underground suddenly aware of the truth between us ...

And then I heard *what* they were whispering.

'... say she walked straight through their magic ...'

'... not a scratch! Not a single scratch!'

'... even more powerful than him ...'

I glanced at Creon beside me, whose face could have been hewn from stone, fathomless eyes gazing into the distance with a blatant disinterest that suggested the opposite below the surface. Those pointy ears tended to be more perceptive than mine. If *I* had heard that last sentence, hissed by one busty vampire to another, he most certainly had.

His expression didn't even twitch in response, scarred eyebrow a fraction higher than the other, unbreakable faint smile around his lips. And yet ...

There was a sense of melancholy about him that even that meticulous shield couldn't hide, a darkness far more pressing than the careless cruelty he hid behind.

'You're alright?' I muttered as we rounded the next corner, leaving the two vampires and their shameless ogling behind.

He lifted one shoulder without glancing my way, a gesture too indifferent to even qualify as a shrug. 'I'm not the one this is new for.'

True, of course. How often had he sauntered through the marble halls of the Crimson Court in much the same way, courtiers whispering with fearful admiration about his latest ruthless feat, forgetting there might still be a heart hidden behind those layers of bravura?

It might not be anything new plaguing him. Gods knew there were plenty of old things left to haunt his every step.

We passed another flutter of saucer-eyed nymphs, pupils in every colour of the rainbow following us down the corridor. The worst part of it, I realised, was not the judgement that might hide behind those unfaltering gazes. It was the way it made me see myself through the eyes of others again: some unknowable creature on a pedestal, like the heroine in a grand and epic ballad, more power than person, more symbol than soul.

'So how do you get used to it?' I said quietly, throwing a quick look over my shoulder to make sure no one was close enough to hear me. 'This feeling that you're just a little too much for the place you're in?'

Creon sent me a side glance, eyebrow quirking up. 'It's too small, you mean.'

'What?'

'Watch out who you're blaming,' he clarified, lips tight. 'You're not too much. The place is too small. Very different problem, very different solution.'

I blinked, waiting until a giddy couple of nymphs with laundry baskets had hurried past. Just like that, he effortlessly understood me again – as if that unravelling conversation on his bed had never even taken place. 'You know the feeling, then.'

'I know the feeling.' He sounded grimly amused. 'Why do you think I grew quietly obsessed with you the moment you started calling me an idiot?'

There's nothing small about you. Had *he* been the one feeling small, those days, for what might have been the first time in centuries?

I hadn't been able to understand so well before. Just a few minutes out here, in this nosey, admiring, intimidated company, and already I was aching for someone to just slap me on the shoulder, invite me for a drink, and call me some unflattering nicknames for no reason but the fun of it.

'Right,' I said sheepishly.

There was a sadness in his brief smile – regret as much as understanding. 'Don't worry too much about it. You'll handle it.'

I scoffed. 'You always say that.'

'Have I ever been wrong?' he countered, then laughed when I found myself unable to produce a more sensible answer than a heartfelt, wordless grumble. Of course he was rarely wrong, damn it. It was just that I couldn't even begin to imagine how I would ever turn this gawking audience into friends again, into people who were at least aware of the very fallible heart beating in my chest.

I would handle it, presumably.

And on the bright side, the opinions of people who were little more than familiar acquaintances were not even close to the first of my worries these days.

Inika's quarter was a little less interested in our every step than the rest of the Underground, although I suspected it was mostly because Agenor's people had better things to do than worry about his unmanageable daughter. They hurried around with characteristic quiet discipline wherever we went, some half-dressed or unarmed due to the rush in which they'd left, clutching the bags that had waited packed beside their doors for weeks. Even so, their hasty conversations fell silent more often than not whenever we stepped around the corner, and their wary glances were divided fairly equally between Creon and me.

Too small.

I gritted my teeth against that thought. Somehow, I *would* find a way to show them I was still human – still capable of feeling small and scared and lost.

It was a relief to finally reach the bright red door near the fields and slip into the library, where few people had bothered to show up on this morning of unrest and upheaval. We passed the empty reading tables and the equally deserted aisles in silence. The rune-covered door to the Wanderer's Wing looked familiar as always, yet I hesitated to step through it – other friends might be inside, Nenya and Cas and Thorir, and what if they would look at me with that same sickening mixture of caution and awe, that look one might aim at a particularly well-forged sword or a legendarily deadly poison?

'Cactus,' Creon muttered behind me, and somehow that one little word said all I needed to hear. No declawing myself. Let me be prickly and deadly and difficult – it wouldn't matter, anyway.

Not to him.

Not to me.

I pushed open the door and strode into the almost-sunlight without allowing myself another thought.

The room hadn't changed, the sight of the faded maps on the walls and the golden alf light of the fields an unexpected reassurance after all the time we'd spent traipsing through unknown territory. Tared and Lyn were standing by the bookshelves, discussing something in hushed tones – no trace of last night's fight to be seen, their rapid exchange as congenial as always. The only other person present, sitting at the table, was Nenya, whose scarred face was an impeccable mask of boredom as she studied her crimson nails and waited.

'Oh, there you are.' Her low, husky voice betrayed little feeling save for a mild irritation at our tardiness, although the way her eyes slid back and forth between the two of us was proof enough that either Tared or Edored must have told her everything. Still, the only comment that followed was, 'I suppose that bird is yours, Emelin?'

Before I could answer, an urgent, excited chirping rose from the fields outside – a sound I recognised intuitively, and not just because I'd known she'd be here, or because there was no other bird to be found in the Underground.

'I think it would be more accurate to say I'm hers,' I said, hurrying to the open arches. Out there, over the endless rows of carrots and cabbages, Alyra was darting back and forth in the alf light that flooded the cave, her feathers a golden white in those unnatural sunrays. She let out a joyous trill the moment she saw me, raced one swift round towards me by way of greeting, then soared away towards the outer ring of water again. 'She's not in anyone's way, is she?'

Nenya huffed a laugh, shaking her long, braided hair over her shoulders. 'She's in my *ears*, Emelin.'

The chirping grew illustratively louder.

'I wouldn't complain about that too much if you value the good health of your eyes and ears,' I said and threw her a bright smile before turning back to the faraway shrieks of my familiar. 'Those talons are pretty sharp.'

She let out a groan. 'What is it with you and murderous things?'

'Thanks, I suppose,' Creon said dryly.

Even Tared let out a chuckle behind me – unwillingly, perhaps, but that only sweetened the triumph.

The scraping of chairs told me they were sitting down; Lyn clambered into her seat just as I turned away from the fields. Between them, the round table with its map of the archipelago inlaid in the surface was covered in small wooden figures, painted in blue and yellow and red. Blue figurines on Tolya and the alf isles – confirmed allies. Yellow on Rhudak and most other nymph isles – likely allies.

Red on Phurys.

The phoenixes. No allies so far.

My stomach clenched at the sight of that single red pawn. It seemed to glare back at me as I sat down.

'Good news first,' Lyn said on the other side of the table, sounding tired. 'It looks like all our allies and probable allies will be in the Underground tomorrow night to discuss numbers and strategies. The alves, vampires, and most of the nymph queens have confirmed they'll be there. The downside of which is obviously that we'll be in some trouble if we don't get the phoenixes to be here by that time, too.'

I swallowed. 'Tomorrow.'

'We really can't wait any longer.' She rubbed both hands over her face, leaving pale streaks below her freckles. 'Now that the Mother is moving, she may attack anyone at any moment, and people above are understandably getting worried. So—'

Explosively interrupting her mid-sentence, a high, familiar voice burst into the room.

'... told you I was just taking a walk! There's nothing illegal about taking a walk! You can't just drag me away from—'

'Morning, Naxi,' Tared wryly interjected without even turning around.

Edored had appeared between the bookcases full of travellers' journals, clutching a wriggling half demon against his chest. With her shark's teeth bared and her nails scraping his forearms, Naxi no longer looked all that innocent, pink dress and blonde curls be damned; rather, she resembled a house cat abruptly gone feral.

'Found her,' Edored said brightly and rather redundantly.

'I was just taking a walk,' Naxi protested again, sounding rather feebler in the face of several sceptical-looking friends. Her feet gave up on kicking, sagging to dangle just above the floor. 'Just ... just stretching my legs.'

'In the old cell block,' Edored helpfully added.

'And then what?' she grumbled and sniffed furiously. 'There are no rules against that, are there?'

'Not at all,' Lyn said, lips trembling as if she wasn't sure whether to laugh or cry. 'There *are* several rules against helping prisoners escape this place, though.'

'And rules against giving prisoners any information they shouldn't be having,' Tared added; the look the two of them exchanged told me that whatever they had fought about in the past few days, this at least was a topic on which they agreed completely and wholeheartedly. 'And against making deals with prisoners on behalf of the Alliance. And ...'

'Basically,' Lyn said, turning back to Naxi, 'we were trying to do you a favour, sparing you the temptation of accidentally breaking those.'

Naxi scoffed, glaring at them like a ruffled pink rag doll against Edored's chest. 'Why in hell would I free her? She can't run from me here.'

'Oddly,' Lyn said with a helpless laugh, 'I'm not fully reassured by that supremely romantic sentiment. Let's see in a few days. And I think you can put her down, Edored darling.'

The alf did, unceremoniously planting his catch back on her feet. Naxi huffed, pulled her dress back into place, and stamped to the nearest empty chair without another word, looking not unlike a child denied her third sweet of the day – a sight that would have been more amusing if I hadn't known she could best most of us with little more than a flick of her fingers.

Edored crashed into the chair next to Nenya, beaming at her with all the unhinged cheer of a particularly loyal sheepdog. 'Did I tell you you're looking better, Nen?'

'Only about six times today,' she said tersely, her glare at him not entirely convincing. 'Thank you, though. Let's get back to the far more sensible topic Lyn was trying to discuss – how in the world we're going to handle the phoenix elders.'

Every sign of amusement abruptly melted from Lyn's freckled face. 'Yes. Please.'

I couldn't help but steal a glance at that bright red figurine again, sitting ominously on the isle of Phurys, just north of the Golden Court. On the other side of the table, Tared was glaring daggers at the same little piece of wood.

Nenya tapped a long red nail against her lips. 'So has anyone come up with another idea, if we're not going to give them the bargain they're looking for?'

'We could just kill them,' Edored said brightly.

'They'll come back to life, Edored sweetling,' Lyn muttered, rubbing her eyes so dejectedly that I could only agree with the storm gathering in Tared's expression. 'And I doubt it will soften their opinion of us if we force them into children's bodies again. If we're unlucky, they'll decide to run straight to the Mother and support her instead.'

I blinked. 'You really think they would do that?'

She was quiet for just a moment too long. Next to her, Tared's face was tight in all the wrong ways – no doubt to be found in his scowl, and that worried me more than even the desperate gleam in Lyn's amber eyes.

Run straight to the Mother. Even in this world of wolves against wolves, even with allies who drank every drop of blood from my friends' veins and welcomed me onto their islands only after divine intervention, I had been under the naïve impression that at least we all shared the same deep-seated hate of the fae empire we were forced to serve. Had even that been too optimistic a thought?

'The problem,' Lyn said, her voice too young and too small, 'is that they really, really don't like to take risks, and they are really, really desperate at this point. You need to keep in mind there were never that many of us in the first place. After the wars and over a century without children, there are just about a few thousand phoenixes left. We're closer to extinction than any other people in the archipelago, and the elders know it.'

That was a perspective I hadn't yet considered. After all those winters of seeing a whole village nearly starve to death, I hated how easily I made sense of it – how easily I understood.

Then again, I doubted the average alf house would ever side with the Mother even if they were down to the last five of their kind.

'And you really think they would ally with her for that reason?' I said, a brand new nervousness stirring in my guts. 'Despite the fact that *she's* the one who brought them to the point of extinction in the first place?'

'It's not that they're terrible people,' she said in a thin voice, then glared at Tared when he scoffed. 'They just prefer to be thorough and certain about things.'

'Insufferable nitpickers,' Tared translated.

She threw him another glower. 'They like rules. They like knowing what they're in for. They really, really like structure and composure and … and … *serenity*. So wars are hardly their cup of tea, and wars they might lose even less so.'

'Cowards,' Tared muttered, grinning at her when she once again sent him a withering look.

Bits and pieces fell into place – the sudden smallness of her otherwise dazzling presence whenever Phurys was mentioned, the depth of the anger in Tared's voice when he'd spoken about them yesterday. *Composure and serenity*. Not the right place for a phoenix with a flaring temper and a heart that felt so, so much. Not a home where anyone would have appreciated her for being … her.

No wonder she had so easily understood the weight on my shoulders.

'So,' I started cautiously, fingers itching, 'if someone were to burst into their meetings without an invitation and shout at them a little, that would be ... frowned upon?'

She closed her eyes. 'Won't work, Em.'

'Are you sure? Because I'm just thinking ...' I gestured at Creon. 'They're afraid to join because they're scared I'm nothing but Creon's puppet and they don't want to risk ending up in a fae empire even worse than the one in which they're currently living. Correct?'

'Yes,' Lyn said wearily, 'but—'

'So if we want them to join, we have two options. Either we have to convince them that Creon is actually a cuddly little sweetheart, which may be accurate but is hard to prove, given his unfortunate tendencies to murder people all over the place ...'

He chuckled next to me. 'Go to hell.'

'... *or*,' I stubbornly continued, ignoring Tared's blink of bemused surprise, 'we have to convince them that even *if* Creon were evil incarnate, I'm not under his thumb at all, and it therefore wouldn't be a problem if I talked to him every now and then. Which sounds a little more doable to me, right?'

'It doesn't work like that, Em,' Lyn said, eyes gleaming with bleak despair. '*They* don't work like that. You can stomp in with Creon on a leash for all they care—'

Creon burst out laughing. Tared dramatically rubbed a hand over his pained face, muttering something about things we could do in our spare time and mental images he had absolutely no use for.

'Oh, come *on*,' Lyn snapped, flinging up her little hands and silencing them both. 'Listen, none of you have the faintest idea of how these people truly operate, alright? They very much aren't alves or fae. You can't impress them by being shockingly brave or vicious, because they don't *care* about courage or viciousness or whatever other quality they consider synonymous with stupidity. All they want is ... is ...'

'Order and obedience,' Nenya muttered.

Lyn slumped in her chair with a grateful look to her side. 'Yes. I think you might get it.'

I didn't want to think about that – how much the place Lyn had called her home resembled the lair of a king who locked the vampires he created in his cellars like cattle to dine on. 'So what do you suggest, then?'

'I don't *know*.' She sounded on the brink of tears. 'If we try to go along with their policies and procedures, we'll have lost the war before we receive their next official response. But bursting in and forcing them to see reason will tell them we're not the sort of people they trust to deliver them victory, and they might just decide that joining the Mother and hoping for her sympathy will be a safer way to get themselves through these months unscathed. Which is obviously not what we're hoping for, either.'

Silence fell. Nenya seemed ready to set her fangs into someone. Naxi was biting her nails with her small, sharp teeth. Tared gave the impression he was itching to fade to Phurys and kick a few locked doors off their hinges.

'And you're sure killing them won't help?' Edored said, looking puzzled.

Nenya let out a groan. '*Edored.*'

'What?' he said indignantly. 'I'm just helping you think. Maybe we could scare them a bit? If they think we'll mess up their libraries if they join the Mother, they might—'

Creon abruptly sat up next to me.

'We're *not* touching anyone's libraries,' Lyn snapped, rolling her eyes so hard I thought she might strain them. 'I have my limits, you heathens, and either way—'

'I wasn't thinking about libraries,' Creon said, throwing her a wry grin.

'Oh, thank the gods.' She sagged a little. 'Any other plans, then?'

'No *plans*, necessarily,' he admitted, sitting straighter, flattening his wings against his shoulders. It was that single movement that abruptly did away with the languid, uncaring manner of the all-powerful fae prince, a gesture that could not have looked more dangerous if he'd slipped his knives from their sheaths in the same breath – sharpening the very air around him in the blink of an eye. 'But I just realised ... Look, we're all focusing on ways to make *not* joining us unpleasant for them, rather than on ways to convince them they'll get what they want if they *do* join us. We might want to try luring them in rather than forcing them.'

'That's lovely in theory,' Nenya said curtly, 'but we don't have anything they want. All we can offer them is risk and likely death.'

Creon shrugged. 'We have Em.'

Oh.

Oh.

'The bindings,' I said breathlessly.

His grin at me was alarmingly alluring – that grin of whirling thoughts, of the Silent Death spinning his spider's web around his unsuspecting victims.

'Yes, obviously they want the bindings,' Lyn burst out, throwing up her arms again, 'but we can't *use* the bloody things yet! We have absolutely no idea which binding belongs to whom! And as long as we don't even know where to start looking—'

'We could promise them they'll be first in line once we know, though,' Tared said slowly. 'Not that I like it much, but from a strategic perspective, that would probably be the first choice anyway. We need those wings.'

'Wait.' I narrowed my eyes at him. 'Did she take their *wings* to bind them?'

'Wings for males, fertility for females. Yes.' His grim smile was utterly joyless. 'So they may very well give in if we can convince them we'll get those things back to them.'

'*If* we can convince them,' Lyn bitterly interrupted. 'Which is currently impossible, because we don't know how to use the gods-damned bindings, and they're not going to believe us on the basis of our pretty blue eyes.'

'Creon has his voice back,' Nenya said, sounding doubtful. 'That could be evidence of what Emelin's new magic can do?'

'Creon is fae *and* technically still bound.' She tugged a wild red curl behind her ear with a groan of frustration. 'He's the very last example they would trust.'

Another silence fell, yet this one no longer seemed nearly so hopeless as the previous ones – it was buzzing with thoughts, with the new ideas bubbling up in me. They came with risks, of course. They came with danger. I would be walking a fine line – but gods, I much preferred that option to not walking at all.

'What if we had just one example?' I said.

'Reading my mind,' Creon muttered. 'I'm just wondering how we'll get Thysandra to talk.'

'Thysandra is very clearly not planning on talking,' Tared said, rubbing the bridge of his nose. 'And if she's used to dealing with demon magic, I doubt you're going to be able to torture the information out of her anytime soon.'

Creon's expression was just shy of an eyeroll. 'Much as it may surprise you, I *do* think about things other than torture every now and then.'

'I could try to convince her?' Naxi suggested hopefully.

'That's about plan F,' Lyn said with a groan. 'Any other ideas?'

Creon shrugged. 'I'm thinking it will be easier to make her betray the location of *one* binding than the general secret of how to identify them. She has a good memory. If she remembered where mine was, she may know where some of the other important ones are kept, too. So if we can offer her something in return ...'

'Like what?' Nenya said, chewing her bottom lip with one razor-sharp fang. 'I don't feel like offering her much, to tell you the truth.'

'She might do it for the opportunity to stick a couple of knives through my wings,' Creon said dryly. 'Pretty sure she's been wanting that for centuries.'

I scoffed, my heart skipping a beat more violently than I liked. The sight of those bloodied arrows still hovered far too close to the surface of my mind. 'Let's not exploit your self-sacrificial tendencies until we've excluded all other options, alright?'

He chuckled. 'So sensible.'

'You're the only person in this room who has ever called me sensible,' I said sourly. 'Not sure I want to know what that says about either of us.

Naxi, is there anything you think she might value enough to give us the information we need?'

'She'd do quite a lot to please the Mother,' Naxi immediately said, blue eyes wide with eager hope – as if Lyn and Tared might change their minds if she was just helpful enough. 'Then again, she may want to *not* please you even more. So it's possible she'll spit in your face the moment you ask for anything.'

I looked at Creon.

Creon looked at me.

Plans seemed to be shaping themselves in the air between us – plans I was strangely, exhilaratingly sure we shared, minds wandering into the same shadowy corners, the same schemes of almost-honesty. I might not be a seasoned general or a warrior with hundreds of battles behind me, but if there was one skill I had honed all my life, it was this one: manoeuvring the opinions of others around me.

He nodded, the faintest hint of a smile on his lips.

'Alright,' I said, drawing in a deep breath as I turned back to the rest of the table. 'Listen.'

And lo and behold, they did.

Chapter 10

The corridor Tared faded us into was long and narrow, pale alf lights hovering near the ceiling to illuminate the rows of cells on either side. The alf steel plates on the doors hinted clearly at the inhabitants they had been intended for – and had been used for, judging by the occasional scratches and dents in the stone and metal around us. Every now and then, some desperate fae must have attempted to fight their way out.

I shivered. I suspected many of the individuals who'd ended up here had never seen the light of day again.

'She's in cell number 104,' Tared said in a low voice, clearly unhindered by the memories this place must evoke. 'Don't tell Naxi, please. Once you're done, you can walk around that corner and left again, and you'll be behind Etele's quarter. I suppose you can find the way back by yourselves?'

We assured him we could. He pressed the key into my fingers and vanished into nothingness, on his way to Phurys to set the next part of the plan in motion. Leaving Creon and me alone so, so easily – it still felt like a miracle.

'It's almost like he suddenly trusts me,' Creon said, studying the cells with the expression of an expert encountering an unusual but impressive piece of work. In the sickly, flickering lights, the scars on his hands and forearms looked like deep, black-bleeding gashes; surrounded by locked doors and traces of violence, he looked more like a fae torturer than he had in a long time. 'Did Ylfreda check him for brain damage after the fight at the Cobalt Court?'

'I'm guessing he just wants to be out of here before I put a leash around your neck,' I said sweetly.

His laughter still sounded like a miracle.

The doors were numbered with small steel signs. We found number 104 at the far end of the corridor – a safety precaution, I assumed, more work for a certain little half demon who'd need to check every single empty cell before finding the one that was currently occupied. I glanced at the key in my fingers, annoyed to find it was trembling despite all my best attempts to believe I knew exactly what I was doing.

'Alright,' I managed to force out before drawing in a deep breath. 'She probably shouldn't see you, don't you think? I'll just go in and leave the door open, and then you can wait around the corner and intervene if things go south – does that work?'

No response.

I looked up to find him leaning against the next steel door, arms crossed and wings folded closely against his back, face tight as he watched me. As if I'd said something catastrophically wrong. As if I'd lethally offended him – again.

My heart flipped in my chest. 'Creon?'

'I may not be able to intervene if she starts causing trouble,' he said, his rough voice low but without a trace of that sharpness with which he'd lashed out in his bedroom. 'If the bindings protected bloody Corydas, they'll protect Thysandra, too.'

'Oh. Right.' I felt my shoulders sag with relief. Gods damn my jittery nerves, reading far too much into simple strategic concern. 'But you have your knives on you, don't you? So you should at least be able to slow her down or drag me out if needed.'

He nodded – a slow, hesitant gesture nowhere near convincing. His frown didn't loosen.

'No?' I said.

'Should work,' he admitted, forcing a brief smile about as genuine as rusting gold. 'I'm just being overly cautious. You could probably manage her on your own either way.'

I narrowed my eyes at him. 'Creon, what is it?'

'Oh, nothing.' He stood straight with an impatient flick of his fingers, wings relaxing a fraction behind his shoulders as he shrugged. 'Nothing of importance, that is. Let's get this business over with, first. We have more to do.'

Edored pretending to understand the intricate complexities of vampire politics had been more credible. I parted my lips to argue, then remembered where we were standing and that I didn't even know whether the door of cell 104 was entirely soundproof – not the safest place to discuss whatever the hell was going on with him. If he didn't even want to tell *me*, he definitely would not want Thysandra to know.

And either way, he was right. If all went according to plan, we *did* have more to do today.

'As you wish,' I forced myself to say, making no effort to look at all convinced. He hadn't done anything to deserve that courtesy. 'Are you ready, then?'

He sank down onto the floor in response, drawing a knife and settling himself against the wall beside the door of cell 104 with a swift nod. As unhurried as his posture might be, I knew he'd be by my side within a heartbeat at the slightest sign of alarm; it was that thought which gave me the courage to turn that damned key in the lock and push the steel-plated door open, left hand against the red skirt of my dress.

There was no need for it. They had chained her in alf steel, the whitish metal gleaming against the dark skin of her wrists in that same sickly light.

Even on the narrow wooden bench of an empty cell, even covered in mud and scrapes, Thysandra stubbornly refused to look like a captive. The glare she sent me was that of an exasperated empress wondering when the peasants would finally stop their ungrateful nagging; her scarred, black-and-gold wings lay curled around her arms and shoulders like unbreakable armour. Someone had brought her food, water, and soap during the night, but she hadn't touched any of it. A blanket lay folded in the corner of the small room, unused.

As if the slightest acknowledgement, even the mere possibility of gratitude, would already be too much of a betrayal.

I hadn't thought I could still feel sorry for her, the sound of Creon's shattering binding still echoing in my ears. But I'd felt her pain with Zera's bag in my arms. I understood what Naxi had told us mere minutes ago. In the end, every comfort she was refusing, every primary need she was denying, was little more than a plea to the Mother – to notice her, to reward her, to love her.

And I doubted the Mother would be all that impressed with this useless show of heroism.

'Morning,' I said, cautiously taking my hand off my dress but leaving the door open behind me. She didn't relax in the slightest, glaring down at me haughtily. 'How are you?'

A scoff was her only response to that question. 'What do you want?'

Somehow, it stung that she was right – that I *was* here because I needed something from her, not out of kindness or compassion. I would have liked to be better than the Mother, at least. Better than the endless dance of favours and debts she knew from the Crimson Court.

Then again, it was a relief that she at least wasn't cowering from me.

'There are a few things I wanted to ask you,' I said.

'A shame,' she said coldly. 'I don't have anything to tell you. If that's all, I'd prefer for you to leave me alone in this hellhole.'

Promising start. I lowered myself into a seat against the opposite wall, out of reach of her chains, and ignored the poisoned daggers in her glare. Compassion or no, we needed her help if we wanted to prove ourselves to our troublesome allies – and if we wanted to have any chance of winning the war, I couldn't, *couldn't* mess this up.

'I would like to know the location of Lyn's binding,' I said.

It came out calm. Confident. As if my hands weren't clammy in my lap, my brain running at red-hot speed trying to plot out every single path this conversation could follow.

Thysandra stiffened, then let out a low, scornful laugh – a laugh that told me she'd rather tear off her own wings with her bare hands than voluntarily hand me any of the information I so desperately needed. 'So that's why I'm not dead yet? Because your sorry traitor friends need me to restore their magic first?'

'You're not dead because we don't want to kill you.' I spread out my hands – deference, an offer of peace. 'Just this one binding. If you can give us that, I'll try not to bother you for the others.'

'Why?' she said sharply.

'Why do we not want to kill you?'

'No. Why Phiramelyndra?' As much as she was trying to look furious, cold, and disinterested, she was unmistakably leaning in a few inches – of course a brain like hers couldn't help but try to make sense of what little crumbs she was given. 'Do you need her unbound magic so badly? Because her offspring isn't going to win you this war.'

'No,' I admitted, resting my head against the wall. *She'll be distrustful of every word you speak*, Creon had said, and so I tried to look trustworthy. Like someone she could, if not like, at least respect. 'But the other phoenixes treated her like shit. One of the elders – Lord Khailan – has been trying for years to punish her for joining the Alliance. I'm trying to make a point.'

She scoffed. 'By getting back her binding and not theirs?'

'Pretty much, yes.' I shrugged. 'The details aren't that important, frankly. Do you know where to find her binding?'

'Of course I do,' she bit out. 'All the important ones. You can tell your darling friends that, and don't forget to pass on that I'd rather spend the next five years in a torture cell than do them the favour of betraying even a single location. Are we done?'

Coming from anyone else, I would have considered that reckless bravura. From her ... She might be speaking the unexaggerated truth.

'I'm not planning to torture you,' I said, rubbing my eyes. 'I could probably do you a favour in return, if you could tell me—'

'Let me go,' she snapped.

I groaned. 'Not that kind of favour.'

'Oh, I see,' she sneered, throwing her head back so that her tangled black-and-gold hair tumbled over her shoulders and red dress. 'You're happy to do me a favour, as long as it's nothing I actually need. Thank you, Thenessa, and once again, *go to hell*.'

'Please,' I managed, voice soaring. 'There must be something I can do for you, even here. Tell me what you want, and—'

'Or what?' she interrupted, biting out the words. 'If I don't give in to your blatant bribery, what will you do? Bring in the golden boy and his knives after all?'

The golden boy. I'd never heard anyone refer to Creon like that, not even the alves in their most furious of rants – was this an old Crimson Court nickname, from before he lost his voice? Or was it just her own animosity speaking, from whatever murky past it might be rooted?

'Once again,' I said, struggling to keep my voice level, struggling not to ask for details, 'I'm not planning to torture you.'

She scoffed. 'You'd be mad.'

I shrugged. 'Maybe I am?'

'Oh, no.' Her dark eyes narrowed. 'You're not playing that game with me again, little dove. You may be a treacherous bitch, but if you survived to this point, you're *nowhere* near mad – so what are you playing at, then?'

This was the Crimson Court talking, I supposed – no words without double meaning, no offer without hidden poison. Did it matter how trustworthy I tried to look? I wouldn't prick through centuries of habits and experiences that way.

So maybe the truth was my best bet.

'You offered me your help, once,' I said slowly. 'Back at the court. After the Mother took Creon. That was kind of you, and I don't see what it would have won you.'

Her lip curled a fraction. 'And see what has come of it.'

'But you *were* honest. I'm trying to be honest, too.' That was, strictly speaking, a lie. I wasn't telling her why I was asking for Lyn's binding. I wasn't telling her why I needed to make an impression on the phoenixes so badly. Then again, my despair was fully, genuinely sincere. 'Thysandra, I just need that one binding. Just something to make the elders regret being such stubborn arses. What do you want? I could allow you to send a letter to the Crimson Court?'

For one brief moment, it seemed like she was doubting, and my heart skipped a beat. Then the vicious suspicion was back in her eyes, sharper than ever before. 'Stop trying to charm me, little dove.' Her voice was just a fraction unsteady. 'My loyalty can't be bought.'

'Everyone's loyalty can be bought,' I retorted, choosing my words with painstaking care even below the throwaway arrogance. 'I'm just trying to figure out your price.'

Was that too much? Her dark cheeks turned even darker, a furious blush in the cold, pale light; her voice hit me like the lash of a whip. 'How *dare* you, you little—'

'Please, Thysandra.' I leaned towards her, emphasising the plea. My last chance. My finishing move. 'Just one binding – just something to make bloody Lord Khailan swallow his pride. I'm *begging* you.'

'I'll give you your one binding,' she spat, half coming up from her plank bed. 'Khailan's is the twenty-third orb in the fifth west aisle. A boon you don't need in return for your useless offers. Now get *out*.'

I could have cried.

Instead, all I said as I scrambled to my feet was, 'I hope you'll come to appreciate us more during your stay.'

'I hope you drown in your own chamber pot,' she snapped, eyes blazing. 'Get out of my fucking sight. And if you want me to ever speak another word to any of you' – she drew in a deep breath, words suddenly wobbling a little – 'you'd better keep Anaxia away from me.'

I turned in the doorway, sliding my gaze over her one last time – hands clenched to fists, muscular forearms bulging against her alf steel chains, breasts heaving with agitation under her torn red dress. Her gaze met mine with roaring fury and something that was perhaps a hint of ...

Fear?

'I'm very sorry,' I said, stepping out. 'I truly don't think anyone down here is that powerful.'

Her curse was the last thing I heard as I slammed the door behind me.

And then there was just Creon's laughter, a sound that made me forget in the blink of an eye about festering hatred and unruly allies – a reward far more glorious than even success itself, echoing through the bleak corridor in bursts of gravelly, infectious triumph.

Lord Khailan's binding.

Step one, at least, I'd managed.

Step two burst into the Skeire home after breakfast the next morning.

I was just setting the last stitches to finish my adjustments to the dress I'd pilfered from Lyn's extensive adult wardrobe – a billowy, velvet creation in such a deep red I could blow up half a city with it – when Cas arrived, faded straight into the living room by a crook-nosed alf female I didn't know by name. The phoenix was blushing with agitation, his awkward not-long-but-not-short-either hair tousled in a tell-tale sign of sleepless nights.

'Emelin,' he panted, collapsing into the nearest armchair as if he'd run all the way from Phurys to the Underground. 'The elders have agreed to see you. In *half an hour*.'

Deafening silence answered him.

I stared at the flustered young male before me, my needle frozen in my fingers, the implications of his words taking an age to land. Next to me, Creon had stiffened over his hastily sketched map of the halls of the Cobalt Court. *Agreed to see you* – but in half an hour?

That was not an agreement. It was hardly an invitation.

Rather, a summons.

Sitting at the table, Tared broke the silence with a slow, heartfelt curse.

'I'm sorry,' Cas stuttered, wringing his hands as he turned his gaze to the alf. 'I passed on the message you gave me – that Emelin wanted to discuss their proposal and had some confidential news on her magic to share with them – but I didn't expect—'

'They're grasping for control,' Creon interrupted, pulling his feet from the chair where they'd so leisurely rested while he puzzled over potential organisations of the bindings. His voice was a little better this morning – husky rather than hoarse – but the anger in it was no less cutting. 'Do they have any other conditions?'

'She's supposed to come alone,' Cas said hurriedly. 'The alves can bring her to Phurys, but she's to take no one with her into the Fireborn Palace. *Especially* no fae company.' His grimace at Creon was half apology, half nervousness. 'They seem to be a little uneasy about you.'

'Can't imagine what I did to deserve that,' Creon muttered, turning to me. 'Is half an hour enough?'

I shrugged. 'I'm always ready.'

That drew a small smile from his lips. 'You could refuse to come running, though.'

'They're capable of making us wait another three weeks,' Lyn said through her fingers, staring miserably at the table. 'Is our annoyance really worth that much?'

Tared groaned. 'Possibly, yes.'

'Look at us, agreeing,' Creon said, sending him a sour grin that was answered in kind. 'If this is the sort of allies they plan to be, I'm starting to think I'd rather have enemies.'

'We never expected them to be kind and welcoming about it,' I said and rolled my eyes at the both of them. 'And I can't make them swallow their pride if I never get to see them in the first place. So I'll just go and politely suggest they try a different tone in their future communications, alright?'

Cas threw one look at the wine-red dress in my hands and swallowed audibly.

'If you could just take someone with you ...' Tared started.

'I'll bring Alyra. Don't suppose they said anything about murderous birds.' I got up, holding up the dress to inspect my last stitching. 'If someone could go look for her while I wrestle myself into this thing, I'll be ready to go in ten minutes at most.'

Tared grumbled another curse but exchanged a glance with Lyn and stood as well. 'I hope you know what you're doing, Em.'

I had not the faintest idea what I was doing – at least, not beyond the plans and counterplans we'd discussed at length the previous day, not beyond the portraits I'd studied until late at night, the names I'd memorised, the floorplans I'd pored over until I knew half the Fireborn Palace by heart. But I was angry. I was hungry. And gods, it felt good to just run with the ideas bubbling up in me, to make my choices and own them – for better or for worse, but at least they were *mine*.

'Don't worry,' I said, making for my bedroom. 'I'm an expert when it comes to changing stubborn immortal minds, as you know.'

Tared sent me an impolite gesture but faded away without further objections.

In the end, it took me even less than ten minutes to prepare, donning the velvet dress and the jewellery I'd collected over the course of our preparations the day before. Two obnoxiously large pearls on my fingers, an emergency source of iridescence. Smooth, gleaming gold around my neck, and more of it in my hair, keeping my brown curls pinned in place. Most important of all, the gold and mother-of-pearl bracelet Creon had fabricated after we returned from our short trip to the Cobalt Court yesterday, using yellow magic I was no longer capable of wielding.

The prettiest, deadliest armour.

I felt like a glittering spectacle by the time I made my way back to the living room, and that, too, felt better than it should have. If I had to be a symbol, at least I'd be a memorable one.

Tared had found Alyra in the meantime; she soared through the room in wide, excited circles, leaving tufts of down behind at every abrupt mid-air turn. The moment I stepped into the room, she let out a shrill squeak and fluttered to a perch on the backrest of a chair, peeking at me with thinly-veiled eagerness.

'You'll have to be careful and do exactly as I say,' I told her, shutting the door behind me. 'We're going into a place where many people recently lost their wings, you see.'

She cowered with another outraged shriek, then glared at Creon when he sniggered.

I allowed myself half a smile and turned to Tared, who stood leaning against the nearest wall, sword in his hand in a silent declaration of war. 'I suppose you're taking me there?'

His grin rivalled Alyra's most violent looks. 'Thought you'd never ask.'

'Be careful, Em,' Lyn muttered at the table, sounding about to burst into tears. 'And *please* don't do anything to anger them if you can help it, alright?'

'But if you can't help it,' Creon said dryly, 'at least make sure you anger them thoroughly.'

I laughed and hugged him, ignoring the panicked little stutter of my heart at the unimaginable publicness of it – but no one said a word as his strong arms closed around me and pressed me tightly against his chest, drowning me for one blissful moment in the scent of spiced honey and the slow thud of his heart. His lips brushed over the crown of my head, lightly, so as not to mess up the careful arrangement of my hair.

'Keep yourself safe,' he said quietly.

I nodded against his shoulder, and he let go of me far too soon, stepping back with a last tense smile. His look at Tared was an obvious warning – *And you'd better keep her safe, too.*

Another drop of venom seemed to vanish from the air between them as Tared curtly said, 'Will do.'

'We have about fifteen minutes left,' Cas said nervously.

Tared groaned a sigh, holding out an arm to me. 'Ready?'

'Ready,' I said, gesturing for Alyra to follow as I stepped around the table to join him. Her small talons dug into my shoulder even through the firmer patch of fabric I'd added to my dress, and I couldn't help a wince as I grabbed Tared's elbow.

The room blurred around me. The silence of the Underground broke into a sudden cacophony of sound.

Time for our final step.

Chapter 11

For six long heartbeats, there was just the whirlpool of light and noise, the blue of the sea and the gold of ripe grain flashing by, the oddly warped sounds of voices and wind and crying seagulls. Then, with a shock, a whole new world took shape around us, brightly coloured buildings and lush, flowering gardens as far as the eye could see.

I hadn't known what to expect from Phurys, but I sure as hell hadn't expected *this*.

It seemed the largest phoenix isle was twice as sunny as any other place in the archipelago I'd visited in my life – golden light glowing on the plastered sandstone buildings and the colourful mosaics that framed the doors and windows, turning the wide square on which we had arrived into a summer scene even in late autumn. Fountains gurgled around us. Palm trees rustled between the houses. Scents of baked herbs and roasted meat wafted towards us from the market stalls on the far side of the square, where red-haired males and females in long robes had gathered to eat and drink and talk.

And on the nearest side …

I turned. A mere fifty feet away from me, rising proudly over the golden square, stood the Fireborn Palace.

I'd seen paintings and drawings and sketches of it yesterday, dozens of them, and none of them had prepared me for the dazzling glory of the building towering over me – the official heart of Lyn's people. A broad flight of stairs led up to a reddish-brown façade, intricate gold filigree and gleaming gems lining the walls and windows. A gate gaped before us, granting access to a wide hall covered in colourful, geometric tiles. Slender towers reached into the sunny summer sky, their parapets covered in crystals like dewdrops, and behind that imposing front, a golden dome gleamed decadently in the sunlight, the structure higher and wider than the house in which I'd lived the first twenty years of my life.

It looked like wealth and knowledge, this castle. Like the endless libraries Lyn had told me about, like the work of people who had lived and died more times than I had seen summers in my whole life.

For the first time, I found myself doubting the details of the plan we'd worked out over yesterday's evening meal.

'Don't let yourself be intimidated,' Tared muttered, hand closing around the shoulder that didn't contain a bristling, fluffy bird. 'It's all show and very little substance.'

I felt like a similarly hollow show myself, I almost said, a little unbound mage wrapped in gold and pearls under the watchful eye of this building older than anyone I knew ... Then again, a little unbound mage was what they expected. That was the girl the Mother had told them about, innocent and naïve and easily susceptible to the treasonous influence of her feared and hated executioner.

The mother-of-pearl bracelet hung heavy on my wrist, a shimmering reminder of the weapons I was bringing.

Softness for movement. Smoothness for mind. Iridescence for magic.

'Thanks,' I forced myself to say, drawing in a deep breath. Heads were turning around us, the first passing phoenixes noting the unexpected arrival of outsiders. 'Anything else I should keep in mind?'

'I'll wait here.' Tared let go of my shoulder, ignoring our growing audience with an enviable lack of concern. 'Send Alyra my way if you need help. Send her my way if you'll be gone for longer than an hour, too, with one of your rings to signal that you're safe and alright. I'll come and get you otherwise.'

'Will do.' Sweat was pearling between my shoulder blades; I wasn't sure if it was the heat of the bright morning sunlight or the prospect of whatever was waiting for me inside. 'Don't kill any phoenixes while I'm gone.'

He grinned at me. 'Don't worry. I'm leaving them for Lyn.'

Alf gallantry really was a phenomenon of its own. I managed to more or less answer his smile, steeled my spine, and walked without looking over my shoulder, sun and watching eyes burning into my back. In this lion's den, I would be a fool to look like I was hoping for anyone's support or approval on my way inside.

No one stopped me as I climbed the broad stairs stretching along the full width of the palace and strode through the wide-open gate with my head held high. Either the phoenixes in their long, elegant robes had known I would be here, or they saw no reason to keep a lone, human-looking girl from entering.

A spacious hall opened up behind the gate, the many intricate niches and pillars covered in more of those same blue and gold tiles. *Walk straight on*, Lyn had said, drawing the route on one of the many floorplans of the palace, *through the wooden gates with the golden dragons, up the stairs, and then to the right until you see a door flanked by two enormous vases. Someone will probably try to stop you there ...*

My footsteps echoed menacingly as I walked, the hem of my velvet dress fluttering around my knees, Alyra's talons digging into my shoulder. As impressive as the palace looked on the outside, I hardly met anyone walking through the corridors – a ghost of a place, a shell of former glory inhabited by five powerful rulers and the handful of people left to serve them.

They're desperate.

I understood it now, noticing the spiderwebs behind half-closed doors, the cracks and flaking paint behind strategically placed furniture. What must it be like to walk these halls day after day, watching the ship sink ever so slowly and being unable to do anything to keep it afloat?

Then again ...

Lyn had been trying to keep them afloat. And they'd cast her out over it all the same.

I walked a little faster.

Alyra grew tenser with every step, her little head shooting from left to right as if she was waiting for the wing thieves to show up. But she held perfectly still when finally, by the door with the vases Lyn had described to me, two tall phoenixes stepped forward and commanded me to stand and wait, speaking the most archaic version of my native language I'd ever heard from anyone's lips.

There was something unnerving about it, two males who looked to be in their thirties yet sounded like they were half a century older than the oldest inhabitants of Cathra and Ildhelm. It told me all I needed to know about their contact with the rest of the world since losing the Last Battle.

'Morning,' I said, granting them my coldest smile. 'I have an appointment with the elders.'

The one on the left – meticulously curled beard, gem-set golden earrings, and a sword the size of a grown man in his hand – narrowed his eyes. 'Emelin of Agenor's house?'

It took all I had not to sweep into a dramatic bow. 'That's me.'

He looked me up and down twice, as if he had expected at least ten more inches and a pair of velvet wings, then exchanged a quick look with his colleague – smooth-shaven, thin-lipped, and holding a loaded crossbow. 'Where is your alf?'

'Outside,' I said, raising an eyebrow in my best imitation of Creon's look of haughty annoyance. 'I was asked not to bring anyone, so I didn't. Of course, if you'd rather see him after all ...'

The hurry with which they assured me they had no desire to see any alves at all would have been amusing if not for my jumpy nerves. 'And the bird?'

'The bird,' I said even more coldly, 'is coming with me.'

Another look went back and forth. 'The invitation—'

'The invitation did not specify anything about non-humanoid companions,' I interrupted, 'only about alves and fae, and in any case, I'm not sure if Alyra would be considered a companion in the strictest sense of the word. As my familiar, she is more or less part of me. I don't suppose your elders are so frightened of visitors they would hide away even from a *bird*?'

They looked a little sheepish. 'No, but—'

Alyra puffed out her chest on my shoulder, releasing a hissing sound.

'Really,' I said, 'you'd cause yourself and the elders more trouble by keeping her away from me. She doesn't take that sort of interference lightly.'

'But the protocol—' started the thin-lipped one on the right.

To hell with it, then. I pressed my left hand to my dress and drew a whiff of the magic it contained – *softness for movement*. A throwaway twirl of my right fingers, and the high wooden gate behind them flew open as if by itself.

The two guards whipped around at the creak of the hinges. 'What—'

'Much obliged,' I said with deeply insincere cheer, striding forward before either of them could regain their composure and stop me.

Quite as I'd hoped, they did not raise their voices or run after me as I made my way into the hall beyond. No phoenix would voluntarily make a scene and admit defeat, Lyn's stories had suggested: much more in line with the national character to swallow their confusion and pretend all was well, even in the face of abundant evidence to the contrary.

The octagonal hall with its domed mosaic ceiling was enormous.

Illuminated by sunlight falling through thin slits beneath the dome itself, the room was an outburst of splendour, a memorial of better and more powerful times. Mosaics on the walls portrayed mythical beasts writhing in flames and blazing wings against dark, starry skies; rows and rows of intricately carved wooden seats allowed access to more phoenixes than might currently be alive in the world. At the far side of the room, an enormous chandelier hovered above a gilded stage, dozens and dozens of scented candles spreading the heavy fragrance of incense through the room.

They sat below that chandelier, the five of them.

Two females. Three males. Some red-haired, others greying, one old enough to have gone bald. They had positioned themselves in a semi-circle on their throne-like seats, richly embroidered silk robes shimmering in the dusty sunlight – watching me as I marched down the deserted central aisle, keeping so quiet that even the soft sound of my footsteps seemed a booming drum to my ears.

A sixth seat, a simple wooden chair far humbler than the thousands I was passing on either side of me, had been placed at the foot of the stage before them.

For the bloody gods' sakes.

Don't anger them, Lyn had said, but this was *not* how we were going to play this game – me sitting demurely before them like a suspect waiting for the jury verdict. It took three steps to assess the situation. Three more steps to make my decision. Then, without slowing down, I kept my left hand against my dress and swung my right hand forward again, aiming for the chair this time. Another burst of softness from the velvet, and the simple seat floated calmly up into the air, settling itself gently on the stage opposite the five elders.

Their widening eyes and thinly veiled gasps alone made it worth the risk.

I strode on as if nothing had happened, ignoring their uneasy glances as I climbed the steps that looked like a later addition to the gilded monstrosity. No more wings for the males. They'd been able to fly up the platform before their bindings.

I might have felt sorry for them if not for their brusque summons, or their treatment of my friends, or their fuckery with the seating arrangements.

'Good morning,' I said as I reached the top of the narrow stairs, smoothing my crimson dress with my politest, most meaningless smile. 'You were expecting me, I believe?'

That was, of course, a lie. They had expected the Mother's witless little dove. They had expected Agenor's barely grown daughter. They had *certainly* not expected a mage who'd walk in with a furious tiny falcon on her shoulder and perform impossible magic tricks before even speaking her first word – a mage who would smile at them with just as much venom as they wielded themselves.

The female sitting on the left was the first to recover, the corners of her painted lips twisting mechanically upwards while the others were still sending concerned glances back and forth. 'Emelin, I presume?'

'You presume correctly,' I said and sat down, ignoring her sharp intake of breath that would, presumably, have led to an invitation to do so. 'Lady Yndrusillitha, I take it?'

There. I hadn't been browsing all those damned portrait books for nothing.

'Ah. Yes.' Her humourless smile turned even more mechanical. Lady Yndrusillitha, Drusa for closer acquaintances. A former friend of Lyn, I'd gathered from our conversations yesterday, although Lyn had stubbornly avoided every mention of what had ended that friendship; my suspicions did not make me look at Drusa's tightly pinned white hair and sourly pursed lips with any more fondness.

Neither did her honey-sweet, 'We are glad you could make it to this meeting, Emelin.'

Had they hoped I wouldn't be able to show up in time? I inclined my head, careful not to make the gesture look anything like a bow, and said, 'I'm grateful you could receive me on such short notice.'

The fact that I wasn't swinging more chairs around seemed to reassure them a little; the others were sitting straighter now, faces pulled back into masks of perfect composure. Directly opposite me, at the centre of their little circle, was the male with the braided red hair and razor-sharp jaw whose portrait Lyn had shown me before any of the others – Lord Khailandakhsyr-something-something, known as Khailan to anyone who didn't feel like memorising the thirty syllables of his full name, and oldest phoenix alive. Powerful mage. Accomplished archer. Lauded poet.

Also, currently wingless.

The sharp edges of the bracelet pressed reassuringly into the flesh of my forearm.

'We have met with your father,' Khailan told me, voice a polished drawl that set me on edge from the very first syllable. 'Lord Agenor.'

They'll want to make small talk for a while. Discuss mutual acquaintances. The weather. The splendour of the hall in which you have gathered. Lyn's words echoed in my mind. *Getting straight to the point will be considered the height of impoliteness.*

'I know who my father is, thank you,' I said icily, smiling back at the male opposite me with an insincerity that matched his own. 'He told me about your meeting. If I recall correctly, you were suggesting a bargain of some kind – something to do with my communications with Creon Hytherion.'

Their scandalised glances were subtle, but still scandalised.

'Ah,' Khailan said stiffly. 'Yes.'

'So I thought it would be easiest to just visit you in person and decide the matter once and for all,' I continued, leaning back in my chair and crossing my legs with another bright smile at him. 'I'll keep it simple – that bargain is not going to happen. As glad as I would be to have you by our side in the upcoming war, this is not a price I'm able to pay. But I will be happy to discuss acceptable alternatives, of course.'

The short male to Khailan's left cleared his throat – Mydhar, I recalled, or at least, that was the sensible part of his voluminous name. 'A rather surprising decision, Lady Emelin.'

'Is it?' I said politely.

'And as older and wiser allies, we must urge you to reconsider.' His sing-song voice managed to be sharp and syrupy at the same time. 'You may not be aware yet, but there have been *worrying* rumours concerning the nature of your relationship with the Silent Death. A refusal from you to decisively disprove those rumours …'

He didn't finish his sentence, allowing it to die away in a tone that suggested all had been said.

'Yes?' I said, raising my eyebrows.

'We cannot join a war if we cannot trust the primary instigator of the conflict,' Drusa said, her voice as sharp as her thin nose. 'Your father, an intelligent male, understood that without question.'

I was beginning to see where things may have gone awry between Lyn and her.

'My father,' I said, 'an intelligent male, trusts me.'

That shut her up for a moment.

'Your father is also fae,' Khailan said coldly. 'We cannot expect him to fully understand the danger you or your ... accomplice ... may pose to the continued existence of our people. Neither, does it seem, do you, Lady Emelin.'

'Bold,' I said, 'to tell a half human who's nearly starved to death several times in her life that she does not understand the threat posed by the fae empire, Lord Khailan.'

'A human would not hesitate to denounce Creon Hytherion,' he retorted.

'Creon Hytherion is not the core of our argument,' I said coolly, and in the face of all his pompous viciousness, it sounded far truer than when I'd lain awake last night, practicing the sentence to myself. 'It's whether I'll allow anyone to wield that sort of power over me. Have you considered the precedent we would be setting, Lord Khailan?'

He cocked his head at me, slowly turning one of his golden rings around his finger as he stared me down. 'How many other fae torturers do you count among your acquaintances?'

'It's not a matter of torturers,' I said with a shrug. 'My father, as you just observed so sharply, is both fae and a former supporter of the Mother. What if, say, one of the vampire kings whose islands were attacked under Agenor's command asks me to swear a bargain never to speak with him again? Am I supposed to never exchange a word with my own father for the rest of my life, then? I can hardly refuse such a thing if I already agreed to it with another ally.'

Khailan remained silent, slender jaw clenched tight. Next to him, Drusa looked as if she'd swallowed a lemon whole.

'Here's what I propose,' I added, leaning forward so that Alyra hastily had to readjust her weight on my shoulder. 'I can bargain I will never attempt to keep Phurys under any sort of fae rule. That I won't be complicit in, assist with, or stay silent about such an attempt if I know about it. But my contacts and conversations are my own to choose.'

'You will be too easily manipulated that way,' Khailan said sharply. 'Do you truly expect us to share any details of our defences or weak spots with you when we know every crumb of information may well end up in Hytherion's hand the next moment?'

I shrugged. 'Do I strike you as easily manipulated?'

'You are a child,' he said with a derisive flick of his hand. 'A young girl in the clutches of a monster. You've barely seen your twentieth summer, for goodness' sake! You'd never seen a magical isle until a year ago! In a few decades, you will look back and understand—'

'In a few decades,' I interrupted, 'we might all be dead if you continue like this.'

A scoff. 'And that is how you hope to convince us to join your desperate war? A war you don't even believe you will win yourself?'

An echoing silence fell, his dulcet voice reverberating back from the colourful mosaic walls around us. Drusa sat stiff as a disapproving grandmother. Mydhar, the short man between them, cleared his throat and cleared it again. On the right side of the semi-circle, the red-haired girl called Thyvle and the bald old man who had to be the much younger Evrun I'd seen on portraits sat watching me with obvious hostility in their eyes.

'I can win this war,' I slowly said.

'You don't have the faintest idea what you're up against,' Drusa said, a trace of shrill laughter in her voice. 'The war won't be won until the Mother is dead, and one little girl will never be able to—'

For fuck's sake. 'Did you notice what I was doing with that chair a moment ago, Lady Drusa?'

She abruptly snapped her mouth shut.

'Here's what none of you understands,' I added, and hell take me, it was hard not to make that sentence the sneer they deserved. 'While you were sitting here and making impossible demands, I was travelling the continent. I was looking for the gods. I *found* them – Zera, that is, but I know at least Inika and Orin are still alive as well.'

Five pairs of eyes shot to Alyra on my shoulder. She huffed, pretending to be extraordinarily busy scratching her neck.

'Are you saying ...' willowy Thyvle started, eyes widening.

'This is ridiculous,' Drusa snapped. 'The gods are dead. And even if they aren't, are we supposed to believe Zera would swear in a *child*?'

'No,' I said, beaming at her. 'Excellent point. I think the core of the matter is that Zera would not swear in a child at all.'

'Any halfwit can put a tame bird on her shoulder and claim to be sent by the gods themselves,' the bald Evrun to my right said brusquely. His voice was a low, rumbling drone. 'Are some tricks with gravity the only evidence you are bringing us, young lady?'

'Not at all,' I said and pressed my left fingers to the mother-of-pearl bracelet around my right wrist.

A bracelet, more specifically, that had been a fragile glass orb twenty-four hours ago.

Creon had changed its shape and material after we'd taken it from the shelf Thysandra had given us and returned to the Underground – but it was still the same binding, and it still contained the magic and sacrifice the Mother had forced Lord Khailan to give up all those years ago. Those things I pulled out now, using the iridescence I drew from the mother-of-pearl surface. Those things I swept back into their former owner's chest with a single offhand turn of my wrist.

Fire roared.

Blinding light split my field of vision in two.

In an explosion of flames, two giant wings burst from Khailan's shoulders – blazing towards the ceiling in the blink of an eye, burning with a heat that sent the mosaic tiles cracking on the wall behind him. Drusa screamed. Mydhar and Thyvle scrambled backwards, away from the fire. At the heart of their semicircle, dollops of fragrant wax began dripping down as the incense candles melted from the chandelier above, leaving scorch marks on the gilded stage.

'Khailan!' Evrun bellowed. 'Restrain yourself!'

I wasn't sure if Khailan even heard, eyes rolling up in their sockets with almost orgasmic bliss as he burned and burned and burned. His wings unfolded wider, sending out twirls of smoke into the dusty room. Six feet on either side of him – a magnificence Lyn's smaller, child-sized wings had nowhere near prepared me for.

Rooted to my spot, I finally understood why Agenor had insisted time and time again that we needed these forces.

'*Khailan!*' Drusa shrieked.

Finally, the fiery feathers began sizzling out, sparks dwindling to the golden platform and dying there. Khailan still didn't move. Against the background of cracked and blackened tiles, he merely continued to stare at me with wide and unseeing amber eyes – as if the fire had not just reduced his objections to ashes, but his good senses, too.

Around him, the four other elders in their smoke-stained robes took their first cautious steps back towards their chairs, like survivors returning to the homes they'd fled.

'You ...' Drusa began breathlessly, looking from Khailan to me to the chair she'd kicked back in her hurry to get away from the blazing inferno. 'You can unbind people?'

I smiled at her. 'As you see.'

'Oh, gods.' Her wrinkled hand flew to her chest. 'Oh, *gods*.'

It wasn't relief, the undertone below those gasped words. It certainly wasn't gratitude either. Fear, perhaps ... but fear tempered by something far uglier, something I knew we needed but couldn't help but hate all the same.

Greed.

'Does that mean you can unbind me, too?' she added, voice soaring, before I could figure out how to respond. 'Can you unbind *all* of us?'

'I have the magic.' Zera help me, I hated to admit it to her – to any of them, with their hungry eyes and their vicious pompousness. 'And I have the physical objects in which the bindings are contained. The one thing we do not yet have for most of those objects is the identification – we cannot determine which binding belongs to which person. Once we have figured out that last step, I'll be able to unbind you all.'

Khailan had sagged to his knees before me, hands grabbing over his shoulders as if to confirm the charred silk his unchecked magic had left behind. He didn't seem to hear a word of what I was saying, his eyes glazed over with delirious shock.

'How long will that take?' Drusa said hoarsely in his place.

'I'm not sure,' I admitted. 'But I can promise you – and I'm willing to make a bargain on it, too – that as soon as I have a means of identification, I will prioritise phoenix bindings, except when individuals of other peoples urgently need their magic for strategic reasons. It's up to you whether that is enough to convince you.'

They were wavering. I could see it in their eyes, shooting back and forth between me and Khailan's smouldering figure – hope, doubt. Shock, joy. Greed, and again ... fear.

'Of course,' I added, 'if you decide to sit back and wait to see who wins the war first, I will likely prioritise everyone else before I have time to unbind you. And I cannot guarantee the bindings will remain whole in the process. The Mother will probably destroy what she can as soon as she hears what I'm able to do, which means we may run out of time at some point.'

Thyvle gasped, a sound that made her look even younger than her fourteen or fifteen physical years. 'And that would mean the magic is lost?'

I shrugged. 'Yes. And everything she made you sacrifice, too.'

'But then ...' She had a deceptively gentle voice, like spring flowers and freshly spun wool – a sound far too sweet for the blistering panic rising in it. 'But then we'll be taking an enormous risk, allying with you! Of *course* the Mother will find out – do you really think you can keep a secret like this for long enough to unbind hundreds of thousands of people? And as soon as she knows, we'll be lost. We'll be *lost*, do you understand?'

The atmosphere turned so swiftly the words evaporated on my lips. 'Wait. No, I didn't mean—'

'You don't understand!' she interrupted shrilly, swinging a hand at the blackened wall behind Khailan. 'You're a *larger* danger to us if you're godsworn and able to unbind us. Without that power, you would just be an ally we couldn't trust. Now, you may just be a reason for the Mother to destroy our last hope once and for all – have you even thought about that at all, Lady Emelin?'

'No,' I tried again, not sure where I was going, 'please, that's not—'

Drusa snapped something in their own language, rattling on too fast for me to catch more than loose shreds of words I thought I might understand. And at once they were all shouting and gesticulating wildly at each other, as if I was no longer even there – my offer forgotten, my bargain magic reduced to yet another threat.

Fuck.

Fuck, fuck, *fuck*.

It was happening too fast, all of it, my careful plan turned on its head with such merciless terror that for two breathless moments I could only just stand and stare at them, my mind a blank sheet. What to say? What to do? The facts wouldn't reassure them, not when they were so stubbornly determined to think the very worst of me – and hell, were they even wrong about the facts? It *was* a risk, joining the Alliance. And as much as I needed them to take that risk, could I in all honesty try to convince them they would be safe as newborn babes on our side?

So what was I supposed to say now?

Did I have any tricks left to play, if they'd just decided my most valuable trump card was a losing bet?

'Please,' I tried again, not sure what the next word would be but well aware I would soon be out of opportunities to use any words at all. 'Please, listen—'

'I'd say we *have* listened to you a great deal, Lady Emelin,' Drusa bit out without even looking my way. Her white hair was escaping its pins, loose tendrils falling messily around her face. 'And all you have done is shown us what a grave danger we're in from the side of those who claim they wish to save us. So thank you, and we know what to do – we know *exactly* what to do.'

Which wasn't joining the cause, judging by the sideways glances they sent me, the undeniable spite in their gazes.

Which meant...

Oh, gods. They did not have *that* many alternatives.

Run straight to the Mother. I stood paralysed below that mosaic dome, the memory of Lyn's voice barraging over me – but if they did that, if they waited for me to turn my back and flew straight to the Crimson Court the moment they thought we wouldn't notice or realise ...

They knew I could break bindings, now.

And if they told the Mother, they'd doom every other magical creature in the archipelago to extinction in their eagerness to save themselves.

Would they be that mad? Lyn had thought them that mad, and who was I to think I knew better after all the years she'd spent in their artful company?

'No,' I managed.

Drusa merely scoffed. 'No? We aren't asking for your permission, girl.'

'No.' My lips were shaping the word all by themselves – a mindless prayer, my last plea to the world to turn itself around. 'No, you can't do this. Do you really not give a damn about the others you'll hurt in the process – the others you'll *kill*?'

'Oh, look at that,' she sneered. 'Like little Phiramelyndra all over again. Telling us to care about the rest of the world, telling us to sacrifice ourselves for those illiterate barbarians of hers … But tell me, Emelin, if we don't take care of ourselves, then who else will do it? Hm?'

Lyn.

Poor, dear Lyn, who must have tried so, so hard.

It was the memory of her gleaming amber eyes that moved me, rather than the thought of those rows and rows of brittle crystal orbs. The way she'd pressed those chubby, freckled hands to her face as if she was fighting not to vomit, rather than the vague and abstract weight of the world's fate on my shoulders.

My left hand slipped to the smooth gold around my neck.

My right hand swept up again.

Smoothness for mind. The magic came to me instinctively, spurred on by the fire of my anger. I threw my every spiteful thought into it, every nugget of persuasion left in me – *You're happy to join us. You're ready to fight. You're prepared to die for your freedom.*

They fell silent, eyes turning glassy.

You wish to bargain with me. My hands were trembling, but the magic flowed and kept flowing, a silky cobweb line between me and the five phoenixes in their gold-covered robes. *You wish to offer me secrecy and all your military support, in return for my promise to unbind you as soon as I'm able to. You're glad to do so.*

'Yes,' Khailan droned, his voice unnaturally flat as he rose, wobbled towards me, and held out a long, perfectly manicured hand. 'We will support the Alliance during the war, Lady Emelin. I can guarantee the discretion of every phoenix under my command. A small price to pay for our wings and children, Lady Emelin.'

My stomach rolled, unexpectedly and violently.

Would it even hold, a bargain created by magical manipulation? I forced myself to extend my own right hand, making sure the flow of smoothness was never interrupted – *you want to bargain, you want to bargain, you want to bargain.* My words felt filthy on my lips as I pushed them out. 'It's a deal.'

It should have been a triumph, the blinding light igniting between our palms. This was what I'd set out to achieve here, wasn't it? We had their armies. We had our winged forces. I even had the smallest bit of revenge for all Lyn had suffered at their hands, and wasn't that the very least they deserved after all this time?

But that quivering hand in mine ...

I had expected them to hate me, and I would have welcomed it. This – this outright cheating, their sickening fear – was not what I'd prepared for.

Was this who I wanted to be? The villain in their story?

The bargain magic sizzled out between us, and I yanked back my hand as fast as Khailan did, barely noticing the brand new, golden mark on the inside of my wrist. Was this what Zera had feared I would do, those days when she'd refused to grant me godsworn powers? Had she known I'd be manipulating my allies with fear and suffering within days of my return to the civilised world?

My brusque movement had finally interrupted my magic. Standing before me, Khailan blinked like a sleepwalker shaken from his dreams – then blinked again, gaze clearing. Then jolted two steps back, gaping at the golden bargain mark on the inside of his wrist.

The sound that fell from his lips was just short of a whimper. 'What in the world—'

'Thank you,' I interrupted in a flash of blinding panic, managing something that might just pass for a confident smile to untrained eyes. 'I'm very glad we could all agree on this subject. I look forward to working with you to free the archipelago from the Mother's rule.'

Did they even remember the bargain he'd made? They must have. The look in Khailan's eyes was one of confusion rather than surprise – he knew exactly where he was, just with no clue of how he'd allowed himself to end up there. Drusa was trembling. Mydhar was staring at my wrist with narrowed eyes. Thyvle flinched as my gaze slid past her, as if my attention alone might be lethal.

'Yes,' Khailan managed, with an audible, commendable effort to sound like he had the faintest idea of what was happening. 'I ... I suppose ...'

'Much obliged,' Drusa stammered, trying to smooth over his hesitation. 'If there is anything we can do to help you decipher the situation with the bindings, or if there's anything else you need from us ...'

'There will be a council of war tonight.' Short sentences. Simple facts. My nerves wouldn't allow me to get more than that past my lips; my stomach was rolling, moving all over again with every glance at the wrist Khailan was still clutching in his other hand. 'You're warmly invited. I'll send the alves to pick you up.'

'Of course,' Khailan said weakly. 'Of course.'

None of them asked so much as a single question. None of them exchanged even the briefest confused glance. The national character, again – order and obedience, and they'd rather cling to their pride and pretend all was well than admit even to each other that they did not have the faintest idea of what had just happened between the six of us.

Which made them the perfect victims.

Which made me the perfect villain.

'Thank you,' I forced myself to say, held in place only by Alyra's talons piercing through my dress and into my shoulder. 'Is there anything else I should clear up for now?'

They were quiet – a loaded silence. Yet no one spoke a word, shoulders straightening on all sides as they determinedly pulled themselves together despite their confusion. Drusa pressed her lips into a hollow smile. Evrun nodded and nodded again, looking like he'd been caught in a conversation of which he didn't understand a single word, but was trying to seem like a fellow expert all the same.

'Excellent.' My voice didn't sound like my own. The incense-heavy air seemed to be crawling into my lungs, smothering me from the inside out with the scent of viciousness. 'Wishing you a pleasant day, in that case.'

I didn't wait for their response as I turned on my heel, hurried off the stairs with unsteady feet, and fled their golden hall.

Chapter 12

'Creon?'

I couldn't keep my voice from cracking as I floundered through the Skeire corridor, panic urging my feet forward. My heart still hadn't stopped thumping against my ribs. Telling Tared that I was fine, that no one had attacked me, and that the phoenixes would be at the gathering tonight was all I'd been able to manage in this state of self-afflicted horror; I'd left Alyra in the living room with him and wormed myself out of his requests for details with some blatantly flimsy excuses on tiredness and wanting to make sure Creon would not be worried.

Which wouldn't work forever.

So what was I supposed to do when they asked again – tell them what I'd done? Tell them what I *could* do, the full sickening, horrifying extent of it?

I flung open the door to Creon's room, staggering in like a drunkard. He was sitting in one of the chairs with his notes and calculations, attempts to find some sort of system behind the Mother's organisation of the bindings based on the two locations we had – but he dropped his pen and parchment the moment I barged in, my distress undoubtedly washing over his demon senses like the emotional equivalent of the pungent stench of fire.

'Em?' His eyes narrowed abruptly. 'What's wrong?'

I slammed the door behind me and erupted.

The elders. Their arguments, their refusals. Khailan's wings, their change of heart, and my last, unthinking act of despair – *smoothness for mind*, their hollow eyes, their trembling hands, the bargain that should not have happened except for my dangerous manipulation. The words gushed over my lips like vomit, a winding, rambling confession, until I finally ran out of thoughts and just stood there panting and shaking, waiting for his judgement. Waiting for him to agree that I had gone too far, that Zera would never approve of this, that I *was* becoming the evil I was fighting after all ...

'Right,' he said.

And that was all.

Just that one word, slow and pensive, with that melodious lilt that even now made my heart skip a beat. His gaze didn't release me, observing me closely as I blinked, frowned, and stammered, 'Right?'

'That sounds like a success.' It *had* to be deliberate, that calculated eyebrow he quirked up – an evident challenge for me to disagree. 'Or at least it's pretty much what you set out to achieve, isn't it?'

'No!' I burst out, voice soaring. *Nothing* was successful about this – about the filthy, gluey sense of wrongness sticking to every inch of my skin, like guilt but more physical, the awareness of my crime slithering through every fibre of my body. I'd killed before, had ended dozens of lives with the tips of my fingers, yet somehow this seemed more heinous. More heartless. The fae who'd died had at least attacked me knowingly. This, on the other hand, taking away all free will, reducing proud, powerful individuals to marionettes on the strings of my magic ...

I wanted to scrub that bargain mark off my skin. Wanted to burn the mother-of-pearl bracelet and the gold in my hair to ashes.

And even that might not be enough.

'Ah,' Creon said, still so pleasantly conversational – as if I had admitted to dropping a plate, not to worming my way into the minds of others to bind them to life-threatening promises. 'I see you're starting to understand why I tried to hide that demon magic from you.'

For a split second, I forgot to be disgusted with myself. 'What?'

'Blood-curdling, isn't it?' From the tone of his voice, he could have been talking about the weather. 'Really not the sort of powers that were ever supposed to be wielded by creatures with any empathy or sense of morality. It gets a little better over time, if it helps. Never exactly *fun*, though.'

I stared at him, jaw sagging.

He smiled back – a cheerless, tired smile – and began gathering his notes, sorting them into a neat little pile before dropping them onto the ground. Seasoned, familiar gestures, accompanied by the equally soothing rustle of parchment – as if nothing had happened.

As if nothing had changed.

I was no longer sure what to think.

'So,' he said when finally all notes and pens had been satisfactorily relocated, looking up and sinking back in his chair to cross his legs. 'Are you going to insist on thinking of yourself as a monster? Because I'm afraid you'll have to extend that qualification to me, too.'

Oh.

Oh, gods.

The fire had been sapped out of me, the violent need for punishment and consequences. I floundered two steps back, dropped down on the edge of his bed, and buried my face in my hands, staring blankly at the floor between my fingers. My thoughts seemed to be settling like dregs fluttering down in a glass of wine.

'Possibly the most life-changing thing you ever taught me,' Creon added, unmoving, 'is that monstrous powers alone are not enough to make a monster. So I'll be damned if I let you drag yourself down that same path, cactus. You did what you had to do, and you did it well. There's nothing evil about that.'

'It *feels* evil,' I managed. 'It ... it ...'

He huffed a laugh. 'Evil would have been forcing them to kill their children. Or possibly making them slit each other's throats and dissolving the bodies in acid. Which would have been amusing in its own way, but—'

I jerked up my head. '*Amusing?*'

His smile was devilish, that expression that sent a chill down my spine and heat into my belly all at once. 'I didn't say I would actually *do* it.'

'No, but ...' A dazed laugh escaped me. 'Good gods. Perhaps I shouldn't have come to you for a chat about ethics.'

'Oh, quite the opposite,' he dryly said. 'Nothing creates an awareness of ethics like walking on the wrong side of the line for most of your life. I may not be *good* at morality, but I've definitely *thought* about it.'

A hundred and thirty years to think about it, while torturing innocent humans and playing the Mother's loyal weapon ... I shivered. Really, spelling a handful of pompous, selfish rulers to stop them from ruining the future of every other magical people was hardly *that* much of a crime in comparison. I hadn't tortured them to death. I hadn't killed their children before their very eyes. I hadn't murdered a full village of their innocent subjects.

All things the Silent Death was whispered to have done ... and I had forgiven Creon quite easily all the same.

But I imagined walking out and proudly informing Tared of exactly what I'd done. I imagined telling Lyn, with her sweet heart and her deep feelings. I imagined the news spreading through the Underground, in whispers and gasps, in grim mumbles behind secretive hands ...

I might be able to forgive myself, if I made the effort – but could they do it, too?

Hell, I'd seen those wary eyes as we walked through the corridors. I'd heard the conversations pausing around me. *She walked straight through their magic*, they'd whispered, such a bloody harmless feat, and that alone had been enough to make them watch me like a wildfire about to combust. How would they ever exchange a normal word with me if they had the faintest clue of what my magic could do to them, if they knew they might not even remember what my magic could have done to them?

'But the others …' I faltered, struggling to find words for the waking nightmare unfolding before my mind's eye. 'They … they'll think …'

His eyes darkened. 'Em.'

'Even if they're happy enough with the results' – I was jabbering, yet he seemed to understand me without effort, watching me motionlessly as I wrestled with my own cursed thoughts – 'the way I did it … the things I *could* do …'

'It won't be a problem to all of them,' he said, the narrowing of his almond eyes spoiling the illusion of unworried calm his voice was spinning. 'Agenor has dealt with significantly worse for centuries. Lyn will be more concerned about you than herself, and Tared will probably laugh for a week if he hears what you did to the elders. None of them is going to condemn you for doing this.'

'They still won't like the fact that I'm able to do it,' I said bitterly. 'Don't you remember how shaken they were when they found out I could bind others? And these are the people who are supposed to know and trust me. Most others consider me a aberration already.'

He hesitated. 'Well—'

'You *know* they do.' I wrapped my arms around myself, fingers tightening into my sides. 'Don't try to reassure me like I'm some frightened child – we both know exactly how they feel about magic they don't understand. I can't even make them overlook my binding powers. I don't think any damn thing I could come up with is going to make them overlook *this*.'

Again that hesitation. Why was he hesitating? He knew their opinions of his own powers – knew that they might accept his presence for the sake of victory, but that they would never do so happily. Knew that they would never consider themselves safe around him, no matter how many of their enemies he killed, and that they would never see his face or hear his name without remembering the threat of his demon magic first.

He changed hearts. I changed minds. I doubted anyone would consider it that much of a difference.

Of all people, he should know.

'So …' My voice wavered. It felt empty, suddenly, the world outside this dusky, parchment-packed bedroom – a cold and unwelcoming void. 'So I should just keep quiet about this, shouldn't I? Pretend that I persuaded the elders through brilliant argumentation and hope the bastards never open their mouths about what really happened? Then if I never repeat anything like this, I might just get away with—'

'Em,' Creon interrupted, crossing his arms over his chest as he leaned back. 'Dare I point out that you're trying to make yourself small again?'

I abruptly fell quiet.

That had been the source of his hesitation – not what I was saying, but what I was doing. Going down that same tired road. Making myself invisible, holding myself back, trying to deny the power that lived beneath my skin. As I'd done so many times before … but was I doing it for the comfort of others or for my own sake now? Was this a cowardly attempt at avoiding consequences, or just a sensible way to allow myself some hard-won peace?

Perhaps it didn't matter. Perhaps the only answer of importance was that this dilemma existed in the first place – that even the Alliance, even this hidden shelter in our world of wolves against wolves, was not a place where I could be fully and truly at home.

A headache was growing behind my eyes – sharp and piercing, like a whetted blade repeatedly pushing itself into my skull.

'The problem is,' I muttered, the words coming out hollow, 'that I don't know if there's a place in the world big enough for me if I stop keeping myself small.'

The room was so very silent. Just the two of us and nothing else – not the blissful peace of not needing to worry about others, but rather the gnawing sense of *having* no others to worry about. I had my friends, of course. I had Agenor and Lyn and Tared, and I knew they would care. But they were rooted in their own little worlds all the same, and here I was, drifting in between – like a little seed blown around by the breeze, unable to settle and grow my own roots in the hard, hostile earth.

Creon had closed his eyes, that beautiful, sharp-lined face suddenly a maze of shadows.

'You have thought about this, too.' There was no other way to interpret his expression, the exhaustion etched in the lines around his lips. 'About where in hell we should go when all of this is over, if we don't want to spend the rest of our lives surrounded by people who'll never feel completely comfortable about us.'

'A little.' It came out reluctantly, like a confession, and when he hesitated, I couldn't help feeling as though he was swallowing something he'd almost have said. Then he opened his mouth again, and it faded. 'But only recently. Before these months … well, I never really assumed the future would be that relevant to me.'

My breath caught. 'Because you assumed you wouldn't survive the war?'

'That.' He shrugged, opening his eyes. There was an apology in the night-black of his irises, in the joyless twist of his lips. 'Or else I assumed I wouldn't survive peace.'

The war is in his blood and bones.

I couldn't breathe for a moment – couldn't move a single muscle in my body as the sight of those blood-stained arrows returned to me with undulled sharpness. The questions I'd managed to ignore for a day reared their deadly heads again, demanding answers I wasn't sure I wanted to hear.

'Please tell me that wasn't the reason you threw yourself at the Moon fleet.' The words tumbled out of my mouth, tasting like bile. 'Because you were scared of—'

'No!' He shot up straight, eyes widening abruptly. 'Good gods, Em. No. I worry about the future, but not so much I'd rather end myself – nothing like that. You'd march straight into hell to drag me back out anyway, and I'd rather spare you the effort in the first place.'

I should have laughed but couldn't – the boulder in my stomach wouldn't let me. 'Even … even if …'

'Oh, fuck. Em.' He rose in one supple motion, holding out a slender hand as he took two steps toward the bed. 'Listen to me. No, I don't have the faintest idea of where I want to end up in life. Yes, in the past, I spent most of my days being violently unhappy, and yes, I *have* wondered at times if it was even worth going on. But I'm happier now than I've ever been, do you understand? Every morning that I wake up with you in my arms, you change the world all over again, and I want *more* of that – more of everything you make me see and feel. So I'm not going anywhere – not as long as you're with me. Do I need to make that any clearer?'

Again my lungs refused service, an entirely different feeling tightening around my heart this time. All that managed to leave my mouth was a breathless, feeble, 'Oh.'

He knelt before me, interlacing our fingers – my smaller, lighter hand so very vulnerable against the calloused, ink-scarred bronze. 'Tell me what you want.'

'Home,' I whispered.

He waited, eyes seeing straight through me as I wrestled down my fears, my memories, the barbed thorns that surrounded the sound of that single word. *Home.* A place where no one stared or whispered. A place where I couldn't embarrass anyone, too. But the future had to be more than a mere collection of things it *wasn't* – more than a flight from all that had ever hurt me in the past.

So what did I want?

'The sea.' I didn't know why it was the first thing that popped into my mind – Cathra's pale beaches, the hours and hours I'd spent playing in the surf, running through the dunes. 'I'd like to be close to the sea again.'

'Well, that should be doable.' A hint of a wry smile returned to his lips. 'Plenty of shore to choose from, I'd say.'

I somehow managed to scrape half a chuckle from the bottom of my soul. 'If you want something more specific, perhaps you shouldn't be leaving all the thinking to me, Your Highness. What do *you* want?'

'Oh, gods.' He rose, pulling me with him so that I ended up standing flush against him, his free arm around my waist. 'Does it count if I just want to bury you in silks and watch those pretty seamstress hands of yours while you work?'

'I suppose it's a start.' My thoughts were coming more easily at that image, somehow – a blurry vision of sun and azure water, of freshly baked bread and ink-stained fingers browsing scribbled pages. 'I ... I think I want a library.'

'A *library*,' he repeated, the amusement in his voice the warmest, most addictive medicine. 'But of course. Let's go get ourselves a library. Any particular requirements?'

'It should have a secret door somewhere,' I said, burying my face against his shoulder, 'and behind the secret door should be *another* library, where I can collect all my favourite filthy novels without Agenor ever laying eyes on them. And ...'

He was laughing openly now, wrapping both arms and wings around me. 'Could I request a few shelves for my books on astronomy, or is that too much to ask?'

'You can have all the shelves you want.' I lifted my head to meet his gaze, but found myself pressed so close against his muscular body that I saw little but a pointed ear and a sharp-edged jaw; his arms didn't budge. 'And I want large windows with stained glass, just like you had at the pavilion. And a balcony where we can have breakfast in the sun. And ...'

'I would appreciate having a decent kitchen,' he admitted, sounding thoughtful, as if the concept had never occurred to him before. 'An icehouse, too. I've missed having one when I lived at the pavilion.'

My heart clenched with almost painful affection. 'Excellent. I'll dig you an icehouse with my own bare hands if I have to. How do you feel about those closets that are practically entire rooms to walk around in?'

'Utterly ridiculous,' he said dryly. 'Let's get one.'

There was no stopping my laughter – giddy, breezy chuckles bubbling out of me, driving away the lingering darkness. It wasn't taking *shape* yet, that home in my mind – it wasn't a shape at all. It was a collage of loose impressions, of beauty and joy, and somehow all the more tangible for that reason. 'We could get a cat?'

He choked on his amusement. 'Em, you have a bird familiar.'

'Two cats, then,' I amended. 'That way they might stand a chance. We could call them Chicken and Egg and teach them to chew on the shoes of people we dislike. And—'

'I'm *not* going to name my cats Chicken and Egg,' he interrupted, chest shaking against me. 'I'm not that eager to get rid of my frightening reputation yet.'

I snorted. 'We could name them after your bloody philosophers.'

'That I can approve of.' He kissed my temple. 'Can't wait to hear you shout at Alyra that she should leave Irythion Thenes and Likothea the Younger alone. She'll probably try to kill them for those names alone.'

Tears were welling in my eyes now, and *still* I could not stop laughing, snotty sniffles and sticky cheeks be damned. The billowing relief was almost too much for my body to contain. I felt like I might have floated off if he hadn't been holding me, the lack of roots to keep me in place suddenly a liberation rather than a deficiency – curiosity rather than uncertainty, excitement rather than apprehension.

Damn him and his demon eyes; he'd managed it again.

'I love you,' I blubbered, clutching my arms around his waist as I looked up again. 'I love you so, so much.'

He kissed me in response.

It said everything words never could, that kiss – a question, a promise. The war might be in his blood and bones, the language of his lips told me, and the gods knew it would take him time to unravel them again ...

But I was in his heart.

And his heart would never falter.

I melted into that kiss with all I had, the room fading around me, his soft, sensual lips the only touch anchoring me to reality. Our tongues found each other, exchanged the meekest touch, and pulled back again – probing, testing, exploring. He tasted of starless nights. He tasted of danger and heady pleasures to come.

Clasping my hands around his shoulders, I came up on my toes and kissed him harder.

He hummed a murmur of approval against my mouth, rough hands circling my waist, locking me closer against him. I slid my hands through his hair, savouring the silky strands between my fingers, and brushed a thumb along the rim of his pointed ear – another moan, and shivers of anticipation rushed down my spine, pooling hot and hungry at the core of me.

I was no longer thinking about cats and malicious bargains.

Really, I was no longer thinking about anything.

How had we slipped past this threshold so easily, past this point of no return? I didn't know. No longer cared, either. His mouth trailed down into the hollow of my neck, kissing and nibbling, and I arched into his rock-hard body, craving oblivion as much as pleasure, craving the illusion of a place to belong. With a low growl, he wrapped his arms around me and lifted me. His lips never abandoned my skin even as he strode towards the bed and lowered me into the messy blankets, hands plucking at my dress, at my rings, at the gold in my hair; I closed my eyes and surrendered with an eagerness bordering on the desperate, hooking my legs around his hips, kissing every bit of skin I could reach—

A bang burst through the symphony of our ragged breaths.

Knuckles. I froze in the sheets as the realisation rose, a slow and supremely unwelcome understanding – those were *knuckles* tapping against our door, cautious yet pressing, a rhythm reminiscent of sleepless nights.

For the bloody gods' sakes.

Not *again*.

Creon had stilled kneeling over me, one hand on my thigh and the other on the collar of my dress, wearing the look of a male at war with his own baser instincts. His eyes never left me as he drew in a strained breath and yelled, 'What is it?'

His tone had just an edge of a threat to it – as if that sentence was waiting to be finished with an ominous *and you'd better make it worth my while*. I lifted a hand and ran my fingertips down his temple, his jaw, the lightly pulsing vein in his throat, begging, *praying* that whoever was standing at the door would take the hint and decide to go bother literally anyone else instead.

They did not.

'Oh, thank the gods, you're here.' Lyn, sounding on the brink of tears. 'Is Em with you?'

Gods damn all of this.

The horny, obstinate brat in me was tempted for a moment to shout that no, I definitely wasn't anywhere to be found, and I wouldn't be for the next two hours either. Didn't the world owe me half a minute of peace after days of frantic preparation, after bloody battles and near-death and the looming loss of the one person I needed more than anyone else?

Then I remembered where I'd just come from. What I'd just done, what I'd been planning to hide from her, and all arousal sizzled out like a bonfire in a spring downpour, as misplaced as jollity at a funeral.

'I'm here,' I yelled, closing my eyes. Under my fingertips, Creon was too tense — good sense battling overwhelming desire, duty battling lust. 'What happened? Please don't say we started another accidental battle.'

'Oh, no.' Her chuckle sounded watery despite being muffled by the thick layer of wood between us. 'Just ... Tared said you seemed upset. Is there anything I can do for you?'

Right.

Tared.

I should have known I couldn't storm off like I had and expect him to sit on his thumbs for two hours, waiting for me to reemerge in gods knew what state. Consulting Lyn had likely been the compromise between his concern and his promise not to come between Creon and me — and with her history with the elders, could I really blame her for wanting to make sure nothing terrible had befallen me inside the Fireborn Palace?

'I'm fine,' I said, my voice hollow. 'It's only that they were about as unpleasant as you warned me they would be. And I'm ... tired, I suppose.'

Already? she should be saying. *We have been fighting this war for centuries, you whiny little child, and do you hear any of us complaining about tiredness?*

But this was Lyn; of course she didn't say any such thing. 'We were planning to discuss our strategy for the meeting tonight, but I don't think you absolutely *need* to be there? We can just tell you what we came up with later today, if you prefer.'

The meeting.

The Alliance's council of war.

Where we would have to present at least a suggestion of a strategy, something to give the gathered kings and queens the impression we could win the war – which meant we would need to tell them what role I would play in that war, too. As tempting as it was to stay here and let Creon have his way with me, did I really want to leave it to Agenor to tell me in a couple of hours how I was supposed to make my way to the Mother and end her?

I was making my own choices, damn it. A few hours of oblivion weren't worth turning myself into a pawn without agency.

Creon was already moving, rolling himself away from me, holding out a hand to help me up. I grabbed it with a long-suffering groan and allowed him to haul my aching, yearning body from the blankets despite every fibre screaming at me to stay exactly where I was.

'Be with you in a few minutes!' I yelled at the door.

Lyn's reply sounded grateful and worried at the same time. Her small footsteps tottered off into the distance, back to the living room, where Tared would no doubt be waiting.

I sagged against Creon's chest, not sure if I wanted to curse or apologise.

'It's alright, Em,' he muttered, lips against the crown of my head. 'There'll be quieter moments later.'

Later. Always later. I squeezed my eyes shut, willing myself to calm down – but gods help me, how long could the future keep inserting itself into the present before the progress of time started blurring into itself?

'Come,' Creon added, a little firmer now, as if he was reading my thoughts and had decided he'd had enough of the wallowing. A little nudge against my shoulder was enough to put me back on my feet. 'Time to get to work, cactus. Think of it this way – we can't get our cats if we die on the battlefield.'

Like a soap bubble, the spell of dread popped within me. I pulled the remaining golden pins from my hair, dragged my shoulders straight, and said with grave and solemn dignity, 'An excellent point, Your Highness. To war, then?'

'To war.' He swept a dramatic gesture at the door. 'For Irythion Thenes.'

'And Likothea the Younger,' I added, following him outside, bursting out laughing when he did.

For an unimaginable moment, even the prospect of battle almost seemed enjoyable.

Chapter 13

They started arriving just after dinner, the rulers of our allies above the earth – grim faces and stiff shoulders as they were faded into the grand hall in the heart of the Underground, where the chalk map on the floor was now finished and surrounded by a large circle of chairs. Lanterns and alf lights twinkled in the shadowy darkness above our heads. Along the smooth walls, the little balconies were packed with Underground inhabitants following the spectacle from a distance; on the floor below, only a few handfuls of us had gathered to welcome the newcomers.

The alves came first, about a dozen of them, all tall and blond and armed to the teeth. Some of them greeted Tared and Valdora with what seemed like genuine warmth, while others appeared to struggle to get even the iciest of greetings over their lips – alf politics I didn't want to spend too much thought on. They were here, at least. As long as they agreed to fight the Mother with us, they could throw as many tantrums as they liked in private.

The others started trickling in soon after, brought in by Underground alves fading back and forth across the archipelago. Helenka was one of the first nymph queens to arrive, dressed in royal, glittering green. She and her colleagues looked much like dew-covered flowers between the earthy colours of the alves and the stark black in which most of the vampires arrived, all lace and leather and the occasional velvet cloak; the groups mingled reluctantly, most of the attendees clearly preferring the company of their own people, even at this gathering intended to solidify our mutual commitment.

The phoenixes showed up last. Just two of them – Khailan and Drusa.

Lyn was suddenly extraordinarily busy chatting with two stern-looking vampire kings on the other side of the hall.

I couldn't help holding my breath as the gazes of the two elders swept around the company and found me, every muscle in my body prepared for roars of anger and vehement accusations. But Khailan merely gave me a stiff nod, and Drusa's watery smile was clearly an attempt at politeness – they still hadn't realised what had happened, then.

And how could they, if they had no idea such a thing as smooth magic even existed?

I still couldn't get my heartbeat to settle.

Once the group was complete, Agenor and Tared wasted no time getting everyone to sit down, and the conversations broke off around me as more and more people made for the circle of chairs. I plopped into the seat next to Creon, which was so high that only the tips of my toes reached the ground, and ignored the meaningful glares sent my way by several representatives as I beckoned Alyra to join me.

'You might want to find yourself another spot if you don't want them to get the worst possible first impression of you,' Creon muttered as my familiar fluttered down to take her place on my shoulder. If anyone in the hall hadn't been glancing at me yet, they certainly were now. 'They're having enough opinions about my presence as is.'

'I'm sitting here,' I said with a small huff. 'I think that'll give them exactly the right impression.'

He drew in a sharp breath and nodded just too quickly as he averted his gaze – the smallest crack in the otherwise immaculate shield of uncaring boredom he'd raised around himself. I would have squeezed his hand if Agenor hadn't sat down three chairs away from me at the same moment — or, more specifically, if the tiny green snake in his chest pocket and Alyra hadn't been glowering at each other with such obvious murder in their beady eyes.

'Don't you dare,' I muttered at her, and she harrumphed and grudgingly turned away, aiming her glare at Khailan instead.

The chairs between my father and me remained empty. So did the four chairs to Creon's right, and the alf in the fifth still looked a smidge uncomfortable about the spot necessity had forced her to take. With the rest of the circle filled to the last seat, we were a glaring little island — feared, barely trusted, and isolated.

The right impression, indeed.

I absently brushed one of Alyra's feathers from my indigo dress — blue enough to look peaceful, dark enough to contain plenty of red — and ignored the looks wandering in our direction.

'So,' Tared broke the strained silence. 'Shall we get started?'

The first part would be a matter of routine, Lyn had warned me that afternoon, a repetition of what had become convention in the decades before the Last Battle. Rulers named their armed forces — a hundred alves here, a thousand vampires there. Two nymphs from the Underground rushed back and forth to plant little wooden cubes on the chalked floor map, every single one representing a hundred warriors.

The island of the Crimson Court was barely visible underneath the mountain of wood already piled on top of it.

I stared at that pile for most of the first half hour, trying not to think of the swarm that had surrounded us in the courtyard of the Golden Court. The numbers being mentioned around me started blurring within minutes and barely registered in my mind, leaving little impression but the creeping awareness that they were not high enough.

Not *nearly* high enough.

They were all thinking the same thing; I could see it in the deepening frowns and tightening fists around the circle, all gazes following those little wooden blocks across the floor as if sheer will could double their numbers. The last queen to speak sounded almost apologetic as she told us she had a hundred and fifty-two nymphs to spare.

'I know it's not much,' she added hastily, as if anyone would jump up in the silence at the end of the list and accuse her of treason, 'but frankly, we just don't have the population we used to ...'

'No one has,' Lyn said, her voice flat. 'Thank you, Kiska.'

Kiska nodded, silver-scaled hands unclenching ever so slightly in her lap.

As if by command, all eyes turned back to Lyn and Tared on the other side of the circle, the first perched on the edge of her chair, the latter lounging in his seat with deceptive nonchalance. They had to feel the weight of the collective attention but didn't exchange so much as a single glance — knowing each other's thoughts as always. Knowing the plans we'd made that afternoon, the strategies we'd agreed upon, the conclusions we wanted this group to reach.

'Considering the numbers,' Tared slowly said, nodding at the map where the last little wooden blocks had just been placed on Kiska's island, 'I'd say a long campaign to exhaust the empire isn't going to help us much. The Mother would retaliate as soon as we made our first attack, and we clearly don't have the forces to protect every community around the archipelago.'

Mutters of agreement went up around the circle. A vampire with three missing fingers huffed and said, 'Betting all we have on a single battle doesn't seem that attractive either when we're outnumbered, Thorgedson.'

'Nothing about being outnumbered is attractive,' Helenka said tartly. The little pile on Tolya was one of the largest among the nymph isles; I wondered how many of the nymphs she was bringing had not yet been warriors a week ago. 'But we've seen she won't hesitate to burn entire islands to the ground to keep the others in line, so I'm not looking forward to seeing what she'll do once she truly wishes to eradicate us. Strike once and well, I'd say. It may be the only chance we'll get.'

The group went quiet at that. More than a handful of people were staring daggers at that pile on the south side of the map — the Crimson Court, heart of the empire, impregnable stronghold.

'We would have to aim for the court, then,' one of the alves finally broke the silence — reaching the conclusion we, too, had reached during hours of frantic preparations that afternoon. I saw Lyn's shoulders loosen a fraction out the corner of my eye. 'Unless we think we can get her to move and leave the castle unprotected, but—'

'Not a chance,' Agenor said grimly, and no one even tried to argue.

'The Crimson Court, then.' Helenka was flexing her claw-like fingers, as if she couldn't wait to rip down the walls with her bare hands. 'Any suggestions on how we're going to break through those defences, Lord Protector?'

The title was a dig and an acknowledgement of authority at once – she wasn't going to forget the times they'd stood opposite each other on a battlefield, it reminded us, but neither would she deny the small advantage his knowledge of the empire's military could offer us. Agenor's nod was a response to both at the same time, somehow. *I remember*, it suggested, *and trust me, I like it as little as you do.*

But all he said was, 'Their usual defences may not be the worst of our problems. Our newest intelligence suggests the bindings may be the first thing in our way – that harming either walls or warriors that Achlys and Melinoë prefer to keep intact is enough to indirectly harm them personally, and therefore enough to prevent us from using magic. We saw very strong signs of it at the Golden Court yesterday.'

No mention of Creon's name. I was oddly grateful for it; the hissed curses and thunderous looks were bad enough without having them aimed directly at the male beside me.

'So we'll need an unbound mage, then,' Helenka said.

And then all the eyes were on me anyway.

I gave a small smile, remembering just in time not to shrug with Alyra on my shoulder. Four chairs away, Agenor drew in an audibly unhappy breath but said, 'Yes.'

'One mage against the entirety of the Crimson Court?' a gruff-looking alf barked, his frown distorting the crude wolf tattoos drawn over his face and neck. 'Even if she's godsworn' – a few people flinched at that – 'that seems a little ambitious to me.'

'I wouldn't dream of confronting the Mother head-on,' I said, unpleasantly aware that this was the first time many of them heard me speak. It added too much weight to every word leaving my lips, no matter how hard I tried to sound like addressing the collective leadership of the immortal world was something I'd done on a daily basis in the twenty-one years of my life. 'And it would be at least two of us. Creon knows the court better than I do.'

And just like that, the first impression was ruined.

It was barely a silence, the heartbeat of speechlessness that followed. It was too full of sharp inhales and curling lips to ever be counted as such, a hundred furious objections rising in that moment stretching from my last syllable to the first snarled response. I steeled myself, ready for the inevitable – *fae whore* or some version of it, every ugly rumour and shred of truth that had been circling the archipelago for weeks—

'And if I need to refresh anyone's memory,' Tared cut in, sounding bored, 'Creon's help was instrumental both in saving Tolya and in winning our first battle at the Golden Court. I suggest we don't go down this path of discussion *again*.'

The bite in that last word was unmistakable, and I saw several around the circle wince as they shut their mouths.

A strained silence fell. More than a few alves gave the impression they'd rather hand over their swords than agree with this madness, and yet none of them responded, save with a few deadly glares that Tared ignored with enviable indifference. Those cold greetings at the start of the evening ... How many houses had he angered and offended just to get them to agree to Creon's presence at this meeting?

'Thank you,' he dryly added when the hall remained quiet, and if he was at all bothered by the same question, his unhurried posture didn't show it. 'Please continue, Em.'

I forced a smile. 'Much appreciated. Where were we?'

'You mentioned you weren't planning to charge at the Mother directly,' Helenka said, pupil-less green eyes narrowed and aimed at me with ruthless sharpness. 'So what are you thinking of? I doubt you'll manage to sneak in through the back door.'

'It's a sentient back door,' I said. 'That might help.'

She stared at me as if I'd lost my mind.

'Here's what I've been thinking,' I continued, which was, strictly speaking, a lie – some of these thoughts were Creon's or Agenor's ideas that had been bounced back and forth and honed by hours of deliberation this afternoon. But I'd informed them from the start that I wasn't going to sit here as a weapon to be wielded by the rest of the world, and they obligingly stayed silent now, allowing me to set out my course as if no one but me had been involved in the plan. 'We don't have the forces to *win* against the Mother's, especially with the bindings still in place. But I'm pretty sure we have the forces to distract her for a few hours, and if I can make use of that, it might be everything we need.'

'The Labyrinth,' one of the nymphs whispered, looking at Lyn. 'You said she escaped through the Labyrinth, didn't you?'

Lyn's smile was like the midsummer sun – so bright it turned deadly.

'It's pretty friendly, assuming you're polite to it,' I said, and now Helenka was not the only one visibly doubting my sanity. 'It saved my life when I escaped the court a few months ago. I'm reasonably sure I can convince it to help me through again, and then we'd be right at the heart of the court, immediately below the bone hall.'

The murmurs picking up around me might have sounded doubtful, but it was the right sort of doubt – the sound of people hesitant to hope rather than people determined to be unimpressed. A white-haired vampire king leaned over as if to bite me and groused, 'And you think your godsworn magic will be enough to attack her?'

Attack. Not even *kill.* They'd all stood before that blue- and black-eyed horror while she locked away their magic and their future; they'd all felt the extent of her power. Was it so strange they had trouble imagining the harm I might do?

'I managed to blind her without any divine help at all,' I said. Couldn't hurt to remind them. 'I do think I'll be able to deal her at least a few blows, yes. And there's still that throne she refuses to leave alone for a moment – depending on how much damage we can do by targeting *that*, we may not even need to face her directly at all.'

'But we don't know what exactly her throne does.'

'We don't.' I hated the fact itself more than having to confess it – hated that even after speaking with goddesses and reading several bookcases' worth of histories, I still hadn't figured out the answer to that one essential question. 'But her protectiveness suggests it can't hurt to smash it to pieces.'

They were silent for a moment as they considered that. I dared to glance at Creon for the first time. Eyes dark, face unreadable, he lounged in his seat with all the lethal grace of a panther curling up for his afternoon nap, the perfect predator in his natural element. Only his fingers moved between us as my gaze slid his way, almost imperceptible twitches, forming the shapes I knew so well ...

Love you.

It took every bit of self-restraint I possessed not to smile as I turned back to our audience.

'So, say we do it the way you suggested ...' an alf with half-shaved hair began, the light around his tall frame flickering worryingly. They wouldn't like to be kept away from the real action, Tared had warned us that afternoon, even if they would understand why sending a godsworn, unbound mage ahead was the only sensible choice. 'What do you propose the rest of us do in the meantime? Just storm the court and kill every single bastard we get within sword range?'

Someone to my left huffed, '*Alves.*'

The half-shaved male veered up as if a wasp had stung his bottom. 'Oh, do you have any better suggestions, Vivesha? If our magic is useless, your tree tricks won't be—'

'Freydur,' Tared interrupted sharply.

'Tree tricks?' the nymph queen who'd spoken shrieked in the same moment, soaring to a pitch that could have broken glass. 'Our sacred magic – *tree tricks*? Should I be calling those swords of yours brute lumps of steel, if you—'

'*Vivesha!*' Lyn snapped.

'Would anyone mind,' Agenor said, his deep voice unaffected but just a fraction louder than usual, 'if I answered the question Freydur posed before we started murdering each other on the empire's behalf? You'll never be more useless than when you're dead.'

Freydur and Vivesha abruptly fell silent, glowering at each other like squabbling children pulled apart. More than a few others deflated and sunk back in their chairs. Lyn sent Agenor a look of gratitude and tartly said, 'Thank you. Do I need to remind anyone of the semantics of the word *alliance*, or can we all behave like adults by ourselves?'

I wasn't sure what was more amusing: to hear those words from the mouth of a seven-year-old or to see several alves wince a little at the sting. Next to me, the tremble of Creon's lips betrayed the first hint of emotion he'd shown since the meeting had started.

Agenor patiently adjusted the cuffs of his sleeves, then, when no one else interrupted, looked back up again, still the epitome of dignified politeness. 'Much obliged.'

'So you're saying you have a plan?' Freydur said brusquely.

'Not a plan, necessarily. Thoughts, more accurately.' The modest lightness in his words fully ignored the fact that even his most jumbled collection of thoughts would be closer to a plan than anything the average alf would come up with after a week of ruminating. 'I wouldn't dare call it a plan until I'd heard your opinions on it.'

Leave it to my father to be perfectly diplomatic about his schemes and strategies. I strongly suspected they would all end up following his proposals to the letter, even if none of them would fully realise it themselves.

'Well, tell us your thoughts, then,' Helenka said impatiently.

'I would recommend we aim to improve our range, first of all.' There was something hypnotic about that low voice of his, twelve centuries of battlefield experience spinning themselves into those self-assured, reassuring words. 'Our opponents may be mages, but very few of them can work magic effectively over a distance of thirty feet or more. Any arrows, fire-bombs, or other projectiles we can fling at them will do damage before they are able to use the advantage of their magic.'

'We have several hundred trained archers,' Khailan said – the first time he'd opened his mouth all night. 'They are at your disposal, of course.'

It was all I could do not to rub my fingers over the bargain mark at my wrist, an aching blemish on my skin. *Of course.*

It was worse that he believed those two words himself.

'How about alf steel?' one of the vampire kings suggested, gesturing at the row of alves with a hand gloved in black leather. 'If we can create any sort of weapon that launches, say, sharp little fragments of alf steel, we could limit their magic even if we don't manage to take them down completely.'

That suggestion was welcomed with a handful of enthusiastic nods and murmurs of agreement. Vivesha shook her green-and-copper curls over her lithe shoulders and said, with more than a hint of spiteful triumph in her voice, 'We would be happy to contribute by producing poisons for archers and other long-range weapons. That happens to be one of the *tree tricks* for which we do not need magic at all.'

'Excellent,' Lyn hastily said, because it was clear that Freydur was ready to retaliate, and five others with him. 'Thank you, Vivesha. And Tilmur, if your tinkerers could look into the alf steel idea, I'm sure we can find you the projectiles to use.'

'Our alf steel supplies are shrinking by the day,' the wolf-tattooed alf said gruffly before the vampire king in question could reply. 'We may not have much left to waste on experimental methods.'

'Then we'll make sure the method is no longer experimental by the time we're going into battle,' Lyn retorted, waving that objection aside. 'This is hardly the moment to let conservatism get in our way. Other suggestions, anyone?'

'Didn't you use something interesting at the battle of the Golden Court this summer?' the vampire with the missing fingers said, cocking his head at Agenor. 'I've heard rumours of some explosive substance you used to hold back the Mother's army that day.'

My heart skipped a beat.

'Etele's blood.' Agenor sounded suddenly breathless. 'Gods and demons, I'd forgotten about it. I suppose if we can find a way to launch some of it at the court, we could—'

My stomach rolled without warning.

'No!' It burst from my lips before I even fully knew where the objection was coming from, the memory of that pulsating, syrupy fluid filling me with a dread far greater than good sense should have allowed. Gazes shot back to me. Surprise, scepticism, annoyance, and still I found myself fumbling on. 'No, we shouldn't be using that blood. We ... we ...'

'Em?' Lyn said, amber eyes round with worry. 'What is the matter?'

What in hell was the matter?

I parted my lips, wavering – unsure for a moment why my stomach rebelled so violently at the thought of that smothering hot day at the Golden Court, the way a little bottle of Etele's cursed blood had annihilated half a battalion. Was it mere squeamishness? An ill-timed sense of religious devotion? The memory of Zera's face when she'd told me she did not know whether her sister was alive at all?

But I *wasn't* squeamish or overly devout or even so very sentimental. And yet, the vision of that golden poison slamming into the Mother's island, seeping deep into the sun-burned earth ...

Oh.

Oh, gods.

'It's divine magic,' I managed to choke out, and suddenly I understood, my thoughts stepping back in line only as the words on my lips forced them to. 'The destructive powers of Etele's blood, I mean. Which means they're dual in nature – that they may destroy everything at first, but they'll nourish other things at the same time. Agenor, didn't you tell us you found worms as large as arms in the soil where our attacks hit at the Golden Court?'

The bewildered looks around me only deepened. A blue-eyed vampire started, 'Fine, but even if we render the island permanently uninhabitable—'

'It's not the *island* I'm worried about,' I interrupted with a frustrated gesture. 'The trouble is—'

'The Labyrinth,' Creon finished, tensing beside me.

The audible gasps from the circle suggested the news of his returned voice had not yet made the rounds among most of our allies.

'Em?' Agenor said sharply.

I sucked in a terse breath. 'Do you really want to know what cursed divine magic could do to a pre-divine entity like the Labyrinth? It's unnervingly powerful already. If—'

'Pre-divine?' a honey-blonde nymph queen with wasp-like antennae interrupted, her tiny nose wrinkled in disbelief. 'What are you talking about? Everyone knows the gods are eternal.'

'Not according to Zera.' I felt like some ridiculed prophetess, seeing her delicate face crinkle up tighter as I spoke. 'Look, I know it's not what common wisdom says, but there are plenty of clues that—'

'You know what?' Lyn hastily intervened, her slightly panicked look a shrill contrast to the soothing tone of the words. 'Let's not turn this into a theological discussion. I think Em's point is relevant no matter how old the gods are – the Labyrinth clearly has powers of its own, and—'

'We're talking about a *mountain*, yes?' the tattooed alf snapped.

'We're talking about a sentient magical entity that may or may not predate the birth of the gods and is in any case closely linked to them,' I said, and no matter how hard I tried to sound patient and understanding, it emerged from between clenched teeth as if I was ready to sink my canines into him. How had I gone from the girl who barely knew magic existed to the girl who knew more about its history than even the average immortal ruler did? 'And whatever it's capable of doing, it's powerful enough that bloody Korok himself decided to build a court on top of it to siphon off some of its magic. I have absolutely no idea what would happen if Etele's insanity somehow infects it, and I have very little desire to find out, too.'

'But that's all hypothetical doom and gloom, isn't it?' the waspy nymph said, her large shimmering eyes narrowing dangerously at Agenor as if *he*, not me, had offered the objection. 'That blood could save thousands of lives. Just because *she* says it's a bad idea ...'

She. The tone of that one word said all that needed to be said – I was barely even a living being in her mind. Just a collection of powers. Just an inconvenient obstacle between her and the basin full of Etele's pulsing blood.

I could feel Creon's displeasure before he spoke – a sensation like the weight of gathering thunderstorms that hung heavy in the air between us. But the drawl of his rough voice was alarmingly amiable as he leaned forward, settled his elbows on his thighs, and said, 'And when did you last have breakfast with Zera herself, Olshona?'

On my shoulder, Alyra let out a trill that I could only interpret as a peal of laughter.

Oh, gods. It was slipping from my grip like a shred of slippery silk, this debate – all the old feuds and grudges we'd prepared for, all the arguments and counterarguments we'd worked out, yet never in my wildest dreams had I imagined anyone would propose to drop a mad goddess's curse onto the most powerful magical being I'd met in my life. That anyone would *want* to. But the disgruntled murmurs were swelling around me, unsmiling scowls flashing our way from all directions – as if I was objecting just to be contrary, not to save them from something that might become worse than even the Mother herself.

Wolves against wolves. They were so caught up in that bloody fight that they refused to see the dragons that might rise and devour us all.

'Having seen firsthand what the Labyrinth can do,' Agenor said, in that poised, self-possessed voice that made it impossible *not* to listen to him, 'I agree that we should not be feeding it any nefarious powers if we can at all avoid it. We won't be using that blood.'

A nymph queen scoffed. 'Are you just agreeing because she happens to be your daughter, Lord Protector?'

Creon slowly sat up straighter – a measured, menacing movement I could only describe as the physical manifestation of the word *danger*. But Agenor merely drew up his brows and pleasantly said, 'Of course I'm listening to her because she's my daughter. I know where she got her brains, you see.'

Tared burst out laughing on the other side of the map. Next to him, Lyn was fidgeting frantically with her hair, darting glances around the circle of chairs like a small rabbit trying to determine where the predator growls are coming from.

Olshona stared at us in a moment of stunned rage, then drew in a barely restrained breath and spat, 'So how are you planning to give my people a fair fighting chance, then? Or are we nothing more than dispensable pawns to you, in true fae fashion?'

'Olshona ...' Lyn whispered, pleading.

'Well, she is asking a fair question, Lyn,' the white-haired vampire said, worrying his leathery bottom lip with a razor-sharp fang. 'We all agreed to join this fight because we believed there to be at least a chance of victory. If our strategists don't even care to explore all possible weapons before throwing us to the hounds ...'

It took all I had not to curse. 'We *did* explore this weapon. We just decided it was too dangerous to be used, especially at the Crimson Court.'

'So what about other places?' Helenka immediately shot back, with that uncompromising efficiency of hers that I was starting to get used to. 'If we lure part of her army elsewhere and shower it with Etele's blood there – are there any concerns associated with that?'

Plenty, I wanted to say, the first of which was that even *thinking* about the blood made me feel sick to my stomach ... but Agenor spoke before I could, in that voice that sounded like it had never snapped or shouted in its entire existence. 'Baiting her elsewhere is an excellent strategy, I would say. If we could pull even a few units to the other side of the archipelago on the day of the battle, that means a few less units able to defend the court for several hours.'

Not a word on whether we would or wouldn't be using Etele's blood in that secondary battle, I noted. No one else seemed to pay attention to that little detail.

'We started this meeting by concluding we did not have the manpower to defend ourselves in multiple places,' Olshona said, eyeing the wooden blocks on the map. 'Do we have the forces to fight two battles at once?'

'I assume we wouldn't be fighting two battles,' a weather-beaten alf with a missing ear piped up. 'Just stage a threat to get them there, then fade all our people back to the Crimson Court the moment they arrive. They can't fade. Would give us an advantage of a few hours while they have to fly back.'

Olshona's nose wrinkled again. 'But that would leave the other location unprotected.'

'We could just pick a fae isle?' one of the vampires suggested.

'None of the fae isles are several hours of flying away from the court.' She glowered at the map of the archipelago. 'So that would mean we'd need to lure them to another island. To one of *our* islands.'

Deadly silence followed.

'Well, I damn well hope it won't be a nymph isle,' Helenka said with a blistering chuckle. 'We've lost enough of our trees already. Also, the alves and vampires are farther to the north.'

'Alf isles are arguably easier to evacuate,' a vampire king suggested, more than a little haste in his throaty voice. 'If we just pick a small house and make sure to move all the more vulnerable inhabitants elsewhere in time ...'

I just caught Tared closing his eyes.

The next moment, every single alf around the circle was standing.

It was hard to make out any particular words, with a good dozen voices bursting out in indignant shouts all at the same time, but the general gist was crystal clear – that there was centuries of history in every fucking wall of even the smallest alf home, that no alf with a single grain of family pride in their body would stand for this madness, and since vampires all insisted on living in dank holes in the ground, why not send the fae *there* instead of—

'That's *enough*!' Tared snapped.

Miracle of miracles, they did go silent at that.

'Sit down.' He hadn't opened his eyes, a grimness around his lips I hadn't seen there all evening. 'And pull yourselves together, for Orin's fucking sake. You *know* I'm not sacrificing anyone's houses for some smoke screen, and neither is anyone else in this room as long as I have anything to say about it. Do I really need to elaborate?'

The house of Skeire, wiped off the face of the earth in a single vengeful attack. Several of the alves swallowed audibly as they sank back into their seats, hands still much closer to the hilts of their swords than I liked; one or two went so far as to mutter an apology. But their glares at the velvet-clad vampire king who had made the suggestion were as loud as their furious voices had been, and the silence from his side spoke volumes on his opinions, too.

'May I advise we take a break?' Agenor politely suggested, as if nothing had happened – still the epitome of well-bred civility in his gold silk shirt and his polished leather boots. 'We've been at this for a while. You could all set matters in motion at home and start the production of whatever poisons or other projectiles you have available. We'll consider the numbers and come up with a plan that doesn't endanger anyone's homes, and we'll reconvene to discuss once we have a solid proposal on the table. Can we agree on that?'

They did agree, but grudgingly and grouchily, and not without a last few grumbled warnings: that they wouldn't be sacrificing their people to any reckless fae games, and that we'd better show up with a damn good plan at our next council of war. Those who had arrived with lukewarm greetings left with frigid nods. Those who had arrived with frigid nods left without any greetings at all.

So much for the semantics of the word *alliance*.

I sat in my seat and wanted to scream and scream and scream.

Chapter 14

'I should probably have kept my mouth shut about your brains,' Agenor mumbled to me as he sank down at the table in the Wanderer's Wing, sounding uncharacteristically rueful. 'Should have known jokes wouldn't mollify them in that state.'

We'd withdrawn to this deserted corner of the Underground after the last of our guests had left, each of us grim and subdued, occupied with our own wretched thoughts. The room itself didn't do much to lift my spirits. The alf lights over the fields outside the library had gone dark after nightfall, and in the resulting gloom, even the fiery red of Lyn's hair managed to look cheerless. Naxi, usually the brightest presence in any company, slipped in behind us, appearing equally small and sullen.

Creon was little more than a shadow by my side, hair and wings blending into the night. But his voice emerged unaffected from the darkness as he said, 'It was the most amusing thing you've said in a century, though.'

Tared chuckled, sauntering back and forth between table and window. Naxi let out a high-strung, unnatural giggle. Agenor closed his eyes, sagged back in his chair, and muttered, 'At least we'll die diverted, then.'

'No one is dying yet,' Lyn said irritably, strutting around the room and flinging small balls of fire into the glass lanterns placed along the walls. 'Although I hadn't expected *you* to start causing trouble, Agenor. I figured you would have plenty of experience shrugging off the occasional jab during meetings.'

'Jabs at me, yes.' He rubbed his face, the tired lines showing again. 'Turns out I have very little experience with jabs aimed at my daughter. My apologies.'

She glanced over her shoulder, expression mellowing. 'Ah.'

'Your daughter appreciates the sentiment, impractical as it may be,' I bleakly said as I fell into a seat as well. Even without a single wooden block in sight, I couldn't look at the map etched into the table surface without seeing those numbers in my mind's eye – that pile of wood eclipsing most of the outlines of the Crimson Court. 'And I should have kept my mouth shut about the Labyrinth, too. Should have known they wouldn't understand.'

Creon scoffed. 'The only reason they don't understand is because they can permit themselves the luxury of not understanding. They aren't the ones who would take the blame if the island turned itself into some eldritch horror.'

I shivered. 'Still ...'

He threw me a look. *Stop making yourself small*, the flicker in his black eyes said, accompanied by something resembling a threat – a gleam that suggested he wouldn't mind shutting me up by kissing me to the point of wordlessness if I made the mistake of arguing this particular point.

I snapped my mouth shut. My father was sitting in the same room, after all.

And if I was honest ...

What would I have won by biting my tongue? I knew what I knew. If the kings and queens and rulers of houses were unhappy with that fact, we'd better deal with it now rather than halfway through a gruelling military campaign.

Creon sent me the briefest smile as he sat down next to me. Somehow, I managed to produce one in response.

'There's no taking back the discussion anyway,' Tared said at that moment, shrugging as he turned at the window. 'The best we can do is think very hard, come up with a decent plan, and then shout at some people a little. Do we really want to try and trick part of the Mother's army into moving away, or was that a desperate suggestion on the spur of the moment?'

'I was mostly trying to draw the attention away from Etele's blood,' Agenor admitted with a grimace. 'Don't get me wrong, it would probably help a *little* if we could lure some of the army to an uninhabited part of Rhudak, but Achlys and Melinoë won't be mad enough to send a truly significant part anywhere. They know as well as we do that we'll have to come for the court sooner or later.'

Tared groaned. 'Yes. Any other suggestions, then?'

'I suppose it would help if we could figure out the bindings,' Lyn sourly said, stomping towards us from the last lantern she'd lit. In the glow of her phoenix fire, the room looked a little cosier, a warm sanctuary rather than our last desperate hideaway. 'Any luck with your calculations, Creon?'

The tightness of his jaw suggested that his failure to solve the puzzle bothered him more than his shrug implied. 'Too many options. If we had three or four more locations of individual bindings, we could likely deduct some rudimentary patterns, but as it stands …'

'So we need Thysandra to talk?' Naxi said eagerly.

Lyn cursed. 'Yes, and also, *no*.'

Naxi deflated like an undercooked pudding.

'No to what?' Agenor said, frowning at the two of them. 'I'm open to most suggestions to get her talking, as long as you aren't planning to torture her.'

'Oh, no,' Naxi said gloomily, rosy fingers fidgeting with her fuzzy pink scarf. 'I tried torture ages ago. Didn't work. I'm pretty sure I could break her if you gave me a few more days to talk to her, though.'

Tared let out a desperate laugh as he plopped himself on the windowsill. 'Look, as romantic as that may sound—'

'As *what?*' Agenor sputtered.

It was in that moment – as we all stared at my father and my father stared at Tared like a male confronted with a language he'd never heard before – that I realised I had never discussed the peculiarities of Naxi's amorous obsession with him, and that it seemed rather unlikely any of the others had done so, either.

Which meant that he knew the story of the Last Battle only from Thysandra's reports.

'Oh,' Lyn said, the breathless laughter in her voice proof of the same dawning understanding. 'Oh, gods. Brace yourself. Where do we start, Naxi?'

'Look, there's no need to make a *spectacle* out of this,' Naxi grumbled, glowering at us from beneath pink-blonde curls. 'Just because she happened to like me last time we met—'

'Beg your pardon?' Agenor's eyes were well on their way to popping from his face. 'Because she— Did I hear you say she *liked* you?'

Naxi's hands tightened in her scarf. 'Yes?'

'She ...' He blinked once, twice. '*Thysandra?*'

'Yes, Thysandra,' she snapped, baring her small teeth at him like a cat about to hiss. 'So?'

'So— Look.' His befuddled laugh suggested he was hoping – *waiting* – for someone sane to intervene and admit we were just messing with him, a poorly timed practical joke. 'We're talking about the same Thysandra who almost killed you during the Last Battle, yes? Who has been known as bloody *Demonbane* for decades since?'

More glowers were the only reply he was granted.

'I suppose they didn't kill each other in the end,' Lyn said, sounding unwillingly amused as she clambered into the lowest chair of the bunch. 'One could consider that a sign of some feelings, presumably.'

'But ...' I'd rarely seen Agenor look so utterly befuddled, glancing around the table as centuries of assumptions fell apart behind his eyes. 'Couldn't it be ... well, a misunderstanding of some sort?'

'I'm a demon,' Naxi said, scowling. 'I don't misunderstand.'

'No,' he blankly said. 'No, I suppose you don't, but—'

'Am I really that unlikable to you?' The tremble in her voice was unexpected. Her fingers were plucking at her scarf more and more frantically, sending flutters of pink wool into the air. 'Is it so impossible to believe—'

'No!' he burst out, wings flaring with agitation as he jerked forward. 'Good gods, that's not what I was saying at all! It's just that Thysandra is hardly known for her warm and sentimental nature, and if there's *anyone* I would consider devoted to the Mother above everything else …'

Creon scoffed under his breath.

'Oh, don't be a brat,' Agenor snapped, whipping around to face him. 'Even your wounded pride should allow you to see some reason here.'

'Wait, what?' I said.

'Nothing of importance.' His glare at Creon was a stern warning. I rarely gave much thought to their age difference – immortal was immortal, after all – and yet something in that look made it suddenly easy to imagine an already jaded Agenor sending a chubby half demon toddler to bed without dinner. 'Old history. Thysandra didn't come out of the whole thing in the best shape.'

I blinked at Creon, who seemed to be biting back several less-than-diplomatic rejoinders, and warily said, 'Out of *what* thing?'

'Me committing the crime of being born.' It *sounded* bored and uncaring, yet the slight twitch at his jaw told an entirely different story. 'She never quite forgave me for it.'

'But why would she—'

'She used to be Achlys and Melinoë's favourite pupil,' Agenor interrupted, sounding like he couldn't wait to leave this subject behind us and return to the more comfortable topic of war and looming death. 'Then Creon was born and she was … more or less forgotten. So there's some bad blood there.'

The golden boy.

I stared unseeingly at Creon's scarred hands as the puzzle solved itself, pieces I hadn't even known were pieces falling together in the blink of an eye. Was *this* why Thysandra had decided to make a name for herself by learning to withstand demon magic – because that same magic was the one thing Creon had always refused to touch, the one playing field where she might still be able to beat him?

All that work, all that suffering, just so the Mother would see that *she* was most worthy of her doting adoration ... and the Mother never had.

'And so she's *jealous* of you?' My voice cracked a fraction. He was just a little too vivid in my mind's eye, that small half demon boy – not yet ten summers old and already wearing the first inked cuts in his skin, the first marks of pain and failure. 'Would she rather have been the one tortured in the name of training?'

Naxi huffed. 'What would you have done to get Valter and Editta's approval?'

Fuck.

'Below the belt,' I managed. It stung, that question. Had I been robbed of my parents' love not by my own insufficiency, but by the appearance of another, worthier recipient ... would I have hated that innocent child with the same deep passion? I couldn't exclude it. Not entirely. 'But point made, I suppose.'

'All I'm trying to say ...' Agenor rubbed his eyes, fingers stiff with exhaustion. 'There are plenty of people at the Crimson Court who play the game for no reason other than the love of bloodshed, and then there's Thysandra. Try to show some empathy.'

Was that scolding aimed at me? At Creon? At all of us together, just in case anyone was about to propose to torture her until she told us all she knew about the bindings?

I glanced at Creon. He met my eyes for the briefest moment, a flicker of understanding passing between us – that he *did* feel empathy, couldn't help but feel empathy, and that he'd had just as little choice in burying all of it beneath layers and layers of cruelty and haughty indifference. Had he cared, as a child? Had he ever tried to win her friendship, young Thysandra with all that hatred in her heart, as he staggered home bleeding from the training fields?

Magic was burning under my skin, hot and red as my anger, itching to wreck the Mother's pale, porcelain face.

'I'm more than willing to be empathic,' Tared was saying by the window, 'but it doesn't change anything about the bloody fact that we need her to open her mouth. Is there any approach we haven't tried yet? Any bargain we could offer her that we haven't thought of?'

A bargain.

I stared at the golden mark on the inside of my wrist and felt the floor sink out from below my feet – held Khailan's shaking hand in mine again, smelled the stench of blackened tiles again. *You wish to bargain with me.*

I'd done it once. Could I do it again?

It *would* work. It would be so very simple – a little smooth magic, a little push in the right direction, and the secret of the bindings might be ours before the sun rose again. It would make a world of difference, that knowledge. Hell, it might just be enough to win us the war.

So perhaps the question was rather … could I afford *not* to do it again?

My stomach rolled violently, remembering the sickening emptiness in those phoenix faces. On the edge of my sight, Creon was watching me with narrowed eyes – knowing, without doubt, exactly what I was thinking.

'Em?' he muttered.

Was that a warning in his hoarse voice? An encouragement? *Stop making yourself small* – but what if I wished for nothing more than to be small now?

What do you want?

I wanted to win the war. I wanted to save lives. Surely a little personal discomfort was not a pressing enough reason to let thousands die without functioning magic?

'I … I suppose I could go have another chat with her.' The words felt like thick, clumpy porridge on my tongue – like something I'd just retched up. 'There are a few things she said in our last conversation that I could work with. If I dug a little deeper …'

'You look tired as death,' Agenor interrupted, rising to his feet with a firm shake of his head. 'If you want to see her again, get some sleep first. Does anyone mind if I pay her a short visit now? At least she once trusted me – she may be willing to give me *some* clues, even if she still tries to scratch my eyes out.'

I should have objected. Trust was nothing to godsworn magic, after all, and why was I sending my weary, overburdened father out on some doomed mission if I could achieve all we needed with a flick of my fingers?

But I just nodded, guts tangled with dread, and let the guilt wash over me.

We lingered in silence after he and Tared faded out, sitting in the candlelit dusk like mourners waiting for sunrise. Lyn stared at her feet, looking small and conflicted. Naxi seemed on the brink of tears. Creon alone moved after a few minutes – squeezed my hand, then ambled off to rummage around the bookshelves. When he returned, he was holding a bag that turned out to be filled with the small wooden figurines I'd seen on this table before, used to indicate the locations of our allies.

For a while, nothing broke the silence except the soft thuds of wood against wood as his nimble fingers rearranged them on the map again, numbers roughly matching those we'd seen in the hall, colours matching species. Green for nymphs. Black for vampires. Blue for alves. Yellow for phoenixes.

Red for fae. *Destruction.*

I stared at the measured motions of his hands, at the familiar patterns the figurines were shaping on the wooden surface – the outlines of islands I could dream by now. In between the flocks of colour, some parts of the archipelago remained strangely empty. Human isles. No magic to be found there, save for the occasional half fae in hiding.

Something was itching against the back of my mind – not a thought yet, but a seed that might grow into a thought if I just knew how to water it.

Tared and Agenor returned before I'd managed.

One look at their faces was enough to send the shame rising in my throat again – tight lines around their lips, shadows in their eyes. Tared's shrug contained a world of meaning: *we tried to get her to talk*, that gesture said, *and we'd probably stand a better chance trying to drain the ocean tomorrow*.

I averted my gaze, fixing it on the map again. I couldn't stand seeing the self-blame in Agenor's eyes.

'She demands to be freed and sent back to the court without any constraints on what she can tell the Mother,' he said flatly as he sat down and settled his wings against his back. 'Specifically regarding the fact that we found the bindings. When I pointed out she can hardly expect us to give up our best chance of survival, she reminded me she can hardly be expected to help *us* survive, either. Which I couldn't really argue against.'

Naxi let out a deep, shuddering sigh.

'At least you got her to eat,' Tared said, dropping into the chair next to Lyn and folding his legs. 'As long as she's not starving, we—'

'She wasn't *eating*?' Naxi shrieked.

'Well, she is now.' Tared's skewed smile lacked its usual genuine assurance. 'Don't worry. We'd have let you know before she was dead.'

The way Naxi's lip curled up suggested there was plenty of reason to worry, for *our* health specifically; her small hands twisted into claw-like shapes, mere twitches away from scratching that smile off Tared's face. 'You could have *told* me.'

He sighed. 'And what would you have done with the information, except feel more miserable?'

Her hands abruptly loosened. The air escaped her lungs in a single breathy sob as she curled up in her chair and buried her face between her arms, rocking back and forth like a little child trying to chase away the dark.

The glance Lyn and Tared exchanged didn't escape me. There were many, many hours of deliberation in that look, and just as many doubts.

'Don't get me wrong,' Agenor broke the tense silence, jaw clenched and shoulders stiff, 'I'm glad she's not starving, but we don't have the time to spend weeks convincing her to talk. Achlys and Melinoë know we're moving against them. They could strike any of our allies tomorrow, for all we know.'

Tared spread his hands. 'What else do you propose?'

'I wish I knew.' A joyless huff. 'We're running out of options, if I'm honest. The simple fact is we need our magic, and if we don't have our magic, we need many, many more people to make up for it. Even if we called upon all allied rulers to see if they could conscript a few more of their subjects ...'

'You wouldn't win much with it,' Lyn said bitterly. 'There simply aren't that many of us left, and begging would only give them another reason to doubt whether we stand any chance at all. They may pull out entirely.'

Agenor let out an uncharacteristically vulgar curse.

My head ached as I stared at that map, the carved bits of coloured wood staring back at me mockingly. *Just get up*, I tried to tell myself. *Just tell them you need to see Thysandra again. Just use the damn smoothness and be done with it.* More magic or more people, and people we couldn't get – so this really was the only chance we had, wasn't it? I'd just have to live with it, turning myself into something far too close to the horrors of which I was trying to rid the world; I had reasons enough not to pick the path of spotless ethics.

Reasons are easy to come by, Zera had said. *It's wisdom that creates the true challenge.*

What was wisdom?

More magic. More people. And if the first could be achieved only at the cost of my conscience ...

More people.

I stared at the figurines on the table as that little seedling of a thought exploded in my mind, growing roots and branches in less than the time it took to gasp. Empty stretches on the map. Entire islands left unaccounted for—

'Em?' Lyn's voice reached me from ages away.

'*Humans.*' It fell from my lips like the answer to a prayer. 'The human isles. Is there any particular reason we haven't asked them to join us yet?'

I looked up from the table to find three pairs of eyes staring blankly at me.

Lyn's had widened. Tared's had narrowed. Naxi didn't appear to have heard me at all, rocking back and forth in her little bubble of misery. Agenor, on the other hand, blinked and blinked again, as if someone had whacked him over the head from behind and he was still trying to figure out where his memory of the last two minutes had gone.

But next to me, without missing a beat, Creon got to his feet and leisurely picked up his bag again. More and more figurines settled on the map under his quick fingers, filling the gaps between the clusters of blue and black and yellow and green – white ones, this time.

White. No magic at all.

'They don't have any of our powers,' Agenor said as the thought was still forming itself in my mind, his voice sharp with exhaustion. 'It would be rather heartless to drag them into a battle of magical peoples if they barely stand a chance of survival.'

A laugh was rising in me – the triumphant, violent kind, a laugh that could tear walls apart. 'You don't have functioning magic either at the moment.'

He blinked again. 'No, but—'

'And they have the numbers.' I felt almost dizzy, nodding at the batches of white forming under Creon's hand – so, so much white. 'There are more humans on Rhudak alone than there are vampires in all of the archipelago. And then there's the northern islands. Ildhelm and its neighbours. The cities on Orthune. If you take all of that—'

'*If*,' Tared said slowly, leaning forward in his seat. 'But even if they're all willing to join, there's no central authority of the sort most magical peoples have. We could waste weeks we don't have trying to convince every little village to send a handful of their people.'

'No, that's true. Officially, at least.' Somehow, the fact didn't slow down my mind in the slightest. My thoughts were spinning all over that map, digging deep into memories I'd buried with the life I'd left behind – village politics, votes on the market square, every island and every city fending for itself. 'But even if they're not formally allied, every single human will be looking at what the White City is doing. If we could get *their* support, we'd be halfway there.'

All gazes shot to the northernmost edge of the archipelago, where Creon was stoically planting white figurine after white figurine – so many of them, all clustered at that coveted east side of their island.

The city.

The high-walled paradise I'd dreamed of every frightful day and every hungry night, in a life that seemed an eternity behind me already.

'Yes,' Agenor admitted, 'but—'

'And they don't all need to join.' My thoughts were racing at breakneck speed, entire lines of argument springing out of nowhere, fully formed and ready to defend themselves. 'Even if, say, a quarter of the human isles agreed to help us, that would make a significant difference, wouldn't it? Imagine if a quarter of her empire suddenly refuses to hand over the food tributes. She'll *have* to send people after that, no matter how much she needs them at the Crimson Court.'

'But they would have to take an enormous risk to rebel like that,' Agenor murmured, rubbing a hand over his chin. 'The White City has always refused to get involved. So why would any of the human isles suddenly stick out their necks for us if—'

Creon's hand landed on the table with a hollow thwack. '*Suddenly?*'

Even Naxi jolted, juddering away from his tall figure with dewy blue eyes and an audible gasp. I whipped around to find him stiffened in his place beside me, bag still dangling from his left hand, wings flaring out behind his shoulders – signs of crumbling self-restraint if his gritted jaw and terse breath had not yet spoken for themselves. Around his right hand, figurines rolled away from his fingers, the faint, scratching sound all that broke the abrupt quiet that had descended over us.

Creon didn't seem to notice. His gaze had fixed itself upon Agenor with the sting of a thousand daggers, burning holes into my father's skin.

'Creon?' Lyn whispered. 'Creon, are you—'

He didn't seem to notice her, either.

'You *idiot*.' He hurled the words into Agenor's face with a fury that stole the breath from my lungs – gloriously genuine, no princely indifference or cruel delight in sight. 'It's been that easy for you, hasn't it? To sit in your office all day and read the fucking reports, nod at the fucking numbers, and give your fucking commands? *That* easy to pretend it was peace you were living in, not a war you had simply moved out of your sight?'

Ringing silence filled the room.

Agenor's eyes had widened, a shock on his face that would have been comical if I hadn't been fighting a similar expression. What in the world was happening? This wasn't the threat of the Silent Death, ruthless and confident and lethally elegant. This was the raw, barely suppressed anger of the bruised and broken soul below, a glimpse beneath the mask I hadn't even dared to *dream* of a week ago, and what in the world had sparked this outburst in a company he rarely even allowed to see him smile?

'What—' Agenor started.

'They have *always* rebelled.' And suddenly I understood what was going on – what festering open wound my father had accidentally prodded with one thoughtless remark. 'But you could simply send me and forget about it, and *I* was the one who had to go there and slit their throats and feel their fear as they bled to death at my hands. Do you understand just how frightened they were, every single fucking time they took up arms again? How many times they *have* taken exactly that risk you're talking about?'

He fell silent, breathing heavily in the stunned quiet. On the other side of the table, Lyn had pressed her freckled hands to her mouth, amber eyes gleaming unnaturally in the firelight. Next to her, Tared gaped at Creon as if he'd never seen him talk before.

'The question isn't *if* we'll get them to revolt,' Creon hoarsely added, sinking back into his chair with restless, shivering wings. 'The power of the entire bloody empire couldn't stop them from revolting. The question is whether we'll get them to trust us enough to make them revolt *with* us, and as Em says, we probably need the White City for that. But don't you dare blame it on cowardice if they refuse. It's the gods-damned opposite.'

Another silence fell. Naxi, unexpectedly, gave a ruthless little giggle.

'Right,' Agenor said, sounding dazed, and then again, as if to convince himself, '*Right.*'

'The White City will be a challenge in itself, though,' Lyn smoothly broke the deadlock – an abrupt return to the matter of strategy, but I suspected she was doing it mostly to spare Creon the embarrassment of lingering on his outburst. 'They're not too fond of magic over there. To put it lightly.'

'Yes,' Tared said, making a valiant attempt to sound like he wasn't doubting every single thought that had passed through his mind in the past century, 'but then again, if they know we're mostly *fighting* the magic in this case ...'

I shifted in my chair, reaching for Creon's hand beneath the table. He didn't look my way as his fingers curled around mine, squeezed, and let go again – a quick reassurance, and an equally clear sign that this was not the moment for concerned questions.

Fine. He'd get them later.

'... a little hypocritical,' Lyn was grumbling on the other side of the table, 'for them to make such a fuss about magic when the Mother would long ago have seized the city if not for their magic defences ...'

I dragged my thoughts back to the matter of human allies. 'So that part of the stories is true? About the walls being magical in some way or another?'

'Oh, yes.' Lyn sat straighter with a little snort, fumbling with her curls. 'They're impossible for magical creatures to cross. It's divine magic, of course – do the human stories still mention that? Another stronghold the gods built during the war, around the same time as the Underground.'

I shrugged. 'There's about ten million different human stories about the city. I'm sure a handful of them mention the gods at some point.'

Her laughter sounded a little wobbly. 'Well, in any case, the bit about the walls is correct. The only way for us to enter would be through the gates, but then there's their laws—'

'—which forbid them from opening the gates to non-humans,' I finished. That part I knew; it had filled my long winter nights with desperate hope, the dream that one day, in a far and wonderful future, I would never have to see those hated fae ships appear on the horizon again. 'Do we know what the laws have to say about half humans, by any chance?'

Silence, again.

'You'd have to go on your own, if they even let you in,' Creon slowly said, eyes trained on that cluster of white figurines as if he could read their minds through the wood. More likely, I figured, he just wasn't feeling like looking anyone else in the eye. 'There's no chance in hell they'll allow any of us to even come close to their walls if they can help it.'

I glanced at the dark fields outside, to where Alyra had vanished the moment we'd stepped into this room. 'Do you think the walls will stop godsworn birds from flying over them, too?'

A wry smile tugged at his lips. 'Don't tell her I forgot to consider that.'

'I certainly won't,' I said earnestly and patted his thigh. 'I happen to like you better with your nose still attached to your face. And either way, even if the walls *would* stop Alyra, it still shouldn't be too dangerous for me to go, should it? Worst case, they'll just refuse to help us. It seems unlikely they'll try to kill me.'

'It's not your physical safety I'm worried about,' he muttered. 'You could raze the entire city to the ground if you wanted to. Just ...'

He didn't finish the sentence. He didn't need to.

Just the people waiting for me.

Valter. Editta. All of Cathra – every single human he'd paid off and sent on their way that night the village had burned to the ground. I swallowed something thorny, scanning the fields again to hide the sting in my eyes – not tears, not yet, but that itch of emotion came closer than I liked all the same.

When I turned back to the others, two heartbeats and several resolute blinks later, they were all politely studying maps and nails, looking up only when I cleared my throat and managed to force out a reasonably composed, 'Do we have any other options?'

Another silence. It was almost starting to become a comfortable routine.

'Nothing that would solve so many of our problems at once, as far as I can see,' Agenor said, a tightness in his voice I couldn't fully pinpoint. Was it Creon's outburst? The prospect of sending me anywhere alone? Or the mention of the people who had raised me in his place? 'Assuming they allow you access *and* agree to help, that is.'

Assuming I wouldn't crumble at the sight of what might have been my future. Assuming I wouldn't run into Valter and Editta between those famous white walls and shrink back into the helpless little girl I'd been in their home.

But if the alternative was Thysandra and the sickening workings of smooth magic …

I drew in a deep breath. 'Let's try, then.'

Creon's gaze was a brand in the corner of my eye, all that predator focus aimed at whatever he'd found in the whirlpool of my feelings. But he remained suspiciously silent as the others nodded and muttered words of agreement – not the moment to challenge me and dig into my motives, not with four others around who did not have the faintest idea of what had truly happened at the Fireborn Palace.

Instead, all he said was, 'You'll have to write to them for permission to enter. I suppose the alves will be able to deliver a letter to the gate?'

That devastatingly swift mind again, already three steps into the plan while I was still coming to grips with the prospect of this journey. I glanced at Tared, who nodded, and then back at Creon, who aimed his gaze at the colourful arrangements on the map without another word. Only his hands moved in his lap, out of view from the others around the table—

Sure about this?

My heart gave a little twinge. 'Yes.'

To everyone else, that little word would be nothing but my agreement with the necessity of letter-writing … but the way Creon's wings loosened a fraction behind his back told me he knew exactly what question I'd responded to. His quick nod was an assurance, even with his eyes focused elsewhere. 'We probably shouldn't wait too long, then. I have no idea how long they'll need to respond.'

'I'm happy to assist writing that letter,' Lyn hurriedly said. 'If you need any help explaining to them who you are and what you're capable of—'

'No! No, none of that.' I let out a joyless laugh, sagging back in my chair. 'Telling them what I can do would be the worst way to go about this. They *hate* fae and magic, remember? If I waltz in and introduce myself as Emelin Thenessa of Agenor's house, godsworn and unbound, every self-respecting human will slam that door in my face and run.'

She looked a little crestfallen.

'The lot of you understand humans the way wolves understand sheep,' I added, wrapping my arms around myself. 'Nothing you can say will sound at all reassuring to them. Just let me think. I'll come up with something and have that letter ready tomorrow morning, alright?'

'As you wish.' Tared's quick smile wasn't entirely free of worry, and it faded as he met Creon's eyes. 'I suppose we can leave any additional safety measures to you?'

An outstretched hand if I'd ever seen one. Creon's nod was curt yet resolute, not a word to reassure any anxious family members that I truly was in good hands … but the tightness at his jaw suggested that a hundred god-built walls wouldn't be enough to keep him out if I was truly in danger.

Even Agenor didn't object.

'Excellent,' Lyn said with a brave attempt at cheeriness. 'Let's try to get a few hours of sleep before dawn, then.'

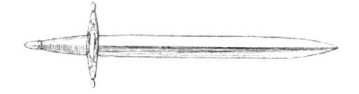

I wrote my letter at Creon's desk in the end, in the smoky, blue-grey glow of his faelights, surrounded by piles of astronomy books and the occasional hurried charcoal sketch of the night sky. Phyron's *Treatises* lay in my lap, Agenor's old copy with my mother's notes in the margins. Reading her words somehow made it a hundred times easier to remember what it was like to be human – short-lived and vulnerable, but so very angry all the same.

Once I closed my eyes and thought of Cathra, the letter frankly wrote itself.

It was brief. It was simple. It was so full of truth, too, that I only allowed Creon to read it before I folded it shut, sealed it, and shoved it beneath Tared's bedroom door – a little piece of my soul I wasn't sure I could share with anyone but those it was meant for.

To the city consuls –

My mother first told me about the White City when I was five winters old and starving. I dreamed of travelling north for fifteen years, until I learned of my fae ancestry and understood I would never be allowed to set foot within your walls.

Faekind took many things from me, but my future is the one I mourn most.

As I'm writing this letter, I'm preparing to fight a war on behalf of every human crushed beneath the heel of the empire – a war I'm not fully sure I'll win. Your support and assistance could tip the scales. It would mean the world to me to work with you, and while I know it will never be possible for me to live in the city, I would be honoured and grateful to be allowed to visit you for a few days and plead my case.

I'm well aware my fae blood would make this a breach of your laws. I can only hope my equally human blood may persuade you to make one temporary exception; I'll gladly comply with every safety requirement you consider necessary.

Thank you, from the bottom of my heart.

Yours,
Emelin of Cathra

Chapter 15

I woke early the next morning and didn't manage to go back to sleep, no matter how temptingly soft wings and strong arms whispered at me to close my eyes and tuck myself back into Creon's embrace. The restless guilt tingling in my limbs wouldn't allow me to – the simple, undeniable fact that I could already have solved most of our troubles and simply … hadn't.

For the sake of scruples.

For the sake of my own already blemished conscience.

Such a wafer-thin excuse, flimsy to the point of silliness. Really, it was madness, betting the future of the world on my rather volatile sense of morality. If the consuls of the White City didn't write back …

Three days, I told myself, ignoring the violent twisting of my stomach as I stared unseeingly into the dark. If we hadn't heard from them in three days, I would walk into Thysandra's cell and make her talk, damn the costs and consequences, damn the sensation of filth spreading below my skin at the thought alone. Until that time, I would do whatever else I could and pray it was enough.

And then we might still lose the battle.

I scrambled upright in the blankets, unable to lie still a single second longer as the anxiety crawled into every toe and fingertip.

Creon didn't move as I untangled myself from his arms and slid to the foot of the bed, where I would not need to climb over him to escape. Even as I looked for clothes in the impenetrable darkness, my mind was a whirlwind of sounds and flashes of more and more pressing images: piles of wooden blocks, sharp voices and sharper glares, arrows protruding from bloodied skin ...

'Cactus,' a sleepy voice rasped behind me.

I froze, then turned, blinking against the darkness as my eyes fought to make sense of shadows and silhouettes.

The rustle of wings against fabric told me he was sitting up. Another whisper of motion, and the faelights lit up around us, silvery rays flooding the room and revealing the exquisitely sculpted, extremely naked body I had left behind in the blankets a moment ago.

Gods help me.

No matter how hard I willed myself to be sensible, no matter how familiar the view after all this time, my heart still skipped a beat at the sight of that raw male glory – rendered all the more tantalising, somehow, by the vulnerability of his half-woken state. He truly didn't know how *not* to be irresistible. Even fogged with sleep, he oozed beauty and power; when he yawned and propped himself up on his elbows, muscles flexed in unfairly ravishing ways, sending his chest and abdomen rippling like liquid gold in the dusky light.

Some of the tightness in my belly turned into an entirely different sort of tautness, spreading like wildfire through my veins.

'Must you?' I managed, suddenly achingly aware of my own nakedness. 'I'm trying to get things done.'

'Ah.' He rubbed a hand over his face, wiping the sleep from his eyes. 'Making an attempt to rinse the guilt from your system by running around all day and slaving away on tasks dozens of others could be doing in your place?'

I stared at him.

His eyes were still a tad bleary, his words sluggish in an oddly endearing way ... but none of that softened the crisp edge of his point in the slightest. He didn't have the *right*, damn it, to be so painfully perceptive before he'd even set a foot out of bed; how was I supposed to quietly beat myself up if he insisted on looking straight through me even while asleep?

'Thought so,' he added when I stayed silent, sitting up straighter with a small groan. His wings strained wide behind him, as if to stretch out the stiffness of the night. 'Wasn't writing that letter enough?'

'I could be doing more,' I said weakly, crossing my arms over my bare chest. 'You know I could be.'

I hadn't even mentioned the possibility of smooth magic to him last night, exhausted and occupied by the White City spinning around my head – but of course he knew exactly where my thoughts had run. There was no surprise in his shrug. 'Yes, but *should* you be doing more?'

I scoffed. 'It would save lives.'

'It would destroy you,' he pleasantly pointed out.

'Then maybe I shouldn't be such a squeamish bloody coward, should I?' I bit back, unable to help myself. Of course he was right. It was *worse*, somehow, that he was right. Just like it was worse to know I'd done this to myself, that Zera had refused me and warned me and *still* I'd asked for these damned powers I couldn't possibly have grasped – powers that made me feel like something dark and putrid was digging its roots beneath my skin.

He arched an eyebrow, running a hand through his tousled hair. 'Ah, yes. Just become someone else. A brilliant solution that has always worked well for you in the past.'

If I'd had anything red within reach, I might have obliterated the bed he was sitting on. As it stood, I couldn't come up with anything more intimidating than a couple of Alvish curses Edored had taught me during a particularly lively card night.

Creon burst out laughing. 'Don't let your father hear you.'

'It's not funny!' I snapped, flinging up my hands. 'I could have unbound half of the Underground by now if I'd just used my stupid magic yesterday – you *know* I could have. Do you really care so little about that?'

He sobered up so abruptly that I startled. 'What?'

It came out too harsh, that one word. Too brusque.

I opened my mouth, closed it again, got out an unpleasantly defensive, 'I mean—'

'Of course I care about the bindings, Em,' he interrupted sharply – much too sharply, the bite in his voice a flawless match to the sudden bitterness twisting his lips. As if I'd mortally offended him. As if I'd crossed some invisible line no one had ever pointed out to me. 'You know damn well I want to win this war as much as anyone else. I just want you safe and happy first. Do you really expect me to care more about everyone and their mother's bindings than I care about your sanity?'

I stared at him numbly, feeling myself grow just a fraction smaller, just a fraction stupider.

My sanity. Which would have been a heartwarming reassurance if not for that look on his face, for the way he'd thrown his question at my feet as a reprimand rather than a declaration of love – such a sudden shift from his careless amusement that I found myself repeating the conversation two, three times in my mind, trying to find my mistake. Fine, I'd been pushing. I'd been arguing. But there was no need for this merciless retaliation, was there – as if I had been trying to attack him in all earnestness?

He knew that I knew that he cared, didn't he?

My head spun. My words came out in a pathetic stammer. 'I— No, but—'

'So of course I want you to unbind them all,' he added before I could gather my thoughts. Why that fierce emphasis, though, as if this would be news to me? 'But not at the cost of *you*, do you understand?'

I understood.

And I also didn't.

This was the second time in three days he was lashing out at me over nothing, making me feel like a fool, snapping at me when he could so easily have made the point in his usual leisurely manner – things he'd never done before in all the time I'd known him. Just tired, I'd told myself the day before yesterday. Just hurt or sick of the world pushing us to our limits. But to hell with that – I *knew* what he was like when he was tired and hurt and sick of the world, and none of it involved losing his temper with me.

So what in hell had gotten him so touchy about reckless battle strategies and broken bindings?

'Yes,' I made myself say. 'Yes, I understand, but ...'

He waited without speaking this time, shoulders straining, wings furling and unfurling in restless little twitches. As if he was bracing himself – the look of a male caught red-handed and desperate to talk his way out of it.

Gods help me. Telling him that he was being ridiculous in this state sounded like guaranteed trouble.

'I'm honestly not sure how we got here.' I sucked in a long breath. Best to move the conversation elsewhere, then. 'Don't get me wrong, I'm glad to hear you won't blindly sacrifice me to save the world, but ...'

His sharp-edged features mellowed as he tilted his head, eyebrow coming up a fraction. 'But you'd still prefer to sacrifice yourself?'

And all of a sudden there was no trace of that haunted vigilance left on his face. The soft lines deepening around his eyes instead were so radically different that I wondered for a moment if I hadn't simply misjudged his expression in the dusky light – what if it was nothing more than a misunderstanding, all of this, some spectacularly poor reading of tone and body language?

But for goodness' sake, I wasn't mad, was I?

'Well, I would *prefer* not to sacrifice anyone,' I said, allowing myself a cautious huff by way of experiment. His expression didn't change – thank the gods. 'But right now, my alternative is letting down all the people who rely on me to save them, and how am I supposed to justify holding back in that situation? Hell, even *Zera* expected me to ... to ...'

To save the world. To do the job I promised her I would. I didn't manage to finish the sentence; it tasted far, far too much like failure.

Creon shoved his blankets aside and swung his legs out of bed, revealing every last inch of that chiselled fae body with an uncharacteristic lack of dramatics. 'And you're telling me that you truly believe Zera would want you to use your godsworn magic in this way? After all the doubts she had in the first place?'

I swallowed, lips pressed tight together. I didn't dare to trust that my voice would come out steady.

'Yes,' he said, mirthless smile tugging at his lips. 'That's what I would think, too.'

How had he morphed back so easily into this version of himself, no more sudden sharpness, nothing but all-seeing tenderness? I wanted to ask. I *needed* to ask. I couldn't let these outbursts keep gnawing at the back of my mind. And at the same time, I wanted to bury the question six feet deep and forget about it – why risk getting an answer if the problem had mysteriously solved itself already, if this was simply my own Creon again, the male I knew and understood and loved so much it hurt?

'But what if we're wrong,' I whispered, swayed by the lure of the easy way out. 'What if she *does* want—'

'Em, she didn't give these powers to whoever you wish you could be.' His eyes burned so piercingly sharp between the deceptive softness of his lashes; his low, rough voice was the gentlest punch in the gut. 'She gave them to you. *Because* of the choices you would make with them. *Because* of the empathic capacity and moral compass that you showed her. So why are you trying to get rid of those very things now, as if you're failing her by doing exactly what she trusted you to do?'

My knees were trembling. I wasn't sure when they'd started.

'You don't want to use the damn magic,' he added wryly, sending me a slight, one-shoulder shrug. 'So don't use it. Do something better instead. You're allowed to keep it that simple, cactus.'

It sounded like a lie, all of it – not because *he* was a liar, but because it seemed unreasonable for the truth to be so convenient. 'But if Thysandra never talks ...'

'Sooner or later, she will.' He closed his eyes for a brief instant. 'I did, too, in the end.'

After the Alliance first captured him. After Lyn talked to him, for days and days and days on end, until finally he'd come to realise that he'd spent his life on the wrong side of this war, that the Mother he'd served had never loved him and never would.

He's served his purpose.

A familiar flare of hot anger burned through me.

'But you had been very explicitly abandoned,' I said, turning away in a desperate attempt to keep my scattering thoughts in line. Thinking clearly was somehow much easier without the distraction of his naked body on that bed. 'So at least you couldn't cling to the fantasy of being her cherished son anymore, could you?'

His curt laugh spoke volumes. 'No.'

'While Thysandra ...' I sucked in a breath between my teeth. 'Well. Thysandra.'

'I'm not the objective voice of reason you might need when it comes to Thysandra,' he said under his breath, head in his hands when I turned back to him. 'As Agenor said – bad blood. I may understand her, but it's hard for me to sympathise with the person who insisted I was living the life of her dreams while I was throwing up from pain and being sent right back into the training ring for the fifth time that day.'

A shudder ran through me. 'Yes, I thought it might be something like that.'

'You were right, as usual.' He sighed, looking up. 'That said, my old grudges are a terrible reason to let her rot away in a cell if we need her to help us out in the end. So ...'

'So we need to figure out something better.' I wandered over to the wardrobe, where piles of my underwear had slowly claimed several of his drawers for themselves. 'Trying to make her open up is probably the wrong approach altogether, don't you think? You changed your mind those days because Lyn kept talking to you, not because you were being besieged by people who needed something from you.'

This time he didn't answer.

I glanced over my shoulder as I snatched my underwear from its drawer, heart skipping a beat – had I said something wrong again? But there was no anger in his expression, no unexpected sharpness. He sat motionless on the edge of the bed, wings draped loosely over the blankets but a frown on his face that looked not nearly so leisurely – a look that was at once a puzzle and a solution.

Our gazes met.

And just like that, I knew exactly what he was thinking.

'How much do you trust her?' I said slowly. 'Naxi?'

His wry smile told me I'd hit the mark on my first try. 'I trust her to know what she wants, at least. So if we can make sure that doesn't involve, say, destroying any more bindings ...'

There was no need to finish that sentence.

Gods help me, it was *addictive*, the way our thoughts intuitively found each other and took solid shape in the empty space between us. The wicked twinkle in his eyes. The sudden clarity of my mind. It was no longer the fear of shameful failure that drove my limbs to move; instead, it was the rush of knowing exactly what to do.

'Lyn and Tared ...' I started.

Creon shrugged. 'They have good reasons to be cautious.'

'They'll try to stop us.'

'Probably,' he admitted dryly.

'So then it's probably best if I go alone,' I said, stepping into my underwear and striding to the chair where I'd chucked my clothes last night. 'They'd forgive me much more easily than you if they were to find out.'

He looked like he wanted to object, but remained silent as I slipped into the indigo dress I'd worn last night. It still smelled of ink and bird. I shook my messy curls over my shoulder and plopped down onto the armrest to put on my socks, looking up again only once I'd finished that task.

He still hadn't moved. He still wore that troubled look – the expression of a male torn between two unpleasant choices.

'You don't want me to go alone,' I concluded, grimacing.

With a joyless chuckle, he slumped on the edge of the bed, shaking his head. 'I feel you're doing more than enough on your own already.'

'So are you.' I hopped off the chair, walked over to the desk, and pulled the key Tared had pressed into my hands two days ago from the smallest drawer. 'I'll be fine, I promise. And you *really* don't want to be found doing anything that could be interpreted by unhappy allies as an attempt to free Thysandra, no matter what your true intentions may be.'

His lips quirked into a smirk that made my stomach feel too tight for my guts. 'Whereas it would be perfectly fine if you were caught doing any such thing?'

I glared at him. 'You know what I mean.'

'Oh, yes. You mean you're determined to do everything by yourself again.' This time, that skewed little smile *had* to be deliberate, the devilish gleam in the black of his eyes. It might look innocent enough, the way he casually stretched his legs in front of him – but I'd be damned if he didn't know exactly what it did to the toned lines of his muscles, or how the motion mercilessly drew the eye to the half-hard masterpiece between his thighs. 'One condition, then.'

'I don't make blind deals with fae,' I said with a snort.

'There's nothing blind about this,' he dryly informed me. 'You're seeing exactly what you're getting.'

'That's the condition?' It would have been more satisfying if my voice had sounded convincingly outraged, rather than choked and a fraction wobbly. 'Fucking you?'

'Oh, dear,' he said primly – how in the world did he manage to look *prim*, sitting stark naked on a tousled bed with his cock well on its way to a bludgeon-like state? 'Do you have to put it like that? Rather vulgar, Thenessa.'

I huffed. 'But am I *wrong*?'

'Depends.' He flicked his tongue along his lips, gaze dropping to my neck. 'The condition I was about to suggest is that you get back here as soon as you're done and take a break before you throw yourself headfirst into the next task. How you spend that free time ...' A chaste flutter of his lashes. 'Well, that is entirely up to you, of course.'

I tried to swallow. My mouth had abruptly gone dry.

His smile was pure seduction, dripping with sin.

'Bastard,' I managed to get out, crossing the three steps to where he was sitting. 'As if I can't—'

With inhuman speed, his hand shot out, locked around my wrist, and dragged me closer. I half tumbled, half jumped into his lap, straddling him; the warm, silky steel of his cock prodded my thigh, and I forgot how to breathe or think for one blissful eternity.

His lips came down on mine, hot and so impossibly soft I couldn't help but whimper.

It happened too fast for me to react with anything but greedy instinct. His fingers tensed around my nape. My mouth opened to his, and he made his claim with savage intensity, tongue taking possession of me, drinking in the next moan that escaped me. I found his lean shoulders under my fingers and held on with all that I had – not enough, not nearly enough, to soften the painful need for his skin against mine ...

The next moment, he pulled away.

I was left flustered and panting in his lap. Lips aching. Skin burning. A throbbing fire licking slowly through my veins. He pressed a torturously tender kiss to my jaw, then sent me a saintly smile that somehow made me feel all the more debauched – the innocent curl of his lips an agonising contrast to the lust unfurling beneath my skin.

'Made my point?' he murmured sweetly.

'You certainly made *a* point.' The breathless quality of my words said all I wasn't willing to admit. My thoughts were slowly caving in to the easy way again – how bad could it really be to stay here and hide a little longer? It couldn't do *that* much harm, could it, if I allowed myself to drown in this world of pleasure and oblivion for a while, before I ventured back into the world of never-ending obligations ...

But already I could feel it tugging at my consciousness again – the heavy awareness of work to be done. Knowing us, we could waste half a day fucking our brains out. With the Mother bound to strike any moment, could I afford it?

'Go do one thing, cactus,' Creon said softly, demon eyes reading every line on my face. 'Just one. Enough to not feel lazy and useless at the end of the day. Then get back here and let me fuck you senseless. You deserve it.'

Gods help me. My body was easy prey to that low purr in his voice; the sound strummed across every hidden part of me, heating the blood in my veins, turning my knees to wobbly mush. In a last desperate attempt to regain my dignity, I pushed myself a few inches away from him and managed a stiff, 'I'll ... consider the invitation.'

'Oh, I strongly suggest you do.' His smile was more animal than fae. 'I'll find you if you don't.'

It truly was a miracle I didn't drop to my knees the moment I crawled off him, my legs unsteady with need. I had to keep my gaze trained on his face as I smoothed my dress; if I strayed down for as much as a glimpse, I wasn't quite sure I'd ever leave the room again.

'I'll try to be quick,' I managed.

'Good.' The satisfaction in that rough drawl alone could have had me climaxing on the spot. 'Because I definitely won't be.'

I turned and fled. If I'd stayed a heartbeat longer, a night of self-reproach would have started to look like a pretty reasonable price for just one more taste of his lips.

Chapter 16

The Underground was no longer as fidgety as it had been after the evacuation of the Golden Court, that restless atmosphere of an anthill under attack. Instead, an eerie calm now permeated the air. Alves and nymphs and vampires moved with grim resolve wherever I looked, few of them paying attention to anything but their own duties; some were running around with letters or books, others dragging baskets of food or weapons from here to there. Every now and then, I passed a small centre of coordination, where tired-looking individuals were counting resources or doling out tasks. 'Two more pounds of willow bark,' I heard a nymph mutter to herself as she inspected a pile of baskets others had brought in, 'and clove extract …'

Willow bark. Cloves. Herbs for pain relief.

Already the guilt was rearing its ugly head again.

But Zera had trusted *me*, not whatever ruthless creature I might one day become; I clung to that thought as I walked on, clenching my fingers around the key in my pocket. I wasn't leaving them to fend for themselves. I had written my letter to the White City, and I would be taking care of Thysandra, too. Just not with the bloody mind magic.

Anything but the bloody mind magic.

Guilt, arousal, and relief made for an odd brew of emotions all at once.

Most of the people I passed ignored me, and those who didn't seemed determined to avoid me. As a consequence, it took a while before I found a nymph willing to pause and tell me where to find Naxi's home. The place turned out to be located on the far side of Zera's quarter, so I spent ten more minutes weaving through the maze of narrow corridors before I finally found the door that had been described to me: golden oakwood, gnarled handle, a bushel of dried lavender hanging from the frame.

I knocked and received no answer.

Hardly unexpected: if every single soul in the Underground was running around preparing for battle, I should have known Naxi would not be lounging in her bed waiting for me. Still, I had to bite away a curse or two as I trudged back to the central hall of the Underground, fielding apprehensive glances at every corner I rounded.

Several desks had been set up where the circle of mismatched chairs had stood last night. Alves faded back and forth at dizzying speed, like fireflies blinking in and out of sight; bent over the tables, a handful of Agenor's fae furiously scribbled down their messages, shouting instructions at others to move or add wooden models on the chalk map. It took a while before I caught sight of Agenor himself. Deep in conversation with Doralis and a bedraggled Thorir, he didn't give the impression he had much time to join the search for wayward demons.

I asked a few other nymphs instead. None of them had seen Naxi since last night, not even after she'd left the Wanderer's Wing with us.

Unhappy suspicions were starting to solidify in my mind.

I slipped out of the hall without drawing too much attention to myself, insofar as it was possible for me to ever be inconspicuous – but at least no one came after me and no one asked why I was slipping away in the direction of Etele's quarter. After a handful of wrong turns and detours, I managed to retrace the path we'd walked a few days ago on our return from Thysandra's cell. Past the rows of sombre vampire front doors, past the training halls and washing rooms …

Into that grim, sickly-lit corridor with its alf steel-plated doors.

Where a small, dishevelled heap of pink skirts and fuzzy wool lay curled up against the stark white walls, face hidden behind a tangle of blonde and pink curls.

Fuck.

'Naxi?' My voice echoed as I hurried into that deserted corridor, towards her crumpled form. 'Naxi, are you alright? Did anyone—'

She shot up with a shriek, staring at me with bewildered, red-rimmed eyes.

'Oh, thank the gods,' I blurted, staggering to a standstill. My heart was pummelling my ribs. 'You were just sleeping? You're not sick or wounded or—'

'Who in hell would wound me?' she grumbled, and then she burst out crying.

It was no pretty crying – no civil, elegant shedding of tears, the way a well-bred girl might show her sorrow after a lover's quarrel. This was ugly, snotty, and raw. Gut-wrenching sobs shook her entire lithe body with an intensity that made me flinch; she curled back up on the floor, buried her face in her ruined scarf, and bawled like she'd been at this for hours and might continue for just as long again if no one stopped her.

Against the harsh backdrop of those cell doors, she looked small and frail and pitiable. Had anyone told me this was one of the Underground's deadliest allies now, I might have laughed in their face.

'Um,' I said, wits and good sense abandoning me as I stood there and stared at her. Would it be dangerous to pat her on the shoulder in this state? 'Naxi ...'

'She's here, isn't she?' she sobbed, barely intelligible through the scarf. 'I can *feel* her – I *know* she's here ...'

Oh, Zera help me.

'Um,' I said again, thoughts rapidly adjusting. This was hardly the rational situation in which I'd hoped to find her – but damn it, I'd make do with it somehow. 'Well—'

'Oh, I know,' she blubbered, jerking up to glare at me with bloodshot blue eyes. '*I know*. You can't tell me and I might kill you all if I knew and—'

'*Would* you kill us all?' I cautiously interrupted, which seemed a relevant question to start with.

She furiously wiped her nose with a slip of her skirt. 'Not very likely. I still need you to get rid of the Mother.'

Lyn and Tared's reserve started making more sense to me by the heartbeat.

'Well, that is extremely reassuring,' I said wryly, sinking down on the floor next to her. The alf steel was icily cold against my back. 'And if the Mother were to be dead already?'

'It's not that I *want* to kill anyone,' she grumbled, sounding like a disgruntled child denied a second helping of dessert. 'I'm not a monster. It's just that you're all being extremely unhelpful, and I want … I want …'

'Thysandra?' I suggested.

She uttered another plaintive wail, sagging against the wall with closed eyes as if the name alone was too much for her heart to bear.

She knows what she wants, Creon had said; the trouble was *I* still wasn't fully sure what in the world Naxi wanted, and making blind deals with demons sounded about as unwise as making blind deals with fae. I tucked my knees into my chest, lowered my chin onto them, and said, 'Why her?'

Naxi's eyes flew open. 'What?'

'Why Thysandra?' As light as I kept my voice, I made sure to let my left hand rest on the indigo surface of my dress – ready to draw red the moment I needed it. I had no ambitions to get killed by a volatile demon in some shadowy corner of the Underground, and that hysterical gleam in her eyes suggested she might be closer to an accident than both of us appreciated. 'It's been almost a century and a half. So what about her makes it worth thirteen decades of pining, exactly?'

Her lips curled as if to bite out some blistering retort, then faltered – a flicker of vulnerability crossing her face as she blinked at me and slowly let go of the breath she'd drawn so brusquely. The violent fury sunk from her eyes bit by bit. As if she'd woken from a nightmare, dazed and disoriented, but now finally recognised me again, remembered who she was and what she was doing here.

A few seconds ticked by before she averted her eyes and let out a long, spiritless sigh. 'Actually, you might understand it better.'

I frowned. 'Better than who?'

'The others.' She fluttered a weak gesture at the world beyond these prison walls. 'Because you love him, you see.'

The matter was growing more and less comprehensible at the same time. 'Is this about people who fall in love with demons?'

'No,' she said wistfully, letting out another sigh so deep it had to come from the pits of her soul. 'About people who aren't scared of them.'

I blinked at her. She didn't elaborate, staring at the wall opposite us with a wobbling bottom lip ... but at least she'd stopped sobbing out loud and no longer gave the impression she would sink her teeth into my face if I asked the wrong question.

'Is that so rare?' I asked warily.

She snorted. 'You're scared of me.'

The hand on my dress seemed to be mocking me all of a sudden. 'Admittedly, but—'

'Oh, I know,' she interrupted, spitting out a laugh. 'You like me. You'd call me a friend. You're happy enough to fight alongside me. They're *all* like that – it's just that it doesn't change a damn thing about the fact they're all scared of me, too.'

Right.

'And it's very sensible,' Naxi added with a laconic shrug. For a moment she sounded like her own light-hearted self again, that familiar, cheerful ruthlessness. 'I *am* quite dangerous. But it still stings at times, you see?'

I did see.

Truly, how could I not understand exactly what she was telling me? I had at least been granted the small mercy of not *feeling* the discomfort around me; all I noticed were stares and whispers, and those hurt enough already. I'd seen Creon destroy himself over his demon senses. I should have known hers wouldn't come without a price either.

'You don't feel empathy, do you?' I said.

'Oh, thank the gods, no.' She huffed a laugh. 'It's tiresome enough to feel everyone's emotions. It would be torture if I had to have my own emotions about them, too.'

It was hard to return even the most watery chuckle at the memory of Creon's empty eyes, the shadows deepening every line of that sharp-edged face. Torture, indeed. 'But you do feel loneliness?'

'I feel …' She hesitated, running the pink tip of her tongue along her lips as if to taste the options. 'I feel outsiderness.'

My heart twinged a little.

'Oh, yes,' she lightly said, throwing me a look of understanding. 'I thought you would.'

For fuck's sake. I didn't want any of this to make so much sense. I didn't want any of this to be about *me*. None of my own troubles were where I needed this conversation to go; I could ponder the many different flavours of loneliness well enough on my own, and meanwhile I wasn't getting any closer to my one useful task for the day.

We still had a war to win. And Creon … Creon was still waiting for me.

'So you decided Thysandra is the solution for you?' I said, resting the back of my head against the cold alf steel door. 'To your outsiderness, I mean.'

'Well,' Naxi said, face darkening as she pouted, 'at least she's devoted her heart and soul to people without a moral compass before, hasn't she?'

It almost sounded like a plea – as if she needed me to agree. As if her future depended on my approval.

I rubbed my face, suppressing the urge to groan. 'Right. And she isn't scared of you.'

'Not of me.' A long-suffering sigh. 'Just of what she feels around me, really.'

You'd better keep Anaxia away from me, Thysandra had snapped as I was leaving her cell, and whatever the emotion in her voice had been, it had more closely resembled fear than anger. I shook my head, not sure who'd win the title of most insane participant in this entire history, and said, 'Well, that sounds like a solid basis for love.'

Naxi couldn't have looked more revolted if I'd pushed a rotting apple under her nose. 'I don't feel love.'

'Oh, apologies,' I said, taking the risk of rolling my eyes at her. 'I didn't know the word was offensive.'

She snort-laughed at that.

'So what is she to you, then?' I added. 'If love doesn't have anything to do with it?'

'Oh, I have decided it would vastly improve my quality of life to have her,' Naxi said without a moment of hesitation. Her tone was dreamy, her tug at the shawl around her shoulders strangely brusque in comparison. 'To the extent that I think I might need her. Not that you should tell her that, of course – she'd run away screaming.'

I managed a laugh. 'Can't in all honesty say I'd blame her.'

Her grin was wolfish. 'Good thing she's chained down, then.'

Gods have mercy. For the first time, I felt a stab of guilt for what I was about to do – not for Lyn and Tared and their unjustified trust in my discretion, but rather for Thysandra and the utter insanity I was about to inflict on her. Then again …

Whenever I closed my eyes tight enough, I could still see Creon's binding shatter on the rocks of the Cobalt Court.

Perhaps she deserved a little insanity for that alone.

'So,' I said, voice lighter than my heart, 'how about a key?'

Naxi's head whipped around to me.

And it was in that moment that I understood exactly why Lyn and Tared hadn't trusted her with the same proposal – why they hadn't been willing to let her come anywhere near the cell in which Thysandra was spending her captivity. The look in those wide cornflower eyes … Like a starving wild animal catching a first glimpse of its prey, thoughts behind that bright blue façade narrowing to nothing but the hunt and the kill. Primal. Instinctive.

And terrifying.

A second realisation clicked in my mind as I sat there and held her gaze, grateful now for the hand I'd pressed against my dress: that I did not need to hold back. That there was no need now for me to be decent and empathic and fair, because the pink, sharp-teethed little creature before me was none of those things and cared about none of them, either – that *I* could be terrifying too, and she would never hold it against me.

If anything, I figured it might amuse her to no end.

'A key?' she repeated, and the tone in which she spoke the words sent a shiver down my spine, low and hungry and full of warnings. 'To her cell?'

'Hm-hmm,' I said.

'For *me*?'

'Yes.' My smile was like one of Miss Matilda's exquisite accessories – crafted with military precision to dazzle and impress. 'With a few conditions, of course.'

She let out a sharp-edged, impatient peal of laughter. 'Oh, do you want to bargain?'

'Not in that way,' I said slowly. 'People would see the mark, and I don't have permission for any of this. We might both get in trouble once they figure it out.'

Her eyes narrowed. 'Lyn and Tared don't know?'

'No.' I gave an apologetic shrug. 'Because Lyn and Tared are extremely decent people who want only the best for you and all of us, and I strongly doubt they would agree to actually threaten you in order to keep the Underground safe. So they'd rather keep you away and make sure there's no need for any of that unpleasantness, I suppose.'

'Yes.' Again she laughed. 'And you're not that decent?'

I thought of Khailan's bland eyes – of the hand trembling in mine – and couldn't suppress another shiver. 'I'm starting to find out I might not be.'

'Good,' she said, that little tongue flicking past her lips again as if to taste the change in the air between us. '*Good*. We won't win the war with decency. Tell me what you want.'

'You can visit her,' I said. This, finally, was the part for which I'd prepared, the part I had actually thought about in the time it had taken me to find her. 'You can talk with her as much as you want, about anything you want. But she is not to leave her cell, and you won't make any bargains or deals with her without asking me or Creon about it first. If you violate any of those terms ...'

Her lips parted a fraction as I paused, as if she could bite the truth out of me.

'You said you expect Thysandra to vastly improve your quality of life.' The words sounded so strangely calm from my lips – as if this was a daily routine for me, threatening desperate little demons in prison halls. 'Trust me to vastly diminish it if you hurt anyone in the Underground for her. And if you're now thinking it's worth some unpleasantness as long as you have Thysandra in the end, keep in mind I may as well remove *her* from your life, too, if you cross the line. Permanently, if I need to.'

A heated blush rose on her girlish face. But whatever she saw in my eyes, she did not laugh or object; there was no resentment or self-pity in her curt nod. 'Understood.'

'Good.' I drew in a deep breath and slid my hand into my pocket, then hesitated a last time as my fingers found the smooth steel of the key. I should just give it to her and get it over with, of course. I'd done what I'd come here to do. *One thing*, Creon had said, and wasn't this plenty to qualify?

But Creon ...

'One more thing,' I heard myself say. 'I was wondering ... do you have any idea ...'

'What's the matter with Creon?' she finished, letting out another of those merciless giggles as she saw my face. 'Can't tell you, Emelin. Gossiping is against my rules, remember?'

To hell with her rules. 'But you're saying something *is* the matter with him?'

'You had already reached that conclusion yourself, hadn't you?' Her grin – shark's teeth, predator eyes – was hardly reassuring. 'Just talk to him. He's not going to learn to use his own big boy words if I keep communicating on his behalf.'

I wished that didn't sound so reasonable. 'But—'

'Emelin,' she cut in, voice strained. 'Am I getting that key?'

Well.

End of conversation, presumably.

I steeled myself and drew the little trinket from my pocket, trying not to wince at the frantic eagerness with which her eyes followed the silvery gleam of the metal. The moment I opened my fingers, she snatched it from my palm as if it was a medicine she required to live.

'What cell?' Her voice was laced with urgency. 'Where is she?'

'104.' I pushed myself to my feet, nodding at the alf steel door in question. 'Say hello from me. Or maybe don't.'

She laughed out loud – a laugh so triumphant it made the hairs in my neck stand up. For one moment, I was overcome by the urge to grab the key from her hands and run ... but then we'd be even farther from a solution to the Thysandra problem, and I would have a whole new problem to deal with, too.

I knew what she wanted – Thysandra. She knew what was at stake – again, Thysandra. Our deal should hold water.

'Thank you, Emelin.' She almost sang the words, that familiar melodious cadence. 'I'll let you know when she tells me anything important.'

'Thank you.' I forced myself to smile. Too late to turn back, now; the best I could do was hope and have faith. 'Have a good day, then.'

'Oh, I'm sure I'll have a *wonderful* day,' she said, laughing again as she skipped towards the door of cell number 104.

Gods help me.

And gods help Thysandra, most of all.

I avoided the heart of the Underground on my way back home. It meant I had to navigate my way through narrow, winding corridors I'd never seen before, taking me ages longer than a straight path through familiar territory would have been – but at least the extra time was time spent in absence of thinly veiled looks, and some wandering around didn't seem too bad a price to pay to escape the ogling and whispering of my allies.

I was in no hurry, I reminded myself with every step. My one task for the day had been completed. My letter had been sent. For a few hours, I could simply consider myself *done* – could lock myself in a quiet bedroom with Creon, get him to use his big boy words, then reward him appropriately for the effort once he had told me what was bothering him. No ambitious expectations. No political games to play.

For the twenty minutes it took me to walk back to the Skeire home, I was free.

Then I pushed open that rune-covered front door and found both Tared and Creon waiting in the living room beyond – sitting quietly with three chairs between them, both staring grimly at the floor. They emanated the air of males bracing themselves for an unpleasant task ahead, a look of unhappy but unanimous resolve.

My heart skipped a beat.

Fuck. Had anything happened? Did Tared have any idea what I'd just done, or had the two of them managed to get themselves entangled in some brand new feud in the hour that I'd left them to their own devices? Had the Mother attacked some innocent island, or—

'Oh, there you are,' Tared interrupted my frantic thoughts as he veered up.

And only then did I see the folded parchment he was holding. Not my letter. This was a new message, on expensive-looking vellum, sealed with the same white wax I'd seen on Valter's correspondence with northern patrons.

The city.

Already?

'They were unexpectedly quick,' Tared said, reading my widening eyes correctly. 'Didn't need more than an hour or two to make their decision.'

Which could hardly be good news – I heard the unspoken thought in the bleak undertone below his words. I floundered towards him as if in a dream, holding out my hand. The wax of that carefully folded letter hadn't been broken yet; no one else was going to let me down easy, then.

My fingers trembled as I fumbled with the seal, too aware of Tared and Creon's eyes on me. Perhaps I should have given the consuls every single title and qualification I held, I considered, useless thoughts that I couldn't stop thinking all the same. Perhaps I should have aimed to sound impressive rather than like a lost, flailing child. That way, they might at least have thought a little longer before rejecting me – might not have laughed and written back the moment my message hit their desk.

Two hours. An embarrassment.

My eyes flew over the text as I unfolded the letter, words written in the quick, regular hand of someone who'd spent half their life with a pen between their fingers.

Emelin,

We've been hoping you would reach out to us. The White City is pleased and ready to welcome you. If it suits, watchmen will be waiting for you by the gate at sunrise tomorrow; no bargains are required, but please make sure no companions of yours approach the city walls too closely.

Sincerely,
Rosalind,
Consul of the White City

Chapter 17

'Mind if I take a look at that letter again?' Creon muttered as soon as I shut the door of Lyn's wardrobe behind me – rather, her wardrobe chamber, as her collection of clothes from several full lifetimes occupied a full bedroom next to the one in which she was sleeping. 'Something about it is bothering me.'

I handed him the folded parchment without question, running my gaze over the packed shelves and racks around us. In the pale alf light, the shimmers of silk and organza gleamed their invitations at me, making my hands itch with old seamstress habits – but no, I had to restrain myself on this occasion. I knew the impression I needed to make; arriving at the White City in an extravagant ball dress would only be slightly less foolish than arriving in layers of black and crimson.

What I needed was white. Pale gold. Eggshell blue. Sweet, innocent colours for this trip, dresses to underline my declaration of peace.

I stepped around a pile of ancient hatboxes and made for the shelves to my right, where a few promising glimpses of ivory had caught my eye. Behind me, I heard Creon sink onto the low footstool that even an adult Lyn would need to reach the highest shelves, followed by the rustle of fingers over parchment.

'Do you have any idea what about it is irking you?' I asked, rummaging through the piles without looking over my shoulder. It was still odd, conversing with him while I couldn't see his face or his hands. 'The tone of her writing? The name? The conditions?'

He let out a joyless laugh behind me. 'What conditions?'

I pulled a face, cautiously freeing a simple linen dress from where it had been crammed away. A little outdated, with that silly row of buttons on the front, but then, perhaps I would look all the more harmless for it.

Draping it over the hat boxes, I turned and admitted, 'I suppose they're not imposing a terrible number of conditions, no.'

'There's exactly one of them,' Creon said wryly, crossing his legs as he leaned back against the wall. 'Namely, that *I* don't come anywhere near them. Nothing about you – about the colour you're bringing or any alf steel you might be wearing—'

'I don't think they know about alf steel,' I said, heart twinging. 'The White City sent a representative to Cathra to witness the experiment with the iron, and he didn't suggest any better alternatives at the time.'

Creon let out a muttered curse, scanning the message again with restless wings and the smallest line between his brows. 'They could at the very least have required a bargain.'

They could have. Hell, they *should* have. I didn't recall much of the White City representative who had arrived in our village on that sun-drenched summer morning, but I was quite sure he had been the one expressing the gruff opinion that magic was a blemish on the face of our world, better to have eradicated entirely. Even if the consuls had heard of me before, even if they knew what I was trying to do …

Why would *any* human with a grain of good sense throw their doors wide for me without even the slightest of security measures?

I didn't want to think the thought that welled up in me as I turned to peruse another pile of clothing, fingers brushing unthinkingly over soft wool and exquisite embroidery. What was the sense in deluding myself with even the smallest spark of false hope? But it wormed its way into my conscious mind no matter how hard I tried to press it down, like water seeping in between my fingers—

Because if the consuls were so swift to trust me, they must have a reason to think well of me.

And there *were* people in the city who knew me.

Was it that mad to think Valter and Editta might have spoken up in my defence? Or that they had at least not slandered my name too much? No pleading letter from my side, no matter how humble and genuine, would have persuaded anyone to let me in if the people who'd raised me were calling me a dangerous little monster and an embarrassment – would it?

The piles of linen before me blurred at the edges.

Damn it all. I squeezed my eyes shut, counted to five, and looked up again, blinking the last of the moisture away. I was being uselessly sentimental, I scolded myself. There might be other reasons for the consuls to be so unusually lenient; for all I knew, the truth might be far less pleasant and far more dangerous. Walking through that gate full of dewy-eyed optimism would be silly at best and reckless at worst.

And I really couldn't afford recklessness when there would be no one around to save me.

'So, do you think it's a trap of some sort?' I said, fighting to suppress the faintest wobble of my voice and soldiering on with my search. 'That they're only welcoming me inside for some hidden reasons of their own?'

'Doesn't make sense either.' The frustration in his voice was palpable. 'I can't see why they would want to harm you or trap you inside the city. You're not a threat to them, and they should know it would cause them a damn lot of trouble with the rest of us.'

I pulled a greyish-blue frock from the shelves and cursed when two others tumbled out with it. The dress was fine, at least: a simple, innocent-looking blouson model I could easily adjust to fit my own measurements. I threw it over the hatboxes with the buttoned white one and glanced over my shoulder. 'It's also pretty unlikely they made a deal with the Mother to hand me over, isn't it?'

'About as unlikely as any alf house making a deal with the Mother,' Creon said, shaking his head at the letter. 'Even if the city-born part of the population would not care all that much, I doubt the part that has fled there during their lifetime would stand for any such thing.'

'Right.' I clambered past a messy clothing rack and over two trunks full of shoes in pursuit of the next fleck of white I'd noticed. Lyn did not make a habit of wearing pale colours, it turned out. 'So what other possibilities are there? Any chance they want to take me hostage to get something from the Alliance?'

He groaned. 'Can't imagine. From what I know of their history, the Alliance has regularly offered to work with them, and the city has always been the side keeping their distance. They should know they don't need blackmail to get our help.'

I freed and unfolded the white piece of clothing I'd spotted – loose, frothy trousers that looked comfortable enough but were guaranteed to cause a stir in more conservative human company. The baby blue dress below it was perfect, on the other hand. I absently retied one of the bows on the sleeves and said, 'So can we conclude that whatever is going on, at least it's unlikely to put me in any serious danger?'

He didn't reply. When I turned back to him, he sat staring at Consul Rosalind's letter as if it might spontaneously combust any moment.

'Creon?' I said cautiously.

'I don't *think* you'll be in serious danger,' he muttered in that slow, rough voice that sent shivers down my spine even now. He still wouldn't meet my gaze, his frown contorting the inked scar through his eyebrow to a grisly gash. 'But something is off all the same, and I wish we could figure it out *before* you have to walk into that city on your own. I hate leaving you to deal with this by yourself.'

Which sounded sensible enough. And then again, that darkness in his eyes ...

It was more than simple worry, that look. More than suspicion or puzzlement. Something far more problematic was festering behind the starless night of his irises, that troubled expression I'd caught before whenever he thought I wasn't watching him – something he wouldn't tell me for whatever unholy reason. *I'm not the one this is new for*, he'd said as we passed the whispering inhabitants of the Underground, and I'd left it at that. *It's nothing of importance*, he'd said before Thysandra's cell, and I hadn't believed it but had ignored it all the same.

Yet the issue had not solved itself.

So perhaps it was time I stopped allowing him to escape so easily.

'And that's the only thing plaguing you?' I said, making my decision in the blink of an eye as I sank down on one of the shoe trunks and clasped my arms around my knees. 'You seem bothered by something.'

From anyone else, the hesitation wouldn't have been noticeable; it was just that his perfectly measured, fluid movements made every contrast so very jarring. He was silent for a moment as he folded the letter and slid it into his pocket, gaze still locked on some distant point beyond the colourful piles of clothes. Only after two, three heartbeats did he say, in that quiet, raspy voice, 'I'm ... thinking.'

The most uninformative of answers. If I hadn't believed he was hiding something yet, I would have been certain of it now; had he been thinking anything he wanted me to know about, I'd already have heard it. 'About what?'

'Anything we might be able to do to minimise the risk.' His half-smile was so obviously forced I wasn't sure why he even made the effort. 'I doubt demanding a hostage from them in return would improve the situation, though.'

'Well, it would be better than you fighting your way in through the gate after me,' I said with a snort, 'but significantly worse than pretty much every other option. What else?'

He quirked up an eyebrow. 'What else what?'

'What else are you thinking?' It took all I had to keep the edge of impatience from my voice. *Just talk to him*, Naxi had said, but gods help me, how was I supposed to talk to him if he insisted on evading my every attempt to get to the bloody point? 'You're not going to convince me you're looking that broody about nothing but a little abducting. What is it?'

Again that hesitation. 'Em ...'

I cocked my head at him, waiting.

It should have become easier, communicating with him, now that he was in possession of his voice again. Yet somehow it seemed I had gotten *worse* at reading him since that night at the Cobalt Court – missing the subtle clues I'd learned to pick up from his gestures, missing the way his expression would speak for him in the silence. What in the world was the tension in his wings and shoulders trying to tell me now?

Fear? Anger?

'I just …' He wavered, averting his eyes – sharp jaw clenched so tightly that the edge could have been sculpted from stone. His words came out hesitant, with deliberate precision. 'I'm trying to figure out what I can do to help you. And what in hell I'll be doing the next few days, if you decide you'll indeed travel to the city.'

If he hadn't looked so antsy about it, I might just have believed him.

But if none of this was more than a little apprehension, why would he have to pick and measure his words so cautiously, as if one mistaken syllable might mean death? And either way, he'd been wearing that gloomy look for days. Neither of us could have predicted I would soon be visiting the White City when we were standing in front of Thysandra's cell; reasonably speaking, his sombreness in that moment could not have had anything to do with it.

So he was not getting rid of me that easily.

'Could you elaborate?' I said, narrowing my eyes at him.

'Just trying to make myself useful, cactus.' A curt, almost snappish tone was seeping into his words. A warning I was digging too deep – a last attempt to push me away from whatever secret he was trying to protect. 'It's not that important.'

'Not that *important*?' I hadn't planned to erupt so easily, but the words burst from my lips all the same – sharp and unavoidable. 'When you've spent days looking like you're waiting for the gallows? I may have kept quiet, but don't insult me by pretending I'm blind enough not to notice – so what *is* it, Creon?'

He closed his eyes. 'I said—'

'That you're trying to figure out what you'll be doing in the coming days.' I gestured wildly at the rest of the Underground, almost knocking over one of Lyn's clothing racks. 'Which doesn't make a lot of sense, does it? Ask Agenor for some task, and I'm sure he'll be happy to run you ragged from dawn to dusk. As long as you're not throwing yourself headfirst into any fae armies again—'

'Counting swords and stirring poisons?' he sharply cut in, lips curling into a sneer that was every inch the spurned, furious fae prince. Like a snake coiling to strike, an animal backed into a corner of its own making. 'Is that really what you want me to be doing, then? Sitting around below the earth for days and wasting my time on jobs any fool could do, while you're out there risking your life and sanity to save the world?'

It echoed in the sudden silence, that last sentence – and something twisted sideways in my brain.

No. No, what was I thinking? Not Creon – not *my* Creon, who loved my sharp edges and my brashness, who had watched me decimate a whole damn fleet and laughed in triumph. Gods help me, none of this was making sense. And yet, the way he was sitting there, tense as if poised for a fight, lips tight with something a hair's breadth removed from spite ...

Is that what you want me to be doing?

'Creon ...' The hairs on the back of my neck were prickling. 'Creon, are you *jealous* of me?'

Had I slapped him in the face, he could not have frozen more abruptly. 'What?'

'Is that what you're trying to avoid telling me? That you're unhappy I now have powers you don't have?' The words spilled from me like poison, burning on my lips – as gut-wrenching as the shocked bewilderment exploding on his face, and still I kept talking. The claws of fear wouldn't let me shut up. 'You've been behaving unlike yourself since the moment we got back home – that reckless nonsense at the Golden Court, looking all miffed when people were whispering about me ... So is this the bloody problem? Are you really just—'

He shot to his feet, wings snapping out with unbridled force. 'Em, *stop.*'

It did not matter I'd had no intention of stopping. It did not matter my thoughts seemed to be crowding my tongue, jostling to be next out the gate. His command came out with all the raw authority only the world's deadliest creature could wield, cutting through the tangle of my thoughts like a freshly whetted knife; my tongue obeyed instinctively, falling silent mid-word. I swallowed and swallowed again, staring up at him with my breath in tatters – trying to make sense of the war waging behind his ink-black eyes, and failing miserably.

Gods help me, was that *fear* darkening his features?

'But—' I started.

'No,' he interrupted, voice sharp and urgent as he crossed the three, four steps between us. 'On every last crumb of honour I have in me, cactus – *no*. You're the very last person in the world I would ever begrudge anything, powers or otherwise. I'm in awe of all you're achieving. All I want is for you to get *more* of it, and I'd rather hand over my own magic to you than deny you a single bloody thing you deserve. Jealousy has nothing to do with any of this. Please.'

Please.

My lips would no longer move.

He towered over me, six solid feet of magic and muscle – a stark, elegant shadow against the colourful cacophony of Lyn's wardrobe, and yet his eyes were darker still. They held my gaze with that unnerving mixture of shock and anguish, some emotion that was vulnerable before it was anything else – as if a single word more from my lips might shatter him. As if my questions *had* already broken something deep within, snapped him like a thread of delicate silk, and left him bleeding out behind that devastating façade.

There was no deception in that look.

Whatever he'd been lying about in these past few days, whatever truths he'd tried to evade and bury beneath indifferent counterquestions – this at least was the full, heartbreaking truth. No envy. No bitterness. If I needed him to give up every single weapon he'd ever wield, he would do it without thinking and never for a minute regret the choice he'd made.

Which I should have known.

And then again, what else was I to make of that harsh, almost spiteful outburst?

'So what is going on, then?' I whispered, head tilted back so I could look up at him. 'It's clear enough that there's *something* you're brooding on. Hiding it from me really isn't going to make anything better.'

He sighed and held out a hand to me, palm up – an offer and request at once. I grabbed his wrist, and he tugged me to my feet with a single smooth motion, wrapping his free arm around me to haul me against his chest.

His shoulder was tense below my forehead. His fingers dug into the small of my back with too much force, as if he was holding on to something he was bound to lose, something that might just slip through his fingers the moment his attention strayed for the blink of an eye. Not jealousy, perhaps, but I'd sooner believe the Mother meant no harm than accept his stubborn insistence there was nothing for me to worry about.

'Creon?' I breathed, closing my eyes.

'I'm having trouble watching you do all you need to do and not being able to take anything off your plate,' he muttered, breath warming the crown of my head as he brushed his lips over my hair. 'I'm not used to it – being powerless. Drives me mad to watch you drive yourself to the edge of insanity without being able to do anything about it.'

The little tremor in his voice was unmistakable. No lies here, either; it sounded too much like him not to be true. Then again …

Was it the full truth?

I clasped my arms around him and buried my face in the hollow of his neck, trying to string my whirling thoughts together. Could this be the entire reason he'd thrown himself at the Mother's army at the Golden Court so recklessly – because he'd believed it would somehow take a burden off my shoulders, one less task to worry about?

That didn't make sense. He should have known it would be a risky operation to say the least, a mission that might very well end in death or danger. He should have realised, too, that a desperate attempt to save his life would not be beneficial for my mental wellbeing in the slightest. So this could not be all of it, could it?

Yet I found myself faltering, the pointed questions welling up in me crumbling to dust on my tongue as I imagined how he might react.

I knew how he'd lashed out last time I'd pressed him for the truth of his motivations that day. I remembered how he'd snapped at me, too, when I'd made the mistake of saying one wrong thing too many about the bindings – even though I still wasn't fully sure *what* the mistake had been. If I stepped into the same trap again ...

I would be leaving at sunset tomorrow.

So did I really want to press this matter now, when I might not see him for days after tonight? What if I hit a sore spot and provoked him all over again – what if we were forced to spend the next few days caught in some unstable truce, worrying about the next time we'd see each other? The White City would give me trouble enough even with my sanity fully intact. Arguing about armies with consuls while my heart was slowly disintegrating in my chest ... that sounded like a vicious hell of its own.

I swallowed my questions. Swallowed the danger. Kissed the smooth, warm skin just above his collarbone and muttered, 'You're doing plenty already.'

He hissed in a slow breath, fingertips tightening on my lower back. 'If you say so.'

'Oh, don't do that thing,' I grumbled, glowering up at him. If I was going to these lengths to keep the peace, the least he could do was keep his own peace, too. 'You're the only person keeping me sane these days, Your Highness. I'd have gone stark mad and probably evil without you – so even if you're determined to loathe yourself, you should at the very least be able to see how much you're contributing to the cause.'

'It's not that I don't believe you.' A lie. I could see it in the artificial blandness of his expression, hear it in the overly restrained quality of his voice. 'I'm just still worried about you.'

'But then *what* are you worried about, if—'

He lowered his face before I could finish the question, mouth brushing over mine with gentle, persuasive intent.

I had not wanted to gasp but gasped nonetheless, the sensation too sudden, too compelling for me to control myself. His lips were firm, in the softest, supplest way. They moulded themselves to mine so easily, tempting, beguiling – whispering at me to let go of all those worrisome thoughts, to trust and have faith and believe him, to let him take care of me in all the ways only he knew. Half my mind obeyed. The other half of it stuck stubbornly to the course it had set out for itself, clinging to the words I'd planned to speak – because I couldn't give in, I *needed* to know …

My head jerked itself back, tearing away from our kiss. Every other fibre of my body cried out in outrage, following my treasonous thoughts down the path of least resistance.

'Creon—' I managed.

'Hush,' he muttered, the rough sound of his voice curling around me like a warm, heavy blanket enveloping my shoulders. His fingers wrapped around my nape, tugging me closer. 'Let me keep you sane, then, love. I promise I'm fine. Stop worrying yourself when there's nothing to worry about – I promise.'

Love.

I should not be listening, I should not give in so easily – but Zera help me, the way he spoke that one coveted word … The reverent twist of his lips. The heat of his breath on my cheek. The soft rasp of that melodious baritone, trailing down my spine like the tender scrape of nails, setting skin and blood on fire …

I promise.

A lie. I knew it was a lie.

But it was such a sweet one, and I would be so glad to believe it …

I was still leaving tomorrow. The rest of this day would be nothing but preparation, nothing but discussions and strategies and well-intended pieces of advice; the night would be too short, and I'd need every minute of sleep I could get. Yet *here* we were free, in this small hideaway with its sparkles and splashes of colour. Here I could surrender to the battle-forged body in my arms, give in to my own selfishness for these few stolen minutes; here I could be just Emelin, not a symbol, not a weapon.

This might be sanity, or it might be the opposite. Hell, it might be both.

I no longer cared to figure it out.

'Don't make me regret this,' I whispered, hands snaking up to his chest, his shoulders. 'Please.'

He kissed me again.

There was a despondency in his touch, an edge of roughness I hadn't felt before – as if he was trying to consume me to the last drop, to take in all of me and leave nothing behind. I knew I should worry. I knew I should ask. But his grip on my nape tightened, his lips tasted like sin and summer nights, and I caved without another thought – arched into him as his mouth moved feverishly on mine.

I'd ask and worry later.

Right now, I just wanted to drown.

I opened my mouth to him, matching the sharp need of his invitation, tangling our tongues together. His growl was a feral warning. I clawed my nails into the straining muscles of his chest, and he let out another sound like liquid hunger; one of his hands grasped my bottom, shoving me roughly against his rock-hard body, kneading my aching flesh. The other knotted in my hair and angled back my head *just* so, holding me still as his lips trailed a slow, ravenous path down my jaw, my throat. I gasped his name, and his fist tightened around my curls.

It hurt. It felt like ecstasy.

I ground myself against the hard bulge of his cock and received a frayed hiss of pleasure in return.

Damn whatever secrets he was keeping, whatever lies he was telling. *This* was true. In this shameless world of teeth on flesh and nails on skin, I did not need to ask questions, did not need to dig and argue; our bodies spoke for us, and there was no deception in these frantic, hungry touches. I lowered my hands to his waistband, fumbling with the fastening. He gripped my buttock with bruising strength. I loosened one, two buttons, then gave up on the measured approach and slipped my hand between skin and linen, desperate to feel him, starved for the sensation of his bare, hard cock against my palm.

Like a brittle chain breaking, the last of his self-restraint snapped at the first touch.

With a vicious snarl, he spun the both of us around in one blisteringly swift motion, pushing me backwards with the weight of his body. I stumbled past leather trunks and fallen dresses until my shoulders thudded against Lyn's shelves, colourful clothing bulging out on every side of me, fingers slipping over silk and velvet as I tried to find my balance. Creon wouldn't let me. He'd seized my wrists before I'd recovered, pinning them over my head with infuriating ease; one hand keeping both of my arms in place, the other lowering to his trousers. Two flicks of his fingers were all he needed to unfasten his buttons. His erection sprang free the next moment, thick and throbbing, dark veins patterning the deep bronze length of him.

I let out a breathless laugh, wrestling to extricate myself from his grip. He held me in place without effort, wrapping his free hand around his shaft instead.

'No,' I whimpered, writhing. There was no taking my eyes off him – it was almost hypnotic, the sight of his scarred, calloused fingers tightening around that glorious cock of his, giving one excruciatingly slow pump. 'Don't you *dare* ...'

'Hmm?' he murmured, then did it again.

'No. *No*.' I tried to arch against him, desperate for his touch, *any* touch, no matter how insufficient; he inched away from me with perfect feline grace, wings flaring out to maintain his balance. Another mewl of frustration escaped me. 'You can't— I can't—'

He leisurely flicked the pad of his thumb over the smooth pink head, smearing a drop of moisture over that sensitive skin.

'Creon.' Just like that, he'd reduced me to a pleading mess, the needy heat burning below my skin as unbearable as physical torture. 'Creon, *please*. I need you ... I ...'

He let go of himself suspiciously easily, left hand still securing my wrists in place. His fingers tenderly cupped my jaw. His thumb brushed over my bottom lip, then pressed into my mouth, a hot, insistent intrusion, bringing the musky taste of his pleasure with it.

I bit down on his thumb and sucked hard, lapping every last trace of that salty sweetness off his skin before I let him go again.

He laughed, dragging his wet thumb across my lip a second time, pulling back when I tried to follow. 'Hungry, cactus?'

'Bastard,' I panted, struggling against his hold. 'As if you don't know ...'

He leaned towards me, so close that I could feel the heat of his tall body through our clothes. The weight of his cock settled against my lower stomach, and I stilled against the shelves, not daring to struggle, not daring to risk him pulling away and robbing me even of that small mercy. My body was achingly hollow, craving his invasion, yearning for that blunt girth to lay me bare and fill me deep. If only I could *move* ...

'What do I know?' he murmured, teeth scraping the rim of my ear. His voice was dark, low, an intoxicating poison I drank down so, so eagerly. 'How wet you are? How desperate you are? How much you'd do just to get my cock inside that sweet little slit of yours?'

'*Please*.' The word was a sob, the despair in my voice nothing short of pathetic. I bucked against the cage of his fingers, to no avail – he didn't yield the slightest fraction of an inch.

'Unbearable, isn't it?' he whispered, kissing my temple as I fought. 'Feeling useless?'

I barely heard him, let alone registered the words. His free hand was finally trailing down my side, a feathery touch but a touch all the same, and every sliver of my mind abruptly forgot to notice anything else, chasing after that sensation and the agonising relief it offered. Down to my hip. Down to my thigh. Closer to that burning spot that wept for his attention, a need so urgent it grew close to pain.

'Tell me you need me.' Another inch down. Ripples of pleasure spread wherever he touched me, as if my body was the still surface of a lake and he was the night breeze itself, leaving no part of me unstirred. His husky voice sent uncontrollable shudders down my spine. 'Tell me you can't do this without me.'

'I *need* you— Oh, gods.' His fingertips had slipped past the hem of my dress and reached the bare skin of my thigh, sending a flurry of sparks into the darkest, deepest core of me. Another sob fell from my lips. 'I'd do anything – *anything* – just to have you—'

In one swift stroke, his hand lay between my thighs.

I almost came at the first touch, the blissful relief of his fingers sweeping over that sensitive spot just once – finally. *Finally*. Without wasting time, he slid beneath my underwear, parted my slick lips with two fingers, and plunged the third deep into me with so much force I cried out, knees buckling. If not for his hand keeping my wrists pinned above my head, I might have toppled over under the flood of sensation, the pressure, the *fullness*, the perfect, maddening rhythm of his strokes as he drew back and thrust two fingers back into me …

'More.' I barely recognised the sound of my own voice. 'Please, Creon. More.'

'So hungry,' he purred, thumb strumming the little bud between my lips. His fingers drove deep again, then pulled out in an excruciatingly slow slide, leaving cold, abandoned flesh behind. 'What do you want, Thenessa? My tongue? My cock? Or are we going to see just how many fingers you can take before you're blowing apart?'

Gods help me, I would never be prepared for this – rough voice, filthy words, twisting together and winding me up so expertly I barely remembered how to move my lips. 'Cock— I need—'

His fingers slipped out of me.

He released my wrists at the same moment, so suddenly I staggered against him. Strong arms caught me before I could cry out, hands around my waist, lifting me, pressing me against the overstuffed shelves. I frantically bunched up my dress as I wrapped my legs around his hips. The length of his shaft slid along my soaked underwear, as hard as I was wet, and I could not bite down another whimper.

'Hard?' he muttered, cupping my buttock with his left hand to keep me in place as he moved back a fraction. His right fingers peeled away the last barrier of drenched linen between my thighs, and then his blunt head lay against my entrance, a promise that radiated into the tip of my curling toes. 'Or harder?'

'Harder,' I breathed, grabbing his shoulders. '*Harder*.'

He grinned and slammed into me.

I arched against him with a stifled cry, sparks firing behind my eyelids at that first brutal thrust – yes. *This*. The rigid steel of his cock, thick and hot and perfect, stretching me wide, claiming every inch of me ... I let my head roll back against the shelves and surrendered. Unintelligible moans were spilling over my lips, cries of pleasure, pleas for more – and more he gave me, devastating stroke after devastating stroke, until I could do nothing but hold on for dear life and *feel* as he fucked me closer and closer to the edge ...

I still reached it far too soon.

My orgasm tore through me with violent intensity, blurring the brightly coloured room as I tensed to the tips of my toes around him and shattered. Creon buried himself in my convulsing body one last time, then followed with a guttural growl. His muscular weight collapsed into me as I gasped and shuddered in his arms, and for one limitless moment, we were one – our bodies fused, our pleasure tangled together, a single savage creature locked in one all-consuming pulse of ecstasy.

The world around us returned slowly, as if even reality itself was loath to disrupt what had just happened.

Around me, green and yellow and orange clothes had tumbled from their shelves, yanked out by my thoughtless hands as I grasped for grip and balance. A leather trunk had fallen over. Shoes had spilled out over the dark floor, and the dresses I'd selected lay rumpled amidst the mess, like unwanted rags too old to be worn.

'Oh,' I got out, breathless and boneless, and again, '*Oh*.'

Creon slipped out of me and lowered me to the ground so gently, arms wrapping around my shoulders and pressing me against him as soon as I regained my footing. His wings swept around us as he buried his face in my hair, breathing in my scent as if he'd never smell anything like it again.

'You'll destroy me one day, cactus,' he whispered, and I couldn't tell whether it was laughter or some other emotion choking his voice. 'You'll be the utter ruin of me, and hell take me, you'll be worth every moment of it.'

That little tremor ...

I should ask.

I should worry.

But tomorrow was close and only coming closer. His strong arms held me like nothing was wrong with the world, and right now, I wanted so badly to believe it – to sink into this brief, sweet state of oblivion and linger there, because gods knew when we'd next have a moment of peace again.

So I tightened my grip on his torso. I buried my face in his chest. I breathed the sweet, musky, summer scent of him and didn't allow myself to wonder or ask questions, to assume anything but that what he'd promised me was true—

That he was fine.

He was *fine*.

Chapter 18

'Did you pack your toothbrush?' Lyn immediately enquired as I appeared for breakfast the next morning, eyeing the modest dimensions of the bag I carried with me. 'Plenty of clean underwear? And something warm for—'

Having just dragged myself out of bed an hour before sunrise, it took an effort not to groan. 'I've packed bags before, Lyn. And morning.'

I received a muttered greeting from Tared, whose mouth was full of bread and eggs, and from Hallthor, who sat bent over some sword design again and seemed much too busy to concern himself with the contents of my luggage. The empty plate by the latter's side suggested that Ylfreda had been here until she was called away to deal with some injury elsewhere, no matter the time of day; Beyla was nowhere to be seen, and Edored was presumably still sleeping at this ungodly hour.

I couldn't entirely blame him.

'Yes, I know,' Lyn said, looking pale and tired beside her bowl of yoghurt and berries, 'but this time I won't be able to send an alf after you if you've forgotten your coat. You *do* have a coat, don't you?'

'I've nicked one of yours,' I said, plopping my bag into the nearest corner and making for the dining table. 'The only one I had down here was red. Don't worry, though – I'm bringing my own underwear.'

She let out a watery laugh. By her side, Tared swallowed his mouthful of food, threw me half a grin, and said, 'I assume you packed a knife?'

'Three of them,' I said.

'A compromise,' Creon wryly added, stepping into the room behind me with his shirt three-quarters buttoned and his hair bound into a messy bun. 'I was aiming for eight, but her ladyship seemed to think—'

'That the consuls might disapprove of me striding in like a walking armoury?' I finished, sinking into a free seat and rolling my eyes at him. 'Odd notion, I know.'

He chuckled but made no further attempts to change my mind – wisely so, since we'd cycled through the same discussion about five times over the course of the previous day and never arrived upon a different outcome. 'It's your head on the line.'

'And a very pretty one, at that,' I said, nodding. 'Could someone pass me the bread, please?'

Tared was a little slow to grant the request, a mild disorientation in his expression that abruptly made me realise it was not just Creon he'd never seen in the context of our honest relationship before. Lyn's quiet smile suddenly looked significantly more genuine.

For a few moments, nothing broke the silence except Creon sitting down and Hallthor's pencil scratching over parchment. I buttered a slice of bread, took a bite, and couldn't help but throw another glance at my bags despite knowing exactly what I'd packed – clothes for four days, daggers, the mother-of-pearl bracelet in case I needed any iridescence ... Toothbrush. Hairbrush. A small purse of gold. Nothing out of the ordinary, everything I'd need. The only unconventional choice I'd made was to slip Agenor's copy of the *Treatises* between my dresses before tying the bag shut: a risk, perhaps, to take that precious little book along, but few things reminded me so effectively what it was like to be human.

And I suspected I might need those memories more than I would need any blades between the god-built walls of the city.

I'd just finished my bread when Creon lowered his cup of tea, sank back in his chair, and slowly said, 'One last thing I wanted to ask. It's been a while since I've been anywhere near the city – how was the refugee situation at the gate yesterday?'

Tared shrugged, not looking up from the last crumbs of egg he was skewering onto his fork. 'Bad.'

'Refugee situation?' I said, frowning at the two of them.

'People who come to the island without the money to buy their way into the city,' Tared clarified with a half-hearted gesture north. 'Either because they lost it on the journey there or because they're hoping to rob others once they get to the place. There have been more of them since rumours of war started circulating, unsurprisingly.'

I stared at him in mute horror. One needed money to get into the White City – that much I'd always known. Few people *had* the money – that was a simple fact, too. But this was an outcome I'd never thought of or heard about, no matter how easily it followed on from the truths I was aware of: gods knew how many humans stuck in the no man's land between empire and city, between servitude and freedom.

'How many?' I got out, voice hoarse.

'A few hundred, usually,' Tared said grimly. 'People tend to either die or return home after a while, so the group rarely grows much larger. Right now, I think it's a little over a thousand camping near the walls.'

The aftertaste of the bread had turned sour in the back of my throat. 'Fuck.'

He shrugged, stuck the last bits of egg into his mouth, and swallowed without chewing. 'Might ask if they're interested in joining an army, seeing as they haven't got anything better to do.'

'As long as you don't let me do the recruiting, you might stand a chance,' Creon said dryly. 'Mind if I come along to drop Em off, though? I'd like to make sure they don't try anything ugly when the gate opens.'

'I can defend myself,' I said indignantly. 'I have three whole knives with me.'

He quirked up an eyebrow. 'And you want those same consuls who would disapprove of a sensible number of blades to first lay eyes upon you while you're slaughtering a few dozen human refugees right outside their gates?'

An annoyingly good point. Then again ... 'Would it be any better if you were the one slaughtering them?'

'To be fair,' Lyn said, grimacing, 'if the poor sods out there have even the tiniest grain of good sense in their noggins, I doubt Creon will have to make a single kill to keep them on their best behaviour.'

Right.

Because I was human-sized and human-shaped, young and dressed in innocent blue, no trace of magic on me but the two easily overlooked bargain marks on the inside of my wrist. To the hopeful observer, I would look like prey.

Creon, on the other hand ...

Even lounging at an alf table, an earthenware mug in his hands and traces of sleep in his eyes, he didn't fully manage to look harmless. No human refugee, no matter how reckless or desperate, would take a look at him, scarred and winged and equipped with more blades than fingers, and decide this was a manageable obstacle between themselves and coveted freedom – not if there existed an alternative of staying really quiet and really careful and possibly making it out alive.

He *would* make it easier to reach the gates without trouble. So why did I feel that faint tremor of discomfort at the suggestion?

The bloody public opinion, again?

The world would know he'd been there with me, in full view of an audience of hundreds. The consuls whose approval I needed would know. Valter and Editta would know, too, and somehow that prospect stung deepest of all.

Then again ... Hadn't I decided the public opinion could go fuck itself?

He was here. I loved him. If the human world could not get past that fact, perhaps it was better if they knew it from the start; it would be much more inconvenient for us if they started rebelling *after* we'd persuaded some of their islands to join our side.

'Alright,' I said, and even though I had barely hesitated, even though the thoughts had shot through my mind in an eyeblink or two, I could see Creon's wings relax ever so slightly in the corner of my sight. 'Good point. Let's go preserve my virtuous image.'

Virtuous? his fingers signed at me below the table. *You?*

I glared at him, trying not to blush as the heat of the previous day's activities clawed its way back through me. He had already averted his face to innocently sip his tea and study Hallthor's sketches – as if he hadn't deliberately replanted those memories in my thoughts, hands pinned to the wall, skilled fingers luring every last drop of sanity from my body.

Gods, I was going to miss him. Already I could feel it tightening in my lower belly – the looming absence of every tender, infuriating, arrogant, broken bit of him.

'Time to go look for Alyra, then,' Tared said, interrupting my thoughts as he hauled himself up from his bench with a look of regret at his empty plate. 'I suppose she'll be around the fields? And I'll let Agenor know we're leaving in a bit.'

'Out of general decency, of course,' Lyn added dryly.

'Exactly.' He grinned at her. 'Not at all because he threatened to disembowel me if I allowed his daughter to sneak out before he'd woken up. Back in a minute.'

He'd faded before I could figure out how literal that depiction of Agenor's fatherly sentiments was. Something about Lyn's smile suggested it had not even been that much of an exaggeration.

I ate my next slice of bread a little more happily.

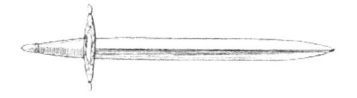

Tared returned just as I finished my breakfast, a loudly excited Alyra on his shoulder. A sleepy-looking Agenor arrived at the Skeire home five minutes later to tell me to be careful and let them know immediately if something seemed off inside the city walls, and also, had I brought a warm coat for the colder northern nights?

My affirmative answer hardly appeared to reassure him. It seemed Creon was not the only one worried about the consuls' intentions, even though I'd summarised the contents of their letter to my father as optimistically as possible.

But no one spoke up to share their concerns and no one stopped me as I checked the contents of my bag one last time and swung it onto my shoulders. Lyn nervously reminded me to send Alyra over the wall with a message at least once a day. Agenor told me to shout at the consuls as convincingly as I could. Hallthor finally shoved his sketches aside and gave me a wordless slap on the shoulder by way of goodbye, and Ylfreda, returning from her patient with bloodied fingers, grumbled something about please not returning with any broken limbs or bones sticking out of me.

I told her I'd try my best. Like Agenor, she didn't seem terribly impressed by that resolution.

And just like that, we were ready to go – no luggage left to pack, no tasks left to be completed. It was only then that my nervousness surged, suddenly and violently – enough to make my mouth go dry. With nothing else to focus on, I had no choice but to face the truth of just what I was about to attempt: walking into a city where my very existence was a breach of the law, bringing word of war into a place where peace had ruled for centuries, and somehow convincing the civilians that this was the moment to step back into the ugly, grief-ridden world outside. A lunacy, frankly. Had anyone asked me a year ago whether the White City would ever go to battle, I would have laughed in their face.

Then again, blinding and escaping the Mother had been impossible, too.

So I steeled my spine, pasted a smile onto my face, and said, 'Time to leave, then?'

Alyra screeched and plummeted to her seat on my shoulder. Tared held out his hand without another word, his sword already on his back. I wrapped my fingers around Creon's black-clad elbow first, then took that offered alf hand with a sensation eerily similar to the moment I'd put the key to cell 104 into Naxi's hungry fingers – a fluttery feeling in my stomach that reminded me that there would be only one direction to go from this point on, and that was forward.

The subtle tug of fading magic behind my navel did not help.

The world went blurry before I could blink, dissolving into the usual disjointed jumble of impressions – flashes of a peachy pink sunrise, the smell of dew on grass, the warm, comforting yellow of grain ready to be harvested. My pulse thundered in my ears. One, two, maybe three heartbeats, and yet it seemed an eternity had gone by when the world pieced itself back together around us, colours and sounds and smells sliding into a landscape I'd dreamed of but never seen with my own eyes before.

A rocky coast.

A stretch of summer-dry grass, covered in messy tents.

And beyond that quiet morning vision, glowing with an almost unearthly gold sheen in the light of the rising autumn sun, the fabled white walls of the world's last bastion of freedom, stretching out on either side of us and twisting like a ribbon between the island's misty, shrub-covered hills.

It was ... *enormous*.

I'd known – rationally, at least – that the White City was more than just the town that made up the heart of it. There was farmland behind those walls, enough of it to survive years of siege, if need be. There was the harbour. There had to be some decent source of fresh water, too, lakes or rivers, anything that the Mother hadn't been able to drain during her past attempts to get rid of this last little blemish on her universal and absolute power.

Yet even in my wildest dreams, I'd never been able to imagine much beyond the scale of Ildhelm's cities, the largest settlements I'd seen in my life. Some humble fields, I'd unthinkingly assumed. A little haven like the one we used to have at home, just enough for a dozen fishing boats and the occasional fae ship coming to demand the empire's tributes.

Nothing like *this*, a walled area more expansive than double the surface of Cathra.

And this ... this could have been my home?

It was that thought, more than even the sheer size of the complex before me, that kept me glued to the rock-strewn earth for a few moments longer than I'd have liked. These walls, house-high and unnaturally white even after over a thousand years of summer sun and winter rains, should have been my final destination in life, a goal leaving nothing else to strive for. And instead, I stood here as an illegality, vessel to a power the world hadn't yet found a place for, human and at the same time ... not human at all.

Not like the small, ragged shapes rummaging around between those mucky tents, waiting for their chance – their only chance perhaps – to escape their fleeting existence of work and hunger and fear.

The twinge of my stomach made me regret having eaten breakfast at all.

Creon and Tared were silent by my side, waiting for me to act. And I *should* be acting – I should say my goodbyes and start walking to that towering gate on the other side of this dry, sandy field, where the watchers would surely be waiting for me, ready to follow their consuls' orders. War was coming, we had no time to lose – I *knew* this was not the moment to dawdle.

But I did not manage to draw my eyes away from the small, pale shapes moving through the human camp, looking so strangely small, so strangely colourless. The wail of a child rose from behind those brown and grey tent-clothes as I stared. A dog barked. Someone shouted at it to shut up; the baby cried harder, and an agitated woman's voice did away with the last illusion of serene morning quiet.

Like home. Like all I'd ever known before my village had burned and a world so much greater and stranger had opened up around me – a cruel, deadly world, yes, but a world of such agonising beauty, too, of places and creatures and colours not even a painter's daughter could ever have imagined.

Only now did I realise I had not met a single living human after the morning we'd fled the Crimson Court.

And here were hundreds of them. *Thousands* of them.

'I'm sorry,' I stammered, not knowing what the rest of my point would be – knowing only that I had to say *something* before the two males beside me started thinking I'd left my voice and wits in the Underground. 'I ... I think I'd forgotten what humanity looks like.'

'In all fairness,' Creon dryly said, keeping his voice low, 'you've had better things to look at.'

I whirled around to glare at him, the paralysis broken. He blinked back at me with unconvincing doe eyes and added, in the indignant tone of a misunderstood innocent, 'Like fae courts and sentient mountains and divine forests ...'

Next to him, Tared looked unsure whether to laugh or commit bloody violence as he chewed silently on a handful of dried apricots. A loud scream rising from the camp behind me suggested our presence had finally been noticed.

'Right,' I said, unsuccessfully suppressing a laugh. 'I think I should be going.'

'Possibly,' Creon admitted, and although I couldn't see the tents without turning, the sudden clamour and his narrow-eyed gaze over my shoulder did not give the impression the humans were reacting well to the sudden appearance of a fae murderer, an armed alf, and a human-like girl who had not been standing in this spot three minutes ago. 'Just walk and keep walking. We'll handle them, if need be.'

I nodded tensely, turning to Alyra's warm, fuzzy weight on my shoulder. 'See if you can fly over the walls. If I can get you in without telling the city about your existence, I'd prefer to keep you as my secret weapon.'

She puffed out her chest at that, lovingly pecked my ear, and launched herself into the brightening morning air. I turned to watch her soar towards the walls, closer and closer and ...

Past them.

Good.

I nodded at Tared, then smiled at Creon – not the moment for passionate kisses, I suspected, no matter how much I wished for one. 'See you in a couple of days.'

I didn't allow myself to wait for their replies. If I had to linger here for a single moment more, my nerves might just get the better of me.

The camp had indeed woken up, explosively so, people in half-buttoned shirts and crinkled dresses crawling from their tents wherever I looked as I strode past. Some appeared to be nothing more sinister than innocent, desperate families, gaunt little children clinging to their fathers' legs or half-hiding behind their mothers' skirts. But then there were plenty of bald, burly men with the neck tattoos I knew were fashionable among Rhudaki gangs. Unshaven sailors openly wearing their clubs and daggers. Worst of all, a handful of individuals who emerged from their tents perfectly groomed and immaculately dressed and not looking afraid in the slightest; I did not want to know what sort of person could manage to maintain a proper standard of life in these barren, desperate circumstances.

Old memories stirred, rising from what seemed like nowhere.

See that man, Emmi? Editta's hushed voice echoed in my mind, so clear she might have been standing behind me. *If someone looking like him ever approaches you, I want you to run and find me. Do you understand? Get away from people like that ...*

I had been frightened that day, five years old and sailing on a ship for the very first time. Why in hell was I thinking of it now – of the woman who had unwillingly called herself my mother all those years?

Did she know I would be visiting the city? Had the consuls been considerate enough to warn her and Valter so they could ...

Do what? *Hide?*

Useless, painful thoughts, and yet I did not manage to shove them back into the pit they'd come from as I walked closer and closer to the gate that the two of them must have passed through all those months ago. To my left, the silent rows of humans watched me without attacking. Before me, the heavy wooden doors cracked open the first two inches – not enough to let even a newborn child pass into the city.

A deep voice with a strong northern accent yelled, 'Emelin of Cathra?'

Again my heart twinged. Did they realise, as I did, that I would never truly be Emelin of Cathra again?

But I shouted a confirmation, and the gate opened another fraction, enough to reveal a small battalion of armed men and women waiting for me. Any movement among the refugees stilled immediately – a larger protective force than usual, I concluded, and it was hardly a surprise. The man leading the group was tall and dark-haired, not in the dazzling, mind-clouding fae way but in the plainer, much more comfortable human sense – not looking that different from me, even though he had a full head of height on me.

None of them looked that different from me, really.

No fangs or scales or wings anywhere in the company that stood waiting on the other side of the wall, no purple hair or crimson eyes, no pointed ears or flickers of alf light ... It was strangely disorienting, the familiarity of the scene before me. When over the last few months had I become the sort of person to consider claws and wings normal appendages, and to be amazed by round ears and soft pink fingers and hair that didn't range beyond the simple shades of blond and brown and black?

'Miss Emelin?' the leader said as I approached within a few feet of him, holding out his hand to me. A tanned, weathered hand – *plough hands*, Editta would have said, and damn it all, why was I thinking of Editta again? 'My name is Delwin. It's a pleasure to welcome you to the White City on behalf of the consulate and our people, Miss Emelin.'

Did he actually mean that? Or was he just being polite, or worse, deceptive?

Questions the fate of the world might depend upon, and presumably I wouldn't find the answers by standing on his doorstep for hours.

I scraped myself together and took my last step forward, across the threshold no magical creature had passed before. Delwin's hand was firm and determined around mine, betraying no nervousness at the sight of an armed alf and the Silent Death himself within earshot. An honest man's handshake – or was I just thinking so because I *wanted* to believe it?

His voice seemed to come from a hundred miles away. 'We weren't sure if you were used to riding, Miss, so we've brought a small chaise with us to take you to the city proper ...'

I heard myself thank him, reassuring him that I had been in the saddle before, but that it had been a while and the chaise was most welcome – all the things a humble human girl ought to say, and they still fell from my lips as if I'd never been anyone else. My mind, meanwhile, continued to spin without pause. Was it just kindness, this helpful gesture? Were they putting me in a chaise because I could not run off so easily that way?

It could not be *dangerous*, could it, accepting the offer?

The gate was already croaking shut behind my back. I threw a last glance over my shoulder, just in time to catch one more glimpse of Tared and Creon near the shore – the first with his arms crossed, the latter with his hands in his pockets, neither of their nonchalant postures enough to hide the wariness in their unblinking gazes.

Then the iron-plated doors slammed back together.

The sound of an impenetrable fort – or, if one was standing on the other side of the walls, of a perfect prison.

Unease crawled up my skin. But the gate watchers were already hauling bolt after bolt back in place behind me, and Delwin's people were mounting their horses; no way out now, not unless I wanted to thoroughly ruin my chances with the consuls forever. And anyway, wouldn't it be a little cowardly to run before anyone had even spoken a single unkind word to me?

So I gingerly stepped into the elegant two-man chaise Delwin had provided for me. I smiled and nodded and shook hands with the members of my escort. Like Valter and Editta's troublesome daughter, desperate not to embarrass; like Miss Matilda's promising apprentice, paid to flatter even the most unflattering clients.

Emelin of Cathra, back in the company of humans.

Chapter 19

The men and women in their shining city armour were quiet around me as we left the gate behind and rode down the meandering sand road, the plodding of hooves and clinking of the stirrups all that broke through the serene silence of dawn. Low hills and boxwood hedges on either side of us restricted most of my view of the surrounding area. The air, however, carried the sweet, comforting fragrance of ripe wheat and dewy grass; there had to be farmland nearby, perhaps just a stone's throw away.

So it was not the grain itself that surprised me when the landscape finally opened up around us and I could see the miles ahead.

It was the *amount* of it.

Like a blanket of gold covering the hills and plains in between, rippling in the clean morning breeze – acres and acres of it, stalks bending under the weight of their bursting ears. On the horizon, I could just distinguish the darker green of orchards. To my left, a field of cabbages was basking in the golden light; to my right, a small irrigation canal cut through swathes of even more grain, the water crystal clear and sparkling, reflecting the coral-coloured clouds spreading across the sky.

Shreds of mist still hovered over the fields here and there, lending a dreamy, almost unearthly quality to the scene. As if we had stepped into the fairytale illustrations of Valter's most expensive book, the one with hand-painted pages showing a world I'd thought could never truly be.

It didn't look like magic. It just looked like happiness.

And if this was a prison ... gods, at least it was a gilded one.

'It's beautiful, isn't it?' Delwin said, riding next to me, and only then did I realise he must have been watching me carefully as we'd rode out from the shelter of the boxwood.

'It's gorgeous.' The breathlessness in my voice was entirely genuine. 'And ... and it's all yours to keep, too?'

He must have come from the world outside; he understood that remark with a grim ease that could only have been nurtured by tribute season after tribute season. 'Miraculous, isn't it?'

'Utterly unbelievable,' I said, and again I meant every word of it.

We rode on in a slightly more comfortable silence, past the lush fields of grain, past a ring of fallow land, past another irrigation canal and a field of leeks ready to be harvested. So much food, and none of it would ever be loaded into fae ships under threat of death and violence – it truly was a challenge to wrap my head around it.

The world was waking up around us. The farther we progressed, the more people came driving in the opposite direction; ox carts full of burly young men, the occasional workhorse pulling wagons containing empty crates. Every single person looked well-fed and content, cheeks rosy from the fresh morning air; they laughed and chatted among themselves, not a trace of fear or tension to be found as they went about their daily work. None of the harried urgency that I knew from the farmers of Cathra. None of that ever-present awareness in the back of their minds that one mistake too many would mean death, either through punishment or starvation.

I wanted to cry.

I wanted to smile so much it hurt.

Two or three times, I thought I saw a familiar face in the groups passing us by, but each of them turned out to be a stranger upon closer inspection. Still, my heart jumped every single time I caught sight of some familiar haircut, a familiar shirt, a familiar pair of broad shoulders – they were *here*, after all, the people I'd once called mine, and surely they couldn't all avoid me for days if we were walking around in the same damn city?

Could they?

I squashed another shiver of nervousness.

And then we rounded a last bend in the road, passed the ridge of a low hill covered in chestnut trees ... and there it was, peaceful and bustling, sprawling out between a small lake and a stretch of vibrant pasture where hairy cows and goats stood grazing.

The city.

Thousands upon thousands of flint and thatch roofs, separated by a spiderweb of streets, surrounded by a low, broad rampart covered in snowy white lilies. Trails of smoke spiralled from chimneys wherever I looked. From our slightly elevated position, I could see market squares and city halls, parks and an open theatre; the pentagonal shape of a temple rose above the roofs at the centre of the town. Not too far from it, an ornate marble building stretched along the long side of a square – the seat of the consuls, I suspected, who would be ruling the people who'd chosen them from behind that grand façade.

Even from this distance, I could hear shouting voices and the coppery boom of a bell counting the hour. The sounds of a living, thriving city. More than that – of a *safe* one.

I swallowed an unexpected twang of envy.

'There we are,' Delwin said and slowed his horse next to me, as if I might have missed my first glimpse of the town that had featured prominently in my every daydream for three quarters of my life. 'I know it's not a fae court, but—'

'Thank the gods it isn't,' I blurted.

That startled a laugh out of him.

We rode on faster, down that hill and across the last meadows that separated us from the city's open gates. Passers-by cheerfully greeted the guards accompanying me and glanced at me with curiosity rather than wariness; I wondered how much they knew, whether the news of my identity had already made the rounds. Perhaps it had. Perhaps this was what magic was to people who had no reason to loathe or fear it – an exotic, exciting rarity rather than a terrifying weapon.

Gods, to live in a world like that …

But I had no time to marvel at the notion. We were fast approaching the gate of the city proper, and I was once again reminded just how long it had been since I'd last seen a human settlement up close – it was so stunningly *normal*, all of it. No jewel colours wherever I looked, no magical light glittering down upon us. Just plastered brick houses and muddy streets that suggested recent rainfall. Dogs and children running around. Signs swinging from storefronts, advertising everything from shoes to fresh bread. It all looked tidy and prosperous, not wild and decadent like the Crimson Court but rather quietly abundant, a place where no child would ever cry themselves to sleep over an empty stomach.

Not magic. Just happiness.

Had they felt the same breathless disbelief upon arriving here, Valter and Editta? Had they thought of me – had they felt guilty at all? Or had they happily blended into their new life, glad to have left the burden of their unruly fae child behind, without worrying what would become of me in the clutches of the monster who'd destroyed their home?

I tried to stop looking out for them as we navigated the maze of broad streets and narrow alleys, riding at a walking pace now – tried to keep my eyes from hooking themselves onto every greying dark braid, every balding head. But my heart skipped a beat all the same whenever we rounded a corner and happened upon some woman in a vaguely familiar floral dress, and I found myself scanning for a signature every time we passed a mural or a portrait proudly displayed in a shop window.

Would Delwin know them? Could I just … ask about them?

I decided not to, in the end. He would doubtlessly report everything to the consuls, and I really did not need them to think of me as a sentimental child.

It took some fifteen minutes before we emerged from the neighbourhoods of farm workers and craftspeople and arrived in what had to be the heart of the city, where the paved streets were broader and the houses had a more lavish air to them. Here were the parks and the markets and the open-air theatre; here, for the first time, we passed others on horses and even the occasional coach. Delwin was greeted wherever we went. Clearly, I concluded with a sinking feeling that was the very opposite of surprise, the consuls hadn't sent just anyone to pick me up from the gate.

And finally, after rounding a last corner on which a dragon-shaped fountain happily gurgled in the brightening sunlight, we reached the marble building I'd seen from the hilltop outside the city, looking twice as large now that I was standing in front of it. Judging by the similarity to the buildings I'd seen in the dead landscape of Lyckfort, it had to be old – as old as the city itself, perhaps. And yet the façade was still a pristine white, the lily engravings around the doors and windows sharp-edged as if they'd been carved a week ago.

Magic or money. Perhaps a little of both.

'The White Hall,' Delwin announced, as if he was the sort of travel guide Valter had told me his rich clients would hire when they could not be arsed to do their own exploring. 'The consuls have their living quarters and guest rooms in the east wing of the building. You'll be staying there, too, during your visit.'

Better than an alf steel cell. I climbed from the chaise, still half-prepared for the guards to seize me and drag me into some hidden, sinister dungeon ... but they did no such thing, and I forced myself to loosen my shoulders as well as I could. I'd talked this through with Creon, damn it. Whatever the intentions behind that unexpectedly amiable invitation, there was no decent reason for any of the consuls to want me dead, locked away, or otherwise disposed of. As long as I made sure not to break any laws here—

'Miss Emelin?' Delwin said, a note of concern in his deep voice, and only then did I realise he must have asked me to follow him inside a moment before.

'Oh, yes,' I hurriedly said, swirling around and rushing after him with a weak wave at the other guards. Some of them smiled as they returned the gesture. 'I was trying to take in the city. It's a little overwhelming, frankly.'

He held the door for me without an immediate answer, his other hand on the short sword he carried at his hip. His right little finger was missing, I noticed. Training accident or fae punishment – I didn't know what option seemed more likely.

We walked in silence down the corridor beyond that main gate – grand, but not *magically* grand, red velvet and marble pillars rather than gem-paved floors and colours so vivid they made you feel like you were learning to see all over again. Only as we climbed a broad flight of stairs to a slightly humbler second floor did Delwin say, 'I'm surprised to see you so affected, I must admit. I had expected you to find the city quite boring, after flitting from fae court to nymph isle for weeks.'

So they *had* gathered intelligence on my movements in the world outside. I filed that little crumb of information away to consider in a calmer moment.

'It's the furthest thing from boring,' I said cautiously, scanning the corridor around us as I spoke. No way out but the stairs and the window – I ought to remember that, just in case. 'The magical islands are beautiful, but they also tend to be rather deadly. It's mind-blowing to me that there are parts of the world where people just … spend their time growing cabbage and mending shoes without having to worry about violence at all.'

He smiled. 'Ah. That I understand.'

'You're not city-born either, then?' I guessed, hoping that would not be too nosy a question.

'My parents sent me and my sister here when we were fifteen.' He pointed to a smaller corridor to our left, where the only decoration was a series of paintings I suspected had been made by a former consul – it seemed the only reason to put the monstrosities anywhere near the main veins of the building. 'That way, please.'

His tone remained calm, but there was a finality about the last words that suggested no more questions on his own past would be welcomed.

Just him and his sister. I wondered where his parents were, now – if he even knew, if he had tried to save up money to allow them to pass through the gate, too, but been too late to save them.

None of that, I supposed, was information he'd share with a little half fae mage he did not trust entirely, even in the most optimistic scenario.

I remarked upon the paintings instead, and he informed me they had been created by the wife of the late Consul Lowell, beloved for his support of the city's artists. Our path subsequently led through a dark corridor that seemed too narrow for its surroundings – 'This shortcut has only been here for a few decades' – and past a barely legible memorial plate – 'The only consul who was ever murdered died here' – to finally arrive at a locked wooden door. Delwin drew the key from his pocket without hesitation, confirming my suspicions that he was certainly not the first guard they'd happened to find available.

'The private wing of the consuls and their guests and families,' he explained, gesturing for me to go first.

This part of the building was cosier than anything I'd seen so far, no cold marble but gleaming old wood, candlelight, and a worn, slightly dusty hall rug guiding our way. I struggled to keep my bearings as we walked up a winding staircase, went left, left, and right again, stepped through a door that looked like all the others and ended up in yet another corridor, until finally my guide slowed down and gestured at a side passage to our left. A faint glimmer of daylight was visible around the corner; whatever side of the building we were on now, there had to be a window there.

'Your rooms are here,' Delwin announced, again politely stepping aside to let me go first. 'I've been instructed to wait here with you until—'

His mouth snapped shut.

And only then did I notice the woman standing beside my guest room door.

She'd taken up position just next to the window at the dead end of the corridor, so that my eyes had been drawn to the bright world outside first and the shadows had concealed even her stark white robes for a moment. Like a thief trained to hide, except everything else about her rendered that stray thought utterly ridiculous – she could not have looked *less* like someone with malicious intentions, this small woman with her dignified clothing and her delicate features and the first strands of grey streaking her dark brown hair. Nor was there anything sinister about the smile that appeared upon her face as she turned towards us, warm and kind and sparkling with just the slightest hint of mischief.

'Ah, thank you, Delwin.' She sounded the way she looked – gentle, but with a core of steel below that tender surface. 'Fast as always, of course.'

'And yet you seem to be even faster,' he said, with a gesture that lay somewhere between a nod and a bow – respectful, but the respect exchanged between equals who appreciate each other's competence, rather than the unconditional reverence demanded by so many of the rulers I'd met in the past few months. 'Happy to report we did not run into any complications. Do you need me here for anything else, or shall I move on to the rest of the list?'

'The rest of the list, thank you.' Her eyes flicked towards him for a moment as she spoke, then darted back to me – inspecting me, undeniably, no matter how courteously she went about it. 'I'll let you know if anything comes up, but if not, I'll see you at the assembly tonight.'

Delwin just nodded again, turned on his heel, and marched out with perfect military efficiency, leaving me in that wood-and-sunshine corridor with the white-dressed woman whose identity I was rapidly developing strong suspicions about. The lily brooch on her chest alone was a glaring hint – too close to the city crest.

Neither of us spoke as the thudding of his heavy boots died away. She took her time sizing me up, not unlike Miss Matilda taking stock of her new clients, assessing all that could be fixed and improved about them. My small bag. My two bargain marks. My harmless blue dress and slightly worn boots …

I waited. Something about those clever blue eyes told me she'd see through my guise of the humble, innocent human girl the moment I opened my mouth.

'So there you are,' she said as she finally lifted her gaze back up to my face – speaking the words slowly, thoughtfully, as if to taste every letter of them. 'Emelin of Agenor's house.'

There was a knifelike precision to that greeting. *I know who you are*, the crystal-clear message between the lines said. *I know* what *you are. Signing your letter as a human did not fool me for half a second, girl.*

As she was right, I decided not to insult her intelligence by correcting her.

'A pleasure to meet you,' I said instead, which I suspected would either turn out to be true or farther from the truth than anything I'd said today. She looked capable of making one's life extremely uncomfortable, if given reason to. 'Consul Rosalind, I presume?'

'Oh, just call me Rosalind,' she said, waving that point away with a single, resolved flick of her wrist. 'The title makes me feel old. Glad to finally meet you, Emelin.'

It sounded genuine. And yet …

We've been hoping you would reach out to us, she'd written in yesterday's letter. Now that I had seen the city she called her home, it seemed even more implausible that that was the full truth: who in the world would be *hoping* for the stench of war to finally creep into this peaceful corner of the archipelago?

But I could hardly ask her to her face, my wariness likely to reinforce her efforts to keep whatever secrets she was keeping.

I settled for half a smile and said, 'I'm grateful you could receive me so swiftly. It's been wonderful to see a little of the city.'

'I'm glad it's been to your liking so far.' There was a strained quality to the smile she returned, not so much insincerity but rather the sense of an underlying emotion she was doing her best to suppress. 'Would you like to see more of it, or would you prefer to have a cup of tea in a calmer part of the Hall? After all you've been up to in the past weeks, I imagine a quiet morning would not be unwelcome.'

I stared at her.

She cocked her head, one lock of brown hair escaping its pins. 'Or, of course, if you'd rather spend your morning in any other way …'

'No!' I blurted, surprise getting in the way of politeness for a moment. 'No, I'd love to see— I just didn't expect— Don't you have more important things to do than show guests around the city? Like ... rule the place?'

'Reading three hundred complaints about the flowerbeds we removed from the Sailors' Park versus having a chat with the young woman preparing to confront the enemy who has been intent on eradicating us for centuries?' This time, the smile tugging at her lips looked entirely genuine. 'I have to admit, it was a difficult choice to make.'

A laugh burst from my lips – I couldn't help it. 'Alright, but ...'

'I'm in no hurry,' she added, smile evaporating. 'If you'd prefer to quickly refresh yourself first, I'm happy to meet you downstairs in a bit.'

'Oh, no.' I gestured sheepishly at my spotless blue dress, not a wrinkle to be found. 'I got here by alf and carriage, so there's nothing to recover from. Just ... Are you sure it will be fine if I start striding around the city? Considering that I'm not technically supposed to be here ...'

'Ah.' She sighed, averting her gaze in what looked suspiciously like an eyeroll in disguise. 'Yes, about that. The short answer is: given that you're here with our permission, you are free to go wherever you wish. The long answer is that, per my colleagues' request, we would ask you not to discuss politics without any government members present in their official capacity and not to use any magic within the walls of the city. Considering that half of our inhabitants have never seen fae powers before at all and the other half have lost friends and family to them, it might cause a bit of a stir, you see.'

And that was all?

I swallowed, suppressing my questions. This was much, much too easy, again – why were they trusting me on my word to not cause any of the catastrophic upheaval I could cause while roaming around unsupervised? Why had Delwin not been asked to shadow me every hour of the day? My letter may have been good, but it had not been *that* convincing, and either way, the people who had kept this city safe from the Mother for all these years should know better than to trust every innocent-looking stranger to come knocking at the gate.

So why was one of their consuls standing here, doing exactly that?

'Yes, of course,' I managed, mind spinning furiously. She was too clever by far to be so dewy-eyed about me, moving letter or not. So either she was playing some bigger game – luring me into an unwise action I couldn't yet foresee, or even just observing what I would do with my apparent freedom – or ...

Or she had some other reason to trust me.

I really had to stop thinking about my gods-damned parents.

'Excellent,' she said lightly, and if not for those razor-sharp eyes monitoring my every word and movement, I might have thought she hadn't noticed my inner turmoil. 'Would you like to leave your luggage here, then?'

I quickly agreed that would be the best idea, glad for a moment of pause to recover and gather my wits again.

The guest room assigned to me was a light, spacious room with high windows and a bed large enough for four. I dropped my bag beside the door, then threw a quick glance outside in an attempt to reorient myself and identify potential escape routes. Unfortunately, street level lay some thirty feet below the window, but at least the sight was familiar – the square on which we had arrived.

Front side.

Which meant Rosalind had not just stood there loitering. Rather, she'd been watching me as her guards escorted me to the building, observing me from the first moment I set foot in her territory.

Nervousness prickled up my spine. No, this whip-smart consul was *definitely* not naïvely letting me run free in the city, and whatever game she was playing, I'd better figure it out soon – before I broke the rules I didn't even know existed and lost my chance, my freedom, or worst of all, a war.

I'd been dazed and overwhelmed for long enough, I decided, turning for the door and steeling my shoulders. It was about time I found some answers.

Chapter 20

A SMALL CROWD HAD gathered near the front gate of the White Hall, erupting in a flurry of urgent whispers the moment I stepped outside with Rosalind by my side.

Heavy lead sank into my stomach without warning.

Nothing about the situation was markedly different from the nervous giggles of nymphs passing me by in the Underground, and yet somehow, the lack of bright pink curls, horns, and scales in this group of onlookers raked up memories of a much older and more unpleasant nature – the children of the village quietly inching away from me as I tried to join their games. Their mothers whispering with Editta in our living room, then turning to glare at me accusingly. Signs I should have understood long before Creon forced the truth of my fae blood upon me ... but then again, should I have realised that the people I'd thought of as family would have kept a truth of that magnitude from me?

'... or the gardens,' Rosalind was saying next to me, and I jolted, realising only then I had missed at least half a sentence from her lips.

'I ... I'm sorry.' Hell's sake, I ought to be paying attention – those answers I needed wouldn't patiently wait for me until I was ready to notice them. 'I was distracted for a moment. What did you say?'

'I suggested we walk to my favourite tearoom,' she said, and while she might have looked amused on the surface, the slight narrowing of her eyes was evidence enough she had already added this small hiccup to her list of questions to answer. 'Very charming historical attic. Lovely gardens. Excellent tea, most important of all.'

I forced a smile. 'I'll gladly follow your lead here.'

'Wonderful.' She nodded at the dragon fountain I'd seen before. 'That way, then.'

The curious audience by the gate didn't follow us, but plenty of other heads turned to catch a glimpse of me as we made for the alley with the flower garlands she had pointed out. Rosalind ignored the wariness in their looks entirely, exchanging cheerful greetings with anyone whose path we crossed. If this small sample was anything to go by, it appeared she knew about three quarters of the city population by name.

'Well, they voted for me,' she dryly said when I asked her, granting a passing woman and her toddler daughter a fond smile. 'It seems polite to know who they are in turn. And admittedly' – her smile grew just a fraction wicked as she turned back to me – 'it's significantly easier to make people do what you want them to do when you know what they're called.'

Again a laugh escaped me. How in hell did she do it, appearing unreserved and amiable even while she was admitting just how damn shrewd a politician she was? It made it hard *not* to like her. Which was in itself evidence of her skills, and all the more reason to be wary ... but perhaps, just perhaps, it was a reason to be honest, too.

She already knew I was not a poor human girl, caught up in conflicts too big for her to comprehend and in dire need of assistance. So if she was showing her hand here, was there any reason left for me not to do the same?

'Some would call that shameless manipulation,' I said as we left the woman and her daughter behind, and I took care not to make it sound like an accusation.

'Oh, of course it is,' Rosalind said and chuckled. 'But we wouldn't get anywhere if we let the people think for themselves all the time, and if I'm to be manipulating them anyway, I'd rather do it shamelessly than shamefully. Saves me a lot of headaches.'

Gods help me, it was *really* hard to dislike her. 'So are you manipulating me right now?'

'Hmm.' She threw me a side glance, steps never faltering on the smoothly paved street. 'No more than you are manipulating me, I would say.'

I should have seen that coming.

'In that case,' I said, drawing in a deep breath, 'would you mind terribly if we ignored etiquette for a bit and moved straight on to the blunt questions? I'd be more than happy to leave the game for what it is and just get right to the point, if it's all the same to you.'

She laughed. 'Ah, points. I'm very fond of those. It truly is a shame so few politicians seem to agree with me.'

'Thankfully I have no ambitions whatsoever to make a name in politics,' I said, unable to keep down a grin. 'It makes many things in life significantly easier. So, as a first question: if you don't mind me asking, what exactly are we doing here?'

'Besides moving in the direction of tea and cinnamon biscuits, you mean?' she said, looking entertained rather than hopeful about the deflection.

'As much as I would appreciate good tea and cinnamon biscuits,' I said, 'somehow it seems unlikely that you broke centuries of city laws and risked getting involved in a, frankly, deeply unpleasant war just to have a drink with me. So I assume there's something else you're looking for. I would like to know what it is.'

'Excellent.' She seemed to mean it, smile sliding off her face but eyes bright with the eager delight of a woman confronted with an interesting challenge to tackle. 'In short, before considering any formal proposals regarding a cooperation between your Alliance and the city, the consulate wants to have a clearer impression of whether you are the sort of person whose proposals we should be welcoming at all. So it has been agreed that I would first have a word with you to better understand where you stand on certain issues that have been, let's say, reason for doubt among the better-informed citizenry, and that we will continue to more concrete negotiations if and only if we feel there is any use in doing so.'

She rattled off the words so easily, so openly — a woman used to matters of policy and strategy, and more than a little skilled at finding the right twists and turns of phrase. Was she speaking the truth? It sounded like it *could* be the truth, but then again, she would be capable of making a lie sound just as believable.

And there was no proper reason this first exploration could not have taken place through written correspondence. Even less reason for her to have so much faith in my harmless intent, if the city government was apparently not even convinced I could be trusted to enter any civilised negotiation.

'I see,' I said.

'Yes,' she said, raising a quick hand to greet a guardsman strolling past. 'I thought you would.'

Honest flattery, or all part of the same smoke screen? I decided it didn't really matter for the next step of this conversation.

'So what are these reasons for doubt you're alluding to?'

'Oh, there are several,' she dryly informed me. 'Your apparent connection, or friendship or whatever it may be, with Creon Hytherion, just to name one.'

It took me a moment or two to figure out what part of that question did not fit the rest of the conversation.

Creon Hytherion.

Not *the Silent Death*, like every other human I'd ever heard referring to him. And she had pronounced that fae title so easily, her accent so fluent; she had to know the language rather well. Was that common, for people to speak Faerie in this most fae-less part of the world?

'You call him by his name,' I said slowly, well-aware I was not answering her question.

'What? Oh, yes.' She shrugged. 'There's enough nonsense making the rounds about individuals like him. I'm not inclined to add to the mythology by turning him into some faceless nightmare – if I must be frightened, I'd rather be frightened of a person.'

Good gods.

Had anyone – *anyone*, even in the Underground – ever so effortlessly grasped the concept of Creon as a real living being with a real beating heart in his chest? Lyn, probably. Naxi, if I ignored the fact that she seemed to consider the matter a fun game half of the time.

Apart from them ...

Consul Rosalind of the White City, of all people.

'Of course,' she added before I could regroup my wits and send them back into battle, 'you don't appear to be that frightened of him at all, from what I've heard.'

It was an uncharacteristically unsubtle request for more information, that question – an optimistic invitation to tell her exactly what my relationship to Creon Hytherion encompassed. Would a woman like her really be that transparent? I felt like she was spinning the conversation around me, a clever thread here, an innocent question there, and I wouldn't notice where she was truly going until she started tightening the net around me.

'I would say,' I said, choosing my words with painstaking care, 'that it's generally rather useful to have some frightening allies on our side.'

The unfulfilled quirk of her lips told me that was not the answer she had been hoping for. But she merely pointed to an alley on our left, pursed her lips, and said, 'Would you say your father falls into that category, too?'

I shrugged. 'Agenor is powerful enough, but I'm not sure I'd call him frightening.'

'He's been on the Mother's side for a while, though,' she retorted – without even a moment of pause, as if this was a part of the conversation she'd prepared well in advance. 'That in itself seems to be an ominous sign, wouldn't you say?'

'Oh, I wouldn't dare to claim he's not an idiot,' I said, and that elicited an unexpected chuckle from her. 'But I'm fully sure that he no longer supports the Mother or the fae empire in general and hasn't done so in my lifetime.'

'Hm.' She seemed to consider that, studying the buildings we passed on her side of the street – small restaurants, an expensive-looking tailor. Most shops were still closed and empty. 'Then how come you did not grow up with him?'

'The Mother was keeping him prisoner while I was born. Apparently, she realised he was developing a little more sympathy for her human slaves than she was comfortable with.' There – that should be a convincing enough argument in favour of his good intentions, shouldn't it? 'By the time she released him and he returned to the Crimson Court, both my mother and I were gone.'

Rosalind was silent for a moment, staring ahead with a small frown on her face as she walked. 'And you believe his story?'

'Yes.'

'Hm,' she said again, and I couldn't tell whether she pensively agreed or thought me unbearably naïve. With her gaze aimed at the small tearoom looming before us, it was hard to read her expression. 'Well, that is clear enough. We're left only with the mystery of you, then – but let's find ourselves a table, first.'

The tearoom, which was called *The Jasmine Vine* and had walls covered in little painted jasmine flowers, was run by a woman who looked old enough to personally remember the Last Battle and hauled kettles of boiling water around as if they were feather pillows. She huffed grumpily when Rosalind asked for a table without eavesdroppers, but sent us into the garden with the promise she would keep the rest of her clients indoors as much as possible.

'That was easy,' I muttered as I followed Rosalind outside into a small and very charming garden crammed between three other houses, every square inch covered in flower garlands and iron lanterns and colourfully painted wooden birds. A flutter of movement in the corner of my eye had me turn my head – Alyra, taking up position between the reddening leaves of the courtyard's only tree.

I smiled. She looked as if she was suppressing a triumphant shriek.

'Half of politics is knowing what people owe you,' Rosalind was saying in the meantime, paying little attention to any tiny falcons suddenly appearing in our surroundings. 'She makes half her yearly income off me at this point. Take a seat – the sun will be creeping into that corner in a few minutes.'

I installed myself at the table she'd pointed out, on a little wooden chair that creaked like it was about to collapse underneath me. The old lady came sailing out of the building at the same moment, carrying a steaming teapot, two cups covered in more jasmine flowers, and a plate full of cinnamon biscuits.

'You know me so well,' Rosalind said fondly.

The only response was another snorted huff, but this one sounded a little more affectionate.

'So,' Rosalind continued once our host had vanished inside and inched the door shut behind her gnarled back. 'About you, Emelin.'

The mystery of you, she'd said before we'd reached our destination. I shifted a tad uncomfortably in my chair – more desperate creaking ensued beneath me – and said, 'There really isn't anything mysterious about me.'

'Hmm.' She picked up the steaming teapot and poured us each a cup of deep golden tea – smelling not just of tea, somehow, but of almonds and orange too, and a hint of ... was that cardamom? 'Young woman no one's ever heard of before, showing up in the heart of the Crimson Court to blind the Mother, only to subsequently vanish from the surface of the earth again for weeks. Reemerging at the Golden Court a little later, damaging the empire's army badly with an unknown poison no one has ever heard of. Vanishing for months again, then turning up at a nymph isle to destroy *an entire fleet* singlehandedly—'

'I had a little help,' I said modestly.

Rosalind gave a chuckle. 'And if I substitute "half a fleet", clearly all my questions have been answered at once.'

I snorted a laugh and picked up a biscuit, wondering just how much I could reasonably be expected to tell a woman whose existence I had not known of until two days ago. 'Most of it sounds more dramatic than it was in the moment, honestly. The core of the story is I'm trying to kill the Mother, and I think that *does* answer most of the questions in one way or another.'

She watched me without answer, eyebrows drawn up a fraction, waiting for more.

I took a bite to win myself some thinking time. The biscuit was sinfully delicious, sweet and spiced and crispy; it took an effort not to let out a content moan.

'Look,' I said after I'd swallowed that first bite, suppressing the urge to stuff the rest of the plate into my mouth as well. 'Don't get me wrong – I would be overjoyed to work with you, and if we *are* working together, I'll be happy to fill you in on every little detail of the past few months. But some of these answers come with information the Mother would be extremely interested in, and even though I appreciate your company—'

'You know very little about my intentions or allegiances in this conflict,' she finished, looking oddly … proud? Content?

As if this, too, had been some test. As if this was the answer she'd been hoping for.

'Yes,' I said, because it seemed a safe thing to say.

'Sensible and understandable.' She brought her teacup to her mouth, blew the steam off it, and watched the rippling surface for a thoughtful moment. Then, slowly, she added, 'Let me explain where I stand.'

This time I was the one to wait.

She put down her cup, visibly searching for words as she parted and closed her lips, fingers fidgeting with the cuff of her robe in the first outward sign of nervousness I'd seen from her. It made her look younger, somehow. Less like a consul. More like a …

Friend?

Hell, I had to stop liking her so much. Was I so desperate to fit back into the human world that I would imagine myself an instant friend of the first woman who smiled at me and offered me a kind word or two?

'They took me at fourteen,' she said brusquely, and all other thoughts evaporated.

'The fae?'

'Yes. To work for them.' A slow, constrained breath in. *Work*. I really, really should not be thinking about what that labour might have entailed. 'By the time I escaped and tried to return home, I found most of my family were dead. Retribution for some minor rebellion.'

The cinnamon had gone dusty and greasy on my tongue. 'Fuck. I'm so sorry.'

'Thank you,' she said, looking up for the first time with her lips pressed tight together. 'So was I. And angry. So ... Well, long story short, I decided I was going to bring them all down. Travelling to the White City seemed a good place to start, for lack of other human strongholds.'

I folded my hands around my cup, unwilling to interrupt her. The fine earthenware was smooth and almost unbearably hot against my palms, a sensation on the edge of pain; I held tight anyway. Like anger, it focused my thoughts.

'The trouble with the city,' Rosalind continued, speaking faster now, back in her politician's skin, 'is that we're divided into two camps, really, and they're about as far apart as can be. There are those who feel it's our duty, as the last bulwark of freedom in the world, to help as many of those outside as possible, to do what we can to support any opposition against the empire. And then there are those ...'

She hesitated.

'Who don't want to give up their safety,' I said slowly.

'Exactly.' She grabbed another biscuit and chewed on it aggressively for a moment. 'Generally speaking, it's the city-born population that is more than content to pretend the outside world doesn't exist, and it's the refugees who are desperate to help their friends and family outside. But there are newcomers too who have been so scarred by the violence that they only want to drown in their illusion of peace, and there are third- or fourth-generation city-dwellers who can so little imagine what it's like outside that they're full of idealistic ambition to spread their wings and free the world.' A joyless chuckle. 'As long as they don't actually have to *risk* anything, of course.'

I thought of Cathra, slaving away year after year; I thought of my friends, watching their loved ones die on the corpse-white battlefield of the Last Battle. It was hard to keep the stab of fury from my voice as I said, 'Of course.'

She gave me that mirthless smile again. 'Yes.'

'So you …' I let go of my teacup to rub my face. 'So you've been doing … what, exactly?'

'Building.' She shrugged. 'When I arrived here, the extent of the city's world-saving ambitions was a programme that allowed fifteen children to move here for free every year. Not with their parents, of course – that would be too much of a good thing. Just the little ones. And they would come here and tell us how grateful they were, and everyone would shed some tears and congratulate themselves on having done their duty towards humanity for the year. I'm sure you can imagine what a moving affair it was.'

She spoke so calmly, her voice still pleasant and restrained. But I saw the way her fingers clenched around her teacup, knuckles white, and I wondered if there were any particular necks she was imagining in place of that earthenware.

'So I've been growing the network,' she added, eyes cast down. 'Finding allies. Accumulating power. Nurturing any support I could find for outward involvement, any understanding that even the White City's peace might not be forever, and hoping I would be ready by the time change came around and someone – *anyone* – began moving against the Mother.'

Anyone.

It was as if I was back at that birchwood table in the pavilion, cold and vulnerable in my flimsy nightgown, still smelling the smoke of my home burning to the ground. *What were you waiting for?* I'd asked, and Creon had written down that one word, full of more meaning than I could ever have comprehended in that night of utter destruction—

You.

Goosebumps were crawling down my neck, my spine, cold despite the gentle autumn sun.

'So,' I forced out, willing my voice not to tremble, 'are you ready, now?'

'It could be worse,' she said, closing her eyes with a deep breath in. 'It could also be better, though. There's three of us consuls – I presume you know that much. Halbert is as far on the other side of the scale as I am on this side. "We paid and worked hard for our peace; tough luck for the people out there, but what would it help if we were to add *our* suffering to the grand total of the universe?" That sort of rhetoric. He was, I'm sorry to say, likely voted into his position *because* of me. Some people got nervous.'

I managed a smile. 'That's a compliment, I'd say.'

'A bloody unfortunate one,' she muttered, but the corners of her lips twisted up an involuntary fraction. 'The third member of the consulate is Norris. He's more moderate. He's the one we'll need to convince, if we want any chance of getting the city involved in the conflict.'

The sort of strategy I'd expected to need to figure out on my own, handed over to me like a cup of tea and a plate of crispy biscuits. It felt too easy, but no matter how hard I looked for it, I couldn't find any hidden schemes behind her words.

'And that would be enough?' I cautiously said. 'You don't need a unanimous vote from the consulate for a decision of this magnitude?'

'Oh, we do,' she said dryly. 'But two out of three is enough to escalate the matter to a city-wide popular vote, if we want. And depending on the exact proposal we made, we would stand a chance there.'

'*Oh*.' City-wide votes. I hadn't even known they existed. 'Well, good thing I wasn't going to suggest sending out every firstborn son into a deadly war.'

She laughed. 'What would you need?'

'The city's stamp of approval, mostly,' I admitted, rubbing my eyes. Damn it, she could have the details of our plans. 'We've been thinking of visiting the other human isles, persuading them to rebel and create unwelcome distractions for the Mother. Bad moment for her to have issues with her supply chains of food and fuel. It would force her to send out people she'd really want around during the fighting itself.'

Her eyes had narrowed. 'Is this one of your father's ideas?'

Not a bad guess, in light of Agenor's reputation. I felt a little sheepish as I shrugged and said, 'Mine, mostly.'

'Dear gods.' Again that laugh, a little more incredulous now. 'I see. So the thought is that you'll stand a much better chance at convincing the humans out there to trust you when you have the weight of the White City behind your requests?'

'Yes, exactly,' I said, relieved despite myself that she did not seem to think it a ludicrous thought. 'You wouldn't have to send *people*, I think. Some money would work. Food. Weapons. Anything that enables us to go there and tell them the city is supporting our efforts.'

She leaned back in her rickety chair, tapping a fingernail against the table. 'And that we could probably get from a public vote. People will feel vaguely guilty about not going out there and fighting the good fight. Giving them a way to buy off that guilt without actually risking a single hair on their heads … I have a feeling that would be a popular option with some of the circles in here.'

A grin was growing on my face, defying all my attempts to remain business-like and pragmatic about the matter. It was oddly exhilarating just to see her *think*, pieces slotting into place behind those clever blue eyes; if she was genuine, if I had judged her correctly …

Then this was the sort of ally I hadn't even dared to dream of.

'Alright,' she said firmly, veering back up and snatching another biscuit off the plate with a swift, energetic motion. 'We have our weekly general assembly tonight with the consuls, the treasurer, the guardmaster – that's Delwin – and a few others. I'll try to gauge where we stand with Norris and let you know. In the meantime, just don't do anything that would ruin your reputation with the general citizens, alright?'

'No dramatic shows of magic,' I said. 'Understood.'

'A fast student.'

I let out a sour laugh. 'I've had two decades to learn that lesson.'

She took a bite and chewed thoughtfully for a moment, examining me with that same assessing look with which she'd welcomed me up in the White Hall. A look of almost *academic* interest – as if she'd read a dozen books devoted to the study of me and was now making a conscious mental effort to match the image she'd constructed in her mind with the living, breathing, scheming individual sitting before her.

I sipped my tea. In cases of doubt, I'd found, that was rarely a disadvantageous decision.

'I know this is technically none of my concern,' Rosalind finally said, and the words came out a little strained, as if she had thought about them too hard to get them over her lips in a remotely natural fashion, 'but would it be terribly impolite for me to ask you for a little summary of those two decades? And the last year, too, if possible? If I have to convince a room full of sceptical colleagues of your good intentions, some knowledge of your background may come in useful.'

I hesitated. 'And that's the only reason?'

'Oh, no,' she admitted with a wry, fleeting smile. 'I'm just nosy, too.'

Had she denied it, I might have kept my cards close to my chest – still the little girl trained to keep her shameful secrets hidden at all costs, still the prisoner who'd survived a fae court by little more than wits and the small advantage of information. But this small, cunning woman before me was not Valter or Editta. She was not the gossiping villagers. She was not the dagger smiles of the Crimson Court.

Rather ... an ally.

And maybe, just maybe, a friend.

'Could you pour me some more tea?' I said. 'I think I'm going to need it.'

She did, with a flicker of relief on her face I couldn't fully make sense of, then refilled her own cup, too. Again, the scent of almonds and orange filled the morning air, mingling with cinnamon and jasmine and the lingering fragrance of dew on leaves.

I hadn't known peace had its own smell until that moment, and now I didn't think I'd ever forget it.

'There,' she said, putting down the teapot and resting her chin in her hands – the epitome of an attentive audience, and judging by the hint of a smile on her lips, it was fully deliberate. 'We're all set. Please start at the beginning, Emelin of Agenor's house.'

So I did.

We'd finished our tea by the time I had summarised the twenty years in which I'd lived as a human, or in which I had at least desperately tried to do so – a period in my life I had always believed overwhelmingly dull, and yet somehow Rosalind's earnest questions made even my stubborn dove-chasing seem diverting. She laughed about my stories of village politics. She winced sympathetically at the tale of how I'd lost my apprenticeship with Miss Matilda. She went still – very, very still – at the description of my last morning in my parent's house, the feast I had not been allowed to attend, the shame and embarrassment.

The ancient owner of the teashop brought us more tea. I told Rosalind how Cathra had burned, how I'd tried to kill Creon, how he'd dragged me off to the Crimson Court all the same. Told her about the Mother's different-coloured eyes and the hounds and the unexpected beauty of the pavilion, the earth-shattering revelations Creon had presented to me, the bargain we'd made.

For some reason, she was smiling broadly at that last point.

I skipped over that kiss inside the Labyrinth but *did* tell her about the mountain's sentient nature; I mentioned the fae ball but concealed that we'd ended up fucking against a wall by the end of the party. Next came Creon's demon powers. Our fight. My flight into the Labyrinth and Ophion waiting for me by the exit to parade me before the Mother as his evidence of her son's treason.

The hellish night after – Creon dangling by his wings, me desperately hauling horses and hay through the Labyrinth's gem-lit tunnels.

We'd finished our second pot of tea by that time and both urgently needed a bathroom break. Rosalind settled the bill while I relieved myself in the small, pink-tiled bathroom that smelled penetratingly of sandalwood; she was waiting for me outside when I returned, looking almost ethereally serene in the sunlight, her white robes fluttering lightly in the breeze.

'I thought we should walk a little,' she said brightly. 'The Sailor's Park is beautiful around this time of the year.'

'Despite the flowerbeds you removed?' I said, and she laughed out loud.

As we sauntered down tree-lined avenues and the occasional towering marble statue, I told her about the Underground, leaving out any details that could be used to locate the Alliance's hideout. Told her how Creon had left, how he'd warned me, how we'd followed him to the Golden Court and run straight into a twelve-hundred-year-old fae male with snake familiars and infuriatingly polished manners who also, impossibly, shared my eyes. I recounted how my newfound father had tried to stop me from finding Creon ('*Men,*' Rosalind muttered), how I'd found him anyway (a heartfelt '*Excellent*'), and how we'd won the battle against the empire's superior force with a bottle of cursed divine blood and an unexpected show of demon power. She laughed again when I told her how I'd stuck a knife through Ophion's wings, and it was the triumphant laugh of a woman who celebrates all allied victories as her own.

We arrived at the Sailor's Park at that point, which turned out to be a memorial for all those lost at sea, heroic statues included. With its vivid red trees and its fields of crocuses, it was a vision of autumnal beauty, and we spent a few minutes admiring the landscaping while Rosalind exchanged cheerful greetings with passing citizens. I wondered if she'd brought me to this busier spot on purpose, if she was quietly demonstrating my harmlessness to the wider public this way. It did seem the sort of thing she might be capable of.

I didn't ask. We had plenty of more pressing matters to discuss.

So I told her of our journey across the plague-cursed continent, of Zera's temple and the island outside time where I'd found the goddess herself. Even then, she did not bat an eye. She had heard of godsworn magic before, it turned out. The story of the battle at Tolya had already reached the White City, too. Only the news of the bindings at the Cobalt Court made her whip around and blink at me for a moment or two, followed by another one of those triumphant laughs – albeit a more bewildered variety this time.

'You've *found* them?'

'We just can't use them yet,' I said wryly, wondering for the first time that day how Naxi was doing and, consequently, whether Thysandra had gone insane yet. 'We need to find out how to match them to the bound individuals first.'

Rosalind blew out her cheeks and kicked a small pebble off the path, into the pond we were passing. It gave a satisfying splash. 'Now I see why you wanted to be sure I would not run off and tell the Mother about your endeavours.'

'Or the rest of the city,' I said hastily. 'You know how news spreads. If even one merchant has a glass of wine too many and forgets to keep quiet ...'

'Oh, yes. I'll be silent as the grave.' Her grin at me still looked a little dazed. 'Can't let the people think for themselves, once again. But if you agree, I can tell the assembly you're working on a way to deal with the disadvantage of the bindings – Halbert won't like that, which means it's almost guaranteed to be good news.'

I laughed. 'I'll let you tell them whatever you think will work.'

'Pragmatic. Very good.' She closed her eyes for a moment, drawing in a lungful of the crisp morning air. 'Let me stew over it a little. I'll come up with something.'

We walked in amiable silence for a minute or so. Rosalind seemed to be brooding on something beside me, and I saw no reason to interrupt her; the city was diverting enough on its own, with its bustling abundance and its odd lack of fae traces. No warehouses for tribute food, untouched even while people were starving. No one-handed or one-eared victims of punishments. This, I realised, was what the continental cities must have been like before the Mother unleashed the plague upon the land and sent the surviving humans fleeing to the islands – a bitter, chafing thought, with the charred corpses in Lyckfort still in the back of my mind.

Finally, the impressive marble façade of the White Hall loomed before us, and Rosalind jolted from whatever thoughts had occupied her to say, 'Is there anything else you'd like to discuss, Emelin?'

A polite but clear sign that we were nearing the end of our walk. I suppressed the one question that hadn't stopped itching since the moment I'd passed through the city gate, instead saying, 'Would you mind showing me the way to the guest wing one more time? I tried to memorise it this morning, but ...'

'Lots of rooms. Yes.' She did not seem at all annoyed by the request, even though she must have better things to do than play lackey to visitors – even to visitors attempting to change the world. 'Just follow me.'

We navigated the maze in silence as I imprinted every twist and turn on my mind's eye – the ugly paintings, the memorial, the winding staircase. Far too soon we stood in that dead-end corridor with the window again, and still I hadn't figured out whether I should speak or stay silent, whether my questions would be silly and sentimental or entirely understandable.

I shouldn't take the risk. I needed her good opinion too much; the world needed this alliance.

I bit my tongue once again.

'There we are,' Rosalind said, slowing to a halt with another probing glance in my direction. 'Do you think you'll find it by yourself next time? If you're in any doubt ...'

'Oh, no, no,' I hastily reassured her – not entirely confident that I would be able to repeat the walk without any delays or detours, but more than sure that my pride could do without another round of instruction. 'This will be fine, thank you so much.'

'Alright.' She did not look fully convinced. 'In that case, please don't spend your day locked up here – as I said, you're free to go wherever you want. I'll let you know about the outcome of the assembly as soon as possible.'

'Yes, thank you.' I forced a smile. 'Good luck convincing them, then.'

She laughed and turned – moving *just* a fraction too slowly, as if she, too, was waiting for me to say more. As if she had already felt the questions crowding my tongue. It was all my heart needed, that little hesitation as she moved away – the realisation that soon, perhaps as soon as tonight, I would leave the city and never see her again and live without answers for what might be the rest of my immortal life.

Good sense and caution crumbled.

'Rosalind?' It sprung from my lips with a force that shocked even me. 'I'm sorry, I just thought— Could I ask you one more thing, perhaps?'

'Yes, of course.' She turned back again, nothing but saintly patience in those blue eyes. 'Ask away. What is it?'

'I – I was just wondering ...' Gods help me. How could a question I'd thought *so* much about still emerge so stuttered, as if I still hadn't mastered the art of speaking full sentences after twenty-one summers of existence? 'If you can't tell me, I fully understand, of course ... I just wanted to ask ... did you by any chance ever meet Valter and Editta? My ... my adoptive parents, I mean?'

And at once she no longer looked so saintly.

It was just a flash, the flicker of something dark and bitter passing across her face – the smallest tightening of her lips, the subtlest narrowing of her eyes. But the hollow silence that followed was just as meaningful, and her carefully crafted unreadable expression could not conceal the simple fact that her smile had gone dull and lifeless: an answer in itself, and not a happy one.

Whatever the master painter and his wife had told her, she had not been glad to hear it.

'Yes,' she said, and the aversion in that one, drawn-out word was palpable. 'We've met, as it so happens. Twice.'

My guts clenched with something that was hope and dread at the same time.

'I visited them a few months ago,' she continued, stepping back to lean against the wall as if she was bracing herself for something. Her voice remained strangely, artificially flat. 'We heard about their connection to you when the news of your antics at the Crimson Court spread, and I try to stay informed. So I wanted to know what they had to say about you.'

I swallowed, nodded. I should have seen that coming.

'And then ...' She closed her eyes, face pale against the faded floral wallpaper. 'Then I went to see them again last night. I wanted to let them know you would likely be visiting the city soon.'

My heart stopped beating for an endless second.

'They ... they know?' The cracking sound that escaped me was barely recognisable as my own voice. 'They know I'm—'

'Yes,' Rosalind interrupted, still not opening her eyes. 'They do. And I wish I did not need to tell you this – I had hoped to meet you with better news – but they have requested not to see you and for you not to be informed about their current whereabouts. For all intents and purposes, Valter told me, it should be to you as if the two of them are not currently living in the city at all. I'm sorry. Believe me when I say I tried to change their minds, but ...'

She did not finish her sentence. The thin line of her lips suggested the remainder of her thoughts would have violated multiple rules of civil conduct, were she to voice them. *They wouldn't hear of it.*

The fucking idiots wouldn't hear of it.

I stared at her, unseeing, unhearing. Outside, children were shrieking and laughing. Horse hooves clattered over the broad square, the rattle of wheels in their wake. Yet my mind was back inside Creon's pavilion, stained glass and the briny scent of nearby sea, a letter trembling in my hands – *Do not write to us.*

How did news I'd heard before still dare to hit so deep, as if this was happening for the first time all over again?

'Alright,' I somehow managed to get past my lips, even though it was *not* alright, would never be alright, could not be further from alright. Old reflexes took over. Don't cry. Don't embarrass. 'That ... that is clear. Thank you for letting me know.'

She sighed. 'I'm sorry, Emelin.'

There didn't seem anything else left to say – nothing, at least, that I could reasonably say to the woman I'd met two hours ago and knew as little more than a strategical acquaintance. I swallowed and swallowed again, fumbled with the doorhandle to my room, and somehow dragged the corners of my mouth into something that might distantly resemble a smile. I had not known it could be physically painful to smile, but this one ... I felt it like a claw in the guts.

'Don't let me delay you any longer, then.' A pathetic, flimsy excuse. 'Let me know what the assembly has to say, and—'

'Emelin?' she interrupted, opening her eyes.

I fell silent.

For a moment I thought she might hug me, the way her fingers clenched and unclenched at her side, like pent-up impulses barely held in check. But she only stood straighter. Only tucked a lock of hair behind her ear and hurriedly said, 'Please remember that you are not to blame for their judgement, will you? You did not scare them. You did not turn them into cowards. Plenty of humans would have been proud to call themselves your parents – you were very, very unlucky, that is all.'

The air in my lungs turned to ice.

'Just thought I should mention that,' she added, averting her eyes with restless motions. 'Well, I should really get back to work – enjoy your day, and I'll let you know as soon as there are any developments …'

I heard myself reply something – something sufficient, presumably, because she did not look at me like I'd gone insane but rather smiled at me one last time and hurried off. And then it was just me in that old, sun-streaked corridor, where no one could see the tears dripping down my face – where I could just be small and lost and broken for one endless moment, and very, very unlucky indeed.

Chapter 21

Alyra was waiting for me on the windowsill when I finally scraped myself together and slipped into the guest room, pecking vexedly at the glass to inform me of her displeasure. The moment I opened the window, she shot inside, a storm of down and feathers, squeaking loudly in obvious but rather unexplained triumph.

'Alyra!' I hissed, gesticulating at her in an unsuccessful attempt to quiet her – how many floors down would they be able to hear the noise? 'Please – you're supposed to be a *secret* weapon. What in the world is the matter?'

A tangle of images washed over me.

Rosalind, seen from my familiar's perspective as she perched on the branches of that chestnut tree in the tea garden. Something to do with the Crimson Court. And most confusing of all, the crystal-clear vision of a bird's nest – braided twigs, soft moss and leaves, small blue-flecked eggs.

'What?' I said.

Alyra hopped up and down impatiently on the foot of the monumental bed.

'*Eggs?*' I plopped down on the blankets, shaking my head at her with a bewildered laugh. 'I'm not sure where you're going with that, I'm sorry. What is the matter with Rosalind?'

The equally confusing image of a worm dangling from a bird's beak was added to the mix, emerging with an odd blend of my own disgust and Alyra's fond early memories. A *worm* – did Rosalind make a habit of feeding the fledgling birds around the city's parks? Did she enjoy fishing in her spare time?

But then why in the world were we thinking of the Crimson Court and eggs, too?

'Alright,' I said weakly, because it was clear Alyra was expecting an answer of some sort – I just did not have the faintest clue *what* answer she needed. 'I'll … consider it?'

She let out a shriek of despair and dropped herself onto her back on the mattress, wings spread and claws up in the air like a dead bird. I needed no additional clues to interpret that little piece of communication – *you idiot*.

'Look, I'm *trying*.' The irritation bled into my words no matter how hard I tried to keep it out. 'You could be clearer, too, don't you think?'

Her glare said she absolutely could not be, and that even a little fledgling still wet from the egg would have been able to make sense of her perfect clarity. As it seemed unlikely she was going to change her mind on that point, I just grimaced and added, 'Are you trying to tell me I'm in immediate danger?'

That didn't seem to be the case.

'Well, then I'll figure it out later.' I glanced at the open window. 'Could you fly back to the outer city gate and let whoever is waiting there know that I'm alive and well so far? They're probably a little tense, and I don't want them to worry any longer than necessary.'

She brightened immediately at the prospect of something useful and important to do. I dug one of my simple white ribbons from my bag – the signal we had agreed upon to let the Alliance know I was not in any trouble – and handed it to her; she curled her talons around the smooth silk as if it was a precious jewel.

'Good luck,' I said, and she soared out of the open window with a last little trill, the ribbon fluttering after her like a banner of victory.

I watched her until she was no more than a tiny dot in the bright blue sky, then sighed and turned back to my room with a mixture of relief and anxiousness. At least Creon would know I had arrived safely at my destination … but there was still the image of that little nest, five blue-and-grey eggs on a soft bed of moss, and Alyra's excitement suggested the message had to be of some importance.

Separated from my friends and allies by ancient divine magic, this was a terrible time and place to feel like I was overlooking something.

It had been about Rosalind, hadn't it? So what if the consul wasn't all she seemed, just after I had told her all about the bindings and my godsworn magic? What if I'd been too quick to trust her and she'd happily betray me to the rest of the consulate? What if …

I shoved that first inkling of a developing panic aside with a heartfelt curse. Alyra had at least said I was not in danger, and either way, there was no undoing the things I'd done. Waiting and hoping for the best was all I could do.

Which admittedly sounded like a miserable way to spend the rest of my day.

I managed to fill a whole five minutes unpacking my bag, hiding my daggers underneath my pillow and in the desk drawers, and exploring the adjacent bathroom. By the time I was done, the sun still hadn't moved any farther across the sky, and Alyra hadn't returned from her mission; it left me with little else to do but stand at the window and stare at the city below, watching the citizens walk by with their carts and their children and their groceries. People who had never needed to hold a weapon in their life. People who would never lose their limbs or bleed to death on a battlefield.

Easy prey, Creon would have said if he had been here to see them, in that rough voice of which even the *thought* sent shivers down my back, and it would only have been half a joke.

He would not have been wrong, either.

What an enviable thing, to be powerless and unimportant, a replaceable piece of the puzzle in this peaceful little corner of the world.

And damn it, what was I doing, standing here moping and staring at what had once been the world of my dreams? The city was expecting me. Rosalind had said I could go wherever I wanted. This was my only chance to experience that life, if only for a few hours; did I really want to return home having seen little more of this place than my own bedroom?

It could hardly be dangerous, going out. Either people would know who I was and think twice before attacking me, or they wouldn't recognise me and have no reason to hurt me. But just in case …

I stepped back from the window and snatched up the dagger I'd slipped into the desk drawer. Two of the white ribbons were sufficient to strap it securely to the inside of my thigh.

There. Even without magic, I wouldn't be a helpless victim.

Now that my plan was made, the thought of spending a single minute more in this lifeless silence suddenly seemed unbearable. I tossed my small purse into my backpack, gulped down a few mouthfuls of water, and slipped out, heading down the winding stairs. The maze of rooms was already starting to look familiar. I found the route out more easily than expected, resisting the urge to snoop in some of the abandoned rooms I encountered on my way – Rosalind was supposed to be taking care of the politics for now, and either way, getting caught with my hands in a clerk's drawers would likely not endear the other two consuls to me.

No one granted me more than a glance of acknowledgement as I stepped out the door and descended the marble stairs to street level. The crowd had vanished, perhaps disappointed I'd failed to kill anyone or blow up the White Hall; I crossed the square feeling remarkably like I had the day I'd arrived on Ildhelm for my apprenticeship and realised that not a single soul in that city knew my name. There was a certain lightness, a sense of freedom, that came only with utter anonymity.

Where to go, if I could go anywhere I wanted?

I turned left, the side I hadn't walked with Rosalind. Stately mansions lined the road before me, surrounded by small but lush gardens where gardeners were tending to the flowerbeds. Around the corner, I discovered a row of shops that obviously catered to the richest inhabitants of the city – a jeweller, an antiquarian, a perfumery. I passed a window full of stately portraits and was annoyingly relieved to see they were not painted in Valter's style. Next came a dressmaker's shop showcasing some cornflower blue creations that could rival the fae designs I'd seen at the Crimson Court, all silver and pearls and frothy organza – and good gods, was that a piece of needle lace I glimpsed in the back of the workshop?

Old habits took over. I slowed down, despite knowing that even the cheapest of these dresses would cost ten times the money I was carrying with me.

In the reflection of the shop window, I could see a man on the opposite side of the street skid to a halt.

I faltered, momentarily distracted from even the mouthwatering designs displayed before me. From what I could see in the smooth glass, the stranger did not have a particular reason to stop there – no shop windows to study, no other passers-by about to run into him. Only after a heartbeat or two did he start rummaging around in his pockets, as if he had belatedly realised he was supposed to have an excuse to be standing still.

Odd. Odd enough to call for further investigation, really.

With a sting of regret, I turned away from the dresses and tentatively sauntered on to the next shop. So did the figure on the other side of the street, having suddenly found whatever he'd been looking for in the pockets of his patched-up jacket.

I paused again. So did he.

Fuck.

That settled it, then – so much for anonymity. Was this a guardsman, following me on the consulate's orders? But he was so bloody clumsy I'd noticed him within five minutes, and what I had seen from Delwin so far did not suggest he'd set such a poorly trained individual on my tail if he did not want me to know he was keeping an eye on me.

So what were the alternatives? Nervous civilians? Supporters of Halbert, hoping to catch me in the act of … well, anything forbidden?

I ambled on, mind whirring, making sure to look as innocent as possible. Was it really a *problem* if someone was following me? I wasn't planning to commit any crimes. If watching me was the worst they would do, that was annoying but not necessarily dangerous. The question remained, though ...

Was it the worst they would do?

Something about the glimpses of a broad-necked, scruffy-bearded man following me down a luxury shopping street did not inspire great optimism about his motives.

Which meant I needed a way to get rid of him. I kept my pace deliberately leisurely as I strolled down the street, around the corner, and around another corner, my shadow never more than forty feet behind me; hard as it was, I took care not to glance over my shoulder or acknowledge his presence. I would likely get only a single chance to shake him off. As soon as he realised I was aware of him, he'd be twice as alert.

Finally, three blocks away, I found the opportunity I'd been looking for – a small, not too formal-looking restaurant, not yet open to guests but with staff already moving inside. The door stood ajar. Good enough for the half-plan taking shape in my thoughts; I wouldn't get any closer to a full strategy anyway, in this unfamiliar territory.

I swivelled off-course at the very last moment. The reflection in the polished wooden door told me my pursuer was knocked off-balance for a moment, staggering to a halt as I nudged open the door and slipped into a white-and-green dining room smelling of fried garlic and fresh bread.

'Miss?' a middle-aged server called from the other side of the room, a tray of clean glasses in her hands. A woman. Good. 'I'm sorry, we're not open yet. If you'd like to make a reservation ...'

'Oh, no, no,' I hurriedly said, tiptoeing awkwardly towards her. 'No, I was wondering— I'm so sorry, this is very embarrassing— Do you perhaps have a bathroom I could quickly use? It's, er, a bit of an *emergency*, if you ...'

'Oh, dear,' she interrupted, deducing the nature of the emergency with the swift feminine intuition I had hoped for. Her glance at the tiles around my feet didn't escape me – as if I'd be bleeding all over her freshly mopped floor. 'Yes, of course. Back of the room and up the stairs; there's a sign on the door.'

I thanked her profusely and hurried off, risking one glance out the window in passing. The bearded man had acquired an equally broad-shouldered companion in the meantime. Judging by their glares at the door through which I'd just entered, they were impatiently waiting for me to come out again.

A shame I had no intention of doing any such thing in the foreseeable future.

Up the stairs I climbed, scanning the dark but tidy attic hall with a rattling heart. There was the door with the bathroom sign – clearly visible, and not what I needed. It would be the first place they would look. The broom closet was far too obvious an option, too, and a quick investigation told me the other doors were locked. I could use magic to open them, of course, but the bastards might notice, and wasn't that exactly what my opponents would be hoping for?

Which left about one option.

Humans never look up, Creon had once signed during a long day of magic training, discussing the tricks and pitfalls of fighting fae. *It's the wings, I suppose. They never seem to realise the danger could be coming from above.*

'You'd better be right,' I mumbled at him, clambering onto the banisters to reach for the sturdy roof beams. 'I'm really not in the mood to murder anyone.'

I could have sworn he was laughing somewhere, somehow.

Hauling myself onto the beams was not an elegant affair: they were dry and dusty, and my legs insisted on flailing in all possible directions as I moaned and groaned my way up onto the wood. At least the damn things were broad enough to hide most of me if I took care to tuck my skirt beneath my legs. I rested my head on the beam and closed my eyes, waiting – ear pricked for any sound coming from downstairs.

They did not make me wait long.

Five minutes, perhaps. Then the shocked shrieks of the middle-aged server rose from below, telling me exactly what was happening. The conversation came through muffled, only shreds distinguishable.

… consuls themselves … most irregular … will have no part in …

The footsteps thundering up the stairs left no doubt on the outcome of the discussion, though.

I held my breath as one of them yanked open the bathroom door and bit out a string of heartfelt curses. Another door flew open. Rummaging sounds, brooms falling over each other, and then a hissing voice – 'She's *gone*!'

'Yes, I can see that,' the other man bit out in that same hushed tone. 'The question is where the hell she's vanished to – has she flown out through the fucking walls?'

'Might be magic,' the first one muttered, even more quietly.

They were both silent for a moment. The sound of their searching had grown significantly more doubtful, as if neither of them truly believed they would find me anymore; a piece of furniture scraped over the floorboards, a pile of blankets or towels thudded over. I lay staring into the dusky darkness, skin prickling with the awareness of their nearness – mere feet below me, a single sharp-eyed glance away.

They seemed too occupied with their own worries to think of glancing up.

'Halbert will have our heads if we tell him we lost her,' one of them hissed, so close I could hear the strain in his voice, and no matter how hard I was biting my tongue, I nearly let out a gasp.

Halbert *himself*?

Not a group of concerned civilians, not a few supporters taking matters into their own hands – no, the bloody consul of the White City was having me followed, and unless Rosalind had deliberately concealed the fact from me, he hadn't even told his own colleagues about it. Which did not suggest the most lawful of intentions. Which meant I would have to be really damn careful around here – the battle was far from over yet.

'Well, he can't blame us if she used magic, can he?' the other man grumbled under his breath, accompanied by the sound of boots hitting a wooden wall. 'If she made herself invisible or … or …'

'Damn right,' the first hurriedly agreed. 'No sense in making a fool of ourselves here. We can wait on the corner of the street and see if she shows up ...'

Their voices died away as they plodded down the stairs again. I heard them snap some curt yet unintelligible words at the staff in the dining room, then the door slammed. I waited ten breaths, wary of tricks and ruses ... but the footsteps did not return, and the dark murmurs rising from below suggested the restaurant's employees felt free to speak again.

Holding my breath, I threw a glance down. The landing below my beam was deserted.

I cautiously slid from my hiding place, landing as quietly as I could. My light blue dress was streaked with dust, unseemly smudges in brown and dark grey all over my back and stomach; making my decision in a heartbeat, I slipped into the bathroom, locked the door behind me, and undressed myself. Cold water and a dust cloth I found in a discreet bathroom cupboard were enough to render my clothes mostly presentable again.

Dusted off and dressed, I took the risk and descended the stairs. Two servers and a cook stood huddled between the small round tables, mouths snapping shut as if by command the moment they caught sight of me.

For one fraught moment, the clatter of pans and tools in the kitchen was all I heard.

Then the same middle-aged woman who had originally helped me cleared her throat, cleared it again, and cautiously said, 'Those were ... not guards, were they?'

So that was the game my pursuers had tried to play. Ballsy, given the rather obvious contrast with the well-groomed, immaculately disciplined guards in their shining city armour who had accompanied me between gate and White Hall.

'No,' I said, deciding in a split second lies could only cause me more trouble here. 'I'm so sorry for involving you in this. They are after me for other reasons.'

'You're the fae girl,' she concluded without a moment of hesitation.

There was no fear in her voice, not a tinge of hysteria. A simple observation. Fae girl, hunted girl, girl with an emergency regarding her monthly – she gave the impression it was all the same to her. Had she ever met a magical creature before? The way she scanned me, almost eager for clues and shocking discoveries, suggested she had never learned to fear my kind that much.

Next to her, the cook and younger server looked like I was a glass of water on fire.

'Yes,' I admitted, unable to suppress a hint of awkwardness. 'Emelin. Pleasure to meet you?'

My conversation partner let out a high laugh – the kind of laugh that said, *I've slept too little and I still have seventeen tables to set, and now there's a fae girl standing in my restaurant.* 'Good gods. Did you do magic?'

'Oh, no,' I said, taking care to make it sound like the suggestion was little more than a harmless joke to me. 'I promised the consuls I wouldn't use magic within the walls of the city, so I climbed onto the roof beams. The gentlemen didn't think of looking up.'

That evoked muffled chuckles from even the cook and the younger girl, who still hadn't dared to speak a word. My conversation partner scoffed and said, shaking her head, 'Well, they were talking of waiting for you at the end of the street. Would you like to use the back door?'

More helpfulness than I had expected, after my lies. 'If you really don't mind ...'

'Oh, please,' she said with a faint smile, beckoning me to follow her. 'I voted for Rosalind for a reason.'

I made a mental note to thank Rosalind for her indirect assistance.

The restaurant's back door opened into a little courtyard, from where a narrow crack between houses and gardens ran all the way to the other side of the block. I professed my gratitude two more times, promised I would do nothing to get the establishment in any trouble, and took off, my backpack bouncing against my shoulders as I hurried between fences and plastered walls.

Where to go next?

With one narrow escape during my first half hour alone in the city, the wisest decision was doubtless to turn back and make for the White

Hall. At least Halbert could not accuse me of magically harming citizens there, and if he wished to quietly kill me, at least I wouldn't harm any bystanders while defending myself. Staying in the city meant taking a risk, one I was not fully sure I could afford.

Then again ...

Old, selfish stubbornness stirred within me – a most welcome guest. To hell with Halbert and his scheming. To hell with the greater good. I was spending a few short days in what had once been the city of my dreams, and was I really considering letting one tricky consul and some dumb muscle lock me in my room all that time?

I reached the end of the alley, hands clutching the straps of my bag, and threw a cautious look around the quiet street that lay beyond. No looming danger to be seen.

Damn them, then.

I drew in a last deep breath and trotted to the next side street, slipping around the corner within mere heartbeats. Deeper into the city. Deeper into the unknown.

Free again, for these stolen hours.

I passed a small group of stonemasons at work, some mothers with children, a merchant expertly steering a cart full of firewood down a narrow alley. There were no glares, no whispers. Some of them even greeted me in passing, with the careless, absent-minded air of people who haven't experienced anything remarkable in years. The city went about its business wherever I walked, unbothered by my presence. I found a theatre announcing its next play in fat, gilded lettering, a horse seller loudly praising his own wares, servant girls gossiping on street corners. If the news of a fae visitor had caused any unrest or civil disagreement, the consequences weren't visible to an outsider.

Perhaps, I considered, Halbert was a lone dissenter, digging for trouble no one else had bothered to worry about. Or perhaps he had just wanted to keep an eye on me to make sure I didn't sneak off and hurt any of his people.

Could I really disagree with that, all things considered?

Around me, the rows of narrow houses abruptly receded to give way to a broad market square: a couple dozen colourful stalls, surrounded by small groups of citizens who chattered merrily amongst each other as they inspected their prospective purchases. No meats and grains and vegetables, as far as I could see. The merchants here sold wares that must have been imported from elsewhere in the archipelago – Rhudaki lace, southern dried flowers, illustrated books from the scriptorium on Furja. No magical items. The ships from the White City might sail anywhere, but it seemed they wouldn't trade with alf smiths or phoenix scribes.

I tiptoed between the stalls, feeling not unlike a child in a pastry shop – finely woven silk here, fragrant incense there, a wide range of paints and dyes next ... Each successive stall heightened my awareness of the heavy purse of gold in my bag. I lingered near a stall with a wide array of stunningly forged daggers, wondering if I should buy the set with mother-of-pearl and obsidian hilts for Creon – he'd like them, doubtlessly, but buying weapons of any kind might not be the wisest choice if I wanted to convince two consuls of my peaceful and harmless intentions.

With a small sting of regret, I left the daggers behind.

Pens and ink. Vellum of a quality that made my hands itch. More Rhudaki lace, and at the next stall—

I let out a small gasp.

Astrolabes.

I'd only ever seen illustrations of the instruments, in the long and incomprehensible foreword to the *Encyclopaedia of Stars*. They were used to measure angles and make calculations – that much I had gathered – and then there were passages on things called dioptras and planispheres and I had given up on making sense of the matter. But they *were* stunning, these intricate contraptions with their drop-like shape and their elegant rings and their engravings of heavenly bodies ...

No one could draw any unhappy conclusions about me based on an innocent interest in astronomy, could they?

And gods help me, Creon *would* be happy with one.

I'd swivelled around and made my way to the stall before I could think through the consequences of drawing attention, my bag already in my hand.

The merchant, who'd stood smoking his pipe until that point, bared his yellowed teeth in a grin as he saw me approach. 'Interested, Miss?'

There was no suspicion in his voice. No one turned a head around me – they must have no idea of who I really was.

'I'm developing a bit of an interest in astronomy,' I merrily told him, sliding my eyes over the range of instruments – some the size of dinner plates, others small enough to fit in the palm of a hand. I pointed at one of average size, made out of copper and engraved with constellations along the edges. 'How much are you asking for that one, for example?'

'Excellent choice,' he said with an earnest nod, making it sound as if he would never have said the exact same thing should my preference have been different. 'Very solid design, that one, was already used by the Elderburg astronomers before the plague. I usually sell it for seven florins, but since you're just getting started …'

His discounted price was still eye-wateringly high, as I had expected. I slid into the game as if I'd never done anything else, remembering how Editta had gone back and forth, back and forth, with merchants for every stretch of linen and every bottle of ink she'd bought – that subtle dance of flattery and feigned indifference, circling that final price that could satisfy all parties. I was not as good at it as she had been. The four florins and three silverlings on which we finally arrived was likely still too much money for what I was getting – but to hell with it, I *had* the money, and if we were all going to die on a battlefield soon, what was the sense in holding on to it?

The merchant turned away to wrap my purchase in strips of linen as I dug my purse from my bag and began counting out the agreed price. Four golden coins hit the wood surface of the stall with satisfying thuds. I felt around for the smaller shapes of silverlings – there was one of them, and a second, and—

'Hey!' someone shouted behind me.

The merchant and I whirled around as one.

A broad man came elbowing through the peaceful crowd, making his way towards us – no to *me*, his hostile gaze burning holes into my face. The way he jutted a stubby finger at me reeked of accusations.

'She's using fae gold!' he barked, loud enough for every single soul in the square to hear him. 'I saw her enchant it behind your back – she's that fae girl!'

And only then did I recognise his voice.

I'd heard it beneath me, half an hour ago, as I lay frozen on a dusty wooden beam.

Fuck. Heads turned around me, too many of them to keep count; conversations stilled with ominous swiftness. *Fae gold.* Stone or mud, enchanted to fool mortals but guaranteed to turn back to worthless dust the next morning – hadn't we all heard the stories about it? Only now did I realise the myth didn't make the least sense, not if yellow magic could just as easily turn earth into gold permanently ... but good gods, how was I going to convince a horde of sceptical humans of that?

It wouldn't help me anyway. Halbert's pawn would just accuse me of using yellow magic instead, and that was equally forbidden.

'Wait,' the pipe-smoking merchant said, every trace of his scruffy grin vanished as he looked back and forth between me and the bearded man closing in on us. 'You're the *fae girl*?'

Was there any sense in denying it?

'Um, yes.' The glares around me were too sharp. Why in hell had I sent Alyra away – why had I been so stupidly thoughtless to venture so far away from the White Hall on my own? 'But the gold is true gold, on my word. The consuls asked me not to use magic, so—'

'I *saw* it,' my accuser bellowed again, drowning out my stammered defence. *Deliberately* drawing attention, I realised – making sure that every single person in our vicinity knew exactly what was going on. 'Those were *pebbles* you pulled from your purse. How dare you come here and dupe our honest traders! Is that how you repay our hospitality?'

Oh, *fuck.*

What to do? What to say? I could tell them I was unable to use yellow magic without draining the colour elsewhere, and since no such thing had happened, clearly I had to be innocent – but I knew how much the average human knew about magic. My argument would have to come with a lecture, and no one would care about it. Which meant ...

I had to use what they knew.

I had to use all *I* had known, a few feeble months ago.

'The light must have fooled you,' I said, and bless years upon years of pretending I was doing just fine; it came out with all the slightly amused surprise of a spotless conscience. My mind was a whirlwind, combing through twenty years of human memories. 'Why in the world would I come here and start using fae tricks against you all of a sudden? I'm trying to *fight* them, not spread their evil.'

Disconcerted murmurs thickened around me. Bystanders inched backwards, ushering their children out of my reach. It left me and my accuser opposite each other, five feet between us, like professional wrestlers about to pounce on each other; only the merchant and his half-wrapped astrolabe remained close, caught with us within the bounds of that artificial arena. The gold lay before him, untouched.

'I know a pebble when I see one, Miss,' the broad-shouldered man growled, and around him, the whispers seemed to agree – surely no one could mistake that fat, gleaming gold for stone if it hadn't *been* stone a minute ago?

As Halbert had imagined, no doubt. After all, who would hand over the city's resources to a suspected liar and thief?

If I hadn't been so furious, I might have appreciated the ingenuity of it.

'Well,' the merchant started, calloused hands pulling the first linen strip off the astrolabe. Ready to put it back between his wares. Ready to send me off. 'In that case—'

Oh, damn it all.

I took the leap.

'Does anyone have any iron to hand, then?' I interrupted, making sure to weave just a hint of laughter into my voice. *A silly misunderstanding*, I willed my tone to say. *We'll have it cleared up in a moment.* 'Just a little bit will do – a nail or a key is plenty.'

Several dozen pairs of dumbfounded eyes stared back at me mutely.

'Oh, come on.' I threw a guileless glance around – the height of righteous innocence. I almost started believing myself. 'Someone must have some iron on them, yes? There's no reason why we should stand here bickering if we can very easily put the accusation to the test.'

'Iron ...' a young woman whispered behind me, loud enough to be heard by most of the group. 'Because it blocks fae magic?'

As I had once believed. As we had *all* believed, betting our lives on that stupid ward around the island.

'Yes, of course,' I said brightly. 'Best way to distinguish fae gold from true gold – didn't you know?'

And *that* they could accept. I could see it in the nods around me, hesitant but without much suspicion: close enough to common human wisdom, to the rules of the world as they knew it. My opponent had gone quiet – stunned into paralysis. Did he know that I was lying through my teeth, or did he believe in the anti-magic properties of iron himself?

Either way, he had to know what was about to happen.

'I've got a key!' a red-haired young man announced with the triumphant aplomb of an investigator solving a murder, holding out the object in question. 'Pure iron, I'm pretty sure!'

'Wonderful,' I said and beamed at him. 'Would you mind just tapping it against the coins a couple of times? If they're enchanted, that should break the spell immediately.'

I could not have wished for a better assistant: he fulfilled the task with a theatrical exaggeration that drew some sniggers from the audience even before the iron made contact, touching key to gold with a dramatic flourish and a loud clink. And a second touch. A third. The gold continued to gleam smooth and buttery in the sunlight, spectacularly unaffected.

'That settles it, doesn't it?' I said before my opponent could speak a word, and it was all I could do to keep looking like I hadn't worried for a minute as the murmurs around me turned relieved and approving. 'Must have been the light.'

My pursuer gave off the air of a man who's bet his house in a game of cards and lost it. His attempt at defiant scepticism came out like childish obstinacy – 'But if the iron wasn't as pure as we're thinking ...'

Endorsing, indirectly, the power of iron as a diagnostic tool.

I huffed a laugh, meaning it this time, and said, 'Well, if the coins miraculously turn into mud tomorrow morning, I'm sure every single person in this city will know where to find me. Really, I hardly picked the most convenient location to start my criminal career.'

Open laughter around me, now; his broad, unshaven face reddened dangerously. 'But—'

'Look, it's fine,' I interrupted, waving the start of that objection away. 'We all make mistakes, don't we? It's wonderful you're looking out for your fellow citizens. Can I buy you a drink to compensate, maybe? I'm sure we'll get along just fine if given the chance.'

He stared at me in disbelief for half a second, then snapped around and strode off with long, brusque steps, cursing under his breath. Laughter stilled in his wake as onlookers stared after him, unsure what to make of so much anger over what seemed to have been nothing but an unfortunate blunder.

No one thought of asking how he'd even known I was *that fae girl*, if I hadn't actually performed any magic tricks.

It was the astrolabe merchant who broke the deadlock in the end, bending over with a groan and scooping my gold into his palm in an unspoken decision. His grin at me was a little nervous but not unfriendly as he said, 'I've never traded with fae before. You look rather human, do you know that?'

By the time I'd explained the details of my ancestry to him and answered the red-haired man's barrage of questions on magic and fae courts, most of the lingering onlookers appeared to have classified me as a rather harmless curiosity, not entirely human but polite enough to make up for it. No one accused me of anything further as I shook hands and chuckled at jokes about my lack of wings. A few children scuttered towards me, and their mothers did not drag them away. And when I finally put my brand-new astrolabe into my bag, said my goodbyes, and began walking back to the White Hall, no one seemed to be following me – no muscular men sneaking around corners, no shadowy individuals pausing whenever I slowed down.

But at the entrance of the White Hall, Delwin stood waiting for me.

I staggered to a halt, wondering for one heart-stopping moment whether the news of my suspected magic use had already reached the consuls ... and then I saw the letter in his rough hand, parchment sealed with stark white wax.

'Assembly outcome,' he said as he gave me the message with a quick nod. 'They asked me to make sure you got it.'

And so he had resolved to take care of the task in person – not a man for doing things by halves, I was starting to discover. I broke the wax seal and hastily unfolded the letter, finding a short note in Rosalind's familiar hand inside.

Emelin,

We would like to meet with you tomorrow to formally discuss the possibility of a collaboration between your Alliance and the city. Please join us in the Great Hall at 10 in the morning – we will send someone to show you the way.

R.

No other information. Either she hadn't seen an opportunity to include it, or she had put everything she'd wanted to say in these few sentences.

I scanned the letter again, faltering midway through this time.

'The Great Hall.' Merely speaking the words was enough to fill me with unpleasant suspicions. 'Does that mean ...'

'Ah, yes,' Delwin said, and although his face remained strictly neutral, I imagined hearing a touch of disapproval in his voice. 'The public will be allowed to attend the meeting tomorrow. Halbert in particular insisted upon that condition.'

Halbert in particular.

That sounded like a warning – Halbert, who hadn't wanted me here in the first place. Halbert, who had tried once before to wield an audience as a weapon against me ... so what was he planning this time?

'Interesting,' I said cautiously.

'Yes,' Delwin said, the lines of his tanned face deepening a fraction. 'Rosalind and I thought so, too.'

It had been a warning, then. Which meant Rosalind didn't know what the bastard was up to, either. Which meant she agreed with me he must be up to *something*, and likely nothing that would better our chances at that confrontation.

'Thanks,' I said, bracing myself. 'I will be ready at ten, then.'

No faster way to figure out Halbert's game, after all.

Chapter 22

Surpassing my worst expectations, it appeared half of the White City had taken a morning off to witness my meeting with the consulate.

Despite the dagger against my thigh, despite the magic in my fingertips, I was quietly glad for Delwin's unflappable presence beside me as he guided me to the open doors of the Great Hall. Around us, the crowd pulsed with excitement, that dangerous atmosphere of dry hay waiting for a single spark. But even the most zealous onlookers struggling to squeeze themselves into the packed galleries receded to let the city's guardmaster through, and in his more illustrious company, most didn't even seem to notice me until we had already passed them by.

Is that her? the hissed whispers echoed behind me, sharp and shameless, as if I was so little like them that the sound of their voices would not even reach me. *No, that can't be her. She's so tiny ...*

I imagined Creon's face if he heard about that particular reasoning, and had to press my lips together a little tighter not to smile.

Before us, the last row of bodies parted, and finally the Great Hall revealed itself to me – a stately, rectangular room with marble walls and marble pillars, sunlight pouring in through the high windows just below the ceiling. The galleries ran the full length of the hall on either side, already filled to the last seat; behind them, tall statues lined the walls, their sculpted robes a clear hint that these were former consuls watching over the proceedings. On the far side, a sail-sized banner covered most of the short wall, embroidered with a silvery lily crest that must have taken a couple dozen seamstresses a while to finish.

Below that banner, on a low stage, the three living consuls had already taken their seats.

I recognised them in an instant, a single glance enough to link names to faces. Rosalind was sitting on the left, legs crossed and head cocked, by the look of it listening to a conversation taking place among the audience. Next to her, a large, bearded man with the round, jovial face of a jolly grandfather was smiling faintly as he glanced back and forth around his surroundings – that was Norris, without a doubt. And on the right, dark hair slicked back and smooth-shaven face moulded into an expression that oozed prosperity, a slender man lounged in his high wooden chair – watching me approach like I was something the cat had retched up during his dinner.

Halbert, I figured.

I smiled politely at him as our gazes met. His thin upper lip curled ever so slightly in response.

There was no seat for me, not entirely to my surprise; I was a supplicant, after all, not an equal partner in the conversation. I followed Delwin until he slowed down and nodded at me to stay where I was. Then I just stood there, in my frilly white dress, chin up high and hands politely interlaced behind my back, as the guardmaster retreated to the side of the hall and the crowd gradually went quiet around us. Norris finally met my gaze for the first time, granting me a warm smile. Rosalind winked at me, then averted her eyes again.

An expected silence stretched itself around us, until even the muffled curses and hissed requests at the entrance died away.

I felt suddenly naked under the weight of all those eyes.

'So,' Norris broke the quiet, with a booming voice that perfectly matched his outward appearance. In all likelihood, I considered, he had been assigned the role of main speaker because his two colleagues had vetoed each other for the task. 'A pleasure to meet you, Emelin. We have, of course, heard a lot about you.'

Regrettably, Halbert's expression said on the right.

'Thank you,' I said, returning a nervous little smile that did not require any great acting skills. 'And that is mutual, of course.'

Norris inclined his head a fraction, giving a chuckle. A few members of the audience followed his example. Most of them remained dead silent, though, waiting for the meat of the conversation – waiting, possibly, for me to start looking a little less tiny and a little more magical.

Rosalind was still smiling faintly. I took that to be a hopeful sign.

'You have of course already spoken with our esteemed colleague here,' Norris continued with a quick nod at the woman beside him, 'but we would very much like to hear your request from your own lips, Emelin. What exactly have you come here to ask the White City? Please take your time – we appreciate any information you're able to give us.'

The *we* seemed to include only him and Rosalind. Halbert was staring at the ceiling, twiddling his thumbs.

Prick.

'The short version of the matter is I'm going to kill the Mother', I said.

To my satisfaction, that made even Halbert's eyes snap back to me as the audience erupted in a flurry of agitated whispers.

'The long version ...'

They immediately became quiet again.

'The long version,' I repeated, my voice echoing through the hushed hall, 'is that we have managed to unite all magical peoples against the empire for the first time since the Last Battle – vampires, alves, phoenixes, nymphs, and a handful of fae who are sick of the Mother, too. Which means we are in a unique position – a position that will likely never be repeated – to actually do some damage to the Crimson Court.'

You could have heard a needle drop against the marble floor.

'And then there's me.' It sounded oddly ... tired to my own ears, that sentence. 'The Mother has not managed to bind my magic like she's bound the magic of every other inhabitant of the empire. Which means

I am able to harm her. I managed to blind her, last time we met. If I can get that close to her again, I plan to do a whole lot worse this time.'

A muffled cheer rose from somewhere to my right, followed by irritated hushing sounds. Again Rosalind's lips twisted up ever so slightly – like an encouragement for my eyes only. Halbert had already averted his eyes again. Norris sat listening attentively, even though nothing I was saying could be news to him.

'The main issue,' I said slowly, 'is getting that close to her again.'

I had thought this part through a thousand times last night, practicing sentences in front of a grumpy Alyra until I could dream every syllable of them. What to ask for? What *not* to ask for? I needed something big enough to be useful, yet small enough to be acceptable. Something that wouldn't sound too easy to be trusted, but nothing that sent them running and hiding behind their god-built walls.

I had gone with Rosalind's advice in the end. *Giving them a way to buy off that guilt without actually risking a single hair on their heads ...*

'The Mother has many, many warriors,' I said, spine straight, head high, voice unwavering, 'and our numbers are, unfortunately, more limited. That means we will have trouble actually entering the Crimson Court, *unless* ...' I waited a moment, just a small pause for dramatic effect. 'Unless we can force her to send part of her army elsewhere, to deal with *other* urgent trouble we have created for her.'

The murmurs picked up again. They sounded vaguely disconcerted.

'That doesn't mean I want her to attack the city,' I quickly added, because it seemed the audience needed that reassurance; indeed, a collective sigh of relief went around the gallery. 'Quite the opposite, really. I'm not going to endanger the last safe place in the archipelago. But we have been thinking of staging a revolt on one or several of the human isles out there, and to do that, we would need some help.'

Norris sank a little lower in his chair, eyes narrowing. With glimpses of shrewdness emerging in his appearance, he suddenly no longer looked nearly so jovial anymore, or so grandfatherly.

'I lived on a human isle for most of my life,' I said and wondered – with such sudden vehemence that it took all I had not to whirl around and take a look – whether any of my fellow villagers might be sitting in the audience. Hell, what were the chances *none* of Cathra's inhabitants had been curious enough to come here today? 'I believed myself to be human for most of my life. I remember – I *know* – that none of us would have dared to take a risk like actively luring an army towards us without some very firm reassurances for our safety, and I am hoping the White City might help me to offer people that safety. That might mean, for example, food for those who will lose their homes and livelihoods to the violence. Medicine for the wounded. A safe haven for their children, perhaps.'

Anything that will allow me to drop your name. Anything that will help me win their trust. It seemed wiser not to inform them of that part.

'I know you've worked hard for your peace and prosperity.' A little nod to Halbert's followers – I had decided last night it couldn't hurt to offer them a small acknowledgement. 'And you must be wary of allowing any war to disturb that peace – rightly so. But I'm hoping this might be within your capabilities, and your help may truly change the world. So I hope – I really hope – you will honestly consider it. Thank you.'

Again someone whooped behind me, a different voice this time. Rosalind didn't smile, but her almost imperceptible nod was enough – *well done*.

It made me feel like glowing, to a troubling extent.

'Thank you,' Norris said, and he sounded genuine as he sat a little straighter again, white robes pulling tight around his sizeable belly. 'That is very clear. You do not mind if we ask you a couple of questions, do you?'

I braced myself. Surely this was the moment where Halbert would stand up and bury me in biting commentary.

'Please do,' I said.

Halbert, shockingly, did not move.

'My first question is whether you have any particular islands in mind already,' Norris said, pressing his fingertips together before his stomach. 'And if not, what *sort* of an island you are thinking of. We can more easily support, say, a small mining community rather than an entire city on Orthune, for example.'

So he was considering it?

He was really, actually considering it?

Only then did I realise I had hardened my heart against guaranteed rejection, against failure and disappointment, from the very first moment they opened their mouths. It was a challenge not to sound too breathless. 'It would be a smaller island, yes. I hate putting anyone in danger at all, and I *certainly* don't want to haul a whole city into the crossfire.'

Theirs included. Even without that being said out loud, there was a hint of relief to the whispers in the hall – the growing realisation that I really was not asking them to send their children into a bloody battle.

Halbert still didn't even uncross his legs, staring into nothingness with an expression of heartfelt boredom on his slick face.

'Excellent,' Norris said, nodding slowly. 'And I assume it is not a problem if the exact nature of our assistance is determined at a later point – that is, once we know what island you are working with and how many people need help, exactly?'

'No problem at all, of course.' I hoped that was true, but Rosalind didn't show any sign of alarm amidst her regular narrow-eyed glances at Halbert. 'Specifics can be decided together. The main thing to determine is whether the city is willing to work with us at all.'

'And this is only about providing support to fellow humans, correct?' Rosalind said, leaning forward with such a convincing look of interest on her face – as if she didn't know damn well it was only about fellow humans, as if this wasn't a point she was making solely for the benefit of those listening to us. 'We're not paying to support homeless nymphs or orphaned phoenixes here?'

'Only the humans.' I allowed myself a little laugh. 'The others will be able to save themselves. I just don't want those without magic to be forgotten.'

There. A little appeal to their consciences. *Save them, since no one else will.*

From what I could glimpse of the galleries out the corners of my eyes, it was working better than I could have dared to hope. And still Halbert wasn't moving – as if this entire conversation was none of his concern anyway, as if he had merely been dragged in here because of his status and couldn't wait until he was allowed to leave again.

Perhaps he had simply betted that I would fold under the pressure and blunder myself to incoherence in the glory of this hall? He couldn't know I had survived bone halls, too.

'A very good point,' Norris was saying, nodding amiably at Rosalind. 'We certainly ought to be supporting humans only. But if that is clear, and if we agree that we can decide upon the exact budget allotted later …'

He hesitated, and my heart skipped an eager beat.

He was going to agree? *Already?* But then we had what we needed – two out of three, enough for that popular vote, no matter how hard Halbert might whine and complain. Then all we needed was to convince the rest of the city that their tax money would be put to decent use, but already people were nodding and smiling in the galleries …

'I have one last question,' a drawling voice interrupted.

My heart plunged into my stomach so swiftly I almost choked on it.

Now Halbert *was* sitting up straight, suddenly, smooth and sophisticated and handsome in a way that made my skin crawl. His smile at me was about as genuine as his non-existent fae gold, and just as fleeting. Around us, the audience had abruptly gone silent – a few hundred excited humans, all realising at the exact same time that *something* was about to happen.

If only I had the faintest idea what it was.

'Yes, Halbert?' Norris said, looking like the only person in the room blissfully unaware of the tension. The look Rosalind and Delwin exchanged did not escape me; the latter's hand suddenly lay a few inches closer to the sword at his hip.

'I was just wondering …' Halbert *savoured* the words, this frozen moment in which everyone's breathless attention lay focused on him and him alone. Slow. Theatrical. Full of honey-sweet venom. 'Could you tell us a little more about your exact relationship with the Silent Death, perhaps, Emelin?'

A sharp, collective intake of breath around me.

'I don't see how that would be related to the matter at hand,' Rosalind said, with the sharp impatience of a woman dealing with a nagging toddler. 'He's not the one asking for help, is he?'

'No,' Halbert admitted, still with that ominous sweetness lacing his words as he smiled at her and then back at me. 'No, he isn't. But we are basing our decision on the assumption that the young lady here is of sound mind and a trustworthy messenger in general, and the ... well, let's say, *rumours*' – he gave an amused little wiggle of his head – 'coming in from the Crimson Court do admittedly cast some doubt on that point. So if you don't mind, Emelin?'

Rumours. My act as Creon's witless little pet. The meal I'd spent in his lap. The ball where he'd all but torn my dress off me in the bone hall, right under the nose of the Mother herself. How much of it had made its way north – how much of it could this smirking man before me possibly have heard?

How much, I wondered with a stutter of panic in my chest, could Valter and Editta possibly have heard?

Best to play it safe. 'Do I correctly understand that you're asking me what reasons I have to trust Creon Hytherion?'

Judging by his smug expression, that was not what he was asking at all, but he said, 'That would be a good start, yes.'

'In that case,' I said slowly, 'do you know what demons are?'

The hall remained icily quiet. Judging by the infinitesimal faltering of Halbert's smirk, the answer to that question was negative.

Good.

'They're creatures capable of affecting the feelings of others,' I continued, voice deliberately flat. 'Whatever a demon makes you feel, he will feel the opposite. Alternatively, if a demon *stops* you from feeling something, he will feel the sensation instead.'

On the left, Rosalind's eyes widened abruptly – of course she had realised where I was going long before I actually arrived there. But she remained silent, did not interrupt my monologue or the breathless anticipation surrounding it.

'Creon is half demon,' I said.

More than a few people gasped behind me.

'I know all the same stories you do – I hated him as much as you do, at the start. Until he returned from one of his assignments on the brink of death and I realised – I finally understood – why no one ever screams under his knives. They don't feel the pain. He is the one feeling it all, instead – the one who has felt it all for almost a century and a half.'

It had become impossible to separate the gasping from the urgent mutters behind me, the shock rippling across the galleries on either side of the hall. The corners of Halbert's lips had not so much sagged as stiffened – the look of a man holding on to his plans and composure by his fingertips.

'So when I realised he'd done all that to *himself*,' I said with a shrug, 'that he stuck the burning pokers into his own eyes and flayed the skin off his own back, for the simple reason that he was the only one at her gods-damned court who would ever show such mercy to the people she wanted dead ... Well, after that I couldn't really go back to hating him, could I?'

Rosalind had clasped a hand over her mouth, as if that physical barrier of flesh and bones was all that could stop her from blurting out words she desperately wanted to speak. Norris muttered something beside her, looking a little nauseous.

'I see,' Halbert said, and something about his tone told me the fight wasn't over yet. Like an archer taking aim. Like a poisoner counting the drops falling into an innocent drink. 'So that is why you jumped into his bed – to comfort him?'

The hall erupted in outraged cries.

'*Halbert!*' Rosalind snapped, eyes shooting back and forth between the spectators and me with disconcerting urgency. 'This is not—'

'But it *is* relevant, esteemed colleague.' Oh, the unholy glee in his eyes – I wondered if the war even mattered to him at all, if this wasn't just a game between him and Rosalind to his mind. 'It's relevant to everyone in this room. We've all lost friends to that monster, haven't we? We've lost family to that monster?'

Her expression was just shy of an eyeroll. *Did you really?* that look suggested. *You, city-born to affluent parents?*

But all she said was, 'And as Emelin clearly explained a minute ago, there's a little more to those executions than—'

'Emelin is suspiciously silent, though, isn't she?' He turned to me, grinning like a man who's just scored the winning point in a particularly exciting game of hearts and bells. 'Almost as if she's trying to hide something. Tell us, Emelin – are they true, the rumours? Did you fuck him?'

There was one split second to deny it.

One last moment to lie – as one half of the hall broke out in furious objections to his language and the other half cheered and laughed – to pull an indignant face and tell him I would *never*, and did I really look like the kind of girl who would throw her honour away like that?

But I was not lying about Creon again.

I'd sworn I would never lie about Creon again.

'You make it sound like a crime, Halbert,' I heard myself say, and somehow my voice was still bright and clear over the roar of the audience, my words carried swiftly to the back of the hall by dozens of eager whispers. 'You do realise it's a rather common activity between adults in love, don't you?'

One moment of baffled silence.

On the left side of the stage, Rosalind closed her eyes.

And then the howls and the shouts were back, louder than ever before – clamouring for the meeting to end, for Rosalind to take back her vote, for me to be thrown out of the city. There were other voices in there, too, arguing stubbornly that my private choices really didn't matter as much as my ability to do away with the fae empire ... but they were few and far between and not nearly as brash as Halbert's zealous supporters.

I wondered, with a pang of vicious scepticism, if he'd paid for them to be here and shout.

'Well,' Norris said, glancing around somewhat nervously. 'I do suppose that changes things, if ...'

A defeat – but gods help me, somehow my heart refused to feel defeated. A brand new fight came bubbling up in my chest as I stood there, scorn and fury raining down around me; it rose with a stubborn spite that surprised me as much as anyone, a resolve I hadn't known I possessed. Damn them, but I would not slink out of this hall like a beaten old dog, tail between my legs. I would not show shame for *loving*.

'Changes things?' I said coolly, and the noise died down a little – even the most vehement of onlookers too curious to miss a single word. 'Why? Because I'm prepared to be honest with you? Would you have preferred for me to lie?'

'We would have preferred you not to be spreading your legs for a man with human blood on his hands,' Halbert cut in, rising from his seat with a swagger that drew a new round of cheers from the audience. He was clearly starting to enjoy himself. 'We would have preferred for you to possess a modicum of self-respect, rather than—'

'That's *enough*,' Rosalind burst out.

Be it from shock or obedience, the hall instantaneously fell silent again.

'This is beyond the pale even for *you*,' she spat, rising to her feet as well – a head and a half shorter than Halbert, but the cold fire burning in those sharp blue eyes made up for every inch of it. 'You're supposed to be a consul of the White City, not some lecherous gossip milking matters of life and death for scandal!'

'And you,' Halbert returned, still smiling gleefully, 'are equally supposed to be a consul of the White City, rather than a champion of little fae whores without a grain of—'

She moved so fast I didn't even see it coming.

Three, four steps. A blur of white as her arm swung up, and then the *smack* of her palm against his cheek, reverberating through the stunned hall like a thunderclap, drawing startled gasps from the audience around us. I cried out in wordless shock. On the edge of my sight, Delwin was reaching for his sword.

'*Rosalind*!' Norris panted, jerking back in his chair as if she might be coming for him next.

She didn't seem to hear any of us.

'Don't you *dare*.' Her voice had gone low and hoarse, the words spat into Halbert's face as he dazedly prodded his reddening cheek. Her hands had balled into white-knuckled fists. 'Don't you dare call my daughter a fae whore *ever again*, you fucking *swine*.'

The world stuttered.

Stiffened.

Or perhaps it was my own mind grinding to a crawl, too paralysed to absorb the gasps and gulps around me, too paralysed to string two thoughts of sense together.

Daughter.

Had she really just said ... *daughter*?

But then—

Then—

'What?' I heard myself say.

'What?' Halbert said in the same moment.

'Oh, and yes, I did the same thing,' she bit out, breathing heavily as she stepped away from him and wiped her palm on her robes. 'Spread my legs for a man with human blood on his hands. So are you going to spit on me, now? Are any of you?'

Rosalind.

Allie.

My thoughts wouldn't move swift enough, nimble enough, to wrap themselves around whatever the hell was happening.

'Here's what you don't understand,' she added, turning away from Halbert and his sagging jaw, her voice loud and clear in the breathless silence. 'What *none* of you understands. This isn't about liking or disliking. It isn't about spotless morals or clearly drawn lines. It's about *survival* – of you and me as much as of anyone trying to live outside these walls.'

She was speaking to the galleries, to the hundreds of bewildered eyes blinking at her from above. To the majestic statues. To the marble pillars and walls, the high windows and the sunlight dazzling through them to illuminate every speck of dust whirling around in the silence.

To everything, really, except for me.

Gods help me, why wasn't she looking at me? I hadn't *dreamed* it, had I, that she'd said ...

My daughter. My daughter. The words pulsed through my skull like a persistent headache, numbing every other sound around me.

'The Mother's empire is only getting stronger,' Rosalind continued, her sharp words reaching me from miles and miles away – marching on, unaffected, as if the floor wasn't sinking away beneath my feet. As if she hadn't just upended my entire existence with a single resounding slap and a few snapped words. 'The rest of the world is only getting weaker. If they don't kill the bitch now, they *never* will – and once she's done away with that bigger threat between our borders, where do you all think her eyes will wander next? Do you really believe she'll contently sit down on that throne she built from *our* bones and gladly accept there is nothing left to conquer?'

You seem to have inherited your mother's talent for shouting rather convincingly, Agenor had said, and gods help me, I could see it now – the paling faces as her words sank in, the shocked murmurs rippling through their ranks.

Rosalind didn't move, didn't flinch. The words kept spilling from her lips.

'I stood before that throne, twenty-two years ago,' she said, and all I heard was that number, the weight behind it. Twenty-two years. *Just before you were born.* 'I know exactly what her magic is capable of. So trust me, by the time she's able to devote a century or two to this city, by the time she no longer has any magical enemies to worry about … The walls *will* fall. Sooner or later, I promise you they will.'

Someone had started crying behind me – quiet, muffled sobs.

'So don't be idiots,' she finished and turned to Norris – ignoring Halbert entirely, in a wordless but crystal-clear message that he'd likely fail that simple assignment anyway. 'Fight her while we still can. It might be the last chance humanity will ever have.'

I realised I wasn't breathing.

That *had* to be enough, surely? No one with an ounce of sense in their minds could refuse a plea like that, could they?

But Norris hesitated, dumbfounded gaze travelling from Rosalind to me to the audience that had just shouted at him so vehemently. His lips moved erratically without producing a single sound.

'This is hardly the moment to start worrying about your re-election, Norris,' Rosalind added impatiently.

That broke the spell. 'But ... but we can't ...'

She scoffed. '*We?*'

'Well, *I* can't just— We have no idea—'

'Is that a no?' she cut in, voice so sharp that even I flinched on the other consul's behalf. 'Are you going to refuse to act?'

'Look, we're talking about *murderers*,' he sputtered with an incoherent gesture at me. 'How can we trust the ... your ... Emelin – hell, how can we trust *you* – if—'

'I see.' There was no hint of disappointment in her voice – just cold, factual observation. But her fingers trembled as she lifted her hand to her chest and yanked off the lily brooch pinned to her white robe. 'Thank you. That's clear enough.'

'Wait,' Norris blurted. 'Wait, what are you—'

The silver lily clattered against the marble floor in response.

'I'm resigning,' she pleasantly informed him, bunching up her robe to pull it over her head. A slim, blue-grey dress appeared below; she chucked the robe into a shapeless heap next to the brooch and smoothed her skirt back in place. 'I'm sick of catering to cowards. Time for war. Let's go, Em.'

It came out quieter, that last sentence – softer, perhaps. I stumbled half a step back, feeling the walls folding in on me, and stammered, 'But ... but we ...'

But we have failed. But we still need to convince them.

And only then did she meet my eye, stepping off the low stage in the numb, tense silence. *There* was the emotion, finally, every feeling her words had lacked; her eyes gleamed with age-old hurt, with regret and apologies, with a plea I felt down to the tips of my toes.

'Please.' She mouthed the word as she passed me, one hand brushing over my upper arm in a gentle, hesitant nudge. 'Come.'

Heart trumped duty again.

I turned mechanically, marvelling at the way my knees held steady, the way my feet carried me after her and towards the doors without crumbling beneath me. I half expected the gaping masses at the exit to block our way out, but they parted as if by command as Rosalind approached, letting us pass in palpable silence.

In the hall behind me, the first whispers picked up.

I could no longer care. I pushed the failures and consequences away, blocked every muttering voice from my mind, as I followed Rosalind up the stairs—

No.

Zera help me – as I followed my *mother* up the stairs.

Chapter 23

Following her through the maze of corridors felt like walking deeper and deeper into a dream – the situation growing more surreal by the step, somehow, even as the pieces of the puzzle began falling into place.

Emelin of Agenor's house, she'd said.

And she would know, wouldn't she?

I could tell myself it made sense, yet it didn't – that this was the same woman whose hand had scribbled those notes in Agenor's books, the woman whose wrist had once borne the other half of that bargain mark he still carried. The woman whose nameless face I'd dreamed of for months on end, now suddenly *here* and *tangible* and so very much a person it made me feel dizzy with disbelief.

Had it been just as overwhelming for her, to watch me step out of that chaise from her vantage point behind the window?

I might have asked her if I'd had the faintest idea how to address her now.

But I did not, and she did not turn around, striding up the stairs and down the corridors as if she'd never move again if she made the mistake of faltering for even a moment. So I drifted after her in silence, unable to stop turning every word she'd spoken over and over in my thoughts …

Is this one of your father's ideas?

Just a little too much intimate knowledge of Agenor's mind – like an inside joke, almost. She *knew* those ideas. She knew them because *she* was the one who'd punched him from his lethargic state of existence twenty-two years ago and made him see—

'Here we are,' she said quietly.

That was enough to yank me back into the here and now.

The door she opened led into a light, spacious room, decorated with little more than a few potted plants and a host of knitted pillows. Most of the available space was taken up by piles and piles of parchment – books and letters and maps and scrolls, all stacked haphazardly on every available surface, cluttering shelves and chairs and three quarters of the dining table. Two packed bags stood next to the couch, partially buried beneath more documents. They must have stood there for a while, then, my remaining sensible thoughts deducted; she must have been prepared to leave.

Had she known this would likely be the outcome of our meeting? Or would she have resigned her post no matter what had happened?

My daughter. My daughter. My daughter.

'Tea?' Rosalind said, closing the door behind me and brushing past me to head for the kitchen.

'Yes,' I said blankly and then hastily added, 'Please,' because it seemed proper to show some manners when meeting your mother for the first time.

The sound of a running tap emerged from around the corner, followed by the thud of a kettle onto a stove. I stood and waited, trying to make myself say something and failing miserably – how in the world would I make the unfurling chaos of my thoughts fit into something as small as words? She'd been so easy to talk to, a mere twenty-four hours ago. Now every secret, every lie and expectation, lay like lead on my tongue – what did you say to the stranger who'd held you in her arms before anyone else in the world?

'Milk?' she yelled from the kitchen. 'Honey?'

I swallowed. 'No, thank you.'

Rosalind returned to the living room the next moment, a steaming teapot in one hand, two mugs in the other, a look of cautious apology in her eyes. They were nothing like mine, those eyes – I couldn't help but notice. Her nose, though ... Vaguely familiar, perhaps. The colour of her hair. Those thin wrists. My gaze had become a scavenger, hunting for clues – for certainty, for facts that could not be masked or twisted by lies.

'So,' she said, voice tired. 'Apologies, first of all. Not how I was planning to tell you – I got a little carried away. Bastards.'

Something laugh-like escaped me.

She waited another moment, as if she expected me to say more, then slowly added, 'I imagine you might have some questions.'

Yes.

Questions.

Is this a dream? I wanted to say.

Why didn't you tell me? I wanted to say.

I missed you before I knew I was missing anything, I wanted to say, *needed you more than I needed even food in that small, barren place where I was always the problem, always too much – and you wanted me, didn't you? You got me here? So where were you when I was told I cried too noisily, or when they locked me in my room whenever guests came over? Where were you when my world burned down?*

Instead ...

Instead, the first thing I heard myself say out loud was, 'Who in hell shortens Rosalind to *Allie*?'

'Oh.' With a nervous chuckle, she turned to put the mugs down on the dinner table; she seemed more than happy to keep her gaze on her hands as she poured the tea, steam whirling from the cups. 'Family name – they were forced to get creative. We had hordes of Rosies and Sallies and Allies and the occasional Lindie around.'

Agenor's voice echoed in my ears, speaking of my name. *A fae equivalent of one of your mother's family names or the human equivalent of one mine ...*

Good gods. Why had I never asked what those human traditions had entailed – what my name would have been if I had been born with pointy ears and wings?

'I see,' I managed.

She put down the teapot, watching me expectantly with those bright blue eyes.

Zera help me, it couldn't be this hard, could it? Tell me what you've been up to for the past twenty years – that was a reasonable question to ask. *Tell me why you never wrote to Agenor. Tell me what game you're playing now, giving up all you've built here for a losing war.* But the words felt hollow and insufficient on my lips – what if those were not the questions she wanted to hear, not the questions she had expected from me?

Talking to Consul Rosalind had been easy. Hell, the worst I could do with a political ally was lose her. A mother, though ...

A mother, I could *disappoint*.

'Um,' I started, desperately. 'Um, I suppose you could perhaps—'

A sharp, ticking sound interrupted me.

I whirled around, alarmed – were the walls crumbling down? Had masses of furious citizens gathered to throw pebbles at the windows? But all I found, sitting small and fluffy on the sill ...

Alyra.

Glaring at me with little dagger eyes as she pecked ferociously at the glass.

'Oh, good gods,' Rosalind said, a breathless laugh in her voice – like a sudden release of tension. 'Is it here for you?'

'Um, yes.' I grimaced, stepping over a pile of books to make my way to the window. 'Her name's Alyra. You see, when Zera swore me in ...'

'Yes,' she said. 'I wondered about that. At least it's not more of those bloody snakes.'

I laughed despite myself, swinging open the window. Alyra shot in with a shriek of excitement, landed on the back of an empty chair, and stayed there, hopping impatiently up and down – her thoughts flooding my own once again, more urgently now. *Dangling worms. Warm, soft wings. Again that little nest, blue eggs on a little bed of moss* ...

Oh, gods help me.

Eggs.

'You had already figured it out?' My voice shot up a little. 'You knew who she was and you tried to tell me by showing me *eggs?*'

Obviously, she informed me with a roll of her beady eyes. How else was I supposed to learn that I had crawled out of Rosalind's egg twenty-one years ago? Granted, she wasn't sure what human eggs looked like, but that seemed a rather minor detail; and had I really not seen the link between those lovely, tasty worms and whatever this woman had fed me in my earliest hours?

Right.

'Very clever,' I numbly said, because this seemed an inopportune moment to teach my familiar about the intricacies of human procreation, and either way, I just wanted her to stop chirping at me so shrilly. 'Look, could you fly back to the others and let them know I'm still alive? I'll probably be back with them within ... well, soon.'

Alyra either didn't notice the hint of defeat or didn't care about it; she hopped up and down once more on her improvised perch, waiting patiently. I reached below my skirt, clumsily untied one of the ribbons that held my dagger in place, and handed it over.

She snatched it from my fingers and took off, soaring out of the open window with a cry of goodbye.

'Don't see a snake doing that anytime soon,' Rosalind dryly said as I shut the panes.

I managed to choke out a laugh. When I turned back around, she had sat down on one side of the moss-green couch with her cup of tea in her lap, the other half of the seat conspicuously empty – as close to an invitation as one could get. It would be so very easy to sit down beside her, to curl against that lithe, frail body and find out if her scent was still familiar to me ...

My legs didn't move.

'You didn't tell me.' It was easier to speak now that Alyra had reminded me how to move my tongue. The accusation in the words was unintentional, though. 'Why didn't you tell me the moment I walked into the White Hall? Was there some test I needed to pass before you—'

'No!' Her voice shot up. 'Please, Em. None of that. I just ... well ...'

A small silence. She sat fidgeting with her mug, lips hesitating around three, four versions of whatever she was about to say.

'I just wanted to be sure I could trust you,' she finally finished, quietly.

'*Trust* me?'

'Or more specifically, that I could trust Agenor.' A joyless laugh. 'And since he found you first ... Well, I figured I should first find out what game *he* had been playing in the past two decades.'

Because she knew as well as I did that my father was usually playing *some* sort of game. It was unnerving, for this almost-stranger to understand so much of me, so much of my history; it made me feel like my mind was running twenty years behind hers.

'You considered the possibility that he might be manipulating me?' I said slowly.

'I considered many things.' She briefly closed her eyes, running a slender fingertip over her temple. 'He— You know what, let's start at the beginning. I suppose he gave you a rough outline of what happened, those months before you were born?'

I grimaced. 'You stole his stuff and called him an idiot, he found out he *was* an idiot, and then things escalated?'

She burst out laughing. 'Concise yet accurate. Anything else?'

'He told me the Mother lured him away and arrested you. And then you bargained with her and outsmarted her, and because the bargain forced her to keep you alive, she had to keep Agenor away for a while and put him in chains – is that all correct?'

'Well, the last part is new to me,' she said wryly, 'but otherwise, yes.'

I stared at her.

She took a sip of tea, grimacing at the heat, and added, 'The Mother was not so charitable, of course, as to explain to me *why* I suddenly found myself abandoned at the heart of a failed resistance effort with a child due in five weeks.'

'You didn't know?' It came out hoarse. 'Before I told you yesterday that she'd kept him captive, you didn't *know* ...'

'Well.' A painful smile. 'No.'

I realised a moment too late my jaw had started sagging.

'I wasn't even sure whether he was alive when she banished me after you were born,' Rosalind added, staring at the whirling steam over her mug. 'Or when I dropped myself off that ship with a large wooden shutter at night and swam to the nearest island. But by the time I arrived on Furja and found out that my father and little brothers had been killed years ago, the only news I managed to scrounge also said Agenor was back at the Crimson Court and by all accounts still obligingly serving the Mother. So ...' She looked up at me, raw hurt in her eyes. 'I knew he wouldn't have been able to actively betray me – that our bargain wouldn't have allowed him to. But I did strongly consider that he might deliberately have looked away while the Mother went after me, yes.'

I staggered my way through the three steps to the dinner table, sinking into a chair with wobbly legs. 'So that's why you never sent word to him? Even though you were technically safe here?'

'I was,' she said, voice strained. 'You weren't.'

Something violently clenched in my throat.

'I had no idea where you'd gone, you understand?' The tremble was unmistakable now. 'I didn't even know whether you'd been smuggled out by humans or magical beings. The only reason I agreed to it was because the alternative was you staying in that hell for the rest of your life, and I couldn't ... I *couldn't*—'

She gasped in a breath, tucking a lock of dark brown hair behind her ear with shaking hands. I grabbed for my tea blindly, took a single minuscule sip; the scorching hot water wasn't enough to wash away that thorny little catch.

'So it was like looking for a drop in the ocean, looking for you,' she added, audibly fighting to collect herself. 'But I knew Agenor would have resources I didn't. Our bargain protected me, not you. And if he was still on her side, if he was just going to hand you over to her to be bound the moment he found you ...'

Again she faltered a moment.

'You couldn't be forced or tricked to give him any information as long as he didn't hear from you?' I somehow got out.

She drew in a deep breath. 'Yes.'

'And in the meantime ...'

'I was looking.' An almost apologetic shrug at the maps and letters around us. 'You should have heard me drivel on about orphans and foundling children and the programmes we might set up to help them. Told them I needed all caretakers of such children to write to me, in order to make an estimate of the extent of the problem, spent years tracking every single child of hazy parentage I received letters about. And then after twenty years – after *twenty fucking years* – some painter arrived here with his whole village and claimed that his adopted daughter Emelin had been abducted and taken to the Crimson Court.'

My heart skipped a beat. 'He told you?'

'He had no idea who I was, of course.' A bitter laugh. 'I about died on the spot – all that effort to keep you away from the gods-damned island, and then they'd taken you there anyway? But then the news came that someone had burned the Mother's eyes right from her face and I *knew* – oh, I knew *immediately* that that had been you.'

Celebrating all victories as if they had been her own, I'd thought yesterday, and only now I understood – because in a way, through twenty years of heartache and fear, the victory *had* been hers.

'And then you still didn't write,' I said.

'Oh, I tried.' She shook her head. 'But as far as the news suggested, you had vanished into nowhere. And it's rare for any magical creatures to show up at the gates – my predecessors have refused any sort of coalition too often for them to keep making the effort. As much as I would have liked to ask them about you, I needed a contact I could trust first.'

That made so much sense I wasn't sure why I hadn't thought of it myself.

'And then the battle at the Golden Court happened,' she added, 'and it turned out Agenor still had his wits about him after all – but when I tried to write to him, he was surrounded by fae warships. Bloody hard to get a letter through under those circumstances.'

The Moon fleet. I thought of the arrow in Creon's back and couldn't help but wince – hadn't Agenor himself said that no one but alves had been able to reach the court after that siege had started?

'I'd been dispatching messages to all human islands,' Rosalind said sheepishly, 'asking them to look out for magical visitors and tell them to contact the White City. I was *that* desperate. And then out of nowhere ...' She swallowed. 'Your letter.'

We've been hoping you would reach out to us.

Something was stinging the back of my eyes.

'I wrote back before I told the others,' she added with a joyless laugh. 'Figured that if they tried to stop me, at least you would still be here the next day. Then packed my bags. Then tried to figure out how in the world I'd tell you all of this.'

I snorted a laugh. 'And the plan on which you arrived was to blurt out the sordid facts at some arsehole of a consul with the whole world watching?'

'Oh, no. That was all divine inspiration in the spur of the moment.' She wiped her eyes with the back of her hand, corners of her lips trembling. 'No, I was thinking I'd wait until we had the political games behind us – figured it would all be overwhelming enough and ... well ... you were clearly trying to focus on the matter of strategy ...'

It hit me, then.

An understanding of such perfect clarity, again, that it truly was a marvel it hadn't occurred to me the very first time she'd hastily averted her eyes.

'You were *scared*,' I said.

She froze. 'Oh, gods help the mothers of clever children.'

Laughter escaped me, a surge of relief. 'And that's all? No tests or expectations? You just didn't dare to—'

'Yes, of course I was scared!' she burst out, shoving her tea aside with such a brusque gesture that it splashed onto her bluish grey dress. 'Maybe you wouldn't even care! Maybe you'd be disappointed in me! Maybe the last thing you wanted was *more* parents, after those ... those ...'

Her voice drifted off into the territory of sheer unspeakability.

Plenty of humans would have been proud to call themselves your parents.
'Oh,' I managed, throat constricting again.

'I could have *killed* them, Em.' She bit out the words without any of that casual fae cruelty, that joyful bloodlust of alves, that indifference towards murder that came with life in a world of war. These were the words of a woman whose violence *meant* something. 'When I first spoke with them and they kept telling me how they'd finally gotten rid of you, how they hadn't wanted you in the first place, as if they expected praise for being heartless cowards ...'

My chest was drawing tighter, tighter, tighter. Breathe, I had to *breathe*, but the air escaped my lungs in squeaking gasps, and my throat felt like coarse sand – and yet the pain was different this time, not that gaping hole in my heart. It was closer to anger, this feeling. Closer to fire.

It burned behind my eyelids, too, threatening to spill over.

'I couldn't make sense of it,' Rosalind whispered, unseeing eyes trained on the floor between our feet. 'I still can't, truly. How dare they get what I so desperately wanted and then handle it so poorly? How dare they refuse so heartlessly what I could hardly bear to give up?'

I no longer felt my fingers. I no longer felt my feet.

'I held you for half an hour. After you were born.' Her voice was barely audible now. 'The most beautiful minutes of my life, and then I had to let you go without knowing if I'd ever see you again. And now you're *here*, Em, and I can barely make sense of that either—'

And just like that, the fog shattered.

Just like that, it was real.

Gone was the paralysis, that dreamlike haze clouding my mind; I stood without thinking, moved without thinking. Who needed reason, after all? Who needed thoughts when instinct took over with such brilliant clarity?

I fell into the seat beside her as if I'd never done anything else. Curled up against her shoulder like a small, scared child and clutched my arms around her willowy frame, soaking up the soft jasmine scent of her body, the quiet strength of her touch, the soothing, unmistakable warmth of living human skin. She let out a choked sound and cradled me in her arms, forehead bumping against the crown of my head – my mother, holding me.

A hot tear dripped onto my temple, and then another one.

'My baby girl,' she whispered, voice shaking on the edge of sobs. 'Oh, my darling, darling baby girl ...'

And then, finally, I was crying too.

Chapter 24

We were halfway through a late and rather teary lunch of scrambled eggs, slightly stale bread, and a wrinkled apple from the back of the pantry when the letter was slipped underneath the door.

Rosalind flipped it over, scanned it, and handed it to me with a heartfelt scoff. The note was short, just a few scrabbled lines:

Please tell the girl she'll have to leave the city tomorrow morning. If you wish to go with her, we can make arrangements.
- Norris

'Arseholes,' Rosalind said, one cheek bulging with egg.

I stared at those few short sentences and tried to squash the sense of failure creeping back up on me.

As easy as it was to ignore the fact between these walls, sitting in my mother's small yet tidy kitchen and exchanging stories of our respective times at the Crimson Court ... The world outside hadn't changed. The war hadn't been averted. Soon I'd be back in the Underground, having won a parent but lost the dream of a human army, and then what would we do?

Smooth magic, after all?

Those hollow eyes ... My stomach clenched violently.

'It might not be so bad,' Rosalind said, watching me closely. 'Perhaps I'll be able to help. Some of the human communities out there might feel reassured that a former consul of the White City is joining the cause.'

They might. And then again ... they might not.

'Yes,' I said, forcing myself to shove Norris's letter aside and pick up my fork again. 'We'll see.'

She gave me a small, encouraging smile. 'So, what were you saying about the Mother's throne before we got interrupted?'

We spent the rest of the afternoon that way – first with more tea, then with a bottle of wine Rosalind pulled from somewhere and that she claimed was too good to be left behind. She told me about Furja, the island where she'd lived until her father had unwisely argued for lower tribute rates in a bad year. I talked about Ildhelm, about Miss Matilda, about the dresses. She treated me to a decade of political city gossip, until we were both crying with laughter over the consul who had, three years ago, resigned after his mother marched into a confidential meeting and threatened to spank him for his poor treatment of his wife.

She did not speak a single word about Agenor, and I did not ask.

Evening fell. We dined on leftover parsnips and soft-boiled eggs, for lack of motivation to go out and get some more proper food. Outside the building, some clamour arose around nightfall, but it died away swiftly; the dusk offered no clues as to what it might have been. While footsteps passed through the corridor outside our door ever now and then, no one was brave enough to knock and disturb us.

We finished the wine. It had to be past midnight by that point.

I ought to have been on my way to bed, I knew; I was supposed to leave the next day, and Halbert likely wouldn't be happy to let me sleep until noon. But it was so blissfully easy to sit there and talk and talk and talk to a mother who looked like me, who thought like me, who knew the human world *and* the fae world like me ...

The building had gone eerily silent by the time our conversation began to ebb, hours past midnight. I was yawning, curled up on the couch with a blanket. Rosalind, her hair sagging from its pins and her voice a fraction slurred by wine or tiredness or both, threw a glance at the window as if she only now realised the sky had gone dark outside.

'Might be time to go to sleep,' I mumbled.

'Yes,' she admitted, rubbing her eyes with a sigh. 'Might be.'

So I disentangled myself from the blanket, hugged her a last time and a *really* last time, and tiptoed out into the dark corridors, feeling my way up the stairs and around the corners by touch and luck more than anything else. The door I finally pushed open turned out to be my own, thankfully; I slipped in, shut the lock behind me, and stared at the large guest bed for a few bleary-eyed moments. It looked ... cold, more than anything. It looked empty.

Outside, on the front side of the building, incoherent shouts were rising from the square every now and then, contrasting sharply with the peaceful silence of the previous night. When I squinted out between the curtains, though, there was little to be seen but the faint flicker of torches around the corner.

The sense of approaching doom didn't soften.

I told myself not to exaggerate as I brushed my hair and undressed, and then jumped anyway when another chorus of bellowing erupted close by, my heart thumping against my ribs at twice its usual speed. I checked the lock three times. I put a dagger on my nightstand and one below my pillow. I searched the bathroom just to make sure no one was lying in wait for me in the bath, and then somehow I felt even *more* anxious as I finally crawled beneath the blankets, staring wide-eyed at the ceiling as my pulse continued to race.

Would Rosalind be asleep already?

I doubted it, somehow. She had looked tired but far from drowsy. And if she, too, was hearing the irregular bursts of activity surrounding the White Hall ...

Oh, to hell with it.

The decision made itself. I rolled out of bed, groped around for my dress in the darkness, then found my backpack and chucked my daggers back into it – no sense in lying here waiting for dawn to come if I wasn't going to sleep anyway. At least I had kept most of my belongings in one place. Even in the depth of night, I was reasonably sure I'd managed to pack everything when I finally swung my bag over my shoulder and ventured out into the dark maze of the building again.

Around the corner and another corner. Down the stairs.

A thin line of candlelight was still visible in the chink beneath the door.

I knocked, keeping my voice hushed. 'Rosalind?'

She opened the door within moments, almost as if she'd been waiting for me to return – not yet asleep, then, although she'd changed into her nightdress. Her eyes were just a little red in the candlelight. Her smile, though quiet and wistful, was no less radiant for it.

'Of course,' she said softly before I could even open my mouth. 'Come in.'

And so I found myself curling up in my mother's bed minutes later, the daggers left in my bag this time, the bathroom unsearched. She blew out the candles, then joined me. In the dark, her slow breathing was a soothing lullaby to my ears – we had no army, no magic, and yet that quiet, even sound reassured me time and time again that all would be well in the end.

'Good night,' I whispered.

Her hand brushed over the crown of my head, as soft as her voice. 'Good night, baby girl.'

This time, I fell asleep within minutes.

I woke to an explosion of noise.

Bellowing voices, clattering horse hooves ... I shot up in the blankets, half-expecting a mob to break through the bedroom door in the same moment, ready to remove the unwanted fae guest from the city by any means necessary. Only after blinking the dreams from my mind did I realise the sound was too distant to be inside: close, yes, but at least outside the walls of the White Hall.

Somehow, that wasn't much of a reassurance to my pounding heart.

'Good gracious,' Rosalind blearily said next to me, rolling over. 'What is going on?'

'It's *your* city,' I said.

She laughed, combing her hair from her face with her fingers as she sat upright; it was unmistakably a tense laugh, though. 'Not anymore, I'm afraid.'

'Do you think …' I swallowed, glancing at the curtains covering the window. Judging by the pale sunlight brushing the heavy fabric, the sun had barely risen. 'Do you think they're here for me?'

'Hope not,' she said sourly.

That was not nearly the comforting answer I'd have preferred.

We dressed in a hurry, without speaking much. Outside, the commotion did not subside; quite the opposite, it sounded as though whatever was happening was only escalating. I tried to find some answers through the windows, but they overlooked the garden behind the White Hall, where I couldn't spot anything unusual going on. Which meant the sound was coming from the *other* side of the building. Which meant there had to be an even larger crowd to produce a roar this loud.

Hundreds, if not thousands of people … and there weren't that many reasons for them to gather there, now, on this morning, were there?

Had Halbert drummed up his supporters to offer me a fitting goodbye?

Worse, had that particular segment of the citizenry decided the little fae whore wasn't leaving fast enough for their taste?

'Come,' Rosalind said as I braided my hair with trembling hands. 'There's a common drawing room nearby that looks out over the square.'

I snatched a dagger from my bag before following her.

Whatever was happening didn't leave the rest of the city government unaffected; a few doors away, just outside the living area of the consuls, clerks were shouting urgently at each other. But no one seemed to have thought of informing us what was going on, and we did not run into anyone as we made our way to the cosily furnished sitting room. I almost stumbled over the edge of a rug as I hurried to the windows on the other side, yanking the gauzy curtains aside with so much force it was a surprise they didn't come down.

The square outside was packed with people.

People, more specifically, carrying weapons.

My heart gave a panicked stutter – hundreds and hundreds of men and women standing at our doorstep, carrying swords and bows and the occasional pitchfork, their laughter and rough voices filling the air. If they tried to hurt me ... Zera help me, I'd have to use magic. Lots of it. And if I was forced to mow down a horde of fae-hunting humans, then how would anyone ever trust me again in the non-magical world? How would we ever—

'They're not here to hurt us,' Rosalind said, squinting at the crowd beside me.

I blinked.

And only then did I realise she was right.

Weapons, yes ... but if I looked closer, the gathered group did not exactly resemble a furious mob in any other way. There was no shouting at the consuls, no chanting for me to come out and defend myself. There were no rallying speeches. They were loud, yes, but if I studied the faces I could make out two floors down, it was a lively, excited sort of loudness – the merry raucousness of men and women about to set off on an adventure.

I blinked again.

An adventure.

No. No, those were nonsensical thoughts welling up in my mind, driven by desperate hopes and dreams rather than by clear and logical observation. Of course they had some other reason to stand here, armed and buzzing with excitement. Of course they weren't here to ...

Gods help me.

Were they here to come *with* us?

Unlikely. Impossible.

But some of them had brought horses – why would anyone bring *horses* to lynch a fae girl and her treasonous mother? And many of them, I registered only now, were carrying large backpacks on their shoulders. Which once again only made sense if—

'Dear gods,' Rosalind whispered. 'Dear *gods*.'

An incredulous smile was trembling around the corners of her lips when I glanced at her, inching closer and closer to a victorious burst of laughter. It was that smile that finally pushed me over the edge – impossible, yes, but if *she* believed it …

We had an army?

We had a bloody *army*.

I turned back to the square below, a breathless laugh releasing itself from my lips at the sight. Zera help me, an army. They must have heard Rosalind's speech, these hundreds and hundreds of people, or perhaps they'd heard about it from friends who had been there. They must have started whispering about it, quietly at first – *So do you think she was right? Do you think we're in danger?*

And at some point, the first of them must have said it out loud. After dinner, I imagined, and emboldened by a pint of beer: *Damn it all, I'm going with them.*

Those bursts of excitement I'd heard outside my window last night had not been threats. The opposite. I'd heard the news spread around me, going from door to door, from family to family – hell, I had unknowingly witnessed the first mass mobilisation in the history of the White City.

War had crept into this corner of the world after all.

I stared blindly at those beaming faces outside and wanted to laugh and cry at once.

'Let's go down,' Rosalind said, a soft hand on my shoulder. 'I imagine some people are waiting to hear from us.'

Yes.

Armies needed symbols, after all.

'Let's get our bags,' I said, irrationally eager to delay the moment another two minutes.

So we got our bags and then left our wing of the building, venturing into the chaos that had taken hold of the White Hall. Past the panicked clerks, who were frantically browsing lawbooks and shrieking things about principles of self-determination; past tense flocks of guards, who paced the halls in their pristine white uniforms and toyed with their swords. No one quite seemed to know what to do with us. Most people seemed wary of even meeting our gaze as we passed their offices – as if it was some mind-clouding spell, that eagerness to go out and fight, and they too might just jump to leave their spouses and children the moment our eyes found each other.

Far too soon, we'd reached the last broad flight of stairs.

Two men stood in the middle of the hall below, surrounded by a few dozen guards as they gesticulated wildly at each other – white robes, red faces. Norris and Halbert.

The former looked close to tears. The latter looked closer to an exploding stove than I'd thought any healthy human being could possibly look.

'... can't possibly *let* them!' he was snapping, his fists balled. 'What for the gods' sakes is a human citizen's business on a magical battlefield? They're barely trained to fight. They have no idea what they're in for. If we see a quarter of them back alive, I'll consider it a positive surprise, for the bloody gods' sakes!'

'Look, you *know* I agree with you,' Norris hissed loudly, his broad chest heaving – and for a single flinching moment, I found myself agreeing, too. 'But they're grown adults, aren't they? We don't have any laws to stop them, and as long as the third consul hasn't been elected, we can't *make* any laws either ...'

It was then that they simultaneously noticed us.

Norris grew even redder. Halbert, on the other hand, paled to a rather unflattering shade of grey at the sight of Rosalind – the look of a man who knows himself defeated by an opponent he considers decidedly beneath him.

'*You!*' he bit out, and that one word contained half a decade of mutual loathing.

'Morning, colleagues,' Rosalind said coolly, and although she looked perfectly unflappable, the hint of sharpness below the surface was unmistakable. 'Interesting developments, aren't they? Is there any reason why we shouldn't go out and have a word with the people waiting for us, from a perspective of general security?'

'Security?' Halbert spat, jutting a sharp, trembling finger at her. '*Security*, Rosalind?'

She arched up a single elegant eyebrow. 'Do you take issue with the concept?'

'You'll murder them, you *witch*!' Droplets of spittle were flying out with the words, landing on the empty battlefield between us. 'Is your pride worth that much? Two thousand people out there, and you'll lure them all to a senseless death with your lies and your ... your ...'

'My leg-spreading?' she dryly suggested.

Halbert glared at me, then saw the dagger in my hand and gulped.

'Odd as the notion may sound to you,' Rosalind added, smiling even more icily, 'some people have principles for which they are willing to make sacrifices. If you are determined they need their minds changed, you're free to make an attempt yourself, of course.'

Halbert turned purple.

'He tried to speak to them,' Norris whispered from behind his hand, as if his colleague wouldn't notice. 'They *laughed*.'

Despite myself, I had to suppress a snigger at that.

'Did they?' Rosalind said, lips twisting. 'Well, that quite settles the matter, doesn't it? In that case— Oh, Delwin!'

We all whipped around just in time to see Delwin slip in through the high front gate and shut it behind his back again. There was a grimness to his expression that told me *he* knew exactly what the crowd outside was headed towards, but all he said was, 'I've given my people orders to clear the route to the city gate. Don't want any bystanders caught up in the masses.'

'*Clear the route?*' Halbert burst out, striding towards the guardmaster with long, snappish steps. 'Without asking the consulate beforehand? Have you gone insane? We're not going to *help* them leave or pretend their government *agrees* with this absurdity – reverse that order right now and then—'

'Ah,' Delwin politely interrupted, hands behind his back. 'No.'

Halbert faltered. 'What?'

At my side, Rosalind swallowed an audible giggle. I stared at Delwin's long, melancholic face, now graced by just a hint of a smile, and suddenly realised what was about to happen.

'You forget your place, guardmaster,' Norris barked, puffing out his chest. He, clearly, did *not* realise. 'If the consulate orders you to make a change, you—'

'Well, yes,' Delwin interrupted, as mild as ever. 'I agree that would be the case if I were still your guardmaster. Unfortunately, I'm resigning. Please send the remainder of my salary to my sister's account, and I'd recommend appointing Armaud as my interim successor – I think that's all we need to arrange before I leave?'

Disconcerted whispers were rising among the guards around us; some were openly casting glances of doubt at the two sputtering consuls. Delwin, on the other hand, did not grant his former employers so much as a last goodbye as he efficiently took off a brooch I had not noticed before on his uniform, brushed his shirt back in place, and turned to Rosalind and me.

'I'd come and take a look outside, if I were you,' he said.

Outside.

Two thousand people, waiting for us to lure them to their death.

But a couple of guards muttered half-baked apologies to Norris and Halbert and began making their way towards the gate, clearly expecting us to follow. Rosalind was already moving, too. And we *needed* that army – *a force from the White City is joining us*, we could tell dozens of other islands around the archipelago, and gods, that would make an impression on human villages as I knew them ...

I started walking.

Delwin smoothly took his place beside me, with that trained guard's skill to somehow look threatening and invisible at the same time. Another handful of his people followed in his wake. We stepped into the morning sunlight like that, a circle of armed men with me as the precious symbol at the heart of it – the sort of protectiveness that almost made me forget I could best all of them together with a few well-aimed blows of magic.

Then again, perhaps it was better if the people on that square forgot about it, too. Perhaps it was better they did not yet realise what they were up against.

A deafening cheer rose from the crowd the moment we emerged – a *cheer*, for the gods' sakes, as if we were the heroes in some triumphant story of human perseverance rather than two generations of fae whores bringing death and destruction. Next to me, Rosalind was all graceful amiability, waving at familiar faces amongst the throng. I smiled until my jaws ached, unable to look any of them in the eyes – the desolate white hills of the Last Battle seemed to have taken root in my mind, a vision that hurt next to these optimistic-looking men and women saluting me with their spotless swords.

They didn't yet know.

And far, far too soon, they would.

The uproar died away, finally. Silence rippled out from the steps of the White Hall as more and more of our recruits lowered their swords and fists and stared at me expectantly, waiting for me to tell them … what? That we were going to win? That it was going to be glorious? That they would return home unscathed in two months with heroic stories to tell and continue to live their lives as if nothing had changed?

Take a good look at the place on your way out, I wanted to say. *Etch it into your memory. You'll long for the days when nothing much happened soon.*

Then again …

They were humans, not children. Mortal, not weak. It was their world that was suffering, too, and as I'd told Agenor myself mere days ago, why shouldn't they be given the chance to fix it with everyone else?

So I straightened my back in the eager silence. I smiled, and this time it felt real, with a first fizzle of the excitement I read on so many of the faces around me.

'Let's go kill the bitch, then,' I said.

And another wave of ecstatic clamour sent the windows trembling in their panes around us.

Chapter 25

Some seven people offered me their horse before I reached the other side of the square with Delwin and Rosalind by my side. I politely declined every single time, told them I was more than happy to walk with everyone else, and received several startled faces and nods of surprised approval in return.

'Clever,' Rosalind murmured next to me once we'd finally moved out of general earshot.

I hadn't even tried to be clever. It just felt obscene to be robbing people of their horses if I might already be robbing them of their lives, too.

Enough of Delwin's guards were joining us that we immediately had a command structure of sorts in place; he directed a few men to this part of the crowd and a few others to that part, until he seemed satisfied that nothing catastrophic would happen without us being aware. Then we walked, us at the head of the procession and the two-thousand-and-something members of our brand new army in a long stream after us, through the broad avenues of the city that had indeed been cleared of onlookers.

I couldn't help but wonder, glancing at the tidy houses we passed, how much Valter and Editta had heard of yesterday's events. If they were regretting all they had told Rosalind. If they were relieved I was leaving, or if there was a small, minuscule part of them that regretted they hadn't seen me – if it weighed on them like I couldn't help but let it weigh on me, the simple fact that I was now leaving their city behind for good.

That I would really never see them again.

In all likelihood, I had to admit with a last twang in my heart, they were just relieved.

It was infuriating that it still hurt, even with Rosalind beside me. How deep had they dug that hole in my heart, that even my mother's radiant smiles couldn't fill it yet?

But people were laughing and singing behind me, Delwin was more talkative than I'd ever known him to be, and soon we reached the outer rampart of the city proper; I shook off the wallowing thoughts and made myself pay attention to the conversation beside me. Rosalind was listing the human isles we should visit next to recruit. Delwin countered that some of those would take a week of travelling to reach, and since we were pressed for time already—

'Oh, travel won't be an issue,' I said. 'We can just ask some of the alves to fade us.'

It turned out neither of them had heard of the concept. So I told them about fading and then about the phoenixes not being birds; Rosalind wanted to know if we had any allied vampires in the Underground, and Delwin turned out to be particularly interested in fire magic. We spent most of our first hour of walking in pleasant conversation on the different corners of the magical world, interrupted every now and then by guards passing on questions. Were we going to set up camp right outside the walls? What were the plans for dinner? Would weapons be distributed among those who hadn't brought any?

'I'll ask the others outside to take care of it,' I kept telling them, smiling my most reassuring smile time and time again. 'Agenor has plenty of experience with this sort of logistics.'

That generally did the trick.

'Your father, isn't he?' Delwin said after the fifth of them hurried off to pass on my message. 'Agenor?'

I nodded. He threw a glance at Rosalind, whose smile suddenly had a decidedly nervous edge to it – an answer to all the questions we weren't asking.

I decided to keep my mouth shut. As much as I wanted to know what she was planning to tell him, the specifics of their love life were hardly my concern.

Alyra joined us after about an hour and a half of walking, prompting another educational conversation on gods and godsworn magic. By the time I'd told Delwin about Agenor's snakes, my feet were aching a little and the gleaming white walls of the city's wider territory were looming up before us, still half-hidden behind hills and forest. The people behind us were audibly getting nervous at the sight, and Delwin announced he was going to make a quick round of the ranks to make sure no one would be panicking when confronted with their first full-blood magical being.

I sent Alyra on her way with all my remaining white ribbons – the clearest sign I could think of that all was well and I would soon be back from my journey. Then it was just Rosalind and me, walking the last mile in silence as behind us the expectant laughter grew quieter and quieter and finally died away entirely.

The guards at the gate appeared to have been warned: they looked grim but unsurprised as we approached. I waited while they hauled away bolt after bolt, wondering suddenly how many of the people behind me had never even seen the world on the other side of that wall – did they know what the sea looked like, the plains and forests stretching out to the west of the city?

The near-absolute silence suggested that at least some of them did not.

There were some gasps behind me when the gate finally swung open.

The field between city and sea was surprisingly empty – no more tents or desperate refugees, only some squares of browned grass showing where the camp had been three days ago. Only as I cautiously stepped past the wall did my gaze fall on the group that had come in place of those unlucky humans: a handful of alves lingering around a small campfire, a single low tent, and at the very right side of their gathering—

My heart skipped a beat.

Creon.

I forgot for a moment about my mother beside me. Forgot about the humans pouring through the gate at my back, whispering urgently amongst each other.

Damn the aching feet – I ran.

He broke away from his alvish company at the same moment, striding towards me with rapidly widening eyes. Something to do with the unannounced army emerging behind me, possibly. Something to do with the forty-something-year-old woman who might look just a bit too much like me to the observant eye. As he came within hearing distance, wings flaring in agitation, he started a slightly bewildered, 'Em, what in the world have you—'

I flung myself around his neck before he could finish.

He went silent.

Near the gate, a few people cried out in shock. Closer, an alf whistled suggestively. But I breathed in the sweet, sweet scent of him, and only then did it truly hit me how much I'd missed him even in these short few days – how much I had craved his touch and his smiles and the rough warmth of his voice.

So much for the peace and the politics and the people who looked like me; this was where I'd unknowingly been going since I stepped through that gate three mornings ago.

'*Em*,' he repeated as he wrapped his arms around me, a hint of baffled laughter in his voice. 'What exactly are these people—'

'That's our army,' I said into his shoulder, my voice muffled by lean muscle and linen. 'Don't worry, they were a surprise for me, too.'

'Ah.' He cleared his throat. 'You realise they're looking at us?'

'Oh, probably.' I tightened my grip, just in case he was thinking of releasing me. 'Can't blame them. You're pretty pleasant to look at.'

This time his laughter was unmistakable. 'Yes, and I wouldn't dare begrudge them the delight, but I've been told my presence is a little divisive. If you don't want to chase your new followers back into the city before they've seen a single battlefield ...'

I shrugged. 'I already told them.'

He stiffened in my arms.

'My least favourite consul decided to accuse me of spreading my legs for murderers during a public meeting,' I added, letting go of his neck to lean back and meet his eye. As expected, his face had gone tight at once. 'So if they could handle that, I suspect they'll survive the sight of a hug, too. And either way, I'm not planning to stop hugging you.'

He seemed torn between relief and murderous ambitions. 'And the consul in question?'

'Got satisfactorily slapped in the face,' I said dryly and stepped out of his embrace. 'Speaking of which, I need you to meet someone. Rosalind?'

She turned from where she'd stood looking out over the sea some twenty feet away – quite possibly the only human present who had not been staring at Creon and me. An unexpectedly mischievous smile rose on her face as she came walking towards us. I was granted maybe five seconds to wonder what in the world she was so amused about – and then Creon froze beside me.

'Wait.' His voice suddenly had a decided urgency about it. 'Wait – *you* again?'

'What?' I said.

'Good morning, Your Highness.' My mother switched effortlessly to fluent Faerie. 'Been a while, hasn't it?'

He stared at her for another stupefied moment, then blinked at me, blinked back at her, and let out the sort of curse I was rather sure no dictionary would ever include.

'Oh, gods,' I said, slowly catching on. 'You've met before? At the Crimson Court?'

'His lordship very kindly didn't kill me,' Rosalind said, biting down a grin that told me she was rather enjoying the dramatics of the moment. 'Which was a surprise, really, given that I was making an obvious attempt to escape the island. I've wondered about that for the past twenty years.'

'Twenty-two,' Creon muttered, closing his eyes. 'Which I suppose means—'

'Oh, yes,' she dryly said. 'It does.'

I glanced back and forth between them, gaping, suddenly feeling infuriatingly young. Knowing Creon had an advantage of three centuries on me was one thing. Knowing that meeting my pregnant mother was still a recent event to his mind was somehow something else entirely, and by the pained look on his face, he rather agreed with me on that.

'Should probably have connected the dots,' he murmured, shaking his head. 'Then again …'

'You looked like you had more important things on your mind at the time,' Rosalind said, head tilting ever so slightly in innocent but razor-sharp curiosity. 'Which I have also wondered about – but I presume those were the effects of demon powers and torture, rather than an unfortunate flu?'

Good gods. That look of shock on her face, the moment I'd told Halbert the truth about Creon's silent murders – how many questions had been answered for her in that moment?

Creon did not even bother to respond – just glanced at me with a slightly frenzied look that said, *I suddenly understand exactly how you came to be the person you are, and gods help me, now there are two of you.*

'Do you happen to know where Agenor is?' I said, grinning back at him.

Rosalind's smile stiffened. I pretended not to notice.

'In the camp we set up a few miles to the west,' Creon said, his expression similarly devoid of all curiosity, even though I knew his sideways glance must have led to the same observation. 'Tared had the rather bright idea to recruit the humans waiting here, if you recall. Children and their mothers are in the Underground; the others are in the camp. We thought the city might get nervous if we settled an army right outside the walls.'

Rosalind's chuckle was almost convincing. 'Wise, yes.'

'Did you just call one of Tared's ideas *bright*?' I said, squinting.

He sent me a wry grin. 'Don't tell him.'

'Can't make any promises,' I said and jumped back to avoid the swat of his wing. 'I'll find an alf to fade us there, then. Can I leave this army to the rest of you? You might want to find Delwin and discuss matters with him – he's sensible.'

Creon shrugged, a hint of a smile twitching at the corner of his mouth. 'We'll be fine. I'm pretty sure I've survived less manageable humans.'

'*Half* human, thank you very much,' I said indignantly, and he chuckled and ruffled my hair before sauntering back to the alves he'd been keeping company before. I expected some remark from Rosalind as he moved out of hearing distance, but she was silent beside me – suspiciously so, really, given that there was plenty of material to remark upon.

I turned to her. She bravely attempted a smile, looking not unlike a convict about to face the gallows.

'Shall we find an alf, then?' I said firmly.

'Probably best if we do,' she admitted, rubbing her eyes. 'Before I run.'

I snorted and grabbed her wrist, dragging her along to the first blond head passing by. The alf – one of Valdora's people, I thought – greeted me cheerfully and eyed Rosalind with obvious curiosity, but did not ask questions when I told him we'd like to be faded to the newly formed army camp.

The journey was so short the world hardly had time to blur around us. Within a heartbeat, the white city walls had dissolved and moved over for a rugged stretch of grass covered in large and small tents, set up in a meticulous grid of the type I imagined my father would prefer. Fae and humans were carrying baskets of food around; between the tents, I noticed other small groups of humans sharpening swords and mending clothes.

They didn't even look up as we appeared out of nowhere. After three days of alves, I supposed they were getting used to it.

'Thanks,' I said, releasing both our guide and a disoriented-looking Rosalind. 'Do you happen to know where exactly I can find Agenor?'

'Red tent over there, I expect.' The alf grinned, giving me a mock salute. 'Anything else, Your Ladyship?'

I glared at him. He chortled and faded, vanishing into nothingness again.

'Good gods,' Rosalind said weakly.

'It'll become normal faster than you think,' I said, hooking my arm through hers just in case she did indeed try to make a run for it. 'Red tent, then?'

She let out a quiet, desperate moan. 'Em, what if he's angry?'

'Then he'd be an idiot,' I said patiently, 'which means it's technically a possibility, but which also means that you'll be able to talk sense into him soon enough. And if you can't, I will. And if neither of us manages, I promise we have plenty of pretty men with wings around to distract you. Is that—'

She burst out laughing. '*Em!*'

'Just laying out the options,' I said dryly.

'I don't *want* any other pretty men with wings,' she said in a melodramatic, exasperated tone. 'I just want ... well ...'

'Him,' I said.

She let out a deep sigh, and it sounded like a surrender. 'Yes.'

'In that case I *definitely* recommend we take a look at that red tent,' I said, ignoring the small twinge of my heart at the memory of Agenor's quiet despair, 'because I think avoiding him for the rest of your life is hardly a winning strategy towards that goal, wouldn't you say?'

'Gods help the mothers of clever children,' she muttered, but she allowed me to pull her along between the tents without further protest.

The red tent was one of the largest in the camp, square and high enough for a tall fae male to stand in. No voices emerged from it as we came closer. I drew in a deep breath, trying not to feel the nerves itching in my own stomach now, and yelled, 'Agenor?'

'Oh, Em?' His voice had that absent-minded air to it that suggested he was sitting knee-deep in administrative tasks, mind lost to a labyrinth of ink and parchment. 'Glad you're back. Do you have a minute? I'll quickly finish this and—'

'No, that's fine,' Rosalind wryly said next to me, in Faerie again. 'I could come back next week, if that fits your schedule better, Lord Protector?'

Deafening silence answered us.

I had to bite my lip not to laugh out loud. 'Agenor?'

The tent cloth was ripped aside without warning, so violently the frame nearly came down in its entirety.

My father emerged from the shadowy interior like a man possessed, eyes wide, wings unfurling behind his shoulders – gaping down at us as if we were two ghosts from his dreams, suddenly standing before him in the flesh. His baffled gaze travelled from Rosalind to me and back to Rosalind, lips parting and closing without a sound.

'Hello, Agenor,' she said brightly, and had she not been threatening to flee a few minutes ago, I would not have recognised the nervousness in her voice. 'Lovely to see you again. Thought it might be time to see how you were doing on this side of the walls.'

He opened his mouth again. This time, a breathless, strangled sound escaped, too incoherent to be wrangled into words.

'Oh, dear,' she said, a mirthless smile tugging at the corner of her lips. 'Worse than I thought, it sounds like.'

Agenor blinked, as if trying to clean a stubborn speck of dust from his eyes. She did not move, and he blinked again and again, as though if he just tested his sight enough, sooner or later this madness would turn out to be too good to be true and he would open his eyes to find her gone after all.

Not being an alf, Rosalind stayed where she stood.

Finally, his voice rough and unsteady, he managed a bewildered, 'Al?'

It cut straight through my heart, the helpless, unfiltered vulnerability in that one word. From the look on his face, he might have forgotten I was standing next to my mother. Hell, he might have forgotten the camp was standing around us, too; his eyes clung to her without pause, an eager, almost desperate hunger in his gaze, as if the smallest detail of her appearance might save his life.

I decided it was about time to get the hell out of here.

'Should I ask Doralis to take over whatever task you were working on?' I said, trying to sound as tactful as possible.

'Oh.' Agenor gave the impression he'd forgotten about the existence of the tasks too, his gaze fixed on the fragile figure of my mother. She did not speak, waiting with what I suspected was nervousness rather than some cruel test of his feelings. 'Yes. Please. That would be ...' He faltered, visibly trying to regain track of his sentence. 'Very helpful. Thanks, Em.'

'I'll do that, then,' I said, stepping back with a quick smile of encouragement at Rosalind. She looked like she might need it. 'Anything else I can do?'

'No. No, I think we will be...' Only then did he lift his gaze from my mother for a fraction of a second, meeting my eyes with a look that was both an apology and a cry for help. 'We'll be just fine?'

Zera help me.

They were grown adults, I told myself as I reluctantly started turning away from them. They could probably sort this out themselves, and no matter how much I felt like interfering, it likely wouldn't help anyone much if I stepped in and physically smashed their heads together like I very much felt like doing.

'See you later, then,' I said instead.

They were already staring at each other again. Neither of them answered; really, I suspected neither of them had heard me at all.

I walked. Behind me, I heard Rosalind say, 'Shall I come in, then?'

Agenor's answer was indistinguishable. She did not speak again. But when I glanced over my shoulder a few seconds later, the tent cloth had been folded shut and both of my parents were gone.

Chapter 26

I FOUND THE CENTRAL command tent without having to ask a single person: it was the tallest structure in all the camp, eye-catching with its white and azure stripes and a golden banner flying from its highest point. A tent one might find in a storybook illustration. A tent, no doubt, that would fill the recruits from the White City with fiery, valiant feelings, the pleasant sensation of being a hero and having the world treat you as one.

I swallowed something bitter as I ducked through the opening.

The tent looked even bigger from the inside, lit by sunlight filtering in and a single alf light hovering just below the ceiling. A square table occupied most of the available space, the surface covered in maps of the archipelago and the Crimson Court; a pile of banners in various colours had been chucked into one corner, while a messy trunk full of writing materials stood in another.

On the farthest side of the tent, Doralis and Beyla stood discussing something that looked like a rather bedraggled sketch in hushed tones. Next to them, Lyn was sitting cross-legged on the table, furiously browsing a leather-bound atlas and drawing pencil lines on yet another map before her.

'Morning?' I said, and only then did they collectively look up to notice me.

'Em!' Lyn veered off the table, brightening abruptly – genuine relief, and yet I couldn't help but notice that she looked much too pale beneath her freckles. 'Oh, thank the gods you're back. How was your visit? Did you have any success with the consuls?'

'Not so much with the consuls,' I admitted. 'The people themselves seem to have liked me better, though. We accidentally convinced about two thousand of them to come with us, so the camp may need to …'

Next to Lyn, Doralis let out a choked sound. '*Two thousand*?'

'Yes.' I grimaced. 'It wasn't entirely planned.'

'Gods have mercy,' she muttered, dropping her notes onto the table and hurrying towards the tent exit, her violet wings shivering with agitation. 'We're going to need more fireplaces and latrines, in that case. Please tell me some of them have brought their own tents – I have no idea where we'd get a thousand tents on such short notice, even if—'

'Most of them had bags,' I hurriedly cut in. 'I think at least some people must have had the bright idea to bring their own equipment.'

She let out a muffled curse under her breath and strode out, vanishing around the corner before any of us could have gotten in another word. Her voice rose outside a few moments later, issuing commands to whatever fae or humans she encountered.

Lyn and Beyla exchanged the swiftest glance of doubt – *should we help out?* that look said – then seemed to decide simultaneously that Doralis would be more than equipped to deal with the challenge on her own. Beyla picked up her notes again. Lyn sent me another smile and said, in a voice that tried just too hard to appear cheerful, 'Well, that's good news, isn't it?'

Wasn't it?

The answer ought to have been positive, presumably … but that stubborn attempt at optimism on her pale face was the fastest antidote to any sense of triumph. So were the lines of worry around Beyla's eyes, turning her usual reserved expression into the look of a female bracing herself for the worst.

'Did anything happen?' I slowly asked, and it felt as if my mind finally followed my body out the gates of the White City with that lethal little question, out of that eerily peaceful dream and back into the deadly reality of the rest of the world. Three days without news. Three days in which half the archipelago may have burned without me knowing – good gods, how had I ever believed I would return from my trip and find the world utterly unchanged?

Lyn's smile twisted into an apology as she deflated a few inches. 'Not yet.'

'But?'

'I faded to the Crimson Court this morning and managed to sneak a few miles through Faewood,' Beyla quietly said. 'Got quite close to the harbour. A couple of fae discovered me there and left me no choice but to fade out again, but it looks like the Mother is finally preparing her warships. They'll be ready to sail out before the end of the day, from the glimpses I caught.'

I stared at her, the last traces of triumph sizzling out like dying sparks.

'We only just heard,' Lyn added, small fingers frantically fidgeting with her curls. 'So we're waiting for Agenor to come this way, and then ...'

Oh.

Oh, fuck.

'Um.' My voice came out too high – Zera help me, why hadn't I asked around *before* dragging Rosalind into my father's arms? 'I should probably have told you this immediately, but I don't think Agenor will be coming this way anytime soon. I could try to get a hold of him if you really think it's necessary, but ...'

Lyn's amber eyes narrowed. 'What's wrong?'

Everything. How dare the world plunge me right back into war so easily – how dare it make such a mockery of these few days of respite? I'd felt so bloody close to optimistic, fifteen minutes ago. I'd found my mother. I'd found an army. We were on our way to acquire the human support we needed, and even if we didn't have it yet, at least there would be no need for me to force Thysandra into talking – not if we were just given a few more days to prepare and forge alliances while the Mother gathered her forces.

And now ...

War ships.

And even Rosalind had suddenly become a liability.

'My mother,' I whispered.

Even Beyla stared at me as if I'd grown wings.

'She was in the White City.' *Still in love with him and unable to trust him for twenty long years* – gods, I didn't *want* to interrupt them. 'I just delivered her to his tent, and he didn't look particularly in the mood to think about strategy and warfare when I last saw him. Nor did she, really. So even if we forcibly drag them into the discussion now ...'

'Your *mother*,' Lyn repeated dazedly – as if the rest of my words had slipped past her entirely. 'Oh, Em, that is amazing!'

'Well, yes,' I helplessly said, 'but—'

'We'll manage,' Beyla cut in, her faint voice unusually impatient. 'We've survived without any fae strategists for centuries – I'm sure we'll keep ourselves afloat until he decides to emerge again. And take a seat, Emelin. You look like you've been on your feet for a while.'

I wordlessly slid my heavy backpack off my shoulders and onto the ground, shoved it beneath the table with my foot, and collapsed into a chair beside them. The map Lyn had been drawing on, I saw now, depicted the entire archipelago. Her pencil lines depicted several possible sea routes from the Crimson Court to other locations of strategical importance, with estimates of the sailing times jotted next to them.

According to those scribbled numbers, the Mother could arrive for attack just about anywhere she wanted before the next twenty-four hours had passed.

Twenty-four hours.

I forced myself to take a few very deep breaths, staring at the familiar outlines of the islands I knew.

'Creon probably has some reasonable ideas on the Mother's strategies, too,' Lyn was saying, her young voice tired. 'But we need information more than anything else now – it's too risky to fade back to the Crimson Court in the next few hours, presumably?'

'They'd be idiots if they weren't waiting for me,' Beyla said. 'I could fade a few of Agenor's fae to an island nearby and ask them to fly closer, though. A few extra pairs of wings might not draw as much attention as an alf showing up, especially from a distance.'

'Still a risk,' Lyn said with a pained moan. 'If they're discovered ...'

Beyla sighed. 'It's war, Lyn.'

They were both quiet for a while, Lyn staring miserably at her maps, Beyla going over the buckles of her swords, adjusting them ever so slightly before she straightened her shoulders again. She did not look impatient. She just looked as she always did – ready to disappear.

'Alright,' Lyn finally murmured. 'See if you can find any volunteers.'

With a nod, Beyla vanished into nothingness.

We sat in silence together for two, three minutes, Lyn and I, while the world outside grew steadily noisier as more and more humans were faded into the camp. Voices clamoured about tents and firewood. Bursts of laughter broke through the clanking of shovels and axes. Blissfully unaware, all of them, that on the other side of the archipelago, the Mother was loading up her ships and preparing to maim and kill, perhaps before the sun set tonight.

Already, the sun-streaked peace of the White City felt an eternity away – settling back into its old role as an unattainable dream, an escape I would never be allowed.

'Shouldn't we be sending alves to the most likely targets?' I eventually said, forcing myself to glance at the map again. My eyes slid past the Fireborn Palace, past Tolya and the other nymph isles, past the alf houses in the north. 'If we aren't able to follow her ships, at least that way they can sound the alarm as soon as anything problematic appears on the horizon.'

She closed her eyes. 'Yes.'

It sounded like there was a *but* about to follow; she didn't speak it out loud.

'But?' I said.

'But the question is what we should do once we know where she's headed,' Lyn mumbled, climbing off the table to plop down into a chair and bury her head in her arms. 'Which I wish was as easy as—'

The tent cloth was brusquely yanked aside before she could finish her sentence, and Edored's habitually overexcited voice burst in. 'Nose-breaker!'

I nearly jumped head-first through the ceiling cloth.

The alf came trotting in with a worryingly broad smile on his face, his leather coat snapping around his legs – looking like he was the tirelessly determined dog and I was the stick he had been looking for since sunrise. His exalted 'There you are!', far louder than the distance between us required, did nothing to soften that impression either.

Next to me, Lyn muttered a long-suffering prayer for strength as she closed her eyes.

'Am I?' I said cautiously.

'Well, you don't look like you're anywhere else,' Edored said without the faintest trace of irony in his face-splitting grin. 'Do you have a moment? We've got something for you.'

'Oh, gods,' Lyn said, opening one eye for the sole purpose of throwing him a devastating glare. '*Now*, Edored?'

'When else, Phiramelyndra?' he returned, rolling his eyes at her. 'When we're all dead and in our graves? Also, don't blame me. The others came up with it.'

'The ... others?' I said even more cautiously.

He pulled a face. 'Can't tell you.'

I blinked at Lyn, who shrugged apologetically at me but didn't say anything, and then at the tent entrance behind Edored's leather-clad back, which was deserted. *The others* – who in the world was he talking about? The family? Him and his drinking friends? Hell, the Underground as a whole?

'Look, I'm rather busy,' I said weakly, gesturing at the maps before us. 'If your secret could possibly wait until we're sure the Mother isn't about to wipe the Fireborn Palace off the face of the earth ...'

'Oh, this is more important,' Edored brightly informed me.

Zera help me. 'Then at the very least give me another hour to—'

'No, no, no.' He shook his head, still grinning broadly. 'You don't get it, Noisy Death. This can't wait another hour. I have instructions to bring you to' – he interrupted himself, clearly having been on the verge of blurting out some monumental secret – 'to *somewhere* immediately, and if I have to drag you there, then it will be my pleasure.'

The whole business was getting more ominous by the heartbeat. I threw another look at Lyn, holding on to some desperate hope that she would burst out laughing and admit that they were all just pulling a prank on me – but Lyn only mouthed a silent apology and Edored was now impatiently hopping from one leg to the other.

'Is anyone in danger?' I guessed, more and more befuddled. 'If people are dying, just tell me and I—'

'No danger!' he interrupted, waving that notion aside with an exasperated snort. 'But if danger is going to make you move faster, I'm more than happy to hold Fury against a couple of throats, Nosebreaker. Whatever works for you.'

Good gods.

'Oh, *fine*,' I muttered, rising from my chair to grab his wrist. 'But it better be very damn urgent. And —'

We were already fading.

It took longer than I'd hoped. The world blurred and kept blurring, one endlessly long heartbeat and then another; wherever we were going, we definitely weren't staying in the vicinity of the White City. Pine green mingled with a sooty black around us. The spray of waves hit me in the face. I smelled musty earth, fish, dew on leaves. Then, finally, the world started piecing itself back together, the smell of the islands I knew replaced by ...

Smoke.

I managed to suck in one deep breath before the thick, metallic vapour settled itself into my lungs and nostrils, sending me doubling over in a fit of coughs. Next to me, Edored had wisely tugged the collar of his shirt over his mouth and nose, looking down at me a little crestfallen as he helplessly patted me on the back.

'You do need to keep breathing, Emelin,' he told me helpfully as I retched and heaved. 'When I told you no one was dying, I didn't mean *you* were supposed to take on the role of—'

'Where *are* we?' I sputtered, spitting the words out between coughs. 'If you're trying to drag me into hell ...'

Someone laughed – a familiar female voice I didn't manage to identify immediately through my own grating breath. Hallthor – yes, that really was Hallthor – dryly said, 'I wasn't aware I was labouring under *such* dire circumstances.'

That laugh had been Ylfreda's, I realised belatedly.

I forced myself to stand up straight, sniffling the tears from my eyes. We had arrived right in the middle of a cloud of smoke, it turned out; the rest of the room, while all but clear, at least offered enough oxygen to keep breathing. In the firelit dusk, Tared and Ylfreda sat lounging on a long wooden work table littered with scorch marks, the both of them grinning at me with an air of excitement I would almost describe as giddiness. Hallthor leaned against an anvil of impressive size, arms crossed and expression amused as he watched my laborious attempts not to suffocate on the spot.

Slowly, understanding rose. The smithy in the Underground. The place where Hallthor spent most of his working days before returning home with brand new soot marks on his leather apron and fragments of molten steel in his hair. Doubtless a place of importance to the family, and I didn't mind seeing it from the inside for once – but was a visit to Skeire's smithy really important enough to justify hauling me off under threats of violence and abduction?

'We're about to go to war,' I managed, clearing the last lingering wisps of smoke from my throat. 'Did you really have to drag me away while I—'

'We had to drag you away *because* of that looming war,' Tared dryly interrupted, still smiling way too broadly for my nerves. 'Had to get it done before the fighting starts, you see.'

It took all I had not to take a swing at him. 'To get *what* done?'

'Good question.' He raised his eyebrows. 'I understand that Edored actually managed to keep a secret for longer than a minute this time?'

'Hey!' Edored protested, dropping himself next to Ylfreda on the edge of the table. 'I am the pinnacle of secrecy, you smug—'

'Yes, yes,' Ylfreda interrupted. Even she was looking unusually cheerful, though there had to be plenty of people to be stitched up in times like these. 'You did an excellent job. Shall we get to the point, then?'

At least there was one sensible person to be found in this room.

'Please,' I said, unable to keep the edge of despair from my voice entirely. 'I would very much like to know—'

'We have a gift for you,' Tared said, as if that would explain everything.

I was getting closer and closer to the point of violence. 'Yes, Edored said that much, but I don't suppose you went to the effort of collecting the whole family together just to give me a new pair of socks, did you?'

He chuckled. 'No.'

'So then what in hell ...'

He turned to Hallthor with a sweeping gesture. 'I'll leave the honour to you.'

The smith just smiled, taciturn as always, and pulled something wrapped in a woollen blanket from behind that boat-sized anvil. He handed me the package as if he was handing over his firstborn child, a sudden earnestness on his face that seemed directly opposed to the air of giddy lightness that had hung in the room a moment ago.

Even then, the pieces didn't click into place.

I peeled the wool off the object, slowly, all too aware of the four pairs of eyes following my every movement. A gleam of metal reflected back at me, almost golden in the light of the smouldering fires. The earthy smoothness of polished leather. Silvery mother-of-pearl. And ...

The sharp edge of a blade.

I froze.

I blinked.

Someone chuckled, a few feet away.

No – no, this couldn't be what I was stupidly thinking it was, could it? In a burst of confusion, I tore off the rest of the blanket, an attempt to put a stop to my fanciful imaginations rather than a matter of impatience ... but it really *was* a sword, and a stunningly beautiful one at that. Pommel and cross-guards inlaid with mother-of-pearl. A razor-sharp alf steel edge. The hilt itself seemed to have been made for fae, common steel where it wasn't covered in leather: no risk that I would accidentally block my own magic while holding the blade.

While holding ...

My blade.

I stared at the weapon in my hand as the sound of those two words slowly sank in.

'You ... you're not joking, are you?' They didn't look like they were joking, the absolute opposite really – but good gods, a *sword*? I knew perfectly well how they felt about their weapons. *Lose it and I'll kill you*, Beyla had told me at the Golden Court, and I'd believed her – believed, at least, that she would have made a good attempt or two before anyone would have been able to talk her into settling for some broken bones and lifelong shunning.

And now they were putting one of those same swords in *my* little fae hands?

'The proper reaction, at least,' Ylfreda said, smiling contently at me. 'Of course we're not joking, Emelin. Why would we?'

'But it ... it's an *alf sword*.' What in the world was I arguing for – for them to abruptly realise they had made a colossal mistake and yank the weapon from my hands again? And yet my lips refused to stop moving, unable to trust, unable to fall and let the net catch me. 'And I'm not an alf. So—'

Tared quirked up an eyebrow. 'Aren't you?'

Oh.

One of us.

Zera help me, he'd *told* me, word for word, in the training hall in Orin's quarter. Had reassured me I would always be family, then gone off to tell the others about Creon – or so I'd thought ...

But hadn't I found Hallthor engrossed in sketches the very next morning?

Already the heat of tears was burning in the corners of my eyes again.

'I ... I don't know what to say,' I managed, returning my gaze to that slender blade just so I had an excuse to blink the wetness from my eyes.

How many hours of work had he put into this, to get it done so swiftly? 'Thank you. Thank you so, so much. I ... I'll take very good care of it, I promise.'

'I hope it'll take good care of you, too,' Hallthor said, watching the sword with something I could only describe as gentle fondness. 'But don't fight with it until you've named it, of course – I hope Tared told you that much?'

I blinked. 'What?'

'Bad luck,' he clarified. 'Fighting with an unnamed sword.'

'Yes, yes, I get that part, but ... *name* it?' I glanced at Tared, who smiled back at me with just a little too much satisfaction. '*I'm* supposed to name it?'

'Yes, of course,' Ylfreda said, clucking her tongue. 'Who else did you think was going to do it for you? The bloody gods?'

'Bold of you to assume I was thinking at all,' I said, a little panicked, looking from the sword to her and back to the sword. It gleamed at me rather ... expectantly. 'How in the world does one name a sword?'

'You think very hard ...' Tared started.

'Or you get very drunk,' Edored helpfully supplied.

'A tried and true method as well, yes,' Tared admitted with a wry grin. 'Either way, you get your brain going somehow, and then sooner or later, you'll ... know.'

I narrowed my eyes at him, somehow less reassured than I'd been a moment before. 'I'll *know*?'

'It's not as vague as it sounds,' he said dryly. 'You'll know when you know, I promise.'

'You're not helping, Tared.' I took two steps back and sank down on a little wooden stool, the sword nameless and heavy in my hands. *One of us*, perhaps – but right now, I felt the absence of a few decades of alvish culture from my life more deeply than ever before. 'I barely know what you people would consider proper names for a sword. Fury is Fury, of course, and I know Beyla's swords, but ...'

'Beyla didn't name her own swords,' Ylfreda said softly. 'That's not the example you want to be looking at.'

'Right.' I rubbed my eyes. 'Did you ...'

She nodded, tapping the hilt of the short sword on her back. 'She's called Mercy.'

A healer's sword, intended to bring death only when it was the kindest option left. I swallowed, nodded, and glanced at Hallthor, who jutted a thumb at the sword standing against the wall in the corner of the room. 'Whisper.'

Ah, yes. The rarity of an even-tempered alf – a quiet male raised in a world of raucous chaos. I turned back to Tared, rubbing my face with my free hand, and said, 'Does Lyn have her own sword, too?'

'Oh, yes, of course.' He grinned. 'You just won't see her wielding it for a few years. It's about as tall as she is right now. It's called Kenaz.'

I frowned. 'Kenaz?'

'It's a rune. Symbol of knowledge.'

'*Oh*.' Lyn and her books – what else could she reasonably have come up with? 'Of course.'

'See?' he said, crossing his legs with the air of a male who's made his point. 'That's what you're looking for – that name that will make everyone around you nod and say, yes, of course this is what Em would have chosen. As I said, you'll know.'

'So why Heartfall, then?' I gestured half-heartedly at the weapon on his back. 'It sounds more obsessed with merciless triumph than you usually are – is there some scandalous past of yours that I'm missing?'

Ylfreda laughed before he could answer. 'It's named after a sword from a story.'

'*Some* people,' Tared immediately shot back, with the sort of tired amusement that proved this was far from the first time a disagreement had arisen on this particular topic, 'including the maker of the sword himself, are of the opinion it *is* the sword from—'

Edored snorted so loudly it echoed through the underground room. 'You forget to tell her that Uncle Ingved was as nutty as a fruitcake.'

'Well—'

'He thought someone came sneaking through his orchard every autumn!' Edored interrupted, his voice rising. 'To steal the bloody leaves from the trees!'

'He was still bright enough when it came to his work, though,' Hallthor said mildly. 'Could tell you exactly when and for whom he'd made every single sword in his workplace until the very last day.'

'He thought I was a pixie!' Edored protested, looking mortally offended. 'He once tried to lure me outside with a glass of milk!'

'In his defence,' Tared said, grinning more widely than I'd seen him do in a long time, 'you did show up with a different black eye every single time we visited him. I can see where the misunderstanding was coming from.'

'Alright,' I interrupted, because it was abundantly clear that Edored was about to unleash a response that wouldn't allow for any sensible conversation for several minutes, and I still hadn't received a proper answer to my questions, 'a sword from a story, you said?'

'Oh, yes.' Tared looked almost regretful about having to give up on nettling Edored as he turned back to me. 'It used to be my favourite story as a child—'

'For utterly unfathomable reasons,' Edored interrupted gleefully.

'Edored,' Ylfreda groaned.

'He sacrifices his sword for her!' The fact that they must have had this conversation a thousand time before did not render his genuine indignance any less passionate; neither did the fact that the events were likely to be entirely fictional. 'I don't care that she turns things into diamonds! What godsforsaken idiot leaves his *sword* behind to—'

'Tared, you *romantic*,' I said, pretending to be shocked.

He threw me a withering look. Next to him, Ylfreda laughed out loud, patting him comfortingly on the shoulder.

'Either way,' Hallthor said, not tempted into anything more than a quiet smile as usual, 'Ingved insisted this was the same Heartfall that was given up in the story. Gave it to Tared when he was old enough, and Edored was not jealous *at all*.'

'Jealous?' Edored bristled. 'Over some sword that was discarded for a woman?'

'Not at all,' Ylfreda agreed placidly.

He huffed triumphantly, apparently missing that she was biting her lip to the point of bleeding to keep her face straight.

'The main conclusion to draw here,' Tared said with a look of pained patience, 'is that like Beyla, I did not name my own sword and am a terrible example. Don't use me as a guideline here.'

'Ah, yes,' I said earnestly. 'You mean I should not be naming my sword after the singing candlestick in the ballad of Molly and the Three Bears? Good to know.'

A chuckle escaped him. 'Well, you can technically do anything you like, of course—'

'As a matter of fact,' Hallthor dryly interrupted, 'I just realised you can't. Name my work after candlesticks and I may just duel you to get it back under my own care – I have my limits.'

And even though I knew it was a joke, even though I had never expected to own a sword until five minutes ago and surely should not be getting used to having one already, I couldn't deny the swift sting of panic I felt at the thought of losing the weapon in my hands.

Good gods. Perhaps there was magic hammered into this steel after all.

'I won't name it after singing candlesticks,' I promised, 'and I won't fight anyone with it until I know what I'm mysteriously supposed to know, and thank you all so, so much for ... for ...'

For the sword. For the stories. For the warmth and the laughs and the good-natured ribbing – for the message beneath the surface, most of all.

One of us.

They seemed to understand without another word from my lips; hell, even Edored sent me a radiant grin before I could figure out how to turn the fuzzy glow in my heart into proper grammar. 'Want me to take you back to your busy life in the north, then, Nosebreaker?'

Oh.

Fuck.

The Mother's bloody warships.

It was miraculous, really, how easily they'd made me forget about the mess waiting for me above the earth – the attack hanging over our heads, the armies readying themselves for the bloodshed to come.

'Might be better to go back, yes,' I made myself say, even though I couldn't think of anything I wanted less than to return to that camp full of hopeful humans, to the choices of life and death waiting for us there.

Hallthor bent over and pulled a brand-new leather sheath from behind his anvil – perfectly tailored to size, the buckle gleaming in the firelight. My muttered thanks as he handed it to me felt ridiculously insufficient, but the laughter wrinkles around his eyes told me he understood.

'I'll be coming with you,' Tared said as I fastened the sword onto my back, rolling my shoulders to adjust to the new weight. 'Sounds like there's plenty for all of us to do. Did I hear you brought an entire army with you, Em?'

'Accidentally,' I said, grimacing.

The conversation rolled on for a few more moments, small talk back and forth until Edored got sick of it and announced we were leaving now – but my mind lagged behind, wondering despite my own better judgement how much of a scandal I would cause by picking *Accidentally* as my sword name.

It did have a certain ring to it, really.

Chapter 27

The blue-and-white tent at the heart of our army camp had filled up significantly since Edored had faded me out half an hour ago. Nenya was standing beside Lyn now, pencil between her blood-red lips, hair braided into complex horn-like structures this morning. And on the other side of the tent – my heart gave a little jump – Creon sat lounging in a chair that did not look designed to be lounged in but had inevitably surrendered to the Silent Death's wishes, allowing him to leisurely curl his wings around the backrest as he scanned the atlas Lyn had held before.

He looked up the moment we appeared beside the table. Edored, meanwhile, let go of my wrist and burst out in an excited, 'Nen!'

There was just a fraction of warmth in her long-suffering sigh. 'Morning, arsehole.'

Lyn threw them a small eyeroll, jumped off her chair, and trotted towards Tared to report the details of Beyla's findings. I decided they would be able to discuss the worrying news perfectly well without me and slipped around the other side of the table, to where Creon had already shoved his atlas aside and nudged a second chair back with his foot. At the sight of the sword on my back, he smiled more broadly than I'd dared to expect.

'You're an alf now?'

'So I've been told,' I said as I loosened the sheath buckle and carefully settled the weapon on the bundle of discarded banners in the corner. Pulling my hands off it felt oddly similar to putting a newborn child in its cradle and having to trust it would continue to breathe on its own – an unexpected itch of protectiveness. 'Hallthor made it.'

'I figured.' He ran his eyes over the mother-of-pearl cross-guards, the slender length of the sheath. 'It's beautiful work.'

I dropped myself into the chair next to him, glanced aside to check whether Tared and Edored were still occupied elsewhere, and whispered, 'I'm supposed to somehow find a name for it. If you have any suggestions ...'

'Call it Cactus,' he dryly offered.

'That's my title,' I mumbled, pulling a face. 'I feel like there can only be so many cacti around at any given time without causing confusion. Nosebreaker and Noisy Death are out of the question for the same reason.'

He laughed. 'And you're not in the mood to embrace the good alf tradition of boastful ambition and call it Queenslayer, either?'

'I suppose I could, but it's so ...' I hesitated. 'So violent.'

As if that was the side of me I preferred above all else – the side that blinded High Ladies and left blood-soaked battlefields behind. As if that was what I wanted my audience to think about, every single time I drew my weapon: not Emelin, saviour of humanity, but Emelin, godsworn mage carrying death on every fingertip.

Creon sent me a mirthless smile. 'Yes. I know.'

Of course he did.

'Perhaps I should follow Edored's advice after all and get mind-numbingly drunk first,' I said sourly. 'Might do wonders for my creativity.'

'Alternatively,' he said, face straight, 'you might wake up from your mead stupor and find you named your sword Creon's Glorious Biceps, which I would of course approve of, but which would probably not be very happily received by certain alves in particular.'

I huffed a laugh, trailing my eyes down over his torso. 'Tared would be lucky if your biceps were the first body part I'd think of.'

The edge of wickedness in his grin could have sent me to my knees. As if we weren't sitting here on the brink of war – as if the weight of the world wasn't weighing on our shoulders. Small moments of reprieve that I craved like sunlight and oxygen; it was all I could do to suppress a groan when Lyn turned towards us on the other side of the tent. 'Creon?'

He sobered up immediately. 'What is it?'

'Do you still need those maps?'

To figure out where the Mother was sending her ships, what innocent lives she'd declared forfeit this time around … The boulder sank back into my stomach.

Choices to be made. It always came down to the same thing in the end.

Creon wordlessly shoved the atlas across the table to Lyn, then slowly said, 'We might at least get an idea of their direction by posting some people as lookouts on nearby islands. If we know whether she takes the east or the west straits …'

'Yes,' Lyn said, drawing out the word with obvious hesitation. 'Yes, we should, but …'

She faltered.

'But the question is what we'd do with the knowledge?' Tared finished.

A groan. 'Exactly.'

'Defend the place she's planning to attack?' I said, a little puzzled by the grimness of their expressions. This was the self-evident part, wasn't it? We could argue about *how* to defend the intended victims or *who* exactly would take the task upon them … but that seemed rather secondary, a matter of details. 'As soon as we know where she's going, we can—'

'With what army?' Tared grimly interrupted me.

I frowned. 'Beg your pardon?'

He muttered a curse as he dropped into his chair and stretched his long legs. 'If she's sending out a fleet of the size Beyla's observations suggest, we're going to need more than a few alves from the Underground to stop them. And the one thing all our allies did seem to agree on was that we would not be fighting multiple battles.'

It took a moment for that to sink in.

'So then what would you suggest instead?' They had all become worryingly quiet around me – even *Creon* didn't smile or nod when I glanced his way. 'You're not saying you don't want to defend whoever her target is at all, are you?'

'It's hardly a matter of wanting,' Nenya muttered, arms crossed, long red nails tapping impatiently against her lace sleeves. 'Rather of what we can afford.'

'Yes.' The tightness in Tared's voice was unmistakable now. 'She could probably wipe out half of us with just the group she's sent on its way today, and even if we took half of *them* with us, she'd barely bat an eye. Taking her bait before we have either worked out the bindings or found the human allies we need is a madman's bet at best.'

I wasn't sure what was worse – his words or the silence that followed, the eloquent absence of objections. Lyn gloomily chewed on her curls. Nenya absently scratched the scars marring her cheek. Edored looked like he was still working out the numbers Tared had presented, but even *his* face was unusually glum – ready to accept the conclusions, as puzzling as they may be to him.

And Creon …

Taut jaw. Bottomless eyes. But he didn't look up from the table and he didn't speak – not a word of protest.

'No,' I said breathlessly, not sure what I was denying – the Mother *did* have the advantage of numbers and the bindings, and hell, of her defences, too. But she may be planning to wipe a whole nymph isle off the face of the earth, just as she'd tried to do with Tolya before, and how could anyone just blankly accept those hard facts if they all knew the consequences?

'Em …' Lyn started, her voice a fraction choked.

'We stopped the Sun fleet at Tolya. All of it, with just the two of us.' I felt more and more like some frantic, drivelling lunatic as I glanced at Creon and received nothing but the faintest headshake in response. 'Why couldn't we try again? Even if there's a few more of them this time ...'

'It's not just the numbers, Em,' he interrupted, his voice low and rough. 'They've seen you work at the Golden Court and lived to tell the tale. Your godsworn powers are no longer a surprise like they were at Tolya. She'll know very damn well you might show up again, and you can bet a good amount of money that her army will be prepared this time.'

I swallowed. 'But—'

'And even if you come out of it alive this time,' Nenya stiffly added, 'you'll have shown her that she can lure you out this way.'

Giving her all the reason in the world to attack again and again and again, more viciously every time to make sure I'd keep taking the bait ... Until eventually, inevitably, something would kill me. The Mother knew as well as I did that every fight was a roll of the dice in a way; for all my magic, for all my strategy, I *had* been lucky to escape my brushes with death so far.

And I only had to be unlucky once for it to all be over.

My mouth was starting to go dry. I understood every argument they were making – couldn't help but accept every single one – and yet the rational conclusion that followed refused to seem even remotely reasonable. If we didn't take the bait ... then we'd just sit here. Wait here. Stay quiet and safe on the one island the Mother wouldn't bother to attack in this war.

And people would hurt and suffer and die.

'So what else do you suggest we do, then?' I managed. 'Nothing?'

'We should make haste reaching out to the bigger human isles and cities,' Lyn said, her expression pleading with me to restrain myself. 'And we should let our allies know to be on guard. If anything happens ...'

'Yes.' Tared sighed. 'Least we can do is evacuate as many people as possible once we know where she's headed.'

'But if she attacks a whole city,' I said, and there was no helping the crack of shrillness, no matter my best attempts to stay calm and collected, 'there's no way in hell you'll manage to get everyone out of there in time, is there? And if she attacks an alf house or a place like the Fireborn Palace, people won't even *want* to get out of—'

'Em, we *know.*' It was Lyn's turn now to lose control of her voice for a moment. 'And we like it as little as you do, trust me – but we've seen this happen before, all of it, and every single magical ruler joining the cause knew exactly what they signed up for. We can't ...'

'She might not even attack a magical community,' Creon quietly said.

Edored let out a befuddled breath beside the entrance of the tent. 'Why in hell would she attack *humans*?'

'Spite.' Creon shrugged – an attempt at indifference wholly negated by the bitter twitch at the corner of his lips and the tension in his wings. He knew that spite far too well, I realised. He'd been the instrument to execute it for hundreds of years. 'She presumably knows Em visited the White City by now. You shouldn't underestimate how petty and vicious she can get when she feels offended, and I suspect that the city breaking its laws for her current foremost enemy must have offended her plenty.'

Her foremost enemy.

I'd never been granted a title I'd so gladly have lost.

'Orin's bloody arse,' Tared muttered, raking a hand through his hair. 'But she wouldn't win anything by attacking a human city. Do you really think she'll be vengeful enough to set all strategy aside and make her decisions based on her grudges alone?'

'Depends on whose advice she is listening to, at the moment,' Creon said sourly. 'Usually when she came up with plans like these, Agenor and Thysandra would have been the ones to talk her out of it. With one of them on our side and the other sitting in a cell ...'

He didn't finish his sentence. Not even Edored seemed to need the rest of his point. Hell, if Ophion was her main choice of advisor right now ...

I suppressed a shiver.

'And,' Creon added, cocking his head at the maps on the table, 'she may get some advantage from attacking humans, in the end. If she has guessed we're looking for alliances in that direction, it's a brilliant opportunity to show the world once again what happens if you dare to turn against her.'

'Which is that people die,' I mumbled, the words on my tongue sour like bile.

He closed his eyes. 'Yes.'

'And we're ... we're really just going to let them die.'

This time, no one responded.

A sickening dread settled in my stomach, a sensation far too close to the memory of Khailan's hollow eyes, his trembling hand in mine. The best option, I tried to tell myself, the only thing we could do – but how could the best option still feel so decidedly *wrong*?

'I'll just start writing messages to the human cities,' I managed to whisper, feeling like a coward for even speaking the words out loud.

Tared's shoulders sagged a few inches on the other side of the table. 'Good. I'll start looking for the best places to send scouts.'

All the right plans, all the right decisions – and yet death loomed closer and closer and closer.

I didn't allow myself a single minute of pause for the rest of that hellish day – not a single minute to start thinking all over again, to start wondering whether it would be *that* bad an idea to find an alf willing to fade me to wherever the attack would take place and face the brunt of the Mother's wrath on my own ...

I knew what the answer would be.

I just didn't *want* to know.

So I made long lists of human islands to reach out to, then wrote polite letters to all of them. I found Alyra staring down an eagle ten times her size and cautiously managed to persuade her to leave the larger bird alone. I finally gave Creon his astrolabe and was rewarded with an expression remarkably similar to that of a young boy just handed his very first toolkit; it was the only thing that could bring a smile to my face that day.

The fae Beyla had sent out to take a look at the Mother's fleet did not return. I worked even harder trying not to think about what might have happened to them.

The day blurred into tents, faces, letters, and more letters. People asked questions — so many questions. Alf scouts set out to keep watch over other islands. Towards the end of the afternoon, when I passed one of the many cooking fires sprinkled throughout the camp, a firm human woman pushed a bag of onions into my arms and told me to make a start on peeling them if I didn't have anything better to do; to spare her the embarrassment, I spent the next half hour chopping onions, wiping tears from my eyes, and wondering how Tared would react if I were to name my sword Paring Knife.

Emelin Thenessa of Agenor's house, Onionbane. So many names no one had bothered to bestow upon me yet.

By the time the sky had gone a deep indigo, I was almost too tired to eat. I managed to choke down a single bowl of soup, then found myself leaning hazily against Creon's shoulders as around me alves faded back and forth to report their utter lack of information, an empty sea here, an island dozing peacefully there ... There was nothing I could do but sleep now, and yet I couldn't bring myself to cross the few dozen feet to the tent we'd been assigned — not if each next alf to arrive might just be the one to bring the news we were all hoping not to hear.

Still nothing on Nuesh — the king has called for arms anyway ...

They didn't pass Cape Dread yet ...

If Livosha is still quiet, they should be safe, right? The ships wouldn't have taken that long to get there?

Ever so slowly, the jumble of voices blurred into dreams.

I woke up one last time, drowsy and disoriented, as Creon was tucking me into bed, the tent cloth around us dimly lit by a waxing moon and the glow of distant campfires. My attempt at protest came out groggy with exhaustion and died a swift death as he slid below the blankets beside me, silky skin and firm muscle soothing me into silence.

'It's alright, cactus,' he muttered, arms wrapping around me. 'They'll wake us up if anything happens.'

If.

When.

But his body was warm against mine, and I was so very tired ...

I sank into feverish dreams of burning towns and screaming children, waking at every rustle and creak for the rest of the night.

I woke for what felt like the hundredth time when the first sunrays came filtering through the tent cloth above our heads. By that time, I was more than ready to leave my blankets – not because I was feeling in any way rested, but rather because every inch of my back had become far too intimately acquainted with the rocky earth after hours of dozing off and jolting awake again.

Next to me, Creon was still fast asleep. I wormed myself into a fresh dress and slipped out of the tent as quietly as I could, determined not to deny him these precious moments of peace.

The camp was still eerily quiet, no one but a handful of sleepy alves tiptoeing between the tents as I made my way to the latrine and then to the blue-and-white command tent. After the feverish activity of last night, the silence was jarring now; I found only Tared in a chair in the most shadowy corner of the tent, a bundle of blankets in his lap from which only some plucky red curls were sticking out at the top. He sent me a tired smile as I snuck in, gesturing at me not to speak too loud.

'Any news?' I breathed.

He shook his head, a slight frown on his face, as though he was feeling the same mixture of relief and suspicion about that fact. No attack – not yet. But the ships *had* gone on their way, and by this time, they should have arrived somewhere, unless the Mother was holding them back for some reason ...

And that reason could hardly be a positive one.

'Did Agenor and Rosalind show up yet?' I whispered, because there was little sense in discussing the thousand-and-one unhappy possibilities around a sleeping Lyn, and either way, I doubted we would have anything new to say to each other.

Tared shook his head again.

'Well.' I suppressed a sigh, fighting the unsettling apprehension creeping up on me – the feeling that we were overlooking something, that danger was looming just out of sight, and that it might come up to devour us far, far too soon. 'I'll go and see if I can drag them out of bed, in that case.'

He gave me a joyless grin. 'You rather than me.'

He was lucky Lyn let out an adorable little snore in his lap at that moment. I might have thrown something at him otherwise.

I found Agenor's red tent fastened shut, not a sound emerging from behind the sturdy waxed cloth. I threw a quick look over my shoulder to make sure no one was listening and said, voice hushed, 'Good morning?'

No reply followed for five, ten, then fifteen seconds.

'Hello?' I added, a little louder now. 'Anyone awake?'

This time a rustle and a groan-like sound emerged from inside the tent, followed by a dull thud that might have been a foot against the earth. Then, finally, Agenor's drowsy voice – 'Em? Is that you?'

'Ten points for you,' I said. 'Can I come in? There have been developments, and I think it's about time we start asking for your opinions again.'

He was silent for a moment or two, then managed a rather groggy, 'Right. If you could give us a moment ...'

Us. A tiny knot of tension loosened itself in my stomach.

'Happy to,' I said, moving my weight to my other leg. For a moment – a small but blissful moment – I almost laughed, ominous movements of the Mother be damned. 'You know patience is my greatest virtue. I hope I'm not arriving at an inopportune moment?'

'Never,' he said with a groan, followed by more thudding around the tent and then the suppressed sound of Rosalind's laughter. 'But for both your and my sakes ...'

'He's looking for trousers,' Rosalind helpfully translated, sounding a whole lot more awake.

I snorted a chuckle. 'Happy to wait, in that case.'

'Thanks, Al,' my father grumbled, voice muffled by the sound of the clothes he was pulling over his head. 'There goes the last of my parental authority.'

'Rest assured,' I said, 'you didn't have a lot of it before.'

Rosalind laughed again. The tent was opened from the inside a moment later, revealing a sloppily-dressed Agenor — bare feet, half-buttoned shirt, hair that could not have seen a comb anytime in the last twenty-four hours. His smile was apologetic and slightly fogged with sleep ... but something about him seemed softer, too, than I'd seen him in all these months.

No — *younger*.

Gone was that persistent weariness, the bitter lines burned around the corners of his eyes and lips by twelve hundred years of war and grief. His eyes were brighter, clearer. As if he'd woken up this morning and found that every fear and responsibility had abruptly lifted off his heart — as if he'd suddenly learned how to laugh again.

I'd come here to talk about war and strategy, and gods help me, now there was nothing I wanted to talk about less.

But he said, 'Developments?', and it seemed unlikely that he would agree to let it go if I told him to forget about it and to focus on his newfound happiness instead.

'It's the Mother,' I said, unable to suppress a smile when Rosalind let out a just-too-loud curse behind him. 'She's been sending out ships, but they haven't arrived anywhere so far, and we aren't sure where they would be arriving in the first place. So I thought ...'

His eyes narrowed abruptly at something behind me.

At the same moment, an alarmed cry went up at the edge of the camp.

I spun around, grabbing reflexively for the red tent cloth. What was wrong? No fae above us, no magic lighting up the sky as far as I could see …

But there, below the ridge of the hills, a lone grey horse came hurtling down the slope towards us, a small rider crouched over its back.

I had already started running.

Agenor caught up with me within seconds, boots on his feet and coat around his shoulders now – a speed honed by twelve hundred years of battle instinct. Neither of us spoke a word as we hurried to the edge of the camp together. In the morning quiet, no one but a handful of human guards had noticed our visitor approach, and they seemed more than happy to hand over the matter to us; the group of them watched quietly from a distance as my father and I strode out into the empty field, to where the horse was limping to a halt.

The poor animal foamed at the mouth, its grey coat shining with sweat and clots of blood. As soon as it thudded to a standstill, panting and heaving, the small human on its back let go of the tangled mane and started sliding, sliding, sliding …

Agenor's flash of yellow was just fast enough. The earth went soft and pliable a fraction of a moment before the rider hit the ground; with a few gentle bounces, their thin, bloodied body landed face-down in the grass and stayed there, motionless.

I swallowed a curse. 'Hello?'

No reaction followed.

I exchanged a quick glance with Agenor, then cautiously tiptoed forward when he nodded. The rider still didn't move when I knelt beside them and prodded a shoulder; my next attempt at a greeting went unanswered, too.

Not an ambush, then? I decided it was time to believe it.

Holding my breath, every muscle in my body tense, I wrapped my hands around those bony upper arms and rolled the limp figure over. The rider landed on their back with a dull thump … and only then did I see the battered face that emerged from below a grubby hood, a swollen black eye and a nose so crooked it must be broken. Short brown hair fell over a split eyebrow – a man's haircut, I would have said, and yet that face it stuck to …

A familiar face.

The realisation rose in me like a memory from a lifetime ago.

But that … that was *impossible*. I stared at those gruff, scrawny features and felt the grass sink away beneath my knees – no doubt about it, even below the disfigurement of her injuries. This was the same face that had scowled at me in the shadows of a dusky stable once. The same face that had furiously snapped at me to get the hell out of her sight while I cowered between the hay bales, desperate for a way to escape.

But that had been at the Crimson Court.

And humans at the court were *bound* to the island.

Cold goosebumps rose over my back and shoulders. She shouldn't be here. She *couldn't* possibly be here … not unless …

'Finn?' I breathed.

A swollen, purple-green eye opened.

'*Finn.*' My voice broke. She looked like someone had made earnest attempts to bludgeon her to death for hours, and yet that stubborn fury in her gaze remained – meeting my eyes with instant recognition and something almost like relief.

Chapped lips parted, releasing a hoarse croak. 'The city …'

'What happened?' I was close to shrieking now. 'Who hurt you like this? Did you—'

'The White City,' she rasped, interrupting me with the urgency of a dying plea. Her bloodied, claw-like hands came up to grab the front of my dress, holding on for dear life. 'Emelin, the Mother … the Mother has taken the *city*.'

Chapter 28

'That's impossible,' I heard myself say.

The words had left my mouth before I could think twice about them, blunt and brusque in the soft morning air. I hadn't meant to call her a liar, the girl who'd once risked her life to help me free Creon from the Mother's clutches. I hadn't meant to doubt her sanity. But my mind heard the words and failed, utterly and completely, to connect them to the realm of reality as I knew it ...

The Mother.

Taking the city.

But the city was *safe*. Wasn't that the one thing we could be sure of – that those walls, built and protected by gods, had kept all traces of magic outside for hundreds of years? So unless the consuls had opened the gates to her, it couldn't be. And the two men we had left behind wouldn't be *that* desperate, would they?

Would they?

'I *saw* them,' Finn defiantly rasped, her eyes wide with horror. 'She made me go on that ship to take care of the horses – she broke my binding to the island to put me on that ship – and then when they finally let us out, I saw the walls of the city and all of them flying right over them. They sent me after them with the carts and when I got there ...'

She choked up, hands clutching my dress as if she was trying to tear it in half.

'Good gods,' Agenor muttered behind me. 'Good *gods*.'

I stared at the wounded girl in front of me, mind not so much spinning in thought as spinning out of control – unable to turn my shock into a coherent line of reasoning, to hear her and believe her and *understand*. So Norris and Halbert hadn't opened the gates. A relief, in a way, and yet it was worse, too – because if it hadn't been the gates, then what in hell had happened?

Right over the walls. Which the Mother had tried before, hadn't she? Tried it and never managed – so why would those god-forged defences suddenly give in now, at the worst possible moment, if they'd held fast for hundreds and hundreds of years?

The only thing that had changed in the meantime ...

The breath stopped dead in my throat, frozen in absolute certainty.

'How did you get here?' Agenor was asking, his deep voice incomprehensibly calm behind me. 'Did they let you go?'

'I tried to escape,' she whispered. 'Tried to sneak out with one of the horses. And then they caught me.'

I stared at her injuries, the purple contusions on her face and the bloody scrapes covering her hands and wrists, and wanted to throw up.

'They were going to kill me.' An audible memory of pain and fear haunted her rough voice. 'But then the Mother made them stop and told them I could be useful. And then she sent me here to tell you ... to tell you ...'

Her damaged lips moved, not a sound coming out.

'Finn?' Agenor said, and I vaguely realised he must have learned her name from me. Had she even been born yet when he left the Crimson Court some twenty years ago?

And hell, did it matter?

'I have to tell you ...' She aimed her gaze back at me, voice faltering to a barely audible whisper. 'I have to tell you that if you surrender yourself to her, she will let the people in the city go. Alive and unharmed.'

Behind me, Agenor cursed.

I couldn't bring myself to speak. Finn was still holding my dress, and the desperate urgency in her look said she wasn't done speaking yet – that she hadn't gotten to the worst of it yet.

'But if ... if you don't ...' she breathed.

And it was in that moment that I knew exactly what she was about to say.

I watched her lips shape the words with an uncanny sensation of recognition, a familiarity so strong that I could have spoken the words aloud with her – the only thing the Mother's vicious mind could have come up with, a trap so perfect that some sick, twisted part of me couldn't help but admire it even as it closed around me.

'If you don't surrender yourself to her by tomorrow night,' Finn whispered, and a first furious tear came trickling down her cheek, 'she will kill every single one of them.'

The entire city.

All those people who had never needed to be warriors in their lives. All those children who had never even seen a magical being up close. Everyone, for hell's sake, who had opted to stay at home and not involve themselves in a gruelling war.

Easy prey.

It felt like a betrayal, that thought. As if it made me just as bad, the simple act of having thought it. As if I should have seen it coming and ignored it, an oversight that did not make me an accomplice but that at least assigned me part of the guilt.

They *were* easy prey, the people of the White City. The only defence they had was the magic of their walls, and that ...

That had failed them.

Three days after I had walked through their gates, the first wielder of magic to visit the city since it had been built.

Agenor was saying something behind me. The words never reached my ears.

'Make sure she sees a healer,' I heard myself say, my voice so unimaginably crisp and clear against the primal scream rising in my head. My fingers pried Finn's away from my dress, and surprisingly, she obliged without protest. 'And do ... do whatever else you think is necessary. You know better than I do.'

The ominous silence behind me spoke volumes.

Then my father's voice again, sharper now. 'Em?'

I got to my feet and walked.

'Emelin!' That was real, gut-tearing fear in his voice, a rare crack of the polish. 'Emelin, where are you going? Don't you *dare*—'

I started running.

Uneven earth below my boots, ankles twisting painfully with every step, and I barely felt it – couldn't care about something as trivial as pain as my world rapidly folded in, mind somehow empty despite the avalanche of thoughts barrelling in. Away – that was where I was going. Out of here – the only destination I could wrap my head around. And if that road happened to lead east, towards the city ...

Maybe it was for the best if the choice made itself for me.

We'd all seen what happened when making the decisions was left to me, after all.

If only I'd just used my magic when I first thought of it. If only I hadn't been so stupid, so desperate, so stupidly, desperately reckless, to try and break those age-old laws I should have known were there for a reason – to believe myself above the rules by which all other mortals and immortals had to abide. I could have stayed at home, and tens of thousands of people would still be sleeping safely in their beds. I could have done my duty, and no children would be captured, maimed, killed.

Instead ...

Tomorrow night.

Too soon. We needed more time than that if we wanted any hope of survival to cling to – there was no sense in charging mindlessly at the Crimson Court without our human allies, without our poisons and alf steel projectiles, without the bindings figured out. Which Agenor knew. Hell, which every halfwit on our side knew.

Which meant we weren't going to attack in time.

Which meant the White City was going to die. That the friendly server in that restaurant was going to die, and the astrolabe merchant, and ...

I couldn't allow myself to think the next two names on that list. *Dying, dying, dying.*

Hills and forests swallowed me. My breath was a ragged mess in my throat, my heart was pounding painfully against my ribs, and still I kept running, unable to think of anything else to do. What was the alternative – going back to the camp? Facing two thousand humans whose parents and siblings and friends had stayed behind in the city, brand new little toys for the Mother to play with?

Pain was better.

Pain at least allowed me to think.

I had to do *something*, that was the one thing I could be sure of. If I had ruined humanity's last safe refuge, I was the one who should go and fix it – a simple matter of justice, of actions and consequences. So what options did I have? Begging the rest of the alliance to join my madman's quest and help me save the city?

It's hardly a matter of wanting, Nenya had said yesterday. *Rather what we can afford.*

They couldn't afford an unprepared attack.

And they were right, but that cold, ruthless calculation didn't change anything about the guilt that kept my feet moving and moving and moving, the unforgivable mistakes that were mine and mine alone. It didn't scrub the sickening images from my mind's eye, the quiet, peaceful streets and the swarms of wings eclipsing the starry skies.

So perhaps going east was the best I could do. Perhaps—

A shadow fell over me.

And no matter the guilt, no matter the urgency driving my limbs forward, twenty years of prey instinct were enough to make me freeze on the spot as the sunlight drew the rough shape of wings on the grass around me.

Creon landed next to me a moment later, inaudible save for the last slap of his wings, which sent a gust of air into my face even from ten feet away. He couldn't have been awake for more than ten minutes, and already he looked perfectly ready for war – knives at his belt, hair bound back, that icy coldness in his eyes that came with the prospect of blood to spill.

The perfect predator ... yet all he did, after finding his footing on the uneven ground and folding his wings against his shoulders, was smile a razor-sharp smile at me. 'Morning, cactus.'

I stared at him, frozen like a panicking rabbit, too out of breath to get a sensible word past my lips.

It didn't matter how casual he made that greeting sound. It didn't matter how leisurely he stood there between the pine trees and the wild grass, hands in his pockets, wings deceptively relaxed. He trailed his gaze over me just once, that piercing, all-seeing demon gaze, and I knew he knew exactly what had just happened, the threats, the promises. He knew the thoughts whirling through my mind, too, and somehow that was worse – to know not just that I had failed, but to have it laid open like this, a bare wound for the world to see.

But all he said, still so dangerously calm, was, 'So what do you think you're doing?'

I wrapped my arms around myself, jutting my chin forward defiantly. 'Something.'

'Ah.' His expression neither sharpened nor softened. 'I see. And that *something* does not, by any chance, include an attempt to hand yourself over to her, does it?'

I didn't reply.

I had no idea what to say to him – not to *him*. To anyone else I could have lied. *No, I just need a little time for myself. No, I'm just trying to think.* But he wouldn't believe me, and somehow that made even the thought of trying a nauseating one – unthinkable, to betray his trust that way.

'Em ...' he said.

There was a layer of disappointment in that one word that made me wince.

'Do you even fully realise what happened?' I managed – a desperate effort to explain myself, to myself as much as to him. 'The walls should have stopped her – should have stopped all of them. The only reason I can think of that they didn't—'

'Is that the laws of the city weren't a formality but rather codified instructions from the gods themselves?' Creon finished, still so unfathomably unmoved. He hadn't even pulled his hands from his pockets. 'Yes. I figured. She must have known the true meaning of that law, for her army to be here so swiftly.'

The Mother, who had lived with the gods – who had known more of their secrets than anyone else in the world ... She must have made her plans the moment she heard I'd travelled to the city. Most likely, she'd laughed herself to shambles all the way through, too.

Had she hoped to catch me there, still enjoying the consuls' ill-advised hospitality? Or had she deliberately waited until I'd left, helpfully taking every battleworthy citizen with me, and then swept in to destroy the last little hope humanity had left?

So much for killing the bitch.

So much for saving the world.

'So they wouldn't be facing death if not for me, right?' I creaked. 'They would all still be fine if not for me.'

He raised one eyebrow a fraction. 'Yes, I suppose one could make that argument.'

An agreement, of sorts, and yet it didn't sound like he agreed with me at all. I took a single wobbly step backwards, as if a few more inches between us would change anything about the way his words sent my mind even more wildly awhirl, and managed, 'So I messed up really, really badly, don't you see?'

'Oh, I see.' It wasn't annoyance in his voice. It was tiredness. It was the smallest, softest sliver of sadness. 'As did your mother for letting you into the city, I would argue. As did Agenor for not realising just how the magic of those walls operated despite having had several centuries in the company of both the Mother and the gods to figure it out. They are blaming themselves plenty right now, in case you were wondering.'

I didn't want to admit I hadn't even thought of wondering about that. 'But I was the one who came up with the plan. I was the one who walked through those gates and ruined everything.'

He sighed. 'So what?'

'So I have to fix it.' I let out a shrill laugh, the sound teetering on the edge of hysteria. 'Or are you going to tell me I should just let these people die as well, like all of you were planning for any other place she might have attacked?'

I was lashing out – I knew I was, and yet I didn't seem able to stop. Perhaps I would feel better if he got angry with me for *this* reason, if he refused to do it because of my deadly failures; perhaps he would turn his back on me and allow me to do whatever reckless things my heart was aching to do.

He did not get angry.

He did not turn his back on me.

'Em.' So dangerously calm. So treacherously gentle. 'We both know you're not here to fix anything. You're here because you're trying to punish yourself again. You should know by now that I can tell the difference between those two things, even if you stubbornly insist on confusing them.'

I stared at him.

'So is this really how you want to go about this?' he continued, and the lethal little tilt of his head was all he needed to keep me rooted to the spot, unable to lift those feet that had been so eager to flee a minute ago. His gaze was like a dagger to the heart. 'Doom us all to an inglorious defeat by throwing yourself into her hands, so you'll feel like you've at least suffered appropriately for your crimes? Just because you've lived all your life believing that no mistake may exist without retribution and—'

My hand jerked itself forward – as if I could silence him by clenching my fingers over that merciless mouth. 'Stop it!'

'No, *you* stop it, Em.' And there was the anger, finally – a tremor of something dark, a sudden sharpness to the words spilling violently from his lips. It didn't make me feel better. It felt much, much worse instead. 'You can go around expecting flawless perfection of yourself, you can beat yourself up over every little misstep if you think it'll make you happier, but I'm drawing the line here – you're not going to hand yourself over to her like some spineless coward because you're still trying to please some phantom voice it's not possible to please. You're not going to turn yourself into some useless martyr for them.'

Them.

A punch to the gut.

'Or what?' My voice soared, throwing those two words into his face with whip-like sharpness – all I could do to keep him away from those deepest parts of me, from something I'd rather protect with every last drop of my strength than take even a single look at. Anger was easy. Anger was safe. The feeling stirring just below the surface, a jagged, damaged thing that chafed and abraded ... it was neither. 'If I *want* to be a spineless coward, what are you going to do about it? Stop me?'

'Oh, I'll fight you,' he coolly informed me.

That shut me up for a moment.

He merely sent me another joyless smile – but there was no doubt in the gesture, no trace of jest. Six feet of scars and muscle, hardened and honed. Magic his body could barely contain, with all the black he needed at his fingertips. I may be unbound and godsworn, may wear the unwanted title of the Mother's foremost enemy ... but I was standing there in nothing but a light blue dress, and that look in his eyes promised me he wouldn't hesitate to take advantage of my every weakness if he thought it necessary.

'I might beat you,' I said weakly, because I had to say *something*.

'You might,' he conceded, apparently unbothered by the possibility. 'Or you might not. We never really tested it out, did we?'

'And you ...' It was becoming harder and harder to find words, to keep speaking as my chest constricted dangerously. *Fight you.* I couldn't tell whether it was a promise or a threat. 'You might hurt me.'

A shrug. 'Not nearly as much as the Mother would.'

'Oh, for fuck's sake – Creon, *please*.' I struggled a single step away from him. *Dying, dying, dying,* sang that same phantom voice I didn't want to think about, *and it's all because of you.* 'I'll think of something. I won't be stupid. I just need to—'

His hand closed around my forearm.

His other arm swept around my waist.

Like a child, I was lifted off my feet and dragged with my back against his chest – the Silent Death, stealing me once again. Constraining me. *Dying, dying, dying*, and they wouldn't stop dying either, would be left to their own devices as the Mother counted down the hours, until tomorrow's sun sank below the horizon and she gleefully, ruthlessly unleashed the horror of her magic upon the first blameless citizens ...

Something broke within me.

I had allowed the reins to slacken once before, standing barefoot on the mother-of-pearl tiles of the Golden Court – had reached out to find my magic and found it willing to come to me from places I had never looked before. But there was no reaching out, this time. The power threw itself onto me instead, and all I did was lose control – all I did was fail to stop what I'd set free as the colours surged through me and roared out of me like a wild creature breaking free.

It was the black of his shirt, pressed against my upper arms.

It was the brown of my hair, curls brushing over my scalp.

It was the bronze of his fingers on my skin, the grey on the inside of my boots, every impossible little fleck of colour I should never have been able to draw, and I soaked them up like I was starving, unable to fend them off as my world turned red and my mind turned red and everything I smelled and heard and felt turned red ...

Someone shouted my name, and even that sound had a crimson edge to it. *My fault. My fault.* They were all dying, children and elders and those two people whose faces I couldn't even bear to think of, who had to know by now, who had to realise that they would die and I was the reason, that the curse on their household had come to haunt them yet again ...

And just as abruptly, with a cold sting of metal against my wrist, it was over.

I came to my senses in a world nothing like the one in which I'd stood a moment before – no more pine trees, no more piles of boulders, no more ferns and moss and knee-high grass. We were standing in a wasteland, nothing but splintered wood and shattered stone as far as the eye could see, and the colours ...

Creon's skin had paled against mine. So had his scars. The red had bled from his shirt, leaving a muddy green behind; the locks of hair curling over my shoulders had turned an even sicklier greenish brown.

The blade of his alf steel dagger lay pressed flat against my arm, gleaming whiter than anything else around us.

Slowly, ever so slowly, reality stitched itself back together in my mind.

'No.' A breathless, powerless plea. 'No ... no, I didn't mean to ...'

Creon's rough breath behind me was enough to interrupt that sorry excuse for a sentence – not a laugh, not a sigh, not a groan of despair. 'In control again, cactus?'

'Yes,' I whispered, unable to look away from the devastation around us – the devastation *I* had caused. Trees that had witnessed centuries, snapped like twigs. Solid stones, cracked like hearts. The firestorm of red had washed my anger away with it. And now that broken, agonised monster below was rising to the surface after all, demanding to be seen, demanding to be felt – worming its way into the tips of my toes and fingers until there was nowhere left for me to hide ...

'It's alright, Em,' Creon muttered against the crown of my head, slipping his dagger back into its sheath. His voice, that rough, golden voice, was like a caress, like the softest woolen blanket around my shoulders. 'It's alright.'

A first tear broke free.

Then a second one.

I sagged against his chest and crumpled as the last of my shields disintegrated – folded into some helpless, powerless creature, all grown up and still so very small, godsworn mage and still not good enough. He scooped me into his arms without another word. I curled up against his shoulder and bawled like a baby into his shirt – cried for every wound I couldn't heal, for every gap I couldn't fill, for every heart I couldn't force to beat again. For the hours counting down. For all I had lost and all I stood to lose.

'Em ...' Creon whispered.

'What is the bloody use of it?' I sobbed, words a snotty, indistinguishable mess. 'Why do I have these bloody powers if I can't even save people with them – if I can't even save ... save ...'

He carefully sat down, arms cradling me, lowering me into his lap. 'Even if you can't be everyone's hero, that doesn't make you a villain, cactus.'

'I don't feel like a villain,' I blubbered. 'I just feel like a failure.'

'Oh, for fuck's sake.' His lips brushed the crown of my head, tender and chastising at once. 'Emelin Thenessa, love of my life, you're farther from a failure than anyone I've ever met in this world. Don't try to argue. It will win you nothing but more declarations of my heartfelt admiration, and they will be *elaborate*.'

But it was easy for him to admire me, wasn't it? He wasn't living between those corrupted walls, waiting for the end to come. He hadn't fed and raised a child through twenty years of near-starvation, only for the wretched creature to come back and kill him.

'You keep trying to be perfect, Em.' As if he had read the thoughts playing through my mind. 'You keep trying to be the flawless hero. But I truly don't think it's perfection that will save us in the end. It's persistence. It's digging your heels in the sand and refusing to give up until things are finally as they are supposed to be – and mistakes or no, you've always been frighteningly good at being stubborn.'

A small whimper escaped me, pressed against his shirt. 'She controls the entire known world now. Things couldn't be *less* like they are supposed to be.'

'And so you give up?'

A challenge, that question. I was too exhausted to accept it – too exhausted to do the hard work of hoping and having faith when there was so very little left in the world to have faith in.

'Our army is too small,' I whispered.

He sighed. 'I know.'

Not what I had expected him to say – not the obligatory optimism I thought one was supposed to feign under these circumstances. The surprise made my next sentence come out more defensive than I'd planned. 'And we still can't use our magic properly, either.'

'Absolutely true,' he admitted, with not a moment of hesitation, and somehow he sounded almost ... amused about it?

That didn't make sense. I tilted up my head to look him in the eye, forgetting for a moment to feel lost and defeated – but good gods, he really *was* smiling, brightly and mischievously, as if the persistent existence of the bindings was a wry joke rather than a disadvantage that might kill us.

Madman.

There was something annoyingly alluring about that smile.

'And ...' My voice came out more firmly now. Damn him, but I could take this challenge; how many reminders of our dire situation did I have to throw at him to wipe that impossible amusement off his face? 'And she's holding tens of thousands of hostages that she won't be afraid to kill.'

He didn't sober up in the slightest. 'Yes, she is.'

This was some stupid game, wasn't it? Simple, transparent bait and nothing else? And yet I couldn't withstand the temptation to sit straighter, sniff defiantly, and say, 'So we can't really win this war anymore. Whatever we do, she has us in a corner.'

'Yes.' He shrugged, scarred eyebrow a fraction higher than the other. 'So let me repeat the question – are you giving up?'

A question.

Because I still had a *choice*.

It was so easy, the idea of accepting my failure at this point – so easy I had overlooked the fact that I might still have other options. Surrender was simple. At least if I had committed the ultimate failure, I had no mistakes left to make. At least if I suffered enough in their place, bloody Valter and Editta would know I had not failed lightly.

But I would doom Creon in my attempts to absolve myself.

I would deny my friends their last hope of victory.

And I would never see that house by the sea, with its icehouse and its stained-glass windows and its library within a library. We would never get those stupid cats.

The prospect of going on, of risking all those lives and knowing we'd most likely fail to save them ... It was like staring down a solid brick wall, miles high and impossible to scale. Impossible enough to almost send me running. Impossible enough to make me want to break down crying and never even try.

Then again ...

I knew what lay on the other side of that wall.

I just had to keep knowing that.

'No,' I whispered.

Creon tilted his head, something wicked flickering back to life in his eyes. 'Say that again?'

'No,' I croaked out again, a little louder now. 'I ... I'm not giving up.'

'Are you sure?' The innocent flutter of his long lashes could have fooled me — that saintly expression on his sinfully handsome face, so close to true sincerity. 'You could make it sound more convincing, you know.'

'Oh, go to hell,' I burst out, and suddenly I knew how to fight again, how to survive again — hell, how to *want* again. 'Fine! We're not giving up! We ... we're going to try and save the city, and if we can't save the city, we're going to kill her, and if we don't manage that either, at least we're going to die bravely and with our weapons in our hands. There. Is that what you wanted to hear?'

His lips curved. 'And there's my cactus again.'

I wanted to slap him. I wanted to laugh. I wanted to kiss him until neither of us could string a coherent word together and the city and its dreadful fate were all but forgotten.

'You're a horrible, horrible person, have I told you that?' I grumbled instead.

'You may have mentioned something once or twice,' he dryly admitted, lifting me with him as he rose to his feet, then planting me back on my own in a single effortless movement. His hand came up, brushing a feathery line down my temple, tucking a stray lock of hair behind my ear. 'So far the pretty face seems to compensate for it, though.'

I punched him.

I *tried*, at least, and got within five inches of his face before his larger hand wrapped around my knuckles and stopped me in mid-air — holding me in place so easily, as if I hadn't spent months swinging weapons around, growing stronger than I'd ever been in my life. Infuriating … but that smirk spreading across his face only strengthened the budding determination within me, a brand new feeling as reckless as it was addictive.

We might not be able to win this war.

I might not be good enough to win this war.

But if I had to lose, I could lose *obstinately*, as stubborn as that fist trying to push its way through a hand that would never let it. And if that was the best option I had left …

I yanked back my arm, away from Creon's hand, and drew in the deepest breath I'd taken all day. It wiped something clean within me, that breath, not unlike the way my storm of red magic had levelled the forest around us – cutting through obstacles rooted so deep I hadn't thought it would be possible to move them at all.

Damn it all.

If this was my best option, then stubborn I *would* be – through war and devastation, until my very last breath.

Chapter 29

The army camp was in an uproar.

Even as we flew over it, it was clear that the news of the White City had spread between the tents: the serene peace of that morning had been cruelly disturbed, and the sound of sobs, desperate shouts, and demands for answers rose from every corner of the camp. From above, I spotted Delwin, gesturing reassuringly at a small group of yelling men. His own sister had stayed behind in the city, I recalled – how much longer would he be able to stand it, pretending it was all under control and would be solved soon?

Better not to wait for that moment.

Creon's tense arms around me told me he was equally prepared to defend us against sudden human rebellion.

But in good wingless tradition, no one looked up to see us fly over, and our arrival at the command tent was witnessed only by the small crowd that had gathered around it, desperately waiting for news or strategies. I told them I didn't have any new information yet, then hurried towards the entrance of the tent – feeling like a coward as they hurled more and more questions after me, but unsure what else I could do before I had spoken to the others. At the very least, I could make sure to be out of the way before any of them could decide that more answers might just be worth a meeting with Creon's knives.

The tent cloth must have been infused with magic. I didn't hear so much as a whisper, even when I stood a single step away from the entrance, yet the moment I parted the strips of waxed linen, Agenor's voiced washed over me. Sharp and impatient – the sound of my father pushed to the very edges of his self-restraint.

'... severely outnumbered,' he was just saying as I slipped in. 'As heartless as it sounds, waiting and growing our forces before attacking—'

'No one is going to join our forces after they hear we allowed the White City to be slaughtered to the last child,' Rosalind cut in, her tone even more biting. 'Not a single human will. You'd be abandoning the city for— Oh, *Em*!'

There was a relief in the sound of my name, an abrupt loosening of tension, that made me want to cower and crawl into her arms at the same time.

Every single one of them had to notice my greenish hair and the obvious evidence of red pulled from Creon's shirt – and yet no one breathed a word about any of it. Lyn sent me a watery smile from the other side of the table. Tared managed to make his muttered greeting sound like I'd never been anywhere I wasn't supposed to be. Finn, sitting hunched and purple-faced next to Rosalind, threw me a grateful look that suggested she had not been prepared to be roped into a heated meeting of magical creatures.

Only Agenor gave a slight grimace on the edge of my sight, mouthing a silent *thank you* at Creon as he followed me into the tent.

I could forgive him for that, though.

'Look,' Lyn said to Rosalind as we sat down, as if we had never interrupted the discussion at all. I was strangely grateful for the pretence of normalcy. 'I see your point – I really do. The last thing I want is to leave the city to its own devices. But I've tried to battle the Mother in a rush before, and that ...'

She swallowed. The rest of her sentence hung in the air between us, bitter and smelling of rot and blood – the white battlefield of Sevrith, the thousands and thousands who'd found their deaths between those hills. A defeat that had doomed most of the magical world to slow extinction, that had forced her to spend her next hundred and thirty years hiding beneath the earth, praying for the impossible to happen …

Never again, her menacing silence said. *I'd rather die.*

I believed it, too.

'And we don't even know if Achlys and Melinoë will still be here tomorrow,' Agenor added, voice low, jaw gritted so tight his strong face seemed all angles and lines. 'If they have any sense left, they should be returning to the Crimson Court as soon as possible to wait for our response. And if we only get a single chance to attack, we shouldn't exhaust ourselves trying to take back the city while they're sitting safely on the other side of the archipelago.'

Rosalind scoffed. 'Apparently she's planning to stay for long enough to collect Em tomorrow.'

'Can't be sure about that,' Lyn said, an edge of apology to her voice as she glanced from me to my mother. 'She may feel nervous enough about Em to leave it to someone else to chain her up and ship her to the Crimson Court – I'm sure she'd have plenty of volunteers. Nor does she need to stay here to act on her threats, for that matter.'

Her threats.

To kill tens of thousands of harmless, defenceless people.

I understood every single one of their doubts, understood every single argument, and yet I refused to believe that their conclusions were true – that we should wait and give up on those lives, that we would serve the greater good by leaving the White City to die. But Rosalind was silent. Tared seemed to be chewing on his own thoughts. Finn, face clean but still distorted by injuries she must not have allowed the mages to heal, looked closer to tears than I'd ever seen her before.

I glanced to the side to meet Creon's eyes – *see*, I wanted to say, *see why I had to run and solve it all by myself?*

But Creon wasn't looking at me. Sprawled in his seat, wings draped loosely over the backrest with an air of casual invincibility, he'd narrowed his eyes at Finn – focus sharpening his features into an expression I knew all too well, that thrill of a predator finding spoor to follow. A look that promised either brilliance or danger. His eyes didn't betray which of the options it might be, dark pools of ink reflecting nothing of the mind behind.

I dared to assume it wouldn't be a suggestion to leave the city to die, though.

'Creon?'

Now he did glance my way, a swift turn of his head. 'I'm thinking about her throne.'

'Her— *Oh*.' I veered up straighter and whirled back to look at Finn, small and grubby by my mother's side. 'You said you were made to assist her with the transport, yes? Did you by any chance see that damned throne of hers anywhere, on the ship or near the wagons?'

She flinched as six pairs of eyes suddenly swept towards her, her gruff voice little more than a whisper. 'The ... the bones?'

'Yes. Did you see it?'

Her gaze darted towards Creon and back to me, sharp with all the suspicion of a girl born and raised at the Crimson Court – trained to distrust fae and their words before she'd learned to walk. She didn't speak.

'Finn?' I said quietly.

Her nod was barely more than a single, involuntary twitch of the head. But it *was* a nod, and Tared's slow, meaningful hiss was proof enough I was not the only one who'd seen it.

'Well, there you have it,' Creon said, sending Agenor a mirthless smile as he leisurely began rolling up his left sleeve – revealing a muscular bronze forearm, marked by the map of inked scars I could have drawn blindly. Such a calm, unthreatening gesture, and yet it somehow brought to mind the sharpening of a blade. 'My bet is she intends to stay for a while, in that case. Transporting the bloody thing isn't that simple.'

A brief silence settled over the table as that point sank in.

I couldn't help but imagine that stately white room with its statues and the lily banner that must have taken years to complete – imagined Ophion gloatingly smashing the marble consuls off their pedestals, imagined that monstrous pile of bones erected in the place where Rosalind had smacked Halbert in the face two mornings ago. From the feverish gleam in her eyes, my mother was seeing very similar visions play across her mind.

'Why in the world would she stay?' Lyn muttered, looking nauseous. 'She has everything she'll ever need at the court. Why would she go to these lengths to turn those poor people's lives into a living hell?'

'They would like the symbolism of it, I think,' Agenor said, bleakly rubbing his temples. 'The last place capable of resisting them, finally made to serve them. It sounds like something they'd find amusing.'

'Oh, yes,' Creon muttered, and the bitterness in his voice made me wince. 'Absolutely hilarious.'

The look of understanding that went back and forth between the two of them was a rare one – a glimpse of centuries of mutual history, of shared memories that not even the deepest grudges, disagreements, or dislike could ever erase. How many times had they sat with her in that hall of bones and heard her forge these same vindictive plans, hating every word from her lips yet unable to do anything to stop her?

'Honestly,' Creon added, averting his gaze to finish the work on his second moss-green sleeve, 'if she brought her throne, I wouldn't be surprised if she's planning to turn the place into a fourth court. One for every point on the compass. The Marble Court, or ...'

'My bet is on Alabaster Court,' Tared said, wry gallows humour lacing his voice. 'Has a more dignified ring to it.'

Creon's snort came suspiciously close to a laugh. 'Ten silverlings.'

'*Boys,*' Lyn hissed, glancing ruefully at Rosalind. '*Please.* It's hardly relevant what she's naming the place when we just need to get her out of it.'

'Fifteen,' Tared muttered under his breath at Creon, then barely dodged the small fireball Lyn flung at him. I would have laughed if not for Rosalind, whose tight lips and paling knuckles suggested she'd left just a few too many friends and acquaintances behind to appreciate any attempts at lightness right now.

The glance Agenor sent her didn't escape me. Nor did the hand he lowered behind the table to squeeze hers, or the shivery breath that escaped her in response.

My heart constricted a little.

'Court names aside,' I said before anyone could break the silence with more sensible but unbearable arguments about delaying our attack, 'wouldn't it be more beneficial for us to strike as soon as possible if we know she's likely staying there? At least the city is still mostly unfamiliar to her now, and our human army knows it very well. Might be a small advantage.'

Agenor hesitated. 'Yes, but—'

'She also will have left a considerable force behind at the Crimson Court,' Creon smoothly interrupted, his wings unfurling a fraction as he sat straighter. 'More of them might come this way in the coming days or weeks. I'd personally prefer to attack before they arrive – especially if we have little hope of growing our own army, as Rosalind argued.'

'Before they arrive, perhaps,' Agenor said sharply, 'but *tomorrow*?'

Creon shrugged, a small smile tugging at those soft lips. 'We might surprise her *and* ourselves.'

'Much more likely, they'll obliterate us.' A joyless laugh. 'I don't have to tell *you* this is a madman's gamble, do I?'

'Did that ever stop me before?' Creon dryly said.

My father's overly restrained inhalation gave the impression his self-control was hanging by a last fraying thread, and his sanity, too. 'Must you?'

'Someone has to do it.' And in the blink of an eye, that nettling amusement had melted off his face – no more princely provocations, that flippant arrogance reminding every single soul around him that even the deadliest battles had rarely been more than a game to him. In its place a cold ruthlessness arose, the Silent Death calculating his path to victory. 'The simple fact is she's only growing stronger and we're only growing weaker. So you can do what you always do and wait for certainties and guarantees until half of us are cold in the ground—'

'Oh, see?' Rosalind muttered, a pale smile flickering over her face. 'Hearing it from someone else for once.'

Agenor fell back in his chair, cursing under his breath. 'We may lose more people on the battlefield than we'll save by acting quickly.'

'Which is true for any battle,' Creon countered without flinching. 'So unless you're waiting for her to surrender—'

My father gave another mirthless huff. 'Please. Fae wars don't end in surrender.'

'Oh, I know.' His smile said he did, indeed – a smile that could have won a small battle in its own right. 'So then fight.'

Agenor looked close to the point of strangulation.

'We might not even get all our allies to show up on such short notice,' Lyn said, and as much as she was fighting to keep her voice composed, the small sparks dancing in and out of existence on her fingers and forearms betrayed her mounting anxiety. 'Last time they heard from us, we promised them a convincing strategy to get through this alive. There are some who might resist a call to arms for something they have no reason to believe will be a winning battle.'

'I'm more than happy to duel the head of any alf house causing trouble,' I generously offered.

She whimpered. 'Em …'

'Much as I appreciate the violent spirit,' Tared said wryly, 'I suggest we try some alternative solutions first. A decent strategy will likely go a long way to convince them, too.'

'Which we don't have,' Agenor muttered.

'Oh, good gods – stop *wallowing*, Lord Protector.' Rosalind's withering glare was a masterpiece – a look that abruptly made me understand exactly how she'd managed to turn his world inside out in the span of just a few weeks, all those years ago. 'Imagine we forced you at knifepoint to attack tomorrow. What would you do? You used to be rather good at this sort of thing, so unless the years are finally creeping up on you …'

He groaned. 'Below the belt, Al.'

'All's fair in love and war,' she retorted, snatching one of the maps from the centre of the table – a hastily sketched overview of the White City, the rough shape of walls and a lake suggested. 'Here you go. What do we do?'

Agenor parted his lips as if to object – then seemed to think better of it and sagged in his chair with nothing but a ragged groan, fingers rubbing over the cuff of his sleeve in restless, aimless circles. 'So do I understand ...' His voice, deep and polished, gave way for a moment. 'Gods and demons, is the conclusion that we are, in all seriousness, going to try and topple the empire on an unknown battlefield and with not even twenty-four hours of preparation?'

A madman's gamble, indeed.

I should have been afraid. Somewhere, in a dark, neglected part of my mind, the fear was trying to make itself heard, clamouring to be noticed – trying to make me realise, fully realise, that I might lose half of my family tomorrow, that tonight's sunset might be the last I'd ever see. But the impatient thumping of my heart drowned out most of those thoughts, smothered the sharpest of my nerves; what was the sense in lingering on any of it, after all, if I wasn't stopping anyway?

I'd prepared for this day since the first time I'd set foot on the fae isles. The thought of finally looking the Mother in her damaged eyes again came with more twisted eagerness than anything else.

'I'm ready to go,' I said.

It seemed ridiculous they were still listening to *me* – the very person whose opinions had landed them here in the first place. But Rosalind's eyes flickered with satisfaction as she leaned back in her chair. Lyn and Tared exchanged a short look, then both nodded – his face grim, hers wide-eyed and anxious.

Next to me, Creon just smiled – that glass-edged smile promising violence.

Agenor let out a long sigh, eyes closing briefly. But all he said was, 'Very well.'

And just like that, a plan was made.

Tomorrow. Impossibly close, suddenly, after months and months of hiding; I couldn't even begin to imagine how the others must have been feeling, realising that a century of clandestine rebellion was abruptly coming to an end. Yet there was no theatrical gravity to their expressions, no sense of dramatic despair. Even Lyn managed the most watery of smiles as she settled her little elbows on the table surface, wiped the messy curls from her face, and said, 'I would still like to have a strategy, though.'

That broke the strange, expectant stillness.

'The rough plan we had in mind for the Crimson Court still holds, of course,' Agenor muttered, pinching the bridge of his nose. 'Emphasis on weapons with a greater range. Find some way to distract the bulk of their army while Em and Creon try to reach Achlys and Melinoë in their throne room, wherever it is now. It's a shame we don't have the Labyrinth here to smuggle them in belowground, but—'

'There are the tunnels, though,' Rosalind unexpectedly interrupted. 'If you need another way in, those might just come in handy.'

We all stared at her.

'They're supposed to be a secret,' she added, snatching the sketched map away from Agenor with sudden feverish excitement. 'Known only to the consuls and a handful of guards. They were created as an escape route after Consul Millard was murdered as he tried to flee to his bedroom.'

I blinked. 'The one from the memorial?'

'Same one.' She firmly planted the pencil on the map, ignoring Lyn's muffled objections, to draw a straight line from the White Hall to a spot on the west side of the city. 'There are two of them, as far as I know. The first one ends up at a small door in the inner city wall, and this one' – another line, now drawn to the east – 'this one ends up next to the lake. Both of them give access to the basement of the White Hall, although the doors opening into the building are of course securely locked.'

'Locks that could withstand a little blast of magic?' I said.

She gave me that mischievous grin. 'No.'

'The west entrance will be easier to reach, by the look of it,' Lyn said, peering at the parchment. 'On the east, we'd have to fight our way over a rather narrow strip of land between water and wall, is that correct?

Which is easier to block if they have any idea where we're going. If the west is open farmland, that will be easier to reach from every direction.'

The way Agenor narrowed his eyes at the map was more meaningful than any word of agreement could have been. 'Any buildings around?'

'A few farming sheds.' Rosalind shrugged. 'Won't be much of a problem if they get damaged.'

Agenor nodded agonisingly slowly, thoughts spinning behind his eyes. 'And that door – how visible is it?'

'I regularly walked past it for fifteen years and never wondered what it was until I was voted into office and they told me,' Rosalind said dryly. 'It's very inconspicuous.'

We were all silent for a moment as the possibilities sank in.

It was astonishing, the way those two pencil lines could change the atmosphere around the table – from a gloomy, fatalistic tension to something that contained a fraction of hope. We didn't have the numbers. We didn't have the bindings. But if we could reach that tunnel, if Creon and I could make it through, if I could find the Mother and somehow end her ...

At least we wouldn't have to fight our way through her army all the way to the centre of the city.

So many ifs. And yet ... we had *something* to aim for.

'We wouldn't have to win that way,' Lyn whispered, chin in her hands. 'We would only need to reach that door and then buy time so Em and Creon could sneak in unnoticed. It might even be enough to distract her by withdrawing and attacking a few times – some strategy that will kill as few people as possible yet keep her properly busy.'

A restlessness was spreading through the tent – minds and limbs itching to get to work, to start setting the plan into action and doing everything, *anything*, to keep ourselves alive. Tared rose to his feet and muttered something about informing the allies. Rosalind announced she was going to let Delwin and the other human recruits know. Agenor didn't seem to hear either of them, his mind engaged in some imaginary battle on the prospering grain fields of the city.

I glanced at Creon, and Creon glanced at me – something dangerous in his gaze, like the coiled energy of a caged panther about to break free.

A hundred and thirty years, and as well as he might hide it in his words and movements, that look in his eyes told me he hadn't forgotten about a minute of that torturous, never-ending wait. He was ready. He would have been ready an hour ago.

He hadn't just argued for a swift attack for my sake, I realised.

I just hoped he had lowered his shields enough to feel my gratitude.

But all he said, leaning over to me, was a quiet, 'You may want to have a quick word with your human friend. I don't think she trusts anyone but—'

The entrance of the tent burst open.

In a whirl of sunlight, Naxi stormed in – blue eyes bright with excitement, blonde curls dancing cheerfully with every step. She didn't seem to hear the shocked cries of the humans waiting outside. Without so much as a question or a greeting, she bounced to a standstill by the table, threw a look of what looked like breathless delight around the gathered company, and airily inquired, 'I suppose you're all worrying terribly about civilian deaths at the moment, aren't you?'

Rosalind turned a worryingly green shade of pale.

'Naxi!' Lyn hissed, wincing in sympathy. 'If you want to help, this is hardly the moment to—'

'I'm being *empathic*,' Naxi protested, defiantly blowing out her cheeks as she draped herself over the nearest empty chair. 'As you *told* me to be. Anyway, I heard the news and I want to make a suggestion. To save lives.'

Even Agenor had looked up now. Finn and Rosalind were exchanging puzzled glances, as if they both felt the need to confirm *they* hadn't abruptly gone mad; I considered quickly introducing the concept of demons without empathy to them but decided it might be better to hold off on that lesson until Naxi had moved far out of hearing distance. Beneath the superficial brightness of her cornflower eyes, she didn't look in a mood to be delayed.

And if I was honest, I wasn't in the mood to delay her either.

'A ... suggestion,' Lyn repeated, suspicion dripping from every syllable. 'I see. Please tell me it's not about Thysandra.'

Naxi beamed at her. 'Oh, it absolutely is about Thysandra.'

Lyn closed her eyes.

'No, *listen*,' Naxi hurried, fluttering her little pink hands at us. 'It's brilliant, I promise. You're worried about the people in the city, yes? Why don't we offer to return Thysandra to the Mother, provided that she makes a bargain not to hurt anyone until tomorrow night? She might bite, and then we won't need to worry about her taking out her frustrations on those people if Em waits a little longer to show up. Or if we attack in the meantime, for that matter.'

At least I wasn't the only one blinking at her in baffled surprise.

'What?' she said, wrinkling her nose at us. 'It makes all the sense in the world, doesn't it? Thysandra wants to go back. We want to keep the citizens alive. Everyone wins. Well, except the Mother, hopefully, in the end, but—'

'Naxi,' Tared interrupted.

She snapped her mouth shut. 'Yes?'

'Are you …' He faltered, raked an aimless hand through his blond hair, and started over with a mirthless chuckle. 'Are we supposed to believe that you're happy to just hand Thysandra over to the empire again? After the lengths you went to to get and keep her here?'

Naxi looked even more innocent. 'There are lives at stake, aren't there?'

Lyn's eyes had narrowed to such thin slits now that I doubted she could still see anything, and Tared's eyebrow was creeping closer and closer to his hairline. I looked at Creon and found him studying Naxi with an unexpectedly dark frown on his face, his eyes black as the night, his jaw hard with some unspoken worry. He did not look my way to meet my gaze.

Something nervous stirred in my guts, but Rosalind hesitantly said, 'I suppose we could send a message to the city and see what they say, at least?'

'Oh, no, no,' Naxi brightly cut in, all honey-sweet pink and cornflower blue as she threw us another bright smile. 'No, I think the best option would be to bring her here first and *then* send a message. That way we can hand her over immediately and spare everyone outside the agony of even more uncertainty. Lots of grief happening in this camp right now, you know?'

'Naxi ...' Tared seemed unsure whether he should laugh or give her a good shake before wasting another word on the matter. 'Are you very sure you are not trying to help her escape again?'

'Yes!' She gave a little pout. 'I'm trying to help you, I swear. On my ... on my tits.'

Finn burst out in mildly hysterical giggles. Tared, exchanging a baffled glance with Lyn, repeated, 'On your *what*?'

'Well, you're supposed to swear on something dear to you, aren't you?' Naxi merrily said, returning his look of suspicion with a perfectly innocent one. 'I'm not planning to betray you all to the Mother, Tared. I'm a *demon*, not a traitor.'

An abrupt understanding rose on Rosalind's face.

'You're hiding something all the same,' Lyn said, eyes narrowed. 'And this would hardly be the first time you're making questionable choices where Thysandra is considered. So as long as we don't know how harmful you're actual plans may be—'

'They're not', Creon curtly interrupted.

I wasn't the only one who whipped around to look at him. His expression hadn't loosened, an odd tightness there that only emphasised the sharp edges of his jaw and cheekbones ... but there seemed to be no doubt in his features, nothing but that oddly grim resolve.

'Creon?' Lyn said, frowning.

'We should give it a try, at least.' He was trying – very clearly trying – to sound casual and conversational about the matter, and I wasn't sure if anyone else realised how hard he was failing. 'The Mother might not be interested, but if she is ... It would make our job tomorrow much, much easier if a bargain forbids her from using her hostages as a human shield.'

'Yes, obviously,' Lyn said, rubbing her eyes, 'but Naxi ...'

'... is fine,' he finished with the most meaningless shrug in the history of shrugs. 'Just play along. We all have the same goal here.'

Naxi beamed at him. Lyn's glower turned even more suspicious; Agenor looked like a male about to come up with a long and exhaustive monologue of objections. But Tared rose from his chair before anyone could speak, threw Naxi a mildly exhausted look, and said, 'In that case, I'll just go and get Thysandra while you demons play your demon games.'

Tared? Trusting *Creon?*

I forgot to worry about demon scheming for a moment.

'Lovely', Naxi cheerfully said, pretending not to notice his annoyance. 'Do you mind if I'm coming along?'

Tared huffed a laugh, grabbing his sword from the table before offering Lyn a hand. 'I'd take the Mother herself with me before bringing you along to that cell. And maybe the rest of you should make a start on reaching out to our allies in the meantime, if we want them to be here before tomorrow morning.'

The next moment, the he and Lyn were gone.

Chapter 30

Something was going on.

If Creon's silence hadn't been enough of a sign, Naxi's decidedly conspiratorial smiles at him would have solidified even the vaguest of suspicions. She skipped around the tent looking oddly like Edored trying to keep a secret, giggling in response to every question asked of her. I tried to get something out of Creon and received nothing but some murmured platitudes on those damn demons and this one in particular – nothing that could begin to explain the haunted look that refused to leave his eyes even after his endorsement of the plan.

Had we been alone, I would have pressed. But my parents were sitting next to me, and even if they hardly qualified as parental figures in any traditional sense, I felt like it would be rightly frowned upon if I were to climb into my lover's lap right before their noses and kiss him into compliance.

It wouldn't do much, anyway. Creon never became more talkative in my father's company.

So we collectively wrote a letter to the Mother instead, debating every word and period of the bargain she would have to make in order to receive Thysandra back into her entourage. Having finished that task, we set to listing the many magical rulers we'd have to reach out to, just to make sure we didn't overlook even a single name in the chaos of the day; we hadn't even finished the first half when Tared and Lyn returned, a stoic-looking Thysandra in alf steel between the two of them.

Rosalind had the presence of mind to quickly pull the map with the tunnels drawn in beneath the table.

They had already explained the gist of the plan to our captive, it turned out. Tared faded out with our letter immediately, and then we waited – unable to discuss anything of importance with Thysandra sitting next to us, and getting more and more disgruntled about the fact as time ticked by. Thysandra, to her credit, looked just as mystified about our reasons to take her from her cell before an agreement had been reached. Naxi had to be very well aware of the glares sent her way with increasing frequency, but she sat in her chair and kept on smiling, humming monotone songs to herself as outside our tent the noise of the camp grew louder and louder.

Five minutes passed, then ten.

Delwin showed up, had a short, whispered conversation with Agenor, then left again to pass on the preliminary conclusions to the humans waiting for news, taking Finn with him. My parents followed soon after with the list of magical rulers – off to find some alves to deliver the first calls to arms, I suspected.

Lyn was visibly getting antsy by that point, fidgeting feverishly with pencils and parchment, glaring at the sun to move along the sky faster. Thysandra took care to equally divide her furious glares between Naxi and Creon. I stared at the latter, tried to figure out how and why his lazy confidence had so suddenly morphed into this barely controlled dread tightening his lips and fingers, and failed miserably.

Five more minutes went by.

It was just before the twenty-minute mark that Tared returned – an eternity, and yet so surprisingly fast that I was fully prepared for him to report the empire's guards had refused to accept the letter at all. But he was holding a new sheet of parchment, and beneath the obvious tension, his smile carried a hint of triumph.

'It's addressed to you,' he informed me as he handed me the message. 'Thought I'd be polite and leave the honour to you.'

The Mother's foremost enemy.

I swallowed something thorny as I broke the seal.

It was infuriating, the way those written words made me remember the porcelain sound of her voice all over again – as if she had slipped the memory itself into the letter, silvery and amused, laughing at me from a few miles away—

Little dove,

Thank you for your generous offer. Unfortunately, we must reject it. It turns out Thysandra is perfectly redundant to our court; if we bargain with you, it will be over more than a traitor's daughter.

Send our regards to your father. For his sake, we hope he's dead before we meet again.

Fondly,

The Mother,
High Lady of faekind,
Empress of all the known world

I stared at those treacherous lines for a mindless moment before a heartfelt '*Fuck*' escaped me.

'Bad news?' Tared said sharply.

'You could call it that.' I scanned the message one more time, then looked up to find four pairs of eyes staring at me with varying levels of eagerness and apprehension. Only Creon hadn't even bothered to look up, resting his head back in his chair with his eyes closed and ever-deepening lines tightening around his lips. In the white-and-blue light filtering through the tent cloth, the shadows sharpened his cheekbones to knife-edges, his scars to bleeding gashes.

He's served his purpose.

My heart twinged. Had he known this would be her response – so close to a repeat of the day he almost died, burned and bleeding, in the mud at the Golden Court?

'Em?' Lyn's voice pulled me back to reality. 'Does she reject the bargain?'

'She ... she does, yes.' I threw her a slightly helpless look, unsure how many details I should add with Thysandra still in the same tent. 'She—'

'Does she make a counteroffer?' Thysandra bit out – the first full sentence she'd spoken since her arrival. It burst from her lips as if it had been aching to escape for the full twenty minutes of our wait. 'Is there anything else she will do for ... for ...'

Me.

She did not finish the sentence – afraid, it seemed, to claim even that much recognition for herself.

I hesitated for a fraction of a second, trying to find a kinder way to deliver the news but unable to settle on anything better than, 'She doesn't, no.'

Thysandra stared at me. 'She doesn't?'

'No.' *She calls you a redundant traitor's daughter* – as little as I liked her, I had no desire at all to rub those words in her face. 'She, um, doesn't give the impression she is open to further proposals, either.'

For a moment, she sat frozen.

Then, so swift that none of us could have had any hope of catching her, she lunged forward, chained hands stretched out in front of her – aiming not for me but for the letter I was holding, snatching it from my fingers as if it was her last chance to live.

My cry of protest came far, far too late.

Thysandra staggered backwards, dark eyes flying over the words. Half a heartbeat, and she stiffened, staring at the message in her hands as if it was a death sentence – as if the parchment itself was all thorns and fangs, its poison spreading through her veins already.

The colour drained from her face.

I thought for an instant she might pass out, the way she went ashen before my very eyes – a hue I'd only ever seen on corpses before. But she stood, albeit swaying on her feet. Her lips parted, then faltered, soundlessly shaping the words as her gaze slid over the message one last time; then, with a shuddering breath, she dropped it.

The parchment fluttered to the ground like a dying butterfly.

'No,' she whispered hoarsely, and shattered binding or no, the sound of that one word cut through my soul with merciless jaggedness. '*No.*'

None of us spoke.

Her gaze travelled from face to face, beseeching, begging quietly for anyone to stand and admit that this letter was a fabrication, just a cruel joke ... but Tared gave only a grim sigh. Lyn's eyes were gleaming. Naxi laconically spread her hands, looking oddly satisfied, and I had to fight the urge to apologise, not sure what in the world I'd be apologising for.

But it was Creon – *Creon*, of all people – who looked up when she finally turned towards him, sighed, and flatly said, 'Hurts, doesn't it?'

I couldn't tell if it was smugness or sympathy in his voice. He'd gone strangely, eerily blank – as if a mask had slipped over his face, still flawlessly beautiful but wholly devoid of life.

'What?' Thysandra spat.

'Being discarded like that.' A nod at the crumbled letter on the ground. 'As if you wouldn't gladly have died for her a hundred times over. As if you haven't lived your entire life to serve her – as if she doesn't know you have.'

She gaped at him – not so much frozen in shock, I suspected, as too furious to react.

'If it helps,' he added, lips twisting into a curve of bitter self-contempt, 'nothing you could have done would have prevented this. It's the way she lives, using and discarding, and you simply ended up on the wrong side of—'

Her face twisted with rage – raw and explosive. 'And what in hell would *you* know of it, little prince?'

My breath caught.

Creon didn't so much as blink.

'She loved you,' Thysandra snarled, scarred, black-and-gold wings twitching with uncontrolled hostility as she staggered towards him. Her dark skin flushed with colour again. 'She adored the fucking ground you walked on, and then *you* were the one to throw it all away and betray her – don't pretend you have the faintest idea what I've gone through when you so easily—'

'She left me behind to die,' he interrupted, still in that strangely flat voice – like he was bored, and yet his tone lay further away from boredom than a tone ever could, taut with pressure like a stone about to shatter. 'I don't suppose she ever told you that? Left me lying in the mud with my chest burned out and told the world I had served my purpose, then ran and saved herself.'

She fell icily silent, gaping at him as if he was telling her he *had* died on that cursed day and risen from the grave soon after. 'You— What?'

Creon just shrugged. His eyes had gone so very black – as dark as the memories themselves. The colour of emptiness. Of bleeding hearts.

'No,' Thysandra stammered. 'No, she wouldn't ...'

But she no longer looked like she might pounce on him any moment. She no longer gave the impression she wanted nothing more than to scratch his eyes from his face.

'She didn't love me, Thys.' Cold, simple facts, yet I knew that even I could scarcely imagine the hours upon hours of despair that lay beneath those words. 'She was never going to love you, either. We were never more than tools to her, and tools don't complain when they are finally declared redundant. Tools just cease to exist and stop bothering her. As she no doubt expects you to do now.'

She gasped in a breath, chest heaving. 'Don't *look* at me like that.'

He raised an eyebrow. 'Like what?'

'With ... with *pity*.' She took a wobbling step backwards, none of the usual lethal grace to her movements as she balled her fists at her sides. Her laugh was a shard of broken glass. 'I wanted to *kill* you when you were born, damn you! I wanted to smother you in your cradle and drop your wretched little corpse into the sea!'

'I know.' A mirthless smile spread over his face. 'You would have spared a lot of people a lot of trouble if you had, frankly.'

She lurched forward.

Lyn cried out. Naxi shrieked. Tared and I jumped at the same time, each of us catching another muscular shoulder; still, it took all of our combined strength to drag her away from Creon, back to her chair, as she swore and spat threats at him. Only as we hauled her into her seat did she give up on struggling. Her curses blurred into gasps as she folded over, then into sobs – quiet, heart-rending whimpers that once again almost made me forget about the fragile glass of that binding shattering on the rocks.

A traitor's daughter.

How many years had she slaved to free herself from that blemish?

'Perhaps,' Naxi said, innocently fluttering her eyelashes at us as she finally jumped up, 'this would be a good moment for me to have a word with Thysandra?'

Only then did it hit me.

Zera have mercy – *this* was what she'd been planning to happen, wasn't it?

But you had been very explicitly abandoned, I'd said to Creon mere days ago, just before handing Naxi the keys to cell 104. She must have come to the same conclusion since, over the course of whatever conversations had taken place. She must have realised she wasn't getting anywhere as long as Thysandra believed the Mother was impatiently waiting for her, expecting the return of a loyal servant. And so, with characteristic ruthlessness …

She'd staged the abandonment she needed. Using us as her unwitting accomplices, hiding her true intentions to make us play our roles with full authenticity.

Had Creon realised what she was aiming for, the moment she first made the suggestion of that bargain? Was that why he'd looked like a male bracing himself for the world to end – past hurt creeping back up on him?

'Good gods,' Lyn said with a shivery laugh, apparently coming to the same realisation. 'If you think it will do any good at this point, have any conversation you like – but for the love of the gods, *don't*—'

'Oh, don't worry,' Naxi purred, hooking her arm through Tared's without waiting for further questions. 'She's not going anywhere.'

The next moment, the three of them were gone, back to the Underground – taking the sound of Thysandra's sobbing with them, and Naxi's devilish smiles, too.

The day passed in a haze, yet seemed to last an eternity; by noon, I could have sworn I'd been awake for a full twenty-four hours already.

Yesterday, I hadn't stopped working because I didn't want to feel the fear. Today, I couldn't have stopped working even if I'd wanted to. There was no end to the list of people who, for some unimaginable reason, wished to have a word with me: humans begging me to save their loved ones, envoys from magical rulers who once again wanted my reassurance that it was possible for me to best the Mother, and most baffling of all, several handfuls of Underground alves who wanted to know if I had named my sword yet. I didn't have the heart to tell them that sword names were about the last problem on my list right now, but by the time number eleven showed up with the same question, my patience was wearing very, very thin.

I told him I was considering naming the blade Silence, after my greatest wish of the day. That seemed to get the message across.

Just after noon, the first magical armies started arriving, and that prompted a whole new wave of panicked questions. I spent an hour running around with Rosalind, trying to convince our human army that no vampire would be sneaking into their camp for a midnight snack; then I wasted equally as much time calming down two vampire males who had been accosted by a number of stake-wielding humans. It was almost a relief when five hundred nymphs were faded onto the field next, giggly and sparkly and scantily dressed. Admittedly, the looks going back and forth between their division and some human men spelled trouble of an entirely different sort ... but then again, it wasn't my concern who would be sleeping in what tent tonight, and at least it seemed unlikely people would be complaining about this.

I was willing to overlook the most egregious violations of army discipline by that point, as long as no one bothered me about it.

While I was running myself ragged, Agenor, Lyn, and Tared spent most of their time in the big command tent, shuffling wooden figures across maps and appeasing the allied rulers stamping in with questions. Delwin was handing out weapons and armour whenever I came across him. Finn made herself useful with the horses, and Creon ...

I wasn't fully sure what Creon was doing.

The few times I caught a glimpse of him, he was talking to Agenor's fae, an attentive look on their faces that suggested he was explaining something of urgent interest. But as far as I knew, there wasn't that much to explain, and most of the time he was nowhere to be found - not that unexpected, I tried to convince myself, for the male who had spent decades working entirely on his own and still struggled to cooperate with anyone.

Yet his absence became more and more striking as the hours went by. Because he may have had trouble working with others, but he'd never had trouble working with *me*. And he had to know there was plenty to do – so why wasn't he here so we could do it together?

I spotted him again later that afternoon, talking with one of the newly arrived vampires on this occasion. But by the time I'd wrestled my way towards them through the throng, only the vampire was left where the two of them had been a moment before, and she couldn't tell me where Creon had gone except that he had suddenly remembered he had something urgent to do.

Something *urgent*?

I stood dazed and confused on the trampled grass as the vampire female excused herself and strode off – but he hadn't looked hurried at all, had he, when I'd caught sight of him a minute or two ago? And it was not at all like Creon to forget about anything urgent, not unless he *wanted* to spontaneously recall something at a convenient moment.

So if he had unexpectedly vanished just as I was approaching him ...

Was he *avoiding* me?

That did not make sense in the slightest – not after the way he'd followed me into the forest that morning, ready to fight me if need be. But then there was that strange darkness on his face when Naxi had suggested her bargain, and the way he'd slipped off before I could ask him what was bothering him. What if the conversation with Thysandra had prodded more than unhappy memories of the day the Mother had revealed her true nature to his dying ears?

It didn't sound logical at all. Then again, I couldn't come up with any more logical explanations, either.

For another hour, I tried to tell myself it was just my own overburdened mind messing with me, seeing unnecessary cause for alarm in the most innocent of clues. But I ran into Delwin six times in that hour and passed Rosalind twice – and still, not a glimpse of Creon.

By the time the phoenix army arrived and began setting up camp – staying a few hundred feet away from everyone else's tents – I decided I was sick of worrying and doing nothing.

It took a few minutes of asking around and stubbornly fending off everyone else's questions, but in the end, I found him - between some alvish tents, of all places, surrounded by a small group of Underground alves. Like the fae I'd seen before, they stood listening to him unusually quietly. None of them noticed me until I advanced within hearing distance, just close enough to catch a shred of Creon's last sentence – '... find maps in the central tent ...'

It was then that a gangly alf interrupted him with a bright, 'Oh, Nosebreaker!'

Creon whipped around.

For a single moment, I thought he'd run or fly or grab the nearest alf to fade out; there was a flicker of shock on his face, there and gone too swiftly for me to be sure of it. But the smile curling around his lips the next moment was his usual one, lazily graceful and sensual in a way that could make an army camp look like a den of sinners; if Naxi's schemes were still haunting him in whatever way, he was hiding it very, very well.

Good gods. I really was working myself up over nothing, wasn't I?

He turned to say something to the alves, and they faded out with some last quick greetings, leaving only the two of us between the tents. Close by, shouts and the clattering of steel against steel suggested a final training session before hell broke loose tomorrow. But in this corner of the camp, the world was jarringly quiet – nothing but grass and endless rows of man-high linen tents, the pale autumn sun shining down upon us.

'Hey,' I said sheepishly, feeling suddenly awkward as the last tendrils of anxiety slithered from my veins, leaving only breathless trepidation behind. He looked so very much like himself, standing there. Bronze skin almost aglow in the sunlight. Long hair bound up, loose strands tucked behind his pointed ears. All loose-winged, loose-shouldered casualness – the very last person in the world to ever do something as dramatic as *avoid* me. 'Good to see you. What have you been doing all morning?'

He shrugged in that careless way of his – a shrug that blithely denied we were standing in the middle of an army, on our way to a likely death within twenty-four hours. 'Oh, a couple of things. Trying to prepare, just in case.'

It took me half a moment to realise that was not, in fact, an answer. 'Things?'

'Things,' he nonchalantly repeated, nodding as if it had been a request for confirmation rather than for the substantial information that was very much lacking, his expression so perfectly unconcerned it could hardly be real. 'You?'

'Reassuring panicking humans about vampires,' I said, squinting at him. Perhaps the worry had not been as misplaced as I'd thought, after all. 'So what sort of situation have you been preparing for, exactly?'

He faltered.

Just one miniscule slip of the mask, smile stiffening for a fraction of a moment – but a slip meant that there *was* a mask, and at once every spark of worry came roaring back to life, the fire I'd so determinedly squashed flaring up to claim its new fuel. Had he been doing things I wasn't supposed to know about?

Had he been avoiding me?

'Creon?' It came out more sharply than intended.

'You know.' An unfocused gesture; his wings fanned out a few inches in half-hearted evasion. 'The whole story with Thysandra.'

Any other time, it would have been convincing enough, the wry, self-deprecating smile that quirked around his lips. Just a topic he preferred not to linger on. Just a small distraction of little importance. Had I not been confused already, it would have worked flawlessly, that hint of a scar he'd rather not prod on a day like this.

But I *was* confused and wary, and he knew it, too.

Which made this a nonsensically empty response.

Which meant that it was the only way he *could* respond – that this was the shield he'd built around whatever lay behind, and he had no choice but to hold it up so stubbornly there was no way to let go of it. Those unhurried shoulders, loose and lean … They weren't a reassurance at all. They were armour as much as the knives in his boots and the restored black of his shirt and trousers.

I cocked my head, frowning. 'What are you hiding?'

The flash of emotion that slid over his face was all the confirmation I needed. No surprise. No confusion. Just that same, strange stiffening – the look of a male caught red-handed, despite his most desperate efforts.

His chuckle came too swiftly to be convincing. 'I—'

'Creon.' I stepped closer, lowering my voice – gods knew who might be hiding in these tents, listening to every word spoken. 'Do I really need to remind you that you're not the only one who notices when something is wrong?'

And why was he looking at me like that as the last shadows of his smile melted off his face, as he parted his lips and closed them again – with such forlorn intensity, as if he'd shut his eyes the next moment and never see a single glimpse of me again?

It took no more than a heartbeat of his silence for a thousand alarming possibilities to storm my mind all at once. 'You … you haven't been organising some suicidal mission into the city, have you? Or made funeral arrangements? Or—'

'No!' His shock, at least, looked fully genuine. 'Hell's sake, Em. I promised I wouldn't do that again.'

Not without telling me, at least. My heartbeat didn't come down, the sound of that arrow smacking into his back still perpetually repeating itself in some dark and unforgiving corner of my mind.

'So then what are you—'

'Cactus.' His voice quivered ever so slightly – *quivered*, that golden sound with its veneer of hoarseness. 'Can I just ... Could you just let me hold you for a moment?'

What in the world?

But I wasn't going to refuse him a single thing, not when he was looking at me like that – like he might crack at the slightest unkind touch, shatter like his binding had shattered. And his arms were robust as always as I stepped into his embrace, wrapping around me with such tender strength, pressing me against his chest with such gentle urgency ... He lowered his forehead to mine. I slipped my arms around his waist, cautious to avoid his wings in this just-too-public spot, and his nails dug into my back in response – primal, possessive, a touch like a claim.

As if someone might try to drag me from his arms in the next moment.

But who in the world would be mad enough to try any such thing? And where had this fear come from so suddenly, if I hadn't seen the slightest trace of it when he'd followed me into the forest or even that bloody blue-and-white tent? Naxi's proposed bargain, then, or Thysandra's collapse, but *why*?

'Creon ...' I whispered, burying my nose into the hollow of his neck.

'You know I'd do anything for you, don't you?' he rasped, a sudden haste in his words, as if his time was counting down to minutes, seconds. '*Anything*. You know that? You won't forget?'

'Why in the world would I— *Creon*.' I pulled back my head to look up at him. His dark eyes bled despondency, an expression pleading with me to understand. 'What has gotten into your head, that you—'

Shrill, urgent chirping exploded behind me.

I had no time to do anything but jump back. No time to tell Creon to stay where he was and give me five short seconds to deal with this. Alyra crashed down onto my shoulder with such force she almost sent me to my knees, making enough noise to render any sensible conversation impossible; before I could tell her to get the hell out of here, Naxi's melodious voice added itself to the cacophony, sounding no less excited.

'Emelin! *Emelin!*'

I snapped around, far too tempted to grab Creon's black sleeve in the same movement and fire off a few warning bursts of red. It was all I could do to instead grit out, 'Could I get back to you later, Naxi? This is really not the moment for—'

'Can't wait,' she interrupted, dancing out from between the pale tents. She was blushing so feverishly her round face was almost as pink as her dress. 'Emelin, she's talked! We know how to use them! We need you at the Cobalt Court right now to—'

'We— Wait, what?' With the hollow misery in Creon's eyes still burned into my mind, it took a few frantic moments to understand what she was even talking about. 'The *bindings*?'

'Yes!' Naxi panted, clutching a sheet of parchment to her chest as she stumbled to a standstill next to me. She must have been sprinting after Alyra, in so much of a hurry to find me that she didn't seem to have noticed one of her hair ribbons had fluttered off. 'We have no time to lose – I have the ones she wrote down right here, and—'

'Alright, *alright*.' I held up my hands in a desperate attempt to slow the onslaught of words. This was good news, my rational thoughts tried to tell me, this was *wonderful* news, and yet the elation refused to even come peeking around the corner. 'I'll have a quick word with Creon and then—'

The rest of the sentence froze on my lips as I turned to where he'd been standing.

The clearing between the tents was no longer empty. A small but rapidly growing circle of onlookers had gathered around us, drawn in by the combined noise of my familiar and the little half demon rattling loudly at me: nymphs and vampires and phoenixes, gaping at us with sagging jaws and eyes gleaming with far too much hope.

But the heart of the circle was empty.

He'd stood beside me a moment ago – yet now, like an alf fading out without leaving a trace, Creon had quietly vanished.

Chapter 31

'But where *is* he?' I snapped for what felt like the twentieth time at the group of dazed creatures around us, ignoring Naxi, who was tugging at my arm with all of her minimal weight. 'Did he fly off? Did anyone try to stop him?'

'He ... he just walked away,' one of the nymphs squeaked. 'That way. He looked ... *angry*, I'd say?'

Which was presumably an answer to my last question, because who in the world would be so stupid as to risk his life trying to stop an angry Silent Death from going exactly wherever the hell he wished to go?

I only barely swallowed a curse.

'*Emelin,*' Naxi repeated for what was also likely the twentieth time, yanking at my arm with so much force I almost dislocated a shoulder. 'We don't have *time* for his dramatics. If you want to unbind as many people as possible before tomorrow morning ...'

'I'm not unbinding anyone!' I snapped, realising only as the group around me collectively gasped that perhaps I could have chosen my words more carefully. But damn it all – something was very, very wrong, and if he was running from me again, that only suggested he needed help more urgently. 'Look, you can start preparing logistics for me, alright? It will probably take a while to get a team of people together, and in the meantime, I'll just figure out wherever the hell he went and—'

'The team's already here, Nosebreaker,' a voice with a strong Alvish accent interrupted me.

I whirled around yet again.

Some fifteen alves had gathered between the tents to my left, in leather and linen, swords on their backs and determined lines around their lips. Some of them were holding drawings – *maps*, I realised after a moment, and more particularly ...

Was that a floorplan of the Cobalt Court, with those two enormous halls and the many aisles of bindings sketched in between the walls?

'Beg your pardon?' I said.

'He's instructed us about the organisation,' the alf who had spoken before said – pierced eyebrow, tattooed temples, a nose with no fewer than three pronounced crooks in it. 'Hytherion, I mean. We're ready to go the moment you need us.'

I stared at him.

Only now did his eyes narrow in confusion, frowns and scowls around him mirroring the surprise. 'He said you knew about it. About the plans.'

What in the world?

'I ... I didn't know about anything.' Zera help me, was *that* what he had been doing, those few times I'd caught sight of him around the camp – instructing various groups about their tasks in the hypothetical case Thysandra finally spilled her secrets? 'Who did he ask? Just the lot of you? Or—'

'Oh, no, there's a few fae, too,' the alf said, with the thinly veiled eyeroll that seemed to be a traditional obligation among alves when mentioning my father's people. 'Should I go and fetch them?'

I swallowed. 'I suppose that would be—'

He was already gone.

They were looking at me with so much expectant confusion, the rest of them – and gods help me, could I blame them? A hundred and thirty years without their fertility, wings, memories, and whatever else the Mother had taken from them ... and here I stood, the solution to their every problem, stammering and stalling rather than doing what needed to be done.

My team was ready. Time was running out. So what excuse did I have to *not* go on my way and get to work?

Was that what Creon had wanted me to do, since he'd made these preparations? Was that why he'd run – some twisted attempt not to distract me while I had better things to think about?

The world was starting to blur around me a little.

'Could ... could someone go and find him?' I no longer cared how pathetic it must sound – unbound fae, godsworn mage, begging for someone to run after her wayward lover in her place. They would be gossiping anyway. 'Tell him I need to have a word with him as soon as possible. Just fade him to the Cobalt Court if I'm there. Please.'

By the looks on their faces, no one was particularly excited about getting close enough to a volatile Silent Death to fade him anywhere.

'*Please,*' I said again, as if that would make a difference. 'I would very much appreciate—'

'Oh, I'll go look for him,' Naxi impatiently cut in, still tugging at my hand at regular intervals. 'Are you coming, then? We're wasting time we shouldn't be wasting.'

After weeks of obsessive stubbornness, I'd almost forgotten that killing the Mother might be the one thing Naxi wanted *more* than Thysandra. No sense in objecting, then – she'd sooner bite me than allow me to run off and go looking for Creon now.

'As long as you find him as soon as possible ...'

She rolled her eyes. 'The longer you stand here, the longer it'll take.'

Ruthless – but she wasn't wrong.

I finally allowed her to haul me with her, cursing Creon and his bloody secrets under my breath when it turned out the alves were, indeed, not the only ones he had instructed over the course of the morning. A small battalion of fae had joined that initial group. There were a handful of nymphs and vampires, too, and even a few phoenixes he must have found among the last people to stay behind in the Underground, every single one of them aware of plans I hadn't even caught a single glimpse of yet.

Just in case, he'd said – but he must have had a strong suspicion Thysandra would talk, surely, to go to such lengths to prepare?

'So,' Naxi started breathlessly as she finally let go of my wrist, her every syllable trembling with excitement. 'The easiest way to identify the bindings, Thysandra told me, is to use the catalogue book that is hidden somewhere at the Crimson Court, but obviously that will be a little hard for us to reach right now …'

Grim laughs went up around us.

'But the individual bindings are labelled, too.' Naxi beamed at me. 'Good thing we didn't move them to the Underground, it turns out. The names have been inscribed into the shelves on which they are lying.'

I frowned. 'What?'

'I'm pretty sure there are no labels anywhere,' an alf said on the other side of the circle – one of Valdora's people. He must have visited the hall before with one of the groups she'd sent out to keep an eye on the treasures. 'We would have noticed.'

'You can't even *read*,' an alf next to him mumbled, and again some nervous chuckles went around the group. They were sounding significantly more doubtful this time, though.

'No, of course there are no labels,' Naxi said impatiently, 'because they were first inscribed and then wiped off again with red magic. You see? The trick to making them visible is to use *just* enough blue magic to heal the wood that was destroyed around the inscription, but not so much blue magic that you'll undo the inscription itself, too – so we need some decent mages. I hope all of you fae are decent mages?'

Good gods.

Creon couldn't have seen *that* coming, could he?

It appeared that he hadn't, as the discussion continued for another few minutes: the gathered fae had received no instructions on what they were supposed to do exactly, just a warning that they would likely be needed and ought to be available. Still …

Why hadn't he just *told* me?

He still hadn't shown up by the time the alves started fading us all towards the Cobalt Court. I was too befuddled to object to leaving.

The old halls of the ruins were significantly less gloomy by full daylight; with the sun streaking in around the rows and rows of shelves, the thousands of crystal orbs twinkled in a way a happier person may have called cheerful. But I wasn't in the mood for pretty sights, and I wasn't given time for them anyway. Someone found me a chair, someone else brought me a table with a mother-of-pearl top, and it was there that they instructed me to stay and wait for the people to come to me.

'But—' I started.

'Hytherion's instructions!' an alf bellowed over his shoulder before fading out again.

Gods *damn* it.

The worst part was that it worked flawlessly, the system he'd devised even without any idea of the mechanism that would identify the bindings. Agenor's fae slowly walked down the aisles, restoring inscriptions. Behind them, members of all magical peoples followed – members it turned out Creon had selected specifically for their outgoing social nature, because it was their task to read the newly revealed names and sound the alarm if they recognised anyone they knew to be among our army. Finally, alves faded back and forth between the camp and the ruins in order to pick up the happy individuals who had been found, hand them their binding, and send them my way.

Within minutes, a timid queue of magical creatures had formed before my chair, clutching glass orbs like they were holding their newborn children. Behind them, blue flashes and cries of recognition went up through the giant hall at irregular intervals.

One fae female sat next to me to restore the table surface to mother-of-pearl every other minute – *iridescence for magic*. And so I went to work, pulling binding after binding from fragile glass and returning the magic to its rightful owner – a satisfying process at first, blurring into monotone routine before I'd reached my first hundred unbound creatures.

I stopped seeing faces after a while. Just glass and pearly silver. Just the ephemeral shimmers of magic no one else was able to see, thin threads soaking back into the bodies they had come from over and over again.

Creon, they informed me, was still nowhere to be found.

I resolved to stop thinking about him and failed miserably. There was nothing *wrong* with the fae female by my side – she appeared to be a capable mage for all intents and purposes – but she was not Creon, and she never read my mind the way he would so easily have done. Several times, she was just a fraction too slow refreshing the magic in the table surface. Whenever I had a request for her, I had to complete my whole explanation; she never picked up my intentions within three words or fewer. She handed me food and water when I was in deep concentration, but had to be asked for them when I was granting myself a break – none of them valid reasons for complaints, but all of them jarring reminders that I was not in the company of the one person who would never have started chatting to me while I was in the middle of extracting a particularly challenging bit of magic from its binding.

We reached two hundred unbound people. Through the cracked windows and the holes in the walls, I could see the sky darkening to a peachy pink, then a soft violet; by that time, I had lost all sense of the passing hours.

Agenor showed up in my queue, turning faintly green the moment his magic and the memories of Korok's death were returned to him. Not much later, Tared followed. The next time I saw him, his eyes were a fraction red; the memory of his parents, I recalled, and that little triumph got me through another hour of Creon-less routine.

Lynn appeared for no other reason than to tell me I should be eating more. When I asked her about Creon, she admitted he had still not been found but reassured me he had to be in the camp *somewhere*: there were alves and fae keeping an eye on the hills and sky, just to make sure the Mother didn't show up for any surprises, and if Creon had tried to go anywhere, surely they would have noticed him?

I didn't ask her if she really believed that a handful of guards could keep Creon from sneaking out whenever he wanted. She was making an effort to make me feel better, and the answer to the question wouldn't cheer me up anyway.

When night fell, torches were lit around the halls, and somehow the flickering firelight turned the sight of those endless glass balls into a far eerier view – like maliciously gleaming eyes, glaring at me from all sides. My fae assistant let out a nervous laugh when I remarked upon it, but failed to make the sort of leisurely joke that I needed to hear; once again, I had to push a sting of longing away.

I had just unbound my four hundredth individual – Nenya was number three hundred and ninety-seven – when Agenor appeared again, in Rosalind's company this time. They had, it turned out, decided it was about time to send me to bed.

'I'm a little old for that, don't you think?' I said.

'You could be nearing the end of your fifth century,' Agenor wryly said, 'and that doesn't change anything about the fact that we need you to win a war tomorrow. You can't fight the Mother on three hours of sleep, Em.'

'But—' I tried.

Rosalind was already instructing the fae working in the aisles that it was time to cease their activities.

So I finished unbinding those who had already been waiting with their bindings, bringing the total of the day to four hundred and thirty-seven – a significant difference from an army in which Lord Khailan and I were the only ones able to wield magic against the Mother's forces, and yet it was hard to feel any triumph at the sight of the tens of thousands of bindings still waiting for me. Against an opponent of the empire's size, it seemed not unlike dropping a bucket of water onto a wildfire.

'There's always more that you could have done,' Rosalind said philosophically, helping me out of the chair in which I'd spent the last six hours. 'At some point you need to stop beating yourself up over it.'

That sounded so much like Creon that I almost burst out crying on the spot.

They walked me to my tent together, the two of them, so patently chatting about everything except Creon that I knew they'd heard the story of his disappearance, had discussed it, and had decided that I needed distraction more than I needed edifying advice right now. Instead, Agenor asked if I was hungry. Rosalind enquired whether I had enough blankets for the cold night. Agenor muttered something about stealing extras, and her laughter made my heart feel too large for my ribcage for an inhalation or two – that unmistakable sound of quiet happiness.

It was wonderful and terrible in equal measures. Wonderful, because something about having both my parents by my side made me feel complete in ways I had never quite imagined, an answer to parts of me I'd never even realised were questions. And yet ... terrible, because that was how my whole life should have been. Terrible, because I could think of nothing but Creon and those hollow, hollow eyes. Terrible, most of all, because I had only just found them, and tomorrow I might lose them all over again.

I didn't want to think about tomorrow.

They made me promise I would go to sleep, repeated five more times that I should try not to worry about anything, then left me alone at my empty tent. I watched them walk off together in the fire-lit dark, his arm around her narrow shoulders, the sound of her laughter breaking through the background murmur of the camp ... and gods help me, how was it possible for satisfaction to hurt so much?

If only we could skip this entire bloody battle. If only we could just have a decent grown-up chat with the Mother, talk sense into her twisted brain, and all live happily ever after.

Fae wars don't end in surrender.

He'd know, presumably.

I waited until the two of them were well out of sight, pulled a warm sweater and a scarf from my tent, and went on my way again.

I passed praying humans, crying humans, small groups sitting around fires and sharing bottles of drink. Particular sounds emerging from a handful of tents suggested the nymphs had indeed found their way into this part of the camp. Here and there I ran into alves or fae, but no one recognised me with my scarf wrapped around my head, and no one tried to stop me as I slowly but steadily made my way to the edge of the camp.

Alyra found me there, as if she sensed I would need her. In all likeliness, she had.

'Do you know where he is?' I whispered.

With a small trill, she launched herself from my shoulder and flew westwards.

It was a clear, windless night. As soon as we left the camp behind, the sound of voices died away to a faint murmur in the distance. With nothing but a pale moon to illuminate the landscape around us, I was walking through a world of silhouettes, the outlines of hills and trees my only guides. The air smelled fresher here, no fire and human sweat, but rather pine needles and autumn cold – a precursor to the frost that would soon settle into the grassy earth and not leave until spring.

I thought of the stark white hills of the battlefield on Sevrith. Of the sticky, iron smell of blood, the buzzing of flies, and couldn't help but shiver.

Looking down at the camp from this hillslope, far enough removed to no longer be able to distinguish the separate voices and faces, it looked like a force I could scoop up in the palm of my hand. A laughable, pitiable band against the full might of an empire, doomed to be swallowed whole by the Mother's wrath and never be seen again.

If Creon didn't show up ...

But Alyra flew onwards ahead of me, farther into the hills, and so I followed her until the camp was so far behind us that the glow of the fires was no longer visible. Over a fallen tree, reminding me uncomfortably of the forest I'd mowed down that morning. Through a thorny bush I hadn't seen in the darkness, leaving scrapes on my shins and knees. Soon I'd lost all sense of direction in the maze of shadows; it was just a tiny white falcon and me, walking deeper and deeper into the night.

Finally, after what felt like hours, a small valley opened up before us, the hills covered in pine trees, the rugged earth strewn with large boulders and weathered stones. And there, at the bottom of the slope …

In the dim moonlight, a lonely silhouette was sitting on a moss-draped rock – his back towards me, his head bent, his wings a shard of night even darker than the starry sky above us.

Chapter 32

'Creon!'

I almost broke my neck rushing down the uneven slope, pits and clumps of grass obscured by the pale moonlight.

He must have heard my voice, must have heard the racket of my unsubtle descent, must have felt the swell of my worry and anger and relief washing over him – and yet he didn't turn or even lift his slumping wings a fraction, a statue but for his hair fluttering softly on the breeze. For one blood-curdling moment, I wondered if it even *was* him, if Alyra hadn't mixed up pairs of wings in her impatience ... but no, I'd recognise that slender silhouette anywhere, and besides, who else would be sitting here in silence in the depths of night?

'Creon?' I slowed down, having reached the last, more level stretch of grass. Alyra chose that moment to decide she was no longer needed here, soaring off into the night sky. 'Are you alright? *Creon.*'

Only then did he move, as I half-tripped to a standstill a few steps behind him – a slow, stilted turn, as if it took every crumb of his self-restraint not to jump up and flee me again.

In the moonlight, his face could have been hewn from stone.

But his eyes ... they were alive with something wild, something dark and jagged, glittering feverishly in the shadows as if lit by their own inner fire. The look of a man possessed. A single glimpse and he turned away again – yet that short glance was alarming enough, sinking into my stomach with a boulder's weight. If *this* was what he'd been trying to hide this afternoon ...

I should not have left him alone today.

I had been a gods-damned idiot to leave him alone today.

'Please,' I whispered, and it came out strained, soothing, as I tiptoed my last steps towards him. As if he was a skittish animal, bound to bolt at the first sudden movement. 'Creon, what in the world is the matter? How long have you been hiding here? Why aren't you in the camp with everyone else?'

His wings twitched restlessly behind his shoulders. His hands cramped on the moss beneath him – knuckles twisting white, scars stretching and contorting, fingers not forming a single sensible word.

He didn't speak.

He didn't look my way.

'You *frighten* me.' A miracle, how that passed my lips with only the slightest wobble. I stepped around the last pile of stones, hands shaking, to where I could face him without that veil of dark hair between us – only to find him avoiding my gaze, eyes fixed on the earth before my feet. 'For hell's sake, Creon – *talk* to me. You have a perfectly fine voice now. Could you please use it?'

He dragged out a rough breath – a hollow attempt at a laugh, perhaps. 'I ... I shouldn't ...'

Silence again. Whatever it was he shouldn't, it had run aground in the shallows of his throat; his lips moved without goal or purpose, nothing I could even attempt to read in the darkness.

Zera help me, if only I could take one look into that tangled, shadowy mind, find the thoughts stuck there like thorns in flesh and gently, ever so gently, pick them out again ... But all I could do, helpless and insufficient, was kneel before him, settle my hands on his muscular thighs, and whisper, 'Does it have anything to do with Naxi or Thysandra?'

He shook his head.

'The bindings?'

A hesitation.

'It's the bindings?'

'It's ...' He gulped in a breath as if it might be his last one, straightening ever so slightly on that rock. His wings gleamed like black silver in the moonlight. 'Em, I ... I don't think I should come with you tomorrow.'

I froze.

I had misheard him – I *must* have misheard him. Even though the words had rung loud and clear in the silence of the night. Even though he wasn't scrambling to correct himself. Even though he still refused to look me in the eyes, an expression not of fear but rather of *shame* on his face ...

But it didn't make *sense*, not a single bit of it, and he had to know that as well as I did, didn't he? We were going to find the Mother together. That had been the only constant in every plan we'd made, more reassuring than any new magic or godsworn familiars had ever been – whatever nightmare I might walk into, I'd do it with *him*.

So then what in hell was this supposed to be?

'What?' I said, a whole three seconds too late.

'It doesn't make sense for me to come,' he mumbled, closing his eyes, words suddenly flowing faster. As if he'd practiced this part. As if it was the argument he'd repeated to himself time and time again, slipping away from every other soul – gods help me, had he planned to just vanish and never even *tell* me? 'You have hundreds of unbound mages at your disposal, Em. I'm still very much bound. It would be sentimental insanity to bring me along under those circumstances – I'm utterly useless to you like this.'

Useless.

Useless.

This stronghold of a male before me, muscles like tempered steel, reflexes of a predator, mind sharper than any sword or arrow, a force of nature in the flesh – *useless*? I'd already parted my lips to tell him he'd gone utterly insane ... and then other memories rushed into the void of my confusion, whacking every sensible word I'd been about to speak inside out and upside down in the blink of an eye.

Unbearable, isn't it? he'd whispered against my temple as he pinned my hands against shelves full of clothing. *Feeling useless?*

But that ...

That had been *ages* ago.

'Wait – *that's* what's been bothering you all this time?' My voice soared, mind soaring with it. All those moments of brooding silence. All that sudden anger. Not jealousy, not some ill-timed hunger for glory, but just ... 'Your bound magic? That's why you threw yourself at the Moon fleet so recklessly – because you were trying to prove you weren't as worthless as you feared you had become?'

He flinched at the word *worthless*.

'I'm not saying you *are* worthless, you— Oh, good gods.' A new memory inserted itself into my unravelling thoughts – as if a hundred doors were opening in my mind at once, sunlight flooding in. 'When you lashed out at me because I suggested you didn't care enough about breaking the bindings – you lashed out because I was *right*? Because you *didn't* want the rest of the world to become unbound and gain that edge on you, and you were trying desperately not to admit it to me?'

His heavy silence was enough of an answer.

'And so you told me not to use my magic against Thysandra? Not because you were worried about me but because you didn't want her to—'

'No!' he burst out, jolting with an uncontrolled slap of his wings, so sudden I almost tumbled backwards at his feet. His eyes had snapped open, burning gaze finding mine with a fractured despair I could feel in the marrow of my bones. 'No, Em, please. I wasn't trying to stop you from breaking the cursed things – I know we need them. Just not ... just not at the cost of you. That's all. I swear I wasn't ... wasn't ...'

Wasn't manipulating me to cling to the last advantage he'd have on a battlefield – my heartbeat came down a little as more rational realisations slipped through. He *had* helped me get that key to Naxi, after all. He *had* talked to Thysandra. He *had* set up that flawless plan to get as many bindings into the right hands as possible, even if he'd hated it, even if he could hardly bear to speak about it—

'I want her dead as much as you do, Em,' he whispered as he bent over, hands wrapping around my elbows, ink-black eyes begging me to believe it. Long hair tumbled over his face, and the soft strands tickled my forearms. 'I just ...'

'You couldn't stand to be weaker than others for once?' I finished, trying to keep the bitterness from my voice.

He winced again, grip on my elbows tightening. No answer, again – we both knew the answer anyway, the unspoken words hovering in the crisp night air between our faces.

All my worrying. All my questions. All those conversations with him repeating again and again that of course he was fine, why would I ever think otherwise – while he had known exactly what was wrong from the moment I told him his binding had broken and he'd looked so strangely, unexpectedly grim about it.

'Why in the world,' I managed, voice straining with the effort to speak softly, slowly, 'didn't you just *tell* me about any of this, you impossible idiot?'

'It might never have been relevant at all!' His fingers were almost squeezing *through* my arms now, holding on for dear life – as if once again someone might try and snatch me from his grip any moment. His hoarse voice shook violently. 'Thysandra might not have talked before the war was over. And as long as you didn't realise I was becoming dead weight, did you really expect me to helpfully remind you of it? So you could ... could ...'

He fell silent, his throat bobbing visibly in the shadows.

'Do *what*?' I forced out a cheerless laugh. 'Did you expect me to mock you? Insult you? Throw you out?'

Again he flinched.

No objections. No correction. No explanation of the terrible fate that would have awaited him instead of any of those ridiculous exaggerations – none of the justifications I had expected from him in response.

I blinked, voice lowering. 'Creon?'

The look in his dark eyes ... Crumbling obsidian, bleeding ink. As if he'd just woken up from a nightmare, only to find himself stuck in an even crueller reality – the eyes of a male about to surrender to a long-feared, inevitable doom.

Throw you out.

Oh, dead and living gods help me.

'That was a hypothetical suggestion to make the point of absurdity!' I wasn't sure if I should be laughing or cursing at this insanity, and Zera have mercy, why was he still looking at me in that same forlorn way, as if the next word from my lips might be a goodbye? 'Of course I'm not shoving you aside over some stupid bound magic. Why in the world would you ever think ...'

Oh.

Oh.

My mind abruptly caught up with my mouth.

Like tools. Hell take me, he'd *told* me – word for word, straight to my face, and still I hadn't managed to connect the dots between his memories and the madness of this night. Phantom voices all over again. How could I ever have assumed he wouldn't be hearing them, too, if they were still clamouring so loudly in my own mind?

He served his purpose.

Always the weapon. Always the protector.

'Creon ...' His name trembled on my lips. 'For the love of the gods, Creon, I'm not your *mother*.'

He stiffened. 'No, of course you're not—'

'And yet you assume I would leave you behind as well, the moment you lose your practical purpose?' I shook my arms from his grip, rising on legs that suddenly were no longer shaking. Gone was the confusion, the horror of knowing *something* was wrong but not how to solve it. This I understood. This I could fix. 'You know me better than that, Your Highness. You know I love you more than that.'

He stared at me as if I'd thrown some impossible mathematical question into his lap, paralysed on the moss and stone beneath him. 'Yes, but—'

'*Creon.*'

'—but people fall out of love,' he finished, voice choked and too quiet.

And there it was.

He looked so strangely small all of a sudden, hunched over, wings drooping, chiselled face a battlefield of shadows in the moonlight – just a single shattering fae prince beneath an endless sky, the indifferent forest stretching out for miles and miles around him. I wanted nothing more than to wrap my arms around those rigid shoulders, kiss that haunted face. Press him against my chest and hold him closer, closer, closer – close enough for my love to seep into his flesh and bones and wipe away the memories burned into every fibre of his being.

But he knew I loved him.

Just not, it seemed, *why*.

'Yes,' I admitted slowly. 'Some people do.'

He drew in a slow, shuddering breath. 'So that means—'

'That *doesn't* mean my feelings are conditional,' I interrupted, voice rising. 'That's the Mother's kind of love you're thinking of again. Not mine.'

'But there's *always* conditions – there *should* be conditions.' An entirely new edge crept into that rich, warm voice, suddenly – a brittleness I'd never heard before, cracking along with his heart. 'If I climbed into my bed tomorrow and refused to ever get out again, you *would* get sick of me sooner or later, wouldn't you? So—'

'But that's not what we're talking about here at all, Creon!'

'You were the one who started the hypothetical suggestions,' he managed, breathlessly. 'I'm just trying to make the point that feelings *are* conditional.'

'Fine, they are – on the condition of *you*.' An exasperated laugh escaped me. 'If you never got out of bed again for no bloody reason at all, the problem wouldn't be that you were useless – the problem would be that you were no longer behaving like yourself. Which is an entirely different point from ... from ...'

A bitter twist of his lips. 'Me being unable to protect you the way I always have?'

He threw the words at my feet like a triumphant conclusion. As if I'd gasp and freeze and realise he was right after all. As if I'd suddenly agree that indeed, he should stay at home during the battle tomorrow, and that once I realised I could not count on him to survive, the fire of my love would start quelling itself, all sparks of passion smothered by the growing recognition of his ineptness.

'For the bloody gods' sakes,' I said.

He swallowed. 'Em—'

'No, *listen* to me!' A frustrated gesture silenced him as if I'd slapped him in the face. 'You're operating under the assumption that I love you because you keep me safe – do I understand that correctly? Because you are dangerous and powerful and you *would do anything for me* – you're assuming *those* are the essential parts of you upon which my feelings hinge?'

He could have been a statue, the moonlight playing over his frozen features as he stared at me in bewildered shock.

I wanted to cry.

I wanted to kill something.

'Let me make this very, very clear.' As if I was explaining to a child how to darn a sock, simple step after simple step. The shivers running down my back had nothing to do with the cold autumn breeze caressing my bare legs and face; they were all fury, all heartfelt frustration. 'First of all, you're so far removed from the concept of uselessness that it never even *occurred* to me to think of you in any such way. You've been the only person keeping me sane for weeks. You forced Thysandra to see who the Mother really is. You prepared for her information and saved us hours of organisational trouble. None of that required a drop of magic, and all of it was invaluable for tomorrow's fight, alright?'

The way he closed his eyes told me he was about to object. 'Yes, but—'

'However,' I crisply interrupted, silencing him again, 'none of that is even remotely relevant to the core of the matter, because *I don't care*, Creon. It's not your battle prowess that made me fall for you. It's not your magic or your blades. If you lost your legs and your hands and your wings tomorrow, I would still love you to death – hell, if all you could do for the rest of your life was just *look* at me the way you look at me, that would be more than enough. Do you understand that?'

He was so very quiet, eyes like bottomless pools as he gaped at me – drinking in every word I spoke like a male dying of thirst.

Did he understand? Was he even capable of seeing himself the way I saw him — of defining himself not as the merciless killer with an accidental heart, but as the fractured, many-faced male I'd found beneath that shield, gentle and ruthless and brilliant and brave and always, unerringly, *mine*?

'I know she made you believe you were good for nothing but bloodshed,' I whispered, stretching out a hand, cupping the smooth edge of his jaw. He sucked in a sharp breath at the touch. 'Which isn't a lie just because there's so much else you do and do flawlessly. It's a lie because you don't need to be good for anything in the first place. You just need to be. You just need to love me and feel like home in this world I can never make sense of on my own, and *that*' — I bent over to kiss his forehead, tipping up his face with my hand still below his chin — 'that doesn't have the faintest thing to do with anyone's bindings, broken or otherwise. It doesn't have anything to do with *use*.'

That last word, quiet and treacherous, hung in the air for one fragile moment.

And then he was crying.

Not the single restrained tear I'd seen from him once before, the night he'd returned half-dead and hurting to the pavilion, but raw, broken sobs that tore from his throat like poison, ripping the last of his desperate composure to shreds. I let go of his face, sank down onto the stone beside him. He curled into my lap like a young boy looking for shelter, and for one heartbreaking moment, he was no longer Creon Hytherion, Silent Death and fae prince ... Just the child tortured into becoming a weapon. The child so many had wanted to smother in his cradle before he'd even learned to walk.

I held him tighter, tears soaking my knitted sweater as decades of despair spilled out. Ran my fingers through his long hair again and again, drew gentle circles over his shoulders and the roots of his wings, until finally he went quiet in my arms, shivering slightly in the cold of the night. I wrapped my scarf around his shoulders. He gave a muffled sound of gratitude without lifting his head from my lap.

'And just so you know,' I muttered, bending over to kiss the rim of his ear, 'you're still coming with me tomorrow. I'm not accepting objections to that part of the plan.'

He groaned but hauled himself upright, cheeks glistening in the moonlight. 'Em, we might die.'

'Yes.' I forced a shrug. 'So?'

'So ...' His unfocused gesture seemed aimed roughly at his throat. Voice. Not magic. That choice I'd made in the torchlit night of the Cobalt Court, coming back to haunt me in such unexpected ways. 'So are you very sure it's worth that risk?'

'It's not a risk,' I said softly.

He averted his eyes, rubbing a sleeve across his red-rimmed eyes. 'Em ...'

'I just had to spend six hours with a mage who wasn't you,' I interrupted, voice wry. 'It was a helpful reminder of how absolutely miserable most people are at reading my mind, and I think I'm going to need cooperation more than magic tomorrow. So I truly do believe I stand a better chance at reaching the Mother with you than with anyone else – and even if I'm wrong and we don't manage ...' I swallowed something thorny. 'I'd still rather die in your arms than in anyone else's.'

He was silent at that.

I turned a fraction, tucked myself into the warm hollow between his right arm and torso, and pulled my knees to my chest. His wing wrapped about me almost thoughtlessly, a tight velvet blanket against the cold of the night; his fingers settled on my hip, squeezing me closer against him.

Hours seemed to pass before he finally muttered, 'Then I'll come with you to the gates of hell itself if I need to.'

Some muscle near my heart loosened for the first time that evening.

Again, neither of us spoke for a while. Above us, the sky was clear and bright, uncountable swaths of stars shimmering like diamonds against black velvet. The forest stood its quiet watch around us. I felt the slow rise and fall of his chest, felt the steady beat of his heart where our bodies were pressed together, and tried my hardest not to think about how that same battered heart might go silent forever tomorrow, every single pulse rushing us closer and closer to that final destination of nothing at all.

'Well.' His quiet voice was light on the surface, seething with something far darker below. 'It's been a decent few months, hasn't it?'

I managed a faint chuckle. 'It certainly could have been worse.'

'Much worse,' he agreed, resting his chin heavily on the crown of my head. 'Much, much worse.'

We were silent again.

Was it better, I wondered, to at least have found that one soul who made my heart sing before the bitter end came for me? Or was it *worse*, to die knowing what immortality might have been for me, knowing how much I would have had to stay alive for?

I bit my tongue.

When Creon spoke again, his voice was husky, low. 'Em?'

'Hmm?' I didn't want to talk. Didn't want to be reminded time was still moving as I breathed in his smell and listened to his heart ticking the minutes away. And at the same time, I wanted him to keep talking and talking, to revel in the triumph of his voice as long as I could ... 'What is it?'

'If I were to die tomorrow ...' He paused for a moment to scoop me up from the moist, mossy stone and pull me gently into his lap, wings folding around me again as soon as he'd completed the manoeuvre. 'If I were to die and you to survive ... is there anything you'd regret not having said? Not having asked?'

My heart clenched with a vehemency that wouldn't allow me to breathe for a second.

I shouldn't have been imagining it, his still face in my hands, his hard, warm body gone cold and limp. I shouldn't even have been *contemplating* it. But he'd asked it all the same, and gods, *if* I were to lose him tomorrow ...

I would curse myself forever, not answering the question.

So I cocked my head back against his shoulder, squinted up at him, and murmured, 'Is that supposed to mean there's something *you* would like to ask?'

His quiet laughter alone, tense as it was, was worth the risk. 'Possibly?'

'That's a yes.'

A muffled snort. 'Don't be so bloody clever, cactus.'

'You'll have to forgive me.' I wiggled around in his arms to face him, shivering as the cold air crept back beneath his wings. 'Is it better if I tell you I might have something for you, too?'

He quirked up an eyebrow. '*Might*?'

'Now who's the clever one here?' I muttered and rolled my eyes at him. 'Tell me, then. What did you want to ask?'

'You first.' He didn't look very hopeful about that suggestion.

'No, *you* first.' I scowled as he opened his mouth to argue. 'You started this whole thing, Your Highness. You get to be the brave one. I'm sure whatever you're about to say is not nearly as outrageous as you think it is.'

'Not outrageous. Just …' He averted his face, avoiding my eyes, drawing in a breath for courage. 'Remember when we'd just arrived in the Underground and I was refusing to leave my room because of the demon trouble going on?'

'Vaguely,' I said dryly.

His chuckle was half-hearted at best. 'This thing you did, one of those days – when you sat before my door and just … *felt* …'

'*Oh.*' At once I knew where he was going. 'I never did that again, did I? Do you want me to do that again?'

He hesitated. 'If you don't mind …'

'Why would I *mind*, you dramatic creature?' I nestled my head more tightly against his chest, closing my eyes. 'You'll be glad to know my request is much more shameless and worth being minded. Makes you look perfectly humble in comparison.'

'I'm overjoyed,' he muttered, but the hint of relief in his voice was unmistakable. 'And bracing myself.'

'It's … it's something Lyn once said.' An eternity ago, it seemed, that morning we'd spent between the twisted trunks of the Faewood trees, sharing sweets, looking out over the pearly beach of the Crimson Court.

'That she used to hear you sing sometimes, before you lost your voice. When you thought no one would be listening.'

He tensed beneath me.

'So ...' His silence was alarming. 'So I was wondering ...'

'Yes,' he whispered. 'Of course.'

Of course I'd wondered? Or of course he'd oblige the unspoken request?

Did it matter at all?

I curled up in his lap, face buried in his chest, his heartbeat a strong, just-too-rapid pulse against my cheek. His arms wrapped around me. So did his scent, that musky, summer-sweet fragrance of hazelnuts and sun-streaked forests, carrying the memory of every heated touch between us, every burst of laughter, every tear shed in his arms ...

His fingers combed through my hair. Feathery caresses, soothing like a lullaby.

I thought of the light in his eyes when he smiled.

I thought of the motions of his fingers in a crowded Underground hall. *Love you.*

And just like that, the shreds of memories began flooding me, as if that slightest nudge was all the encouragement they needed ... Velvet wings, folding over me as I slept. Ink-stained fingers, browsing nimbly through piles of parchment. The wry quirk of a scarred eyebrow, the melody of his laughter, the warmth of his lips on mine. The rasp of his voice just as I drifted into dreams – *my love* ...

There was too much of him for a single heart to contain. I felt like I was swelling with it, with everything he was, everything he had ever been, everything he would always be to me ... until it came spilling over the edges of me, the intensity of the feeling flooding the world around me and drowning out all the rest. Until I no longer felt my own skin and bones, my body held together by nothing but that fierce, all-consuming devotion.

Creon held me without a word in the starry darkness. Held me, felt with me, soaking up every surge of love that poured from me.

And finally, on what might be the last night of our lives, he sang for me – a quiet ballad of hope and heartbreak, courage and despair, and a world that would never be the same again.

Chapter 33

Dawn arrived with deceptively peaceful radiance.

I woke at the first glimmer of that golden light touching the tent above me – woke with one hand wrapped around Creon's and the other clenched around the hilt of the unnamed alf sword beside me, as if even my dreams had been bracing for battle.

Neither of us spoke as we rose and dressed in black from head to toe, arming ourselves to the teeth. A brief glance was all we shared before we left our tent, the only acknowledgement I dared to give of whatever had shifted between us last night; I feared that if I lingered on it for even a second, I'd find myself running for the hills, dragging Creon as far away from the city as I could manage. Away from the violence. Away, most of all, from the mother whose voice he still couldn't help but hear, who sat waiting for us on her grisly throne like a spider hovering at the heart of its web.

Ready for us to come and find her.

Ready for us to die.

It was impossible not to think of it as I buckled my sword to my back, as I slipped the mother-of-pearl bracelet onto my wrist, as I opened the tent and let the vibrant glow of the sunrise wash over me – *this might be the last time.*

I strode on all the same.

It was in that same golden light that we gathered at the heart of the camp, grim and subdued, surrounded by the ominous silence that hung like morning mist over the endless numbers of warriors readying themselves. Lyn was there, in loose red tunic and trousers, a curved dagger strapped to her hip. Tared and Edored, blades on their backs, alf light flickering restlessly around them. Agenor, dressed in all-black as well, carrying the broad sword I'd only ever seen him wield during our first battle at the Golden Court, and Rosalind, looking human and delicate and ready to stab anyone who dared to suggest she'd better hide in the Underground and wait for the battle to pass.

If they were at all surprised to see Creon, they hid it well.

'Get something to eat,' Agenor told me in between muttered conversations with vampire and nymph commanders. He'd gone absent-minded the way I recalled from my previous battle by his side, mind already on the grain fields of the city, working out the pieces on the board. 'We're moving soon.'

Moving.

My last breakfast.

There was no banishing that thought, no matter how unwanted.

I barely tasted my bread. Messengers flew and faded back and forth around us as I ate, passing on the last questions and orders; in the distance, the otherworldly silence was broken by the occasional yelled command. Thousands upon thousands of warriors moving into position – all that was left of the magical world, preparing for their last desperate march …

Counting on me to finish the job.

The sword on my shoulder had never felt so heavy before.

The sun had only just risen above the horizon, still shrouding the world in a buttery yellow light, when we began our four-mile march towards the city, our final battlefield.

Only as we scaled the first hill did I realise how much larger our army had grown overnight. More units of magical beings must have continued to arrive even after Creon and I had finally stumbled into our tent, hours past midnight. Around the small elevation on which we stood, a sea of heads stretched out on all sides. On the far left flank, the red hair and golden armour of the phoenixes shone almost as bright as the rising sun, the longbows slung over many of their shoulders proof that fire would not be their only weapon. Next to them, the perfectly straight ranks of vampires marched on with ruthless discipline and efficiency, spears in their gloved hands, hooded cloaks billowing behind them.

The alves walking out ahead of us were a horde of writhing chaos in comparison – a swarm of fur and leather and wolfskin cloaks, and plenty of individuals who were not wearing shirts or coats at all, tattooed torsos gleaming in the morning light.

'That way clothes can't get in the way while they're fighting,' Edored told me when I enquired after their safety, looking like it was the most self-explanatory thing in the world to run into a battle without a shred of protection on one's body.

I didn't even try to argue.

To our right walked the nymphs, with their strange, organic-looking armour and their brightly coloured hair and clothes; behind them, the small group of Agenor's fae was a fleck of stark black against the green-grey hills. The human army, finally, came last, ranks expertly held together by Delwin and his men. They would not be joining the fray until we'd punched through to the city itself, where at least they had the advantage of knowing their surroundings.

And I ...

I would wait, too.

Until we were convinced Creon and I could safely reach that little door Rosalind had told us about, leading us to the heart of the Mother's new territory. No sense in risking our lives before that time, Agenor had sternly informed me; no one would be better off if a stray arrow hit me before I could do the one thing only a godsworn mage could manage.

I understood. I agreed with the theory – I really did.

It was infuriating all the same.

On we marched, eastward. The briny, home-like smell of the sea grew ever more pungent. Twice, a large gull came shrieking past; both birds were chased away by Alyra, who appeared to be of the opinion that any unknown passing creature might just as well be spying on behalf of the Mother. When the sea itself finally came into view, an eternity later, I had to bite down the urge to falter – if we were that close to the coast, it would be mere minutes until the city became visible, too.

They knew it as well as I did, the marching humans behind us. For the first time, they were snapping at the heels of the nymphs and vampires before them – that twisted impatience to see just how bad the bad news would be, just how little hope would be left for the loved ones they'd left behind.

Going home would never be the same, I'd wanted to tell them as we marched out of the city two mornings ago … but none of us had ever expected *home* to change.

The sun stood a hand's breadth above the horizon when we caught the first glimpse of the outer walls, appearing jarringly unchanged, the same pristine white looping through the landscape. It wasn't until we climbed the next flat-topped hill that we finally got our first look at the city itself, nestled at the heart of that once-safe territory.

It had been such a light, lively place, the first time I'd lain eyes on it.

Now there were no farmers in the fields, no city guards on the roads. Instead, the winged silhouettes of fae swarmed between the roofs in the distance, gods knew how many more of them hiding between the buildings. Most of the houses still seemed to be standing, although plumes of black smoke rose from a few spots in the city; there hadn't been much of a fight, then, when the Mother's forces had arrived.

Her war ships – I counted fifteen of them, each bigger than the ships of the Sun fleet at Tolya – had dropped their anchors just outside the entrance to the city's harbour, bobbing on the peaceful waves. More fae might be hiding there, too.

'She's pinned a row of human bodies to the inner city wall,' Tared quietly said next to me, watching the distant city without even squinting against the sunlight. 'Might be a few hundred of them, if she continued around the full perimeter.'

That low earthen wall, covered in white lilies ... I was overcome by a sudden urge to gag. Next to me, Rosalind looked about to be violently sick.

Creon, on the other hand, gave the impression he hadn't expected anything else and was, if anything, relieved she hadn't lined the outer walls with corpses, too. 'Any sign of traps between us and the city?'

'Nothing I can see,' Tared muttered, gaze scanning the area. 'Although there is no telling what she's hidden in those sheds and stables, of course. She must have known we were coming, and it wouldn't be like her not to greet us with a few surprises.'

I swallowed, studying the quiet silhouettes of the buildings scattered across the farmland before us. 'Can't we ask the phoenixes to burn them down?'

'If they can reach them alive, yes,' Agenor grimly said.

I tried to swallow again and found my mouth had gone dry as dust.

An hour ago, I'd thought it would be horrific to finally see her fae army in all its venomous glory – that force that so easily outnumbered ours, even without the disadvantage of our bindings. But somehow this was worse, to not see our opponents at all. To stand here and look out over what could have been mistaken for a peaceful scene, having to guess at the horrors that lay in wait for us ... to not know when she would suddenly rise and strike, ready to wipe us off the face of the earth.

Was it a game she was playing on purpose? Pretending to ignore us entirely, reminding us that we were little more than annoying lice in her pelt?

The unease was spreading – I heard it in the whispers and mutters around us, ranks of warriors allowing their grim composure to slip for the first time, confronted with the strangely empty battlefield before us. Had we misjudged after all? Was the Mother no longer here despite having moved her throne? Were we looking at nothing but the rearguard of the army she'd brought here to take the city the night before last?

But Agenor didn't even blink, squinting at the stretches of golden grain, calculating a thousand and one possible moves behind those familiar green eyes.

'If she's trying to lure us closer ...' Creon muttered.

'Yes.' My father shook his head as if he'd been yanked from his sleep, suddenly all tightly controlled composure again. 'Ask the phoenixes to take down a stretch of the outer wall for those of us who cannot fly. Then send a group of alves inside and tell them to fade back to us the moment anything happens. Do we have a few with enough sense to remember that when things get heated?'

Tared let out a grim laugh; he was already strolling down the hill, to where several of the alves had begun drawing their weapons. Lyn swept out her wings in the same moment. I watched her soar towards the far-left flank in a streak of fire, doubtlessly in search of Khailan, and only barely managed not to hop from one foot to the other as we waited – the serene quiet growing more ominous with every passing minute, the lull before the deadliest storm.

Events unfolded swiftly, as if time itself shared my growing impatience. A small group of phoenixes rose from the left flank not long after Lyn's arrival, wings of flames carrying them to the outer wall. A downpour of fire spilled from their hands, and mortals and immortals gasped around us as fifty feet of that age-old, god-built wall burned to the ground within seconds, the white-hot fire leaving scorched bricks behind on either side of the breach.

Tared seemed to have found his delegation in the meantime. From the teeming ranks of the alves, a dozen individuals came forward, swords loose in their hands as they cautiously made for the smouldering remains the wall had left behind. One step over that blackened line, as the rest of us held our breaths, bracing for a sudden attack. A second step. One more, and still nothing moved near the city proper but for the occasional fae flying back and forth between homes ...

'So what are we waiting for?' Edored loudly said, looking ready to leap after the other alves beyond the wall. 'If nothing is happening to them, shouldn't we—'

Alyra let out a screech above us – a single high-pitched, ear-splitting warning.

The next moment, the alf delegation started screaming.

It was over so fast I barely registered what had happened. One moment the twelve of them were still standing, walking, not a sign of hurt or injury. The next ...

They crumpled simultaneously, collapsed to the ground in a shared outburst of excruciating cries. Limbs twitched and shuddered. Swords dropped from hands. There was blood, suddenly, so much blood, pools of crimson rapidly widening around each of them even though there were no wounds to be seen – two, perhaps three seconds, and then the twelve of them lay dead on the grassy earth, eyes wide open, faces frozen in eternal agony. Only the blood still moved, trickling through the grass around them, soaking into the dark earth below.

A tick of baffled silence.

Then the alf legion below the hill erupted in deafening shouting.

Alyra landed on my shoulder, still shrieking. Even Creon breathed an audible '*Fuck*' beside me. Tared reappeared on the hilltop the next moment, in a furious flicker of light. 'What for Orin's fucking eye—'

'Blood magic, I'm guessing,' Agenor interrupted stiffly. He hadn't paled, not exactly ... but the usual deep bronze of his skin now held a tinge of greyness, and the square lines of his jaw looked substantially squarer than a minute ago. 'Korok's own contribution to her godsworn powers.'

Zera help me.

I stared at those twelve cramped corpses beyond the wall, gall rising in my throat. Godsworn powers ... Was it delusional to wonder if this was a message aimed directly at me – an ungentle reminder that even if I wielded *some* godsworn magic, there were still powers only the Mother possessed? That even if Zera had woken my latent surface magic, Korok had blessed Achlys and Melinoë with both that *and* blood magic of his own?

'... suppose she drew a defence line around all of the territory,' Creon was saying next to me, his face hard, his voice rough. 'She had no way of knowing where we'd try to enter.'

Oh, hell.

What if we couldn't pass through at all? Did the Mother plan for us to lay siege to the city while she waited for sundown and made a start on slaughtering every last human soul between those walls?

'I could go and take a look at it?' The words were out before I could stop them. 'Perhaps if I use my iridescent magic, I can neutralise *her* magic, and ...'

Agenor closed his eyes. 'You're the very last person I'd send to take a look at this mess, Em.'

'But—'

'Agenor?' a sharp voice interrupted before I could finish.

It was Nenya, climbing up the hill in her swirling black cloak, her face even paler than usual thanks to the waxy substance she and the other vampires used to protect their skin from the sunlight. Lyn came trotting after her on her short legs, wings flaring out every few seconds to propel her up a particularly steep part of the slope.

Blood magic.

Vampire magic.

Upon reflection, perhaps I should indeed leave this part of the work to others.

'It's a blood mark,' Nenya added as she came within a few feet, a fraction out of breath. 'Bakaru has used them from time to time. Although I don't want to know how much blood she spilled to set up one of this size, but ...'

'Would a few hundred dead citizens suffice?' Tared grimly suggested.

Her lip curled up. 'Oh, yes. That would do the trick.'

Those poor people pinned to the wall ahead. I glanced at the dead alves again, then at the horde of their living next of kin, who were irately crowding up on the invisible line between our side and the territory the Mother had claimed for herself – mere minutes until some of them recklessly tried to follow and suffer the same fate, I estimated.

If we even had that long.

'Fastest way to remove the mark is to kill the Mother,' Nenya said hoarsely. Her face was too tight – as if she was about to propose cutting off her own leg to solve the deadlock. 'I think Bakaru would be able to undo it, but there's no way in hell you'll convince him to get involved personally. So as far as I know, the best we can try is to temporarily ... subdue it. For long enough that our army can cross the line, at least.'

Edored gave a deafening snort before anyone else could react, scowling at her with a suspicion that surprised me. 'You mean you're going to try yourself, don't you?'

She grimaced. 'Well—'

'And what's that going to cost you, Nen?'

'Blood,' she said defiantly, red lips twisting into a humourless smile. 'Lots of it. Good thing that I've survived it before, being bled dry to the last drop.'

The flash of panic on Lyn's face told me I wasn't the only one who remembered the way she'd shown up in Zera's temple after her last visit to Bakaru, pale as a sheet and wavering on her feet. 'Isn't there someone else who could ...'

'Doubt it,' Nenya said, shrugging. 'You're going to need a strong blood mage, and an unbound one, too, because I figure opening the way to an enemy army rather qualifies as an attempt to harm the Mother. I'm the only member of Bakaru's bloodline who was unbound yesterday. You're not going to find a mage with enough power outside his house.'

Alyra squeaked on my shoulder.

Below the hill, a spine-chilling howl of pain rose from the front ranks of the alves. For a heartbeat, the wave of bodies moved back, and I saw with a gaping hollowness in my stomach that two new corpses had added themselves to the pile, collapsed unceremoniously over the bodies of their fallen comrades.

'If you can temper the magic for long enough to let us pass,' Agenor said, speaking twice as fast as usual, 'I suppose that means we won't be able to cross the line in the other direction either, once you've exhausted your powers? Meaning we won't be able to retreat?'

Fuck.

So much for our plan to attack and retreat as often as possible, buying time with as few casualties as we could manage.

'Yes,' Nenya said brusquely. 'That would be a consequence.'

A single, resounding moment of silence.

'The alternative is packing our bags and leaving, isn't it?' Rosalind said, crossing her arms with an unamused cock of her head.

'She's not going to let us leave alive, anyway,' Creon muttered with a glance at the distant city — at the White Hall, where the Mother doubtlessly sat cackling about the perfect trap she'd set. 'So if there's going to be a fight, we might as well attack first and hope for the best.'

Agenor's shoulders sagged half an inch in resignation. But all he said was, 'Whenever you're ready, then, Nenkhet.'

She turned without another word, striding back down the hill on her knee-high leather boots, that heavy cloak billowing out behind her.

Edored violently elbowed me aside to storm after her. As he caught up, halfway down the slope, I just heard the loud start of another indignant outburst — '*Alone*, Nen? You thought I was going to let you …'

The rest of his sentence was lost to the noise of the clamouring alvish crowd.

They parted to let Nenya through, though.

Gradually, the shouts died down as she knelt a few inches from the charred remains of the wall and drew a small silver knife. Alves shrunk away from her. Only Edored remained, standing two feet behind her with his arms crossed, his rigid posture a clear message not to try anything funny as long as he was around to stop it.

Nenya slashed the knife across her left forearm without a moment of hesitation, leaving a single sharp cut behind.

On my shoulder, Alyra winced.

Nothing seemed to happen for a moment or two. Then Nenya lifted her head a fraction, lips moving, and Edored darted forward without warning, jumping over the invisible line that had killed fourteen others before him.

Tared gulped, grabbing Lyn's shoulder in a panicked reflex.

But his cousin stood and kept standing, turning back to the ranks of alves with a dramatic flourish and a broad grin of triumph. Next to him, Nenya sat hunched over in the grass, more and more blood trickling down her wrist and palm – gods help me, how long could she keep bleeding, if that was what it took for us to cross the line alive?

'Time to move,' Agenor grimly said, as if he'd read my thoughts.

There was no need for commands. At the foot of our hill, the first alves were already pouring through the gap in the wall, charging into the fields with drawn swords and howls for revenge. The vampires marched in after them. The fae and the winged half of the phoenixes took to the air to cross more swiftly, and within minutes, the first nymphs had reached the breach, too, following their allies onto the trampled grain fields beyond.

Creon unfurled his wings beside me, holding out his hand to me.

And it was in that moment – with over half of our army past the blood mark and the remaining part well on its way to joining them – that the first swarm of black-clad fae burst from the nearest warship, eclipsing the morning sky in less than the time it took to cry out a warning.

Chapter 34

There was no way to turn back.

Even if we *could* have reached the alves in time, there was no chance we'd have persuaded them to give up and wait for better chances; worse, with the crowd that was still pressing to make its way through the breach in the wall, the ones who had already crossed had little choice but to keep moving forward. Farther towards the city. Farther towards the hundreds, no, *thousands* of fae launching themselves from the ships, like a flock of hungry carrion birds …

'Are we going in?' Creon sharply said beside me.

Into the tightening noose. Into the cage that would soon click shut behind us.

But the alternative …

Stand here, unable to reach the brunt of our army, while the Mother's forces slaughtered them like animals? They didn't stand a chance to win. All they could do was win time for *me*, and what would be the use of their sacrifice if I wasn't even there?

'We're going in,' I breathed.

His wings swept out while he was still hauling me into his arms.

Alyra screeched and soared after us, a flash of silvery white as she shot past us and over the invisible line of the blood mark. Beneath us, nymphs were still pouring through the gap in the wall. I caught a single glimpse of Nenya between their writhing bodies, still kneeling in the grass, head drooping dangerously; Edored crouched behind her now, hands on her shoulders, holding her upright as she bled and bled and bled.

She would survive, wouldn't she?

He would *make* her survive, wouldn't he?

Before us, the fae army was now growing into a solid wall of wings, obscuring the golden morning light, casting unnatural shadows over the meadows and fields. The alves were still storming forward. The vampires and phoenixes had slowed down, waiting for orders. The nymphs were fanning out behind them, and the first humans were now making their way through the gap in the wall as well, back onto what should have been homeland to them.

A blur of fire shot past us. Lyn's voice – 'To that hill!'

Creon changed course.

We landed on a small elevation just within the wall, the gentle slopes covered in cow parsley and nettles and the occasional scraggly pine tree. Lyn was already there, eyes flaming. Agenor followed a moment later, Rosalind in his arms; I caught sight of Tared between the nymphs, and of Alyra hovering a little farther over the battlefield, looking for eyes to sink her claws into. The first alves were half a minute away from clashing with the fae army and showed no sign of slowing down.

The fae, on the other hand … they seemed to be waiting for something, hovering black and ominous over the city and the fields.

'Let's hope Khailan has the sense to get the archers in position,' Agenor muttered next to me, scanning the field with flickering eyes. 'Those orchards – the nymphs may be able to use the trees. Winged forces—'

Something howled, farther out in the fields.

Something feral and mournful and decidedly non-human.

'Oh, *fuck*,' Creon muttered as in the middle of the alf ranks, a farm shed collapsed and five, ten, fifteen dog-shaped, horse-high creatures broke free from their confinement ...

The hounds.

The Mother had brought the *hounds*.

It was hard to see what exactly was happening, half a mile away – but the screams ... The screams were unmistakable. I saw one of the creatures rip into the ranks of the alves in a spray of blood, dragging corpses along as it snarled and howled and clawed its way across the battlefield. Another hound emerged from the fray with an alf caught between its jaws, ripping the poor male to shreds like he was no more than a slip of parchment.

Around the monsters, more and more alves began fading away, breaking the unified front of their attack.

And *now* the Mother's fae surged forward.

'Lyn?' Agenor said, voice tight. 'How many hounds did you and Tared take down during the Last Battle again?'

She gave a high-strung laugh. 'Think we ended up with nine. Do you want us to see if we can top that?'

A rough exhale. 'Please.'

'Alright.' Her wings flared from her shoulder blades, then sizzled out again as she hesitated and turned back towards us. A strange smile lay on her face, suddenly. There was no joy in it – not a sliver of optimism. 'And if I don't see any of you again ...'

My heart skipped a beat. '*Don't* say that.'

'Dying without saying anything would be worse,' she wryly said, small hand coming up to squeeze mine. Her fingers were so hot it hurt. 'So ... it's been a pleasure, everyone. And for the love of the gods, please make sure the alves don't take over my library if I die, will you?'

And just like that she was gone, without waiting for an answer – shooting into the air in a long streak of fire. I watched her soar towards Tared with eyes that were suddenly misty. My thoughts wouldn't stop hammering the same two words, over and over again: *Last time. Last time. Last time.*

Tared turned as she reached him, raising his hand at us from the distance. A swift, wordless greeting – no, a goodbye.

The next moment, the both of them had vanished.

And the fae ... the fae were positioning for attack.

Strings twanged. A cloud of arrows darkened the sky. Khailan's archers, who had treated their arrow tips with nymph poisons ... but even though a few fae went down screaming, thousands of others flew on unhindered, descending onto our scattered army with wrathful efficiency. Red flickered over the battlefield. Bodies fell wherever I looked, unable to find cover on the open farmland.

And *still* more fae were rising from the city and ships.

I threw a panicked glance over my shoulder. No one was coming through the breach in the wall anymore. On the other side of the blood mark, a few hundred humans had stayed behind, their desperation visible even from the distance; Nenya lay in Edored's arms, head lolling back, arms dangling powerlessly to the earth.

He was holding his wrist to her lips – feeding her his own blood, I realised, thoughts scattering. So she might recover. She might be able to open the line again. But until she did, or until the Mother died ...

We were trapped.

On these few square miles of a battlefield, locked in with fifteen ravenous hounds and tens of thousands of glory-hungry fae and the Mother herself, waiting to wipe out the fragment of our army that accidentally survived those opponents.

The last desperate march of the magical world ... rounded up like deer for hunting, having never stood a chance.

'We should go,' I heard myself say. 'We should go *now*.'

I expected Agenor to object. The risks, the hastiness, the plans we'd made ... but all he said, voice tight, was, 'Stay near the ground. You'll draw too much attention flying.'

And somehow that scared me more than anything that had happened before – because if even Agenor no longer cared about risks and careful planning ...

It had to be bad.

It had to be really, really bad.

'Will do,' Creon curtly said in my place. He looked strung tight like a coil about to snap – the Mother's perfect prince of war, aching to join the fray, every muscle and tendon drawn tight beneath the poised exterior. 'Might help for you to show your face on the other side of the battlefield in the meantime. If we're lucky, they take the bait and forget about Em and me for a moment.'

Agenor sighed, face weary but fingers drifting to the sword on his hip. 'Yes. It's about time I get involved anyway.'

My stomach clenched tight without warning.

Get involved.

He was unbound now, I tried to reassure myself. He'd survived plenty of battles in his lifetime. If *anyone* here could get through this mess alive, it was probably Agenor Thenes, powerful mage and male the Mother had once entrusted with the safety of her court ... But against the backdrop of hissing arrows and howling hounds and screaming warriors, none of those thoughts held even the slightest reassurance.

If I don't see any of you again ...

I might be too slow. Rosalind might be too human, too frail. What if they were lying in their graves next time I saw the two of them – what if these few months, these few days, had been all we'd ever have?

They knew I would care, didn't they?

Had I ever even told them how glad I was I'd found them before the end?

'Em?' Creon said quietly.

Hounds howled behind me.

'Don't die,' I blurted at my parents, words coming out scrambled and not at all like what I'd wanted to say – *thank you*, that's what I should have said, *thank you for being here, and I know we've hardly had the time to try and be a decent family, but I think we could have been pretty damn good at it if we'd only been given the chance ...* Yet all that would leave my lips, as if my mind had simply blocked the path to all feelings in the face of the horrors behind me, was another numb, '*Please* don't die.'

'You're the one who's about to walk into the Mother's hands, Em,' Rosalind said and hugged me, arms drawing tight one last moment before she released me. There was a glimmer of tears in her eyes, but she smiled so very determinedly all the same – a forced, watery smile that desperately tried to hide the fact that dying was far from the worst outcome she'd imagined. 'You'll be careful?'

I managed a nod. More than that, and I might have burst out crying.

'Good.' She stepped back, giving me a last little nudge. 'Then go and show her, baby girl.'

Show her.

Right.

That I could do.

I took a single step, and then I could no longer allow myself to stop moving for fear I'd stand still again. Creon's hand found mine. I exchanged one last glance with Agenor – one last look into those green-gold eyes so very much like mine – and then we were running, side by side, hand in hand, down the slope of our hill and towards the city.

Towards the tunnel that might save the world.

And most of all, towards the rows and rows of fae around it.

The peaceful farmland of the White City looked nothing like farmland anymore, and even less like peace.

The acres of grain we passed had been trampled by hundreds of vampires ahead of us; the low hedges had been torn root and stem from the earth, then snapped and crushed by dozens of passing feet. The territory to the south of the city, the side where I'd arrived four days ago, was now the stage of the fiercest fighting, phoenix arrows and alves making desperate attempts to break through the ranks of the fae. Closer by, wings of fire flared around the bulging shapes of the hounds, whisking in and out of existence – Lyn and Tared, burning and fading.

They were still alive, then.

We ran, not breaking our speed. Creon swung an arm around my waist as we approached a small irrigation canal; a single slap of his wings and we'd crossed it, his strong arms carrying me effortlessly to the other side. No grain on this side, just rows of cabbages. The food wasn't as trampled, here, a little closer to the city; no armies had passed this part of the territory yet.

I saw a glimpse of pink in the distance. Around it, at least two dozen fae fell screaming from the sky.

Naxi.

I would have told Creon if I'd had any breath left to speak.

About a mile ahead of us, the city loomed, half-hidden from view by the fae surrounding it. None of them seemed to have noticed us yet, their attention focused on the greater battlefield – but there, to our left, a streak of black came diving our way …

Red magic flickered towards us, missing me by a hair's breadth and ruining a bed of cabbages instead.

Creon yanked me aside, slowing down – just in time to dodge a second attack. I threw a burst of red back at the fae and hit his wing on my first try, sending him plummeting into the furrows with a cry of agony. Next to me, Creon had already released me and drawn a knife, stepping forward to slit our attacker's throat as I scanned the sky for others.

Swift, efficient cooperation … Or so it would have been, if I'd remembered to watch the ground as well.

The attack came out of nowhere, a snarl and a flash of movement. Something hit me with the force of a sledgehammer, knocking the breath out of me, and then I was flying – flying – flying – an eternity in which I hung suspended in the air, the world reduced to incoherent screams and the penetrating smell of dog and rotting blood …

I slammed like a ragdoll against the earth.

Pain exploded through me a moment later, even my nerves slow to catch up on what in hell was happening. I whimpered and tried to roll over, the world around me staggering back into existence. Moist earth beneath my palms. The sword on my back, cross-guard prodding my neck at every movement. Howling …

Howling.

Abruptly, my muscles regained their senses.

I hauled myself onto my back in a burst of instinct, blinking to turn smudges of colour back into the reality I knew. The dead fae lay sprawled between the cabbages a few feet away from me, blood still gushing from his cut throat. Behind him, seven feet tall, fur knotted with blood and mud and gods knew what else …

A hound.

Snarling at Creon.

My breath caught again.

Inches away from those dripping jaws, Creon slowly sauntered back, away from me. Holding the creature's red-glowing gaze with a look no less dangerous – eyes shining with a murderous fire, sharp lines of his face shifted into the ferocity of a circling hawk. The hound followed, growling but holding back. Sentient enough, it seemed, to recognise danger when staring it right in the face – sentient enough to wait for weakness, rather than charge without a second thought.

Monster to monster. Predator to predator. A delicate dance between fae and beast …

But Creon's magic was still bound.

So when the hound lashed out, would he even be able to defend himself? The fact that the creature was still alive, that he was distracting it rather than having killed it the moment it attacked, suggested he at least doubted it himself.

I staggered to my feet, pain shooting up my left ankle as I put my weight on it. The hound didn't seem to notice me as it yawned, revealing half of a bloodied hand still stuck between its fangs.

Creon didn't even flinch.

I drew from my black shirt without thinking, aiming the full force of my red magic at the vulnerable spot beneath the hound's jaw.

The creature whipped back around, howling in pain … and only then did I realise the mistake I'd made. Because the bleeding gash in the monster's neck didn't slow its movements in the slightest – the opposite if anything – and now that furious bulk of muscle and teeth was charging at me once again, the stench of rotting meat washing over me …

A loud screech behind me.

The whizz of small wings past my ear.

The hound roared as Alyra buried her talons deep into the scurvy skin of its snout. She let go as fast as she'd made contact, spun around in mid-air, and managed to hit an eye on her second attempt, claws sinking mercilessly into that red-glowing darkness.

I pulled myself together enough to send a flare of red after her, hitting the spot just above the other eye. With a howl of agony, the hound reared, claws coming off the ground as it coiled for attack …

That one moment was all Creon needed.

A slam of wings, a flicker of steel, and his dagger dug deep into the monster's exposed chest, staying behind as he jumped back with cat-like grace and speed. Whining, the hound staggered a last step forward, then collapsed, landing with a thump I felt vibrating through the earth beneath my feet.

A last wet growl, and it went silent.

Alyra let out a triumphant squeal and fluttered down to perch on the dead creature's snout.

Only then did I hear my own ragged breathing; it came shrieking from my throat as I stared at that mountain of hair and claws and fangs, covered in raw wounds and festering scabs. Sharp pain lanced through my ankle as I staggered back. The sounds of the battlefield finally made their way to my conscious mind again, a never-ending cacophony of screams and sizzles and clattering metal.

'Are you alright?' Only the hint of roughness in Creon's voice suggested his staring match with a creature ten times his size may not have left him entirely unaffected. His movements were tightly coiled and perfectly controlled as always as he retrieved his knife from the hound's chest and wiped it on a patch of more or less clean fur, then turned to me, gaze shooting down to my ankle. 'Sprained?'

I grimaced. 'Think so.'

He muttered a curse, sliding his knife back into his boot. 'We can't linger here. We're lucky no one else seems to have noticed us.'

Next to the giant corpse of a hound, in the middle of an empty cabbage field … Not the best strategy to remain invisible. I nodded and hobbled one step forward, then nearly collapsed the moment I tried to lift my good foot – a pain as if someone was jabbing a spear into my left leg from below.

With three long strides, Creon stood beside me. 'Come here.'

'What—'

He'd already swept me into his arms.

I clung to his shoulders for dear life as he ran, away from the hound, away from the dead fae, towards the city in the distance. Out of the cabbage fields. Into yet another stretch of grain. The world was jarringly quiet around us, not a soul moving to stop us … But close by, to the south of the city, fae and phoenixes were battling above the throng of bodies, red magic and fire flashing wherever I looked. Clouds of arrows came whizzing over at irregular intervals, but fewer and fewer of them.

And there, in the distance …

Was that Agenor, that lone figure charging an entire unit of the Mother's fae?

I buried my face in Creon's neck and tried to stop thinking, to stop hearing. My ankle throbbed like hellfire. Still, better to focus on the pain than on the cries of dying people out there, those hundreds and hundreds of individuals who wouldn't have been here if not for me – who would still have been alive if not for me.

Creon slowed down.

I jolted up, ready for alarm … but there were no fae to be seen except those surrounding the city half a mile away, like a swarm of deadly insects blotting out the sun. A small shed rose from the meadow before us, however, and it was there that Creon was headed.

Shed.

Shelter.

I couldn't help breathing a sigh of relief.

He kicked open the door without further ado, carrying me into the dimly lit space beyond. The smell of dust and straw filled my nostrils; mice hastily skittered off into the corners as he set me down on a bale of hay and knelt before me. His fingers tenderly prodded the swelling in my boot. Blue magic skidded over my skin, and the pain softened, although it didn't disappear entirely.

'Better,' I whispered. 'Much better.'

A wry smile on his lips. 'I know.'

Bloody demon powers ... but I didn't have the heart to say it out loud, not now, not here. Not as the battle outside raged on, paying in blood for every minute we delayed.

'We should go on,' I breathed.

He didn't rise, didn't take his fingers from my skin. 'Yes.'

For an endless tick of time, neither of us moved, watching each other in the dusky light of that muddy little shed – a moment etching itself in my memory like a carving in stone. His pupils, blooming wide in the unfathomable darkness of his eyes. His sensuous lips, parted a fraction – the only softness in the sculpted austerity of his features. A single loose lock of hair, black on bronze, brushing over sharp-edged cheekbones.

Last time, my thoughts whispered. *Last time.*

Without warning, he rose and leaned forward, lips seeking mine in a hard, desperate kiss.

It was all teeth and nails, that kiss. All the fears we wouldn't let ourselves speak out loud. His fingers tangled in my hair, pulling me closer; I all but threw myself into his arms, hands finding the familiar edge of his jaw, the pointed tips of his ears. A last taste. A last reminder. A single thundering heartbeat, and then it was over; he pulled away as abruptly as he'd lunged at me, eyes wild, lips flushed.

'Time to go?' His voice was rough.

'Time to go.' Mine was barely a whisper.

He squeezed my hand as we slipped back outside. Alyra sat waiting on the windowsill, visibly impatient ... but the reproachful thoughts I expected didn't come.

The city was close enough now that I could distinguish the individual buildings propped against the earthen wall, the shapes of the bodies pinned between the lilies. *There* was the guardhouse Rosalind had told me about, a slender and now partially burned wooden tower that marked the spot of the tunnel door. A single sprint away, nothing but an empty meadow in between.

Creon flicked a spark of yellow magic at me before I could speak, turning the black of my shirt and loose linen trousers into a shimmering, pearlescent darkness.

'Stay close to me,' I managed.

He gave a tense laugh. 'Nothing I'd rather do.'

We ran.

Whatever Agenor was doing on the other side of the city, the Mother's army seemed to have focused its attention on anything but the land they were supposed to guard; there were no shouts of alarm as we sprinted closer, no flocks soaring our way to stop us. Three hundred yards left to go. Two hundred. There was the door, small and grubby, nestled between two blood-soaked corpses and a patch of dying lilies ...

It was as good as unprotected. As we closed the distance, the ranks of fae were moving *away* from us, away from that door, towards the battlefield forming south of the city. No time to lose – who knew when they'd realise Agenor's attacks were little more than a flimsy distraction?

A hundred and fifty yards.

A hundred.

Fifty. Still not a single head turned our way as they hovered there, wings beating wherever I looked, every single one of them focused on the movements to the south ...

Too focused, almost. A twinge of discomfort took root even as my legs kept moving, even as my breath kept heaving through my chest. I'd expected a fight by this point. Wasn't it a little too easy, that not a single soul would glance over their shoulder even once? That none of these guards would think of paying attention to the approach of two very visible mages, coming within thirty yards of the wall they were guarding now?

Almost as if ...

'Fuck,' Creon hissed in the same moment, slowing a fraction, hands shooting to his knives. 'Em, they're not distracted – they're—'

Waiting.

The bastards were *waiting*.

For a single paralysed moment, as they started turning, as we faltered, as the world came to a screeching halt around me, my brain was blank except for a resounding *fuck, fuck, fuck*—

And then they surged forward.

It was so smooth a manoeuvre I couldn't help but admire it, in the last little part of my mind not consumed by acute mortal fear – hundreds upon hundreds of fae, sweeping away from the city in a single coordinated blur, closing in on either side of us. The snare tightened in less than the time it took to curse. A wildfire of red lit up the sky, and I grabbed for my shirt without thinking, hurtling my shield into that attack with all the force of my panic – *iridescence for magic*, but they would be prepared for that now, wouldn't they?

And *we* were far from prepared for an organised attack.

Red crackled and dissolved against my defences. But more was already flashing our way, almost too fast for me to draw, and there on the edge of my sight, a handful of fae were tightening their bowstrings …

Creon's left arm flung around my waist, dragging my feet off the ground as his wings swept out. The whistle of an arrow shot past my temple. I wielded my iridescence blindly, recklessly, flares of red magic exploding into sparks wherever it collided with my godsworn powers; Creon's right hand lashed out beside me, the knife between his fingers flickering in the sunlight as he slapped an arrow off course with inhuman precision. The city wall lay beneath us, the door so close it felt I only needed to stretch out a hand to push it open.

A fae came hurtling towards us, sword swinging. Only the fastest whirl aside saved me from a full-speed collision with that blade – forcing us away from the door again. Again, the arrows came hissing down …

I desperately reached for Creon's wing, drawing some of the softness from that taut velvet to blast the projectiles away from us. Red magic bit me in the shoulder in the same moment, sharp enough that I couldn't help but cry out.

Creon dived.

If his plummet was more controlled than a free fall, it didn't feel like it. Wind whipped my face, slamming the breath from my lungs. Red sparked and crackled around us. Half a second at most and we crashed into the earth together; like a cat, he somehow landed on his feet, his arm still tight around my waist. I stumbled against his strong body, cursing. Above us, the fae ranks were so dense I no longer saw the blue of the sky.

The door – that cursed door – was still thirty feet away from us.

Five humans had been pinned to the wall in the space between, men and women with wooden stakes through their chests, dead fingers still clawing desperately into the clay. Anger blew my next desperate swing of iridescence from my fingertips with too much force: I drew nearly all of the power left in my shirt, and above me, red magic bounced off of my shield and back into the ranks of our attackers. Two of them went down. The gaps were filled before I could blink.

Where were the mind-clouding, forest-levelling outbursts when I needed them? Be it fear or exhaustion, the magic wouldn't break free from me in the same all-consuming way. What would it even *help*, damn it? They were prepared for me to repeat the tricks I'd shown at the Golden Court. Nothing I could do would shock them enough to collectively stun them for a second or three, and we *needed* that time to cross the distance …

'Em,' Creon hissed next to me, whirling around to catch a stray flare of red on the blade of his alf steel knife. Blood trickled down his temple. 'The *corpses*.'

What?

Yellow magic flashed from his fingertips, hitting my dull shirt – but rather than the shimmering pearlescent texture from before, the result was a thick, dark velvet.

Velvet.

Softness for movement.

'You can't— *Creon*.' No. He wasn't in all seriousness suggesting … 'They were *murdered*. I can't just—'

Another flare of red made it through the throng, hitting me hard and vicious on my left eyebrow.

Oh, to hell with the ethical concerns, then.

Soft magic unspooled from me like a net cast wide, sweeping up every target it found along the way. The dead woman next to me, her bloodless lips wrenched open in a never-ending scream. The boy to her right, in his nightclothes, hair still tousled from sleep or violence. The stocky man beside them, the crumpled old lady with her knobbly hands, the gangly youth with his unshaven jaw ... I tugged at my magic, and their limp bodies shuddered up, inch by inch, away from the earthen wall.

More red flashed around me. Pain bloomed in my shoulder, burning down my arm.

I drew every drop of softness from my velvet shirt.

The net swept up, and they went *hurtling* – five dead humans, launched from the lily-covered earth and into the hovering ranks of their murderers like stones thrown by a catapult. Voices cried out in shock. The barrage of red magic faltered. And I was already running, even while I was still pumping the last of my magic into the movement, even while the corpses were still shooting up – grabbed Creon's arm and sprinted for dear life. Twenty feet. Fifteen—

Red magic slammed into the ground behind me.

'The *door*!' Creon hissed.

I smacked my hand against his wing and drew, a burst of soft magic punching not just the door from its hinges but the door frame from its foundation, too.

Around it, the wall started crumbling.

No time to think – no time to hesitate. Before me, a silvery white flash soared through the collapsing tunnel entrance. We jumped after her without pausing, ducking through the rubble of falling stone and earth, stumbling into the pitch-black dark with nothing but our intertwined hands to guide us.

'Follow them!' a voice hollered behind us.

I swung my red back blindly.

Bricks shattered as the magic hit. With an unearthly creaking and groaning, the walls around the entrance caved in entirely, taking clumps of earth along as they collapsed – shutting out the cacophony of the battlefield and taking the last glimmer of daylight with them.

Chapter 35

On the downward sloping floor, it was difficult to stop running. The upper half of my body kept falling forward. The lower half kept catching it. It took a hard collision with a wooden buttress beam to finally bring me to a standstill, my ears ringing, my chest heaving; next to me, I heard Creon sweep out his wings to slow himself down. His hand still gripped mine with painful force, as if in this impenetrable darkness, he might lose hold of me and never see me again.

'You …' I ground out, panting. 'You …'

His free hand clamped unceremoniously over my mouth.

Right.

Everyone and their mother might be waiting for us in the darkness, straining their ears for any clue of our plans or location.

I nodded, and he let go, the motion followed by the soft whisper of a knife being drawn. The most minuscule spark of yellow flashed through the dark, and the dagger blade lit up like a smouldering chunk of coal, hidden from general view by his wing wrapped around it. His face wasn't even visible in that dim glow. Just his right hand, which he cautiously extracted from mine to sign, *Wounded?*

I shook my head, then realised he wouldn't be able to see that, either. *Hardly.* My signs were stiffer than his, not nearly as practised. *Nothing serious.*

If I hadn't had months of practice interpreting even his quietest breaths and motions, I'd barely have heard his slow exhalation. I certainly wouldn't have recognised the relief in it.

You? I added quickly.

Judging by the lift of his wing, he was shrugging. *I'm fine.*

He'd been fine with an arrow in his back, too ... but that seemed an unhelpful point to make right now. Soft thuds were coming from the collapsed entrance behind me, the sounds of fae trying to dig us out. We didn't have time to argue about the exact severity of his injuries.

Instead, I signed, *Do I need to point out how useful you're being?*

His scarred fingers stiffened for the briefest moment. *I only—*

I swatted the rest of his gestures away.

His laughter – just a hitch of his breath, really – said all his hands didn't. *Useful or no, we need to get out of here, cactus.*

Before the army we'd left behind caught up with us. Before we drew the attention of whatever else was waiting here below for us. After all, if the Mother had known we'd be coming this way, if she'd found this tunnel and figured we'd use it ...

Surely she'd done more than post an army in front of it and consider the matter taken care of?

There might be traps. I had to spell out the last word; I had no idea what the sign for *traps* might be. *Or ambushes.*

He hesitated. *They've only had a day to set things up.*

Enough time for a blood mark around the city, I wryly signed.

Means she'll have had less time for anything else. He lifted his glowing dagger a fraction, as if looking for something. *And I think Alyra noticed the blood mark before any of us did.*

A muffled squeal nearby confirmed that.

I held out my hand, and she hopped into the small halo of light and onto my forearm, looking dusty and smug. An impression of empty darkness washed over me, the low corridor seeming enormous from her perspective, and utterly devoid of life.

'She says there's no one near down here,' I breathed.

Creon drew another spark of yellow from the dagger hilt in response, intensifying the blade's luminescence. Finally I could see the buried corridor in which we'd ended up, dry earth floor and brick-covered walls, a tunnel made for nothing but cases of the direst emergency. The path sloped down before us, winding around the corner some twenty strides away. Behind us, an avalanche-like heap of fallen stones separated us from the world outside.

The muffled thuds and shouts behind that heap grew slowly but steadily louder.

'Should we bring down a little more of the tunnel?' I muttered, eyeing the ceiling beams. 'If it delays them ...'

Creon grimaced. 'I have no idea how sturdy the construction is. You could just as easily bury us beneath a whole block of houses.'

Which would admittedly be unpleasant. I gave the collapsed entrance a last quick glance and said, 'Time to move, then?'

'Yes.' He absently swatted a flicker of blue at my bleeding shoulder, then turned to Alyra on my arm and quirked up an eyebrow. 'Want to go first?'

She proudly puffed out her chest and took off, fluttering deeper into the tunnel.

We followed as fast as we dared, shadows shifting ominously around the sturdy wooden beams as the dagger-light moved with us. The place smelled of mud and mould. Like a freshly opened grave, and *that* was a thought I shouldn't have allowed into my mind, with the image of those staked corpses still vivid and the sound of our pursuers growing louder and louder behind us ...

Alyra shrieked.

I froze mid-step, heart skipping a beat.

But there were no sudden armies to be seen, no hordes of fae storming into the tunnel to stop us ... Just my familiar, landing cautiously on the trampled earth floor some five feet ahead of us, cocking her head from one wall to another. A messy impression of her thoughts flooded my mind. The sensation of recent magic use. Sharp edges and treacherous ground. Holes where holes shouldn't be, and a faint association with hunters' snares.

'Alyra,' I hissed.

Ignoring me entirely, she hopped forward.

A loud *clang* tore the silence to shreds, metal bursting into view with such force I jolted back. Dust erupted into the colourless corridor. Behind that swirling cloud of dirt and debris, rows and rows of iron spears had appeared out of nowhere, piercing the empty space of moments before, crossing from wall to wall ... penetrating what would have been my chest, my throat, my face, if I'd unsuspectingly stood in Alyra's place instead.

Even Creon breathed a curse beside me.

Alyra huffed beneath the spears, ruffling her feathers to flick the dirt off her head and wings, then glared at me as if to say, *See how useful tiny friends can be?*

'Yes.' The word came out breathless. It was too easy – far too easy – to imagine what would have happened if I'd stepped onto that trapped spot, jagged tips tearing through skin and bone before I could have raised a single shield. 'Yes, thank you so much.'

With another huff, she tiptoed on into the dark.

I ducked below the spears, swallowing at the sight of their jagged edges. The corridor waiting beyond looked as empty as this one had done, and yet it took every bit of discipline to keep walking forward – step by step, wrestling the urge to inspect every single brick and pebble before moving past it. We didn't have *time* for elaborate inspections, damn it. If it took me three hours to cross the distance to the White Hall, everyone outside might be dead – so I walked, even as every fibre and muscle revolted, around the first corner and then the next, winding deeper below the city ...

'Seems we're following the street plan,' Creon quietly said next to me, studying the ceiling. 'They may have had to avoid the foundations of houses, if they built it more recently.'

'Yes.' I followed his gaze. 'Would it be worth trying to dig our way out on that side? If we get closer and—'

Alyra screeched before us.

Not her usual light squeal, the sound I knew so well – not a simple attempt to draw my intention. This was a cry of fear. Of *pain*. I whipped around so fast I nearly sprained my ankle again, squinting to make sense of the dusky world around us as I hurried forward – undamaged walls, boring sandy floor …

But some ten yards away, below the spot where Alyra was fluttering desperately, that same floor seemed to have … wrinkled.

Like a sheet of parchment folding in.

Panicked flashes of her bird thoughts reached me, interspersed with a burning, throbbing agony I felt echoing in the toes of my own left foot. Creon caught up with me the next moment, red sparking from his fingertips and pulverizing that oddly creased layer of sand. Below, the dark shape of a basin appeared, filled to the brim with a sickly yellow fluid.

Feet. A pliable layer of fake earth, built to fold as soon as anyone placed their weight upon it. That ominous fluid below, steaming lightly …

'Acid,' Creon muttered next to me, his lip curling slightly. 'Inelegant.'

Alyra flapped onto my shoulder with another miserable cry, balancing clumsily on one claw as she held out the other. One of her talons looked oddly raw, the nail bleached pale, the leathery skin peeled back like melting wax. She was hopping about so much that my first two hurried attempts to heal her missed their mark; my third finally found its target, restoring the burned skin while the nail kept its unnatural faded colour.

She collapsed onto my shoulder with a sound strangely like a whimper, curling up in the hollow of my neck. Enough traps for her, her thoughts informed me; if I insisted on traipsing through this hellhole, perhaps Prince Big Wings over there could start pulling his weight and step into the next pit of poison by himself?

Fuck.

I couldn't blame her … but how were we going to get through this swiftly *and* alive without her instincts to keep us safe?

Behind us, I caught shreds of voices, shouting at each other to move.

'Em?' Creon said tightly. 'Could you restore the trap? Very, very small amount of blue, enough to heal just the upper skin of the floor they dug away.'

It took even less blue than I expected. The resulting layer of lookalike earth was flimsy as parchment; I couldn't suppress a shiver at the thought of what may have happened if Alyra had been any heavier.

'Good.' He stepped forward, pressed the glowing dagger into my hands, and hoisted me into his arms without warning. Alyra grumpily fluttered off my shoulder. 'Hold on tight.'

The next moment he'd jumped, with a powerful beat of his wings – enough to reach the safe side of the acid basin, leaving the trap for our pursuers. Then he didn't stop walking. Long, reckless strides, towards the shadows gaping before us, carrying me around the corner so swiftly I barely had the wits to object.

'Creon! Creon, you can't just—'

'I know.' A few more strides and he lowered me to my feet, face tight as he scanned the dark corridor around us. 'Figured they wouldn't do two traps directly after each other, and I wanted us out of mage's reach if anyone steps into that acid bath. What do we do?'

'Try to get out of this tunnel and into the world above?' I wryly suggested.

He looked up, wings twitching with agitation. 'The city will be swarming with fae.'

'But at least it won't have *traps*, will it?'

'No,' he muttered. 'No, but ...'

The look on his face was alarming – a puzzled line between his brows, the same look he'd get when he couldn't figure out a thorny mathematical problem. Right now, that expression made me want to grab him by the shoulders and shake him to hurry up; we didn't have *time* for meticulous thinking, damn it.

'What is it?' I managed.

'These traps.' A curt gesture of his head at the one we'd left behind. 'They don't really seem her style, do they?'

Did they?

Mud, iron, and poison. Nothing like the shield we'd found around the Cobalt Court, impossible to pass without a key or godsworn magic. Nothing like the blood mark, as gruesome as it was effective, another vicious yet sophisticated demonstration of the Mother's unmatched powers.

These traps ... A human could have set them up.

And now that he pointed it out, it seemed unlikely Achlys and Melinoë would ever stoop to using mortal strategies.

'So what are you thinking?' My heart was pounding in my throat. 'That the traps may already have been here before her army arrived?'

He shook his head, shadows playing around the sharp lines of his cheekbones. 'Those were fae spears. But she may have delegated the defence of this tunnel to someone else, or ...'

The sentence finished itself in my mind before he could.

Or she was playing some other game entirely.

Were we going mad? But there was no denying that these traps, deadly as they were, were not at all deadly enough for the Mother at the full force of her wrath. Hell, even I could have done a better job, had I truly wanted to stop someone from coming through this tunnel ... so where, then, was all the damage she could so easily have done?

My hands were going clammy. Were we focusing on the wrong things entirely, while the true threat was hovering just out of sight?

'Perhaps she's just trying to delay us,' I whispered. Was it my high-strung imagination, or did the voices behind us sound like they were coming closer now? 'If we have to throw pebbles at every inch of the ground before we can safely walk on ...'

'She could just have installed a shield like the one around the Cobalt Court,' Creon said tightly. 'She shouldn't know you're able to get through it.'

No arguing with that.

So ...

I saw the question rise in his eyes as it rose in my mind. So did that mean the Mother actually *wanted* us to make it through this part?

That could hardly be good news. Whatever she had waiting for us beyond, it would likely be significantly more unpleasant than anything we'd seen so far. Then again, even if it was, what could we do about it?

Turn around?

The howls of our pursuers didn't give the impression they'd be much more welcoming than the High Lady herself.

'Your iridescent magic,' Creon said, his voice urgent as he undoubtedly reached the same conclusion. 'Do you think it's possible to see traces of other magic with it? Could you use it to find traps, I mean?'

'Iridescence and ... yellow, perhaps?' It was hard to think straight with the unmistakable sound of a horde of fae hurtling closer. 'To change magic into something visible?'

He'd already changed my shirt again.

It wasn't careful, the burst of magic I flung around. It was the opposite of elegant. Glaring, lemony yellow, garishly dazzling pearlescence – like a child's drawing, made up of colours too bright to be true. But my shirt lit up like the sea sparkle that would glow in Cathra's waves on hot summer's nights, and so did the spot on my shoulder that Creon had healed on our arrival in the tunnel.

'Good.' He turned a small slab of wall iridescent – allowing me to spare the yellow in my shirt, which he wouldn't be able to replenish. 'Let's run.'

I drained all iridescence in the wall at once. Nothing started glowing in the sparsely lit tunnel before us.

We sprinted to the next bend.

I lost track of time and direction within minutes. Behind us, voices and footsteps echoed through the tunnel, coming rapidly closer. We darted through the meandering tunnel in a routine that established itself – sprint, corner, magic, over and over again. Every few hundred yards, a spot lit up in the tunnel walls around us, and we'd have to stop to set up a shield and jump through, hoping for the best ... But we managed to pass every trap without touching the magic-worked floors, and left them behind without triggering anything, undoing the sparkling mark before running on.

It was just after passing one such trap that the vengeful shouts behind us suddenly morphed into shrill screams of pain.

'I'm guessing they found the bath,' Creon muttered beside me.

I managed a tense grin. Good news; either our pursuers would progress more slowly, or they'd soon be confronted with the next trap, which had seemed set up to release something from the ceiling upon our passing.

We rounded one more corner, and another one. Passed one more sparkling trap – this one, it appeared, triggered by touching the wall in the wrong spot – and hurried around one more bend in the tunnel.

There, appearing so suddenly before us that I jumped …

A door.

A perfectly common, perfectly innocent door, worn wood and iron lock, beckoning us closer like the answer to a prayer. Had we already come this far – could this really be the place Rosalind had talked about, the locked entrance to the basement of the White Hall?

It didn't seem impossible. We'd been running for a while, and the city wasn't *that* large.

'Could you check it for magic?' Creon said in a hushed tone.

I did. The doorknob lit up in sparkles, but the door and frame itself remained as earthly as they'd seemed before; it hadn't been placed here by fae magic, then, just booby-trapped for anyone who might try to open it.

'There are people beyond it,' Creon added even more quietly. 'Or at least there's a heap of emotions nearby on that side. They're not particularly happy, from what I can feel.'

I bit my lip. 'You think they're waiting for us?'

'Probably.' A shrug. 'They're tense enough to be.'

'Not triumphant? Not feeling like people who are congratulating themselves on their clever trapping work or their brilliant strategy for guaranteed victory?'

He let out a joyless laugh. 'Absolutely none of that.'

We were both quiet for a moment. Behind us, in the distance, our pursuers started shrieking again – something about burning tar this time. Alyra landed on my shoulder, talons flexing. She was very ready to deal with the bastards who had nearly killed her, I gathered from the rather violent flood of thoughts that hit me; there was more detailed fantasising about the gouging out of eyes in her little mind than I'd ever need in my own.

And frankly ...

Was there any reason to make this more complicated? It didn't sound like any alarming strategies were waiting for us. If our welcoming committee was already anticipating a looming defeat, I was more than happy to give them one.

'Ready, then?' I said, quickly checking the buckle of my sword.

His smile dripped with violent intent. 'With you always.'

I lay my left hand against the soft surface of his wing and blew the door from its hinges.

Shocked cries, flaring red, and we'd already leapt into the room beyond, three bodies going down at the first burst of my magic. There were only about a dozen of them. Packed between the rough stone walls of the White Hall's basement, they had no way to flee, no way to take cover; if they ducked away from my magic, Creon's blades were waiting for them, and if they miraculously survived both of us, Alyra's beak and talons were already shredding their wings. It was more slaughter than fight. Like helpless children they went down, unable to break through my shields, defenceless against my magic.

Had these fae not been willing to bestow the exact same fate upon the city's innocent inhabitants, I might have felt pity for them.

It was over within a minute or two. We were left standing in a circle of limp limbs and wings, Alyra circling triumphantly over the fallen bodies, the way to the stairs on the other side of the room open.

Next to me, Creon looked as dazed as I felt.

I could use my magic. His signs came slow with confusion as he gestured at a pale-winged fae on the other side of the room, a bleeding gash across his equally pale face. *I took him down without any trouble. Bindings weren't invoked. So that suggests ...*

That you're not hurting her by killing them? I finished, taking the hint and reverting to signing as well. No way to tell who or what was waiting for us at the top of those stairs; best to make as little sound as possible. *That she sent them here without caring whether they'd die?*

His grimace didn't require any additional signing.

Those unambitious traps. The woefully small group that had stood waiting for us here. My nervousness stirred again, more violently than ever before – something we were missing, some game that was being played over our heads ...

Wings slapped behind me.

Alyra cried out.

I was just a fraction too slow, needed just a fraction too long to drag my thoughts from the tangles of the Mother's mind and back into the deadly, urgent here and now. Before me, Creon began turning. His eyes widened. His hand shot to his knives. Time seemed to slow to a syrupy crawl for a single endless instant, observations dripping into my mind like honey—

Then silk-clad arms yanked me backwards.

And an alf steel knife settled against my throat.

Chapter 36

I FROZE, THE SMELL of wine-soaked breath washing over me. A glimpse of long, pale fingers around a silver hilt, of bluish black wings in the corner of my eye ...

Recognition came like a punch to the gut.

Ophion.

He seemed just a tad unsteady on his feet, his weight leaning into my back with a heaviness that made me want to gag. But the knife on my throat didn't tremble. And Creon ... Creon stood paralysed three steps away from me, hands slowly pulling away from the weapons at his belt, wings flaring out in what I could only read as fear.

It was that sight that sent my heart skipping more than anything – the Silent Death, made powerless.

Was this the end, then?

Hell, what could be easier than for Ophion to slice that whetted alf steel edge through my vulnerable skin and veins in the next moment?

That staircase on the other side of the basement seemed to be laughing at me.

'Ah, little dove,' the Mother's lover purred, slowly, theatrically – as if we had all the time in the world together. As if my lifespan hadn't just shortened itself from eternity into a matter of seconds. 'What a joy to see you again. I've been looking forward to our reunion – haven't you, love?'

There was such venom in his taunting voice. A more tangible reminder than the blade he held that he had neither forgotten nor forgiven that day I'd made a mockery of him at the Golden Court, then run a dagger through his wings to add to the injury – the day Lyn had held him down, not unlike how he was holding me now, arms around shoulders, alf steel to the throat. I wanted to swallow but didn't dare to. His knife was so close I feared I'd slit my own bobbing throat.

'And what a good job you've done.' His slick, self-satisfied drawl crawled over the skin of my cheek and ear; again I had to suppress the urge to retch. 'Making it all the way here so swiftly. I'm sure father-dear would be ever so proud of you, if he lived to hear the tale.'

I shouldn't have taken the bait – shouldn't have shown him I cared, and yet I couldn't help myself. 'Oh, fuck *off*, will you?'

He chuckled, shifting his knife half an inch and tugging the silk cuff of his sleeve back down. 'Oh, I'm so very sorry, Emelin, but the two of us are going to have a little chat first. Well, the three of us, strictly speaking' – another chuckle – 'but our princeling tends to be quiet in conversations, doesn't he?'

So he didn't know.

I met the furious intensity of Creon's gaze and tried to shake my head without moving anything but my eyes. *Don't give the game away just to shock him.* It might not work. It might only motivate Ophion *more* to do away with me, just to keep the bindings safe on the Mother's behalf, and then what chance would we have left to stop them?

Either my frantic eye movements got the message across, or Creon's thoughts had gone down the same path. He didn't move, his stony face unreadable, his eyes burning like obsidian fire. On the other side of the room, Alyra was a fluffy little orb of anger, ready to launch herself at Ophion as soon as any opportunity revealed itself.

Better to keep him talking, before she unexpectedly decided this was the moment.

'What do you want to chat about?' I breathlessly managed, torn between shrinking away from the cold steel edge at my throat and getting as far away from Ophion's tall body as I could.

'A proposal.' He spoke faster, suddenly, no more theatrics. 'To save both of our lives, as it so happens. I assume you might be interested in a discussion to that effect?'

What?

Save *my* life – *Ophion*?

'Please continue.' My voice sounded strangled. My neck was starting to hurt from the unnatural way I bent it to keep myself uncut and alive. 'I'm all ears.'

'As I was hoping, little dove,' he drawled, all slick arrogance again, the reversal just as abrupt as his first change in tone. 'I'm not a fool, you see. I could slit your pretty little throat, and your darling prince would be more than happy to spend the next five months carving me to pieces – he gets rather excited about that sort of thing, doesn't he?'

It didn't seem in my best interests to correct him on that last point. Creon's glass-edged expression suggested the rest of the argument was true enough to make up for it, anyway.

'So?' I managed.

'So I'm offering you a way out.' A small, drawn-out silence. 'I keep you alive and tell you what you'll need to survive the rest of this day. You'll keep me alive in exchange. A lovely bargain for all of us ... so what do you say, little dove?'

I wasn't saying anything.

I'd momentarily forgotten how to move my tongue.

I must have misunderstood him, surely? Must have misheard some part of that smooth-tongued monologue? He couldn't truly be suggesting he'd betray the Mother's secrets and strategies to us if we went along with him – *he*, Ophion Kinslayer, the very same male who'd murdered his own parents and sisters to win her favours during her conquest of the fae isles. The same male who'd taken a god's place in her bed.

Utterly nonsensical ... but something suspiciously like shock was mellowing the sharpest lines of Creon's face, too.

A lovely bargain.

What in the world?

'If you're trying so hard to save your own life,' I rasped, 'why did you bother to attack us at all? You could just have let us pass. We hadn't noticed you. And it doesn't appear you were particularly moved by your loyalty to the ladyship's cause, either.'

'They'd punish me.' He bit out the answer as soon as I stopped speaking. 'I was assigned the responsibility to stop you before this point, and they don't take failure lightly. Ask Hytherion – he knows all about it.'

Creon's eyes had narrowed. I knew that look – puzzles, again.

'But if you were afraid of being punished ...' Could I ask this question? Hell, apparently he needed me alive, and I definitely needed to know before I agreed to any bargains at all. 'Why didn't you just try a little harder to stop us?'

Ophion let out a sharp laugh. 'With what people? With what magic?'

The small group of corpses around us.

The rudimentary traps in the tunnel, lacking all the Mother's godsworn powers.

Something shifted in my mind with the force of an avalanche, understanding barrelling in. Zera help me – did that mean she'd set him up to fail from the start? Given him this order, threatened him with the consequences, then allotted him resources that wouldn't ever hold against the combination of the Silent Death and a godsworn mage?

But *why*?

His defeat at the Golden Court? Had that single misstep dropped him so far down the ranks she'd rather be rid of him entirely?

'Do I understand correctly,' I said, slowly, picking my words with painstaking care, 'that she never actually cared about stopping us? That she *wanted* us to make it this far?'

'They wanted to make sure you didn't bring a host of others with you,' Ophion spat out – so strangely hasty again, as if nervousness had suddenly gotten its hooks into him. His long fingers shifted once more, tugging his sleeve back down his wrist. 'But yes, they seemed to be rather amused by the thought of seeing you again.'

Amused.

Dead and living gods help me.

And Ophion, with his twisted, tricky fae mind, had realised he'd be dead if we made it to the Mother's throne despite him – that he'd be the next on her list once she'd dealt with us. Meaning that his only chance was not just to let us pass in exchange for his own life, but to give us the best chance we had at defeating his former lover before she could turn on him.

So utterly mercenary. So utterly merciless.

I'd seen the traces the Crimson Court had left on Creon's heart. Had held him in my arms while he cried last night, unable to fully grasp a world in which he might be useless and loved at once. And still, it turned out, I hadn't fully fathomed the extent of the lovelessness that had shaped the world he'd grown up in.

'What is she planning to do once we've found her?' I said, forcing myself to stay with the core of the matter, never mind how much I wanted to dive into the deadly intrigue that underlaid this conversation.

'Something with godsworn magic.' The worlds hurtled over his lips; a small pause followed before he added, more nonchalantly, 'I won't tell you anything else without the confirmation of our bargain, of course.'

Of course.

That strange urgency ... it made the smugness that came after sound decidedly forced.

'Do you *know* what she's planning?' I tried, haphazardly.

'No!' he burst out, his knife hand jerking aside. I gasped as the steel edge pressed closer to my throat, but he pulled away again with a movement just as strained, smoothing the cuff of his right sleeve with fingers that suddenly trembled. 'No, she didn't tell me! Are you happy now, you little bitch? Was that all you wanted to know, or do we have to stand here for ten more minutes before we make that gods-damned bargain?'

What?

Creon was staring at us as bewilderedly as I felt.

'I'm not sure ...' I stammered. 'Why ...'

There were too many questions to finish that sentence with, and none of them made it to my tongue. Why he was suddenly being so honest. Why he was lashing out so abruptly. Why he had been so ruthlessly discarded, a change of heart that seemed extreme even for the Mother after a single lost battle ...

That gods-damned bargain.

Wait.

Zera have mercy – *wait.*

That sleeve he kept tugging back over his wrist ...

'We never included an end point,' I whispered, dazed.

Ophion's knife hand was shaking violently now.

'That bargain we made at the Golden Court.' The words spilled from my lips unchecked. *Now* Creon's eyes widened abruptly – understanding what was happening at the same time I did, having only ever heard about the events from me. 'Your answers in return for your life – but we never specified *how long* you had to keep being honest with me, did we? My side of the bargain was fulfilled as soon as you were delivered back to the Crimson Court. Yours ...'

I hesitated, out of breath.

Ophion did not speak.

'Am I right?' I added – like a test, my lips shaping the question so very deliberately.

He jerked forward. '*Yes.*'

'So that's why she threw you out? Not because you lost that battle, but because you were still showing our bargain mark and she knew everything she told you would end up with us if you were ever captured?' A peal of shrill, hysterical laughter was wrestling its way up my throat. 'Oh, if only I'd *known*. I could have spent so many nights cackling myself to sleep.'

'Careful,' he snarled, and the smell of wine seemed to thicken on his breath. 'You have no idea how very much I'd like to feel you bleed to death in my hands, little dove, and the more you tempt me ...'

'I doubt you'll ever love your revenge more than you love yourself,' I retorted, unable to fully catch my breath. Gods help me, my parents would have to survive the battle now, wouldn't they? There could be no conceivable world in which death was allowed to come between them and this story – Ophion Kinslayer, destroyed by one unthinking bargain, fallen from the pedestal for which he'd cut off his dead sisters' fingers. 'And you still need me alive to get out of here in one piece, may I remind you.'

He scoffed. 'If I needed the reminder, you'd be dead already.'

'I appreciate the honesty.' I glanced at Creon, whose burning eyes lay trained on the blade at my throat – following every twitch closer to my skin, every tremble that might lead to my death. 'Fine, then. I'll bargain to keep you alive.'

Creon's lip curled a fraction, but he didn't object. A necessary price to pay for my survival, even if he liked it as little as I did – liked it even less, perhaps, after having spent most of his life sharing a home with the prick behind me.

'Alive *and* out of captivity,' Ophion corrected me, voice sliding back into a semblance of his earlier drawl. 'I'm not spending eternity behind bars, little dove. Might as well kill myself now, if that's the life I can look forward to. And I'd like your assurance that you won't get in the way of any ... let us say, *amusements* I grant myself.'

Amusements.

Like what – fae balls? Hunting pixies? Abducting the occasional defenceless human girl and having his way with her?

I hadn't known it was possible to hate a single person this much. Zera's bag may have instilled some empathy in me when it came to Thysandra, or to Valter and Editta ... but the glimpses I'd caught of Ophion's deepest pain only made me wish *more* of it upon him. And yet, with his knife against my throat ...

Was there anything I could do but give in?

'Would you like a castle, too, by any chance?' I enquired, my voice dripping with sarcasm. 'Daily meals delivered to your doorstep? A flock of pretty fae girls to follow you around and swoon at your every move?'

Apparently, our bargain was capable of differentiating questions to which I didn't need an answer. He just laughed – that snigger that said he knew he had the upper hand and was enjoying it far too much.

It was that laugh – or perhaps the hate it inspired – that sparked the utter brilliance of my next thought.

'Fine,' I burst out, giving myself no time to think things through, no time to hesitate. Either this would work, or the consequences might kill me; no sense in lingering on that. 'Fine, you can have your life and your freedom and your amusements – but let me ask you one more question first, just to be sure.'

'As you wish, little dove.' The triumph oozed into his every word. 'It's not my time we're wasting here.'

'Did you ever regret it?' I said.

He snorted. 'Unlikely – but which of my past crimes are we talking about?'

'Killing your parents. Your sisters.' I kept my voice light as I spoke, even though every muscle in my body was on high alert, ready to fight or flee – this would be his last chance to slit my throat if he wanted to avoid the answer I'd felt with Zera's bag in my arms. 'Did you ever find yourself wishing you hadn't, *Kinslayer*?'

A pulse of silence.

Then he let out a raw cry of pain, knife clattering from his fingers as he grabbed for the pale green bargain mark on his slender wrist.

I kicked the weapon away with a reflex I hadn't known I possessed, then ducked from between his arms, staggering towards Creon. Ophion barely seemed to notice. Hand clenched around his wrist, he bent over where he stood, gasping. 'I ... I ...'

Truthfully and immediately, our bargain required.

And yet ...

Yet no answer came.

Between his pale fingers, the bargain mark glowed brighter and brighter, like a cat's eye in the dark. Ophion's voice rose to a shrill pitch as he tried to force the words out in jumbled wheezes. 'I did n—,' he managed and another flare of pain tensed his entire body, his denial derailing into another screech of pain. 'I never— I—'

Around that pale green agate, his veins were growing purple, then black.

He dropped to his knees, sobbing now, face contorted into a grimace that could no longer be recognised as the Mother's fiendishly handsome lover. I couldn't stop watching, enthralled and revolted at once. The spiderweb of black veins spread over his forearm, below his shirt; he curled up on the floor, clutching that marred wrist like a madman, jabbering incoherent pleas and attempts at denial.

Creon's hand wrapped around mine.

That hand ... scarred with wounds the crumbling male before me had inflicted.

'Did you?' I repeated, a strange calm coming over me – a feeling like I was swinging the axe down as I spoke the words. 'Did you regret it?'

'No!' he wheezed, spitting out the lie with inhuman ferocity. 'I – did – *never!*'

Blinding green light erupted from his bargain mark.

Ophion let out a last howl of agony.

When he became quiet, when the light flickered out, his forearm had gone a deep, scorched black, skin the colour of bubbling tar. Dark veins spread out from above his collar, too. His left fingers continued to cling to his burnt wrist as fiercely as they had done in life, his lips remained curled to reveal blackened gums ...

But his head had lolled back against the floor, blue-black curls stained with the blood of his fallen allies, and his cat eyes had dulled to the glassy void of death.

Chapter 37

Creon did not speak as he wrapped his arms around me and buried his face in my hair, but the cramped strength of his fingers digging into my back spoke louder than a thousand words.

'I'm alright,' I breathed, and only then did my legs start shaking, fear bursting through my veins minutes too late. 'I'm alright, I'm alright, I'm—'

He kissed me.

A hungry kiss, a desperate kiss – a kiss begging for answers in a way I would not have understood before last night. Here he'd stood, watching me on the brink of death. Unable to fight for me, forced to stay silent. Seeing yet another one of the Mother's presumed loved ones cast aside over pragmatism, the perfect example of the life he'd believed to be the universal way of things for far too long …

None of that, the response of my lips said, fingers tightening on his nape to pull him closer. *You're mine. I'm yours. We're not doing this the fae way, and don't you dare tell me I'm wrong either.*

Ever so slowly, the tension in his touch mellowed, the tautness of his muscles loosening under my fingers.

'And I'm still glad you're with me,' I whispered when we finally broke apart, foreheads bumping together. 'In case that needed to be said.'

The tremble in his quiet laugh suggested the reminder was far from redundant. 'I'll never complain about—'

A loud bang from the open tunnel door interrupted him, followed by a cacophony of shocked and agonised voices.

Yet another trap going off in the distance, shattering the brief moment of peace. Creon released me at once, face hardening. Alyra was circling near the stairwell, eager to go up and face whatever the Mother had planned for us above – whatever awaited us in the White Hall itself, the last obstacles between me and that cold heart of hers.

We had to go, I knew. We had nothing to win by postponing that confrontation, and yet ...

Amused, Ophion had said.

A shiver ran down my spine as I forced myself to start walking, stepping cautiously around dead limbs and pools of blood. Already I could hear that tinkling voice again – *Little dove* ...

Wait.

I stiffened in place.

'Em?' Creon muttered.

Little dove. My thoughts unravelled, or rather slammed together in entirely new ways – that cursed nickname, Alyra, Zera's doves cooing around my feet ... and then I was fighting with the buckle of my sword, the new leather of the belt still stiff and unobliging. Even in the dim light of this basement, the weapon's alf steel and mother-of-pearl gleamed white and clear as I shook it into my hands, its weight growing familiar already, its balance perfect.

You'll know, Tared had said.

All of a sudden, that seemed a perfectly reasonable instruction.

'Feather,' I whispered, and it *fit*, somehow – the same satisfying sensation that came with slipping your hand into a perfectly tailored glove, or with mixing a jar of paint to just the right hue on your very first try. Soft and harmless at first glance. Brimming with godsworn magic at a second. All I was, all I wasn't ... 'I'm calling it Feather.'

Really, how had I ever *not* known that would be its name?

'Inspiration through murder,' Creon said, the smallest smile quirking around his lips. 'The alves will be proud of you.'

'Careful.' I glared at him as I fastened the sword back over my shoulders with jittery fingers, ready to grab it and fight. Unnervingly, the weapon seemed lighter than before. 'I'm allowed to draw blood with it now, if you recall.'

'You can duel me all you want once we get out of here alive.' Somehow he managed to make it sound like the most scandalous of propositions; whether he was trying to soothe his own fears or mine, I was grateful for it. 'Unusual as it may be, there are people more deserving of your violence in the building right now.'

I managed a chuckle. 'First time the Mother is actually saving you, then.'

His laughter was equally strained.

We resumed our path towards the stairs, past the fallen bodies, past a few dusty crates of broken bricks that someone must have put here in better times. The tunnel remained silent behind us. Perhaps the latest explosion had finally convinced our pursuers that others would be far better equipped to deal with the trouble of our existence; they may have decided that they'd be of more use by retreating to the battlefield outside and risking their lives against living, visible opponents.

The stairs were eerily quiet, not a soul moving in the pale sunlight falling in from above. The corridor waiting for us at the top was equally deserted, nothing but the rubble of fallen statues and doors hanging askew to bear witness to the violence that had washed through the building in the past twenty-four hours.

Amused.

Where was the trap?

I used some more iridescence to scan the area before us for magic and found nothing but lingering traces of a short fight. So we tiptoed on, through the pressing silence, to the corner at the end of the corridor. Another hall opened up before us, as battered as the one we'd just crossed and just as empty—

No, wait.

It was not empty at *all*.

I only noticed the child on my second glance around, her small body huddled behind a marble pedestal, her dirty white dress blending in easily against that background. She was barefoot, her long dark hair dusty and tangled. There were no parents to be seen anywhere, dead or otherwise – just a handful of blood smudges staining the floor tiles, painting a grim picture of how she may have ended up in this cursed place all alone.

Her shoulders were rising and falling swiftly. Still alive, then, although I couldn't tell if she was wounded.

'Hello?' I tried.

Even my hushed voice echoed through the unnatural silence. The child didn't move – didn't give the impression she had heard me at all.

Good sense made me scan the room with iridescence before stepping forward – no major traces of magic, again, although some sparkles lit up around the little girl's head. Next to me, Creon was watching her with bottomless eyes, strong fingers resting on the hilt of his largest knife in an unmistakable warning.

Can we go closer? I signed.

His nod was too slow for the motion to hold any reassurance. *Her emotions are ... messy.*

I grimaced. *Can't blame her.*

He granted me that point with a grim smile, gesturing for me to go ahead.

Even as I walked towards her, deliberately noisy so as not to startle her, the child didn't so much as lift her head, curled up in her own little world of misery. For a moment, I wondered whether she might be sleeping; when I knelt before her, her breath didn't even quicken, and her face remained hidden behind her arms and those thick, black tresses.

'Hello?' I whispered again.

Her head jerked up.

A face from hell stared back at me.

I recoiled as if I'd been slapped, a choked cry slipping past my lips. The creation before me ... It still had all the elements a face should have – mouth, nose, eyes. But the little girl's lips were a pale blue, the skin chapped and bloodless. Her nose was crooked and likely broken. And her *eyes* ...

They weren't eyes at all.

Where pupils and irises should have been, two smooth stone orbs had been lodged into her eye sockets, sapphire and obsidian, glittering with an unearthly sheen in the faded light.

Sapphire and obsidian.

Blue and black.

I found myself unable to breathe for an endless moment, gaping at those lifeless, inhuman surfaces.

Then her chin jerked up, and I couldn't jump back fast enough – away, out of reach, feet tangling as I fled ... The girl didn't come after me. She just sat there, tiny and vulnerable, staring at me like a macabre doll come to life.

Her lips parted.

I grabbed reflexively for my mostly-black trousers.

'Emelin,' she sang, a bright, clear child's voice, melodious but devoid of all sentiment. 'The Mother is expecting you, Emelin.'

Goosebumps were crawling down my spine, my arms – down every inch of skin I hadn't known could prickle at all. I slowly inched back, closer to Creon. Those sapphire and obsidian eyes followed me with every step, the face around them showing not the faintest trace of emotion – a blank, maimed mask.

Could she attack us? Harm us?

And if she could ... then how in the world would I stop her without damaging the innocent child in whose body she moved?

'You're making them wait, Emelin.' She pronounced my name like some exotic delicacy, every syllable savoured by her grey lips. 'They have a *surprise* for you, Emelin.'

'Ah,' I managed, wrestling against my gag reflex. On the edge of my sight, Creon was prowling closer, a dark, lean shape against the backdrop of white marble. 'This ... this isn't the surprise yet, I suppose?'

She laughed, scrambling up from the floor – a high, unnatural laugh. Her arms jerked back and forth as she ambled towards us, as if her puppet master had not yet learned precisely which strings to pull to move which limbs.

'Stay back,' I snapped, raising my right hand towards her. 'Don't come closer or ... or ...'

'Or what, Emelin?' Again that laugh, sending the hairs rising on my neck. It didn't fit her sweet, childish voice in the slightest. 'Are you going to hurt a poor, innocent little human if—'

Creon shot forward.

He was so fast I could do nothing but cry out in that split second between leap and landing, between blade and target – a flicker of steel in the sunlight and the sickening squelch of a weapon digging into flesh ...

Her little head tumbled to the ground first.

The rest of her body followed a long heartbeat later.

'No!' I gasped, pathetically late – and now I *was* gagging, the sight of her severed neck too much for my unravelling nerves to bear. The girl's corpse barely bled, as if she'd been drained long before Creon's blade came sweeping in. 'No, I could have— I wanted—'

Creon's expression made me fall quiet.

Heal her, I'd wanted to say ... but the barely restrained rage in his dark eyes cut effortlessly through the disgust and the desperate hope clouding my own mind. Hell, what were the chances healing her would even have been possible? The girl's body had been irreparably maimed. Her mind had been at least partly invaded. Even if we managed to kill the Mother ...

How much humanity would have been left in this little puppet?

This swift beheading hadn't just been a way to protect me, the taut edge of Creon's jaw said. It had been a mercy kill too.

I swallowed something bitter, tore my gaze away from the little corpse, and mumbled a choked, 'Thank you.'

He squeezed my shoulder but didn't speak. *Ready to move?*

No.

'Yes,' I whispered.

She was waiting for us anyway.

So we made our way to the other side of the hall, leaving the dead girl behind, following the route through the building Rosalind's sketches had set out for us. Still no sound seeped in through the thick walls. If not for the rubble and dust, one could have forgotten about the battle raging outside, the desperate screams of the wounded and dying.

The only thing disturbing the silence …

A faint, thumping pulse in the distance, growing steadily louder as we made our way through the ruined corridors.

I thought it might be the rhythmic beat of a hammer against wood at first, or a smith battering an anvil. Only as the second, softer thud added itself to the cadence did I realise what we were hearing …

A heartbeat.

The sound of a *heartbeat* was echoing through the White Hall.

It swelled with every corner we rounded, until finally we stepped into the antechamber of the main hall I knew and it had grown loud enough to vibrate through walls and floor, every *thump* another tremor beneath my feet. A human man stood on each side of the hall's entrance, lips grey, blue and black stones in their eye sockets. Their features were so battered it took me a second glance to recognise them – Halbert and Norris.

I had to dig my nails into my palms not to cry out for them.

Their gem eyes followed us as we cautiously crossed the open space towards them, their voices hollow and barely recognisable as their own. 'The Mother—'

'Is expecting me,' I cut in, my voice too high. 'I know.'

They let out forced, mechanical peals of laughter. *Thump thump*, the heartbeat pulsed on, *thump thump*, a little faster now …

As if even that cursed sound knew we were close to the end.

Creon's yellow magic flashed as we neared the open doorway, turning my clothes plush and pearlescent one last time. I faltered and grabbed his hand – one last touch, one last echo of that love I'd follow into hell and back …

'How romantic,' Halbert's almost-corpse croaked.

Creon swung a knife into his forehead without even looking, and the former consul of the White City went down without another sound.

Next to him, Norris did not blink, continuing to stare at us with that utterly vacant expression.

But behind those doors ...

A ripple of tinkling laughter, turning my blood to ice at the first giggle.

Creon's fingers squeezed mine so hard it hurt.

Every muscle and tendon in my body was screaming at me to run, *run*, as far away from that cruel amusement as my feet could carry me ... but Creon kept walking, and so I did too, towards that doorway I'd crossed three mornings ago with Delwin by my side. Into the boom of that thundering pulse, as if the heart of the city had come alive around us.

Into the monster's lair.

Into a hall I barely even recognised.

Gone were the lily banners, the rows of statues, the galleries full of living, laughing citizens. A grave-like silence hung over the room now. The smell of blood and sweet perfume hung heavy in the air. Sapphire- and obsidian-eyed fae and humans stood quietly along the walls, shoulders stiff and faces empty, and there at the far side of the room, rising from the low stage like some ancient horror ...

The bone throne.

Around its base, dozens more humans sat hunched up on the floor, dressed in melodramatic white cloaks like a circle of twisted priests.

And in its seat, lounging in black silk and velvet pillows ... the Mother.

Still pale as marble. Still dressed in sparkling, shimmering slips of fabric. Still spine-chillingly beautiful, with those plush pink lips and that pointy face and those silvery white locks cascading all the way to her perfectly curved hips ...

But where her damaged eyes had been, she, too, carried gemstones instead.

Zera help me, was she seeing *through* the eyes of all those others? Like Orin and his moonstone eye – but so, so much more viciously?

I could sense Creon's roaring disgust without looking at him, as if the intensity of his feelings was reaching my heart through our intertwined fingers. Trying to steady my breathing, I released him – we both ought to have our hands available when the inevitable attack came, and any moment now, she could strike ...

Thump thump, the heart went, quickening ever so slightly. *Thump thump. Thump thump.*

But the Mother only sat and smiled at me, ignoring her son entirely – that flawless, icy smile, an expression dripping with poison and condescension.

'Emelin,' she purred, and it was then that I knew for certain the little girl's mind had not been her own – because the High Lady of all fae pronounced my name in the exact same way, three unhurried syllables, balancing each of them on the tip of her tongue before setting them free. 'Our little dove. What a joy to *see* you again, after all this time.'

So she was seeing, then. I wiped my clammy palms on my shimmering shirt, forcing myself to return her smile despite my racing heart and weak knees, and managed to get out an almost natural, 'The pleasure is mutual, of course.'

She threw her head back and laughed.

I cautiously took two steps forward, Alyra hovering on one side of me, Creon following like a quiet shadow on the other, Feather a reassuring weight on my shoulder. The Mother didn't seem in the least concerned as she tittered and turned back to me, wiping some imaginary tears with her glittering sleeve. 'We *knew* you wouldn't bore us.'

As if this was still nothing but shallow entertainment – her lover dead, her city under attack, and boredom the worst of her troubles. I didn't speak, waiting. If I just refused to play along, sooner or later she'd have to reveal her game ... and as far as my nerves were concerned, sooner would be better.

'But in all seriousness, Emelin,' she added lightly, as if she'd read my mind – leaning forward in her monstrous seat, pressing her fingertips together in elegant eagerness. Creon still didn't receive a single glance. 'We have some things to talk about, don't we? Unbound magic! Godsworn powers! You've been very busy without us, little dove.'

Through the echoes of that booming heartbeat, I thought I heard a choked moan emerge from one of the crouching humans around her throne. But none of them moved, and their faces remained hidden behind their white hoods and hunched-up knees – had it been nothing but my imagination, then?

Gods knew what she might be doing to them. I wasn't sure if *I* wanted to know.

There were so many things I'd imagined I would tell her when we finally met again. So many accusations I'd thought I would throw at her feet before unleashing my magic against her and praying I'd survive ... Agenor's memories. Tared's family. Creon – always, most of all, Creon. *How could you?* I'd have shouted at her. *How did you ever believe any of this could be justified?*

And yet, now that the moment was here ...

I no longer wanted to shout.

I just wanted her to bleed.

'You do realise,' I said, my mouth dry, my voice hoarse, 'that I didn't come here to exchange pleasantries with you, don't you?'

She smiled at me as if I was still that half-witted child I'd been at the Crimson Court – a look that made the colours itch beneath my fingers. 'Oh, little dove, we know. But you're missing some information, of course, and we're rather certain that once you're fully informed, you'll no longer be nearly so inclined to hurt us.'

There was something too meaningful about the way she spoke the words – something unnervingly ... smug?

Fuck. I'd have preferred a direct attack, deadly as it may have been; at least in that case, I'd have had something to fight against.

'I think you may be overestimating your own likeability,' I managed.

She burst out laughing again. Along the walls, the lines of gem-eyed humans and fae forced out spurts of laughter with her – grating, mechanical chuckles rising hollowly from every corner of the hall.

It took all I had to keep breathing calmly, evenly, as the unbearable sound slowly died away. On the edge of my sight, Alyra fluttered sideways, landing on the gallery balustrade and continuing to glare at the throne from that spot.

'Hilarious,' the Mother cooed, white wings flaring behind her shoulders as she curled up more comfortably in her pillows – a gesture that would have looked cosy on anyone else but managed to look like a murder threat with her smile to set the tone. 'Likeability has little to do with it, Emelin. We're talking about what it would cost you to kill us, in the unlikely event you could manage in the first place.'

Even that little jab came out so sweetly, like a well-meaning aunt speaking to her favourite niece. I tilted my head at her, wondering if I wouldn't be better off drawing Feather and charging at her before she could finish her monologue …

But no doubt she'd prepared for that. And as long as she kept talking, I stood a chance of learning what her preparations had looked like.

'And I suppose,' I said, aiming for unimpressed mockery and landing somewhere around breathless defiance, 'you now want me to ask what in hell you're talking about?'

'That would have been appreciated, but we'll gladly volunteer the information.' She looked almost *giddy*, in a way that made my stomach clench; around us, the rhythmic thump-thumping intensified, echoing relentlessly through the room. 'A lovely piece of blood magic, if we may say so ourselves. Do you hear that pulse, little dove? That's the sound of our own heart linked to those of our little guests down here. Which means, if we need to spell it out for you, that *if* you were to accidentally succeed in your rather ambitious intentions …'

Linked.

Oh, Zera help me.

Smirking expectantly, the Mother was clearly waiting for me to finish the sentence … but for one moment I didn't care about resisting her dramatic orchestrations. 'You're saying I'd end their lives, too, if you were to die?'

The cruel quirk of her lips was all the confirmation anyone could need. 'And you wouldn't want that, would you, Emelin?'

Would I?

My heart was pounding at twice the pace of hers now.

Those quiet figures by her feet, drowning in their grotesque white cloaks, their heads bent beneath the hoods … Were they feeling it, the strength of the Mother's magic tugging at their hearts with every beat? How long had they been sitting here, the poor souls – had she dragged them from their beds the moment she entered the city, prepared for my arrival from the very start?

Had they known all this time that they'd die the moment anyone succeeded in saving the rest of their world?

They remained suspiciously motionless. Either they had become too numb to react to anything, or she'd linked more than just their hearts to keep them subdued. Some forty or fifty of them, waiting quietly for death to come – which was monstrous, it absolutely was ...

But if I forced myself to be purely rational for a moment, what was the alternative? Letting them live, allowing the Mother to walk free, and sending a hundred times their number to their graves outside?

'Oh, I know what you're thinking.' The Mother's voice was sweet like sticky, syrupy honey, the sound crawling down my spine. 'A simple trade-off, isn't it? These few lives for your victory? An easy price to pay?'

Easy.

I didn't inform her she had, as a matter of fact, not the faintest idea what I was thinking.

'What's the catch?' I flatly said.

'So impatient, little dove.' But she clucked her tongue at the hunched humans at her feet, as if commanding a flock of well-trained animals. 'Go ahead, then, loves – show your darling Miss Emelin.'

Their Emelin?

And then the first of them obediently lifted their hands to their hoods, and faces began to appear before me – panicked, tear-stained faces, but still alive, still in possession of their own bewildered eyes ...

Faces I knew.

Faces of *home*.

My heart caught in my chest.

No, no, *no* – but there was old Miss Ariella who'd tucked sweets into my palm, and cross-eyed little Edie who was no longer so little at all, and Aldous, the blacksmith's apprentice, whose hand language I'd used to teach Creon ... Neighbours, dozens of them. Family friends. Nephews and nieces, and—

My thoughts stuttered.

And—

There, at the centre of the low stage, positioned right below the Mother's feet with impeccable theatrical precision, sat the two people I'd called my parents for twenty years of my life, clinging to each other, gaping at me in mute, terrified horror.

Chapter 38

'No.'

I barely heard myself say it.

No, no, no – there seemed to be no other word left inside me. The hall, the throne, the rows of fae and humans with their mutilated eyes ... their existence had gone muffled, subdued, as if a heavy fog separated them from my mind and senses. Had the Mother tried to kill me in that moment, she would have managed; I would have forgotten about my own defences until I lay bleeding on the ground.

She didn't.

She sat and watched the spectacle through a hundred eyes at once, cackling at the impact of her perfectly orchestrated blow.

No. Fifty strangers I could have killed. My old neighbours, the people who'd watched me grow from a tottering child into an equally misplaced young woman ... I might have managed to sacrifice them, too. But those two pairs of eyes – those two people who had never needed blades or magic to reduce me to nothing but a fumbling mess ...

Failure, their frightened looks said.

We always knew it, they said.

I'd kill them in the end, just as they'd always feared I would. Just as they'd always expected. Turning me not into the villain of their story, perhaps, but into—

No.

Wait.

I'd seen that thought before.

And at once the mist cleared, at once the storm quieted – because I *knew* this path, had followed it into insanity once before already, and what was I doing, listening to those gods-damned phantom voices again as if I'd never grown into more than a scared, unwanted village girl?

Not perfection, Creon's voice echoed through my mind, even as he stood tense and quiet beside me, unmoving in this moment of deadlock. *Just stubbornness.*

Yes.

Yes.

I *could* be stubborn.

The bitch wanted me to choose between victory and family? Then damn her; I'd get both. I was my mother's daughter, after all, and my father knew where I got my brains – so what was I born for if not this, bargains and trickery, games of wits on the most uneven of battlefields? Achlys and Melinoë might hold the best cards between us, the most powerful magic, the most vicious plans ... but no matter how many eyes they stole, they would never see my thoughts. They would never know my heart.

And my heart ...

Hell, it was ready to play.

'So what do you want?' Gone was the hoarseness, the barely suppressed tremble. I sounded like myself again. Sounded *better* than myself. 'Am I supposed to hand myself over to you in return for mercy? To surrender my own life in order to save theirs?'

'Oh, *please*, little dove,' she purred, twirling a long strand of snow-white hair around an equally pale finger. 'You're not fooling us again with your pretend silliness. No sensible soul would kill herself that way, family or no – we're not wasting time offering you a bargain you're guaranteed to reject.'

What?

It took a fraction of a second for that to land – she'd never even expected me to consider her original demand to surrender in order to save the city?

Then what had it been? Nothing but a nudge for us to attack fast and unprepared, an ultimatum so outrageous no one with a grain of sense would ever accept it? Was *that* what she believed me to be – powerful like her and clever like her, and therefore, by necessary extension, also heartless like her?

But then ... then she didn't understand *anything*.

I had not used my smooth magic. I had not chosen the easy way out.

I was *not* the evil I was fighting.

'So what are you offering me?' It took all I had to keep the elation from my voice, the urge to burst out in hysterical laughter. No cheering until the game was won ... but I'd scored a point here, and best of all, she didn't even have the faintest clue. 'I don't suppose you'll let them walk away if I just smile a little more prettily.'

The Mother cocked her head, the sunlight glinting off the smooth surfaces of her new, inhuman eyes. 'We would like to offer you an opportunity.'

Even better.

'I'm all ears,' I said, crossing my arms.

'Peace.' The word rolled off her tongue with flawless theatrical timing, right in the beat of silence between one thump of her heart and the next. 'A way out of this hopeless race you're running – that's the bargain we'll give you for your people's lives. You'll leave now and never look for us again. You'll never try to hurt us again. In return, we will not harm or bother you either, and within the limitations set, you're free to do as your heart desires for the rest of eternity. How does that sound, little dove?'

Like a lie.

I didn't speak the words out loud.

But it *had* to be a trap, hadn't it? Even Alyra was looking violently sceptical in the corner of my eye. It was far too good to be true, coming from the High Lady who wanted me dead above anything else ... An open door to freedom. Away from the war, away from the hounds and the blood marks and the mutilated children ...

Ridiculous. But she *was* proposing a bargain.

'Why?' I slowly said.

'Because you remind us of ourselves, Emelin.' As if it was a compliment. As if I'd pleaded for her approval like a beggar for bread. 'You're hungry. You're bold. We do respect that, even if you made the mistake of using those powers against us.'

Ah, yes. Because she'd made such a habit of respecting all the other bold, hungry people who had challenged her in the past, rather than killing them outright ...

Oh.

It dawned on me, then – she wasn't sure if she *could* kill me.

So that was the game she was playing? Too dangerous to risk a fight, if I was powerful enough to make it into the city alive ... so this had been her solution, a far cleaner way to render me harmless. Offer me a truce too good to reject. Nudge me to accept it, using hostages I cared about. Damn the people fighting outside, the friends and family risking their lives for me as we were standing here ...

Had it even occurred to her that they might mean something to me? That even a godsworn mage might see her allies as more than a means to an end?

'Here's the thing, Emelin,' she continued, lowering her voice to a conspiratorial whisper – seeing the frozen bewilderment on my face and interpreting it as everything it wasn't: hope, temptation. 'This world was never built for people like you, people like us. To many others out there, you will never be more than an idol. An ideal.'

That hit home.

Her curving lips told me her borrowed eyes were all too well-aware of it.

'So we must support each other when we find each other, little dove.' Spoken with such sweet sincerity – such tempting lies. 'We must carve out a place for ourselves. Look at what we did, our court, our safety ... Don't you want to follow our example? Learn from the two of us?'

The two of us.

I gaped at her, frozen, as out of nowhere my thoughts collided.

A place for ourselves.

There was nothing new about the sight before me – nothing new about the memories sparking violently in my mind. That monstrous pile of bones. Two-coloured eyes, sapphire and obsidian – Achlys and Melinoë. The beat of that thumping heart, *one* heart ...

Nothing new – but at once, I understood.

I understood *everything*.

'I want Creon included in the bargain.' My voice carried bright and clear, plans rolling out with it. I knew what to do, suddenly – knew it with such baffling clarity, as if my mind had condensed days of thinking into a single, blinding flash of insight. 'You will not hurt either me *or* him, nor try to contain or capture us. If I live the rest of my life in peace, I will not do so alone.'

I saw Creon's head jerk around on the edge of my sight. Caught a glimpse of the wide-eyed shock on his face, even if he didn't speak a word – *Em, no!* that look said, and gods help me, could I blame him?

Trust me, I spelled, moving nothing but my fingers by my side.

His breath caught. But his wings sagged a fraction, and he didn't interrupt.

The Mother threw him no more than a single bored glance before returning her gaze to me, a hint of dramatic vexation in her sigh – a female annoyed to be reminded of a small but nagging problem. 'Oh, as you wish.'

She must have prepared for that demand. There was no way she would have made that decision so easily otherwise.

'You said I should leave and never return,' I added, and no matter how feverish my thoughts, my words remained flat and perfectly controlled. Was there anything I was overlooking? Anything else our bargain needed to contain? 'I would like a ten-minute grace period before I go. I have some last things to do here – say goodbye, for one.'

The Mother curled her upper lip at the shivering humans around her throne. 'Five minutes and not a second more.'

'That will do.' I prayed with all my might it was true – but bartering would only make her wonder what I was planning to do in all that time, and I had better favours to ask for. 'And then there's one more thing ...'

She canted her head, waiting.

I drew in a deep breath, focusing my gaze on the blue gem in her right eye socket. Here was the gamble, then, the breaking point, the victory hinging on what I thought I understood. Blue. I was speaking to nothing but that deep, ocean blue – never mind her other eye sparkling at me, never mind the rows of fae and humans by the walls ... *Blue*. 'As my last adjustment, I would like to specify that I will not hurt you *physically*. If I want to call you a vicious bitch, just to name an example, I'd like to retain the right to do so. But I will aim no magic or blades at you, and I'm willing to make a bargain on that.'

Creon's breath was quickening by my side, a testament to the effort it took him to stay silent. The Mother considered me for a motionless moment – *thump thump*, her heart kept pounding – then smiled, nodded.

'Good,' I said grimly, stepping forward. 'Then we—'

Creon grabbed my shoulder before I could finish that sentence, yanking me back a quarter turn with lightning speed.

No need for him to sign or speak a single world. The panicked gleam in his dark eyes contained all he wanted to shout at me – *What are you doing, for hell's sake? What do you think will happen once we fly off into the sunset? Other unbound mages won't get anywhere without godsworn magic to counter hers, and you may not even be able to unbind anyone else ...*

'I know,' I said, holding his piercing gaze, smiling for the benefit of the Mother's many eyes watching us. 'It's for the best, Creon, believe me.'

His fingers twitched on my skin.

But slowly, hesitantly, he let go – moving as if he was dropping me into a ravine and trusting me to fly on my own.

I gave him a last quick smile, the most reassuring one I dared to allow onto my face, and turned, making my way to the low stage and the towering bone throne erected on it. My own pulse echoed in my ears like the Mother's deafening heartbeat around me. Five minutes. Frighteningly little time to do what had to be done, but I'd deal with it – *somehow* I'd deal with it ...

'Don't bother coming any closer, little dove,' the Mother drawled, sitting straighter with a flick of her fingers. 'This will do.'

From her fingertips, a wisp of light broke free.

A single glowing line grew from her skin and fluttered down like a silk ribbon, wrapping itself around my wrist surprisingly gently. I blinked at it, then looked up at her again. The other end of the line had similarly draped itself around her powder-pale arm.

'It's a bargain?' she said, cruel smile broadening.

Five minutes.

Or else ...

'It's a bargain,' I said.

The light erupted.

Blazing white, cold as ice yet burning my skin like the midday sun ... clinging to my wrists like shackles. My heart was all but hammering *through* my ribs now, and still the bargain magic glowed brighter and brighter, shining through skin and flesh and bone until tears sprang to my eyes ...

A biting sting shot through the inside of my forearm, and at once the light dissipated, there and gone in the blink of an eye. Beneath the red and golden gems I already carried on my wrist, a stark white mark had broken through my skin – *white*.

The colour of no magic at all.

The pounding of that cursed heartbeat abruptly went silent. Around me, neighbours and family members shrieked and gasped as the blood magic released their hearts, and those sounds tore me back into the here and now faster than anything.

Five minutes. Starting now.

I didn't have a bloody second to lose.

'Get out.' I grabbed the nearest white-clad arm – old Miss Ariella, her brittle wrist thin between my fingers – and hauled her to her feet with little regard for her shocked stammers. No need for me to be polite.

All I needed was for the lot of them to be gone before the next step of my death-or-glory bet; around us, the others were scrambling up with shaking hands and knees, not nearly fast enough for my own hammering heart. I blindly pulled another one of them to standing. 'Get *out*! Stay together, stay inside the building until the battle is over, and for the gods' sakes, don't ask any questions – is that clear?'

'Emelin—' an old neighbour started as he staggered towards me, hands stretched out.

'Is that *clear*?' I snapped, shoving him towards the exit.

That got the message across.

They fled, looking like a panicked flock of swans in their dramatic white gowns, dragging the limping and the wounded along between them. On the throne, the Mother started laughing – sharp, triumphant howls in *both* her voices, the sounds twisting together in gleeful delight. Just *hearing* that laughter made the colour of my shirt itch sharply under my fingers ...

The thought sent a biting twinge of pain through my right wrist.

I will aim no magic or blades at you.

'I thought you wanted to say goodbye?' Two voices speaking with one pair of lips, their timbre minutely different, their malicious amusement eerily identical. 'Or did you need the time to take your leave of *me*, little dove? I won't be here for five more minutes, I'm afraid – I must go take care of the troublemakers outside you just so happily abandoned ...'

I barely heard her, stepping onto the now-empty stage. My pulse was pounding the seconds away, counting down the minutes. No magic or blades at *her* ...

But we hadn't said anything about thrones, had we?

Red magic bloomed bright as blood from my fingertips. A glorious crackle of magic, lighting up the galleries and the marble walls and the unblinking gemstone eyes around us ... smashing into the towering pile of bones, punching a man-sized hole in its front and sending ribs and femurs and jawbones flying. A long thighbone hit me on the temple, a skull nearly knocked out my legs from beneath me. Above me, the

Mother shrieked in two outraged voices, sweeping out her wings ... but I didn't cower, didn't run.

She could no longer harm me anyway.

And my magic was already reaching out again, softness for movement, draining the velvety plushness from my shirt. Spooling into the hollow inside of that throne. Dragging out, with a single burst of godsworn power, what I'd *known* I would find inside that tomb she never let out of sight ...

The two of us.

The Mother, who discarded even her lovers and children like used rags ... What would she ever guard so fiercely but *herself*?

It looked like it was sleeping, the body my magic yanked out from beneath her seat.

I caught just a single glimpse. Closed eyes. Black wings. Bronze skin and raven-black hair, none of them yet whitened by magic exhausting the colours ...

One glimpse, and then the second half of the Mother smacked into my arms with all the force of my soft magic, her lifeless weight sending us both sprawling on the floor in a tangle of limbs and wings. I landed on bones and fragments of ivory, sharp edges sticking into my legs, my back, my shoulders, the pain blurring my sight for a fraction of an instant.

But I had my hands around her neck.

And below my fingers, her pulse was unmistakable.

'*My body!*' one of the Mother's voices cried out above me, voice ragged with hysteria. '*My body!*'

I rolled over, just in time to see the flash of white as she dove at me – colliding midway with the silvery streak of a throwing knife. Creon. A shrill laugh escaped me as I forced myself upright, hauling Melinoë's body with me – Creon, who may still be bound, but who had made no bargain to keep his blades away from her.

Not useless.

Definitely not useless.

She only just avoided the dagger, landing five strides away from me amidst the rubble of bones and marble. Her face ... Expressions seemed to flicker across her features like dancing flames, two souls fighting for control – fury, fear, desperate attempts to regain composure. Her voice was similarly scattered. 'You— *My body*— Emelin, don't you— *Let go of*— Listen—'

'I didn't fully catch that,' I said, and there was no stopping the maniacal grin growing on my face with my fingers digging into the faint pulse at her throat. 'Could you be a little clearer, perhaps?'

Another of Creon's knives came whizzing her way. She only just managed to slap it from the air in a burst of red magic, even her limbs jerking indecisively back and forth as she spat, 'Leave – our – body – *alone*!'

I reached for Feather in response.

'No!' She had to jump back to avoid yet another dagger. 'No, you can't! You *can't*! You made a bargain – you—'

'To not do bodily harm,' I readily agreed, grinning at her – at that sapphire eye that could pop from her face any moment. *Blue eyes is Achlys*, Agenor had told me months ago at the Golden Court. *Black eyes is Melinoë. They're inhabiting what was originally Achlys's body.* 'No harm to *that* body, more specifically. Didn't you realise I was talking to you, Achlys?'

'You insolent little—' she started, sputtering, and then Melinoë's voice broke through again – '*Get away from my body you—*'

Feather slid from its sheath so easily.

And my bargain mark didn't sting – didn't give the faintest twinge – as I calmly, meticulously settled the alf steel edge against that sleeping throat.

The Mother roared – Melinoë's voice, I thought at first, and only then did I see the knife blooming from her chest, inches away from her heart. She'd been too distracted to dodge it. Was it going to be this easy, then? One more well-aimed blade and—

'No!' she howled, staggering back, yanking the weapon from her chest and dropping it as if the hilt was burning hot. '*Do* something, you fools! If we die, all of you will die with us! If you wish to live ...'

For one moment, I thought she'd lost her mind.

Then the gem-eyed puppets around the wall jerked into movement.

Fuck – how was that even possible? She had bargained not to harm us, hadn't she? And yet dozens and dozens of fae and humans came lurching towards us without any sign of pain, limbs jerking but unblinking gem eyes trained on me … In a panicked reflex, I let go of Melinoë's throat, pressed my left hand against her black wing, and let loose another wave of red magic. A handful of her pawns went down. The others didn't even slow.

A burst of red flashed back at me as the fae among them began firing. Fuck. *Fuck*. I winced as a flare hit my sword arm, thoughts bolting. Apparently I wasn't the only one who could play tricks with words; apparently there was enough of a mind left in her victims that our bargain counted *them* as the attackers … And attack they did, violent intent obvious in every curled lip and clawing finger, even the humans among them looking more like caged animals now.

Alyra soared down, shrieking, claws sinking into every throat and nose she could reach. Creon's blades stopped three, four, five attackers. Still dozens more kept coming, approaching me on all sides – ready to drag the limp body from my arms and tear me apart. I could fight, of course … but I'd have to let go of Melinoë. Of my best bargaining chip.

Fuck.

'Not so clever now, are you?' the Mother snarled, perched on the edge of her damaged throne seat. She was no longer bleeding – she must have healed herself, only her soaked dress still showing where the wound had been. 'Let that body go and we'll call back our people. Your last chance, little dove.'

A last chance … but without a bargain.

Which meant she could break her word.

Which meant she probably *would* break her word, from the way her nails were digging into her scattered velvet pillows. I glanced at Creon – one last alf steel dagger in his hand, blood dripping down his temple, the first staggering humans already between us – and took the leap without thinking, without daring to think.

'Let's do it the other way around, shall we?' I grabbed Melinoë's dark hair, tilting her head back. Baring her throat to the gleaming edge of my blade. 'You call for retreat within five seconds, and I'll keep you unharmed. Wait any longer, and—'

Her laughter interrupted me, shrill and maniacal. Achlys's voice. Achlys's laughter. 'Do as you please, little bitch! Our souls are safe inside—'

She faltered.

Her face shifted as though a mask had slipped off.

'No!' A hollow screech, wrestling over those plush pink lips – Melinoë, again. '*No*! Not my body – not—'

'Four,' I said, ducking to avoid a flare of red shooting past the crown of my head. 'Three.'

The Mother jolted off her throne with a single, staggering slap of her wings – Melinoë, trying to regain control of their shared body, trying to lurch at me. It had to be Achlys who held back, who forced out a choked, 'It's the only way …'

The sound of rolling heads emerged from Creon's direction, the first humans reaching him. Alyra screeched somewhere between their ranks.

'Two,' I coldly said.

'Go ahead!' Achlys snapped at me, and then it was Melinoë again, hands coming up as if to claw out my eyes – 'How dare you? How *dare* you? How—'

I gripped Feather's hilt more tightly. 'One.'

'No!' the Mother howled, and I thought it was Melinoë at first, uttering that wild, desperate animal cry as she dropped to her knees …

But then I saw her eyes.

Colour was leaching from the obsidian in her left eye socket, like paint seeping from a jar. Gods have mercy – was she drawing magic from those gems? But no colour was leaving her pale fingers, and either way, the colour wasn't exactly *vanishing*. Instead …

The Mother's obsidian eye was turning as blue as the sapphire beside it.

Around me, the gem-eyed attackers swayed to a standstill, marionettes whose strings were abruptly left alone.

And beneath my fingers, Melinoë's lifeless body trembled.

'No,' Achlys keened again, fingers clutching furiously at her chest – as if trying to reach something unreachable, to contain something uncontainable. 'No, please! A soul can't leave a body, he said! The body can't bear it! You'll ... you'll ...'

Oh.

Oh, *gods*.

Even Creon was no longer fighting on the edge of my sight, surrounded by frozen fae and humans, staring at his mother as she moaned and begged on the marble floor. Her limbs shook violently. Her wings cramped into painful folds. Her voice rose to shrill heights as her once-obsidian eye turned a deep midnight blue, then paled slowly like a sky at dawn – 'Sister! *Sister!*'

Melinoë's body gulped in a quivering lungful of air.

Achlys's breath caught at the same moment.

'Not you,' she whimpered, hand clawing into her bloodied chest. Nothing remained of her flawless beauty, the cold sneer on her lips, the ancient cruelty gleaming even in her gem eyes; the female curling up on the floor, like an animal crawling away to die, looked *mortal*, suddenly, and dismally broken-hearted. 'Not *you*, too ...'

Lovers. Children. Gods.

And now ... her own sister, abandoning her.

In my arms, Melinoë's limbs twitched. Achlys's body slackened at the same moment, her head lolling to one side as she slumped to the ground; two sapphire eyes gleamed in her ivory face, her lips almost as pale, her white hair fanning out around her shoulders. One last time I heard her voice. '*Please ...*'

Then she went quiet.

Deadly, mortally quiet.

With a loud gasp, Melinoë's eyes flew open.

Ink-black pupils stared out into the world with animal ferocity – *Creon's* eyes, and I hadn't seen the similarity as keenly until this moment, in a face that so much more closely resembled his own. Same high cheekbones. Same deep bronze skin. Even the way her lip curled up was familiar, not sweet and mocking like the Mother I'd known but savage in its fury, the expression of a female prepared to sacrifice *everything* for survival.

Even if it was the sister whose mind she'd shared for centuries.

I almost, *almost* yanked my hands off her when she moved.

She didn't seem able to look at Achlys's body six strides away, at the dead flesh and bones in which she'd moved for so long. Instead, those dark eyes aimed themselves at Creon. Her arms rose from the floor, reaching out for him – slender lady's hands, not a trace of scars or callouses marring the skin.

'My son …' she rasped.

He stared back at her, eyes empty like mirrors, a knife between his unmoving fingers. Around him, her mutilated victims didn't move – silent witnesses of her latest attempt to sacrifice him for her own survival.

'Please.' A wheezing little laugh escaped her trembling lips. 'I'm your *mother*. You can't let her do this to me – you—'

'I don't think you'll get far with that line of argument,' I said brusquely, angling Feather to fit the blade more snugly against her vulnerable artery. My hand in her hair was shaking, and yet my sword hand held perfectly still. 'There's quite a lot that mothers shouldn't be doing to their sons either.'

'Oh, go to hell,' she hissed, voice sharpening in an instant, hands wrapping around my elbow as if to pull me away. I didn't budge even as her nails dug into my skin. 'You *can't* kill me, you little pests. Not if you ever want that voice back. Not if you don't want the rest of the magical world to die out within— *Why are you laughing?*'

Because an unexpected smile was curving around Creon's mouth, wild and as sharp as unsheathed claws. A smile as inhuman as it was magnificent, primal and tightly controlled at once … and just like that, I knew what was coming.

Knew it, and *craved* it.

'Sorry, Mother.' His golden voice was low and deadly – like the sweetest, purest honey, dripping with venom. 'I'm afraid you've rather … served your purpose.'

Her eyes widened.

One frozen instant in which I saw the understanding hit, his voice, his words – one moment of explosive, horrified insight ...

Then I slit her throat.

Chapter 39

She died with nothing but a last, undignified gurgle.

The second half of the Mother, High Lady of faekind, killer of gods and destroyer of continents ... lying dead in my lap, curled up like a child to be comforted.

Her fingers still clawed into my forearm. Her once-beautiful face remained fixed in grotesque contortions. Around us, dull thuds broke the silence – her puppets dropping to the floor as the magic sustaining them died with her. Nothing else moved as I slowly pulled back my sword – nothing but the blood that kept gushing from her throat, dripping onto the marble floor with what seemed like obscene loudness.

So, so much blood, and yet reality only sank in slowly – that she was really, truly dead.

She was *dead*.

She would never hurt another soul again. Would never bind another soul again. Would never let out that blood-curdling little laugh again, would never call me her little dove again ... I struggled to shove the lifeless weight of Melinoë's corpse off me, my hands shaking, my trousers and fingers stained with blood. I'd killed her. I'd *killed* her. Ended the empire. Ended the war. Saved the whole damn world ...

Simple thoughts, simple facts, and yet my mind refused to absorb them.

Still no one moved as I dropped my sword and rose to my feet, as if the world had turned into a gallery of statues around me. The gem-eyed bodies lay scattered around the hall. Alyra had landed on an armrest of the ruined throne, glaring majestically at the mess below. Creon stood frozen, shadows carving his face into razor-sharp angles as he stared down at the body of the mother he'd never known, that stranger's face mirroring his own.

But behind me ...

The softest, quietest whimper broke the silence.

I snapped around.

They stood in the doorway, half-huddled behind the frame but *there* all the same – Valter and Editta, his arm around her shoulders, her hands clutched over her mouth as if to hold back the screams bubbling up from her throat. There was no one else to be seen behind them. The two of them must have stayed behind as the others ran for their lives – morbid curiosity? Or, much more far-fetched ...

They might even have cared whether I made it out alive.

It was strange how flatly that thought arrived in my mind, sparking not the faintest glimmer of hope or elation.

They suddenly seemed so bewilderingly *small*, standing there pale and frightened – so utterly feeble that my mind scrambled to match the sight of them to the parents living in my memories, the people I'd believed I knew for twenty years. So much had changed since I'd last seen them. *I* had changed, most of all, yet only now did I realise that my memories hadn't changed with me – that my mind had somehow frozen the two of them in time as pivotal and powerful figures, those phantom voices that could make or break my world.

And only now, looking at them in their melodramatic white cloaks, at Valter's thinning hair and Editta's time-worn features, did I realise these two had never even managed to break the chains of their own fears.

Let alone anyone's world.

Let alone *me*.

And it was miraculous how easy it was to open my mouth, suddenly, without any fear of saying the wrong thing or looking the wrong way – how effortlessly I smiled at them, bloody and grimy and wounded. 'Still here?'

They flinched.

Making *me* the frightening one between the three of us, all of a sudden.

Although Creon probably didn't help, prowling into the edge of my sight in the same moment – Creon, who they'd last seen burning their village to the ground, threatening them to draw out the secrets they'd kept from me all my life. I glanced at him. The slight narrowing of his eyes said all I needed to know – that he remembered that same night, vividly so, and a single word from my lips would be all he needed to make that point in several elaborate and very unpleasant ways.

I gave the smallest headshake.

A small, tired smile crept around his lips.

'Em ...' Editta started in the doorway, her voice choked with sobs. 'Em, we didn't want ... We never should have ...'

I was so bloody sick of it before she'd even figured out the sentence.

So many times I'd been unable to stop hoping. To stop imagining that one day they might just change their minds and show up at my doorstep to tell me that they'd been wrong, I was right, and I'd done all I could to be the daughter they'd wanted – and yet now that I *had* proven them wrong, now that I *had* shown them I would never have turned against them even at the risk of my own life ...

I found I could no longer give a damn.

All I wanted now was to be *done* with this.

'It's fine.' The most bewildering part of it was that it was true – that I no longer even cared about revenge, about anger, about being right. What did it matter? They would spend the rest of their mortal lives well-aware of their mistakes, and I would live my infinite years and never hear their voices again. 'It's all fine. Hope the shop is doing well. Hope you've found a good place to live here.'

They blinked owlishly at me.

'Go find the others and go home,' I added, flatly. 'I don't have anything else to say to you.'

They seemed to shrink a few inches. Valter's hand – pale fingers, stained with paint – squeezed his wife's shoulder tightly as he started, 'But Em—'

Creon scarcely raised his knife – little more than a twitch of his fingers.

They ran like the wind.

I might have laughed, if there had been any laughter left within me – might have cried, too, if there had been any tears left to shed. But all that remained in their wake was an emptiness – or rather the hollow sensation of emotions too exhausted to be felt – and once again that smothering silence settled over us as the clatter of their footsteps died away, emptier now, and somehow lighter.

Somehow ... freer.

'If either of us has any more parents to deal with,' Creon said, his voice raw and hollow despite the spark of humour below the surface, 'I suggest we ask them to wait until tomorrow, don't you think?'

That broke the spell.

Half a chuckle escaped me as I staggered towards him, over the bone-strewn floor, past my sword and the blood and the corpses; another one as I threw myself into his embrace and wrapped my arms around his slender waist, fingers digging into the muscular planes of his back. His heart thudded against my cheek. His arms and wings enfolded me as he let out a single long, shuddering breath, relaxing the weight of his head against mine – the unyielding warrior, shedding his armour at last.

'Thank you,' he breathed, voice choked. '*Thank* you ...'

And I could have told him it was his victory as much as it was mine, could have told him I would have been dead without him, could have told him every drop of red I'd aimed at her had been drawn in his name and his name only ...

But I had the rest of eternity to find those words.

So I held him tight instead as we stood there in the unnatural quiet – held him and breathed the scent of his solid body and tried to believe, truly believe, that it was over.

It was mere minutes later, just as I was gathering courage to make my way back into the battle raging outside, that my parents swept into the hall – covered in blood but very much alive, the expressions on their faces as good as any victorious blare of battle horns.

Rosalind gave a triumphant 'Ha!' at the sight of the Mother's corpses, hugging me close before venturing deeper into the hall. Agenor, more surprisingly, merely blinked at Melinoë and the gash in her throat, then whipped around to Creon and me with a strange urgency in his expression. 'Who?'

Creon nodded at me before I could figure out what he was even asking. 'Em.'

'Ah.' My father's broad shoulders sagged half an inch as he sent me a smile that was somehow watery and proud at once. 'Good. Good. *Excellent.*'

I wanted to ask what in the world that was supposed to mean but didn't get the chance; Lyn came soaring into the hall the next moment, letting out a fierce cry of triumph as she landed. One of her shoulders was soaked with blood, and claw marks on her other arm suggested hounds and narrow escapes. But she hugged me as if pain did not exist, and the happy tears in her eyes made me believe it for a moment – damn the dead, damn the injured ...

We had *won.*

The full realisation still wouldn't land.

Tared strode in moments after Lyn, sword in his hand, the widest grin I'd ever seen on his face; Naxi bounced through the gates a minute later, sticking out her tongue at corpses at every turn. Rosalind was saying practical things about bringing in the wounded. Agenor was summarising the battle to me or Creon or no one in particular, something about half of the Mother's army defecting as soon as the Alliance's magic was unblocked and made the fae forces realise their High Lady was beyond the point of being harmed by anyone ...

Their voices seemed to slide off me like dewdrops off leaves. As if I was barely even *there*, amongst the bones and the rubble, the ruined remains of the Mother's throne still towering over the hall.

More of our allies came pouring in through the open doorway. Alves faded out to return with straw mats, blankets, wounded bodies. The smell of blood mingled with the atmosphere of dazed triumph, hysterical relief somehow mixing effortlessly with the pragmatic bustle of *more* work to be done; healers appeared out of nowhere, fae with their blue magic and nymphs with their potions, everyone around me seeming to know exactly where they were needed. I caught a glimpse of Rosalind, attending to a group of injured humans. Agenor had vanished to deal with captives or gods knew what else army commanders had to deal with.

I asked a passing fae healer if there was anything I could do to help. She looked at me as if I'd suggested I'd do a little dance to cheer up the wounded and informed me they were managing perfectly well, no need for me to exert myself, and why didn't I find a slightly more pleasant place to enjoy the fruits of my work?

Was that what I was expected to do, now – celebrate while the dead were buried?

I wanted to ask Creon but found he'd left the hall as well. Gone to have a word with some of the Mother's captured army commanders, someone informed me.

I retrieved Feather from a helpful alf who would not stop excitedly shaking my hand for two minutes, then floundered to the exit, past the beds of moaning and howling injured. Delwin was there, missing half a leg, a woman by his side who resembled him so closely she had to be his sister. Thorir lay sprawled out on a mat a bit farther down the aisle, trading quips with his healer as she patiently stitched his guts back into his torso. Helenka, the nymph queen of Tolya, was carried in as I slipped out of the hall, bleeding all over, the hair of a decapitated fae head still clutched in one of her clawlike hands.

In the antechamber of the hall, people sat kneeling by the bodies of their friends and family, sobbing quietly over them.

I didn't dare to look any of them in the eyes as I hurried out.

The world outside was a mess, nothing like the city I'd left behind on my first visit: collapsed walls, scorched flowerbeds, human bodies dangling from the White Hall's façade. Here, too, people were buzzing around wherever I looked, quickly applying bandages, chaining up fae. The humans of our army seemed to be going from door to door looking for survivors and bringing the bittersweet news of the city's liberation; here and there, groups of terrified citizens huddled together as fae repaired the first of their houses with sweeping bursts of blue.

I ran into Edored and Nenya a few corners away from the city centre. He was carrying her through the rubble-filled streets, rambling about his plans to chase down a few fae to make up for missing the battle; in his arms, Nenya was no longer waxen in colour, rather looking like she ought to be quite capable of walking again. They both beamed at me when they noticed me. The blood mark had vanished with the Mother's death, they reported, and more healers from the various magical isles would soon arrive.

'That's wonderful,' I weakly said, unwilling to admit I'd forgotten about that cursed mark entirely.

'All thanks to you, Noisy Death,' Edored said, throwing me a broad grin that looked like a hand-less salute and walking on.

I watched them until their voices died away – Nenya protesting that surely her feet would be able to carry her now and Edored claiming for the first time in his life that he'd rather be safe than sorry – and felt strangely hollow for reasons I couldn't pinpoint entirely.

A column of smoke near the edge of the city drew my attention. Arriving at the lily wall, I found Tared, Lyn, and a handful of other red-haired individuals bustling around a dozen hastily erected pyres, burning the bodies of the phoenixes who had fallen in battle. A child's cry erupted from a smouldering heap of ashes just as I rounded the corner, and Lyn bent over to pick up the newly born phoenix from the embers, swaddling them neatly in a swath of cloth. On the other side of the pyres, people were setting up rows and rows of cribs with quiet efficiency.

Tared noticed me as he turned to haul a new corpse from the rather unceremonious pile by the wall. Shirt unbuttoned, arms and face covered in soot stains, he vaguely resembled a miner after a long day of work – but there was no weariness in his movements as he carried a dead red-haired boy to the nearest pile of wood, then turned, wiping his hands on his equally smudged trousers.

'Afternoon, Em.' His skewed grin hid a spark of concern that barely touched his voice. 'Coming to take a look at the bakery?'

Lyn tossed a handful of fire at him from the other side of the street. He ducked to avoid it without even having looked at her.

'They trust you with their dead even though you're treating their revival like grilling dinner?' I said, glancing at the other phoenixes. None of them even seemed to be keeping an eye on the one alf in their midst – unusual, after the way I'd seen them keep their distance from everyone else in our army camp.

Tared shrugged as he snatched a torch from the ground. 'They know Lyn survived her last twelve deaths.'

When he'd been the one cremating her and picking her small body from the ashes when the fire died down ... My heart clenched violently and without warning.

'You're alright?' he added in a lower voice, watching me closely.

Was I alright?

I *should* have been. I should have been bursting with joy. The world had been saved, hadn't it? The empire had been defeated? This was what I'd worked towards since the day I woke up in my burning village, this was what I'd braved curses and gods and bargains for – and yet ...

Yet the contentment wouldn't come.

Now that the Mother was gone, now that the archipelago was free, everyone would return to their homes and families ... and I?

I knew what I wanted.

I just didn't have the faintest idea where it was.

'I know,' Tared said softly, and suddenly the light flickering around him seemed duller, his smile wry. 'Things will settle. Helps to stay busy in the meantime.'

I swallowed. 'Right.'

He reached out to ruffle my hair, then pointed a thumb at the baby in Lyn's arms, amusement sparking back to life in his eyes. 'You could go say hello to Khailan, for a start. He's never more pleasant than at this stage in life, if you ask me.'

Khailan?

I threw a slightly more attentive glance at the child Lyn was just handing over to another phoenix female. Plump and pink ... but something in the lines of that round, chubby face bore the faintest resemblance to the haughty, sharp-jawed phoenix male I'd bargained with.

'I think I'll pass,' I said and grimaced. 'He might shit all over me if I try to hold him.'

Tared burst out laughing. 'A badge of honour, one could argue.'

I couldn't help a small chuckle. Around us, phoenixes threw uncertain looks our way, apparently doubting whether there would be any sense in telling alf savages or godsworn half fae to behave with a little more civility.

'I should be leaving you to the work,' I muttered, looking away from them. 'See you ... soon, I suppose.'

A mirthless smile. 'See you, little brat.'

I hugged Lyn on my way out, then passed by Khailan's crib as I left the smoking pyres behind. The oldest phoenix alive, now looking no different from any plucky human baby minutes after birth, lay glowering at the sky in his blankets, his chubby little hands balled into fists. The inside of his wrist ...

Empty. Not a bargain mark to be seen.

My heart stuttered as I glanced down at my own forearm and found it equally, flawlessly unmarred, no trace left of the three gems that had adorned my skin when I'd last spent a thought on them.

My bargain with the Mother had ended with her death. So had Khailan's, presumably. But even that small ruby mark I'd shared with Creon, the bargain I'd carried with me since the very first night at the

Crimson Court ... It was gone as if it had never been there at all, my promise to help him end the Mother finally fulfilled.

Why did even that observation feel like a raw, visceral loss?

I walked on and stumbled upon a breach in the city wall, finding myself close to the shores of the lake when I slipped out. On the other side of the water, people were combing through the bodies of the fallen, looking for friends and survivors. But where I walked, half-hidden between rows of apple trees, one could almost pretend the devastating fight had never happened at all, the air smelling of earth and ripe fruit rather than the metallic tang of blood.

As if peace was already here.

As if I might soon be able to feel it, too.

I found myself a spot on the banks of the lake in the end, a little way from the path, shielded from the world by a reedbed and a tangle of weeping willows. There I unbuckled my sword, scrubbed the blood off my hands, and curled up in the grass, staring at the blue sky with a mind that seemed unable to go quiet, flashes of empty obsidian eyes and the Mother's last moments crowding my thoughts no matter how hard I tried to push them away.

The sun drew its slow path over me. Faint sounds reached me from the city every now and then, laments and celebrations, too far away to seem real.

It had to be long past midday when wingbeats finally shattered the quiet, the crackling of twigs beneath boots. A squeak, and then the voice I hadn't realised until that moment I'd been waiting for with every fibre of my being—

'Oh, *here* you are.'

Creon.

Chapter 40

He ducked beneath a low-hanging willow branch to step into view, dark hair unbound now, wings tucked in closely. Alyra was sitting on his shoulder – on *his* shoulder, of all places – looking deeply smug as she chirped a greeting at me. She had been the one to find me, apparently, our godsworn bond more helpful here than even the sharpest pair of eyes.

'Hey,' I said sheepishly.

Creon's smile was soft at the edges and laced with more than a little concern. But rather than returning the greeting, he nudged Alyra off his shoulder and told her, too straight-faced to be sincere, 'Did I mention the alves were very grateful for your help finding fae in hiding? They said you were extraordinarily good at it.'

My familiar seemed to puff up to twice her size.

'I wouldn't dare tell you what to do, obviously,' he added, still in that innocently earnest tone – and only then did I realise what he was playing at. 'But I think the two of us will manage here, so if you want to stretch your wings a little more ...'

She took off with a triumphant cry, soaring over the reeds and back towards the city. Creon's smile went from innocent to devilish as he sank into the sun-drenched grass, stretched out his legs, and dryly said, 'There.'

I managed a laugh. 'Did the alves say any such thing?'

'Oh, no.' He tilted his head towards the sun, letting the light dance across his face. It seemed to set his bronze skin aglow, lighting up the playful twinkle in his eyes. 'But telling her to bugger off didn't appear the best way to get her out of here. I don't think my godlike countenance would be improved by her biting my nose off, for a start.'

Another chortle escaped me. 'Glad to hear saving the world didn't lead to any existential doubts on your side.'

His gaze lingered on me for a moment, too sharp for the loose drape of his shoulders and wings. But his voice was the same melodious drawl as he looked away and said, 'What part of existence is it you're doubting, exactly?'

'Where to start?' I said sourly.

He waited, gazing out over the rippling surface of the lake, undeterred by that half-hearted attempt at dodging the question.

Hell, why was I even dodging questions at all? This ought to be a moment of celebration. We were done; we were free. No more battles, no more life and death choices to get in the way of the life I wanted to live. We could find that home we wanted. I could spend the next few decades buried in books and pretty silks, and Creon could finally let go of the dark fae prince's role and—

Wait.

Prince.

The nameless, slumbering discomfort took solid shape all at once, the core of it crystallising in that single treacherous word.

'Creon?' A small crack in my voice. 'Creon, I ... I can't believe I never thought about this before, but ... if the Mother is dead ...'

He tilted his head at me, a small, joyless smile teasing the corner of his lips. 'Which is no longer a hypothetical matter, I might point out.'

'Yes, thank you.' My laugh inched over my lips, brittle and tense. 'Now that she's dead ... doesn't that mean you're technically the new High Lord of the empire? Being her only living son and all that?'

'Ah.' He cleared his throat. 'Straight to the point.'

'So you *are*—'

'No,' he interrupted, voice calm and measured as he reclined in the grass, resting his weight on his elbows. His wings flattened out behind him, gleaming softly in the sunlight – *almost* convincingly careless, except that his motions were too deliberate, too controlled, to pass for fully nonchalant, and his smile had vanished like a shadow. 'It's not traditionally an inherited title. Noble houses have always gone from parent to child, but the throne tends to play by different rules.'

A relief, if only the reluctance in his voice allowed for any sense of reassurance. Now I felt like I was tiptoeing into some sort of trap as I cautiously said, 'Then how does one become High Lord or Lady?'

He grimaced. 'By killing the previous one, usually.'

It took a moment for that to land.

A long, befuddled moment – several heartbeats in which my overcrowded mind suddenly found itself incapable of producing even a single coherent thought.

'What?' I said.

Creon shrugged. The gesture had a decidedly remorseful air to it – but no trace of mischief, no sign he was simply pulling a misplaced joke on me.

Killing the previous one.

'You mean ...' A sensible conclusion, and yet it didn't *feel* like one – didn't feel like a conclusion at all. 'You mean, like I just did?'

'Well.' His half-smile didn't reach his eyes. 'That would be an example, yes.'

I stared at him.

That little exchange between him and Agenor, right after the latter found us next to Achlys' and Melinoe's bodies ... *Who?* The shortest, simplest question, as if no more explanation was needed. And then my father's relief as Creon put forward my name – because the alternative had been *Creon* taking credit for the kill, *Creon* on the throne of the empire ...

Whereas now ...

My thoughts didn't manage to reach any further than that.

'I'm sorry,' he softly said, sitting up straight again and draping his arms over his knees. His gaze didn't stray from my face. 'I didn't realise you didn't know until a few days ago. And then I figured – with everything you had on your mind already – you might prefer to focus on the fight ahead without having to worry about fae politics.'

That little bit of well-intended scheming barely made it through to my conscious mind. 'But ... but you're not honestly saying ...'

Another apologetic shrug.

'But that's *ridiculous*,' I burst out.

He gracefully tilted his head, strands of dark hair brushing over his sculpted shoulders. The first hint of a challenge glittered back to life in his eyes, that look that told me he was ready to make every opposing point, in twisted and elaborate and potentially pleasurable ways, if I really insisted on arguing the matter. 'Is it?'

'Don't make a bloody game out of this!' I clenched my fists in the grass, soft blades tickling the skin between my fingers. 'Not a single sensible person is going to accept this madness. You know they won't. I'm a *child* in fae years, for hell's sake!'

'Not in human years,' he dryly pointed out.

I barely heard him. 'And I don't have wings! I didn't grow up in the fae isles! I don't even know enough about my own people's history to realise I just accidentally crowned myself! How in the world would I ever—'

'You have me and Agenor and all the time in the world,' he interrupted, unfazed. 'That clever brain of yours has handled itself under worse circumstances.'

'I don't have time if someone sticks a knife in my back tomorrow!' I snapped. 'Which they'll probably try, given that—'

He sighed. 'Who would, Em?'

That was such a reasonable question – such a maddeningly pragmatic question, too – that it took all the wind from my furious sails.

I deflated into the grass, suddenly aware of the lake and the rustling reeds and the balmy sunlight again, and defiantly mumbled, 'Well ... everyone.'

His eyebrows shot op.

'Except for you, of course.' I rolled my eyes. 'And Agenor, I suppose. But there have to be high-ranking individuals from her court who didn't get killed in the fight ...'

'Oh, yes,' he readily agreed. 'Plenty.'

'And I suppose we *could* have them all executed, but the bastards presumably have friends and family who would only be more determined to take revenge and go after me ...'

Creon's face remained suspiciously neutral. 'Mm-hm.'

'But if we keep them alive ...' I grimaced. 'Well, I doubt the war ended their personal ambitions. So what's stopping them from trying to take advantage of the power void the Mother has left behind?'

'It's not a void,' he pleasantly corrected. 'You're very much filling it.'

I flung up my hands. 'You don't get to avoid the very reasonable point I'm making by quibbling about semantics, Creon!'

He accepted that argument with a wry grin, rubbing a scarred hand over his face. 'As you wish. In that case – yes, there are people I would expect to cause trouble if given the chance, and no, I wouldn't recommend killing them all. So why do you think I just spent hours having cosy chats with a few dozen of our captives, exactly?'

I frowned. 'You ... what?'

'Thought it couldn't hurt to be clear.' He tapped the knives on his belt. 'So I've helpfully laid out the situation to them and made it ... sufficiently explicit that I'll be unpleasant about any attempts to contest your right to the throne or remove you from it in more clandestine ways. Took a few drops of blood, but I'm quite confident the message landed firmly enough to get us through the next few months without major trouble, at least.'

My jaw had sagged.

'So.' That conspiratorial smile bloomed on his face again, smug yet oddly soft at the edges. 'Any other concerns?'

'You ... you've been threatening people in my name before even telling *me* ...'

'You gave the impression you needed a break,' he said, grinning at me as if it was the most obvious thing in the world. 'And I figured it might be best not to let any hopeful thoughts take root among the esteemed ranks of our opponents for even a few hours. So ...'

'You *monster*,' I said weakly.

His grin broke through. 'For you always, Your Majesty.'

Insanity. Utter insanity, and yet ... if Agenor accepted the madness, and if Creon did, and if even the scheming and conniving bastards at the Crimson Court would refrain from objecting for a while ...

Could I do it?

Hell, did I trust anyone else to do it?

It made me wince, that thought – too close to the whispering voices that had pushed me away from myself over and over again for months. I'd been the Alliance's unbound mage because no one else could be. I'd been the godsworn symbol, because who else would be able to fill that role? And here was yet another pedestal waiting for me, another world to save, coming with a fight that wouldn't end as long as the fae isles existed ...

No.

No.

What did I want? Creon hadn't even asked the question yet, and already the answer emerged from my thoughts so smoothly, gleaming in my mind like a freshly forged weapon – *not this*.

Not more choices.

Not more responsibility to carry.

I'd fought for *peace*, damn it, not for a lifetime of backstabbing and intrigue and conniving courtiers, for an eternity of looking over my shoulder at every turn. Nothing could be further from the home I'd imagined than the Mother's court I remembered, that twisted, violent place ... And even if I could change it, or could at least try to change it, what would *that* effort cost me?

More than reading books and sewing pretty dresses. More than running down beaches and eating pancakes and fucking Creon on every available surface.

More than I was willing to give.

'So ...' I pulled up my knees, wiggling my toes in the moist grass. It was hard to look him in the eyes, suddenly. 'So what if I don't feel like becoming a High Lady, purely hypothetically?'

A single beat of silence.

And then his voice, softer, suddenly – 'I was hoping you'd say that.'

I jerked up my head. 'You *were?*'

'Much as it may surprise you,' he said, a small, self-deprecating smile twisting around the corners of his mouth, 'the time I spent at the Crimson Court was hardly the happiest of my life. I wouldn't mind not moving back into it.'

Decade after decade of pain and cruelty, of living behind the mask of the male he no longer wanted to be – I should have known. 'But ... but you ...'

'Having a word with her commanders was a necessity anyway.' He hesitated, then added, more cautiously now, 'And I didn't want to influence you too much. If it had been your life's dream to spend the next two hundred years dealing with scheming sycophants, of course I would have come with you.'

'You know very well it's the bloody opposite of my dreams!' An exasperated laugh escaped me. 'Good gods. Can I just ... refuse to do it? Is it that simple?'

'You're the one making the rules now,' he dryly said, and the hint of amusement tugging at his lips almost changed my mind – that glimpse of unlimited possibilities. 'I'm rather sure you can do whatever you like. Assuming you limit yourself to upheaving the fae isles and don't try to build a home in Bakaru's backyard, that is.'

I snorted. 'I was thinking of the Fireborn Palace, but I'll come up with something else.'

His wolfish grin made it harder and harder to keep thinking clearly – but gods help me, I *had* to be smart now, had to make sure I didn't accidentally start a new war in my attempts to avoid one. If I refused to rule the empire in the Mother's place ...

My breath was quickening. If *I* didn't do it, someone else would have to do it. And leaving it to the Crimson Court to choose the next High Lord or Lady from their midst was a guarantee for trouble, the easiest way to have another war on our doorsteps before the end of the century – which meant I'd have to choose someone myself. Someone I trusted, preferably.

But there weren't that many fae who answered that description, and somehow I suspected my mother would be unhappy if I were to send Agenor back to the court she'd so narrowly escaped.

Gods help me. It was too bloody powerful, the empire, that was half the trouble; a single nymph isle or alf house, no matter how inept their rulers, could never cause a fraction of the havoc the Mother had caused over the last few centuries. But for some reason, the fae had to be united in that massive block of power at the south of the archipelago, and—

Wait.

I made the rules now.

So if I didn't like the empire in its current state and shape ...

'What if we split it up?' I blurted.

Only once I noticed Creon's blank stare did I realise he had not necessarily been witness to the past three seconds of my whirling mind.

'The empire,' I added, suddenly breathless. Insanity, and yet ... spoken out loud, it didn't sound like insanity at all. It sounded like brilliance. 'The courts. What if we separated them – turned them into three independent kingdoms rather than the decorative entities they are now?'

He blinked at me. 'I suppose you could, but—'

'No, listen. *Listen.*' It seemed my lips did the thinking now; I barely knew my thoughts myself until I heard them, in a voice that was my own and a stranger's at once. 'There were three fae peoples originally, yes? There's no bloody reason there needs to be one empire at all – it's far too dangerous, far too much of a threat to everyone else. So what if we divide the whole thing again, appoint a different ruler to each court ...'

His eyes had narrowed, the first sparks of interest sharpening the lines of his face. 'You'd have to find three people you're willing to trust, though.'

I shrugged. 'Agenor could get the Golden Court.'

'Ah.' He seemed a fraction annoyed he hadn't thought of it himself. 'Of course. Still, the—'

'And then,' I continued, too absorbed in my own thoughts to listen as the next idea appeared, uncoiled, and settled in my mind within the time it took to draw a breath, 'we could take the Cobalt Court for ourselves.'

He went quiet.

Acutely, utterly quiet.

'I know it's not much of a court right now.' The words hurried over my lips like an anxious crowd – desperate to explain, to plead my case, before he could cut in and tell me I'd lost my mind. 'But it's a very pretty place and you don't have terrible memories of it – you'd never even been there until a few weeks ago, yes? So we could spend the next few centuries rebuilding it exactly the way we like. With an icehouse. And a library. And ... and we could build you an observatory and adopt an army of cats, and our friends could come visit us whenever they liked and—'

'Yes,' he said quietly.

Nothing else.

Just that one word, earnest and breathless, and all of a sudden I'd run out of things to say – of things to *think*.

'Yes?' I managed, and it felt like a sacred vow on my tongue.

'Yes.' A smile tugged at his lips this time – a smile that made my knees feel wobbly even as I sat firmly in the grass. 'How many times are you planning to say it back to me before you believe me?'

My laugh slipped out like the idea itself had done, there and out in the world before I'd had a chance to look at it twice. 'It's just that it's a little ... sudden, isn't it? You might want to think about it for more than half a second before you agree to anything.'

He shrugged. 'I once decided in the span of roughly three seconds I was going to drag you home with me, if you recall. I'm not going to be the one to object here.'

Right.

That dazzlingly quick fae mind again.

'A bout of improvised kidnapping that could admittedly have turned out worse,' I said, aiming for lightness and reaching none of it through the landslides of my thoughts.

'Best decision of my life,' he corrected softly. 'So I'm not too worried about rushed choices here, to tell you the truth. We just need to work out ...'

'What in the world we should do with the Crimson Court?'

A grimace. 'Exactly.'

Because even the serene peace of the Cobalt Court wouldn't last if, a few hundred miles away, the Crimson Court threw itself back into senseless warfare before the decade was over ... And how would we ever sleep soundly in our beds if we knew trouble *would* be coming from that direction sooner or later?

I buried my face in my hands. Somewhere in the distance, a roar of triumph went up – the alves hunting fae defectors, lost in their game, having no idea that a few hundred strides away, in a quiet conversation between the reeds, crowns were being handed around like flower baskets. The Crimson Court ... Unsalvageable, the rational side of my mind informed me. A pit of vipers loyal to no one but themselves. And yet ... hadn't we seen even the most fixed of loyalties waver in the past few days?

Which meant ...

'What if we hand it over to Thysandra?' I said, lifting my head.

Creon's eyebrows shot up half a mile. 'What?'

'We could make Thysandra deal with the Crimson Court.' Now that I heard myself say it, the idea somehow seemed far less outrageous than it had at first spark. 'At least she has *some* sort of moral code, and I'm pretty damn sure she wouldn't do half a job. If she accepted the responsibility, she'd either manage it or die trying.'

'*If* she accepted the responsibility,' he retorted, visibly wrestling with far less nuanced replies. 'As far as Agenor told me, she's locked herself back into her cell after spilling the secret of the bindings and has refused to speak a word to anyone since, Naxi included. I doubt a court is what she's looking for right now.'

'I wasn't really planning to give her a *choice*,' I said, straight-faced.

He huffed a laugh. 'Monster.'

'It's better than keeping her in that cell for years.' I shrugged. 'For all we know a new goal in life might be exactly what she needs, now that she's given up on pleasing the Mother.'

Creon groaned, rubbing his face. 'And if we're unlucky, she interprets that goal as "restoring the Crimson Court to its former glory". I'm not sure if that's a risk you're willing to take, given what she's capable of.'

An even more outrageous thought whispered its way into my mind. 'Do you still think it's a risk if we send Naxi after her?'

He stared at me.

'That is,' I amended wryly, 'I'm not sure anyone could *stop* Naxi from going after her – but if she's going anyway, we may as well ask her to make sure no one tries to turn into a second Mother and—'

His befuddled laughter interrupted me. 'Cactus, how in the world do you keep coming up with these mad suggestions and somehow persuade me to like them, too?'

'It's brilliant, isn't it?' I beamed at him. 'And if it doesn't work out after all ... Well, who knows. We might get bored with the peace. A little scuffle to restore order at the court may be just what we need in twenty years' time.'

'Twenty years?' The gleam in his eyes went suddenly dangerous. 'Oh, you're underestimating in just how many ways I'm planning to keep you entertained for the time coming, Thenessa. Tell me if you need a list.'

My cheeks heated. 'I'm trying to work out world peace, you degenerate!'

'And doing an excellent job of it.' He raked a hand through his hair, the black strands gleaming like silk in the sunlight – a gesture that *must* have been designed to make my mouth go dry, the way it emphasised the sharpness of his features, the grace of his movements. 'So what exactly do you have left to decide now, if I may ask?'

I stared at him, my mind suddenly vacant.

'Because to my humble ears' – the flash of a smile on his face was anything but humble – 'it rather sounds like you've covered everything of importance for now. Other people will be far better suited to deal with the administrative nitty-gritty of it, and either way, that can wait a few days. There are lives to be saved first.'

'Yes, but—'

'Which means,' he continued, as if I hadn't interrupted him, 'that the next urgent point on your list is to take a break and *celebrate*, Em. You just singlehandedly won an entire bloody war on behalf of us all, if I need to remind you. You're done. You're free. So unless there are any other existential doubts we urgently need to discuss ...'

Those doubts.

Those cursed unknowns that had sent me floundering into this hiding place, far away from every enviable person who *knew* where they belonged, every fortunate individual with a purpose to fulfil and a home to return to ... I tried to find them now, festering where the triumph should be, and found ...

An image.

Of long black beaches at dusk, the sky a primrose pink deepening to violet. Of stone arches towering over the surf, a rugged cliff beyond, and crumbling walls rising from its edges, looking out over the crashing waves. Overgrown gardens and the quiet wilderness beyond, beckoning to be explored ...

How had I never thought of it as a place to call home before, when it slid into the blanks of my future so very easily?

'No,' I whispered, heartbeat finally settling. 'No more doubts.'

Not with a place to call ours, a sanctuary in this world that had not been built for us – a home that would not be carved out with blades and magic like the Mother had suggested, but grown and nurtured, like a secret garden hidden from the prying eyes of the world.

Blue for healing.

My heart swelled against my ribs as the thought took root.

'And that,' Creon muttered, leaning over to wrap his arm around my waist and scoop me up from the grass, 'is a lot more like it, cactus.'

A quivering laugh bubbled out of me. 'We really did win, didn't we? We really …'

'We did.' He pulled me into his lap as if I wasn't bloody and bruised and altogether grimy, arms wrapping around me from behind. His warm lips found the hollow of my neck, the sensitive spot just beneath my jaw. 'Or you did, arguably. I was mostly decorative for a significant part of the process, but—'

'Hey!' I made an unsuccessful attempt to glare at him; his arms wouldn't allow me to turn more than a fraction. 'You told me to fling around corpses! You dealt with those traps! You threw a bloody dagger into her chest!'

He nuzzled a slow line down my neck, his breath heating every inch of skin he passed. 'In a very decorative way.'

I scoffed. 'Looking pretty while throwing a blade doesn't make the blade useless.'

'Hmm,' he murmured against my skin, his rough voice vibrating through me. 'A very interesting argument. I can't wait to fight about this for the next hundred and fifty years.'

'You have a week to agree with me before I start getting violent,' I informed him, digging my nails into his thighs, fighting to keep my breathing under control as he kissed my shoulder with slow, languorous lips. 'We can fight about cat names for a century, if you need to be petty about something. Not about the question whether I would have survived until this day without you, to which every halfwit knows the answer is a resounding negative.'

He nibbled at my earlobe. 'Sometimes I truly don't know what I did to deserve you, Em.'

'I think it's the sex,' I said earnestly.

He froze in surprise, then burst out laughing and flipped me over in a single smooth motion, pinning me in the grass, his lean body straddling me. 'Is it, Your Majesty?' His voice had abruptly gone low and husky; his wings swept out on either side of his shoulders, casting shadows over our entangled bodies. 'Because in that case, I'm rather sure I've been neglecting my duties to an outrageous extent. You'll have to excuse me for getting distracted by futilities like battles and strategy.'

It was getting harder and harder to breathe, my suppressed laughter squeezing my throat, the light in his eyes enchanting enough to drive the air from anyone's lungs. Biting my lip was all I could do to keep my face straight and get out an almost unruffled, 'Don't worry, I *might* still forgive you.'

'I'm more grateful for your mildness than you'll ever know,' he muttered, lowering his face to a hair's breadth from mine. His hand drew a leisurely line over my body, feathery fingertips lighting my skin on fire. 'Need me to demonstrate just how agonisingly sorry I am, then?'

I tangled my fingers in his silky black hair and pulled him into a kiss.

He met me in a clash of ravenous desire, lips claiming mine with a hunger that matched my own, tongue taking possession of my mouth in an instant. His fingers clawed into my hip. His weight pressed me into the grass, locking me between him and the earth, and I arched into him instinctively – an unthinking reflex to get closer, *tighter*, as our bodies melded together.

His laughter was almost a growl. 'Looking for something, cactus?'

'Your modesty,' I panted, unable to help myself as I clasped my fingers into his lower back. 'Not very successful so far, but who knows ...'

He tilted his hips in reply, grinding himself against me just once – the bulge in his trousers an unmistakable punishment against my thigh, insistent and promising. I gasped in spite of all my more dignified intentions. He pulled away just as swiftly, allowing a whisper of fresh air to come between us – smirking down at me as he hovered over me, lips flushed red, a wicked glint in his eyes.

'And you're sure that's all?' he muttered sweetly.

Oh, the urge to claw that grin off his face ... And yet *this* finally felt like victory – not the slitting of throats and claiming of crowns, but this simple game of body against body, the world reduced to nothing but the heat under my skin and the taste of sin on my lips. Gone was the rustling of the reeds. The distant shouting. The lake lapping gently at the shore beside us. Each of them belonged to a battlefield that seemed ages beyond me already, and I ...

I was barely even here anymore.

I no longer *needed* to be here, and it was that baffling realisation that sparked the next surge of brilliance – a thought that had me prop myself up on my elbows beneath him and murmur, 'Do you think they would miss us in the city for the next twenty-four hours or so?'

His scarred eyebrow quirked up. 'Ambitious.'

I huffed a laugh. 'I'm nothing if not confident in your superior virility, but I'm thinking you might want to demonstrate it elsewhere.'

'Ah.' He rolled off me with a lazy grin, shoulders bulging as he settled onto his elbows too. His shirt hung loosely around his muscular frame, revealing his collarbone, half an inked scar, a tantalising glimpse of taut bronze chest – as if even now, moving away from me, his body was still whispering at me to change my mind and tear all that unnecessary linen off him. 'I see. So where are we going?'

'Depends,' I said slowly. 'How do you feel about some flying?'

And that, it turned out, was all the information he needed, those dangerous, smouldering dark eyes reading my mind as usual.

'We're going to need more than twenty-four hours, in that case,' he said, sitting up straight in the blink of an eye – suddenly all business again, and yet the way he spoke the words, so deliberately unhurried, turned even a discussion of travel into something unbearably sensual. 'If you want to make it back here and also sleep for a few hours, that is.'

'I was thinking we could fly straight on to the Crimson Court tomorrow.' I cocked my head at him, fluttering my lashes. 'But if you're too impatient to get me into a bed to make the time for travelling, we could just as easily dive into the nearest army tent and—'

'I'm rather sick of army tents, to tell you the truth,' he dryly interrupted, offering me a hand as he rose nimbly to his feet. 'So even though I *am* admittedly rather impatient to get you into ... well, anything vaguely resembling a bed ...'

I swatted at him.

'... I'll show some more of my inhuman self-restraint and get us out of here first,' he finished, unperturbed, sending me a saintly smile as he continued to hold out his hand. 'As long as you know I'll make up for the delay later.'

Damn him and that suggestive little smirk; I almost gave in, the temptation to drop back into the grass and pull him into my arms a blaze beneath my skin. But the alves were still shouting in the background, far too close for comfort. The smell of blood was starting to creep even into this little hideaway, staining the water and the weeping willows. And if I was very honest ...

I just wanted to go home.

'Let's go change clothes first,' I said, pulling myself up by his hand, making a face at my grimy shirt. 'And then I'm going to have a quick word with Agenor.'

Chapter 41

The sun was already sinking towards the sea when we flew back to the city about half an hour later, having found some clean clothes in the deserted army camp. Beneath us, the ruined fields and damaged streets were swarming with people; few of them paid attention to yet another fae soaring over, busy as they were with bandaging the wounded or making some first attempts to restore their houses to their former glory.

Alyra joined us as we swept towards the centre of the town, her talons a little bloody. The flashes I caught of her thoughts suggested she'd chased a satisfactory number of fae from their hiding places – *that's what you get with those big wings*, her grimly pitying look said, *far too visible.*

I informed her of the plans as Creon began his slow descent. She grumbled a little about distance but bristled when I suggested she may want to catch a lift on our shoulders for part of the journey. What did I think she was, some weak little fledgling?

I didn't bother to argue. There was no time, anyway; we had already reached the White Hall itself.

Someone had taken away the dead bodies from the façade of the building, although bloodstains still marred the otherwise pristine white walls. On the square where our hopeful human army had gathered mere days ago, large cookfires had now been erected, and flocks of magical people and awkward-looking humans mingled freely in what was at once a celebration, a vigil, and a public spectacle. I caught a glimpse of Edored in the distance, a jug of beer in his hand, shouting tall stories at a handful of wide-eyed human women. Nenya, on the other hand, was nowhere to be seen.

Silence spread around us as we landed. Fae and humans alike hastily swallowed their conversations, watching us pass with bated breath – the new High Lady of the empire, and who knew when I'd start handing out the first merciless orders to the flesh-and-blood weapon by my side, like every sensible fae ruler would do?

I kindly smiled back at them, making my way up the White Hall's steps.

Somehow, that only seemed to alarm them more.

There was no way to avoid the stares inside the building either, no way to ignore the palpable quiet that fell whenever we rounded a corner ... and yet I found myself unable to care much, the eyes and whispers a mild annoyance rather than the burden they had once been. Let them see a symbol in my place, then. Let them wonder and speculate. I knew who I was and where I was going – I no longer had any phantom voices to please.

A liberation. Apparently, I hadn't just broken the chains on the rest of the world this morning.

We reached the main hall and did not find either of my parents between the rows of broken and bleeding bodies. The only familiar face was Nenya, who came hurrying towards us the moment we stepped inside – looking more rosy-cheeked than I'd ever seen her, her eyes bright and feverish. There was a small trace of blood on her chin that hadn't been there when I'd run into her and Edored earlier, and for a single nauseating moment I couldn't help but wince. Had she been snacking on the injured to restore her strength?

But no – not Nenya, who had been the victim of so much worse in Bakaru's cruel hands. Most likely, it was simply more of Edored's blood.

'There you are!' She sounded uncharacteristically giddy. 'Looking for Agenor and Rosalind, I suppose?'

It came out too gleeful, that question. Next to me, Creon slowly tilted his head at her, looking as suspicious as I felt – proud, stoic Nenya, of all people, was not the first person I'd expected to be buzzing with excitement about my parent's whereabouts.

Odd.

Very odd.

'And if we were?' I said cautiously.

She grinned, baring her fangs. Those, too, were still a little bloody. 'They just left for the consuls' living quarters with a request not to be disturbed. A few things they had to discuss in private, I believe.'

Gods help me. 'The naked sort of private discussion, or—'

'Oh, no.' She considered that for a moment, then dryly added, 'Not yet, at least. I won't spoil the surprise for you.'

More and more ominous … but she didn't give the impression she would elaborate, and Creon was already turning around beside me, ready to set course for the left wing of the building. I took my leave of Nenya with a last suspicious look and followed him out of the hall, Alyra fluttering frantically behind me.

'Any idea what that was about?' I muttered as we finally found a deserted corridor, five corners away from the main hall.

He grimaced. 'You should probably go have a word with them alone. If your dear father is already upset about something, I doubt my presence is going to improve his feelings.'

There was no arguing with that.

We crossed the strangely untainted corridors, climbed the strangely untainted staircase, to the room that had been Rosalind's until a few days ago. There was no need to wonder whether they might have gone anywhere else: Agenor's deep voice was recognisable long before I could make out the individual words, carrying through the closed door between us with disconcerting ease.

'I'll wait for you elsewhere,' Creon said wryly, then added to Alyra, 'Let's find you some fresh air, shall we?'

She seemed conflicted for a moment, then launched herself from my shoulder and followed him in a flash of white and grey feathers – the urge to protect me temporarily trumped by the far more tempting prospect of open blue sky.

I watched them disappear around the corner, then turned, braced myself, and knocked. Inside the apartment, my father's outburst abruptly went silent.

'It's me,' I yelled before anyone could send a bolt of red through the door. 'Mind if I interrupt you for a minute?'

Something sounding like a curse emerged from inside. The door swung open the next instant, though, revealing the unusually dishevelled figure of my father – dark hair ruffled, green eyes wild, his expression more dazed than even when he'd found the Mother's long-lost second body on the floor with her throat slit. Behind him, Rosalind was looking worryingly pale, sitting on the couch – but she beamed at me all the same when I stepped into the room, her lips pressed together in a devilish smile that suggested she was enjoying the quarrel more than she knew she should.

'Is this an inopportune moment to show up?' I said, knowing full well that it was.

Agenor slammed the door behind me without even bothering to politely deny it. 'I just found out your mother has—'

'—in her infinite wisdom—' Rosalind dryly interjected.

'—out of *nowhere*—'

She chuckled. 'After twenty years of consideration—'

'—of which I was *not* informed—'

She swung her legs off the couch, sending me a conspiratorial smile as she pointed at her face. 'He's not too keen on these, Em.'

'On what—' I began, and then she curled up her upper lip.

A choked sound caught in my throat.

Two elongated, razor-sharp fangs protruded from my mother's gums where her canines should have been, glinting unnaturally white in the golden sunlight – *vampire* fangs. And at once it all fell into place,

Nenya's giddiness and the blood and the unmistakable gleam of panic in Agenor's eyes ...

'*What?*' I blurted.

Rosalind grinned even broader. 'Mortality was starting to bother me.'

Of course it was. Of *course*. I staggered two steps back and dropped into the nearest chair, blinking at those slender fangs, my plans and requests forgotten – how in the world had I *not* seen this coming, knowing it was the only possible answer to our horribly mismatched lifetimes? 'So you asked Nenya ...'

'She was most helpful.' Her contented tone was a shrill contrast to Agenor's expression of bewildered exasperation. 'The sensitivity to sunlight is unpleasant, of course, and I'll have to get used to the blood ...'

My father let out a strangled groan. 'Do I need to repeat that you're not getting *my* blood, Al? If you were hoping I'd turn myself into your personal buffet—'

'Oh, don't worry,' she dryly said, waving that point aside. 'According to Nenya, Rhudak is home to plenty of pretty young men who don't mind at *all* being—'

'You're *not* running off to Rhudak to set your teeth into any pretty young men either!' His deep voice was rising again. 'Whatever Nenkhet has been telling you, those ... establishments are not ... not ...'

'Very proper?' Rosalind innocently suggested.

His laborious inhale was an audible compromise between silence and profanity. 'Do you mind if we discuss this without any children in the room?'

'Hey!' I sputtered.

Rosalind chuckled. 'Well, then I'll have to starve to death – a shame, truly, but if all other options are unacceptable ...'

'I'll get you a couple of juicy goats for your birthday,' I said, rolling my eyes at her. She winked back. I threw one look at my father, who still gave the impression he might start steaming from his ears at any moment, and quickly added, 'And while everyone is still alive, mind if I ask you two for a favour? To offer some distraction from the fangs?'

Agenor let out a long-suffering groan as he sank into a chair and buried his face in his gold-flecked fingers. 'Gods and demons. Imagine the two of you allowing me a minute of peace every now and then.'

'You've had twenty years of peace,' Rosalind dryly pointed out, settling herself more snugly into the couch cushions. 'How much did you enjoy those?'

He didn't even bother to answer that question, turning to me with an expression of thinly veiled despair instead. 'What did you want to ask?'

'I was wondering if you could arrange to have everyone of importance at the Crimson Court tomorrow around this time,' I said, and his wings unclenched ever so slightly at the pragmatic normalcy of the request. 'The main members of the Alliance, in any case. Couple of other kings and queens, if possible. Please don't forget to bring Thysandra, and if any other captives want to come along, they're more than welcome as far as I'm concerned. Do you think that would be possible?'

He hesitated. 'Do I understand you're planning to be ... elsewhere, in the meantime?'

'Oh, I'll be inspecting the properties,' I said, face straight. 'I've recently come into an inheritance, I've been told.'

It was hard to decide which was the more satisfying reward – Rosalind's muffled laughter or Agenor's expression, his face frozen in habitual poise, a small, twitching muscle at his temple the only sign of just how hard he was fighting to compose himself. It took two beats of perfect silence before he parted his lips, closed his lips again, parted his lips once more, and finally, carefully said, 'I see.'

'You do?' I said.

'Yes.' The word was strained with a hundred other things I knew he wasn't saying – *these games will hurt you if you're not careful*, and *believe me, the Crimson Court isn't where you want to spend the rest of your days*, and *are you really going to make your decisions with no one but Creon to help you?* But he swallowed them all, every well-intended assertion on my wishes and feelings, leaving nothing but a tense, 'Are you being careful?'

The surge of affection welling up in me was strong enough to catch me off guard – a sudden, almost forceful urge to throw my arms around him and hug those lines of concern off his face. 'I'll be careful. Promise.'

'Good,' he managed, then hurriedly added, 'And whatever you do, keep in mind people will expect gifts and favours in return for their allegiance, will you? Loyalty has always been bought by the crown. You don't need to follow tradition, but be aware that it *is* the tradition, if you—'

'Are you saying you need payment to get people to the Crimson Court tomorrow?' I said, unable to suppress my growing grin.

He threw me a tired look. 'Em, you know very damn well—'

'Because in that case,' I cheerfully continued, ignoring the reproach entirely, 'do you think the Golden Court would suffice?'

He stiffened.

'And the title, I suppose.' I bit my lip in mock-thoughtfulness. 'I don't think I have any use for that, either. So—'

'Em,' he sharply interrupted, disbelief and warning warring for preference in his voice. 'What in the world are you talking about? The empire—'

'I'm doing away with the empire,' I said, shrugging. 'One court is plenty for me. So if you'd like to have the Golden Court back ...'

He stared at me, lost for words.

On the couch, Rosalind was no longer laughing.

'I ...' Agenor's eyes darted towards her, his expression strangely helpless. 'I suppose we'll have to discuss ...'

Rosalind cleared her throat. 'I assume there's enough space to keep some goats at that court of yours?'

He went quiet again.

'Oh, plenty,' I merrily said in his place. 'I think you could keep a few thousand of them on the plains, if you felt so inclined.'

'Excellent,' she said and winced as one of her fangs nicked her lip, leaving a small cut. 'Well, then I'm voting in favour. Unless you have any objections, of course, Lord Protector?'

A mirthless laugh fell over his lips. '*Me?*'

'As I thought.' She sent him another wicked grin, wiping away the blood welling from her bottom lip with the back of her hand. 'That's settled, then. Lovely idea, Em darling. You're taking the Cobalt Court, I suppose?'

'What?' Agenor said bewilderedly.

'You didn't think any daughter of mine was going to spend the rest of her life in that hell in the south, did you?' she shot back, her bright blue eyes gleaming with mischievous triumph. 'Also, I assume it's not a coincidence that only Thysandra was mentioned by name in the list of tomorrow's required attendants?'

'Gods help the children of clever mothers,' I said, sagging in my chair.

And that radiant look she gave me in response ... it was so, so far removed from anything I'd ever seen in Editta's eyes, so incomprehensibly different from everything I'd ever considered motherly love in my life, that I almost wept on the spot.

'Don't mind me trying to catch up,' Agenor said with a sour chuckle, rubbing his temples. His glance at me was wryly resigned on the surface but hid something far softer below. 'As I said, I do know where you got your brains.'

Only then did I realise it – that he had never been talking about himself at all.

'Flatterer,' Rosalind fondly said. 'Are we all done arranging matters, then? Not that I don't want you to stick around, Em, but we still have a fight to finish – and I presume Creon is waiting for you somewhere?'

I snorted a laugh. 'I'll see myself out, don't worry.'

'Oh, no, no.' She jumped up from the couch, holding out her arms to me. 'You know that's not what I mean – we'll see you tomorrow, alright?'

'Yes.' I rose, eyed her outstretched hands with a little suspicion, and added, 'Don't bite.'

She swatted at me, then wrapped her arms around me and pressed me close for a short moment. Even below the blood and sweat and mud, she still smelled like jasmine – that faint, sweet fragrance of peace.

'Go enjoy your break,' she murmured as she released me, hands lingering on my upper arms a moment longer. 'We'll be there.'

I nodded wordlessly and turned to Agenor, who had risen from his chair as well – still looking slightly thunderstruck and entirely unsure what to do with his hands. Ready to give me the usual awkward nod by way of goodbye, that ill-at-ease look of a male a little too conscious of his own dignity and a little too uncertain of the etiquette and conventions prescribed in the handling of daughters ...

Oh, damn it all.

I flung my arms around him before I could think better of it.

He stiffened in surprise but didn't dodge – standing paralysed in my embrace for an endless moment before letting out a dazed 'Oh' and cautiously wrapping his arms around my shoulders. His hands found their place on my back, hesitant and tentative. His palms half-hovered over my skin even then, as if he was afraid a firmer touch might break me.

It was a rather terrible hug. But he'd once been a rather terrible father, too, and even in this dumbfounded state, his arms were strong in a promising, reassuring sort of way; I dared to believe we'd get better at it with a little practice.

'You'll be careful?' he muttered again, voice teetering on the edge of cracking.

'Will do,' I whispered into his shirt, and then, the word slipping out in an even quieter, reckless, unstoppable breath, 'Father.'

He froze again.

Clutched against him, I could have sworn I felt his heart skip a beat.

'You'll be the death of me one day,' he said quietly, releasing me – but he was smiling, no matter how much he was trying to compose himself, an irrepressible smile that lit up his eyes and stripped centuries of weariness from his face. Like magic. No, *better* than magic. 'Off you go, then ... daughter.'

Off I went.

But that last word lingered with me, glowing happily in my chest even as I closed the door behind me and hurried back into the White Hall's cold and empty corridors.

Chapter 42

I found Creon on the rooftop of the building, basking in the sunlight with his back against a chimney while Alyra darted tirelessly around him, chirping without pause, drawing more and more artistic shapes in the air. They both turned as I clambered from the open hatch and nudged it shut behind me.

'Calmed them down?' Creon said, looking rather unconcerned. He, too, had to feel the warmth still pulsing through my veins.

'She turned herself into a vampire,' I said, as if that was an answer to his question.

He snorted a laugh. 'Did she tell him in advance?'

'No.' I grimaced, wiping my dusty palms on my skirt as I made my way towards him. 'Hence the shouting. They were happy with the court plans, though. Are you ready to go?'

'Always,' he said, rising and picking up the bundle of dark fabric beside him – his coat, I realised only as he unfolded it and held it out to me, a motion so smooth I needed a moment to work out why it looked so strangely familiar to me.

The roar of flames. The stench of burning wood and plaster. That very first night in my burning hometown, as different from this clear, sun-streaked rooftop as anything could get.

'What was the line again?' I said, wrapping my fingers around the bunched-up wool. 'I don't need a coat ...'

'And even if you did, you'd rather freeze to death than wear mine,' he finished without missing a beat, laugh lines deepening around his eyes.

I chuckled and draped the piece of clothing around my shoulders – uncomfortably hot in the sunlight, yet I knew I'd be grateful for the warmth as soon as we'd ascended. 'I'm glad my witty conversation left an impression.'

'You started leaving an impression the moment I first laid eyes on you,' he muttered, lifting me into his arms and taking off into the sky.

I wasn't sure how to reply to that, so I didn't speak at all – just quickly bunched my hair beneath the collar of the coat as the wind began whipping the unhelpful strands into his face. He gave a low noise of gratefulness, shoulders straining as his wings rapidly carried us higher and the White City shrunk to the size of a painting below us, the earth a patchwork of farmland and battlefields around it.

It looked not nearly as ruined, somehow, with every trampled meadow and blood-soaked field reduced to the equivalent of a brushstroke.

The people of the city would fix it over time, I told myself. Of course they would. And even if they didn't ...

Well, someone else would surely be more qualified to handle that.

We left the island and its people behind within minutes, the rugged hills and the forests sinking away until they were little more than a grey-green line on the horizon. Below us, the azure sea gleamed golden in the light of the sinking sun; now and then, other landmasses slid past, like a life-sized geography test. Alyra soared along, flapping frantically to keep up but showing no signs of exhaustion yet.

None of us made a sound. The world up here, so high and serene, was too blissfully silent to disturb the peace for even a moment. I rested my head against Creon's shoulder and soaked up the rhythmic, rolling movements of his muscles, watching the archipelago stretch out below us ... the same world I'd risked my life for over and over again, and it seemed both more real and strangely dreamlike as we flew across it, all those islands looking as if they might fit in the palm of my hand.

The sun sank to the horizon on our right, its light glinting off the waves below like scattered gold. Creon's strong arms around me never wavered as the sky transitioned from a vibrant orange to a softer pink and then a deep, brilliant violet; the first stars appeared bright and silvery in the twilight, slowly giving shape to the constellations I knew. And still we flew southward, small and solitary, as the night wrapped itself around us and the moon began its silent ascent into that vast indigo dome.

It was then that the first fire flickered to life beneath us – blazing from the heart of a small coastal town, the surrounding houses visible only by the shine of torches and illuminated windows in the dark.

I gasped.

Far, far away, shreds of howling voices drifted into the night air, the eerie sound breaking hours of silence.

For one moment, I didn't see, just remembered. The orange glow of fire, burning beneath the uncaring starry sky. The cold night air biting my face. The stench of burning wood lingering in my nostrils ... Not again, not *tonight*—

'It's a bonfire, cactus,' Creon murmured, arms tightening around me in a moment of wordless comfort. 'Nothing else is burning.'

The memories stuttered.

And at once, I could see clearly again.

A *bonfire* – not a blaze of death and destruction. Just that single pyre, built on what must be the town square. Those voices crying out ...

Not panic. *Celebration.*

'Do they know?' I whispered breathlessly. 'Do they know she's dead?'

'I'm guessing some alves went around and spread the happy tidings.' He sounded amused, but there was a layer of emotion beneath – neither sorrow nor joy, but something that lay closer to bittersweet melancholy. 'It *is* the news of the century, after all.'

A century during which he'd hated every passing hour, surviving by the barest thread of his will – and yet *he* wasn't there, dancing around the town square, kissing village lasses in shadowy alleys and drinking his way through half a vat of home-brewed beer.

I squeezed his hand.

He squeezed back, no more words needed.

The next bonfire lit up minutes later, a few miles away on the same island. Then a third one, on the horizon to our left, and a fourth and a fifth ... More and more of them as darkness fell, until I could tell the outlines of the islands by the dozens, *hundreds* of flames flickering below, even the smallest hamlets coming together to toast the fall of the empire and the birth of a brand new world. I recognised Ildhelm by its shape, and the smaller islands around it, the little corner of the archipelago I could have drawn with my eyes shut ...

Only Cathra was dark, entirely invisible to the east of Ildhelm's larger presence. The only island that *wasn't* burning tonight – the bitter irony.

And yet, imagining all those hundreds of thousands of people below, filled with hope and incredulous elation for what may be the first time in their short lives ...

It didn't leave much room for grief.

We flew on. Alyra, whose rapid wingbeats had grown more and more agitated as night fell, finally gave in and curled up on my shoulder, where she promptly fell asleep. Creon still never faltered as we crossed into the southwest segment of the archipelago, leaving the human isles behind, finally, and soaring into the territory of the fae.

No bonfires were burning there, unsurprisingly.

In the light of the plump moon, the world below us was all blue and silver, mirroring the starry sky. It was in that same monochrome glow that finally – the constellations shifted, the moon past its highest point already – our destination loomed up from the darkness, grand and desolate at once. Rugged mountains, wild gardens. Crumbled walls and towers, rising from their cliff with the stubbornness of a wounded warrior refusing to die.

The Cobalt Court.

I looked up at Creon and found him smiling – a quiet, fragile smile more beautiful than even the island waiting for us.

Alyra woke up as we descended and shot out from the hollow of my shoulder, making straight for the cliffs in a streak of white. Creon followed more slowly as he carried me down to the dizzying precipice of the cliffs, the same spot Beyla had once brought me to so I could sneak into the ruins through the back door. Little had changed since then – but the faint iridescent shimmer around the court had vanished, that flimsy glimpse of magic I'd caught from the corner of my eye whenever I had visited the castle before.

Ahead of us, Alyra soared into the gardens without any sign of trouble, disappearing into the maze of trees.

'The shield is gone,' I whispered as Creon's feet touched the ground, lightly like a leaf drifting down. 'It must have dissolved when she died.'

He put me down, flexed his arms and shoulders a few times as he folded in his wings, then said, 'There are upsides to being able to access one's home without magic tricks, I suppose.'

Home.

I turned back to the ruins looming before us. Bare, crumbling towers, vines of ivy claiming the weathered stones for themselves ... but then there were the elegant arched windows, glass gone but the ornate carvings around them still recognisable. The wildflowers thriving in the gardens. The cracked marble of the floors behind these blue-grey granite walls, the faded mosaics waiting to be found beneath layers of dust and sand.

It had never stopped being beautiful, this place. Its beauty simply lay dormant, ready for a touch of magic to wake it again.

'So,' I muttered, unable to tear my eyes away from the beckoning walls, 'how about a bedroom with an ocean view?'

Creon let out a low laugh beside me. 'As long as it has a balcony, I'm fine with any view. And that tower on the left would be a good base for an observatory, if we build it high enough.'

Yes. *Yes.* The shapes of restored towers and galleries were drawing themselves in the night air before me, shifting with my thoughts, blooming as my plans unfolded. 'We could put the library in that wing, too, don't you think? And then move all the guest rooms to the other side, so people can read their books in peace even if we have a few dozen alves around. And obviously we need a ridiculously large main hall somewhere …'

'I've seen paintings of an utterly decadent entrance hall,' Creon dryly said. His eyes were shining when I glanced at him, his hair still ruffled from the long flight – a face begging for my hands to wrap around it and pull him in for a kiss. 'It's all gone now, though, so—'

'You're not going to suggest building a *small* entrance hall instead, are you?' I said with mock outrage, tucking my arm through his and pulling him with me as I began hurrying towards the ruins. 'Clearly, the only reasonable thing to do is to make it even larger and even more decadent. Hovering flights of stairs, a house-sized chandelier …'

He snorted a laugh. 'High stained-glass windows depicting your grand and heroic deeds …'

'I was rather thinking of stained-glass windows depicting your face from various angles,' I said as earnestly as I could manage. Under my feet, the old stones creaked with every step, and pieces of rubble and shards of glass crunched. 'Might as well show visitors the best our household has to offer, wouldn't you say?'

His eyebrow quirked dangerously. 'I don't think my face is what you're looking for, then, cactus.'

Gods have mercy – I should have seen it coming, and yet there was no keeping my voice down at that image, the grand and serene Cobalt Court restored in all its glory, proudly displaying a ten-foot glass phallus straight above its entrance. 'We are *not*—'

'Think of what Agenor would say, though,' he interrupted, with a sideways glance suggesting that was a perfectly reasonable argument.

'Reminding me of my father is *not* how you convince me to immortalise your cock in our windows, Creon!'

He looked even more reasonable. 'Who is talking about cocks? I was suggesting putting Alyra's likeness in there – imagine what the snakes would do if they saw her.'

I tried to shove him. Unfortunately, it turned out that even while walking, his muscular body was far too solid to be easily toppled; I all but flung myself to the ground instead, tripping over my feet and an inopportune chunk of marble, and ended up stumbling against his lean chest, held up only by our intertwined arms.

He laughed out loud. 'Are you *that* impatient to get closer to the sculpted glory of my presence, Your Majesty?'

'Oh, go to hell,' I sputtered, making valiant attempts to regain my balance and step back. His arm slipping around my waist wouldn't let me. 'Don't "Your Majesty" me, and also, you can't just describe *yourself* as sculpted and glorious, you arrogant wretch.'

'I can't?' He blinked innocently, eyes gleaming in the moonlight. 'Am I supposed to lie, then?'

It really was unfortunate how closely the feeling of justified outrage resembled the heated flush of arousal, the sudden warmth brewing where we were pressed together. With the thought of his naked body – stained glass or otherwise – still vividly present in my mind, it took all I had to huff and grumble, 'I'd describe your presence as passable at best. Adequate. Perfectly acceptable to look at, if I were in a generous mood.'

'Hmm,' he muttered, arm tightening at the small of my back to press me against his muscular body. His other hand wrapped around my cheek, tilting my head to bring our faces mere inches away from each other – close enough to distinguish his long lashes in the darkness, the sharp shadows playing over his jaw, the dangerous twist of his lips. In the moonlight, his smile was like a whispered secret. 'And I suppose it's that same passable face that makes you think of my cock all day, is it?'

'I do no such thing!' It sounded like a lie, quite possibly because it *was* a lie. His body was too damn hot against me. His smirk too damn suggestive. And I was far, far too familiar with the object of discussion to *not* see it in my mind's eye at the slightest mention, to not feel its phantom weight imprinted in my palms ... 'You're the one who started insinuating all kinds of vulgarities!'

The look in his eyes as he watched me, mouth quirking ... I could almost taste the smouldering heat. 'Are you saying you're not thinking of my cock right now?'

'Of course I'm not,' I lied. My voice had gone infuriatingly hoarse. 'Don't know why you'd think I'd do any such thing.'

'You don't?' His hand on my back sank a few inches, cupping my bottom and shoving me tight against him – tight against the unmistakable hardness pressing into my belly. A gasp escaped my lips, and his grin widened. 'Liar.'

I squeezed my eyes shut so as not to see that dangerous gleam in his dark pupils – another mistake. With my sight gone, my other senses seemed twice as aware, the autumn scent of his body, the thinly veiled desire of his fingers clawing into my sensitive flesh ... His rock-hard erection, most of all, demanding my notice, my attention.

'I could be wrong, of course,' he whispered, lips brushing my earlobe as he spoke, sending a shudder down my spine. 'You might be occupied with entirely innocent thoughts. Just tell me what you're thinking of, love – I'm most eager to hear.'

Eager – gods have mercy, did he *have* to speak that word with such suggestive sweetness, igniting sparks in all the places I wished he'd touch? It took every last drop of willpower to suck in a cool breath and grind out a deeply unconvincing, 'Architecture. I ... I'm thinking about architecture.'

'Oh no, you aren't.' His purring voice grew even more syrupy, fingers crawling down, down, down, over my thigh, towards the hem of his own coat on my shoulders. 'Try again.'

The flaming blush rising on my face had to be visible even in the moonlight. 'What do we have for breakfast?'

'Depends,' he muttered. 'What would you like for breakfast?'

Hell take me. The memory of him in my mouth immediately sprang to life, the thick and rigid feel of him, the musky taste of his flesh vivid on my tongue ... A stab of heat burned through me, and he laughed out loud, a sound of pure indulgence scattering through the deserted garden.

'I still feel what you feel, Em.' His fingers slipped beneath his coat, beneath my dress, then slid up over my bare thigh in ripples of pleasure. Too close to the damp heat soaking my underwear. Far too close to the truth. 'And architecture or breakfast are the last things on your mind now – admit it.'

Zera help me. It would be so, so easy to admit it.

But I was nothing if not stubborn – and damn him, did he really think I would be defeated that easily? I wouldn't let myself be reduced to prey without a fight. If he wanted to turn these games into a hunt …

To hell with it. He could go ahead and earn it.

'Make me,' I breathed.

And ran.

The surprise was my only advantage – a single heartbeat of motionlessness behind me as I sprinted over the uneven garden path, willing my wobbly knees to behave. Then, like a predator unleashed, he bolted after me. His laughter and the sound of my racing heartbeat blended into the night – the moonlit hedges and crumbled statues blurring around me, the world narrowing to nothing but the ruins rising from the earth a hundred feet away. Thorns slashed my legs. Tiles cracked beneath my feet. But Creon was laughing behind me, the sound promising revenge of the most pleasurable sort, and through the smouldering of my body, I barely felt the pain.

There, before me, an open doorway beckoned …

To my right, the faint glow of the bindings lit up the walls and arches, thousands of gleaming orbs I would have to deal with in the years to come. But before me, all was dark, and I didn't hesitate as I barrelled through that gaping hole, into the tempting shadows beyond. Into the maze of corridors I would soon know even with my eyes shut – surprises around every corner now, hiding place and hunting ground at once.

I ducked through the first doorway I found, tiptoeing into the weed-covered room beyond with my back against the wall. Behind me, Creon's voice echoed through the ruins, laced with laughter – 'Want to tell me what you're thinking of now, cactus?'

Your hands – the answer rose in my mind without hesitation. Those strong, graceful hands and the way they would soon be stripping every inch of clothing off me, would soon be wrapping around the inside of my thighs and spreading me wide for—

I swallowed loudly, resting my head against the cold stone behind my back. Next to me, the wall had cracked open, giving access to what must once have been a luxurious atrium.

'Cross-stitching,' I yelled. 'Why?'

Long, purposeful strides moved my way, and I quickly scurried through the breach, suppressing a giggle. Uneven pillars loomed over me, silver in the moonlight – a muddy basin at the centre of the open space, headless, armless statues on either side of the entrances. Above my head, the starry sky stretched over the ruins, twinkling down at me with what almost looked like amusement.

Was that the swift slap of a wing to my left?

I scrambled to move, every sense on high alert, every nerve in my body tingling with white-hot anticipation. What if he was standing there, right around the nearest doorway, waiting for me to walk into his merciless arms? What if I found myself pinned to the wall in two steps, the way he'd pinned me to the wall in Lyn's wardrobe and—

A soft chuckle, far too close. 'Still cross-stitching?'

Oh, fuck.

He could feel those flares of arousal, couldn't he?

'Clearly,' I said haughtily, tiptoeing backwards to the other exit of the atrium, 'you have not the faintest idea how exciting specialty stitches can be.'

Footsteps, again.

I made a run for it.

Through a skewed open arch, around the nearest corner … Before me, a wide space unfolded. A great hall in better times, no doubt, although now the ceiling was gone and only the slender buttresses along the walls hinted at the place it had once been. Moonlight bathed the weathered marble floor in an ethereal glow, and for a moment, my steps slowed as I drank in the strange, shattered beauty of it all …

Only then did I realise the world had gone suspiciously quiet behind me.

I stiffened, then slowly began turning, goosebumps prickling every inch of my skin. But the doorway through which I'd come was empty, no trace of the tall silhouette I'd expected to find waiting …

Something moved above me.

Above me.

I knew before I started running that I was too late.

He didn't even land. The solid weight of his body hit me from behind, and then his arms were around me, catching me as I tumbled forward ... Velvet wings swept out on either side of us. I tried to land on my feet as we half fell, half floated to the floor, but he wouldn't let me; cold marble bit into my knees, my hands, my shins as he lowered me, pinning me to the ground as I struggled against his hold.

'That's *cheating*,' I gasped, trying to elbow his wing.

His laughter brushed over the back of my neck, hot and feathery. 'All you told me was to make you speak the truth, cactus. I didn't hear anything about rules.'

I tried to wriggle from his grasp. He didn't budge, his weight locking me between him and the floor, his hands constraining mine with effortless strength. The cold of the marble was seeping through my dress, numbing my stomach; in contrast, the heat of his muscular body pressing into my back was almost unbearable.

'Want to tell me what's on your mind now?' he muttered sweetly into my ear.

'You bastard,' I panted, which would have sounded more convincing if not for the hysterical laughter spilling out with it. Gods save me, his hard body on mine, raw strength leaving me entirely at his mercy ... how was I supposed to keep thinking at all? 'You're holding me down and tormenting me! Do I look like I have time for deep ruminations on *anything*?'

He wedged his thigh in between mine, forcing my legs apart. 'If you're looking for something deep ...'

'Like ocean trenches?' I managed through gritted teeth.

'Oh, we both know you're not thinking about the ocean,' he informed me, easily transferring both my wrists to his left hand. His right slid below my skirt again, and this time there was no fleeing as he relentlessly, unyieldingly made his way up my thigh, closer and closer to my soaked underwear. 'Unless it's a metaphor for wetness, of course, in which case—'

My hips jerked up against him – I couldn't help it. '*Creon.*'

'No?' he murmured. 'Not thinking about metaphors either? One wonders what *is* occupying your thoughts, in that case.'

Agony. Pure and simple agony, my skin burning under his touch, my body craving that sweet, sweet invasion … His hand was so close now. *So* close to the place where I needed him most, and yet he was stalling, waiting for me to respond – a single bit of truth away from ecstasy.

My lips – my stupid, stubborn lips – moved without my permission. 'Gardening. I … I'm thinking of gardening.'

His rough laugh told me he was enjoying the struggle far too much. 'Are you?'

'How about a maze of boxwood hedges?' I was babbling now, barely hearing myself. He nudged my thighs further apart with his knee between my legs, baring me and the damning wetness at my core to the night air, and my thoughts spiralled into nothing but *need* – nothing but the bulge of his cock pressed against my lower back, taunting me with its nearness. My tongue kept going all the same. 'And a rose garden and an exotic fish pond and … and—'

His fingers ghosted over my underwear just once.

Every muscle in my body clenched simultaneously as sparks exploded beneath that tender skin – clenched around the emptiness far too deep inside me, craving the fulfilment I knew was just a whisper away. He *had* to know, damn him. He could feel my fingers clawing at the cold marble, could feel my body begging for him to take it … But he retracted as swiftly as he'd come, fingers brushing gossamer touches back down my thighs. Refusing to set me free. Refusing to save me from myself.

'And?' he said sweetly, his long hair tickling my cheek as he bent over me.

'Please,' I whispered.

'Hmm?' He ground against me, a slow, torturous stroke, his straining hardness all I could feel even through trousers and coat and dress. Ready to shatter me. Ready to drive me over the edge in all the ways only he could. 'Is there anything you need, love? All you need to do is tell me – your wish is my command, of course.'

That melodious voice, teasing and taunting, curling around me like smoke in the darkness … I gasped in a breath, then another one. His fingers were drawing idle circles on the inside of my thigh, barely-there touches that left trails of fire in their wake; no mercy, those touches told me, no matter how much I might beg. Fae wars didn't end in surrender.

Only defeat would do.

Just tell me ...

'You,' I breathed. 'I'm thinking of you.'

He slipped his fingers beneath my underwear in response.

Warm, firm flesh met mine, tracing the slick lines of my body with cruel gentleness. My hips bucked, trying to get him closer, *deeper* ... and he laughed again, retreating.

'No.' It burst from my lungs by reflex. 'No, please—'

'I'm going to need a few more words,' he muttered, his hand sliding between our bodies pressed together. The rustle of skin on fabric, the release of a button coming loose; a sob of relief almost escaped me. 'What part of my ravishing person are you contemplating, exactly? I would hate to bore you with the bits you don't care about, pretty as they may be.'

'All of it,' I moaned. 'All of you.'

He flicked his finger over the vulnerable flesh between my thighs just once, then began bunching up my dress and coat with maddeningly patient movements – exposing me to the starry sky, messy and defiled, sprawled out over the old marble like a sacrificial offering. 'Did I ever let you get away so easily, cactus?'

A whimper escaped me. The cold autumn breeze nipped my bare skin, the frigid marble was turning the front half of my body to ice ... and yet it was the anticipation that had me shivering above all else, glorious and torturous at once. '*Please.*'

'You stubborn little thing,' he softly said, shifting his body over me, and it was not amusement lending that touch of emotion to his voice. Instead ... fondness? *Admiration?* 'Stop fighting, Em. Start wanting. You've earned everything and more.'

Everything.

His love. His pleasure. All of this court and this night and this madness, all of the future, all of the peace – and I gave in, finally, as his fingers gently scooted my underwear aside and the straining head of his erection settled against my entrance, thick and smooth and incomprehensibly hard.

'That,' I gasped. '*That* is what I'm thinking about.'

He pressed the tip into me, not even half an inch. A warning. A promise. Around him, my body stretched and strained, clenching as if to draw him deeper inside me – failing to get him even a fraction closer to where I so desperately needed him.

'What is?' His own breath was strained now. His hand around my wrists finally let go, settling on the marble floor instead. 'Words, Em.'

'Your cock, damn you!' My voiced lashed into the quiet night like a whip – like breaking chains, and gods, it felt so, so good to lose. 'I need your cock inside me like I need air, and please, *please*—'

He slammed into me.

One ruthless stroke, and I evaporated around him, reduced to nothing but need and desire as his hot, hard length filled me to the brim and then some. A scream ripped from my throat. My nails dug into the marble so hard it hurt. Too much sensation, too much *fullness*, and yet he gave me no time to recover as he pulled back and drove himself deep again, claiming me like a victory. I gasped his name. He slipped his hand between my stomach and the floor in response, fingers finding the little bundle of nerves between my slick lips.

Colours exploded across my vision as he plunged into me at the same moment, too much of that gorgeous friction for my body to contain.

'Is this what you want?' His voice was a rough growl against my ear, each word punctuated by another savage thrust. 'Is this what you need?'

I could no longer talk.

Animal sounds fell from my lips at every stroke into my body. There was no pain. Just that perfect completeness, obliterating any semblance of reason or restraint; his cock and fingers moved in perfect unison, a primal rhythm that sent a storm of devastating sensation roaring through my veins. I lifted my head off the marble, struggling to speak, and his teeth grazed my shoulder, adding *more*.

'Don't hold back,' he snarled, his voice scraping down my nape. 'Don't you dare hold back for me, Em.'

It turned out my body had yet more to give.

I melted like wax around him. Yielded to his relentless desire, to *my* relentless desire, the hunger and the triumph clawing through me and shattering all doubt and resistance in their wake …

The world faded.

The stars above me seemed to blur and burst. The darkness, the ruins, even the cold marble beneath me … they ceased to exist for a single blissful moment as I hung suspended in the void, nothing but my unravelling body and his conquering cock inside me.

Then I went over the edge.

Perhaps I screamed. Perhaps I cried. Perhaps I cursed the gods and every living thing in existence. But I'd won, I'd won, I'd *won*, and I *knew* it then – as pleasure rippled through me and every last drop of strength was obliterated from my body – that I was safe. That I was home. That I would never, *ever* be small again.

Not for anything.

Not for anyone.

And this … *this* was what glory felt like.

I came back to myself on the cold marble, overwhelmed and undone, on my side, my breath in tangles. Creon's arm lay around me, pressing me to his chest. His cock throbbed softly against my bare lower back; his thigh lay between my legs, pressed against my sex – grounding me with every convulsion shuddering through my body until finally, slowly, the last of the madness seeped out of me and left me perfectly, deliciously empty.

It seemed unlikely, I considered with an odd, detached calm, that I would ever be able to walk again.

For this victory, that did not seem too outrageous a price to pay.

'Have I told you,' Creon muttered against the crown of my head, 'how much I'm planning to enjoy the next few centuries, cactus?'

I let out a choked laugh, turning in his arms to meet his gaze. My limbs were floppy as jellyfish. My mind felt even less coherent. Above the ruins, the endless starry sky stretched over us, promising forever. 'The big question is whether we'll ever find time to rebuild this court at all.'

'Five minutes every now and then, perhaps. In between more urgent activity.' His fingers lazily circled my breast, thumb brushing a nipple through my dress, as he nodded at my bunched-up skirt. 'Spread your legs.'

My breath caught. 'What?'

'What, what.' A slow, wicked smile spread over his face as he lowered me to my back, then sat up, raising an eyebrow at me. 'You didn't think I was done making you scream, did you?'

Gods help me. I came up on my elbows, my arms quivering beneath me. 'I don't think there's any air left in me to—'

'Legs, love,' he interrupted sweetly. 'You'll scream exactly when I want you to.'

And damn him ...

I did.

Dawn found us rumpled and sticky, sore and exhausted, in the wild grass of the gardens where we'd tried to go to sleep for a few minutes and failed miserably. At the eastern horizon, the sky paled, then turned a brilliant blossom pink – the very first sunrise in over a thousand years that wouldn't be witnessed by the Mother's eyes.

And gods, it was a gorgeous one.

Next to me, Creon lay sprawled out in the grass, shirt gone, trousers sloppily buttoned. In the blushing morning light, even the sculpted ridges of his abdomen looked gentler, the hard lines of his face mellowed; the colours of the sunrise reflected in his eyes, and for a moment every trace of darkness was gone, every last glimpse of the shields and thorns he'd built around his soul. Just a tired, tousled, dazzlingly beautiful male, soaking up the first rays peeking over the edge of the world. Just ...

Mine.

I didn't seem able to stop smiling.

It was in that rosy light that Alyra found us not much later, soaring out from behind the court's weathered walls. She was hauling a linen pouch along in her claws, flapping furiously to keep herself aloft despite the extra weight; when she dropped it into the grass at my feet, half a loaf of bread, a chunk of cheese, and a wrinkly pear came rolling out.

I stared at it, and only then did I notice my own rumbling stomach. 'You found us *breakfast?*'

She gave me a long, unimpressed look as she landed beside me, beady eyes trailing from my thorn-scratched calves to my sticky thighs to the traces of seed clinging to the collar of my dress. *I did*, the disapproving impression on her face said, *and looking at you now, I regret I didn't pick a bar of soap instead.*

'Just wait until you meet the eagle of your dreams,' I told her, suppressing a yawn behind my hand. 'You'll understand.'

She looked even less impressed by that argument as she hopped off to find some worms for herself to eat.

I tore off a handful of bread, gave the rest to Creon, and spent the next few minutes chewing in drowsy silence, watching the sun rise over the otherworldly landscape of the Cobalt Court. In the peachy light, the black beaches on either side of our cliff glowed a rosy pink. On the rocky plains ahead, the grey-green eucalyptus trees rustled softly in the morning mist, and beyond, quartz veins shimmered in the dark mountain slopes, waterfalls rushing down the jagged rocks like ethereal veils sparkling in the gold and pink morning light.

The Crimson Court and its scheming seemed an eternity away already.

I'd host a summer festival here one day, I thoughtfully decided as I chewed – a long night of roaring bonfires and too much honey mead even for Edored to devour. I'd make my parents come over for dinner every week. And on quiet winter mornings, Lyn might like to visit me, and we'd sit in the library together, gazing out over the chilly sea and sipping piping hot tea as we browsed our books …

Creon was talking to me. I didn't register his voice until several seconds too late – '... should be able to find them ...'

'Wait.' I jolted up, blinking, shaken roughly from my daydreams. 'What were you saying?'

He stuck a last bite of bread into his mouth, nodding at me with an amused lift of his eyebrows. 'I was asking whether you were planning to appear before the gathered kings and queens of the world in this state. Or before your parents, for that matter.'

Right.

An eternity away or no, we *did* still have some matters to settle today ... and perhaps I shouldn't try to settle them with seed stains on my clothes and limbs.

'So what do you suggest?' I lazily stretched out, squinting at the waterfalls in the distance. 'Find a brook and freshen up a little before we leave?'

'As I was saying,' he dryly said, 'there should be hot springs on this island somewhere. I have faith we can find one that allows for more pleasant bathing than mountain creeks.'

I stared at him.

He was already rising to his feet, holding out his hand to me, mud- and seed-stained wings unfolding, without further ado.

We found a cluster of pools at the foot of the nearest mountain's ridge – six smooth, round basins feeding into each other, nestled snugly in between the irregular quartz formations that surrounded them. The first two were too hot for comfortable bathing, too close to their bubbling source. But the third was just right, and the crystal-clear surface rippled invitingly as I dipped in my foot; I couldn't keep down a sigh of relief as I lowered myself into the balmy water and its soothing, comforting warmth enveloped me.

Welcome home, it seemed to be telling me.

And I could see it then, the dozens and dozens of late afternoons we would retreat to this spot, rinsing the stone dust and chalk from our hair as the ruins on the distant cliffs slowly grew into a home again ...

Could see it, and couldn't stop smiling.

We spent a few minutes scrubbing sweat and mud from each other's skin, then curled up in the water together, exhausted and quiet in that most content of ways. Above us, the sky was a palette of pastel hues now, pink and blue and some lingering purple. The minty scent of eucalyptus drifted along on the morning breeze. I lay dreamy and drowsy in Creon's arms and watched the steam twirl from the water's surface in elegant wisps, my mind empty, my heart at ease, my eyelids growing heavier and heavier …

'Em,' he whispered breathlessly.

I jolted from thoughts that may have been dreams.

'Shh.' He rose a few inches, lifting his hand from the water with unusual caution. Against my back, I could feel his heartbeat quicken a fraction; his wings tensed on either side of us. 'Shh, Em – *look.*'

And only then, following his outstretched finger, did I see them. Mere feet away, rummaging around between the gleaming rocks …

Two fluffy, snow-white doves.

Zera's blessing.

My breath caught.

The birds lingered for a few more moments, preening their feathers, cooing softly, as if to offer us every opportunity to notice them. Then they swept out their snowy wings and took off, back to the west, towards the continent and Zera's woods – two inseparable dots of white, flying side by side, blending seamlessly into the lustre of a brand new day.

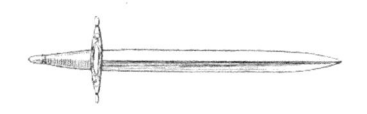

The End

Not yet ready to say goodbye to the Fae Isles world? We'll see Em and Creon – and the rest of the crew – again in the spin-offs!

With Wing and Claw, Fae Isles book 5, is Naxi and Thysandra's stand-alone story. Having unexpectedly inherited the Crimson Court, a shaken Thysandra resolves to restore order in her former home ... but rebellious fae, a grumpy Labyrinth, and the unwanted admiration of a troublesome little half demon make the job a whole lot harder than it ought to be.

Get *With Wing and Claw* here: https://mybook.to/WWaC

Want to stay updated about future releases, bonus content, and other fun stuff? Follow me on instagram as @authorlisettemarshall, sign up for my newsletter at lisettemarshall.com/sign-up, or join my reader server on Discord at discord.gg/HREGt2mAAB.

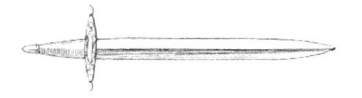

Other books by Lisette Marshall

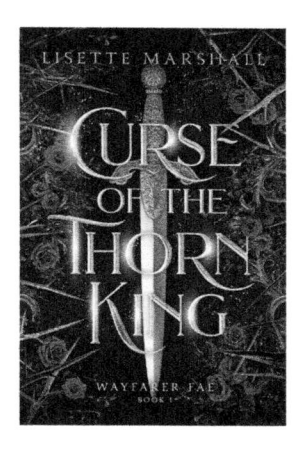

Killing a fae king is hard. Doing so politely is even harder.

Briannis Iavi – well-bred lady and accidental assassin – is so close to securing the life of her dreams. All she needs to do is complete one last job: make her way into fae territory, sneak into the enchanted halls of Rosethorn Keep, and kill the king of Faerie.

But miles away from the respectable life she thought she knew, even her knives and poisons may not be enough to protect her heart ...

Get Curse of the Thorn King through https://mybook.to/thornking

About the Author

Lisette Marshall is a fantasy romance author, language nerd and cartography enthusiast. Having grown up on a steady diet of epic fantasy, regency romance and cosy mysteries, she now writes steamy, swoony stories with a generous sprinkle of murder.

Lisette lives in the Netherlands (yes, below sea level) with her boyfriend and the few house plants that miraculously survive her highly irregular watering regime. When she's not reading or writing, she can usually be found drawing fantasy maps, baking and eating too many chocolate cookies, or geeking out over Ancient Greek.

To get in touch, visit www.lisettemarshall.com, or follow @authorlisettemarshall on Instagram, where she spends way too much time looking at pretty book pictures.

Printed in Great Britain
by Amazon